The sorcerer s_____etted against the firelight ____ _ _____ were live things, embers of scarlet and amber set in his gaunt face.

In the dream—or nightmare—the wizard Balamung spoke: "Lord Gerin the Fox, it's no less than a nuisance you are to me, no less, so I pray you'll forgive my costing you a dollop of sleep to show you what's waiting in the northlands. Would I could be drawing the black-hearted soul of you from your carcass, but there's no spell I ken to do it, what with you so far away."

No spell Gerin knew could have reached across the miles at all. He was nothing, not even a wraith, just eyes and ears bound to see and hear only what Balamung chose to reveal.

The spell the mage used must have been readied beforehand, for when he cried out in the harsh Kizzuwatnan tongue, a stout wicker cage rose from the ground and drifted slowly toward the fire. In the cage, a man struggled vainly to free himself.

"Have a look, Lord Gerin," Balamung whispered, "for your turn is next!" His voice was cold as ice, harsh as stone. And while he spoke, the cage entered the blaze.

Fire cavorted over the caged man's body, but Balamung's evil magic would not let him die. He fought against the unyielding door until his very tendons burned away. His shrieks had stopped long before, when flames swallowed his larynx.

"He was a job I had to rush," Balamung said. "When it's you, now, Fox, falling into my hand, I'll take the time to think up something truly worthy of you, oh indeed and I will!" He made a gesture of dismissal.

Gerin found himself staring up from his bedroll, body wet with cold sweat.

"Bad dream, captain?" Van asked.

BAEN BOOKS by HARRY TURTLEDOVE
The Fox novels:

Wisdom of the Fox
King of the North
Fox and Empire

The Case of the Toxic Spell Dump
Down in the Bottomlands
Thessalonica
Alternate Generals (editor)

WISDOM
Of
The FOX

Harry Turtledove

WISDOM OF THE FOX

This book was previously published in parts as *Werenight* copyright © 1994 and *Prince of the North* copyright © 1994 by Harry Turtledove.

A Baen Book

Baen Publishing Enterprises
P.O. Box 1403
Riverdale, NY 10471

ISBN: 0-671-57838-3

Cover art by Bob Eggleton
Map by Eleanor Kostyk

First printing, November 1999

Distributed by Simon & Schuster
1230 Avenue of the Americas
New York, NY 10020

Typeset by Stacksgraph, Newberg, OR
Printed in the United States of America

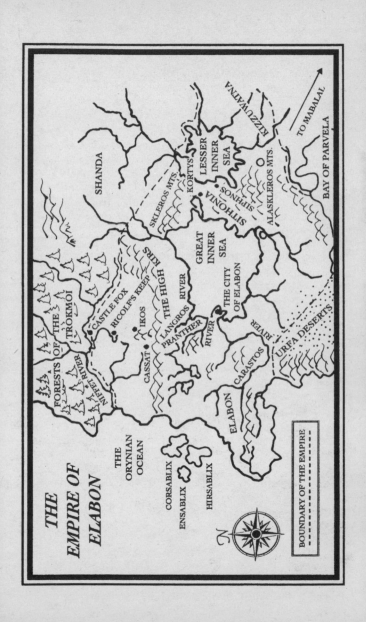

THE
EMPIRE OF
ELABON

BOUNDARY OF THE EMPIRE - - - - - - -

THE ORYNIAN OCEAN

CORSABLIX
ENSABLIX
HIRSABLIX

FORESTS OF THE TROKMOI

NIFFET RIVER

SHANDA

CASTLE FOX
RICOLF'S KEEP
IKOS
CASSAT

KIRS

THE HIGH

LANGROS RIVER
PRANTHER RIVER

SKLEROS MTS.

KORTYS

LESSER INNER SEA

SITHONIA

SIPHNOS

VINONIA

GREAT INNER SEA

THE CITY OF ELABON

ELABON

CARASTOS

RIVER

URFA DESERTS

ALASKLEROS MTS.

KIZZUWATNA

TO MABALAL

BAY OF PARVELA

WERENIGHT

I

"Duin, you're a damned fool if you think you can fight from horseback," Drago the Bear said, tossing a gnawed bone to his trencher.

Duin the Bold slammed his tankard down on the long table. Ale slopped over the rim. "Fool, is it?" he shouted, his fair face reddening. "You're the fool, you thickskulled muckbrain!"

Drago stormed up with an oath, murder in his eyes. His thick arms groped toward Duin. The slimmer man skipped back. His hand flashed to his swordhilt. Cries of anger and alarm rang through Castle Fox's great hall.

Gerin the Fox, baron of Fox Keep, sprang to his feet. "Stop it!" he shouted. The shout froze both angry men for a moment, giving their benchmates a chance to crowd between them. Drago sent one man flying with a shrug of his massive shoulders, but was brought up short by a grip not even his massive thews could break. Van of the Strong Arm grinned down at him. Almost a foot taller than the squat Bear, the outlander was every bit as powerfully made.

Gerin glowered at his fractious vassals, disgust plain in every line of his lean body. The men grew shamefaced under his glare. Nothing would have pleased him more than breaking both their stupid heads. He lashed them with his voice instead, snapping, "I called you here to fight the Trokmoi, not each other. The woodsrunners will be a tough enough nut to crack without us squabbling among ourselves."

"Then let us fight them!" Duin said, but his blade was back in its scabbard. "This Dyaus-damned rain has cooped us up here for ten days now. No wonder we're quarreling like so many snapping turtles in a pot. Turn us loose, lord Gerin!" To that even Drago rumbled agreement. He was not alone.

The Fox shook his head. "If we try to cross the River Niffet in this weather, either current or storm will surely swamp us. When the sky clears, we move. Not before."

1

Privately, Gerin was more worried than his liegemen, but he did not want them to see that. Since spring he'd been sure the northern barbarians were planning to swarm south over the Niffet and ravage his holding. He'd decided to strike first.

But this downpour—worse than any he could remember in all his thirty years on the northern marches of the Empire of Elabon—balked his plans. For ten days he'd had no glimpse of sun, moons, or stars. Even the Niffet, a scant half mile away, was hard to spy.

Rumor also said the Trokmoi had a new wizard of great power. More than once, the baron had seen fell lights dancing deep within the northern forests. His ever-suspicious mind found it all too easy to blame the Trokmê mage for the rude weather.

Duin started to protest further. Then he saw the scar over Gerin's right eye go pale: a sure danger signal. The words stayed bottled in his throat. He made sheepish apologies to Drago, who frowned but, under Gerin's implacable gaze, nodded and clasped his hand.

As calm descended, the baron took a long pull at his own ale. It was late. He was tired, but he was not eager for bed. His chamber was on the second floor, and the roof leaked.

Siglorel Shelofas' son, when sober the best Elabonian wizard north of the High Kirs, had set a five-year calking spell on it only the summer before, but the old sot must have had a bad day. Water trickled through the roofing and collected in cold puddles on the upper story's floor. Spread rushes did little to soak it up.

Gerin plucked at his neat black beard. He wished for carpets like those he had known in his younger days south of the mountains. Study was all he'd lived for then, and the barony the furthest thing from his mind. He remembered the fiasco that had resulted when exasperation drove him to try the book of spells he'd brought north from the capital.

History and natural lore had always interested him more than magecraft. His studies at the Sorcerers' Collegium began late and, worse, were cut short after fewer than a hundred days: a Trokmê ambush took both his father and elder brother, leaving him the unexpected master of Fox Keep.

In the eight years since, he'd had little cause to try wizardry. His skill was not large. Nor did age improve it: his incantation raised nothing but a cloud of stinking black smoke and his vassals' hackles. On the whole, he counted himself lucky. Amateur wizards who played with forces stronger than they could control often met unpleasant ends.

A snatch of drunken song made him look up. Duin and Drago sat with their arms round each other's shoulders, boasting of the havoc they would wreak among the Trokmoi when the cursed weather finally cleared. The baron was relieved. They were two of his stoutest fighting men.

He drained his mug and rose to receive the salutes of his vassals. Head buzzing slightly, he climbed the soot-grimed oak stairway to his bedchamber. His last waking thought was a prayer to Dyaus for fair weather so he could add another chapter to the vengeance he was taking on the barbarians. . . .

A horn cried danger from the watchtower, tumbling him from his bed with the least ceremony imaginable. He cursed the bronzen clangor as he stumbled to a window. "If that overeager lackwit up there is tooting for his amusement, I'll have his ears," he muttered to himself. But the scar over his eyes throbbed and his fingers were nervous in his beard. If the Trokmoi had found a way to cross the Niffet in the rain, no telling how much damage they might do.

The window was only a north-facing slit, intended more for shooting arrows than sight. The little Gerin saw was enough. Jabbing forks of lightning revealed hand after hand of Trokmoi, all searching for something to carry off or, failing that, to burn. The wind blew snatches of their lilting speech to his ears.

"May the gods fry you, Aingus, you tricky bastard, and your pet wizard too," Gerin growled. He wondered how the Trokmê chieftain had got so many men across the river so fast. Then he raised his eyes further and saw the bridge bulking impossibly huge over the Niffet.

It had to be sorcerous: a silvery band of light leading from the northern woods into Gerin's holding. It had not been there when the baron went to his rest. As he watched, Trokmê nobles poured over it in their chariots, retainers loping beside them. Once long ago, Gerin thought, he had read something of such spans. He could not recall where or when, but the half-memory sent a pang of fear icing up his spine.

No time for such worries now. He hurled himself into trousers and hobnailed sandals, buckled on his sword, and rushed down dim-lit passageway and creaking stair to the great hall, where his vassals had hung their corselets when they arrived. That hall was a swearing jumble of men donning bronze-faced leather cuirasses and kilts, strapping on greaves, jamming pot-shaped helms onto their heads, and fouling each other as they waved spears in the air. Like Gerin, most had skin that took the sun well and dark hair and eyes, but a few freckled faces and light beards told of northern blood—Duin, for one, was fair as any Trokmê.

"Ho, captain!" Van of the Strong Arm boomed. "Thought you'd never get here!"

Even in the rowdy crew Gerin led, Van stood out. Taller than the Fox's six feet by as many inches, he was broad enough not to look his height. A sword-cut creased his nose and disappeared into the sun-colored mat of beard covering most of his face. Little hellish lights flickered in his blue eyes.

His gear was as remarkable as his person, for his back-and-breast was cast of two solid pieces of bronze. Not even the Emperor had a finer one. Unlike the businesslike helms his comrades wore, Van's was a fantastic affair with a scarlet horsehair plume nodding above his head and leather cheekpieces to protect his face. Looking more war-god than man, he shook a spear like a young tree.

If his tale was true, he'd been trying to cross the Trokmê forests from north to south, and had all but done it till he fell foul of Aingus' clan. But he'd escaped them too, and had enough left in his giant frame to swim the Niffet, towing his precious armor behind him on a makeshift raft.

His strength, bluff good humor, and wide-ranging stories (told in the forest tongue until he learned Elabonian) had won him a home at Fox Keep for as long as he wanted to stay. But when Gerin asked him his homeland, he politely declined to answer. The Fox did not ask twice; if Van did not want to talk, it was his affair. That had been only two years ago, Gerin thought with a twinge of surprise. He had trouble remembering what life had been like without his burly friend at his side.

The Fox's own armor was of the plainest, leather much patched, plates battered and nicked. The leather was firm and supple, though, and every plate sound. To Gerin's way of thinking, the figure he cut was less important than staying alive himself and putting a quick end to his foes.

The warriors wallowed through thick mud to the stables. It squelched underfoot, trying to suck their sandals and boots into its cold, slimy mouth. The chaos was worse inside the stables, as boys tried to hitch unwilling horses to their masters' chariots.

Gerin strung his bow and stowed in on the right side of his car next to his quiver; on the left went an axe. Like many of the Fox's vassals, Van affected to despise the bow as an unmanly weapon. He bore sword, dagger, and a wickedly spiked mace on his belt.

His shield and the Fox's, yard-wide discs of bronze-faced wood and leather, topped the car's low sidewalls when put in their brackets. Gerin's was deliberately dull, Van's burnished bright. Despite their contrasting styles, the two formed one of the most feared teams on the border.

Gerin's driver, a gangling youth named Raffo, leaped into the chariot. A six-foot shield of heavy leather was slung on a baldric over his left shoulder. It gave Gerin cover from which to shoot. Taking up the reins, Raffo skillfully picked his way through the confusion.

After what seemed far too much time to the Fox, his men gathered in loose formation just behind the gatehouse. Shrieks from beyond the keep told plain as need be that the Trokmoi were plundering his serfs. Archers on the palisade kept up a sputtering duel with the barbarians, targets limited to those the lightning showed.

At Gerin's shouted command, the gatehouse crew flung wide the strong-hinged gates and let the drawbridge thump down. The chariots lumbered into action, trailing mucky wakes. Van's bellowed oaths cut off in midword when he saw the bridge. "By my beard," he grunted, "where did it come from?"

"Magicked up, without a doubt." Gerin wished he were as calm as he sounded. No Trokmê hedge-wizard could have called that spell into being—nor could the elegant and talented mages of the Sorcerer's Guild down in the capital.

An arrow whizzing past his ear shattered his brief reverie. Trokmoi swarmed out of the peasant village to meet his men. They had no mind to let their looting be stopped. "Aingus!" they shouted, and "Balamung!"—a name the Fox did not know. The Elabonians roared back: "Gerin the Fox!" The two bands met in bloody collision.

A northerner appeared at the left side of the Fox's chariot, sword in hand. The rain plastered his long red hair and flowing mustaches against his head; he wore no helm. The reek of ale was thick about him.

Reading his mind was easy. Van would have to twist his body to use his spear, Raffo had his hands full, and Gerin, who had just shot, could never get off another arrow before the Trokmê's blade pierced him. Feeling like a gambler playing with loaded dice, the Fox snatched up his axe with his left hand. He drove it into the barbarian's skull. The Trokmê toppled, a look of outraged surprise still on his face.

Van exploded into laughter. "What a rare sneaky thing it must be to be left-handed," he said.

More barbarians were hustling stolen cattle, pigs, sheep, and serfs across the gleaming bridge to their homeland. The villeins had no chance against the northern wolves. Huddled in their huts against the storm and the wandering ghosts of the night, they were easy meat. A few had tried to fight. Their crumpled bodies lay beside their homes. Sickle, flail, and scythe were no match for the sword, spear, bow, and armor of the Trokmê nobles, though their retainers were often little better armed than the peasants.

Gerin almost felt pity as he drove an arrow into one of those retainers and watched him thrash his life away. He knew the northerner would have had no second thoughts about gutting him.

A few Trokmoi had managed to light torches despite the downpour. They smoked and sputtered in the woodsrunners' hands. The rain, though, made the thatched roofs and wattle walls of the cottages all but impossible to light.

With a wave and a shout, Gerin sent half his chariots after the pillagers. His own car was in the middle of the village when he shouted, "Pull up!"

Raffo obediently slowed. Gerin slung his quiver over his shoulder. He and Van slid their shields onto their arms and leaped into the mire. Raffo wheeled the horses and made for the safety of Fox Keep's walls. The chariot-riders not chasing looters followed the Fox to the ground. Panting footsoldiers rushed up to stiffen their line.

A Trokmê sprang on the baron's back before he could find his footing in the mud. His bow flew from his hand. The two struggling men fell together. The barbarian's dagger sought Gerin's heart, but was foiled by his cuirass. He jabbed an elbow into the Trokmê's unarmored middle. The fellow grunted and loosened his grasp.

Both men scrambled to their feet. Gerin was quicker. His foot lashed out in a roundhouse kick. The spiked sole of his sandal ripped away half the Trokmê's face. With a dreadful wail, the marauder sprawled in the ooze, his features a gory mask.

Duin the Bold thundered by on a horse. Though his legs were clenched round its barrel, he still wobbled on the beast's bare back. Since a rider did not have both hands free to use a bow and could not deliver any sort of spearthrust without going over his horse's tail, Gerin thought fighting from horseback a foolish notion.

But his fierce little vassal clung to the idea with the tenacity of a bear-baiting dog. Duin cut down one startled Trokmê with his sword. When he slashed at another, the northerner ducked under his stroke and gave him a hefty push. He fell in the mud with a splash. The horse fled. The Trokmê was bending over his prostrate victim when an Elabonian with a mace stove in his skull from behind.

Van was in his element. Never happier than when on the field, he howled a battle song in a language Gerin did not know. His spear drank the blood of one mustachioed barbarian. Panther-quick, he brought its bronze-shod butt back to smash the teeth of another raider who thought to take him from behind.

A third Trokmê rushed at him with an axe. The barbarian's wild swipe went wide, as did Van's answering thrust. The impulse of the blows left them breast to breast. Van dropped his spear and seized the barbarian's neck with his huge fist. He shook him once, as a dog does a rat. Bones snapped. The Trokmê went limp. Van flung him aside.

Gerin did not share his comrade's red joy in slaughter. The main satisfaction he took from killing was the knowledge that the shuddering corpse at his feet was one enemy who would never trouble him again. As far as he could, he stood aloof from his fellow barons' internecine quarrels. He fought only when provoked, and was fell enough to be provoked but seldom.

Toward the Trokmoi, though, he bore a cold, bitter hatred. At first, it had been fueled by the slaying of his father and brother, but now revenge was only a small part of it. The woodsrunners lived only to destroy. All too often, his border holding tasted of that destruction as it shielded the softer, more civilized southlands from the sudden bite of arrows and the baying of barbarians in the night.

Almost without thinking, he ducked under a flung stone. Another glanced from his helmet and filled his head with a brief shower of stars. A spear grazed his thigh; an arrow pierced his shield but was turned by his corselet.

His archers shot back, filling the air with death. Spouting bodies disappeared in the mud, to be trampled by friend and foe alike. The Trokmoi swarmed round Gerin's armored troopers like snarling wolves round bears, but little by little they were driven back from the village toward their bridge. Their chieftains fought back, making fierce charges across the Fox's fertile wheatfields, crushing his men beneath the flailing hooves of their woods ponies, sending yard-long arrows through cuirasses into soft flesh, and lopping off arms and heads with their great slashing swords.

At their fore was Aingus. He had led his clan for nearly as long as Gerin had been alive, but his splendid red mustachioes were unfrosted. Almost as tall as Van, if less wide through the shoulders, he was proud in gilded armor and wheel-crested bronze helm. Golden fylfots and the ears of men he had slain adorned his chariot. His right hand held a dripping sword, his left the head of an Elabonian who had tried to stand against him.

His long, knobby-cheekboned face split in a grin when he spied Gerin. "It's himself himself," he roared, "come to be corbies' meat like his father. Thinking to be a man before your ape of a friend, are you, laddie?" His Elabonian was fluent enough, though flavored by his own tongue.

Van shouted back at him; Gerin, silent, set himself for the charge. Aingus swung up his sword. His driver, a gaunt, black-robed man the Fox did not know, whipped his beasts forward.

On came the chariot, its horses' hooves pounding like doom. Gerin was lifting his shield to beat back Aingus' first mighty stroke when Van's spear flashed over his shoulder and took one of the onrushing ponies full in the chest.

With the awful scream only wounded horses make, the shaggy pony reared and then fell. It dragged its harness-mate down with it. The chariot overturned and shattered, sending one wheel flying and spilling both riders into the muck.

Gerin ran forward to finish Aingus. The Trokmê lit rolling and rushed to meet him. "A fine thing will your skull be over my gate," he shouted. Then their blades joined with a clash of sparks and there was no more time for words.

Slashing and chopping, Aingus surged forward, trying to overwhelm his smaller foe at the first onset. Gerin parried desperately. Had any of the Trokmê's cuts landed, he would have been cut in two. When Aingus' blade bit so deep into the edge of his shield that it stuck for a moment, the Fox seized the chance for a thrust of his own. Aingus knocked the questing point aside with a dagger in his left hand; he had lost his bloody trophy when the chariot foundered.

The barbarian would not tire. Gerin's sword was heavy in his hands, his battered shield a lump of lead on his arm, but Aingus only grew stronger. He was bleeding from a cut under his chin and another on his arm, but his attack never slowed.

Crash! Crash! An overhand blow smashed the Fox's shield to kindling. The next ripped through his armor and drew a track of fire down his ribs. He groaned and sank to one knee.

Thinking him finished, the Trokmê loomed over him, eager to take his head. But Gerin was not yet done. His sword shot up and out with all the force of his body behind it. The point tore out Aingus' throat. Dark in the gloom, his lifeblood fountained forth as he fell, both hands clutching futilely at his neck.

The baron dragged himself to his feet. Van came up beside him. There was a fresh cut on his forearm, but his mace dripped blood and brains and his face was wreathed in smiles. He brandished the gory weapon and shouted, "Come on, captain! We've broken them!"

"Is it to go through me you're thinking?"

Gerin's head jerked up. The Trokmê voice seemed to have come from beside him, but the only northerner within fifty yards was Aingus' scrawny driver. He wore no armor under his sodden robes and carried no weapon, but he strode forward with the confidence of a demigod.

"Stand aside, fool," Gerin said. "I have no stomach for killing an unarmed man."

"Then have not a care in the world, southron darling, for I'll be the death of you and not the other way round at all." Lightning cracked, giving Gerin a glimpse of the northerner's pale skin stretched drumhead tight over skull and jaw. Like a cat's, the fellow's eyes gave back the light in a green flash.

He raised his arms and began to chant. An invocation poured forth, sonorous and guttural. Gerin's blood froze in his veins as he recognized the magic-steeped speech of the dreaming river valleys of ancient Kizzuwatna. He knew that tongue, and knew it did not belong in the mouth of a swaggering woodsrunner.

The Trokmê dropped his hands, screaming, *"Ethrog, O Luhuzantiyas!"*

A horror from the hells of the haunted east appeared before him. Its legs, torso, and head were human, the face even grimly handsome: swarthy, hooknosed, and proud, beard falling in curling ringlets over broad chest. But its arms were the snapping chelae of a monster scorpion. A scorpion's jointed tail grew from the base of its spine, sting gleaming at the tip. With a bellow that should have come from the throat of a bull, the demon Luhuzantiyas sprang at Gerin and Van.

It was a nightmare fight. Quicker on its feet than any human, the demon used its tail like a living spear. The sting flashed past Gerin's face, so close that he caught the acrid reek of its poison. It scored a glittering line across Van's corselet. Those terrible claws chewed the outlander's shield to bits. Only a backward leap saved his arm.

He and Gerin landed blow after blow, but the demon would not go down, though dark ichor pumped from a score of wounds and one claw was sheared away. Not until Van, with a strength born of loathing, smashed its skull and face to bloody pulp with frenzied strokes of his mace did it fall. Even then it writhed and thrashed in the mire, still seeking its foes.

Gerin drew in a long, shuddering breath. "Now, wizard," he grated, "join your devil in the fiery pit that spawned it."

The Trokmê had put twenty or so paces between himself and the Fox. His laugh—an unclean chuckle that scraped across Gerin's nerves—made plain his lack of fear. "It's a strong man you are, lord Gerin the Fox"—the contempt he packed into that stung—"and this day is yours. But we'll meet again; aye, indeed we will. My name, lord Gerin, is Balamung. Mark it well, for you've heard it twice the now, and hear it again you will."

"Twice?" Gerin only whispered it, but Balamung heard.

"Not even remembering, are you? Well, 'twas three years gone by I came south, having it in mind to take up sorcery. You made me sleep in the stables, with the reeking horses and all, for some fatgut from the south and his party of pimps filled the keep all to bursting, you said. When the next time comes for me to sleep at Fox Keep—and 'twill be soon—I shan't bed in the stables.

"So south I fared, stinking of horsedung, and in Elabon the town only their hinder parts did the Sorcerers' Collegium show me. They called me savage, and that to my face, mind! After you, it's them to pay their price.

"For, you see, quit I didna. I wandered through desert and mountain, and learned from warlocks and grizzled hermits and squinting scribes who cared nought about a 'rentice's accent, so long as he did their bidding. And in a cave lost in the snows of the High Kirs, far above one of the passes the Empire blocked, I found what I had learned to seek: the Book of Shabeth-Shiri the sorcerer-king of Kizzuwatna long ago.

"Himself had died there. When I took the Book from his dead fingers, he turned to a puff of smoke and blew away. And today the Book is mine, and tomorrow the northlands—and after that, the world is none too big!"

"You lie," Gerin said. "All you will own is a nameless grave, with no one to comfort your shade."

Balamung laughed again. Now his eyes flamed red, with a fire of their own. "Wrong you are, for the stars tell me no grave will ever hold me. They tell me more, too, for they show me the gates of your precious keep all beat to flinders, and that inside two turns of the bloody second moon."

"You lie," Gerin growled again. He ran forward, ignoring the pain that lanced up from his wound. Balamung stood watching him, hands on hips. The Fox lifted his blade. Balamung was unmoving, even when it came hissing down to cleave him from crown to breastbone.

The stroke met empty air—like the light of a candle suddenly snuffed, the wizard was gone. Gerin staggered and almost fell. Balamung's derisive laugh rang in his ears for a long moment, then it too faded. "Father Dyaus above!" the shaken Fox said again.

Van muttered an oath in an unknown tongue. "Well, captain," he said, "there's your warlock."

Gerin did not argue.

The Trokmoi seemed to lose their nerve when the sorcerer disappeared. Faster and faster they streamed over Balamung's bridge, their feet silent on its misty surface. Only a snarling rearguard held Gerin's men at bay. Those warriors slipped away to safety one by one. With deep-throated roars of triumph, the Elabonians swarmed after them.

Like a phantasm compounded of coils of smoke, the bridge vanished. Soldiers screamed as they plunged into the foaming Niffet, the bronze they wore for safety dragging them to a watery doom. On the shore, men doffed armor with frantic haste and splashed into the water to save their comrades. Jeering Trokmoi on the northern bank shot at victims and rescuers alike.

It took two men to save Duin. Impetuous as always, he had been farthest along the bridge when it evaporated, and he could not swim. Somehow he managed to stay afloat until the first rescuer reached him, but his grip was so desperate that he and his would-be savior both would have drowned had another swimmer not been nearby. A few others were also hauled out, but Balamung's trap took more than a dozen.

A plashing downstream made Gerin whirl. Matter-of-fact as a river godlet, Drago the Bear came out of the water, wringing his long beard like a peasant wench with her man's breeches. Incredibly, armor still gleamed on his breast.

If anyone could survive such a dip, thought Gerin, it would be Drago. He was strong as an ox and lacked the imagination to let anything frighten him. "Nasty," he rumbled in a voice like falling trees. He might have been talking about the weather.

"Aye," an abstracted Gerin muttered. At the instant the bridge had melted away, the rain stopped. Pale, dim Nothos, nearing full, gleamed in a suddenly star-flecked sky, while ruddy Elleb, now waning toward third quarter, was just beginning to wester. The other two moons, golden Math and quick-moving Tiwaz, were both near new and hence invisible.

Hustling along a doubled handful of disheveled prisoners, most of them wounded, the weary army trudged back to the keep. Gerin's serfs met them at the village. They shouted thanks for having their crops, or most of them, saved. Their dialect was so rustic that even Gerin, who had heard it since birth, found it hard to follow.

Gerin ordered ten oxen slaughtered, laying the fat-wrapped thighbones on the altars of Dyaus and the war-god Deinos which stood in his great hall. The rest of the meat vanished into his men. To wash it down, barrel after barrel of smooth, foaming ale and sweet mead was broached and emptied. Men who found combat raising a different urge pursued peasant wenches and servant wenches, many of whom preferred being chased to chaste.

At first the baron did not join the merrymaking. He applied an ointment of honey, lard, and astringent herbs to his wound (luckily not deep), and winced at its bite. Then he had the brightest-looking captive, a tall mournful blond barbarian who kept his left hand clutched to a torn right shoulder, bandaged and brought into a storeroom.

While two troopers stood by with drawn swords, Gerin cleaned his nails with a dagger from his belt. He said nothing.

The silence bothered the Trokmê, who fidgeted. "What is it you want of me?" he burst out at last. "It's Cliath son of Ailech I am, of a house noble for more generations than I have toes and fingers, and no right at all do you have to treat me like some low footpad."

"What right have you," Gerin asked mildly, "to rob and burn my land and kill my men? I could flay the hide off your carcass in inch-wide strips and give it to my dogs to eat while what was left of you watched, and no one could say I did not have the right. Thank your gods Wolfar did not catch you; he would do it. But tell me what I need to know, and I will set you free. Otherwise"—his eyes flicked to the two hard men by him—"I'll walk out this door, and ask no questions after."

One of Cliath's eyes was swollen shut. The other peered at the Fox. "What would keep you from doing that anyway, once I've talked?"

Gerin shrugged. "I've held this keep almost eight years. Men on both side of the Niffet know what my word is worth. And on this you have that word: you'll get no second chance."

Cliath studied him. The Trokmê made as if to rub his chin, but grimaced in pain and stopped. He sighed. "What would you know of me, then?"

"Tell me this: what do you know of the black-robed warlock who calls himself Balamung?"

"Och, that kern? Till this raid it's little I've had to do with him, and wanted less. It's bad cess for any man to have truck with a wizard, say I, for all he brings loot. No glory in beating ensorceled foes is there, no more than in cutting the throat of a pig, and it tied, too. But those who go with Balamung grow fat, and the few as stand against him die, and in ways less pretty than having the skins of them flayed off. I mind me of one fellow—puir wight!—who no slower than a sneeze was naught but a pile of twisty, slimy worms—and the stench of him!

"Nigh on a year and a half it is since the wizard omadhaun came to us, and for all we're friends now with

Bricriu's clan and thieving Meriasek's, still I long for the days when a man could take a head without asking the leave of a dried-up little turd like Balamung. Him and his dog-futtering talisman!" The Trokmê spat on the hard-packed dirt floor.

"Talisman?" Gerin prompted.

"Aye. With my own eyes I've seen it. 'Tis squarish, perhaps as long as my forearm, and as wide, but not near so thick, you understand, and opening out to double that. And when he'd fain bewitch someone or magic up something, why, the talisman lights up almost like a torch. With my own eyes I've seen it," Cliath repeated.

"Can you read?" the baron asked.

"No, nor write, no more than I can fly. Why in the name of the gods would you care to know that?"

"Never mind," Gerin said. "I know enough now." *More than I want,* he added to himself: Bricriu's clan and Meriasek's had been at feud since the days of their grandfathers.

The Fox tossed his little knife to the barbarian, who tucked it into the top of one of his high rawhide boots. Gerin led him through the main hall, ignoring his vassals' stares. He told his startled gatekeepers to let Cliath out, and said to him, "How you cross the river is your affair, but with that blade perhaps you won't be waylaid by my serfs."

Good eye shining, Cliath held out his left hand. "A puir clasp, but I'm proud to make it. Och, what a clansmate you'd have been."

Gerin took the offered hand but shook his head. "No, I'd sooner live on my own land than take away my neighbor's. Now go, before I think about the trouble I'm giving myself by turning you loose."

As the northerner trotted down the low hill, Gerin was already on his way back to the rollicking great hall, a frown on his face. Truly Deinos was coursing his terrible warhounds through the northern forests, and the baron was the game they sought.

After he had downed five or six tankards, though, things looked rosier. He staggered up the stairs to his room, arm round the waist of one of his serving wenches. But even as he cupped her soft breasts later, part of his mind saw Castle Fox a smoking ruin, and fire and death all along the border.

II

He woke some time past noon. By the racket coming from below, the roistering had never ceased. Probably no one was on the walls, either, he thought disgustedly; could Balamung have roused his men to a second attack, he would have had Fox Keep in the palm of his hand.

The girl was already gone. Gerin dressed and went down to the great hall, looking for half a dozen of his leading liegemen. He found Van and Rollan the Boar-Slayer still rehashing the battle, drawing lines on the table in sticky mead. Fandor the Fat had a beaker of mead, too, but he was drinking from it. That was his usual sport; his red nose and awesome capacity testified to it. Drago was asleep on the floor, his body swathed in furs. Beside him snored Simrin Widin's son. Duin was nowhere to be found.

The Fox woke Simrin and Drago and bullied his lieutenants up the stairs to the library. Grumbling, they found seats round the central table. They stared suspiciously at the shelves full of neatly pigeonholed scrolls and codices bound in leather and gold leaf. Most of them were as illiterate as Cliath and held reading an affectation, but Gerin was a good enough man of his hands to let them overlook his eccentricity. Still, the books and the quiet overawed them a bit. The baron would need that today.

He scratched his bearded chin and remembered how horrified everyone had been when, after his father was killed, he'd come back from the southlands clean-shaven. Duin's father, dour old Borbeto the Grim, had managed the barony till his return. When he saw Gerin, he'd roared, "Is Duren's son a fancy-boy?" Gerin had only grinned and answered, "Ask your daughter"; shouts of laughter won his vassals to him.

Duin wandered in, still fumbling at his breeches. Bawdy chuckles greeted him. Fandor called, "Easier to stay on a lass than a horse, is it?"

"It is, and more fun besides," Duin grinned, plainly none the worse for his dunking. He turned to Gerin, sketched a salute. "What's on your mind, lord?"

"Among other things," Gerin said drily, "the bridge that was almost your end."

"Downright uncanny, I call it," Rollan murmured. He spoke thickly, for his slashed lip had three stitches holding it shut. Tall, solid, and dark, he ran his fief with some skill, fought bravely, and never let a new thought trouble his mind.

"Me, I have no truck with wizards," Drago said righteously. He sneezed. "Damn! I've taken cold." He went on, "There's no way to trust a body like that. Noses always in a scroll, think they're better than simple folk."

"Remember where you are, fool," Simrin Widin's son hissed.

"No offense meant, of course, lord," Drago said hastily.

"Of course." Gerin sighed. "Now let me tell you what I learned last night." The faces of his men grew grave as the tale unfolded, and there was a silence when he was through.

Duin broke it. Along with his auburn hair, his fiery temper told of Trokmê blood. Now he thumped a fist down on the table and shouted, "A pox on wizardry! There's but one thing to do about it. We have to hit the whoreson before he can hit us again, this time with all the northmen, not just Aingus' clan."

A mutter of agreement ran down the table. Gerin shook his head. This was what he had to head off at all costs. "There's nothing I'd like better," he lied, "but it won't do. On his home ground, their mage would squash us like so many bugs. But from what the braggart said, we have some time. What I'd fain do is go south to the capital and hire a warlock from the Sorcerers' Collegium there so we can fight magic with magic. I don't relish leaving Fox Keep under the axe, but the task is mine, for I still have connections in the southlands. We can settle Balamung properly once I'm back."

"It strikes me as a fool's errand, lord," Duin said, plainspoken as always. "What we need is a good, hard stroke now—"

"Duin, if you want to beard that wizard without one at your back, then you're the fool. If you had to take a keep with a stone-thrower over its gate, you'd find a stone-thrower of your own, wouldn't you?"

"I suppose so," Duin said. His tone was surly, but there were nods round the table. Gerin was relieved. He was coming to the tricky part. With a little luck, he could slip it by them before they noticed.

"Stout fellow!" he said, and went on easily, "Van will need your help here while I'm gone. With him in charge, nothing can go too badly wrong."

It didn't work. Even Fandor and Simrin, both of whom had kept those noses buried in their drinking jacks till now, jerked up their heads. Diffidently, Rollan began, "Begging your pardon, my lord—" and Gerin braced for insubordination. It came fast enough: "The gods know Van of the Strong Arm has proven himself a man, time and again, and a loyal and true vassal as well. But for all that, he is an outlander and owns no land hereabouts, guesting with you as he does. It'd be downright unseemly for us, whose families have held our fiefs for generations, to take orders from him."

Gerin gathered himself for an explosion. Before he loosed it, he saw all the barons nodding their agreement. He caught Van's eyes; the outlander shrugged. Tasting gall, the Fox yielded with as much grace as he could. "If that's how you would have it, so be it. Van, would it please you to ride with me, then?"

"It would that, captain," Van said, coming as close as he ever did to Gerin's proper feudal title. "I've never been south of the Kirs, and I've heard enough about Elabon's capital to make me want to see it."

"Fine," Gerin said. "Duin, you have the highest standing of any here. Do you think you can keep things afloat while I'm away?"

"Aye, or die trying."

Gerin feared the latter, but merely said, "Good!" and whispered a prayer under his breath. Duin was more than doughty enough and not stupid, but he lacked common sense.

Drago and Rollan decided to stay at Fox Keep themselves and leave the defense of their own castles to the vassal contingents they would send home; Gerin dared hope they might restrain Duin. After his other liegemen had gone, he spent a couple of hours giving Duin instructions on matters probable, matters possible, and as many matters impossible as his fertile mind could envision. He finished, "For Dyaus' sake, send word along the West March Road and the Emperor's Highway. The border barons must know of this, so they can ready themselves for the storm."

"Even Wolfar?"

"As his holding borders mine, news has to go through him anyway. But the slug happens to be out a-courting, and his man Schild, though he has no love for me, won't kill a messenger for the sport of it. Also, you could do worse than to get Siglorel here; he has the most power of any Elabonian wizard north of the Kirs, even if he is overfond of ale. Last I heard, he was in the keep of Hovan son of Hagop east of here, trying to cure Hovan's piles."

Duin nodded, hopefully in wisdom. He surprised Gerin by offering a suggestion of his own: "If you're bound to go through with this wizard scheme, lord, why not go to Ikos and ask the Sibyl for her advice?"

"You know, that's not a bad thought," Gerin mused. "I've been that way once before, and it will only cost me an extra day or so."

Next day he decided—not for the first time—that mixing ale and mead was a poor idea. The cool, crisp early morning air settled in his lungs like sludge. His side was stiff and sore. His head ached. The creaks and groans of the light wagon and steady pound of hooves on stone roadbed, sounds he usually failed to notice, rang loud in his ears. The sun seemed to have singled him out for all its rays.

Worst of all, Van was awake and in full song. Holding his throbbing head, Gerin asked, "Don't you know any quiet tunes?"

"Aye, several of 'em," Van answered, and returned to his interrupted ditty.

Gerin contemplated death and other delights. At last the song came to an end. "I thank you," he said.

"Nothing at all, captain." Van frowned, then went on, "I think yesterday I was too hellishly worn out to pay as much attention to what you were saying as I should. Why is it such a fell thing for Balamung to have got his claws on Shabeth-Shiri's book?"

The Fox was glad to talk, if only to dull the edge of

his own worry. "Shabeth-Shiri was the greatest sorcerer of Kizzuwatna long ago: the land where all wizardry began, and where it flourishes to this day. They say he was the first to uncover the laws behind their magic, and set them down in writing to teach his pupils."

"Now, that can't be the book Balamung was boasting of, can it?"

"No. I have a copy of that one myself, as a matter of fact. So does everyone who's ever dabbled in magic. It's not a book of spells, but of the principles by which they're cast. But, using those principles, Shabeth-Shiri worked more powerful warlockery than any this poor shuddering world has seen since. He made himself king as well as mage, and he fought so many wars he ran short of men, or so the story goes. So he kept his rule alive by raising demons to fight for him, and by many other such cantrips. Think how embarrassed an army that thought itself safe behind a stream would be to have it flood and drown their camp, or turn to blood—or to see Shabeth-Shiri's men charging over a bridge like the one Balamung used against us."

"Embarrassed is scarcely the word, captain."

"I suppose not. Shabeth-Shiri wrote down all his most frightful spells, too, but in a book he showed to no one. He meant it for his son, they say, but for all his wizardry he was beaten at last: all the other mages and marshals of Kizzuwatna combined against him, lest he rule the whole world. His son was killed in the sack of his last citadel, Shaushka—"

"Shaushka the Damned? That was his? I've seen it with my own eyes. It lies in the far north of Kizzuwatna, at the edge of the plains of Shanda, and the plainsmen showed it to me from far away: stark, dark, and dead. Nothing grows there to this day, even after—how many years?"

Gerin shuddered. "Two thousand, if a day. But the winners never found Shabeth-Shiri's body, or his book either, and sorcerers have searched for it from that day to this. The legends say some of its pages are of human skin. It glows with a light of its own when its master uses it." The baron shook his head. "Cliath saw it, sure as sure."

"A nice fellow, this Shabeth-Shiri, and I think he'd be proud of the one who has his Book now. It seems all

Kizzuwatnans have a taste for blood, though," Van said. "Once when I was traveling with the nomads—" Gerin never found out about the Kizzuwatnan Van had fallen foul of, for at that moment two hurtling bodies burst from the oaks that grew almost to within bowshot of the road.

One was a stag, proud head now low as it fled. But it had not taken more than three bounds when a tawny avalanche struck it from behind and smashed it to the grass. Great stabbing fangs tore into its throat, once, twice. Blood spurted and slowed; the stag's hooves drummed and were still.

Crouched over its kill, the longtooth snarled a warning at the travelers. It settled its short hind legs under its belly and began to feed. Its stumpy tail quivered in absurd delight as it tore hunks of flesh from the stag's carcass. When the men stopped to watch, it growled deep in its throat and dragged its prey into the cover of the woods.

Van was all for flushing it out again, but Gerin demurred; like rogue aurochs, longtooths were best hunted by parties larger than two. Rather grumpily, Van put away his spear. "Sometimes, Gerin," he said, "you take all the fun out of life."

The Fox did not answer. His gloomy mood slowly cleared as the sun rose higher in the sky. He looked about with more than a little pride, for the lands he ruled were rich ones. And, he thought, the wealth they made stayed on them.

The lands between the Kirs and the Niffet had drawn the Empire of Elabon for their copper and tin and as a buffer between its heartland and the northern savages. Once seized, though, they were left largely to their own devices. Not a measure of grain nor a pound of tin did Elabon take from Gerin's land, or from any other borderer lord's. The Marchwarden of the North, Carus Beo's son, kept his toy garrison in Cassat under the shadow of the Kirs. So long as the borderers held the Trokmoi at bay, the Empire let them have their freedom.

Traffic on the great road was light so near the Niffet. The only traveler Gerin and Van met the first day was a wandering merchant. A thin, doleful man, he nodded gravely as he headed north. A calico cat with mismatched eyes and only one ear sat on his shoulder. It glared at Gerin as they passed.

When night began to near, the baron brought a brace of fowls from a farmer who dwelt by the road. Van shook his head as he watched his friend haggle with the peasant. "Why not just take what you need, like any lord?" he asked. "The kern is your subject, after all."

"True, but he's not my slave. A baron who treats his serfs like beasts of burden will see his castle come down round his ears the first time his crops fail. Serve him right, too, the fool."

After they stopped for the evening, Gerin wrung a hen's neck and drained its blood into a trough he dug in the rich black soil. "That should satisfy any roving spirits," he said, plucking and gutting the bird and skewering it to roast over the campfire.

"Any that wouldn't sooner drink *our* blood instead," Van said. "Captain, out on the plains of Shanda the ghosts have real fangs, and they aren't shy of watchfires. Only the charms the nomads' shamans magic up can keep them at bay—and sometimes not those, either, if most of the moons are dark. A bad place."

Gerin believed him. Any land that made his hard-bitten comrade leery sounded like a good place to avoid.

They drew straws for the first watch. Within seconds, Van was curled in his bedroll and snoring like a thunderstorm. Gerin watched Tiwaz and Math, both thin crescents almost lost in the skirts of twilight, follow the sun down to the horizon. As they sank, full Nothos rose. Under his weak grayish light, field and forest alike were half-seen mysteries. Small night-creatures chirped and hummed. Gerin let the fire die into embers, and the ghosts came.

As always, the eye refused to grasp their shapes, sliding away before they could be recognized. They swarmed round the pool of blood like great carrion flies. Their buzzing filled Gerin's mind. Some shouted in tongues so ancient their very names were lost. Others he almost understood, but no true words could be heard, only clamor and loss and wailing.

The Fox knew that if he tried to grasp one of the flittering shapes it would slip through his fingers like so much mist, for the dead kept but a pallid semblance of life. Grateful for the boon of blood, they tried to give him such redes as they thought good, but only a noise like the rushing wind filled his head. Had he not granted them that gift, or had the fire not been there, they likely would have driven him mad.

He kept watch until midnight, staring at stars and full Nothos and the half-seen shapes of spirits until Elleb, a copper disc almost half chewed away, was well clear of the dark woods on the horizon. No man disturbed him: few travelers were so bold as to risk moving in the dark of the sun.

When Gerin roused Van, he woke with the instant awareness of a seasoned warrior. "The ghosts are bad tonight," the baron mumbled, and then he was asleep.

Van announced the dawn with a whoop that jerked the Fox awake. Trying to pry his eyes open, he said, "I feel as if my head were filled with sand. 'Early in the morning' says the same thing twice."

"An hour this side of midday is counted as morning, is it not?"

"Aye, it is, and too bloody early in the bargain. Oh for the days when I was in the capital and not one of the wise men I listened to thought of opening his mouth before noon."

Gerin gnawed leathery journeybread, dried fruit, and smoked sausage, washing them down with bitter beer. He had to choke the bread down. The stuff had the virtue of keeping nearly forever, and he understood why: the bugs liked it no better than he.

He sighed, stretched, and climbed into his armor, wincing as his helm slipped down over one ear bent permanently outward by a northerner's club in a long-ago skirmish. "The birds are shining, the sun is chirping, and who am I to complain?" he said.

Van gave him a curious glance. "You feeling all right, captain?" he asked, a note of real concern in his voice.

"Yes and no," Gerin said thoughtfully. "But for the first time since I came back from the southlands, it doesn't matter at all. Things are out of my hands, and they will be for a while now. If someone pisses in the soup-pot, why,

Duin will just have to try and take care of it without me. It's a funny feeling, you know. I'm half glad to be free and half afraid things will fall apart without me. It's like running a long way and then stopping short: I've got used to the strain, and feel wrong without it."

They moved south steadily, but not in silence. Van extracted a clay flute from his kit and made the morning hideous with it. Gerin politely asked if he'd been taking music lessons from the ghosts, but he shrugged a massive shrug and kept on tweedling.

A pair of guardhouses flanked the road where it crossed from Gerin's lands to those of Palin the Eagle. Two sets of troopers sprawled in the roadway, dicing the day away. At the creak of the wagon, they abandoned the game and reached for their weapons.

Gerin looked down his long nose at the wary archers. "Hail!" he said. "Would that you'd been so watchful last summer, when you let Wacho and his brigands sneak south without so much as a challenge."

The guard captain shuffled his feet. "Lord, how was I to know he'd forged his safe-conduct?"

"By the hand of it, and the spelling. The lout could barely write. Too late now, but if it happens again you'll find a new lord, probably in the underworld. Do we pass your inspection?"

"You do that, lord." The guard waved the wagon on. Gerin drew sword as he passed the ancient boundary stone separating his holding from Palin's. Palin's guardsmen returned his salute. For long generations the two houses had been at peace. The stone, its timeworn runes covered by gray-green moss, had sunk almost half its height into the soft earth.

Once past the guards, Van turned and said to Gerin, "You know, Fox, when I first came to your land I thought Palin the Eagle had to be some fine warrior, to judge by what his folk called him. How was I to know they were talking of his nose?"

"He's no Carlun come again, I will say." Gerin chuckled. "But he and his vassals keep order well enough that I don't fear a night or so in the open in his lands, or perhaps with one of his lordlets."

"You don't want himself to guest you?"

"No indeed. He has an unmarried sister who must be rising forty by now and desperate, poor lass. Worse, she cooks for him too, and badly. The last time I ate with Palin, I thought the belly-sickness had me, not just a sour stomach."

When the travelers did stop for the night, it was at the ramshackle keep of one of Palin's vassals, Raff the Ready. A blocky boulder of a man, he was very much of the old school, wearing a forked beard that almost reached his waist. His unflappable solidity reminded the Fox of Drago; so, less hearteningly, did his disdain for cleanliness.

Withal, he set a good table. He had killed a cow that day, and along with the beef there was a stew of frogs and mussels from a nearby pond, fresh-baked bread, blueberries and blueberry tarts, and a fine, nutlike ale with which to wash them down.

Gerin sighed in contentment, loosened his belt, belched, and then, reluctantly, gave Raff his news. His host looked uneasy. He promised to spread the word. "You think your men won't be able to hold them at the Niffet, then?" he asked.

"I'm very much afraid they won't."

"Well, I'll tell my neighbors, not that it'll do much good. All of us are looking south, not north, waiting for the trouble in Bevon's barony to spill over into ours."

"There's fighting there?" Van asked hopefully.

"Aye, there is that. All four of Bevon's sons are brawling over the succession, and him not even dead yet. One of them ran twenty sheep off Palin's land, too, the son of a whore."

With that warning, they left early, almost before dawn. They carried a torch to keep the ghosts at bay. Even so, Gerin's skin crawled with dread until the spirits fled the rays of the sun.

He spent a nervous morning hurrying south through Bevon's strife-torn barony. Every one of Bevon's vassals kept his castle shut tight. The men on the walls gave Gerin and Van hard stares, but no one tried to stop them.

Around noon, they heard fighting down an approaching side road. Van looked interested, but Gerin cared far more about reaching the capital than getting drawn into an imbroglio not his own.

The choice did not stay in his hands. Two spearmen and an archer, plainly fleeing, burst onto the highway. The archer took one quick glance at Gerin and Van, shouted "More traitors!" and let fly. His shaft sailed between them, perhaps because he could not pick either one as target.

He got no second shot. Gerin had been sitting with bow ready to hand, and no confusion spoiled his aim. But even as the archer fell, his comrades charged the wagon. Gerin and Van sprang down to meet them.

The fight was short but savage. The footsoldiers seemed to have already despaired of their lives, and thought only of killing before they fell. Cool as usual in a fight, the Fox ducked under his foe's guard and slid the point of his blade between the luckless fellow's ribs. The man coughed blood and died.

The baron wheeled to help Van, but his friend needed no aid. A stroke of his axe had shattered his man's spearshaft, another clove through helm and skull alike. Only a tiny cut above his knee showed he had fought at all. He rubbed at it, grumbling, "Bastard pinked me. I must be getting old."

The triumph left the taste of ashes in Gerin's mouth. What fools the men of Elabon were, to be fighting among themselves while a storm to sweep them all away was rising in the northern forests! And now he was as guilty as any. Warriors who might have been bold against the Trokmoi were stiffening corpses in the roadway—because of him.

"Where you're going makes you more important than them," Van said when he voiced that worry aloud.

"I hope so." But in his heart, Gerin wondered if the southern wizards could withstand Balamung and the Book of Shabeth-Shiri.

He sighed with relief when at last he spied the guard-house of Bevon's southern neighbor, Ricolf the Red. He was not surprised to see it had a double complement of men.

The baron returned the greetings Ricolf's guardsmen gave him. He knew a few of them, for he had spent several pleasant weeks at Ricolf's keep on his last journey to the southlands. "It's been too long, lord Gerin," one of the guards said. "Ricolf will be glad to see you."

"And I him. He was like a second father to me."

"Peace be with you, wayfarers," Ricolf's man called as they drove past.

"And to you also peace." Van made the proper response, for he held the reins. He had been quick to pick up the customs of Gerin's land.

The sun was dying in the west and Gerin felt the first low keenings of long-dead wraiths when Ricolf's castle came into view, crowned by a scarlet banner. Somewhere high overhead, an eagle screamed. Van's sharp eyes searched the sky till he found the moving speck. "On our right," he said. "There's a good omen, if you care for one."

"I mislike taking omens from birds," Gerin said. "They're too public. Who's to say a foretelling is meant for him and not some lout in the next holding who has to squint to see it?"

A boy's clear voice floated from Ricolf's watchtower: "Who comes to the holding of Ricolf the Red?"

"I am Gerin, called the Fox, guest-friend to your master Ricolf, and with me is my friend and companion, Van of the Strong Arm. By Dyaus and Rilyn, god of friendship, we claim shelter for the night."

"Bide a moment." After a pause, Gerin heard Ricolf's deep voice exclaim, "What? Let them in, fool, let them in!" The drawbridge swung down. The lad cried, "In the names of Dyaus and Rilyn, welcome, guest-friend Gerin! Be you welcome also, Van of the Strong Arm."

Ricolf's keep, more sophisticated than Gerin's frontier fortress, had stone outwalls instead of a log palisade. Its moat was broad and deep; limp-looking plants splashed the slick surface of the water. A vile stench rose from the moat. Sinuous ripples made Gerin suspect water plants were not the only things to call it home.

Ricolf greeted his guests at the gatehouse. He was stout, perhaps fifty, with a square, ruddy face and blue eyes. His tunic and trousers were brightly checked and modish in cut, but the sword swinging at his belt was a plain, well-battered weapon that had seen much use. He had more gray in his red hair and beard than Gerin remembered, and lines of worry the Fox had not seen before bracketed his eyes and mouth.

When Gerin scrambled down from the wagon, Ricolf enfolded him in a bearhug, pumping his hand and thumping his back. "Great Dyaus above, lad, is it ten years? They've made a man of you! Ten years indeed, and us not living five days' ride from each other. This must never happen again!"

Untangling himself, Gerin said, "True enough, but I doubt if either one of us had a five-day stretch free and clear in all those years." He explained why he was traveling south. Ricolf nodded in grim comprehension. Gerin went on, "If what traders say is true, you've had your own troubles."

"I did, until I sent my unloving cousin Sarus to the afterworld this past winter," Ricolf agreed. He focused on Van. "Is this your new lieutenant? I thought what news I heard of him so much nonsense, but I see it was just the truth."

"My comrade, rather," Gerin said, and made the introduction. Van acknowledged it with grave respect. His broad hand, back thick-thatched with golden hair, swallowed Ricolf's in its clasp.

"I greet you as well, Van of the Strong Arm. Use my home as you own for as long as you would. Speaking of which"—Ricolf turned back to Gerin—"would you like to scrub off the dust of the road in my bath-house before we eat? You have the time, I think."

"Bath-house?" Gerin stared. "I thought I'd have to shiver in the streams or reek like a dungheap till I got south of the mountains."

Ricolf looked pleased. "So far as I know, I have the first up here. I had it put in last summer, when I sent messages to the unmarried barons of the north-country—and to some south of the Kirs, too—that any who thought himself worthy of my daughter Elise's hand should come here, to let me decide which man I thought most suited to her. My wife Yrse gave me no sons who lived, you know, nor have I hopes for any legitimate ones now, as I've no real intention of marrying again. I had three bastard boys, and one a lad of promise, too, but the chest-fever carried them off two winters back, poor lads, so when I die the holding passes to Elise and whomever she weds. Gerin, you must have got my invitation to join us; I know you're still wifeless."

"Yes, I did, but I had an arrow through my shoulder. It was a nasty one, and I was afraid the wound would rot if I traveled too soon. I sent my regrets."

"That's right, so you did. I remember now. I was truly sorry; you've done yourself a fine job since Duren and Dagref, er, died."

"It wasn't the trade I was trained for," Gerin shrugged. "My father always counted on Dagref; besides being older than me, he was a fighter born. Who would have thought the Trokmoi could get them both at once? I know my father never did. As for me, I'm still alive, so I suppose I haven't disgraced myself."

He changed the subject; remembering his father still hurt. "Now you'd better show me where that bath-house of yours is, before your dogs decide I'm part of the midden." He scratched the ears of a shaggy, reddish hound sniffing his ankles. Its tail switched back and forth as it grinned up at him, tongue lolling out. A half-memory flickered, but he could not make it light.

"Go away, Ruffian!" Ricolf snapped. The dog ignored him. "Beast thinks the place belongs to him," Ricolf grumbled. He took Gerin's arm and pointed. "Right over there, and I'll see to it your horses are tended."

Ricolf's tubs were carved limestone. The delicate frieze of river godlets and nymphs carved round them told Gerin they'd been hauled up from the south, for local gravers were less skilled. Soaking in steaming water, the Fox said, "Ricolf gives the suitors nothing but the finest. I never thought I'd feel clean again."

Van's bulk almost oozed out of the tub, but he grunted contented agreement. He asked, "What is this daughter of Ricolf's like?"

Gerin paused to rinse suds from his beard. "Your guess is as good as mine. Ten years back, she was small and skinny and rather wished she were a boy."

They dried off. Van spent a few minutes polishing imaginary dull places on his cuirass and combing the scarlet crest of his helm. Gerin did not re-don his own armor, choosing instead a sky-blue tunic and black breeches.

"With your gear, you could go anywhere," he said, "but I'd look a mere private soldier in mine. Even this is none too good; the southerners will doubtless have their hair all curled and oiled and wear those toga things they affect." He waved a limp-wristed hand. "And they talk so pretty, too."

"Don't have much use for them, eh, captain?"

Gerin smiled wryly. "That's the funniest part of it. I spent the happiest part of my life south of the Kirs. I'm a southerner at heart some ways, I suppose, but I can't let it show at Fox Keep."

Ricolf led them into his long hall. At the west end, a great pile of fat-wrapped bones smoked before Dyaus' altar. "You feed the god well," Gerin said.

"He has earned it." Ricolf turned to the men already at the tables. "Let me present the baron Gerin, called the Fox, and his companion Van of the Strong Arm. Gentlemen, we have here Rihwin the Fox—"

Gerin stared at the man who shared his sobriquet. Rihwin stared back, his clean-shaven face a mask. His smooth cheeks alone would have said he was from the south, but he also wore a flowing green toga and a golden hoop in his left ear. Gerin liked most southern ways, but he had always thought earrings excessive.

Ricolf was still talking. "Also Rumold of the Long Bow, Laidrad the Besieger, Wolfar of the Axe—"

Gerin muttered a polite unpleasantry. Wolfar, a dark-skinned lump of a man with bushy eyebrows, coarse black hair, and an unkempt thicket of beard that almost reached his swordbelt, was the Fox's western neighbor. They'd fought a bloody skirmish over nothing in particular two winters ago, before Wolfar went to seek Ricolf's daughter.

While Ricolf droned on, introducing more suitors and men of his household, Gerin got hungrier and hungrier. Finally Ricolf said, "And last but surely not least, my daughter Elise."

The baron was dimly aware of Van's sweeping off his helmet and somehow bowing from the waist in full armor. What Elise's long golden gown contained reminded him acutely of how much little girls could grow in ten years. He vaguely regretted she did not follow the bare-bodiced southern style, but the gown showed plenty as it was. Long brown hair flowed over her creamy shoulders.

Her laughing green eyes held him. "I remember you well, lord Gerin," she said. "When last you were here, you bounced me on your knee. Times change, though."

"So they do, my lady," he agreed mournfully.

He took a seat without much attention to his benchmates, and found himself between Rihwin and Wolfar. "Bounced her on your knee, forsooth?" Rihwin said, soft voice turning words in elaborate southern patterns. "I should be less than a truthteller were I to say some such idea had not crossed my mind at one time or another, and I daresay the minds of others here as well. And now we meet a man who has accomplished the fondest dreams of a double hand of nobles and more: in good truth, a fellow manifestly to be watched with the greatest of care."

He raised a mug in mocking salute, but Gerin thought the smile on his handsome face real. The baron drained his own tankard in return. Rihwin seemed to wince as he downed his ale; no doubt he preferred wine. Most southerners did, but grapes grew poorly north of the Kirs.

An elbow nudged Gerin's ribs. Wolfar grinned at him, displaying snaggled teeth. Gerin suspected he had wereblood in him. His hairiness varied marvelously as the moons whirled through the sky. Three years before, when Nothos and Math were full at the same time, a tale went round that he'd gone all alone into the forests of the Trokmoi and slain men with his teeth.

At the moment, he seemed civil—and civilized—enough. "How fare you, Fox?" he asked.

"Well enough, until now," Gerin answered smoothly. From the corner of his eye, he saw Rihwin cock an eyebrow in an expression he was more used to feeling on his own face than seeing on another. He felt he had passed an obscure test.

His belly was growling when the repast appeared. Ricolf's cooks did not have the spices and condiments the Fox had known south of the mountains, but the food was good and they did no violence to it. There was beef both roasted and boiled, fowls fried crisp and brown, mutton, ribs of pork cooked in a tangy sauce, creamy cheese with a firm, tasty skin, thick soup from the stockpot, and mountains of fresh-baked bread. Ricolf's good beer was an added delight. Serving wenches ran here and there, food-laden bronze platters in their hands, trying to keep ahead of the gobbling suitors.

Rihwin and one or two others discreetly patted the girls as they went by. Gerin understood their caution; it would not have done for a noble intent on marrying Ricolf's daughter to get one of his wenches with child. Van had no such worries. When a well-made lass came by, he kissed her and gave her a squeeze. She squealed and almost dropped her tray. Her face was red as she pulled away, but she smiled back at him.

The feasters tossed gnawed bones onto the hall's dirt floor, where Ricolf's dogs snarled and fought over them. Whenever the battles grew too noisy, a couple of cleaned-up serfs in stout boots toed the hounds apart. Even so, the din was overpowering.

So were the smells. The odors of dog and man vied with the smell of cooking meat. Smoke from the torches and the great hearth next to Dyaus' altar hung in a choking cloud.

Gerin ate until he could barely move, then settled back, replete and happy. Everyone rose as Elise made her exit, flanked by two maids. When she was gone, the serious drinking and gambling began.

Wolfar, Gerin knew, was a fanatic for dicing, but tonight, for some reason, he declined to enter the game. "I never bet in my life," he declared loftily, pretending not to hear the Fox's snort.

"I wish I could say that," a loser mourned as his bet was scooped up.

"Why can't you? Wolfar just did," Rihwin said. Gerin grinned at him with genuine liking. In the southlands the smooth insult was a fine art, one the baron had enjoyed but one too subtle for Castle Fox. Rihwin nodded back; maybe he had aimed the remark for Gerin's ears. It always warmed the Fox when a southerner born and bred took him for an equal. They were a snobbish lot on the other side of the Kirs. That Rihwin's target was Wolfar only made things more delightful.

Rihwin had a capacity for ale that belied his soft looks. Gerin valiantly tried to keep up, emptying his mug again and again until the room spun as he rose. His last clear memory was of Van howling out a nomad battlesong and accompanying himself with the flat of his blade on the tabletop.

To his surprise, the baron woke up the next morning in a bed. He had scant notion of how or when he'd reached it. Little wails of delight and Van's hoarse chuckle from the next room told him the outlander had not wasted his night sleeping.

The Fox found a bucket of cold water outside his door. He poured half of it over his head. Spluttering, he walked down the passageway and into the yard. He found Ricolf there, halfheartedly practicing with the bow. Though the older man had not tried to pace his guests, he looked wan.

"Does this sort of thing happen every night?" Gerin asked.

"The gods forbid! Were it so, I'd have been long dead. No, I plan to announce my choice tonight, and it would be less than natural if tension didn't build. For near a year I've seen these men—all but Sigiber the South, poor wight, who got a spear through his middle—in battle, heard them talk, watched them. Aye, my mind's made up at last."

"Who?"

"Can you keep it quiet? No, that's a foolish question; you could before, pup though you were, and it's not the sort of thing to change in a man. For all his affected ways—I know some call him 'Fop' and not 'Fox'—Rihwin is easily the best of them. After him, perhaps, would be Wolfar, but a long way back."

"Wolfar?" Gerin was amazed. "You can't mean it?"

"Aye, I do. I know of your trouble with him, but you can't deny he's a doughty warrior. He's not as slow of wit as his looks would make you think, either."

"He's a mean one, though. Once in hand-to-hand he almost bit my ear off." Something else occurred to the Fox. "What of your daughter? If the choice were hers, whom would she pick?"

It was Ricolf's turn for surprise. "What does that matter? She'll do as I bid her." He turned back to his archery.

Gerin was tempted to leave, but knew his old friend would think him rude to vanish on the eve of the betrothal. He spent the day relaxing, glancing at the couple of books Ricolf owned, and making light talk with some of the suitors.

Van emerged in the early afternoon, a smile on his face. The outlander was rubbing a callus on his right forefinger when he found Gerin. The baron remembered the heavy silver ring he'd worn there. Van explained, "It's only right to give the lassie something to remember me by."

"You, I don't think she's likely to forget."

"I suppose not," Van said happily.

A bit before sunset, a wandering minstrel appeared outside Ricolf's gate and prayed shelter for the night. The baron granted it, on condition that he sing after Elise's betrothal was announced. The minstrel, whose name was Tassilo, agreed at once. "How not?" he said. "After all, 'tis the purpose of a singer to sing."

The evening meal was like the one the night before. Tonight, though, Ricolf opened jugs of wine brought up from the south along with griffin-headed ivory rhytons and eared cups of finest Sithonian ware—beautiful scenes of hunting, drinking, and the deeds of the gods were painted under their glaze. Gerin's thrifty soul quailed when he thought of what Ricolf must have spent.

Rihwin, who seemed to expect his coming triumph and hadn't tasted the wine he loved in a year, began pouring it down almost faster than he could be served. He held it well at first, regaling his comrades with bits of gossip from the Emperor's court. Though this was a year old, most of it was new to Gerin.

The feasters finished. An expectant hush fell on the hall.

Just as Ricolf began to rise, Rihwin suddenly clambered onto the table. The boards creaked. Voice wine-blurred, Rihwin called out, "Ha, bard, play me a tune, and make it a lively one!"

Tassilo, who had looked at the bottom of his cup more than once himself, struck fiery music from his mandolin. Rihwin went into a northern dance. Gerin stared at him. He was sure Ricolf would not like this. But Rihwin found the jig too sedate. He shifted in midstep to a wild, stamping nomad dance.

Ricolf, watching the unmanly performance, looked like a man bathing in hellfire. He had all but beggared himself to provide the best for these men and make his holding as much like the elegant southland as he could. Was this his reward?

Then, with a howl, Rihwin stood on his hands and kicked his legs in the air in time to the music. His toga fell limply around his ears. He wore nothing under it.

At that spectacle, the maids hustled Elise from the hall. Gerin did not quite catch her expression, but thought amusement a large part of it.

In agony, Ricolf cried, "Rihwin, you have danced your wife away!"

"I could hardly care less," Rihwin said cheerfully. "Play on, minstrel!"

III

After that, there was little Ricolf could do. He tried to make the best of the fiasco by proclaiming to everyone that Wolfar of the Axe was his true choice as Elise's groom. Wolfar acknowledged his honor with a gracious grunt, which only disconcerted Ricolf more. There were scattered cheers, including a sardonic one from Rihwin.

Gerin muttered insincere congratulations to Wolfar. Then he left the feast, claiming he wanted to make an early start in the morning. That held just enough truth to make mannerly his escape from his enemy's triumph. Van had already disappeared with another wench and a jug of wine. Ignoring the raucous celebration in the great hall, Gerin blew out the little flame flickering from the middle fingertip of the hand-shaped clay lamp by his bed and fell asleep.

He woke to the sound of someone fumbling at the barred door. Elleb's crescent, just now topping the walls of Ricolf's keep, peeped through the east-facing slit window and sent a pale pink stripe of light across the bed to the door. Sunrise was still two or three hours away.

Head aching, Gerin groped for his clothes. He slid into trousers, but wrapped his tunic round his right arm for a shield. The fumbling went on. Knife in hand, he padded to the door and flung it open.

Whatever outcry he had intended clogged in his throat. "Great Dyaus, Elise, what are you doing here?" he gurgled. He almost had not known her. No longer was she gowned and bedecked. She wore stout boots, breeches, and a sheepskin jacket so baggy it all but hid her curves. A knife swung at her belt. Her long hair was tucked up under a shapeless leather traveler's hat.

For a long moment, she stared at the blade in his left hand. Its nicked edge glittered in the fading light of the hallway torches. Then she brushed past the stunned Fox and shut the door behind them. Voice low and fast, she said, "I need help, lord Gerin, and of all the men here, I think I can only ask it of you. I was willing to try my father's idiot scheme as long as I thought I had some chance of getting a husband I could endure, but Wolfar of the Axe—"

Gerin wished he had not drunk so much. His head still buzzed and his wits were slow. "All the northland knows I have no love for Wolfar, but what do you want of me?" he asked, already afraid he knew the answer.

She looked up at him, eyes enormous in the gloom. "I know you are going to the capital—take me with you! My mother was of a southern house, and I have kin there. I'd be no burden to you. I've been daughter and son both to my father, and I can live from the land like any warrior—"

"Don't you see I can't?" Gerin broke in. "It's impossible. What would my life be worth if someone were to find you here even now?" Alarmed at that, he added, "By the gods, where are your maids?"

"As soon as I knew my father had chosen Wolfar, I put a sleeping powder in their cups. The ninnies were still clucking over poor besotted Rihwin. He wasn't a bad fellow, for all his silly ways."

The baron felt a twinge of annoyance at her mentioning the drunken fool with kindness, but stifled it. He said, "That's one for you, then. But why won't Ricolf think I ran off with you against your will?"

"Nothing simpler: I left a note in my room saying just what I was doing, and why. There are things in it only he and I know; he'd not think it forced from me."

Gerin stared. Women who read and wrote were not of the ordinary sort. *Well*, he thought, *I've already found that out*. But he shook his head, saying, "You have all the answers, it seems. But answer me this: would you have me break the sacred oath of guest-friendship I hold with your father? No luck comes to the oath-breaker; gods and men alike turn from him."

She inspected him. Her eyes filled with tears. He felt himself flinch under her gaze. "You've forgotten the oath you gave me all those years ago, then?" she asked bitterly. "How old was I? Eight? Ten? I don't know, but I've remembered from then till now that you treated me like a real person, not just a brat underfoot. You swore if ever I needed you, there you would be. Is an oath less an oath because given to a child? Am I less a person because I have no beard? You called on Dyaus; by Dyaus, lord Gerin, could you see yourself wed to Wolfar, were you a woman?" The tears slid down her cheeks.

"No," he sighed, understanding what the truth meant but unable to lie to her.

"No more could I. I would sooner die."

"There's no need of that," he said, awkwardly patting her shoulder. He shrugged on the rolled-up tunic and climbed into his cuirass. "What sort of gear do you have?"

"No need to worry about that. I've already stowed it in your wagon."

He threw his hands in the air. "I might have known. You know, Van will call me nine different kinds of fool, and every one of them true, but you'll be useful to have around. You could talk a longtooth into eating parsnips.

"Wait here," he added, and stepped into the hall. He tried Van's door. It was barred. He swore under his breath. He was about to tap when the door flew open. Van loomed over him, naked as the day he was born. His mace checked its downward arc inches from the Fox's head.

"Captain, what in the five hells are you up to?" he hissed. Behind him, a woman made drowsy complaint. In the half-light, the curve of her hip and thigh made an inviting shadow on the bed. "It's all right, love," the outlander reassured her. She sighed and went back to sleep. Van turned to Gerin: "Don't come scratching round my door. It isn't healthy."

"So I see. Now will you put that fornicating thing down and listen to me?"

When the baron finished, there was nothing but astonishment on Van's face. He whistled softly. "I will be damned. Spend two years thinking a man stodgy and then he does this to you." His shoulders shook with suppressed mirth. "What are you standing here gawking for? Go on, get the horses hitched up; I'll be with you in a few minutes." Softly but firmly, he shut the door in Gerin's face.

Blinking, the baron retrieved Elise and hurried down the hallway. The only sounds were faint cracklings from the guttering torches and snoring from behind almost every door. Gerin thanked the gods for the flooring of rammed earth. On planking, the nails in his sandals would have clicked like the wooden snappers some Sithonian dancers wore on their fingers.

"How can I thank you?" Elise whispered. "I—" Gerin clamped a hand over her mouth: someone else was in the hall.

Wolfar, stumbling to his bed, had rarely felt better in his life. He had spent most of the night thinking of Gerin chopped into dogmeat after he took over Ricolf's lands as well as his own; Elise was a tasty baggage, too. Every other feaster had long since either lurched off to bed or slid under the table, but Wolfar, buoyed by visions of glory and mayhem, was still mostly himself after drinking them all down.

He gaped when Gerin appeared before him. "Ah, the Fox," he said jovially. "I was just thinking of you." His piggy eyes went wide when he saw the baron's companion.

Gerin saw Wolfar fill his lungs to shout. He snatched a dead torch from its dragon-headed bronze sconce and broke it over his rival's bald spot. Wolfar sank without a sound, mouth still open. Gerin and Elise darted for the stables, not knowing how long he would stay stunned.

They slowed once they got outside the castle. Attracting the gate crew's attention was the last thing they wanted.

The horses looked resentful as Gerin harnessed them. His fingers leaped over the leather straps. Each had to go in its proper place, lest the whole harness come apart. He expected an alarm at any moment. But the horses were hitched and Elise hidden under blankets in the back of the wagon, and all stayed quiet. Van, however, did not come. Gerin waited and worried.

A footfall in the doorway made him whirl. His hand leaped for his swordhilt, but that gigantic silhouette could only belong to one man. "What kept you?" the baron barked.

"Some things, a gentleman never hurries," Van said with dignity. "You laid Wolfar out cold as a cod; he'll have himself a ten-day headache. Now let's be off, shall we? Ah, you've already got a torch lit. Good. Here, start another. The light may keep the worst of the ghosts away. Or, of course, it may not. I know few men who've gone night-faring, and fewer still who came back again, but now it's a needful thing, I think."

He climbed aboard, took the reins, and set the horses moving. Harness jingling, they rode up to the gate. A couple of Ricolf's hounds sniffed about the wagon's wheels. Van flicked them away with his whip.

The gate guards made no move to let down the draw-bridge. They looked curiously at Van and Gerin. One asked, "Lords, why are you on your way so early?"

Van stopped breathing. It was a question for which he had no good answer. But Gerin only grinned a lopsided grin. He laughed at the guards and said, "I'm running away with Ricolf's daughter; she's much too good for any-one here."

The soldier shook his head. "Ask a question like that and you deserve whatever answer you get, I suppose. Come on, Vukov," he said to the other watchman, "let down the bridge. If they want to take their chances with the ghosts, it's their affair and none of mine."

Smothering a yawn, Vukov helped his comrade with the winch. The bridge slowly lowered, then dropped the last few feet with a thump. To Gerin, the clop of the horses' hooves on it seemed the loudest thing in the world.

Trying not to bellow laughter, Van wheezed and choked. Between splutters, he said, "Captain, that was the most outrageous thing I've ever seen! You've got to promise me you'll never, ever let me gamble with you. I have better things to do than throwing my money away."

"It's ill-done to lie in the house of a guest-friend. If his men choose not to believe, why, that's their affair and none of mine." Gerin shrugged, mimicking the guardsman.

As soon as they left the shelter of Ricolf's keep, the ghosts were on them, keening loss and shrieking resent-ment of any who still kept warm blood in their veins. Without the boon of blood to placate them, they sent an icy blast of terror down on the travelers.

The horses rolled their eyes, shying at things only they saw. Gerin stopped his ears with his fingers in a vain effort to shut out the ghosts' wails. He saw Van work his mas-sive jaw, but no word of complaint passed the outlander's lips. Elise, shivering, came up to sit with them under the scant protection the torches gave.

Ricolf's lands shot by in a gray blur, as if Van thought to outrun the ghosts by fleeing south. The horses did not falter; rather they seemed glad to run. False dawn was touching the east with yellow light when the wagon sped past the little guardpost Ricolf kept on his southern border. Gerin was not much surprised to see the guards curled up asleep inside; fire and blood warded them from the night spirits. They did not stir as the wagon clattered past.

The Fox had been looking back over his shoulder as long as he was in Ricolf's lands. When he saw how Van slowed their pace once past the border, he knew he had not been the only one to worry. He cocked an eyebrow at his friend. "For all his willingness to help carry off the lady," he said to no one in particular, "I seem to notice a certain burly accomplice of mine lacking a perfect faith in the power of her notes to soothe ruffled tempers."

"If all that noise means me," Van rumbled, "then you've hit in the center of the target. It would have been downright awkward to have to explain to a horde of warriors just what I was doing with their lord's daughter."

Elise made a face at him. She, at least, seemed confident there would be no followers. Gerin wondered what it took to put trust in someone unknown for a double handful of years. His mind stalked round the idea like a cat with ruffled fur. He was still astonished any pleading of hers could have convinced him to bring her along.

At last the sun touched the eastern horizon, spilling out ruddy light like a huge hand pouring wine from a jug. The ghosts gave a last frightened moan and returned to whatever gloomy haunts they inhabited during the day.

The morning wore on with no sign of anyone on Gerin's trail, but he still felt uneasy for no reason he could name. It could not have been the land. Save for the High Kirs, now a deep blue shadow on the southern skyline, nothing was much different from what he knew in his own barony.

Meadow and forest alternated, and if there were a few more elms and oaks and a few less pines and maples, that mattered little. The woods did grow closer to the road than the Fox would have liked: south of Ricolf's holding, the highway marked the boundaries of two barons said to be rivals, and to Gerin's way of thinking they should have kept the undergrowth well trimmed so no one could use it for cover.

Once a little stream wound close by the roadway. When Van pulled off to water the horses and let them rest for a few minutes, frogs and turtles leaped from mossy rocks and churned away in senseless terror, just as they would have near Fox Keep. No, the Fox thought as he stared back at a suspicious turtle, the land was not what troubled him.

The peasants seemed much the same, too. They lived in little villages of wattle and daub, the community oxen housed about as well as the people. Scrawny chickens picked around cottages and squawked warnings at dogs, who snarled back. Little naked herdboys guided flocks of sheep and cattle with sticks, helped by the shortlegged brown and white dogs native to the north country. Men and women in colorless homespun worked in the fields, as hard as the draft animals laboring with them.

Not until Gerin lifted his eyes to the keeps could he finger what troubled him. Castles crowned many hills, but here and there the banks of their moats were beginning to crumble into the water. Some lesser barons let stands of trees big enough to shelter scores of warriors grow almost within bowshot of their walls.

Gerin had no desire to claim shelter from any of these nobles. The few he saw on the road distressed him. Their chariots were decorated with inlays of gold and bright stones, but plainly had never seen combat. More than one man wore cloth instead of mail. What cuirasses were to be seen were covered with studs and curlicues of bronze: beautiful to look at, but sure to catch and hold a spearpoint.

The footsoldiers were not much better. They were well armed, but soft jaws and thick middles said they were unblooded troops. Behind the shield of the border, where the Trokmoi were always ready to pounce on the weak, Elabon's northern province was starting to rot.

Van saw it too. "This land is ripe for the taking," he said. Gerin could only nod.

The sun rose high and hot. Gerin felt the sweat trickle

down his back and chest. He wished he could scratch through his armor.

With fairer skin, Van suffered more, tanned though he was. He finally took off his proud helm and carefully stowed it in the back of the wagon, then poured over his head a bucket of cool water from the brook where they had stopped. He puffed and snorted as the water poured down his face and dripped through his beard. "Ahhh!" he said. "That's better, even if I do sound like a whale coming up for air."

"A whale?" Elise said. She had shed her jacket. In tunic and trousers, she was more comfortable than either of the men. Her hat she kept on, for her fairness was not like that of Van, who grew golden under the sun: she would burn and freckle and peel and never really tan at all. She went on, "I've heard the word. Some kind of fish, is it not? I've never seen one."

"Nor I," Gerin said. "The farthest I've traveled is to the capital, and there are no whales in the Inner Seas."

"Well, captain, I'll tell you—and you, my lady—I've seen whales right enough, and closer than I wanted, too. Do you know the land called Mabalal?"

Elise shook her head. Gerin said, "I've heard the name. It's far to the south and east, I think."

"That's the one, captain. And sultry—why, this is nothing beside what it's like there. I thought I'd melt like a lump of wax in a fire. The people are little and dark, and they seem to like it well enough. For all their swarthy hides, the women are not uncomely, and what they do—" Van abruptly broke off. Gerin was amused to see his huge friend could blush.

"But I was talking about whales," Van went on. "They come in all sizes, and the sailors like the little ones, and wouldn't think of harming them. But the big ones hate men, and sink whatever boats they can. Now, one of them had lived outside the harbor at Jalor—that's the capital thereabouts—for years, and he'd sunk maybe twenty ships. He had a reddish skin they knew him by, and they called him 'Old Crimson,' since crimson is the color their kings wear. Five times they'd tried to kill him, and neither of the two harpooners who lived was whole.

"It got so bad the captains wouldn't ship out of Jalor, and if they did they couldn't find a soul to man the oars. Didn't that put a pretty squeeze on the merchants! So they decided to have another go at him, and when one of their big traders, a fellow named Kariri, saw me in some dive, he thought I would make a good oarsman, having more in the way of muscle than his countrymen. I was game; things had been dull since I'd had to leave Shanda, and the price he promised was good. It had to be, to get rowers for that boat! Most of us were foreigners of one kind or another: the folk of Jalor knew better.

"So off we sailed, the only ship in the water, though the docks and beach were black with people watching. Now, in those part the way they lure whales is this: they catch a lot of fat tunny and pickle them with salt in big jars, and when they're nice and ripe, they soak rags in the fish-grease and dump 'em in the water where they think the whales are. The first thing any of us knew of Old Crimson being round was a sort of a loud hiss and a cloud of evil-smelling steam. Whales aren't like other fish. They have to come to the surface every so often to get a breath of air and blow out the old. That's what he'd done, not fifty yards to starboard.

"I tell you, I missed a stroke, and I wasn't the only one. Then he came all the way out of the water, and I never want to see such a sight again. That ruddy hide of his was all scarred and torn from the ships he'd sunk, and I saw three spearpoints stuck in just back of his head, but not deep enough to do more than drive him mad with pain over the years. I don't lie when I say I'd've sooner been elsewhere right then. He was bigger than our boat, and not by a little, either.

"But the harpooning crew knew what to do if they—and we—were going to come home alive. They tossed ten or twelve pounds of that pickled tunny toward the monster, and he snapped it up. It's a funny thing, but the stuff makes whales drunk, and Old Crimson lay still in the water. If he were a kitten, he would have purred.

"Once that happened, the harpooners slipped out of their clothes (not that they wore much, just rags round their middles) and swam over to him, quiet as they could. One trailed his barbed harpoon, the second a little stand for it, and the third, who had more brawn than most men of Mabalal, took a big mallet with him. They climbed up on Old Crimson's head, and he never stirred. We lay dead quiet in the water, for fear of rousing him.

"They set up the harpoon just aft of his head, right behind the others that hadn't gone deep enough to kill. Then the fellow with the mallet swung it up over his head and hit the butt end of the harpoon with everything he had. I swear by all the gods there are that the whale leaped clean out of the water, with the harpooners still clinging to him. They might have screamed, but we never would have heard them. We were backing water for all we were worth, but still I saw that great tail like a fist over the bow.

"When it came down, the ship just went all to splinters. I'm hazy about what happened next, because something hit me right between the eyes. I must have grabbed an oar; the next thing I remember is being fished out of the water by one of the little boats that came out as soon as the people on shore saw Old Crimson was really dead. Thirty-four people were on our boat when we set out, and six of us lived: only one of the harpooners, the fellow with the little stand.

"Anyway, the fishermen who rescued me took me to shore, and the Jalorians took the whale's carcass ashore too, for they valued the meat and oil of it. The head of the merchants' guild kissed all of us who had lived, and gave each of us a tooth worried out of the whale's head: I don't lie when I say it was more than half a foot long.

"But do you know what? I didn't make a copper more from it, for that fat merchant sitting on his arse on the shore just called me a filthy foreigner and wouldn't pay. For all that, though, I drank my way through the grogshops for ten days straight without touching a coin of my own, and to this day no one in Jalor knows how old Kariri's warehouses burned down."

"You know," Gerin said thoughtfully, "if they were to put a line on the end of their harpoons with floats—sealed empty casks, maybe—every hundred paces or so, they could spear their whales without having to climb onto them, and if the wound didn't kill on the spot, the whales couldn't escape by diving, either."

Van stared at him. "I do believe it'd work," he said at last. "Why weren't you there then to think of it? The gods know I never would have." He looked to Elise. "Gerin, I do believe our guest thinks my yarn would be good for making flowers grow, but not much else, though since she's kind as she is fair she's too polite to say so. Hold the reins a bit for me, will you?"

Elise started to protest, but Van was not listening to her. He stepped into the back of the wagon. Gerin heard him rummaging in the battered leather sack where he kept his treasures. After a minute or two, he grunted in satisfaction and emerged, handing Elise what he held.

Gerin craned his neck to look too. It was an ivory tusk unlike any he had ever seen: though no longer than the fang of the longtooth he knew, this was twice as thick, and pure white, not yellowish. Someone had carved a whale and the prow of an unfamiliar ship on the tooth; the whale was tinted a delicate pink.

Seeing the baron's admiration, Van said, "A friend of mine made it while I was out roistering. You'll notice it isn't done, but I got out of Jalor in a hurry, and he didn't have time to finish."

Elise was silent.

Gerin kept the reins. Van had been yawning all morning, and now he tried to snatch some sleep in the cramped rear of the wagon. The Fox was looking for one particular dirt track of the many joining the Elabon Way. Each path had a stone post set beside it, carved with the marks of the petty barons to whose keeps the roadlets ran. It was past noon before Gerin saw the winged eye he sought. He almost passed it by, for the carving was so ancient that parts of it had weathered away; startling red lichens covered much of what remained.

"Where are we going?" Elise asked when he turned down the track. She coughed as the horses kicked up dust.

"I thought you knew all my plans," Gerin said. "I'd like to hear what the Sibyl at Ikos tells me. I stopped there once before, when I went south for the first time, and she warned me I'd never be a scholar. I laughed at her, but two years later the Trokmoi killed my father and my brother, and I had to quit the southlands."

"That I had heard," Elise said softly. "I'm sorry." Gerin could feel the truth in her words. He was touched, and at the same time annoyed with himself for letting her sympathy reach him. He felt relieved when she returned to her original thought: "Where we go matters little to me; I simply didn't know. Any place away from Wolfar is good enough, though I've heard evil things of the country round Ikos."

"I've heard them too," he admitted, "but I've never seen much to make me think them true. This road goes over the hills and through some of the deepest forest this side of the Niffet before it reaches the Sibyl's shrine. It's said strange beasts dwell in the forest. I never saw any, though I did see tracks on the roadway that belong to no animals the outer world knows."

The more prosperous petty barons and their lands clung leechlike to the Elabon Way. A few hours' travel from it, things were poorer. Freeholders held their own plots, men not under the dominion of any local lordling. They were of an ancient race, the folk who had been on the land between the Niffet and the High Kirs even before the coming of the Trokmoi whom the Empire had expelled. Slim and dark, they spoke the tongue of Elabon fluently enough, but among themselves used their own soft, sibilant language.

The road narrowed, becoming little more than a winding rutted lane under frowning trees. The sinking sun's light could barely reach through the green arcade overhead. Gerin jumped when a scarlet finch shot across the roadway, taken aback by the flash of color in the gloom. As the sun set, he pulled off the road and behind a thick clump of trees.

He routed Van from his jouncing bed. Together they unharnessed the horses and let them crop what little grass grew in the shade of the tall beeches.

They had but a scanty offering for the ghosts: dried beef mixed with water. It was not really enough, but Gerin hoped it would serve. Elise wanted to take one watch. The Fox and Van said no in the same breath.

"Please yourselves," she shrugged, "but I could do it well

enough." A knife appeared in her hand and then, almost before the eye could see it, was quivering in a treetrunk twenty feet away.

Gerin was thoughtful as he plucked the dagger free, but still refused. Elise looked to Van. He shook his head and laughed: "My lady, I haven't been guarded by women since I was old enough to keep my mother from learning what I was up to. I don't plan to start over now."

She looked hurt, but said only, "Very well, then. Guard me well this night, heroes." He half-sketched a salute as she slipped into her bedroll.

Van, who was rested, offered to take the first watch. Gerin got under a blanket, twisted until he found a position where the fewest pebbles dug into him, and knew no more until Van prodded him awake. "Math is down, and— what do you call the fast moon? I've forgotten."

"Tiwaz."

"That's it. As well as I can see through the trees, it'll set in an hour or so. That makes it midnight, and time for me to sleep." Van was under his own blanket—the gold-and-black striped hide of some great hunting beast—and asleep with the speed of the experienced wanderer. Gerin stretched, yawned, and heard the ghosts buzz in his mind like gnats.

In the dim red light of the embers, the wagon was a lump on the edge of visibility, the horses a pair of dark shadows. Gerin listened to their unhurried breathing and the chirp and rustle of tiny crawling things. An owl overhead loosed its hollow, eerie call. Somewhere not far away, a small stream chuckled to itself. A longtooth roared in the distance, and for a moment everything else was quiet.

The baron turned at a sound close by. He saw Elise half-sitting, watching him. Her expression was unreadable. "Regrets?" he asked, voice the barest thread of sound.

Her answer was softer still. "Of course. To leave all I've ever known . . . it's no easy road, but one I have to travel."

"You could still go back."

"With Wolfar's arms waiting? There's no returning." She started to say more, stopped, began again. "Do you know why I came with you? You helped me once, long ago." Her eyes were looking into the past, not at Gerin. "The first time I saw you was the most woeful day of my life. I had a dog I'd raised from a pup; he had a floppy ear and one of his eyes was half blue, and because of his red fur I called him Elleb. He used to like to go out and hunt rabbits, and when he caught one he'd bring it home to me. One day he went out as he always did, but he didn't come back.

"I was frantic. I looked for two days before I could find him, and when I did, I wished I hadn't. He'd run down a little gully and caught his hind leg in a trap."

"I remember," Gerin said, realizing why the dog Ruffian had seemed familiar. "I heard you crying and went to see what the trouble was. I was heading south to study."

"Was I crying? I suppose I was. I don't remember. All I could think of was poor Elleb's leg shredded in the jaw of the trap, and blood dried black, and the flies. The trap was chained to a stake, and I couldn't pry it loose from him.

"Hurt as he was, I remember him growling when you came up, still trying to keep me safe. You knelt down beside me and patted him and poured some water from your canteen on the ground for him to drink, and then you took out your knife and did what needed to be done.

"Not many would tried to make friends with him first, and not many would have sat with me afterwards and made me understand why an end to his pain was the last gift he could get from someone who loved him. By the time you took me home, I really did understand it. You were kind to me, and I've never forgotten."

"And because of so small a thing you put your trust in me?"

"I did, and I have no regrets." Her last words were sleep-softened.

Gerin watched Nothos and the stars peep through holes in the leafy canopy and thought about the obligations with which he had saddled himself. After a while, he decided he too had no regets. He fed bits of wood to the tiny fire, slapped at the buzzing biters lured by its light, and waited for the sun to put the ghosts to rout.

At dawn he woke Van. His comrade knuckled his eyes and spoke mostly in sleepy grunts as they harnessed the horses. Elise doused and covered the fire before Gerin could tend to it. They breakfasted on hard bread and smoked meat. To his disgust, Gerin missed a shot at a fat grouse foolish enough to roost on a branch not a hundred feet away. It flapped off, wings whirring.

The track wound through the forest. Trailing shoots and damp hanging mosses hung from branches overhead, eager to snatch at anything daring to brave the wood's cool dim calm. The horses were balky. More than once Van had to touch them with the whip before they would go on.

Few birds trilled to ease the quiet. Almost the only sounds were the creaking of branches and the rustling of leaves in a breeze too soft to reach down to the road.

Once a sound almost softer than silence paced the wagon for a time. It might have been the pad of great supple feet, or perhaps nothing at all. Gerin saw—or thought he saw—a pair of eyes, greener than the leaves, measuring him. He blinked or they blinked and when he looked again they were gone. The rattle of the wagon's wheels was swallowed as if it had never been.

"Place gives me the bloody shivers!" Van said. To Gerin, his friend's voice sounded louder than needful.

The baron thought the day passing faster than it was, so thick was the gloom. He bit back an exclamation of surprise when they burst from shadow into the brightness of the late afternoon sun. He had not realized how much the thought of camping again in the forest chilled him until he saw he would not have to.

The hills cupped the valley in which Ikos lay. Travelers could look down on their goal before they reached it. The main road came from the southwest. Gerin could see little dots of moving men, carriages, and wagons, all come to consult the Sibyl. His own road was less used. The border lords usually put more faith in edged bronze than prophecy.

A tiny grove surrounded the temple. Probably in days long past the forest had lapped down from the hilltops into the valley, but the sacred grove was all that was left of it there. The shrine's glistening marble roof stood out vividly against the green of the trees.

Around the temple proper were the houses of the priests, the attendants, and the little people who, while not really connected with the Sibyl, made their livings from those who came to see her: sellers of images and sacrificial animals, freelance soothsayers and oracle-interpreters, innkeepers and whores, and the motley crew who sold amulets, charms—and doubtless curses too.

Around the townlet were cleared fields, each small plot owned by a freeholder. Gerin knew the temple clung to the old ways. He did not grudge it its customs, but still thought freeholding subversive. A peasant could not produce enough wealth to equip himself with all the gear a proper warrior needed. Without the nobles, the border and all the land behind would have been a red tangle of warfare, with the barbarians howling down to loot and burn and kill.

"Should we go down before the light fails?" Van asked.

Gerin thought of Ikos' dingy hostels. He shook his head. "We'd get nothing done at this hour. From what I recall of the inns, we'll find fewer bugs here."

The evening meal was spare, taken from the same rations as breakfast. Gerin knew those had been packed with the idea of feeding two people, not three. He reminded himself to lay in more. *Pretty sorry scholar you are*, he jeered at himself—*worrying over smoked sausages and journeybread*.

He must have said that aloud, for Van laughed and said, "Well, someone has to, after all."

The baron took the first watch. In Ikos below, the lights faded until all was dark save for a central watchfire. The hills to the southwest were dotted with tiny sparks of light Gerin knew to be camps like his own. In its grove, the temple was strange, for the light streaming out from it glowed blue instead of the comfortable red-gold of honest flame.

Magic, Gerin decided sleepily, or else the god walking about inside. When Math's golden half-circle set, he roused Van, then dove headfirst into sleep.

He woke to the scent of cooking; luckier than he had been the morning before, Van had bagged a squirrel and two rabbits and was stewing them. Elise contributed mushrooms and a handful of herbs. Feeling better about the world with his belly full, Gerin hitched up the horses. The wagon rolled down the path toward the Sibyl.

IV

Gerin soon discovered his memory had buried a lot about Ikos. First of all, the place stank. It lay under a cloud of incense so cloying that he wished he could stow his nose in the wagon. Mixed with the sweet reek were the scents of charring fat from the sacrifices and the usual town odors of stale cookery, garbage, ordure, and long-unwashed animals and humanity.

The noise was as bad. Gerin's ears had not faced such an assault since he returned to the north country. It seemed as if every peddler in Ikos rolled down on the wagon, each crying his wares at the top of his lungs: swordblades, rare and potent drugs, sanctified water, oats, pretty boys, savory cooked geese, collected books of prophetic verse, and countless other things. A fat bald man in greasy tunic and shiny leather apron, an innkeeper from the look of him, pushed his way through and bowed low before the bemused Fox, who had never seen him before. "Count Stoffer, I believe?" he said, back still bent.

Patience exhausted, Gerin snapped, "Well, if you believe that, you'll believe anything, won't you?" and left the poor fellow to the jeers of his fellow townsmen.

"Is this what the capital is like?" Elise asked faintly.

"It is," Gerin said, "but only if you will allow that a map is like the country it pictures."

She used a word he had not suspected she knew.

Van chuckled and said, "It's the same problem both places, I think: too many people all pushed together. Captain, you're the only one of us with pockets. Have a care they aren't slit."

Gerin thumped himself to make sure he was still secure. "If any of these fine bucks tries it, he'll be slit himself, and not in the pocket." He suddenly grinned. "Or else not, depending on how lucky I am."

They pushed their slow way through Ikos and into the clearing round the sacred grove. The sun was already high when they reached it. They bought cheese and little bowls

53

of barley porridge from the legion of vendors. Men from every nation Gerin knew cursed and jostled one another, each trying to be the first to the god's voice on earth.

One lightly built chariot held two nomads from the eastern plains. They were little and lithe, flat of face and dark of skin, with scraggly caricatures of beards dangling from their chins. They dressed in wolfskin jackets and leather trousers, and bore double-curved bows reinforced with sinew. They carried small leather shields on their left arms; one was bossed with a golden panther, the other with a leaping stag. When Van noticed them, he shouted something in a language that sounded like hissing snakes. Their slanted eyes lit as they gave eager answer.

There were Kizzuwatnans in heavy carts hauled by straining donkeys: squat, heavy-boned men with swarthy skins; broad, hook-nosed faces; and liquid, mournful eyes. Their hair and beards curled in ringlets. They wore long linen tunics that reached to their knees.

There were a few Sithonians, though most of them preferred the oracle at Pronni in their own country. Slimmer and fairer than the Kizzuwatnans, they wore woolen mantles with brightly dyed edgings. They scornfully peered about from under broad-brimmed straw hats: though they had been subjects of the Empire for five centuries, they still saw themselves as something of an elite, and looked down on their Elabonian overlords as muscular dullards.

Even an Urfa from the deserts of the far south had come to Ikos. He must have ridden all the way around Elabon's Greater Inner Sea, for he was still perched atop his camel. Gerin looked at its reins and saddle with interest, thinking how fascinated Duin would have been. The desert-dweller peered down at the wains and chariots around him. He growled guttural warning when they came too close. That was seldom; horses shied from his evil-looking mount.

The Urfa was wrapped in a robe of grimy wool. Eyes and teeth flashed in a face darkened by dirt and long years of sun. Save for a nose even larger than the Kizzuwatnans', his features were delicate, almost feminine. He wore a thin fringe of beard and, for all his filth, seemed to think himself the lord of creation.

Gerin had a hard time naming some of the other outlanders.

Van claimed one black-haired, fair-skinned giant belonged to the Gradi, who lived north of the Trokmoi. The man was afoot, and sweating in his furs. He carried a stout mace and a short-handled throwing axe. Gerin knew almost nothing of the Gradi, but Van spoke of them with casual familiarity.

"Do you know their tongue?" Elise asked.

"Aye, a bit," Van said.

"Just how many languages do you know?" Gerin asked.

"Well, if you mean to say hello in, and maybe swear a bit, gods, I've lost track long since. Tongues I know fairly well, though, perhaps ten or a dozen. Something like that."

"Which is your own?" Elise asked.

"My lady," Van said, with something as close to embarrassment as his deep voice could produce, "I've been on the road a lot of years now. After so long, where I started matters little."

Gerin grinned wryly; he'd got much the same answer when he asked that question. Elise looked to want to pursue it further, but held her tongue.

One group of foreigners the Fox knew only too well: the Trokmoi. Three chieftains had come to consult the Sibyl. Their chariots stayed together in the disorder.

They were from deep in the northern woods: Gerin, who knew the clans on the far side of the border as well as he knew the barons warding it, recognized none of them, nor were the clan patterns of bright checks on their drivers' tunics familiar to him. Chiefs and drivers alike were tall thin men; four had red hair and two were blond. All wore their hair long and had huge drooping mustachioes, though they shaved their cheeks and chins. Two clutched jugs of ale to themselves; another wore a necklace of human ears.

Priests circulated through the crowd. Gerin looked with scant liking at the one approaching the wagon. A robe of gold brocade was stretched across his over-ample belly, and his beardless cheeks shone pink. Everything about him was round and soft, from his limpid blue eyes to the toes peeking sausage-like from his sandals. He was a eunuch, for the god accepted no whole man as his servitor.

The tip of his tongue played redly across his lips as he asked, "What would your business be, gentles, with the Sibyl of my lord Biton?" His voice was soft and sticky, like the caress of a hand dripping with honey.

"I'd sooner not speak of it in public," Gerin said.

"Quite, quite. Your servant Falfarun most definitely agrees. You have, though, a suitably appropriate offering for the god, I hope?"

"I think so." Gerin swung a purse into Falfarun's pudgy fist.

The priest's face was blank. "Doubtless all will be well when your question is heard."

"I do hope, my dear Falfarun, it will be heard soon," Gerin said in his suavest voice. He handed the priest another, larger purse, which vanished into a fold of Falfarun's robe.

"Indeed. Yes, indeed. Come this way, if you please." Falfarun neared briskness as he elbowed aside less forethoughtful seekers of divine wisdom. Clucking to the horses, Van steered after him. Falfarun led the wagon into the sacred grove around the temple precinct. Seeing the Fox's success, the Trokmoi pulled off rings, armlets, and a heavy golden pectoral and waved them in the face of another plump priest.

"You gauged the size of your second sack about right," Van whispered.

"Praise Dyaus for that! The last time I was here, I spent three days cooling my heels before I got to go before the Sibyl. I was still too young to know the world runs on gold."

"Was the wench worth looking at, once you finally saw her?"

"Scarcely. She was a wrinkled old crone. I wonder if she still lives."

"Why have hags to give prophesies? It seems to me they'd hardly be fitting mates for whatever god runs the shrine here. Give me a young, juicy lass every time," Van said, drawing a sniff from Elise.

"Biton has spoken through her since she was chosen for him when she was still a child," Gerin explained. "Whenever a Sibyl dies, the priests search among families of the old race; this valley has always been their stronghold. When they find a girl-child with a certain mark—what it is they keep secret, but it's been Biton's sign for ages—she becomes the new Sibyl for as long as she remains a maiden: and her chastity is guarded, I assure you."

The tumult behind them faded under the trees. Images of all-seeing Biton were everywhere in the grove, half of them turned to show the two eyes in the back of his head. Another priest led the Trokmoi along a different path. Far from being struck by the holiness of the wood, they argued loudly in their own language.

High walls of gleaming white marble warded the outer courtyard of Biton's temple. The gates were flung wide, but spear-carrying temple guards stood ready to slam them shut should trouble threaten. Here and there the shining stone was chipped and discolored, a mute reminder of the great invasion of the Trokmoi two hundred sixty years before, when Biton himself, the priests maintained, made an appearance to drive the barbarians from his shrine.

Before they could go in, Falfarun summoned a green-robed underpriest. The fat priest said, "It is not permitted to enter the courtyard save on foot; Arcarola here will take your wagon to its proper place. Fear not, for there is no theft on the grounds of the temple. A loathsome plague unfailingly smites any miscreant daring to attempt such rapine."

"How many are thus stricken?" Gerin asked skeptically.

"The body of the latest is one of the curiosities within the outer walls. Poor wretch; may he edify others."

Sobered, Gerin descended from the wagon, followed by Elise and Van. When Arcarola climbed up, the horses rolled their eyes and tried to rear, feeling the unfamiliar touch at the reins. Van put a heavy hand on each one's muzzle and growled, "Don't you be stupid, now," following that with an oath in the harsh tongue Gerin guessed was his own. The beasts subsided and let themselves be led away.

The Trokmoi came up about then. More green-robes took their chariots. The priest who was leading them drew Falfarun aside and spoke softly with him. The Trokmoi were talking too, and not softly: the argument they'd begun under the trees of the sacred grove was still in full swing. Gerin was about to greet them in their own tongue until he heard what they were quarreling about.

One of the northerners looked suspiciously at the Fox and his comrades. "Not so loud should you make it, Catuvolcus," he said. He sounded worried, and his scarred hands made hushing motions.

Catuvolcus was not going to be hushed. Gerin guessed he was a bit drunk. His eyes were shot with red, his speech slurred. He toyed with his gruesome necklace. "Divico," he said, "you can take a flying futter at fast Fomor." He used the northern name for the quickest moon. "What's the chance we would find someone this far south who speaks the real language?"

"There's no need to take a chance for no purpose."

"But I'm saying it's no chance at all. And if you will remember, now, 'twas your scheme to come here. And what was the why of it? Just to have the privacy we could scarce be getting from our own oracles."

"A proper notion it was, too. I'd liefer not have that Balamung omadhaun know it's less than full faith I have in him. Who is the spalpeen, anyhow, and why should we fight for him? If I go hunting with a bear, why, I want to be sure he'll not save me for the main course."

Listening as hard as he could without seeming to, Gerin barely noticed Falfarun return. He was trailed by the other priest, who was even fatter than he. Falfarun coughed and said, "Good sir, my colleague Saspir"—he indicated his companion, whose smooth eunuch's face belied the years shown by his graying hair and sagging jowls—"and I have decided that these northern gentlemen should precede you to the Sibyl, as their journey has been longer than yours and they have urgent business in their own land which requires them to make haste."

"You are trying to tell me they paid you more," Gerin said without much rancor.

Falfarun's chins quivered. His voice was hurt as he answered, "I would not put it so crassly—"

"—But it's still true," Gerin finished for him. "Be it so, then, if we can follow them directly."

"But of course," Falfarun said, relieved to find him so agreeable. Saspir gave the Trokmoi the good news and took them into the temple courtyard. Falfarun followed, his reedy voice loud in the ears of Gerin, who would much rather have listened to the barbarians. Another golden-robed hierarch conducted a toga-clad noble out from the holy precinct; the man's thin, pale face bore a troubled expression. The nomads from the plains of Shanda came up just as Gerin entered the courtyard. He heard a priest override their loud objections to being separated from their chariot.

Even the Trokmoi had fallen silent in the temple forecourt. They were gawking, necks craning every which way, trying to see everything at once. Gerin thought they looked like so many hungry hounds licking their chops in front of a butcher's shop. He did not much blame them, for the sight of so much treasure affected him the same way. The would-be thief's corpse, covered with hideous raw-edged lesions and bloated and stinking after some days in the open, did little to dampen his enthusiasm. Beside him Van whistled, soft and low.

Only the choicest gauds were on display. Most of the riches Biton's shrine had accumulated over the centuries were stored away in strong-walled vaults behind the temple or in caves below it. What was visible was plenty to rouse a plunderer's lusts.

Chief among the marvels were twin ten-foot statues of gold and ivory, one of the Emperor Oren II, who had built the temple in the ancient grove, the other of his father, Ros the Fierce, who drove the Trokmoi north of the River Niffet and won the land between the Kirs and the Niffet for Elabon. Oren wore the toga and held in his upraised right hand the orb of empire; Ros, mailed, had a javelin ready to cast and leaned upon a narrow-waisted shield of antique design.

Ros' stern craggy face, with its thrusting nose and lines carved deep on weathered cheeks, still brought awe after four hundred years. Gerin shivered when he looked up into those cold eyes of jet.

A huge golden mixing bowl celebrated Biton's triumph over the Trokmoi. Wider even than Van's outstretched arms, it was set upon a claw-footed tripod of bronze, and held the images of barbarians fleeing the god's just wrath—and the prostrate bodies of those his arrows had struck down. On a pedestal of purple marble next to it was a splendid statue of a dying Trokmê. The naked warrior was on his right side, propping himself up with his right arm. That hand still clung to swordhilt. The other clutched a gaping gash in his right side; the red-painted blood streamed down his flank to form a puddle at his hip. His face was turned up to stare at his unportrayed conqueror. Its grimace showed agony and defiance, but not a hint of fear. The statue's features were blunter than those usual among the long-faced, thin-nosed Trokmoi. Probably the sculptor, himself a Sithonian, had used a countryman as model, adding only long hair and mustaches to make clear the statue's race.

There was much else to see: the silver-and-gold longtooth, its leap onto an aurochs frozen by a master artisan of long ago; the chalices and urns of precious metals, alabaster, cinnabar, and multicolored jades; the stacks of ingots and bars of gold and silver, each with a plaque telling which accurate prophesy it commemorated . . . but Falfarun was leading Gerin up to the steps of the temple, and that was a sight in itself.

Oren's architect had tried to harmonize the sparely elegant columned shrines the Sithonians loved with the native brickwork fanes of Elabon, and his effort was a noble one. The sides of Biton's shrine were marble blocks; spacious glazed windows helped illuminate the interior. The front wall was pure Sithonian, with its triangular entablature supported by delicately fluted columns of whitest stone.

Between architrave and overhanging eaves the frieze, carved by a team of workmen from drawing by the creator of the dying Trokmê, showed Biton, hand outstretched, guiding an imperial column against a horde of Trokmoi. Ros, his harsh features easy to recognize, stood in the lead chariot. His men had a tough uniformity in striking contrast to the disorderly foe they battled—and to the barons who had come after them.

Up the seven marble steps they went, Falfarun chattering all the while. When Elise heard statue and frieze sprang from the same man's mind, she asked his name. Falfarun looked shocked and shook his head. "I have no idea," he said. "The work is far too holy to be polluted by such mundanities."

Gerin's eyes needed a moment to adjust to the inside of Biton's shrine, accustomed as they were to bright sunshine. They went wide as he saw the splendor within, for it had faded in his memory.

Limiting himself to simple white stone for the outside of the building, its designer had let color run riot within. Twin rows of crimson granite columns, polished mirror-bright, led the eye to the altar. That was of sandalwood overlain with gold and encrusted with all kinds of precious stone. It threw back in coruscating sheets the light cast on it by dozens of fat candles in three arabesqued chandeliers overhead.

The temple's inner walls were faced with rare green marbled shot with gold. That stone came from only one quarry, near Siphnos in Sithonia. The Fox could but marvel at the sweat and gold needed to haul it here, a journey of several hundred miles over the Greater Inner Sea and the royal roads of Elabon. Like the columns, it was buffed till it gleamed; it tinged niche-set gold and silver statues with its own color.

Chanting acolytes paced here and there, intent on Biton's rituals. Their slippers swished over the floor mosaics, their swinging censers filled the air with the fragrances of aloes, myrrh, and other costly incenses. Folk who wanted Biton's aid but needed no sight of the future knelt and prayed in pews flanking the granite columns. Some kept their heads lowered; others raised them to the ceiling frescoes, as if seeking inspiration from the scenes of the god's begetting by Dyaus on a princess and of his subsequent adventures, most of them caused by the jealousy of the heavenly queen Darza.

Only in two respects was Biton's shrine unlike many even more superb temples in the lands south of the mountains. One was the image of the god behind the altar. Here he was no graceful youth. A square column of rough black stone stood there, drinking in the light and giving back none. Immeasurably old, it could have been a natural pillar, save for the faint images of eyes round its top and a jutting phallus stabbing forward from its middle.

Biton's priests had only smiled when Oren proclaimed their deity a son of Dyaus. In their hearts they knew whose god was the elder. Seeing that image, Gerin was not inclined to doubt them. Biton's power was rooted in the earth, and in the square of bare earth to the left of the altar was a rift leading down below the roots of the sacred grove to the Sibyl's cave, a rift whose like was unknown in the tamer south.

The Trokmoi made obeisance before Biton's altar, the three chieftains on their knees and the drivers flat on their bellies. They rose, dusted themselves off, and followed their guide into the yawning mouth of the cave. One driver, a freckled youth with face tight-set against fear, flexed the fingers of one hand in a sign to avert evil. The other was tight on the hilt of his blade.

Falfarun brought up his charges to take the barbarians' place. All bent the knee before Biton, Falfarun panting as he eased his bulk to the floor. Gerin looked up at the ancient idol. For an instant, he thought he saw eyes brown as his own looking back at him, but when he looked again they were only scratches on stone.

Rising, Falfarun asked, "Would it please you to take more comfortable seats while waiting to meet the Sibyl?"

Gerin sat in the foremost pew. He ignored the puffing Falfarun, who dabbed at his forehead with a square of blue silk. His thoughts were on the Trokmoi: if these barbarians, men from so deep in the forests he knew nothing of them, had allied their clans with Balamung, how many more had done the same? Fox Keep, it seemed, was in the way of an onsalught more terrible than the attack whose scars still showed on the temple forecourt's walls.

He grew more and more jittery until the Trokmoi emerged from the cavemouth. All were grim-faced: they had no liking for what they'd heard. The young driver who had made the wardsign was white as an exterior column, the freckles on his nose and cheeks standing out like spatters of dried blood.

The two chiefs who had been quarreling outside the temple forecourt were still at it. Divico, even more worried than before, waved a hand in front of Catuvolcus' face. "Are you not glad now we came?" he said. "Plain as day the witch-woman told us there'd be naught but a fox gnawing our middles if we joined Balamung, plain as day."

"Ox ordure," Catuvolcus said. "The old gammer has no more wits than teeth, the count of which is none. On all the border there's but one southron called the Fox, and were you not listening when himself told us the kern'd be ravens' meat in no more than days? It must be done by now, so where's your worry?"

Gerin stood and gave the Trokmoi his politest bow. "Begging your pardon," he said, using their tongue with a borderer's ease, "but a wizard's word a coin I'd bite or ever I pocketed it. But if you're after the Fox, I am he, and I tell you this: the raven who'll pick my bones is not yet hatched, no, nor his grandsire either."

He had hoped his sudden appearance would show the barbarians the folly of their way. Instead he saw the rashness of his, for Catuvolcus bellowed an oath, grasped sword from scabbard, and rushed. His five comrades followed.

Leaping to his feet, Van lifted Falfarun over his head as easily as if the fat eunuch had been stuffed with down. He pitched him into the Trokmoi, bowling over two of them and giving himself and Gerin time to free their blades. At the same instant Elise hurled a dagger, then skipped back to safety. The freckled driver fell, throat pumping a torrent of blood round the hilt suddenly flowering there and sword slipping from nerveless fingers.

Catuvolcus ducked under the hurtling priest. He swung up his sword two-handed, brought it down in a cut to cleave Gerin from crown to chin. Sparks flew as the Fox blocked the stroke. His arms felt numb to the elbow. He ducked under another wild slash, edged bronze whizzing bare inches above his head.

His own sword bit into the Trokmê's belly. He ripped it free to parry the lunge of one of the drivers. The northerner seemed confused at facing a lefthanded swordsman. Gerin beat down another tentative thrust, feinted at his enemy's throat, and guided his sword into the barbarian's heart. More surprise than pain on his face, the Trokmê swayed and fell. He gasped for air he could not breathe, tried to speak. Only blood gushed from between his lips.

The Fox looked round for more fight, but there was none. Van leaned on his blade and puffed; he watched the shrilling, scrambling eunuchs with distaste. Half the proud crest of his helm was sheared away. His armor was drenched with gore, but none was his. Red hair matted by redder blood, the head of one barbarian stared glassily at its body. The ghastly corpse lay across another, whose entrails and pouring blood befouled the gentle meadow of the mosaic floor.

Horror on her face, Elise came up to survey the carnage. With a flourish, Van plucked her dagger from its victim's throat and handed her the dripping weapon. "As fine a throw as I've ever seen, and as timely, too," he said. She held it a moment, then threw it to the floor as hard as she could and gagged, reeling back against the pews.

Gerin put a hand on her shoulder to comfort her. She clung to him and sobbed. He murmured wordless reassurance. He was nearly as much an accidental warrior as was she, and recalled only too well puking up his guts in a clump of bushes after his first kill. Now he was just glad he was still among the living, and tried not to think of the ruined humanity at his feet.

He offered his canteen to Elise so she could rinse her mouth. She took it with a muffled word of thanks.

A squad of temple guardsmen rushed down the main aisle, brushing aside the plainsmen (who had watched the fight with interest) and their guide. The guard captain, his corselet gilded to show his rank, shook his head when he heard Gerin's story, though Saspir confirmed it. Tugging his beard, the officer, whose name was Etchebar, said, "To slay a priest of the god, even to save your own lives, is foully done. Surprised am I Biton did not smite you dead."

"Slay?" Van shouted. "Who in the five hells said anything about slaying a priest, you jouncebrained lump of dung?" Etchebar's spearmen bristled at that, but restrained themselves at his gesture. "The great tun is no more slain than you, as you'd find out if you flipped water in his fat face. And if we'd waited for *your* aid, it'd be the Trokmoi you were jabbering with here!" He spat into the pool of red. "Look!"

As smoothly as before, he lifted Falfarun. The priest had still been on top of the inert Divico. Van set him on his feet as blood dribbled from the hem of his robe. The outlander slapped him gently, once or twice. He groaned and clutched his head. He did not seem much hurt, however shaken he was.

Gerin turned all his powers of persuasion on the guard captain and the priest, one of whose eyes was already beginning to blacken. He broke off in mid-sentence when he saw Van stooping over Divico, plainly intending to finish off the unconscious man. The baron made a quick grab for his friend's arm.

"Captain, are you daft?" Van said.

"I hope not." Gerin took Van's place over the fallen Trokmê and shook him.

Divico came to himself with a thunderstorm in his head. He moaned and opened his eyes. That accursed Fox was bending over him, the scar above his eye white against his tan, his square face hard. The Trokmê gathered himself for a spring until he felt the cold kiss of a blade at his throat. He rolled his eyes down until he saw its upper edge, still smeared with blood.

Impotent rage flashed across his face. "I willna beg for my life, if it's that you're after," he said. "Slit my weasand and have done."

"A warrior's answer," Gerin nodded, still speaking the forest tongue with a fluency Divico found damnable. "Can it be you're wise as well?"

He sheathed his sword and helped the bewildered Trokmê sit. The chieftain hissed when he saw his slaughtered comrades.

Gerin waved at them and went on, "You and your friends heard the Sibyl's words, but did they heed them? Not a bit, and see what's become of them now. Sure as sure the same'll befall you and your clansmen if you go following Balamung's war-trumpets. If I give you your life, would you go and tell them that, aye, and others you meet on the way?"

Divico's red brows came together as he thought. At last he said, "I would that. For Catuvolcus and Arviragus I cared not a fart. Poor Togail is another matter, though. Black shame 'twill be to me to tell my brother Kell his son had his lovely throat torn out while I return revengeless. Still, I will do it, to keep the same from befalling all my kin.

Fox, I like you not, but I will. By Taranis, Teutates, and Esus I swear it."

That was the strongest oath the Trokmoi knew, Gerin thought; if it would not bind Divico to his word, nothing would. "Good man!" he said, clasping his hand and helping him to his feet. He almost told the Trokmê he thought like an Elabonian, but judged the proud chieftain would think it an insult.

"A moment," Etchebar said drily. "You have not the only claim on this man. Because of him, blood was shed in the holy precinct, which is abhorrent to our lord Biton." He touched his eyes and the back of his head in reverence. Falfarun nodded vigorous agreement. The guardsmen leveled their spears at Divico, who shrugged and relaxed but kept his hand near his sword.

"I am sure we can come to an understanding," Gerin said, propelling guard captain and priest into a quiet corner. There they argued for some minutes. The Fox reminded them that Divico had opposed Catuvolcus, who started the unholy combat. Furthermore, he pointed out, Biton was able to deal with those who offended him, as he had proved on the body of the luckless thief who was displayed in the forecourt.

Etchebar growled a curt order and Divico was set free. The Trokmê bowed to Gerin and left, one hand still clutched to his aching skull.

Another discreet offering of gold "for the temple" salved Falfarun's bruises. Etchebar was a harder case, for Van's chaffing had wounded his pride. He wanted satisfaction, not gold. Making sure the outlander was not in earshot, Gerin apologized profusely.

Black-robed temple servitors dragged away the dead Trokmoi and began to mop up their spilled gore, which had already attracted a few flies. Eyes still unhappy under bushy eyebrows, Etchebar gathered up his men and led them back to the forecourt. "And now, gentles, to the Sibyl at last," Falfarun said, with quite as much solemn aplomb as he had had before he was tossed about and his gleaming robe befouled.

The mouth to the Sibyl's cave was a black, grinning slit.

Elise, still wan, took Gerin's hand. Looking down into the inky unknown, he was glad of the touch. Van fumed blasphemously as he tried to scrub sticky drying blood from his cuirass.

Falfarun vanished down the cavemouth. "You need have no fear for your footing," he called. "Since the unhappy day a century ago when the cousin of the Emperor Forenz (the second of that name, I believe) tumbled and broke an ankle, it was thought wise to construct regular steps and flooring to replace rocks and dirt. Such is life." He sighed, a bit unhappy at tradition flouted.

The subterranean corridor to the Sibyl's cave went down and down, twisting until Gerin lost all idea of which way he was going. A few dim candles set in brackets of immemorial antiquity gave pale and fitful light, making the flapping shadow of Falfarun's robe a monstrous thing. Cross-branches of the caverns were holes of deeper blackness in the gloom. Elise's grip on Gerin's hand tightened.

Most of the cave wall was left in its natural state. Now and again a bit of rock crystal would gleam for a moment in the candlelight and then fade. A few stretches were walled off by brickwork of a most antique mode which had its origins in the timeworn river land of Kizzuwatna, where men first lived in cities: not truly square like most bricks, these had convex tops and looked like buns of baked earth.

When Gerin asked the reason for the brickwork, Falfarun answered with a shiver, "Behind the bricks are charms of great fellness, for not all branches of these caves are safe for men. As you have seen, some we use for armories, others to store grain or treasure. But in some branches dread things dwell, and men who tried to explore them never returned. Those ways were stopped, as you see, to prevent such tragedies. More than that I cannot tell you, for it was done ages ago."

Imagining the pallid monsters that could inhabit such dismal gloom, Gerin shivered himself. He tried not to think of the tons of rock and earth over his head. Van muttered something that might have been prayer or curse and hitched the swordbelt higher on his hip.

An ancient statue of Biton smiled its secret smile at them as they neared the Sibyl. The candles gave way to brighter torches. The corridor widened to form a small chamber. A gust of cool, damp wind blew past Gerin's face. He heard the deep mutter of a great subterranean river far below.

When Falfarun touched his elbow, he started. "Your gifts entitle you to privacy with the Sibyl, if such is your desire," the priest said.

Gerin thought, then nodded.

Surprisingly, Falfarun's bruised face crinkled into a half-smile. "Good," he said. "Did the answer you received please you not, belike your brawny friend would undertake to pitch me through a wall." Van sputtered in embarrassment. Falfarun went on, "Good fortune attend you, gentles, and I leave you with the Sibyl." He waved at the throne set against the rear wall of the chamber and was gone.

"By my sword," Van said softly, "if I didn't know better, I'd say it was carved from one black pearl." Taller than a man, the high seat glimmered nacreously in the torchlight; crowns of silver shone on its two back posts.

The throne's splendor made the bundle of rags sitting on it altogether incongruous. Though the Trokmoi had called the Sibyl a crone, Gerin hadn't been able to believe the withered body through which the god had spoken ten years before still held life. But it was she, one eye dim, the other whitened by cataract. Her face was a badlands of wrinkles; her scalp shone through thinning strands of yellowish hair.

The mind behind that ruined countenance was still sharp, though. She raised one withered claw in a gesture of command. "Step forward, lass, lads," she said, voice a dry rustle. Gerin knew she would have called his father "lad" had he been before her, and she would have been as right.

"What would you know of my master Biton?" she asked.

For some days Gerin had mulled the question he would put. Still, in that place his tongue stumbled as he asked, "How best may I save myself and my lands and destroy the wizard who threatens them?"

She did not reply at once. Thinking she had not heard, the baron opened his mouth to ask the question again. But with no warning, her eyes rolled back, showing only vein-tracked whites. Her scrawny fists clenched; her body shook and trembled, throwing her robe off one dry shoulder to reveal an empty dug. Her face twisted. When she spoke, it was not in her own voice, but that of a powerful man in the first flush of strength. Hearing the god, Gerin and his companions went to their knees as his words washed over them:

> "Buildings fall in flame and fire:
> Against you even gods conspire.
> Bow before the mage of the north
> When all his power is put forth
> To crush you down, to lay you low:
> For his grave no man will know."

The god's voice and power gone, the Sibyl slumped forward in a faint.

V

Evening came. Gray clouds scudded across the sky. The wet-dust smell of rain was in the air. Grim and silent, Gerin began to help Van make camp. Elise, worry in her voice and on her face, said, "Not three words have you spoken since we left the temple."

All the rage and helplessness the baron had contained since he stalked frozen-faced past Falfarun to reclaim the wagon came out in a torrent of bile. He slammed his helmet to the ground. It spun into the undergrowth. "What difference does it make?" he said bitterly. "I might as well cut my own throat and save that perambulating corpse the work. The Sibyl told me the same thing he did, only from him I hadn't believed it. I was a fool to go to her; I wanted advice, not a death sentence. A plague take all oracles!"

At that, Van looked up. While Gerin stormed, he had quietly gone on setting up camp. He'd started a fire and drained the blood of a purchased fowl into a trench to propitiate the ghosts. "I knew a man who said something like that once, captain," he said.

"Is there a story to go with the knowing?" Elise asked, seemingly searching for any way to draw Gerin out of his inner darkness.

"Aye, that there is," Van agreed. He understood well enough what she was after, and pitched his words to the Fox. Elise settled herself by the fire to listen. "Captain, you know—or you've heard me say—the world is round, no matter what any priest may blabber. I know. I should; I've been round it.

"Maybe ten years ago, when I was at the far eastern edge of this continent, I hired on as a man-at-arms under a merchant named Zairin. He was moving a shipment of jade, silk, and spices from a place called Ban Yarang to Selat, a couple of hundred miles southeastward. The folk are funny round those parts, little yellow-skins with slanting eyes like the Shanda nomads'. It looks better on the women, I must say. Still, that's no part of the yarn.

70

"Zairin was one of those people who have no truck with the gods. Now, in those parts it's customary to check the omens by watching the way the sacred peacocks peck at grain. If they eat well, the journey will be a good one. If not, it's thought wiser to try again some other time.

"There we were, all ready to set out, and Zairin's right-hand man—a fat little fellow named Tzem—brought us a bird from the shrine. He poured out the grain, but the peacock, who probably hadn't much liked traveling slung under his arm for more than a mile, just looked at it. He wouldn't touch it for anything, not that bird.

"Zairin sat watching this, getting madder and madder. Finally the old bandit had himself a gutful. He got up on his feet and roared out, 'If he won't eat, let him drink!' May my beard fall out if I lie, he picked up that peacock, chucked it into the Kemlong river (which runs through Ban Yarang) and started off regardless."

Gerin was caught up in spite of himself. "Dyaus! It's not a chance I'd like to take," he said.

"And you the fellow who curses oracles? You can imagine what we were thinking. Most of the way, though, things went well enough. The road was only a little track through the thickest jungle I've ever seen, so we lost a couple of porters to venomous snakes the poor barefoot fools stepped on, and one more to a blood-sucking demon that left him no more than a withered husk when we found him the next morning. But on a trip like that, you learn to expect such things. Zairin was mightily pleased with himself. He kept laughing and telling anyone who'd listen what a lot of twaddle it was to pay any attention to a fool bird.

"Well, a day and a half before we would have made Selat and proved the old croaker right, everything came unraveled at once. A dam broke upstream from where we were fording; five men and half our donkeys drowned. The customs man Zairin knew at the border had been transferred, and I shudder to think of the silver his replacement gouged out of us. Half the men got a bloody flux. It bothered me for two years. And just to top everything off, old Zairin came down with the crabs. From then on, captain, he was a believer, I can tell you!"

"Go howl!" Gerin said. "I was hoping you'd cheer me

with a yarn where a prophesy turned out wrong. I know enough of the other sort myself. For that you can stand first watch."

"Can I, now? Well, *you* can—" The outlander scorched Gerin in more tongues than the Fox knew. Finally he said, "Captain, fair is fair: I'll wrestle you for it."

"Aren't you the bloodthirsty one? I thought you'd had enough fighting for one day."

Gerin got up and pulled off his tunic. He helped Van undo the leather laces of his back-and-breast. His friend sighed as the weight came off. In kilt and sandals, Van seemed more a war-god than ever. His muscles rippled as he stretched. The forest of golden hair on his chest and belly flashed in the firelight. Only his scars told of his humanity— and his turbulent past. One terrible gash ran from right armpit to navel; every time Gerin saw it, he wondered how the outlander had lived.

Not that he was unmarked himself: sword, spear, knife, and arrow had left their signatures on his skin, and the cut Aingus had given him was only half healed. Seeing Elise's eyes travel from Van's enormous frame to him, he knew he seemed a stripling beside his companion, though he was a well-made man of good size.

But he had a name as a wrestler on both sides of the Niffet. He had learned more tricks from masters south of the Kirs than his neighbors ever imagined, and threw men much bigger than himself. For all that, though, Van's raw strength was enough to flatten him as often as he could finesse his way to victory. When word went out that they would tussle, even Trokmoi came to watch and bet.

Embarrassed that her look had been seen and understood, Elise dropped her eyes. Gerin grinned at her. "He won't chuck me through a tree, girl."

"Who says I won't?" Van bellowed. He charged like an avalanche. Gerin sprang to meet him. Ducking under the thick arms that would quickly have squeezed breath from him, he hooked his own left arm behind Van's right knee and rammed a shoulder into his friend's hard-muscled middle.

Van grunted and went down, but a meaty paw dragged Gerin after him. They rolled, thrashed, and grappled in the dirt. Gerin ended up riding his friend's broad back. His hands had slid under the outlander's shoulders; his hands were clasped behind Van's neck. Van slapped the ground. Gerin let him up. He shook his head and rubbed his eye to rout out some dust.

"You'll have to show me that one again, Gerin," he said. "Another fall?"

The baron shrugged. "All right, but the last one was for the watch." Van nodded. In mid-nod, he leaped. Gerin had no chance to use any of his feints or traps. He was seized, lifted, and slammed to earth with rib-jarring force. Van sprang on him like a starving lion onto a fat sheep.

Thoroughly pinned, Gerin grumbled, "Get off me, you pile of suet!" Van snorted and pulled him to his feet. They both swore as they swabbed each other's scratches with beer-soaked rags. The stuff stung foully.

After supper, Gerin began to regret not having the first watch. He was sure he was too full of troubles to sleep, despite the day's exertions. He tossed, wriggled until a small stone no longed gouged his back, wished the crickets were not so loud. . . .

Van watched his friend's face relax as slumber overtook him. He was not too worried about the baron's dejection; he had seen him downhearted before, and knew he recovered quickly. But the Fox deeply felt his responsibilities. If anything, a menace to his lands hit him harder than a threat against himself.

More and more clouds blew in from the west, pale against the dark blue dome of the sky. Math, a day past first quarter, and mottled Tiwaz, now nearly full, jumped in and out of sight. A couple of hours before midnight, dim Nothos' waning gibbous disk joined them. The wind carried a faint salt tang from the Orynian Ocean far away. Van scrubbed dried blood from his armor and helm, waiting till it was time to wake Gerin.

Rain threatened all through the Fox's watch. It was still dark when the first spatters came. Elise jerked as a drop splashed her cheek; she woke up all at once, like a soldier. Smiling at Gerin, she said, " 'The gods in the heaven send dripping-tressed rain/ To nourish sweet hope in a desert of pain'—or so the poet says, anyway."

He stared at her. The passage of a night had eased much of his gloom; now surprise banished the rest. "Where did you learn to quote Lekapenos? And whose rendering was that? Whoever did it knows his Sithonian well."

"As for the rendering—" She shrugged. "It's mine. That passage always appealed to me. And where else would I learn my letters than from the epics?"

That held much truth. The baron still recalled the godlike feeling he'd had when the curious marks on parchment began to correspond with the verses he'd learned by ear. Thoughtfully, he started getting ready to travel again.

Gerin was glad to exchange the dirt road that led to Ikos for the main southbound highway before the former became a bottomless river of mud. Moments later, he was wondering at the wisdom of his choice. From behind him came a drumming of hooves, the deadly clangor of bronze on bronze, and wheels rumbling on a stone roadbed—a squadron of chariotry, moving fast.

Van unshipped his spear and Gerin began to string his bow. Then a deep voice sounded above the rising clatter: "Way! Way for the men of Aragis the Archer!"

The baron pulled off the road with almost unseemly haste. Ignoring the rain, Aragis' troopers pounded past, brave in surcoats of scarlet and silver. A handful of draggled bandits were their reluctant companions.

Proud hawk face never smiling, Aragis' captain—or maybe it was Aragis himself—raised one arm in salute as his men thundered by. Some of them had leers for Elise, stares for Van's fine cuirass. The bandits looked stolidly ahead. Gerin guessed they could already see the headsman's axe looming large across their futures, and precious little else.

"Whew!" Van said as the chariots disappeared into the rain ahead. "This trip will make a fine yarn, but it's not something I'd like to do more than once."

"Which is true of most things that make good stories," Gerin said. Van laughed and nodded.

From Ikos to Cassat was a journey of two days. To the baron, they were a time of revelation. For years his mind had not reached further than the harvest, the balance of a blade, or the best place to set an ambush. But Elise had read many of the works that were his own favorites and, better yet, thought on what she read. They passed hour after hour quoting passages they liked and arguing meanings.

Gerin had almost forgotten talk like this existed. Over the years, all without his knowing it, his mind had grown stuffy and stale. Now he relished the fresh new breeze playing through it.

Van chimed in too, from time to time. He lacked the background Gerin and Elise shared, but he had seen more of the varied ways of man than either, and his wit was keen.

The purple bulk of the High Kirs, a great rampart looming tall on the southern horizon, came to dominate the landscape. Eternal snow clung to many peaks, scoffing at high summer below. Eight passes traversed the mountains; seven the Empire had painstakingly blocked over the years, to keep out the northern barbarians. In the foothills before the eighth squatted the town of Cassat, a monument to what might have been.

Oren II had planned it as a splendid capital for the new province his father had won. Its great central square was filled with temples, triumphal arches, law courts, and a theater. But fate had not been kind. Birds nested under the eaves of the noble buildings; grass pushed up between marble paving-blocks. The only reality to Cassat was its barracks, squat, unlovely structures of wood and grimy plaster where a few hundred imperial soldiers pretended to rule the northlands. A few streets of horsetraders, swordsmiths, joyhouses, and taverns met their needs. The dusty wind blew mournful through the rest of the town.

The Empire's dragon flag, black on gold, flew only over the barracks. There did Carus Beo's son, the Marchwarden of the North, perform his office; mice alone disputed in the courthouse Oren had built.

Once, Carus had been a favorite at court. He had earned his present post some years back, when the Urfa massacred a column he led. Because of what he saw as exile to the cheerless north, he despised and resented the border barons.

Gerin called on him nonetheless. Few as they were, Carus' men would help hold the border against the Trokmoi, could he be persuaded to send them north. Elise accompanied the baron. Van took the wagon to a leading trader of horseflesh, seeking fresh animals to replace Gerin's weary beasts.

The Marchwarden of the North sat at a well-scuffed desk piled high with parchments of all sizes. He was sixty or a bit over; his yellowish-white hair had retreated to a ruff round his ears and the back of his neck, leaving his pink scalp bare but for a meager forelock. His eyes had dark pockets under them.

His jowls quivered when he lifted his head from whatever bureaucratic inconsequentiality Gerin's arrival had interrupted.

"My man tells me you seek the assistance of the Empire against the Trokmoi. Surely the boldness of the brave holders of Elabon's frontier cannot have declined to such an abysmal level?" he said, looking at Gerin with no liking at all.

Then his narrow eyes swiveled to Elise, and a murky gleam lit them. The Fox saw a liking there, sure enough, but only of the sort that made him want to kick Carus' stained teeth down his throat. Elise studied a point on the wall directly behind the Marchwarden's forehead.

"Surely not," Gerin said. Ignoring the fact that he had not been offered a seat, he handed Elise into a chair and took another for himself. Carus' sallow cheeks reddened. As if nothing had happened, the Fox resumed, "At the present time, however, circumstances are of unusual difficulty." He told the Marchwarden of Balamung and his threatened invasion.

Carus was drumming his nails on top of his desk by the time the Fox finished. "Let me see if I understand you correctly," he said. "You expect the troops of the Empire to get you out of trouble with this wizard, into which you have gotten yourself. Now to justify this request for service, you may point to—what?"

"Among other things, that we border barons have kept the Trokmoi out of the Empire for two hundred years and more."

"A trivium." Carus waved his hand in a languid southern gesture which might have seemed courtly from Rihwin but was only grotesque in a man of the Marchwarden's years and girth. "If I had my way, we would merely send a few thousand tons of stone down behind the Great Gate. That would quite nicely seal off the barbarians for all time."

"Horseballs," Gerin muttered. Elise heard him and grinned. Carus heard him too. The baron had not intended that.

"Horseballs?" Carus' mouth moved in what might have been a smile, but his eyes stayed cold. "Ah, the vivid turn of phrase of the frontier. But do let me return to what I was saying: indeed, I think the Empire would be as well off without you. What do we gain from you, after all? No metals, no grain—only trouble. Half the rebels of the past two hundred years have had northern ties. You corrupt the calm, orderly way of life we crave. No, my good lord Gerin, if the barbarians can eat you up, they are welcome to you."

The Fox had not really expected help from the Marchwarden, but he had not expected outright hatred, either. He drew in a long, angry breath. Elise pressed his hand in warning, but he was too furious to pay heed. He spoke in the same polished phrases Carus had used, and the same venom rode them: "You complain the Empire receives nothing from us? Up on the border, we wonder what we get from you. Where are the men and chariots of the Empire, to help us drive away the northern raiders? Where are they when we fight among ourselves? Do you care? Not a bit, for if we are kept distracted, we cannot think of rebellion. You judge, and rightly, our flesh and blood a better shield than any you might make of stone or wood, and so we die, for nothing."

Bowing to Carus, Gerin stood to go. "And you, my fine Marchwarden, you have gained most of all from our thankless toil. While we sweat and bleed to keep the border safe, here you have stayed for the past twenty-five years, shuffling parchments from one pile to the next and sitting on your fat fornicating fundament!" The last was a roar of surprising volume.

Carus leaped to his feet, fumbling for his sword but finding only an empty scabbard. Gerin laughed mockingly. "Guards!" the Marchwarden bleated. When the men appeared, he gabbled, "Clap this insolent lout in chains and cast him in the dungeon until he learns politeness." His eyes lingered on Elise. He reached out a flabby hand to take her arm. "I will undertake to instruct the wench personally."

The befuddlement on the guards' faces was ludicrous; they had not seen their master so active in years. Gerin made no move for his own blade. He said mildly, "Do you know what will happen if you seize us? As soon as the barons learn of it, they will come down in a body and leave your precious barracks so much kindling. Not long after that, the Trokmoi will be here to light it. I'm almost sorry you won't live to watch."

"What? What nonsense are you spewing now? I'll— *gark!*" Carus' voice abruptly disappeared. Elise was tickling the soft skin under his chin with the tip of her dagger. She smiled sweetly at him. The blood drained from his face, leaving it the color of the parchment on his desk. Moving very carefully, he let go of her arm. "Go," he said, in ragged parody of the tone he had used a moment before. "Get out. Guards, take them away."

"To the dungeons, sir?" asked one, scorn in his voice.

"No, no, just go." Carus sank back into his chair, hands shaking and sweat gleaming on his bald head. With as much ceremony as if it were a daily occurrence, his men conducted Gerin and Elise from the Marchwarden's presence.

The sun was still high in the southwest; the audience had made up in heat what it lacked in length. Gerin turned to Elise and said, "I knew having you along would be a nuisance. Once he caught a glimpse of you, the old lecher couldn't find a way to get me out of there fast enough."

"Don't be ridiculous. I'm a mess." Of itself, her hand moved to brush at her hair.

The baron surveyed her. There was dust in her hair and a smudge of grime on her forehead, but her green eyes sparkled, the mild doses of sun she allowed herself had brought out a spray of freckles on her nose and cheeks, her lips were soft and red, and even in tunic and trousers she was plainly no boy. . . .

Easy there, Gerin told himself: *do you want to make Ricolf your irreconcilable enemy too, along with the Trokmoi and Wolfar?* He gave his beard a judicious tug. "You'll do," he said. "You'll definitely do."

She snorted and poked him in the ribs. He yelped and mimed a grab at her; she made as if to stab him. They were still smiling half an hour later, when Van pulled up in the wagon. He smelled of horses and beer, and had two new beasts in the traces. A grin split his face when he saw how happy Gerin looked. "Himself gave you the men, did he?"

"What? Oh. No, I'm afraid not." The Fox explained the fiasco; Van laughed loud and long. Gerin went on, "I expected nothing much, and got just that. You seem to have been busy, though—what sort of horse do you have there, anyway?" He jerked a thumb at one of Van's newly acquired animals.

Unlike its companion, a handsome gray gelding, this rough-coated little beast was even less sightly than the shaggy woods-ponies of the Trokmoi. But Van looked scandalized. He leaped down and rubbed the horse's muzzle.

A quick snap made him jerk his hand away. Even so, he said, "Captain, don't tell me you don't know a Shanda horse when you see one? The fool trader who had him didn't. He thought he was putting one over on me. Well, let him laugh. A Shanda horse will go all day and all night; you can't wear one down if you try. I like the bargain, and you will too."

"All right, show me." Gerin helped Elise up, then climbed on himself. Van followed. The wagon clattered out of Cassat toward the Great Gate, the sole remaining link the Empire allowed itself with its northern provinces.

It was a long pull through the Gate. Toward the end, the gray horse was lathered and blowing, but the pony from the plains showed no more sign of strain than if it had spent the day grazing. Gerin was impressed.

Though Elabon had not blocked this last way through the Kirs, her marshals had done their best to make sure no enemy could use it. Fortresses of brick and stone flanked the roadway. Watchmen tramped smartly along their battlements, alert against any mischance. The towers' bronze-sheathed wooden gates were closed now, but could open to vomit forth chariots and footsoldiers against any invader.

Wizards, too, aided in defending the Empire. They had their own dwellings, twin needle-like spires of what seemed to be multicolored glass, off which the late afternoon sun shimmered and sparkled. Should the fortresses' armed might fail to blunt an attack, the warlocks would set in motion the thousands of boulders heaped on either side of the pass, and thus block it forever.

The arrangement left Gerin uneasy: what wizardry had made, it could unmake. He cheered slightly when he discovered the warriors in the fastnesses could also start the avalanche by purely natural means: paths led up to the tops of the piles of scree, and triggering rocks there had levers under them. The Fox did not envy the men who would work those levers.

The succession of powerful strongholds awed even Van. "Folk who huddle behind forts are dead inside," he said, "but with forts like these it will be a while yet before anyone notices the reek of the corpse."

A brown and buff lizard chased a grasshopper into the road. It danced madly under hooves and wagon wheels, then vanished into a crevice in the rocks on the far side. Gerin never knew whether it had caught its bug.

Traffic through the Great Gates was heavy. Traders headed north. Their donkeys brayed loud disgust at the weight of the packs they bore. Traders came south. Their donkeys brayed loud disgust over nothing at all. Mercenaries, wandering wise men, wizards, and a good many travelers who fell into no neat scheme—all used the imperial highway.

Nearly two hours went by before the wagon reached the end of the pass. Golden under the light of the setting sun, the southern land spread out ahead like a picture from a landscape master's brush. Field and forest, town and orchard, all were plain to see, with brooks and rivers like lines of molten copper.

"It's a rare pretty country," Van said. "What are the people like?"

"People," Gerin shrugged.

"I'd best keep an eye on my wallet, then."

"Go howl! You'd bite a coin free-given."

"Likely I would, if I planned to spend it."

"Scoffer!"

Just then a warm, dry breeze wafted up from the south. It was sweet and spicy, with the faintest tang of salt from the distant Inner Sea, and carried scents the baron had forgotten.

Like a swift stream breaching the dam that restrained it, long-buried memories flooded up in Gerin. He thought of the two years free from care he had spent in the capital, then of the sterile, worry-filled time since—and was appalled.

"Why did I ever leave you?" he cried to the waiting land ahead. "Father Dyaus, you know I would sooner have been a starving schoolmaster in the capital than king of all the northlands!"

"If that's how you feel, why not stay in the south?" Elise asked. Her voice was gentle, for the fair land ahead had enchanted her as much as the Fox.

"Why not indeed?" Gerin said surpised. He realized the notion had never crossed his mind, and wondered why. At last he sighed and shook his head. "Were the danger behind me less great, I'd leap at the chance like a starving longtooth. But for better or worse, my life is on the cooler side of the mountains. Much depends on me there. If I stay, I betray more than my own men, I think. The land will fall to Balamung, and I doubt it will slake his evil thirst. That may happen yet; the gods have given the northland little enough hope. It's partly my fault Balamung is what he is; if I can make amends, I will."

"I think you will do well," Elise said slowly. "Often, it seems, the most glory is won by those who seek it least."

"Glory? If I can stay alive and free without it, I don't give a moldy loaf of journeybread for glory. I leave all that to Van."

"Ha!" Van said. "Do you want to know the real reason he's bound to go back, my lady?"

"Tell *me*," Gerin said, curious to see what slander his friend would come up with.

"Captain, you'd need more than a wizard to drive you away from your books, and you know it as well as I do." There was enough truth in that to make Gerin throw a lazy punch at Van, who ducked. A good part of the barony's silver flowed south to the copyists and bookdealers in Elabon's capital.

They wound their way down from the pass, hoping to reach a town before the sun disappeared. Gerin was less worried about the ghosts than he would have been on the other side of the mountains; peace had reigned here for many years, and the spirits were relatively mild. For his part, Van grew eloquent about the advantages of fresh food, a mug of ale (or even wine!), a comfortable bed, and perhaps (though he did not say so) a wench to warm it.

The road was flanked by a grove of fruit trees of a kind unknown north of the Kirs. Not very tall, they had gray-brown bark, shiny light-green leaves, and egg-shaped yellow fruit. Both leaves and fruit were fragrant, but Gerin remembered how astonishingly sour the fruit was to the tongue. It was called . . . he snapped his fingers in annoyance. He had forgotten the very name.

As the trees began to thin, another smell made its presence known through their perfume: a faint carrion reek. The baron's lips drew back in a mirthless grimace. "I think we've found our town," he said.

The road turned, the screen of trees disappeared, and sure enough the town was there. It was not big enough to have a wall. The Fox was sure folk living ten miles from it had never heard its name. Nonetheless, it aspired to cityhood in a way open to the meanest of hamlets: by the road stood a row of crucifixes, each with its slow-rotting burden. Under them children played, now and then shying a stone upward. Dogs slunk there too, dogs with poor masters or none, waiting for easy meals.

Some of the spiked and roped criminals were not yet dead. Through sun-baked and blistered lips they begged for water or death, each according to the strength left in him. One, newly elevated or unnaturally strong, still howled defiance at gods and men.

His roars annoyed the carrion birds nearby. Strong black bills filled with noisome food, they flapped lazily into the sky, staring down with fine impartiality on town, travelers, and field. They knew all would come to them in good time.

Van's face might have been carved from stone as he surveyed the wretches. Elise was pale. Her eyes went wide with horror. Her lips shaped the word "Why?" but no sound emerged. Gerin tried not to remember his own thoughts when he'd first encountered the malignant notions of justice the southerners had borrowed from Sithonia.

"Maybe," he said grimly, "I had my reasons for going home, after all."

VI

The town (Gerin learned its name was Fibis) did little to restore the luster of the southlands in the baron's eyes. The houses lining the north-south road were little finer than the huts of his peasants. Only muddy alleys ankle-deep in slops led away from that road.

The sole hostel Fibis boasted was of a piece with the rest. It was low-roofed, dingy, and small. The sign outside had faded past legibility. Within, the smell of old grease fought with but could not overcome the odor of stale urine from the dyeworks next door and the never-absent stench of the crosses.

And the townsfolk! City ways that had been sophisticated to the youth who traveled this road ten years before now seemed either foppish or surly. Gerin tried to strike up a conversation with the innkeeper, a dour, weathered old codger named Grizzard, but got only grunts in return. He gave up and went back to the rickety table where his friends awaited supper. "If I didn't know better," he said, "I'd take oath the fellow was afraid of me."

"Then he thinks you've already tasted his wine," said Van, who was on his third mug. "What swill!" He swigged, pursed his lips to spit, but swallowed instead.

The rest of the meal was not much better than the wine. Plainly, lack of competition was all that kept Grizzard in business. Disgusted with the long, fruitless day he had put in, Gerin was about to head for bed when a cheery voice said, "Hello, you're new here! What's old Grizzard given you to drink?"

Without so much as a by-your-leave, the fellow pulled up a chair and joined them. He sniffed the wine, grimaced, and flipped a spinning silver disk to the innkeeper, who made it disappear. "You can do better than this, you thief," he said. To the Fox's surprise, Grizzard could.

The baron studied his new acquaintance curiously, for the man seemed made of pieces which did not belong together. Despite his heartiness, his voice soon dropped so low Grizzard could not hear what he said. While his mouth was full of slang from the capital, his homespun tunic and trousers were both rustic. Yet his chin sported a gray imperial and his shoes turned up at the toes: both Sithonian styles. The name he gave—just Tevis, without patronymic or sobriquet—was one of the three or four commonest south of the mountains.

Whoever he was, he had a rare skill with words. Softly, easily, he enticed from Gerin (usually as close-mouthed as any man alive) the story of his travels, and all without revealing a bit of his own purpose. It was almost as if he cast a spell. He paused a while in silent consideration, his clear dark eyes studying the Fox. "You have not been well-used by the Empire," he said at last.

Gerin only shrugged. His caution had returned. He was wary of this smooth-talking man of mystery. Tevis nodded, as if he had expected nothing more. "Tell me," he said, "do you know of Moribar the Magnificent, his imperial majesty's governor at Kortys?"

Van, who had drunk deep, stared at Tevis in owlish incomprehension. Elise was nearly asleep, her head warm on Gerin's shoulder. Her hair tickled his cheek. The scent of it filled his nose. But in his mind the stench of the rood was stronger still. Here was the very thing Carus Beo's son had feared most: a potential rebel in the capital of Sithonia, seeking northern help.

At any other time, the baron would have shed no tears to see the Empire go up in civil war, but now he needed whatever strength he could find at his back. He chose his words with care: "Tevis, I don't know you and I didn't ask to know you. If you say one word more to me, you will have spoken treason, and I will not hear it. True, I've had my quarrels with some of his majesty's servants, but if he does not plot against me in my land, I have no right to plot against him in his. I would not have drunk with you had I known what was in your mind. Here, take this and go." He set a coin on the table to pay for the jug of wine.

Tevis smiled faintly. "Keep it," he said, "and this as well." He took something from the pouch on his belt, tossed it next to the coin, and was gone into the night while Gerin still gaped at what he had thrown: a tiny bronze hand, fingers beginning to curl into a fist.

"Oh, great Dyaus above!" he said. "An Imperial Hand!" He propped his chin on his palm and stared at the little token before him. He could have been no more startled had it sprung up and slapped him in the face.

Bristles rasped under Van's fingers as he scratched his jaw. "And what in the five hells is that?" he asked with ponderous patience.

"A secret agent, spy, informer ... call him what you will. That doesn't matter. But if I'd shown any interest in setting Moribar on the throne, by this time tomorrow we'd be on crosses side by side, waiting for the vultures to pick out our eyes."

"Ha! I'd bite off their heads!" Van seemed more concerned with the vultures than the crucifixion that would invite them.

"That's one way of dealing with them, I suppose," Gerin agreed mildly. He woke Elise. She yawned and walked sleepily to the one room Grizzard grudged female travelers. Van and Gerin headed for their own pallets, hoping they would not be bug-ridden. Almost as an afterthought, the Fox scooped up the diminutive but deadly emblem Tevis had left behind.

Though weary, he slept poorly. The quarrel with Carus, his jarring reintroduction to the dark side of the southlands, and above all the brush with doom in the form of Tevis kept him tossing all night. The bed was hard and lumpy, too. When he awoke, half a dozen red, itchy spots on his arms and chest proved he had not slept alone.

Van was unusually quiet at breakfast. "Head hurt?" Gerin asked as they walked to the stables.

"What. Oh. No, it's not that, captain." Van hesitated. Finally he said, "I'll tell you right out, Gerin, last night I almost decided to buy myself a gig and get the blazes out of this crazy country."

Gerin had imagined disaster piled on disaster, but never in his worst nightmares had he imagined his friend leaving. Ever since Van came to Fox Keep the two of them had been inseparable, fighting back to back and then carousing and yarning far into the night. Each owed the other his life several times. With a shock, the baron realized Van was a larger, gustier version of his dead brother Dagref. Losing him would be more than parting with a comrade; part of the baron's soul would go with him.

Before he could put what he felt into words, Elise spoke first: "Why would you want to leave now? Are you afraid? The danger is in the north, not here." She seemed unwilling to believe her ears.

At any other time, the outlander's wrath would have kindled if his courage was questioned. Now he only sighed and kicked at a pebble. Genuine distress was in his voice as he answered, "My lady, look about you." His wave encompassed not just the grubby little hamlet of Fibis and the crosses outside it, but all the land where the writ of the Empire was law. "You've seen enough of me to know what I am and what my pleasures are: fighting, talking, drinking, aye, and wenching too, I'll not deny. But here, what good am I? If I break wind in the backhouse, I have to look over my shoulder lest some listening spy call it treason. It's not the kind of life I care to lead: worrying before I move, not daring even to think."

Gerin understood that well enough, for much the same sense of oppression weighed on him. But Van was still talking: "I was all set to take my leave of you this morning—head north again, I suppose. But then I got to thinking"—he suddenly grinned—"and I decided that if any boy-loving Imperial Hand doesn't like the way I speak, why, I'll carve the son of a pimp into steaks and leave him by the side of the road to warn his scurvy cousins!"

Elise laughed in delight and kissed him on the cheek.

"I think you planned this whole thing just to get that kiss," Gerin said. "Come on, you hulk, quit holding up the works."

"Bastard." Still grinning, Van pitched his gear into the wagon.

The morning was still young when they splashed through the chilly Langros river. Though not as great as the Niffet or the mighty Carastos which watered much of the plain of Elabon, its cold current ran swift as it leaped down from the Kirs toward the Greater Inner Sea.

The water at the ford swirled icily around Gerin's toes and welled up between the wagon's floorboards. Most of the travelers' belongings were safe in oiled leather sacks, but half the journeybread turned to slimy brown paste. Gerin swore in disgust. Van said, "Cheer up, captain, the stuff wasn't worth eating anyhow."

When they stopped to rest and eat, Van turned to Gerin and said quietly, "Thanks for not pushing me this morning. You might have made it hard for me to stay."

"I know," Gerin said. Neither of them mentioned the matter again.

They made good progress that day, passing small farms in the foothills and then, as the land began to level out, going by great estates with splendid manor-houses set well back from the road. When shadows lengthened and cool evening breezes began to blow, they camped by the road-side instead of seeking an inn. Gerin fed and watered the horses as the sun set. In the growing darkness the ghosts appeared, but their wails were somehow muted, their cries almost croons.

Elleb's thin crescent soon followed the sun, like a small boy staying close to his father. That left the sky to the stars and Math, whose gibbous disk bathed the land beyond reach of the campfire in pale golden light. As the night went on, she was joined by Tiwaz, whose speedy flight through the heavens had taken him well past full. And, when Gerin's watch was nearly done, Nothos poked his slow-moving head over the horizon. The baron watched him climb for most of an hour, then gave the night to Van.

The next day gave every promise of rolling along as smoothly as had its predecessor. The promise was abruptly broken a bit before noon. A manor-holder had decided to send his geese to market. The road was jammed by an endless array of tall white birds herded along by a dozen or so men with sticks. The geese honked, cackled, squabbled, and tried to sneak off the road for a mouthful of grain. They did everything, in fact, but hurry. When Gerin asked their warders to clear a way so he could pass, they refused. "If these blame birds get into the fields," one said, "we'll be three days getting them all out again, and our lord'll have our heads."

"Let's charge right through," Van suggested. "Can't you see the feathers fly?"

The thought of a goose stampede brought a smile to Gerin's lips, but he said, "No, these poor fellows have their job to do too, I suppose." And so they fretted and fumed while the birds dawdled along in front of them. More traffic piled up behind.

As time dragged on, Van's direct approach looked better and better. The whip twitched in Gerin's hand. But before he used it, he noticed the road was coming to a fork. The geese streamed down the eastern path. "Can we use the western branch to get to the capital?" he called.

"You can that," one of the flock-tenders answered, so the Fox swung the wagon down the new way.

New? Hardly. Gerin noticed that none of the others stalled behind the geese used the clear road. Soon enough, he found out why. The eastern branch of the highway was far newer. After it was complete, evidently nobody had bothered with the other one again. The wagon jounced and rattled as it banged over gaping holes in the roadbed. On one stretch, the paved surface vanished altogether. There the blocks had been set, not in concrete, but in molten lead. Locals had carried away blocks and valuable mortar alike as soon as imperial inspectors no longer bothered to protect them. The baron cursed the lout who had sent him down this road. He hoped he could make it without breaking a wheel.

The district had perhaps once been prosperous, but had decayed when its road was superseded. The farther they went, the thicker the forest grew, until at last its arms clasped above the roadway and squirrels flirted their bushy gray tails directly overhead.

Soon the very memory of the road would be gone.

Finding a village in the midst of such decline seemed divine intervention. The villagers fell on Gerin and his friends like long-lost relatives, plying them with food and a rough, heady country wine and listening eagerly to every word they brought of the world outside. Not a copper would they take in payment. The baron blessed such kindly folk, and blessed them doubly when they confirmed that the road did in fact eventually lead to the capital instead of sinking into a bog.

"You see, captain? You worry too much," Van said. "Everything will work out all right."

Gerin did not answer. He could not *let* things work out all right; he had to *make* them do so. Backtracking would have cost him a day he could not afford to spend.

The villagers insisted on putting up their guests for the night. Gerin's host was a lean farmer named Badoc son of Tevis (the baron hid a shiver). Other villagers, just as anxious for news, claimed Elise and Van.

The benches round Badoc's table were filled to overflowing by the farmer, his plump, friendly wife Leunadra, the Fox, and a swarm of children. These ranged in age from a boy barely able to toddle to Badoc's twin daughters Callis and Elminda, who were about seventeen. Gerin eyed the striking girls appreciatively. They had curly hair, sparkling brown eyes, and cheeks rosy under sun-bestowed bronze; their thin linen tunics clung to young breasts. As subtly as he could, the baron turned the conversation in their direction. They hung on his every word . . . so long as he was talking about Van. To his own charms they remained sublimely indifferent.

"I wish your friend could stay here," one of the twins mourned; Gerin had forgotten which was which. They both babbled on about Van's thews, his armor, his rugged features, his smile . . . and on and on, until Gerin began to hate the sound of his comrade's name. Badoc's craggy face almost smiled as he watched his guest's discomfiture.

At last the ordeal was over. The baron, quite alone and by then glad of it, went to his bed. His feet hung over the end, for Badoc had ousted one of his younger sons to accommodate the Fox. Gerin was tired enough that it fazed him not a bit.

A woman's cry woke him around midnight. Another followed, then another, long and drawn out: *"Evoi! Evoiii!"* The baron relaxed; it was only the followers of Mavrix, the Sithonian god of wine, out on one of their moonlight revels. Gerin was a bit surprised Mavrix's cult had spread to this out-of-the-way place, but what of it? He went back to sleep.

The next morning he discovered the considerate villagers had not only curried his horses till their coats gleamed, but also left gifts of fresh bread, wine, cheese, onions, and bars of dried fruit and meat in the back of the wagon. A troop of small boys followed him south until their parents finally called them home.

"I almost hate to leave," Van said. Gerin studied him: was he still wearing the traces of a satisfied grin? *What if he is, witling?* the baron asked himself. *Do you begrudge him his good fortune? Well, yes, a little*, his inner voice answered.

The road was a bit better south of the village; at least it never disappeared. Under the trees the air was cool and moist, the sunlight subdued. Gerin felt more at home than he had since leaving Ricolf's keep. He was not alone. He heard Elise softly humming a song of the north country. She smiled when she saw him watching her.

They came to a clearing almost wide enough to be called a meadow, hidden away deep in the forest. The Fox squinted at the sudden brightness. A doe which had been nibbling at the soft grass by the forest's edge lifted its head at the wagon's noisy arrival and sprang into the woods.

"Pull over, will you?" Van said. The outlander reached for Gerin's bow and quiver. Though he disdained archery in battle, he loved to hunt and was a fine shot. He trotted across the clearing and vanished among the trees with grace and silence a hunting cat might have envied.

Sighing, Gerin threw down the reins and stretched out full-length on the sweet-smelling grass. Sore muscles began to unkink. Elise stepped down and joined him. The horses were as glad at the break as the people; they cropped the grass with as much alacrity as the deer had shown.

Minute followed minute, but Van gave no sign of returning. "He's probably forgotten which end of the arrow goes first," Gerin said. He rose, went to the wagon, and emerged with Van's spear. "Carrying this, I shouldn't wonder." Every time he touched it, he marveled at his friend's skill with such a heavy weapon.

He practiced slow thrusts and parries to while away the time, more than a little conscious of Elise's eyes on him. Showing off in front of a pretty girl was a pleasure he did not get often enough. More and more he resented the wound that had kept him from courting this particular pretty girl.

It was not that he lacked for women. If nothing else, a baron's prerogatives were enough to prevent that, though he was moderate in his enjoyment of them and never bedded a wench unwilling. But none of his partners had roused more than his lusts, and he quickly tired of each new liaison. In Elise he was beginning to suspect something he had thought rare to the point of nonexistence: a kindred soul.

He had just dispatched another imaginary foe when a crackle in the bushes on the far side of the clearing made him raise his head. *Van back at last*, he thought; he filled his lungs to shout a greeting. It died unuttered. Only a thin whisper emerged, and that directed at Elise: "Do just what I tell you. Walk very slowly to the far side of the wagon, then run for the woods. Move!" he snapped when she hesitated. He made sure she was on her way before loping into the middle of the clearing to confront the aurochs.

It was a bull, a great roan, shaggy shoulders higher than a tall man's head. Scars old and new crisscrossed its hide. Its right horn was a shattered ruin, broken in some combat or accident long ago. The other curved out and forward, a glittering spear of death.

The aurochs' ears twitched as it stared at the puny man who dared challenge it. The certainty of a charge lay like a lump of ice in Gerin's belly: any aurochs would attack man or beast, but a lone bull was doubly terrible. Drago's grandfather had died under the horns and stamping hooves of just such a foe.

Quicker even than the Fox expected, the charge came. The beast's hooves sent chunks of sod flying skyward. There was no time to throw Van's spear. Gerin could only hurl himself to his left, diving to the turf. He had a glimpse of a green eye filled with insane hatred. Then the aurochs was past, the jagged stump of its horn passing just over him. The rank smell of its skin fought the clean odors of grass and dirt.

Gerin was on his feet in an instant. But the aurochs was already wheeling for another charge, faster than any four-footed beast had any right to be. The Fox hurled his spear, but the cast was hurried and high. It flew over the aurochs' shoulder. Only a desperate leap saved Gerin. Had the bull had two horns, he would surely have been spitted. As it was, he knew he could not elude it much longer in the open.

He sprang up and sprinted for the forest, snatching the spear as he ran. Behind him came the drumroll of the aurochs' hooves. The small of his back tingled, anticipating the horn. Then, breath sobbing in his throat, he was among the trees. Timber cracked as the aurochs smashed through brush and saplings. Still, it had to slow as it followed his dodges from tree to tree.

He hoped to lose it in the wood, but it pursued him with a deadly patience he had never known an aurochs to show. Its bellows and snorts of rage rang loud in his ears. Deeper and deeper into the forest he ran, following a vague game trail.

That came to an abrupt end: some time not long before, a forest giant had toppled, falling directly across the path. Its collapse brought down other trees and walled off the trail as thoroughly as any work of man's might have done. Gerin clambered over the dead timer. The aurochs was not far behind.

The Fox's wits had been frozen in dismay from the moment the aurochs appeared in the clearing. They began to work again as he leaped down from the deadfall. Panting, "I can't run any farther anyway," he jabbed the bronze-clad butt of Van's spear deep into the soft earth, then blundered away into the forest, having thrown his dice for the last time.

Ever louder came the thunder of the aurochs' hooves, till the Fox could feel the ground shake. For a terrible moment, he thought it would try to batter through the dead trees, but it must have known that was beyond its power. It hurled its bulk into the air, easily clearing the man-high barrier—and spitted itself on the upthrust spear.

The tough wood of the spearshaft shivered into a thousand splinters, but the leaf-shaped bronze point was driven deep into the aurochs' vitals. It staggered a couple of steps on wobbling legs, blood spurting from its belly. Then a great gout poured from its mouth and nose. It shuddered and fell. Its sides heaved a last time, then were still. It gave the Fox a reproachful brown bovine stare and died.

Gerin rubbed his eyes. In his dance with death out on the meadow, he had been sure the beast's eyes were green. His own hand came away bloody. He must have been swiped by a branch while dashing through the forest, but he had no memory of it. *Shows how much I know*, he thought. He wearily climbed back over the deadfall.

He had not gone far when Van came crashing down the game trail, drawn bow in his hands. Elise was right behind him. The outlander skidded to a stop, his jaw dropping. "How are you, captain?" he asked foolishly.

"Alive, much to my surprise."

"But—the aurochs . . . Elise said . . ." Van stopped, the picture of confusion.

Gerin was just glad Elise had had the sense to go after his friend instead of showing herself to the aurochs and probably getting herself killed. "I'm afraid I'll have to buy you a new spear when we get to the capital," he said.

Van hauled himself over the barrier. He came back carrying the spearpoint; bronze was too valuable to leave. "What in the name of the trident of Shamadraka did you do?" he asked.

The baron wondered where Shamadraka's worshipers lived; he had never heard of the god. "Climbing those trunks took everything I had left," he said. "The beast was hunting me like a hound—I've never known anything like it. He would have had me in a few minutes. But by some miracle I remembered a fable I read a long time ago, about a slave who was too lazy to hunt. He'd block a trail, set a javelin behind his barrier, and wait for the deer to skewer themselves for him."

Elise said, "I know the fable you mean: the tale of the Deer and Mahee. In the end he's killed by his own spear, and a good thing, too. He was a cruel, wicked man."

"You got the idea for killing the brute out of a book?" Van shook his head. "Out of a *book*? Captain, I swear I'll never sneer at reading again, if it can show you something that'll save your neck. The real pity of it is, you'll never have a chance to brag about this."

"And why not?" Gerin had been looking forward to doing just that.

"Slaying a bull aurochs singlehanded with a spear? Don't be a fool, Gerin: who would believe you?"

Van had killed his doe while the baron battled the aurochs. He dumped the bled and gutted carcass into the wagon and urged the horses southward. None of the travelers wanted to spend the night near the body of the slain aurochs. Not only would it draw unwelcome scavengers, but the spilled blood was sure to lure hungry, lonely ghosts from far and wide, all eager to share the unexpected bounty of the kill.

When the failing light told them it was time to camp, the deer proved toothsome indeed. Van carved steaks from its flanks. They roasted the meat over a fire. But despite a full belly, the outlander was unhappy. He grumbled, "I feel naked without my spear. What will I do without it in a fight?"

Gerin was less than sympathetic. "Seeing that you've brought a mace, an axe, three knives—"

"Only two. The third is just for eating."

"My apologies. Two knives, then, and a sword so heavy I can hardly lift it, let alone swing it. So I think you'll find some way to make a nuisance of yourself."

A nuisance Van was; he plucked a long straw from Elise's hand, leaving the short one—and the first watch—for Gerin. The Fox tried not to hear his friend's comfort-filled snores. His sense of the basic injustice of the universe was only slightly salved when Elise decided not to fall asleep at once.

Gerin was glad of her company. Without it, he probably would have dozed, for the night was almost silent. The sad murmurs of the ghosts, heard with the mind's ear rather than the body's, were also faint: the lure of the dead aurochs reached for miles, leaving the surrounding countryside all but bare of spirits.

For some reason the Fox could not fathom, Elise thought he was a hero for slaying the aurochs. He felt more lucky than heroic. There was precious little glory involved in running like a rabbit, which was most of what he'd done. Had he not plucked what he needed from his rubbish-heap of a memory, the beast would have killed him. "Fool luck," he concluded.

"Nonsense," Elise said. "Don't make yourself less than you are. In the heat of the fight you were able to remember what you had to know and, more, to do something with it. You need more than muscle to make a hero."

Not convinced, Gerin shrugged and changed the subject, asking Elise what she knew of her kin in the capital. Her closest relative there, it transpired, was her mother's brother Valdabrun the Stout, who held some position or other at the Emperor's court. Though he did not say, Gerin found that a dubious recommendation. His imperial majesty Hildor III was an indolent dandy, and the baron saw little reason to expect his courtiers to be different.

To hide his worry, he talked of the capital and his own two years there. Elise was a good audience, as city life of any sort was new to her. He told a couple of his better stories. Her laugh warmed the cool evening. She moved closer to him, eager to hear more.

He leaned over and kissed her. It seemed the most natural thing in the world to do. For a moment, her lips were startled and still under his. Then she returned the kiss, at first hesitantly, then with a warmth to match his own.

You do have a gift for complicating your life, he told himself as she snuggled her head into his shoulder. *If things go on the way they've started, not only will Wolfar want to cut out your heart and eat it (a project he's been nursing quite a while anyhow), but your old friend Ricolf will be convinced—note or no note—you ran off with his daughter for reasons having very little to do with taking her to her uncle. And what is* she *thinking? She's no peasant wench, to be honored by a tumble and then forgotten. And further . . .*

A plague on it all, he thought. He kissed her again.

But when his lips touched her soft white throat and his hands moved to slide inside her tunic, she asked him softly, "Was it for this, then, you decided to bring me south? Have I traded one Wolfar for another?" She tried to keep her tone light, but hurt and disappointment were in her voice. They stopped him effectively as a dagger drawn, perhaps more so. She slipped free of his encircling arm.

Breath whistled through his nostrils as he brought his body back under mind's rein. "I would never have you think that," he said.

"Nor do I, in truth," she replied, but the hurt was still there. The time to remember he was man and she maid might come later, he thought. It was not here yet, despite the cool quiet of the night and the moonlight filtering through the trees.

She was silent so long he thought her still upset, but when he framed further apologies, she waved them away. They talked of inconsequential things for a little while. Then she rose and walked to the wagon for her bedroll. As she passed him, she stooped; her lips brushed his cheek.

His mind was still thought-filled long after she had fallen asleep. Elleb's thick waxing crescent was well set and the nearly full Math, bright as a golden coin, beginning to wester when he woke Van and sank into exhausted slumber.

His dreams at first were murky, filled now with the aurochs, now with Elise. He remembered little of them. He rarely did, and thought strange those who could recall their dreams and cast omens from them. But then it was as if a gale arose within his sleeping mind and blew away the mists separating him from the country of dreams.

Clear as if he had been standing on the spot, he saw the great watchfires flame, heard wild music of pipe, horn, and harp skirl up to the sky, saw tall northern warriors gathered by the fires, some with spears, others with drinking-horns in their hands. *This is no common dream*, he thought, and felt fear, but he could not leave it, not even when black wings drowned his sight in darkness.

Those proved to be the edges of the wizard's cloak Balamung wore. The sorcerer stepped back a pace, to be silhouetted against the firelight like a bird of prey. Only his eyes were live things, embers of scarlet and amber set in his gaunt face.

The barbarian mage was only too aware of the Fox. He turned a trifle and bowed a hate-filled bow, as if the baron had been there in the flesh. The light played redly off his hollow cheeks. He said, "Lord Gerin the Fox, it's no less than a nuisance you are to me, no less, so I pray you'll forgive my costing you a dollop of sleep to show you what's waiting in the northlands whilst you scuttle about the filthy south. Would I could be drawing the black-hearted soul of you from your carcass, but there's no spell I ken to do it, what with you so far away."

No spell Gerin knew could have reached across the miles at all. He was nothing, not even a wraith, just eyes and ears bound to see and hear only what Balamung chose to reveal.

The Trokmoi danced round the fires, tossing swords, spears, aye, and drinking-horns, too, into the air. The baron's disembodied spirit was less terrified than it might have been; the dance was one of those Rihwin had performed atop Ricolf's table. It seemed an age ago. But Balamung surely knew the baron expected him to arm for war. What else had he been summoned to see?

Balamung called down curses on the Fox's head. He hoped they would not bite deep. On and on the wizard ranted, until he paused to draw breath. Then he went on more calmly, saying, "Not least do I mislike you for costing me the soul of a fine fighting man this day. Like a wee bird I sent it flitting out, to light in the body of the great aurochs. Sure as sure I was he'd stomp you to flinders and leave you dead by the side of the road. Curse your tricky soul, how did you escape him? His spirit died trapped in the beast, for I could not draw it free in time. And when it flickered away, his body was forfeit too, poor wight."

No wonder the bull had trailed him with such grim intensity! Maybe he'd been right when he thought its eyes were green, there in the meadow; that might have been some byproduct of Balamung's magic. He had been lucky indeed.

"But sure and I'll have my revenge!" Balamung screamed. Behind him, the music had fallen silent. The dancers stood motionless and expectant.

The spell the mage used must have been readied beforehand, for when he cried out in the harsh Kizzuwatnan tongue a stout wicker cage rose from the ground and drifted slowly toward the fire. Gerin's spirit quailed when he saw it; he knew the Trokmoi burned their criminals alive, and in this cage, too, a man struggled vainly to free himself.

"Die, traitor, die!" Balamung shouted. All the gathered warriors took up the cry. Horror rose in Gerin, who suddenly recognized the condemned prisoner. It was Divico, the Trokmê chieftain whose life he had spared at Ikos. He wished sickly that he had let Van give the northerner a clean death. "Have a look at what befalls them who fight me," Balamung whispered, "for your turn is next!" His voice was cold as ice, harsh as stone.

And while he spoke, the cage entered the blaze. Some minor magic had proofed the wicker against flame; no fire would hold on it. But wherever a tongue licked Divico, it clung, flaring as brightly as if his body were a pitch-soaked torch.

Held there by Balamung's wizardry, Gerin watched in dread as the flames boiled Divico's eyeballs in his head, melted his ears into shapeless lumps of meat that sagged and ran against his cheeks, then charred the flesh from those cheeks to leave white bone staring through. Fire cavorted over the Trokmê's body, but Balamung's evil magic would not let him die. He fought against the unyielding door until his very tendons burned away. His shrieks had stopped long before, when flames swallowed his larynx.

"He was a job I had to rush," Balamung said. "When it's you, now, Fox, falling into my hand, I'll take the time to think up something truly worthy of you, oh indeed and I will!" He made a gesture of dismissal. Gerin found himself staring up from his bedroll, body wet with cold sweat.

"Bad dream, captain?" Van asked.

Gerin's only answer was a grunt. He was too shaken for coherent speech. Divico's face, eaten by flames, still stood before his eyes, more vivid than the dimly lit campsite he really saw. He thought he would never want to sleep again, but his weary body needed rest more than his mind feared it.

The sounds of a scuffle woke him. Before he could do more than open his eyes, strong hands pinned him to the ground. It was still far from sunrise. Did bandits in the southland dare the darkness, or was this some new assault of Balamung's? He twisted, trying to lever himself up on an elbow and see who or what had overcome him.

"Be still, or I'll rend thee where thou liest." The voice was soft, tender, female, and altogether mad. More hands, all full of casual deranged strength, pressed down his legs. They tugged warningly. He felt his joints creak.

All hope left him. After he had escaped Balamung's forays, it seemed unfair for him to die under the tearing hands of the votaries of Mavrix. Why had the wine-god's orgiastic, frenzied cult ever spread outside his native Sithonia?

Moving very slowly, the baron turned his head, trying to see the extent of the disaster. Perhaps one of his comrades had managed to get away. But no: in the moonlight he saw Van, his vast muscles twisting and knotting to no avail, pinned by more of the madwomen. Still more had fastened themselves to Elise.

The maenads' eyes reflected the firelight like those of so many wolves. That was the only light in them. They held no human intelligence or mercy, for they were filled by the madness of the god. The finery in which they had begun their trek through the woods was ripped and tattered and splashed with mud and grime, their hair awry and full of twigs. One woman, plainly a lady of high station from the remnants of fine linen draped about her body, clutched the mangled corpse of some small animal to her bosom, crooning over and over, "My baby, my baby."

A blue light drifted out of the forest, a shining nimbus round a figure . . . godlike was the only word for it, Gerin thought. "What have we here?" the figure asked, voice deep and sweet like the drink the desert nomads brewed to keep off sleep.

"Mavrix!" the women breathed, their faces slack with ecstasy. Gerin felt their hands quiver and slip. He braced himself for a surge, but even as he tensed the god waved and the grip on him tightened again.

"What have we here?" Mavrix repeated.

Van gave a grunt of surprise. "How is it you speak my language?"

To the Fox it had been Elabonian. "He didn't—" The protest died half-spoken as his captors snarled.

The god made an airy, effeminate gesture. "We have our ways," he said . . . and suddenly there were two of him, standing side by side. They—he—gestured again, and there was only one.

As well as he could, Gerin studied Mavrix. The god wore fawnskin, soft and supple, with a wreath of grape leaves round his brow. In his left hand he bore an ivy-tipped wand. At need, Gerin knew, it was a weapon more deadly than any mortal's spear. Mavrix's blond curls reached his shoulder;

his cheeks and chin were shaven. That soft-featured, smiling face was a pederast's dream, but for the eyes: two black pits reflecting nothing, giving back only the night. A faint odor of fermenting grapes and something else, a rank something Gerin could not name, clung to him.

"That must be a useful art." The baron spoke in halting Sithonian, trying to pique the god's interest and buy at least a few extra minutes of life.

Mavrix turned those fathomless eyes on the Fox, but his face was still a smiling mask. He answered in the same tongue: "How pleasant to hear the true speech once more, albeit in the mouth of a victim," and Gerin knew his doom.

"Are you in league with Balamung, then?" he growled, knowing nothing he said now could hurt him further.

"I, friend to some fribbling barbarian charlatan? What care I for such things? But surely, friend mortal, you see this is your fate. The madness of the Mavriad cannot, must not be thwarted. Were it so, the festival would have no meaning, for what is it but the ultimate negation of all the petty nonfulfillments of humdrum, everyday life?"

"It's not right!" Elise burst out. "Dying I can understand; everyone dies, soon or late. But after the baron Gerin"—the Fox thought it a poor time to rhyme, but kept quiet—"singlehanded slew the aurochs, to die at the hands of lunatics, god-driven or no—"

Mavrix broke in, deep voice cracking: "Gerin slew a great wild ox—" The god's smile gave way to an expression of purest horror. "The oxgoad come again!" he screamed, "but now in the shape of a man! Metokhites, I thought you slain!" With a final despairing shriek, the god vanished into the depths of the woods. His followers fled after, afflicted by his terror—all but the lady of rank, who still sat contentedly, rocking her gruesome "baby."

Still amazed at being alive, Gerin slowly sat up. So did Elise and Van, both wearing bewildered expressions. "What did I say?" Elise asked.

Gerin thumped his forehead, trying to jar loose a memory. He had paid scant attention to Mavrix in the past, as the god's principal manifestations, wine and the grape, were rare north of the Kirs. "I have it!" he said at last, snapping his fingers. "This Metokhites was a Sithonian prince long ago. Once he chased the god into the Lesser Inner Sea, beating him about the head with a metal-tipped oxgoad: Mavrix always was a coward. I suppose he thought I was a new—what would the word be?—incarnation of his tormentor."

"What happened to this Metokhites fellow?" Van asked. "It's not the smartest thing, tangling with gods."

"As I remember, he chopped his son into bloody bits, being under the impression the lad was a grapevine."

"A grapevine, you say? Well, captain, if I ever seem to you to go all green and leafy-like, be so good as to warn me before you try to trim me."

At that, the last of the maenads lifted her eyes from the ruined little body she dandled. There was a beginning of knowledge in her face, though she was not yet fully aware of herself or her surroundings. Her voice had some of the authority of the Sibyl at Ikos when she spoke: "Mock not Mavrix, lord of the sweet grape. Rest assured, you are not forgotten!" Gathering her rags about her, she swept imperiously into the woods. Silence fell on the camp.

VII

Taking advantage of the quiet of the ghosts, Gerin decided to leave at once, though he knew mere distance was even less guarantee of safety from Mavrix than from Balamung. No thunderbolt smote him. Before too much time had passed, the rising sun turned Tiwaz and Math to a pair of pale gleams hanging close together in the southern sky.

So full of events had the previous day been that the Fox took till mid-afternoon to remember his dream, if such it was. By that time they were on the main road again, three more corpuscles among the thousands flowing toward the Empire's heart. "So that's why you woke with such a thrash!" Van said. Then the full import of the baron's words sank in. "You're saying the scrawny son of nobody knows where we are and what we're up to?"

Gerin rubbed his chin. "Where we are, anyway."

"I'm not sure I like that."

"I know damned well I don't, but what can I do about it?"

The Fox spent a gloomy, watchful night, fearing a return visit from Mavrix. The oracular tones of the god's half-crazed worshiper had left him jittery. The watch was lonely, too. Van fell asleep at once, and Elise quickly followed him.

That day on the road, she had hardly spoken to the baron. She spent most of her time listening to Van's yarns; he would cheerfully spin them for hours on end. She gave Gerin nothing more than cool courtesy when he tried to join the conversation. At length he subsided, feeling isolated and vaguely betrayed. The left side of his mouth quirked up in a sour smile; he knew only too well that his ill-timed ardor was what made her wary.

The new morning began much as the day before had ended: Gerin and Elise cautious and elaborately polite while Van, who seemed oblivious to the tension around him, bawled out a bawdy tune he had learned from the Trokmoi. So it went till they reached the Pranther River, another of the streams that rose in the foothills of the Kirs and ended by swelling the waters of the Greater Inner Sea.

The road did not falter at the Pranther, but sprang over it on a bridge supported by eight pillars of stone. The span itself was of stout timbers, which could be removed at need to slow invaders. This bridge was no flimsy magician's trick—it looked ready to stand for a thousand years.

Van gazed at it with admiration. "What a fine thing! It beats getting your backside wet, any day."

"It's probably the most famous bridge in the Empire," Gerin told him, grinning; the bridge over the Pranther was one of his favorite places in the south. "It's called Dalassenos' Revenge."

"Why's that, captain?"

"Dalassenos was Oren the Builder's chief architect. He was the fellow who designed this bridge, but Oren wanted only his own name on it. Being a Sithonian, Dalassenos didn't have much use for the Emperor in the first place, and that was too much to bear. So he carved his own message into the rock, then put a coat of plaster over it and chiseled Oren's name in that. After a few years, the plaster peeled away and—well, see for yourself." He jerked a thumb at the pylon.

"It's only so many scratches to me. I don't read Sithonian, or much else, for that matter."

Gerin thought for a moment. "As near as I can put it into Elabonian, it says:

> 'The plaster above? 'Twas nought but a farce,
> And as for King Oren, he can kiss my arse.' "

Van bellowed laughter. "Ho, ho! That calls for a snort." A blind reach into the back of the wagon brought him his quarry—a wineskin. He swigged noisily.

Dalassenos' flip insolence also earned the Fox a smile from Elise; her appreciation was worth more to him than Van's chuckles. "What happened to Dalassenos when the plaster wore off?" she asked. The friendly interest in her voice told Gerin he had been forgiven.

"Not a thing," he answered. "It lasted through Oren's life, and he died childless (he liked boys). His successor hated him for almost bankrupting the Empire with all his building, and likely laughed his head off when he learned what Dalassenos had done. I know he sent Dalassenos a pound of gold, tight though he was."

As they passed over the bridge, Gerin looked down into the Pranther's clear water. A green manlike shape caught his eye. It was so close to the surface that he could easily see the four scarlet gill-slits on either side of its neck.

The Pranther held the only colony of rivermen west of the Greater Inner Sea. Dalassenos had brought the reptiles here from their native Sithonian streams. The canny artificer knew stones and sand propelled by the Pranther's current would eventually scour away the riverbottom from under his bridge's pilings and bring it tumbling down. Hence the rivermen: they repaired such damage as fast as it occurred.

In exchange, the Empire banned humans from fishing in the Pranther, and gave the rivermen leave to enforce the prohibition with their poisoned darts. It was also said that Dalassenos had hired a wizard to put a spell of permanent plenty on the fish. The baron did not know about that, but the rivermen had flourished in the Pranther for more than three hundred years.

Gerin heard the screech of an eagle overhead. Shielding his eyes from the sun, he looked up into morning haze until he found it. It wheeled in the sky, sun striking sparks from its ruddy plumage. Its feathers, he mused, were red as a Trokmê's mustache.

Sudden suspicion flared in him as he realized what he'd thought. "Van, do you think you can bring me down that overgrown pigeon?" he asked, knowing his friend's mighty arms could propel a shaft farther than most men dreamed possible.

The outlander squinted upward, shook his head. "No more than I could flap my arms and fly to Fomor."

"Fomor, is it?"

"Tiwaz, I mean. Whatever fool name you give the quick moon."

"Two years with me, and you still talk like a Trokmê." Gerin sadly shook his head.

"Go howl, captain. What's in your mind?"

The Fox did not answer. He pulled the wagon off the road. The eagle gave no sign of flying away, nor had he expected any. He had never seen a red eagle, and was convinced it was some creature of Balamung's, a flying spy. He climbed down from the wagon and began to root among the bushes by the roadside.

"What are you looking for, Gerin?" Elise asked.

"Sneezeweed," he answered, not finding any. He muttered a curse. The plant was a rank pest near Fox Keep; it grew everywhere in the northlands, even invading wheatfields. When it flowered, those sensitive to its pollen went into a season-long agony of wheezing, sneezing, runny eyes, and puffy faces. The dried pollen was also a first-rate itching powder, as small boys soon learned. The Fox remembered a thrashing his brother Dagref had given him over a pair of sneezeweed-impregnated breeches.

At last he found a ragged sneezeweed plant huddling under two bigger bushes, its shiny, dark green leaves sadly bug-eaten. He murmured a prayer of thanks to Dyaus when he saw a spike of pink flowers still clinging to it. It would serve for the small magic he had in mind.

He ran the spell over and over in his head, hoping he still had it memorized. It was simple enough, and one all 'prentices learned—a fine joke on the unwary. At the Sorcerers' Collegium, one quickly learned not to be unwary.

He held the spray of sneezeweed flowers in his left hand and began to chant. His right hand moved through the few simple passes the spell required. It took less than a minute. When it was done, he looked up and awaited developments.

For a moment, nothing happened. He wondered if he had botched the incantation or if it simply was not strong enough to reach the high-flying eagle. Then the bird seemed to stagger in mid-flight. Its head darted under its wing to peck furiously. No longer could it maintain its effortless rhythm through the air, but fought without success to maintain altitude. It descended in an ungainly spiral, screaming its rage all the while, and flopped into the bushes about twenty paces from the wagon. Van put an arrow through it. It died still snapping at the shaft.

Much pleased with himself, the Fox trotted over to collect the carcass. He had just brought it to the wagon when Elise cried out in warning. Two more red eagles were diving out of the morning sky, stooping like falcons. Van had time for one hasty shot. He missed. Cursing foully, he snatched up the whip and swung it in a terrible arc. It smashed into one bird with a sound like a thunderclap. Feathers flew in a metallic cloud. The eagle gave a despairing screech and tumbled to the roadway.

The other one flew into Gerin's surprised arms.

It fastened its claw on the leather sleeve of his corselet, seeming to think the garment part of its owner. The Fox plunged his free hand at its shining breast, trying to keep its bill from his eyes. It screamed and bucked, buffeting him with vile-smelling wings.

There was a crunch. Van drove the butt end of the whip into the eagle's head, again and again. The mad gleam in its golden eyes faded. Gerin slowly realized he was holding a dead weight. Blood trickled down his arm; that leather sleeve had not altogether protected him.

A gleam of silver caught his eye. The bird wore a tiny button at its throat, held on by a fine chain. The button bore only one mark: a fylfot. "Balamung, sure enough," Gerin muttered.

Van peered at it over his shoulder. "Let me have a closer look at that, will you?" he said. Gerin slipped the chain from the dead eagle's neck and passed it to him. He hefted it thoughtfully. "Lighter than it should be." He squeezed it between thumb and finger, grunting at the effort. "Gives a little, but not enough." He brought down a booted foot club-fashion. There was a thin, hissing wail. Gerin gagged. He thought of latrines, of new-dug graves fresh uncovered, of scummed moats, of long slow evils fermenting deep in the bowels of swamps and oozing upwards to burst as slimy bubbles.

The body in his arms writhed, though he knew it was, knew it had to be, dead. He looked down, and dropped his burden with an exclamation of horror. No longer was the corpse that of an eagle, but of a Trokmê, his head battered to a pulp, fiery locks soaked in blood. But . . . the broken body was no bigger than the bird had been. Grim-faced, he and Van repeated the grisly experiment twice more, each time with the same result.

As he buried the three tiny bodies in a common grave, the pride he had felt in his sorcerous talent drained away like wine from a broken cup. What good were his little skills against such power as Balamung possessed, power that could rob men of their very shapes and send them winging over hundreds of miles to slay at his bidding?

Elise said, "It will take a mighty southern mage indeed to overcome such strength." Her voice was somber, but somehow her words, instead of depressing the baron, lifted his spirits. They reminded him he would not, after all, have to face Balamung alone. More and more, their conflict was assuming in his mind the nature of a duel between himself and the northern wizard, a duel in which the Trokmê owned most of the weapons. But why was he here in the southlands, if not for allies?

"You have a gift for saying the right thing," he told her gratefully. She shook her head in pretty confusion. He did not explain. As the day wore on, he felt better and better. True, Balamung had tried to slay him from afar, but twice now his efforts had come to nothing, and every hour put more miles between him and his quarry.

Late in the afternoon, Van pointed to a hand-sized roadside shrub not much different from its neighbors and said, "You know some plant-lore, Gerin—there's another useful plant for you."

"That?" the Fox said. "It looks like any other weed to me."

"Then you Elabonians don't know what to do with it. It grows out on the plains of Shanda, too. The shamans there call it 'aoratos,' which means it lets you see a bit of the unseen when you chew the leaves. Not only that, they help keep you awake on watch. Like I said, a useful plant."

"What do you mean, 'it lets you see a bit of the unseen'?"

"That's the only way I can explain it, captain. Hold up a moment, and I'll let you see for yourself." Van uprooted the little bush and returned to the wagon. Gerin studied the plant curiously, but it was so nondescript he could not say whether he had seen its like before.

He got to test its properties soon enough, for he drew first watch that night. The leaves were gritty and bitter. Their juice burned as he swallowed. Little by little, he felt his tiredness slip away. As he sat sentinel, the night came alive around him.

The sky seemed to darken; Elleb, just past first quarter, shone with spectral clarity. So, when she rose, did Math, a day past full. The stars also seemed very bright and clear.

But that was the least effect of the aoratos plant. The Fox found he could tell with certainty where every live thing lurked within a hundred yards of the fire. No matter how well concealed it was, its life force impinged on him like a spot of light seen in the back of his mind.

He understood why Van had had trouble talking about the experience—it seemed to use a sense his body did not normally employ. He was even able to detect strange patterns of radiance within the ghosts, though their flickering shapes remained indistinct as ever.

The extra perception gradually faded, and was gone well before midnight. On the whole, he decided, he approved of the aoratos plant. If nothing else, it made ambushes nearly impossible. "Aye, it does that," Van nodded when Gerin told him of his feelings, "but you have to use near half the plant at every dose. The gods know when we'll see another here. I never did find one in the northlands, you know."

Nor did they find another aoratos bush the following day, or the next, or the next. The last of its leaves stripped, the little plant was tossed away and all but forgotten. As the road swung east, down into the great plain whose heart was Elabon's capital, Gerin found he had more important things to think about. The dry warmth of the south, the quality of the sunlight pouring down from the sky, and the bustling people of the ever more numerous towns were calling forth a side of his nature he had had to hide on the frontier, a gentler side his vassals would only have construed as weakness.

Drago or Rollan could never have understood his open admiration of a sunset; his search for verses from Lekapenos appropriate to its beauty; his easy, friendly dealing with merchants and innkeepers, men at whom they would simply have barked orders. He felt like a flower, half of whose petals were seeing the sun for the first time in years.

The presence of Elise beside him was a pleasant pain. She unsettled him more than he was willing to admit, even to himself. He was too conscious of her as a woman to bring back all the ease of talk they had once enjoyed. She stayed warm and friendly, but deftly avoided anything truly personal, seeming content with the inconclusive status quo. Her warmth extended farther than the Fox, too; her laughing responses to Van's outrageous flirtation grated on Gerin's nerves.

Two days out from the capital, the travelers found lodging at a tavern in a little town called Cormilia. The lass who served them there was short, dark, and, though a bit plump, quite pretty; a tiny mole on her right cheek made her round face piquant.

Something about her struck the Fox's fancy. When he raised an eyebrow at her, she winked back saucily. He was not surprised when she tapped at his door later that night. While her thighs clasped him, she seemed hot-blooded enough for any man's taste. But her ministrations, immensely pleasant in the moment, somehow left him less than satisfied after she slipped away.

He knew he had pleased her. Her adoring manner the next morning spoke of how much. But the coupling only showed him the emptiness within himself. He was preoccupied and curt, and breakfasted without much noticing what he ate.

When he and Van went out to the stable to hitch up the horses, he blurted, "You know, when Dyaus created women he must have been in a fey mood. You can't live with them and sure as sure can't live without them."

Though surmise gleamed in Van's eye, he said nothing to that. He knew Gerin was a man who had to work things through in his own mind and often thought advice interference.

A briny breeze from the Greater Inner Sea blew all day. They might have made the capital by evening. But Gerin did not relish trying in the dark to find his old friend Turgis' inn; the great city's maze of streets was bad enough by day.

The coming parting with Elise also wrenched him more each mile he traveled. He was far from eager to speed it unduly. He decided to camp just in front of the last low ridge shielding the capital from sight. As darkness fell, the city's lights put a glow on the eastern horizon and bleached fainter stars from the sky.

In an area so densely peopled, night travel was no longer unthinkable. A brightly lit convoy of wagons and chariots rumbled past the campsite every few minutes, often with a mumbling priest to help ward off the spirits.

Of this Van heard nothing, for he fell asleep almost instantly. But Gerin did not pass his watch in lonely contemplation. For the first time since the night Mavrix appeared, Elise decided to stay up a while and talk. The reason soon became clear: she was bubbling over with excitement and curiosity about the capital and the family in it she had never seen.

She gushed on for a time, then stopped, embarrassed. "But this is terrible! What a loon I am! Here I play the magpie over all I'll see and do in the city, and not a word of thanks to you, who brought me here safe through so many troubles. What must you think of me?"

The answer to that had been slowly forming in the baron's mind ever since he helped her slip from Ricolf's keep. Her rhetorical question but served to bring it into sharper focus. He replied hesitantly, though, for fear of her thinking he was abusing the privilege their companionship had given him. "It's simple enough," he said at last, taking the plunge—the thought of losing her forever filled him with more dread than any Trokmê horde. "After Balamung and his woodsrunners are driven back to the forests where they belong, nothing would make me happier than coming south again so I can court you properly."

He did not know what reaction he had expected from her—certainly not the glad acceptance she showed. "As things are now, I cannot say as much as I would like," she said, "but nothing would please me more." Her lips met his in a gentle kiss that gave him more contentment than all his sweaty exertions the night before in Cormilia. She went on, "Foolish man, did you not know I cried last year when I learned your wound would keep you from coming to my father's holding?"

He held her close, his mind filling with a hundred, a thousand foolish plans for the future. The rest of the watch flew by like a dream, as it would have for any lover who suddenly found his love returned. If Balamung's gaunt figure stood like a jagged reef between him and his dreams, on this night he would pretend he did not see it.

Elise fought sleep until Math rose to add her light to that of Elleb, whose nearly full disc rode high in the south. The baron watched her face relax into slumber, murmured, "Sleep warm," and kissed her forehead. She smiled and stirred, but did not wake.

When Gerin told Van what he had done, the outlander slapped his back, saying, "And what took you so long?"

The Fox grunted, half annoyed his friend had been able to follow his thoughts so well. Something else occurred to him. "We need to start right at sunrise tomorrow," he said.

"What? Why?" Van did not seem to believe his ears.

"I have my reasons."

"They must be good ones, to make a slugabed like you want an early start. All right, captain, sunrise it is."

They topped the last rise just as the sun climbed over the eastern horizon. It flamed off the Greater Inner Sea and transformed the water to a lambent sheet of fire, dazzling to the eye. Tiny black dots on that expanse were ships: merchantmen with broad sails billowing in the fresh morning breeze and arrogant galleys striding over the waves like outsized spiders on oared legs.

Elise, who had never seen the sea, cried out in wonder and delight. She squeezed Gerin's hand. The Fox beamed, proud as if he'd created the vista himself. Van also nodded his appreciation. "Very nice, captain, very nice," he told the baron.

"If that's all you can find to say, you'd likely say the same if Farris herself offered to share your bed."

"She's your goddess of love and such things?" At Gerin's nod, Van went on, "I'll tell you, Fox, that reminds me of a story—"

"Which I'll hear some other time," Gerin said firmly. Straight ahead, on a spur of land thrusting out into the sea, lay Elabon's capital. All his attention centered there.

A thousand years before, he knew, it had been nothing but a farming village. Then the Sithonians came west across the Sea, and the infant city, now a center for Sithonian trade with the folk they deemed barbarous westerners, acquired its first wall. Its inhabitants learned much from the Sithonians. Little by little it extended its sway over the fertile western plain, drawing on ever greater reserves of men and resources. Soon it swallowed up the Sithonian colonies on the western shore of the Greater Inner Sea.

Nor could the Sithonians come to the aid of those colonies, for Sithonia itself, divided into rival confederacies led by its two greatest city-states, Siphnos and Kortys, fell into a century of bloody civil war. All the while, Elabon waxed. No sooner had Kortys at last beaten down her rival than she had to face the army of Carlun World-Bestrider, whose victory ended the Elabonian League and began the Empire of Elabon. A great marble statue of him, ten times as high as a man, still looked east from the shore. It was easy to spy, silhouetted against the bright sea.

Not far away from Carlun's monument stood the Palace Imperial. Gleaming like an inverted icicle, it shot a spearpoint of marble and crystal to the sky. An eternal fire burned at its apex, a guide from afar to ships on the Inner Sea. Round it was a wide space of well-trimmed gardens, so the palace itself almost seemed a plant grown from some strange seed.

Near the palace was the nobles' quarters; their homes were less imposing by far than the Emperor's residence, but most were far more splendid than anything north of the Kirs.

To Gerin's mind, though, the rest of Elabon was the Empire's true heart. Men of every race and tribe dwelt there; it boiled and bubbled cauldron-wise with the surge of life through its veins. There was a saying that you could buy anything in Elabon, including the fellow who sold it to you.

The Fox could have gazed on the city for hours, but from behind a gruff bass voice roared, "Move it there, you whoreson! Do you want to diddle the whole day away?" The speaker was a merchant, a loudly unhappy one.

Gerin waved back at him. "This is the first time I've seen Elabon in eight years," he apologized.

The merchant was not appeased. "May it be your last, then, ever again. You stand gawking, you boy-loving booby, and here I am, trying to make an honest living from tight-fisted nobles and little bandit lordlings, and all my thirty wagons are piling into each other while you crane your fool neck. I ought to set my guards on you, and it's a mark of my good temper and restraint that I don't. Now move it!"

Gerin twitched the reins and got the horses moving. Van chuckled. "Fellow sounds like a sergeant I knew once."

Like any town south of the mountains, Elabon had its ring of crucifixes. Because of the city's size, the crosses made a veritable forest. Bright-winged gulls from off the Inner Sea squabbled with ravens and vultures over the dead meat on them. The stench was overpowering. Elise produced a wisp of scented cloth and pressed it to her nose. Gerin wished for one of his own.

Expanding through long years of security, the capital had outgrown three walls. Two had vanished altogether, their bricks and stones going to swell the growth. Only a low ridge showed where the rammed-earth core of the third had stood.

Gerin took the wagon down the city's main street. The locals affectionately called it the Alley; it ran due east, arrow-straight, from the outskirts of the capital to the docks, and was filled with markets and shops from one end to the other. The Fox drove past the Lane of Silversmiths (a trade Kizzuwatnans dominated), the pottery mart where Sithonians and Elabonians cried their wares, odorous eateries serving the fare of every nation subject or neighbor to the Empire, the great canvas-roofed emporium where wheat imported from the northern shore of the Inner Sea was sold, a small nest of armorers and smiths (the baron had to promise Van they would come back later), and so much else he began to feel dizzy trying to take it all in at once.

Beggars limped, prostitutes of both sexes jiggled and pranced, scribes stood at the ready to write for illiterate patrons, minstrels played on every corner, and, no doubt, thieves lurked to despoil them of the coins they earned. Running, shouting lads were everywhere underfoot. Gerin marveled that any of them lived to grow up. He pricked up his ears when he heard one shouting, "Turgis!" His head swiveled till he spied the boy.

"Snatch him, Van!" He steered toward his target, talking the horses to calm in chaos.

"Right you are, captain." Van reached out and grabbed up a ragamuffin whose first beard was just beginning to sprout.

"You can lead us to Turgis?" Gerin demanded.

"I can, sir, and swear by all the gods and goddesses no finer hostel than his exists anywhere."

"Spare me the glowing promises. I'm known to Turgis. Tell me, lad, how is the old butterball?"

"He's well enough my lord, indeed he is, and generous of food, though sparing of praises. You turn left here, sir," he added.

Within moments, Gerin was lost in the maze of the capital. He did not think Turgis' hostel had formerly been in this district; the old fraud must have moved. His guide, who called himself Jouner, gave directions mixed with shrill abuse directed at anyone who dared block the narrow, winding back streets. The abuse often came back with interest.

Jouner was also extravagantly admiring of his charges—especially Elise. She blushed and tried to wave him to silence, not recognizing that his manner was part professional courtesy. Still, the Fox heard sincerity in the lad's voice, too.

Most of the houses in this part of the city were two-storied, flat-roofed structures. Their whitewashed outer walls defined the twisting paths of its streets. Despite occasional obscenities scrawled in charcoal, from the outside one was much like another. But within the austerity, Gerin knew, would be courtyards bright with flowers and cheerfully painted statuary. Some, perhaps, would be enlivened further by floor mosaics or intricately patterned carpets woven by the Urfa.

Poorer folk lived in apartment houses: "islands," in Elabon's slang. Solid and unlovely, the brick buildings towered fifty and sixty feet into the air, throwing whole blocks of houses into shadow. More than once, jars of slops emptied from some upper window splashed down into the street, sending passersby running for cover. "Watch it!" Van bellowed up. An instant later, two more loads just missed the wagon.

"That's one of the first things you learn to watch for here," Gerin told him, remembering his own experience. "They hold the high ground."

When at last the travelers came to Turgis' establishment, the baron was agreeably surprised by the marble columns on either side of the entranceway and the close-cropped lawn in front of the hostel itself. "Go right in," Jouner said, scrambling down. "I'll see to your horses and wagon."

"Many thanks, lad," Gerin said as he descended. He gave the boy a couple of coppers, then helped Elise down, taking the opportunity to hug her briefly.

"Have a care with that Shanda horse," Van warned Jouner. "He snaps."

The boy nodded. As he began to head for the stable, Elise said, "A moment. Jouner, how do you live in this stench?"

Puzzlement crossed Jouner's face. "Stench, my lady? What stench? Travelers always complain about it, but I don't notice a thing."

Turgis met the travelers at the front door. His bald pate, brown as the leather apron he wore, gleamed in the sunlight. A smile stretched across his fat face, the ends of it disappearing into a thick graying beard. "You appear to have come up in the world a mite," Gerin said by way of greeting.

"Crave pardon, sir? No, wait, I know that voice, though you've had the wisdom to hide your face in hair." Turgis' grin widened. "A cocky young whelp by the name of Gerin, badly miscalled the Fox, not so?"

"Aye, it is, you old bandit. Also Van of the Strong Arm and the lady Elise."

Turgis bobbed a bow. "You have a most lovely wife, Fox."

"The lady is not my wife," Gerin said.

"Oh? My lord Van—?"

"Nor mine." Van grinned.

"Oh? Ho, ho!" Turgis laid a finger alongside his nose and winked.

Elise spluttered indignation.

"Not that either," Gerin said. "It's a long story, and more complicated than I like."

"I daresay it must be. Well, it would honor me if you tell it."

"You'll hear it before the day is done, never fear. Turgis, it does my heart good to see you again, and to know you've not forgotten me."

"I, Turgis son of Turpin, forget a friend? Never!"

Gerin had hoped for that opening. "Then no doubt you recall just as well the promise you made the night I left the city."

The smile disappeared from Turgis' face. "What promise was that, lord Gerin? We both looked into our cups too often that night, and it was a long time ago."

"You won't wriggle out as easy as that, you saucy robber. You know as well as I, you gave me an oath if ever I came this way again I'd have my rooms for the same rate as I had them then!"

"What? You insolent whelp, this is a whole new building—or had your oh-so-perfect memory not noticed that? Are you fain to hold me to a drunken vow? May your fundament fall out! And the way prices have risen! Why, I could weep great buckets and your flinty heart would not be so much as—"

"An oath, damn your eyes, an oath!" Gerin said. Both men were laughing now.

Turgis talked right through him. "—softened. Think of my wife! Think of my children! My youngest son Egginhard would study wizardry, and for such school, nothing less than which is his heart's desire, much silver is needed."

"If he would be a conjurer, let him magic it up, and not have his father steal it."

"Think of my poor maiden aunt!" Turgis wailed.

"When I was here last, your poor maiden aunt ran the biggest gambling den in the city, you bloodsucker. An oath, remember?"

"As my head lives, only a third more would satisfy me—"

"On that your head would live entirely too well. Would you be known as Turgis the Oathbreaker?"

"May all the grapes in every vineyard you own turn sour!"

"Don't own any at all, truth to tell: too far north. Is your memory jogged yet?"

Turgis hopped on one foot, hopped on the other foot, plucked a gray hair from his beard, and sighed heavily. "All

right, I recollect. Bah! The innkeeping trade lost a great one
when you became a pirate or baron or whatever it is you
do. I'm sure you're a howling success. Now go howl and let
me lick my wounds—or do you carry courtesy so far?"

"What do you think, Van?" Gerin said.

His comrade had watched the altercation with amusement. "Reckon so, captain, if your friend can fix me up
with a hot tub big enough for my bulk."

"Who dares call Turgis son of Turpin a friend of this
backwoods bandit? Were I half my age and twice my size,
I'd challenge you for that. As is, however, go down this
corridor. Third door on the left. You might follow him,
Gerin; even your name stinks in my nostrils at this moment.
And for you, my lady, we have somewhat more elegant
arrangements. If you would care to follow me . . . ?"

Turgis led Elise off to whatever facilities he had for
making beautiful women more so. She seemed as much
captivated by the innkeeper as was Gerin himself; though
this was a new building, the same atmosphere of comfort
and good cheer the Fox had always known was here. Other
hostels might have had more splendid accommodations, but
none of them had Turgis.

The bath-house's masseur was a slim young Sithonian
with outsized hands, arms, and shoulders. His name was
Vatatzes. As if by magic, he had two steaming tubs ready
and waiting. He helped Van unlace his corselet. When the
outlander shed his bronze-studded leather kilt, Vatatzes, true
to the predilections of his nation, whistled in awe and
admiration.

"Sorry, my friend," Van chuckled, understanding him well
enough. "Gerin and I both like women."

"You poor dears," Vatatzes said. His disappointment did
not stop him from kneading away the kinks of travel as the
hot water soaked off grime. Swathed in linen towels and
mightily relaxed, Gerin and Van emerged from the bath
to find Jouner waiting outside. "I've taken the liberty of
moving your gear to your rooms," he said. "Follow me if you
would, sirs." He also offered to carry Van's cuirass but, as
usual, the outlander declined to be parted from it even for
a moment.

The rooms were on the second floor of the hostel. They

offered a fine view of the Palace Imperial. A door which could be barred on either side gave access from one to the other. "Don't bother to put things away," Gerin told Jouner. "I'd sooner do it myself—that way I know where everything is."

"As you wish, my lord." Jouner pocketed a tip and disappeared.

Gerin surveyed the room. If nothing else, it was more spacious than the cubicle he had called his own during his former stay in the capital. Nor would he sleep on a straw pallet as he had then. He had a mattress and pillow, both stuffed with goosedown, and two thick wool blankets to ward off night's chill. By the bed were a jug, bowl, and chamberpot, all of Sithonian ware fine enough to be worth a small fortune north of the Kirs. A footstool, chair, and stout oaken chest completed the furnishings. On the chest were two fat beeswax candles and a shrine to Dyaus with a pinch of perfumed incense already smoking away. Above it hung an encaustic painting of a mountain scene done by a Sithonian homesick for his craggy native land.

The baron quickly unpacked and threw himself onto the bed, sighing with pleasure as he sank into its soft stuffing. Van rapped on the connecting door. "This is the life!" he said when Gerin let him in. "I haven't seen beds so fine since a bordello I visited in Jalor. I don't know about you, Fox, but I'm all for sacking out for a while. It's been a long, hard trip."

"I was thinking the same thing," Gerin told him. Yawning, Van went back into his own room. The baron knew he should go down to see how Elise liked her chamber in the women's quarters. Enervated from the hot bath and massage and tired from many nights with little sleep, he could not find the energy. . . .

The next thing he knew, Jouner was knocking on the door. "My lord," he called, "Turgis bids you join him in the taproom for supper in half an hour's time."

"Thanks, lad. I'll be there." Gerin yawned and stretched. He heard Jouner deliver the same message to Van, who eventually grumbled a reply.

It was a bit past sunset. Tiwaz's razor-thin crescent, almost invisible in the pink in the west.

The Fox splashed water on his face, then went rummaging through his gear for an outfit that might impress Turgis and, not incidentally, Elise. After some thought, he decided on a maroon tunic with sleeves flaring out from the elbows and checked trousers of contrasting shades of blue. A necklace of gold nuggets and a belt with a bronze buckle in the shape of a leaping longtooth (Shanda work, that) completed the outfit. Wishing for a mirror, he combed his hair and beard with a bone comb. *I look the very northerner*, he thought: *well, fair enough, that's what I am.* He set out for the taproom.

Folk of every race filled the high-ceilinged hall. Three musicians—flautist, piper, and mandolin-player—performed on a small stage at one end, but they were all but ignored. Every man's attention was on Turgis' cook.

A dark, burly fellow with hooked noise, bushy beard, and black hair drawn back into a bun, he worked behind a great bronze griddle in the center of the room, and in his own way was more a showman than the musicians. He kept up a steady stream of chatter about every dish he was preparing, and knives were quicker in his hands than in those of any warrior Gerin had ever seen. Its gleam reflecting off his sweaty face, bronze danced as if alive, shining in the torchlight, dicing vegetables and slicing meat with a rhythm of its own. No, not quite; with a small shock, Gerin realized the knives were providing a percussion accompaniment to the music from the stage.

A waiter hovering by his elbow, Turgis sat at a quiet corner table. He surged to his feet and embraced Gerin, who pointed to the cook and asked, "Where did you find him?"

"He's something, isn't he?" Turgis beamed. "He's good for business, too. Just watching him makes people hungry." He turned to the server, saying, "Bring me my special bottle. You know the one I mean. Bring some ordinary good wine, too, and—hmm—four glasses."

The Fox's eyes widened. "That can't be the same 'special bottle' you used to keep when I was here before?"

"The very same, and not much lower, either. Where would I get another? You know as well as I that it was salvage from a ship of some unknown land that wrecked itself down in the southeast on the Bay of Parvela's rocks.

Aye, it's precious stuff, my friend—see, I still call you that, highway robber though you be—but then how often do we look upon friends thought lost forever?"

"Not often enough."

"Truth in your words, truth in your words."

The waiter returned. Careful not to spill even one drop, Turgis worked at the cork of the flask they had been discussing. Even that flask was special: small and squat and silvery, like no other glass Gerin had seen. "Here it is," Turgis said. "Nectar of the sun."

Gerin had a sudden terrible fear that when Van came down, he would loudly announce he had traveled with whole shiploads of the brew. By rights, there should be no more than this one miraculous bottle.

At Turgis' murmured invitation, the baron enjoyed the rare drink's rich fragrance. A silence fell over the hall. For a moment, Gerin thought his nose's pleasure had made him ignore his other senses, but the quiet was real. He looked up. There in the doorway stood Van, helm and armor gleaming, crimson cloak over his shoulders matching helm's crest. He was a splendid sight: indeed, too splendid, for Gerin heard a mutter of superstitious marvel. "Come in and sit down, you great gowk," he called, "before everyone decides you're a god."

Van's earthy reply sent relieved laughter echoing through the room. The outlander joined his friend and his host. He looked with interest at the bottle Gerin still held. "Never seen glasswork like that before," he said, and the Fox, too, knew relief.

A few moments later, Elise arrived. The buzz of conversation in the taproom again lowered, this time in appreciation. As Gerin rose to greet her, he realized once more how fair she was. He had grown used to her in battered traveler's hat and sturdy but unlovely clothes. Now, in a clinging gown of sea-green linen, she was another creature altogether, and startlingly beautiful.

Turgis' servitors had subtly enhanced the colors of her eyes and lips, and worked her hair into a pile of fluffy curls. The style became her; it was popular in Elabon this year, and several other women in the hall wore their hair thus. The baron saw more than one jealous glance directed at

Elise, and felt proud to have earned the affection of such a woman.

Turgis was also on his feet. He bowed and kissed Elise's hand. "The sunshine of my lady's beauty brightens my hostel," he exclaimed. When he saw he had flustered her, he added with a wink, "What in Dyaus' name do you see in this predacious lout who brought you here?" Put at her ease, she smiled and sat. Turgis poured a drop or two of his nectar of the sun into each of the four glasses, then resealed the flask. He raised his glass. "To past friendships now restored and successes yet to come!"

Everyone drank. Gerin felt the brew caress his tongue like smooth silk, like soft kisses. He heard Van's hum of approval and was glad his far-traveled friend had found a new thing to enjoy.

Turgis poured again, this time from the local bottle. As Gerin's stomach began to growl, the waiter returned, bringing dinner just in time, he thought, to save him from starvation. The first course was a delicate clear soup, made flavorful by bits of pork and chopped scallion. It was followed by what Turgis called a "meat tile," which convinced the Fox that Turgis' cook was a genius as well as a showman: simmered and sautéed pieces of lamb and veal in a spicy sauce which also featured pounded lobster tail and nutmeats. Whole lobster tails garnished the incredible creation; Gerin had never tasted anything so delicious in his life. He could hardly look at the fruits and spun-sugar confections that came after. All the while, Turgis made sure no glass stayed empty long.

The baron's head was beginning to spin when Turgis announced, "Now I will have the tale of your coming here."

All three travelers told it, each amplifying the others' accounts. Gerin tried to slide through the tale of his fight with the aurochs, but to his annoyance Elise made him backtrack and tell it in full.

Turgis looked at him shrewdly. "Still carrying your lantern with a hood on it, are you?" He turned to Elise: "My lady, here we have the most talented of men, the only one who does not know it being himself. He can sing a song, cut a purse (even mine, the unprincipled highwayman!), tell you what that finger-long bug is on friend Van's cuirass— and the cure for its bite as well—"

Snarling an oath, Van crushed the luckless insect. "No need for that," the Fox said. "It was only a walkingstick, and it doesn't bite at all; its sole food is tree sap."

"You see?" Turgis said triumphantly. The wine had flushed his face and loosened his tongue. "He can conjure you up an ever-filled purse—"

"Of mud, perhaps," Gerin said, wishing Turgis would shut up. The innkeeper's paean of praise made him nervous. Most plaudits did; as a second son, he'd seldom got them and never quite worked out how to deal with them. He knew his virtues well enough, and knew one of the greatest was his ability to keep his mouth shut about them. They were often of most use when employed unexpectedly.

Turgis was not about to be quiet. "Besides all that," he said, "this northern ruffian is as kind and loyal a friend as one could ever hope for"—Elise and Van nodded solemnly—"and worth any three men you could name in a brawl. I well recall the day he flattened three rascals who thought to rob me, though he wasn't much more than a stripling himself."

"You never told me that one," Van said.

"They were just tavern toughs," Gerin said, "and this fellow here did a lot of the work. He's pretty handy with a broken bottle."

"Me?" Turgis said. "No one wants to hear about me, fat old slug that I am. What happened after the aurochs was slain?" The hosteler howled laughter to hear how Mavrix had been thwarted. "Truly, I love the god for his gift of the grape, but much of his cult gives me chills."

The baron quickly brought the journey down to the capital: too quickly, again, for Elise. She said, "Once more he leaves out a vital bit of the story. You see, as we traveled we came to care for each other more and more, try though he would to hide himself behind modesty and gloom." She gave him a challenging stare. He would not meet her eye, riveting his attention on his glass. She went on, "And so it's scarcely surprising that when he asked if he might come south to court me when the trouble is done, I was proud to say yes."

"Lord Gerin, my heartiest congratulations," Turgis said, pumping his hand. "My lady, I would offer you the same, but I grieve to think of your beauty passed on to your children diluted by the blood of this ape."

Gerin jerked his hand free of the innkeeper's grip. "A fine excuse for a host you are, to insult your guests."

"Insult? I thought I was giving you the benefit of the doubt." Turgis poured wine all around. A sudden commotion drowned out his toast. Two men who had been arguing over the company of a coldly beautiful Sithonian courtesan rose from their seats and began pummeling each other. Three husky waiters seized them and wrestled them out to the street.

Turgis mopped his brow. "A good thing they chose to quarrel now. The could have broken Osnabroc's concentration—see, here he comes!"

A rising hum of excitement and a few spatters of applause greeted Osnabroc, a short, stocky man whose every muscle was so perfectly defined that it might have been sculpted from stone. He wore only a black loincloth. In his hand he carried a pole about twenty feet long; a crosspiece had been nailed a yard or so from one end.

A pair of young women followed him. They, too, wore only loincloths, one of red silk, the other of green. Both had the small-breasted, taut-bellied look of dancers or acrobats; Gerin doubted if either was five feet tall.

The musicians vacated the stage and Osnabroc ascended. More torches were brought. Each girl took one and set the rest in brackets. After a sharp, short bow to his audience, Osnabroc arched his back and bent his head backwards, setting the pole on his forehead. He balanced it with effortless ease. At his command, both girls shinnied up the pole, torches in their teeth. Once at the crosspiece, they turned somersaults, flips, and other evolutions so astounding Gerin felt his heart rise into his throat. All the while, the pole stayed steady as a rock.

One girl slid down headfirst, leaving the other hanging by her knees twenty feet above the floor. But not for long—she flailed her arms once, twice, and then she was upright again, going through a series of yet more spectacular capers. Despite her gyrations, the supporting pole never budged. A grimace of concentration distorted Osnabroc's face; sweat ran streakily down his magnificent body.

"Who do you think has the harder job?" Turgis whispered to Gerin: "Osnabroc or his girls?"

"I couldn't begin to tell you," the baron answered.

Turgis laughed and nodded. "It's the same with me. I couldn't begin to tell you, either."

Van, though, had no doubts: his eyes were only on the whirling girl. "Just think," he said, half to himself, "of all the ways you could do it with a lass so limber! She all but flies."

"Speak to me not of people flying!" Turgis said as the second girl slid down the pole to a thunderous ovation. She skipped off the stage, followed by her fellow acrobat and Osnabroc. He sagged now as he walked, and his forehead looked puffy.

Van tried to catch the eye of one of the girls, but with no apparent luck. Disappointed, he turned his attention back to Turgis. "What do you have against people flying?" he asked.

"Nothing against it, precisely. It does remind me of a strange story, though." He waited to be urged to go on. His companions quickly obliged him. He began, "You've told me much of the Trokmoi tonight; this story has a Trokmê in it too. He was drunk, as they often are, and since the place was crowded that night, he was sharing a table with a wizard. You know how some folk, when they go too deep into a bottle, like to sing or whatever. Well, this lad flapped his arms like he was trying to take off and fly. Finally he knocked a drink from the wizard's hand, which was the wrong thing to do.

"The wizard paid his scot and walked out, and I thought I'd been lucky enough to escape trouble. But next thing I knew, the northerner started flapping again, and—may my private parts shrivel if I lie—sure enough he took off and flew around the room like a drunken buzzard."

"A boozard, maybe," Gerin suggested.

"I hope not," Turgis said.

"What befell?" Elise asked.

"He did, lass, on his head. He was doing a fine job of flying, just like a bird, but the poor sot smashed against that candelabra you see up there and fell right into someone's soup. He earned himself a knot on the head as big as an egg and, I hope, enough sense not to make another wizard annoyed at him.

"This tale-telling gets to be thirsty work," Turgis added, calling for another bottle of wine. But when he opened it and began to pour, Elise put a hand over her glass. A few minutes later she rose. Pausing only to bestow a hurried but warm kiss on Gerin, she made her way to her room.

The three men sat, drank, and talked a bit longer. Turgis said, "Gerin, you're no fool like that Trokmê was. You're the last man I ever would have picked to make a sorcerer your mortal foe."

"It was his choosing, not mine!" The wine had risen to Gerin's head, adding vehemence to his words. "The gods decreed I am not to be a scholar, as I had dreamed. So be it. Most of my bitterness is gone. There's satisfaction in holding the border against the barbarians, and more in making my holding a better place for all to live, vassals and serfs alike. Much of what I learned here has uses in the north: we no longer have wells near the cesspits, for instance, and we grow beans to refresh the soil. And, though my vassals know it not, I've taught a few of the brighter peasants to read."

"What? You have?" Van stared at the Fox as if he'd never seen him before.

"Aye, and I'm not sorry, either." Gerin turned back to Turgis. "We've had no famines round Fox Keep, despite two bad winters, and no peasant revolts either. Wizard or no wizard, no skulking savage is going to ruin all I've worked so hard to kill. He may kill me—the way things look now, he likely *will* kill me—but Dyaus knows he'll never run me off!"

He slammed his glass to the table with such violence that it shattered and cut his hand. The pain abruptly sobered him. Startled by his outburst, his friends exclaimed in sympathy. He sat silent and somber, staring at the thin stream of blood that welled from between his clenched fingers.

VIII

After the Alley's hurley-burley, the calm, nearly trafficless lanes of the nobles' quarter came as a relief. Jouner had given the Fox careful directions on how to find Elise's uncle's home. For a miracle, they proved good as well as careful.

Valdabrun the Stout lived almost in the shadow of the Palace Imperial. Despite his closeness to the Empire's heart, the grounds of his home were less imposing than those of many nobles in less prestigious areas. No carefully trimmed topiaries adorned his lawns, no statuary group stood frozen in mid-cavort. Nor did the drive from the road wind and twist its way to his house under sweetly scented trees. It ran directly to his front door, straight as the Elabon Way. The dominant impression his grounds gave was one of discipline and strength.

The baron hitched the horses. Van gave both beasts feedbags, eluding a snap from the Shanda pony. He cuffed it, grumbling, "Poxy animal would sooner have my hand than its oats."

Valdabrun's door-knocker was a snarling bronze longtooth's head. Gerin grasped a fang, swung it up, then down. He had expected the knock to set off sorcerous chimes. Many southern nobles liked such conceits. But there was only the honest clang of metal on metal. After a stir inside, a retainer swung open the door. "Sirs, lady, how may I help you?" he asked crisply.

The man's speech and bearing impressed Gerin: he seemed more soldier than servitor. "Is your master in?" the Fox asked.

"Lord Valdabrun? No, but I expect him back shortly. Would you care to wait?"

"If you would be so kind."

"This way, then." Executing a smart about-turn, the steward led them to a rather bare antechamber. He briefly saw to their comfort, then said, "If you will excuse me, I have other duties to perform." He left through another door; Gerin heard him bar it after himself.

A woman's voice, low and throaty, came from behind the door. Gerin could not make out her words, but heard the steward reply, "I know not, lady Namarra. They did not state their business, nor did I inquire deeply."

"I will see them," the woman said.

The bar was lifted. Valdabrun's man announced, "Sirs, lady, my lord Valdabrun's, ah, companion, the lady Namarra," and went off.

As Namarra entered, Van sprang to his feet. Gerin was only a blink behind. No matter what he felt toward Elise, Valdabrun's companion was, quite simply, the most spectacular woman he had every seen: tiny, catlike, and exquisite. The clinging silk she wore accented her figure's lushness.

Her hair, worn short and straight, was the color of flame. Like a fire, it seemed to give out more light than fell on it. Yet for all that incandescent hair, she was no Trokmê woman; her face was soft, rounded, and small-featured, her skin golden brown. Her eyes, a slightly darker shade of gold, were subtly slanted but rounded as if in perpetual surprise; the strange combination, more than anything save perhaps her purring name, made Gerin think her feline. She wore no jewelry—she herself was ornament enough, and more.

She studied the Fox with some interest, Van with a good deal more, and Elise with the wary concern one gave any dangerous beast suddenly found in the parlor. Out of the corner of his eye, Gerin saw Elise returning that look. He felt a twinge of alarm.

Namarra swept out a lithe arm to point at the baron. "You are—?"

He introduced himself and Van, and was on the point of naming Elise when he was interrupted: "And your charming, ah, companion?" Namarra used the same deliberately ambiguous intonation the steward had applied to her.

Voice dangerously calm, Elise replied, "I am Elise, Ricolf's daughter." The Fox noticed she made no claim of relationship to Valdabrun.

The name of Elise's father meant nothing to Namarra. She turned back to Gerin. "May I ask your business with my lord?"

The baron was not sure how to reply. He had no idea

how much of the noble's confidence and trust his woman enjoyed. He was framing an equivocal answer when a door slammed at the back of the house. Seconds later, the steward reappeared, to announce his master's presence.

"Enough of this foolishness. Let me by," Valdabrun the Stout said as he surged into the antechamber.

Gerin hastily revised his notion of what the noble's sobriquet implied. Valdabrun was edging toward fifty, balding, and did in fact carry a considerable paunch, but the Fox was sure he would break fingers if he rammed a fist into it. Shaven face or no, here was a soldier, and no mistake. Hard eyes, firm mouth, the set of his chin all bespoke a man long used to command. Nor was he slow to see he faced two of his own breed.

The air in the room crackled as the three strong men took one another's measure. Each in his own way was a warrior to reckon with: Gerin supple, clever, always waiting for a foe to expose a flaw; Van, who fought with a berserker's delight and a drillmaster's elegance; and their host, who reminded the Fox of one of Carlun's or Ros' great captains: a man with scant polish or flair, but possessed of an almost brutal indomitability, the very concept of retreat alien to him.

The tableau held for long seconds. Elise shattered it, exclaiming "Uncle!" and throwing herself into Valdabrun's startled arms. The stern expression dropped from his face, to be replaced by one of utter bafflement.

Namarra's face changed, too. Her eyes narrowed; her lips drew back, exposing white, pointed teeth. A cat she was, and feral. She laid a hand on Valdarun's arm. "My lord—" she began.

"Be still, my dear," he said, and she *was* still, though restive. Gerin's respect for him grew. He untangled himself from Elise. "Young lady, you will explain yourself," he told her, still in that tone of command.

She was as matter-of-fact as he. "Of course. As I told your leman"—Namarra bristled, but held her tongue—"I'm Elise, daughter of Ricolf the Red—and your sister Yrse. My mother always said you would know this locket." She drew it up from between her breasts, freed it of its chain, and handed it to Valdabrun.

He examined it at arm's length; his sight had begun to lengthen, as it often does in the middle years. His face softened, as much as that craggy countenance could. "Yrse's child!" he said softly. This time, he folded her into a bearlike embrace.

Behind his back, Namarra's expression was frightening.

Elise introduced Gerin and Van to Valdabrun. "I've heard of you, sirrah," he told the Fox: "One of those who never pay their taxes, aye?"

"I pay them in blood," Gerin answered soberly.

Valdabrun surprised him by nodding. "So you do, youngling, so you do." He exchanged a bone-wrenching handclasp with Van that left both big men wincing, then announced, "Now I will have the tale of your coming here." He visibly composed himself to listen.

As they had the night before to Turgis, the three of them told their story. "I never thought that harebrained scheme would work," Valdabrun observed when Elise spoke of her father's plan to find her a husband.

The noble proved a far more skeptical audience than Turgis had, firing probing questions at Gerin on Balamung's wizardry, politics in the northlands, Mavrix's cultists, and whatever else caught his interest.

"Well, well," he said at last. "The whole thing is so unlikely I suppose it must be true. Child, you are welcome to stay with me as long as you like." He told his steward to take her gear from the wagon, then turned to Namarra, who appeared less than delighted at his niece's arrival. "Kitten, show Elise around while I talk with these rogues."

"Of course. We can talk as we go. Come, child." In Namarra's red-lipped mouth, the word was poisonously sweet.

"That would be wonderful," Elise answered. "I've always wanted to talk to a woman of your, ah, experience." A tiny smile on her face, she kissed Van and Gerin, fiercely hugged the Fox, and whispered, "This will be hard. Hurry back, please!" She followed Namarra out. When the door closed behind her, Gerin felt the sunshine had left the day.

Valdabrun seemed oblivious to the byplay between the two women. That proved again to the baron that he was more used to the field than to the imperial court's intrigues.

After his niece and mistress were gone, he said bluntly, "Fox, if half what you've said is true, your arse is in a sling."

"I'd be lying if I said I liked the odds," Gerin agreed.

"Advice from me would be nothing but damned impertinence right now, so I'll give you none. But I will say this: if any man is slippery enough to slide through this net, you may be that man. Yet you seem to have kept your honor too. I'm glad of it, for my niece's—how strange that seems!—sake." He shifted his attention to Van. "Could I by any chance persuade you to join the Imperial Guard?" His smile showed he knew the question foolish before he asked it.

Van shook his head; the plume of his helm swayed gently. "You're not like most of the popinjays here, Valdabrun. You seem a fighting man. So you tell me: where will I find better fighting than with the Fox?"

"There you have me," Valdabrun said. "Gentlemen, I would like nothing more than talking the day away over a few stoups of wine, but I must get back to the palace. The Eshref clan out of Shanda have forced a pass in the Skleros Mountains, and their brigands are plundering northern Sithonia. His imperial majesty thinks paying tribute will get them to leave. I have to persuade him otherwise."

"The Eshref?" Van said. "Is Gaykhatu still their chief?"

"I believe that was the name, yes. Why?"

"Send troops," the outlander said decisively. "He'll run. I knew him out on the plains, and he always did."

"You knew him on the plains . . ." Valdabrun shook his head. "I won't ask how or when, but I do give thanks for the rede—and when I talk with his imperial majesty, I'll term it 'expert testimony' or some such tripe. Dyaus, what drivel I've had to learn in the past year or so!"

As Van and Gerin drove away from Valdabrun's home, the baron was heavy-hearted over parting from Elise, necessary though he knew it was. Van, on the other hand, was full of lickerish praise for Namarra and lewd speculation on the means Valdabrun, who was certainly no beauty, used to keep her at his side. His sallies grew so unlikely and so comical that Gerin finally had to laugh with him.

"Where now?" Van asked as the Alley's turmoil surrounded them once more.

"The Sorcerers' Collegium. It's in the southwestern part of the city, near the apothecaries' district. I should know when to turn."

But he did not. He never learned whether the building he sought as a marker was torn down or if he had simply forgotten its looks in the eight years since he'd seen it last. Whichever, before long he knew he had gone too far west along the Alley. He turned to passersby for directions.

At first he got no responses save shrugs and a few vaguely pointing fingers. Realizing his mistake, he tossed a copper to the first halfway intelligent-looking fellow he spied. The man's instructions were so artfully phrased, accompanied by such eloquent gestures, that Gerin listened as if spellbound. He had all he could do to keep from applauding. Instead, he gave his benefactor another coin. The man's thanks would have drawn an aurochs into a temple.

Unfortunately, the Sorcerers' Collegium was nowhere near where he claimed. Gerin expended more coppers and most of his patience before he finally found it.

There was nothing outwardly marvelous about the building that housed it, a gray brick "island" not much different from scores of others in the capital. But it was discreetly segregated from its neighbors by a broad smooth expanse of lawn. None of the nearby buildings had a window that faced the Collegium. They only gave it blank walls of stucco, timber, or brick, perhaps fearing the sorceries emanating from it.

Though the Collegium accepted students only from within the Empire, folk of various races called on it for services. Many odd vehicles and beasts were tied in front of it; to his horses' alarm, Gerin hitched the wagon next to a camel some Urfa had ridden up from the desert.

No sooner had he done so than three muscular individuals appeared and asked if the gentlemen in the wagon would pay them to watch it. "I'll see you in the hottest firepit in the five hells first," Gerin said genially. "You know as well as I, the Collegium has spells to keep thieves away from its clients."

The largest of the bravos, a fellow who would have been a giant beside anyone but Van, shrugged and grinned.

"Sorry, boss," he said, "but the two of you looked such rubes, it was worth the chance."

"Now you know better, so be off with you." After exchanging a final good-natured insult with the baron, the ruffians ambled away, looking for less worldly folk to bilk. Gerin shook his head. "When I was a student the same sort of rascals were about, preying on strangers."

Inside the Collegium the ground floor was lit, mundanely enough, by torches. Some of them flared crimson, green, or blue, but that was the simplest of tricks, scarcely sorcery at all, merely involving the use of certain powdered earths. A greater magic kept the chamber free of smoke but let the nose detect the pinches of delicate incense burning in tiny braziers set along the walls and mounted on the sturdy granite columns that supported the Collegium's upper stories.

The procedures on the ground floor of the Collegium reminded Gerin of nothing so much as those of the Imperial Bank. Orderly lines of clients snaked their way toward young mages seated at tables along the north wall. Once there, they explained their problems in low voices. Most were helped on the spot, but from time to time a wizard would send one elsewhere, presumably to deal with someone more experienced.

Van bore queueing up with poor grace: "I don't fancy all this standing about."

"Patience," Van said. "It's a trick to overawe people. The longer you have to wait, the more important you think whoever you're waiting for is."

"Bah." Van made as if to spit on the floor, but changed his mind. It was too beautiful to soil: an abstract mosaic of tiny glass tesserae of silver, lilac, and sea-green, glittering in the torchlight.

The man in front of them finally reached a wizard and poured out his tale of woe like a spilled jug of wine, glug, glug, glug. At last the wizard exclaimed, "Enough! Enough! Follow this"—a blob of pink foxfire appeared in front of the startled fellow's nose—"and it will lead you to someone who can help you." He turned to Gerin and Van, said courteously, "And what my I do for you gentlemen? You may call me Avelmir; my true name, of course, is hidden."

Avelmir was younger than Gerin, his round, smoothly shaved face smiling and open. His familiar, a fat gray lizard about a foot long, rested on the table in front of him. Its yellow eyes gave back Gerin's stare unwinkingly. When Avelmir stroked its scaly skin, it arched its back in pleasure.

Gerin told his story. When he was done, Avelmir's smile had quite gone. "You pose a difficult problem, sir baron, and one in which I am not sure we can render timely assistance. Let me consult here . . ." He glanced down at a scrap of parchment. "We are badly understaffed, as you must be aware, and I fear we shall be unable to send anyone truly competent north of the Kirs before, hmm, seventy-five to eighty days."

"What!" Gerin's bellow of outrage whipped heads around. "In that time I'll be dead, with my keep and most of the northland aflame for my pyre!"

Avelmir's manner grew chillier yet. "We find ourselves under heavy obligations in the near future, the nature of which I do not propose to discuss with you. If you do not care to wait for our services against your barbarous warlock, hire some northern bungler, and may you have joy of him. Good day, sir."

"You—" Outrage choked the Fox.

The battle-gleam kindled in Van's eyes. "Shall I break the place apart a bit, captain?"

"I would not try that," Avelmir said quietly.

"And why not?" Van tugged at his sword. It came halfway free, then struck. He roared a curse. Avelmir's hands writhed through passes. When Gerin tried to stop him, the reptilian familiar puffed itself up to twice its size and jumped at him. He drew back, not sure if it was venomous.

Sweat started forth on Van's forehead, and an instant later on Avelmir's. The outlander gained an inch, lost it again. Then more and more blade began to show. At last it jerked clear. With a howl of triumph, Van raised his sword arm.

Gerin grabbed it with both hands. For a moment, he thought he would be lifted off the floor and swung with the blade. But reason returned to Van's face. The outlander relaxed.

Avelmir had the look of a man who'd fished for minnows

and caught a shark. Into the dead silence of the great chamber, he said, "We must see if a way can be found. Follow this."

A blue foxfire globe popped into being an inch in front of Gerin's nose. Startled, he took a step backwards. The foxfire hurried away, like a man on an important errand. Gerin and Van followed.

The ball of light led them down a steep spiral stairway into the bowels of the Collegium. Gerin's excitement grew; here, he knew, the potent sorceries were undertaken. When he was a student, he had been restricted to the upper floors. As the eerie guide led him down echoing corridors, he realized for the first time how much of the Collegium was underground—and how little he had understood its true extent.

He and Van passed doors without number. Most were shut; more than one bore runes of power to ensure it stayed so. Many of the open ones were innocuous: a smithy, a chamber in which glassblowers created vessels of curious shapes and sizes, a crowded library. But a winged, tailed demon thrashed within a pentacle in one room. It glared at the Fox with fiery eyes; its stench followed him down the hall.

"What do you suppose would happen if we didn't choose to follow our magical guide?" Van said.

"Nothing good, I'm sure."

The foxfire winked out in front of a closed door. Gerin knocked; there was no reply. He lifted the latch. The door silently swung open.

The chamber was far underground and held no lamps, but it was not dark. A soft silvery gleam which had no apparent source suffused it. Behind a curiously carven ebony table sat an old wizard who looked up from some arcane computation when the privacy of his cubicle was breached. His amber silk robes rustled as he moved.

He nodded to Gerin and Van. "If you need a name for me, call me Sosper." That was clearly a pseudonym, for he was no Sithonian. Though his phrases were polished, he spoke with a western accent; he must have been born somewhere on the long peninsula that jutted into the Orynian Ocean. He smiled at Van. "No need to keep hand on hilt, my friend. It will avail you nothing, as I am no child in shaping spells of sealing." The outlander, confident as always in his own strength, tried to draw. His sword was frozen fast. Gerin would have believed Sosper without test; the man radiated power as a bonfire radiates heat.

Gentle but overwhelmingly self-assured, Sosper cut off the baron when he began to speak. "Why do you question Avelmir's judgment? I can give you no aid, nor can the Collegium, until the time he specified. What happens among barbarians is of little moment to us in any event, and less now. You may perhaps be able to deduce the reason, having once studied here. No, look not so startled, my young friend: who knows the chick better than the hen?"

Trying to master his surprise, Gerin turned his wits to the problem Sosper had set him. He found no solution, and said so.

"Do you not? A pity. In that case, there appears to be no need for further conversation. Leave me, I pray, so I may return to my calculations."

"At least tell me why you will not aid me," Gerin said. "Balamung is no ordinary mage; he has more power than any I've seen here."

For the first time, Sosper spoke with a touch of asperity. "I am under no obligation to you, sir; rather the reverse, for you take me away from important matters. And as for your Trokmê, I care not if he has the Book of Shabeth-Shiri—"

"He has. You don't seem to have listened to a word I said."

"How can you know this? Have you seen its terrible glow with your own eyes?" Sosper was skeptical, almost contemptuous.

"No, but I spoke with a woodsrunner who has."

"You accept the untrained observations of a savage as fact? My good man, a hundred generations of scriers have sought the Book of Shabeth-Shiri—in vain. I doubt a barbarian hedge-wizard could have found it where they failed. No, lost it is and lost it shall remain, until the one no grave shall hold brings it back to the world of men."

Gerin had not heard that bit of lore before. It chilled him to the marrow. But his protests died unspoken. The

old man before him had been right for so long, and grown
so arrogant in his rightness, that now he could not hear
anything that contradicted his set image of the world. He
was talented, brilliant . . . and deafened by his own rigidity.

"Leave me," Sosper said. It was order, not request.
Followed close by Van, Gerin left the chamber. Ice was
in his heart. The door swung closed behind them of its own
accord. Like a faithful servant, the foxfire ball reappeared
to guide them back to its creator.

On their return, Avelmir looked to be considering some
remark at their expense, but Gerin's stony visage and an
ominous twitch of Van's great forearm muscles persuaded
him to hold his tongue.

"What now, captain?" the outlander asked as they left
the Collegium.

Gerin shook his head in dejected bewilderment. "Great
Dyaus above, how should I know? Every move I make rams
my head into a stone wall: the Sibyl, Carus, now this.
Maybe Balamung was right. Maybe I can do nothing to
fight him. Still, I intend to go on trying—what else can I
do? And I can do one thing for myself right now."

"What's that?"

"Get drunk."

Van slapped him on the back, sending him staggering
down the steps. "Best notion I've heard in days. Where do
we find a place?"

"It shouldn't be hard." Nor was it. Not five minutes' ride
from the Collegium stood a small tavern, set between an
apothecary's shop and an embalmer—"Where the druggist
sends his mistakes, I suppose," Gerin said. He read the
faded sign over the tavern door. "'The Barons' Roost.' Hah!
Anything that roosted here would come away with lice in
its feathers."

"Someone doesn't seem to care." Van pointed to the
matched blooded dapples and fine chariot tied in front of
the tavern.

"He must be slumming." Gerin slid down and hitched
the wagon next to the fancy rig.

The Barons' Roost had no door, only a splotchily dyed
curtain, once perhaps forest green. Inside, it was dirty, dark,
and close. Its few patrons, from the look of them mostly

burglars, pimps, and other small-time grifters, gave Gerin and Van a wary once-over before returning to their low-voiced talk. "Hemp for smoking?" Gerin heard one say to another. "I can get it for you, of course I can. How much do you want?"

"What can I give you boys?" asked the fat man behind the bar. His hard eyes gave the lie to the jovial air he tried to cultivate.

"Wine," Gerin said. "And quiet."

"The quiet's free. For the wine, I'd see your silver first."

Van laughed at that. "Show too much silver in a dive like this and half the jackals here'll decide they're wolves today."

"They don't seem to be troubling him, do they?" The taverner jerked a thumb at the noble slumped over the far corner of the bar. Three jars of various vintages stood before him; from his slack-jointed posture they were empty, or nearly so.

"For all I know, he's one of them, or their boss," Van said.

At that, the noble slowly swung round. A golden ear-ring caught candlelight and glinted. "Who is it," he asked loftily, "who dares impute me a part of this place in any way save my location?" A swacked grin spread across his face as he focused on Gerin and Van. "As I live and breathe, the wench-stealers!"

"Rihwin! What are you doing here?" Gerin exclaimed.

"I? I am becoming preternaturally drunk, though if I can still say preter—pre—that word, I have not yet arrived. I shall be honored to stand you gentlemen a round: any-one filching so luscious a lass as Elise from Wolfar of the Axe deserves reward. Yet after she was gone, what point to my staying in the north—especially as my welcome had worn rather thin? So three days later, home I fared, and here I am."

Considering it, Gerin decided it was quite possible; Rihwin would have taken no side-trips to delay his jour-ney. With his load of cares, the Fox was glad to see any face he knew. He answered, "You can buy for us if we can buy for you."

"Fair enough." Rihwin turned to the tapster. "A double measure of Siphnian for my comrades, and quickly! They have considerable overtaking to do."

The wine the taverner brought had never seen Siphnos, and the amphora in which it came was a crude local imitation of Sithonian ware. At any other time, Gerin would have stalked out of the dive. Now he relished the warmth rising from his belly to his brain. When the vessel was empty he ordered another, then another.

No amateur toper himself, Rihwin watched in disbelief as Van poured down mug after mug of wine. "Heaven above and hells below!" he exlaimed. "I toast your capacity." The three men drained their cups.

"And I your fine company," Van said. The cups emptied again. Rihwin and Van looked expectantly at Gerin.

He raised his mug. "A murrain take all magicians." He drank.

Van drank.

"All but me," Rihwin said. He drank too.

"What's that?" Gerin was abruptly half sober.

"What's—*arp!*—what? Excuse me, I pray, I am not well." Rihwin's head flopped onto his arms. He slept. Gerin shook, prodded, and nudged him, to no avail. The southerner muttered and whimpered, but would not wake.

"We've got to get him out of here," the Fox told Van.

Van stared owlishly. "Who out of where?"

"Not you too!" Gerin snarled. "Before he flickered out, this candle said he was a wizard."

"A murrain take all wizards!" Van shouted. He drank.

The baron tried to whip his fuzzy wits into action. At last he smote fist into palm in satisfaction. "I'd wager you think you're quite the strong fellow," he said to Van.

"I am that," the outlander allowed between swigs. "And sober, too."

"I doubt it," Gerin said. "In fact, I'd bet you're too puny and too drunk even to carry this chap here"—he indicated the inert Rihwin—"out to the wagon."

"Go howl, captain." Van slung Rihwin over his shoulder like an empty suit of clothes and headed for the door. Gerin paid the taverner and followed.

Van slung Rihwin into the back of the wagon so hard Gerin hoped the noble was unhurt. "Will you own you were wrong?" he said.

"It seems I have to," Gerin answered, smiling inside.

"Pay up, then."

"Tell you what: I'll race you back to Turgis', double or nothing. You take the wagon and I'll drive Rihwin's chariot."

"Doesn't seem quite fair," Van complained.

Privately, Gerin would have agreed. He loaded his voice with scorn. "Not game, eh?"

"You'll see!" Van untied the wagon from the hitching rail, leaped aboard. He cracked his whip and was gone. Gerin was right behind him. Pedestrians fled every which way, tumbling back into shops and displays for their lives.

Rihwin's team was as fine as it looked, but the Fox still had trouble gaining on Van. The outlander, with more weight behind him, bulled through holes Gerin had to avoid. He also drove with utter disregard for life and limb, his own or anyone else's.

They were neck and neck when they reached the Alley. They stormed down it. And then, right outside the wheat emporium, they descended on a great flock of geese being driven to slaughter. Gerin doubted it was the flock which had delayed them on their way to the capital. That one still had to be on the road.

Van never slowed down. He had time for one bellowed "Gangway!" before he was into the middle of the geese, Gerin still a length or two behind. The Fox glimpsed blank despair on the face of one goose-tender. Then the air was full of terrified honking, squealing, cackling, defecating big white birds.

Some flew into the grain market. They promptly began to devour the wheat there. Swearing merchants tried to drive them back into the street, only to retreat in dismay as the birds fought back with buffeting wings and savage pecks and bites.

Half a dozen geese flapped their way through the second-story window of a bath-house. An instant later, four nude men leaped out the same window.

A dun-colored hound contested the right of two geese to a cartload of peaches. When five more birds joined the fray, the dog ran off, tail between its legs. Squawking contentedly, the victors settled down to enjoy their spoils.

Yet another goose seized a trollop's filmy skirt in its beak. The goose tore it from her legs and left her half naked in the roadway. Her curses only added to the turmoil.

Somehow or other, the racers got through. Any pursuit was lost in the gallinaceous stampede. Gerin took the lead for a moment, then lost it when Van, quite by accident, found a shortcut. The baron was gaining at the end, but Van pulled into Turgis' forecourt a few seconds in front.

Plucking a feather from his beard, he walked over to the Fox, broad palm out. "Pay up, if you please."

"You know, we forgot to set a stake. I owe you twice nothing, which, the subtle Sithonians assure us, remains nothing."

Van pondered this, nodded reluctantly. "Then we'll just have to race back," he declared. He took two steps toward the wagon and fell on his face.

The pound of galloping hooves brought Turgis out his front door on the run. "What in the name of the gods is going on?" he shouted. "Oh, it's you, Gerin. I might have known."

The baron lacked the patience to trade gibes with him. He boiled with urgency. "Do you have a potion to sober up these two right away?" He nodded toward Van and Rihwin, whom he had lain beside his friend. The noble had stayed unconscious all through the wild ride.

"Aye, but they'll not be happier for it." Turgis vanished into the hostel. He returned a moment later with a small, tightly stoppered vial. He poured half its contents into Van, gave the rest to Rihwin.

As the drug took effect, the two of them thrashed like broken-backed things, then spewed their guts on the ground. Sudden reason showed in Rihwin's eyes. Wiping his mouth, he asked, "What am I doing here? Where, for that matter, is here? Who do you think you are, my good man?" he added when Van, still in pain, rolled up against him. His voice showed much of his usual cheerful hauteur.

The outlander groaned. "With any luck, I'll die before I remember. There's an earthquake in my brains."

Rihwin rose gingerly. He looked from Van, who stayed on the ground with head in hands, to Gerin, none too steady on his feet himself. "I congratulate you, my friends: practice has made you a superior pair of kidnappers. Tell me, which of you has wed Elise, and which intends to marry me? I confess, I have given little thought to my dowry."

"Go howl!" Gerin said. "Tell me at once: is it true you're a wizard?"

"Where did you learn that, in that horrid dive? How drunk was I? It were better to say I am all but a mage. I completed the course at the Collegium but never graduated, nor was I linked to a familiar."

"Why not?"

"Of what interest is this to you, may I ask?"

"Rihwin, you will have my story, I promise you," Gerin said. "Now tell me yours, before I throttle you."

"Very well. The fault, I fear, was my own. I learned all the required lores, mastered the spells they set me, met every examination, completed each conjuration with adequate results—which is to say, no fiend swallowed me up. And all this I accomplished on my own, for he who nominally supervised my work was so concerned with his own goetic researches that he had scant moments to lavish on his pupils."

"Not the wizard who styles himself Sosper?" Gerin asked.

"Indeed yes. How could you know that?"

"I've met the man. Go on, please."

"Came the night before I was to be consecrated mage, and in my folly I resolved to repay my mentor for all his indifference. He is a man who likes the good life, is Sosper, for all his sorcerous craft, and he dwells near the Palace Imperial. At midnight I essayed a small summoning. When the demon I evoked appeared, I charged it to go to my master's bedchamber, give his couch a hearty shake, and vanish instanter once he awoke. What I ordained, the demon did."

A reminiscent grin lit Rihwin's face. "Oh, it was a lovely jape! Even warlocks are muzzy when bounced from slumber, and Sosper, suspecting nothing other than a common earthquake, rushed in his nightshirt to the palace to inquire after the Emperor's safety. I would have given half my lands to see his face when he found the temblor his private property.

"But it takes a mighty wizard to befool such a man for long, and I, alas, had nowhere near the skill to maintain my appearance of innocence 'gainst his inquiry. Which leaves me here . . . almost a mage, and glad, I suppose, my punishment was no worse than expulsion."

Rihwin's tale was in keeping with the judgment Gerin had formed of him at Ricolf's holding: a man who would dare anything on the impulse of a moment, never stopping to consider the consequences—but one who would then jauntily bear those consequences, whatever they were.

Banking on that mercurial nature, Gerin plunged into his own tale. "And so," he finished, "I found I could get no proper mage, and was in despair, not knowing what to do. Meeting you in the tavern seems nothing less than the intervention of the gods—and on my behalf, for once. Fare north with me, to be my aid against the Trokmoi."

Rihwin studied him, wearing his usual expression of amused cynicism like a gambler's stiff face. "You know, I suppose, that I have every right to bear you ill-will for winning the love of a girl for whose hand I struggled over the course of a year?"

"So you do," Gerin said stonily.

"And you know I find your northern province uncouth, unmannered, and violent, nothing at all like this soft, smiling land?"

"Rihwin, if you mean no, say no and stop twisting the knife!"

"But my dear fellow Fox, I am trying to say yes!"

"What?" Gerin stared at him.

"Why do you think I traveled north a year ago, if not for the adventure of it, and the change? I was stifled by the insipid life I led here; were it not that I am in a bad odor up there, I doubt I should have returned at all."

Van struggled to his feet. "Good for you! Keep the same ground under your feet too long and you grow roots like a radish."

"But—what you said of Elise . . ." Gerin was floundering now.

"What of it? That I lost her was my own foolish fault, and none other's. I was not in love with her, nor she with me. Aye, she's a comely maid, but I've found there are a good many of those, and most of them like me well. I entered Ricolf's contest much more to measure myself against the other suitors than for her sake."

The last of his foppish mask slipped away, and he spoke with a seriousness the baron had never heard from him:

"Lord Gerin, if you truly want my aid, I will meet you here in three days' time, ready to travel. I pray your pardon for not being quicker, but as I'm here, I should set my affairs in order before faring north again. Does it please you?"

Dumbfounded, Gerin could only nod. Rihwin sketched a salute, climbed into his chariot, and departed. His horses whickered happily at the familiar feel of his hands on the reins.

"What do you know?" Van said. "More to that fellow than he lets on."

Gerin was thinking much the same thing. It occurred to him that he had seen Rihwin only on a couple of the worst days of his life; now he began to understand why Ricolf, with longer acquaintance, had thought the southerner a fit match for Elise.

More than once over those three days, the Fox wondered if Rihwin would have second thoughts, but he was too busy readying his own return to waste much time on worry. Van acquired a stout ash spear ("A little light, but what can you do?") and four examples of another weapon Gerin had not seen before: flat rings of bronze with sharp outer edges. Their central holes were sized so they fit snugly onto the outlander's forearms.

"They're called chakrams," Van explained. "I learned the use of them in Mabalal. They're easier to throw straight than knives, and if I just leave them where they are, they make a forearm smash unpleasant for whoever's in the way."

When the baron paid Turgis, the innkeeper put an arm round his shoulder. "You're a good friend, Fox. I'm sorry to see you go. You remind me of the days when I still had hair on my pate. Please note, however, you brigand, I am not so sorry as to make you any rash promises. The last one cost me dear enough."

Rihwin arrived on the morning he had set, and as ready as he had vowed. Gone was his thin toga; he wore a leather tunic and baggy woolen trousers. A sword swung at his hip, armor and a quiver of javelins were stowed behind him, and he had set a battered bronze helm on his curls.

His left ear, though, still sported a golden ring. "It's possible to ask too much of me, you know," he said sheepishly when Gerin pointed at it.

"Rihwin, for all I care, you can wear the damned thing in your nose. Let's be off."

The baron drove the wagon up the Alley. Van stayed in the rear compartment, out of sight. Gerin did not want to be stopped by some irate merchant who'd had his goods smashed or scattered in the wild ride and now recognized one of its perpetrators. He was confident he was immune from being identified so; save for his northern dress, he looked like just another Elabonian. Thus it came as a small shock when someone waved frantically and called his name.

"Elise!" he said. "Great Dyaus above, what now?"

IX

Elise's story was simple enough, if unpleasing. Valdabrun's delight at guesting his unknown niece had faded. The fading quickened when he realized how cordially Elise and Namarra despised each other.

"It all blew up at dawn this morning in a glorious fight," Elise said. She reached into a pocket of her traveling coat and brought out a lock of Namarra's fiery hair. "Black at the roots, you'll notice."

"May I be of service, my lady?" Rihwin asked. "A spell for an enemy's ruin is easy when one has a lock of hair with which to work."

"I know enough magic for that myself," Gerin said, not wanting Rihwin to help Elise in any way at all.

"The hussy hardly merits being blasted from the face of the earth simply because she and I don't get along," Elise said. She asked Rihwin, "How is it you are in the city, and in Gerin's company?"

He briefly explained. She said, "When last I saw you— and more of you than I wanted to, I'll have you know— I would have thought you'd never want to go back to the northlands again."

He flinched at that, but answered, "They hold no terror for me, so long as I am not required to face your father."

"Where shall I take you now?" Gerin asked Elise. "You must have other kin here."

"I do, but I know none of them by name. Nor would it do me much good if I did. My uncle is not a man to use half-measures. He swore he'd make sure I was no more welcome in any of their houses than in his. That leaves me little choice but to travel north with you."

Gerin realized she was right.

"Get moving, will you, and talk later," Van said from his comfortless perch in the back of the wagon. "I feel like an ostrich in a robin's egg."

Once they were out of the city, he emerged from confinement and stretched till his joints creaked. "Let me ride

145

with you a while, Rihwin," he said. "I like the bounce of a chariot under my feet."

"Do you indeed?" Rihwin said. He flicked the whip over his matched dapples. They leaped forward, sending the light car bounding into the air whenever its bronze-shod wheels struck a stone set an inch or two higher in the roadbed than its fellows. Van was unruffled. He shifted his weight with marvelous quickness, not deigning to clutch at the chariot's handrail.

Rihwin gave up after a wild quarter of a mile, slowing his horses to a walk. As Gerin caught up, he asked Elise, "Does he always act so?"

"I've rarely seen him otherwise. The day he came to court me, he stepped down from his car, kissed me, then kissed my father twice as hard! But he has such charm and nonchalance that the outrageous things he does don't grate as they would from someone else."

"What, ah, do you think of him?" Gerin asked carefully.

"As a possible husband, you mean? I could have done much worse." She laid a hand on his arm. "But I could do much better, too, and I think I have."

Guard duty was easier to bear with three men to carry the load. Golden Math, a waning crescent, had been in the sky when Rihwin woke Gerin to stand the third watch. Elleb, three days past full, was nearing the meridian; Tiwaz had just set.

"Tell me, how is it you know sorcery?" Rihwin asked. To Gerin, he seemed to be saying, *How could a backwoodsman like you hope to master such a subtle art?*

The baron had met that attitude from southerners too often during his first stay in the capital. Touched on an old sore spot, he said shortly, "Surprising as it may seem, I spent two years studying in the city, including a turn at the Collegium, though a short one."

"Did you really? What did you study besides magecraft?" Far from being condescending, Rihwin showed eager interest.

"Natural philosophy, mostly, and history."

"History? Great Dyaus above, man, did you ever hear Maleinos lecture?"

"Yes, often. He interested me."

"What do you think of his cyclical notion of historical development? I was so impressed by the peroration he always used that I memorized it: 'Peoples and cities now have great success, now are so totally defeated as no longer to exist. And the changing circuit revealed such things before our time, and will reveal them again, and the revelations will not cease, so long as there be men and battles.' And he would stalk off, like an angry god."

"Yes, and do you know where he'd go?" Gerin said: "To a little tavern close by, to drink resinated wine—how do Sithonians stand the stuff?—for hours on end."

Rihwin looked pained. "You just shattered one of my few remaining illusions."

"I'm not saying he's not a brilliant man. I do think he presents his ideas too forcefully, though, and makes too little allowance for variations and exceptions to his rules."

"I can't quite agree with you there. . . ." All but oblivious to their surroundings, they fenced with ideas, arguing in low voices until Rihwin exclaimed, "Is it growing light already?"

They made good progress the next day, and the next, and the next, reaching the Pranther River at the end of the fourth day out of the capital. They camped near its southern bank.

The night was quiet, save for the river's gentle murmur. Pale clouds drifted lazily from west to east, obscuring now the pale thin waxing crescent of Nothos, now Tiwaz's bright full face, now rosy Elleb, which came into the sky halfway through the midwatch. Gerin, whose watch that was, endured the muttering of the ghosts for another couple of hours, then nudged Van.

His friend woke with a thrash. "Anything happening?" he asked.

"Not so you'd notice," Gerin said.

"Aye, it seems restful enough." Van looked down. "What's this? Look what I've been all but sleeping on, captain—another aoratos plant." He plucked it from the ground.

Gerin eyed it with distaste. "Now that I'm only standing one watch in three I don't need anything to keep me awake at night, and the leaves are so bitter they shrivel my tongue. Throw it away."

"I'd sooner not. I want to see if Rihwin knows of it."

"Suit yourself. As for me, I can hardly keep my eyes open."

It was still nearly dark when Van woke him. "Something moved over by the river, behind that stand of brush," the outlander whispered. "I couldn't quite make out what it was, but I don't like it."

"Let's have a look." Grabbing for sword and trousers, the baron slid out of his bedroll. He roused Elise and Rihwin, told them to give him and Van a few minutes and then to use their own judgment. Then he slipped on his helm and followed Van down toward the Pranther.

As always, the Fox marveled at Van's uncanny ability to pick his way through undergrowth. His own woodscraft was better than most, but once or twice an arm or shoulder brushed a branch hard enough to make it rustle. His comrade made never a sound.

Van froze when he came to the edge of the brush. A moment later Gerin eased up beside him, following with his eyes the outlander's pointing finger. "Trokmoi!" he hissed, hand tightening of itself on swordhilt.

A pair of the barbarians sprawled by the riverbank. Their attention seemed focused on the stream. Their tunics were not checked in the usual northern fashion, but were all over fylfots. These were Balamung's men!

But they did not move, not even when Gerin parted the curtain of bushes and walked toward them. His bafflement grew with every step. He came up close behind them, and still they were oblivious. Then he bent down and prodded one of them.

The Trokmê toppled. He was dead, his face an agonized rictus. In his throat stood an unfletched wooden dart, half its length stained with an orange paste. A matching dart was in his companion's unmoving chest. A fat green trout lay between the Trokmoi, bone hook still set in its mouth.

"What in the gods' holy names—!" Van burst out.

A grim smile formed on Gerin's face. "I do believe the rivermen have done us a good turn," he said. "Can you think of any reason Balamung would send men south, except to hunt us? And here, almost up with their prey, they stopped to do a little fishing—in the one river in all

Elabon men don't fish." He explained how the rivermen had come to the Pranther.

Van shook his head. "Poor damned fools, to die for a trout. But it will make us a fine breakfast." He stooped to pick up the fish.

Gerin grabbed his arm and stopped him. A reptilian head was watching them from the river. No expression was readable in the riverman's unwinking amber eyes, but he held an envenomed dart ready to throw.

"All right, keep the blasted thing!" Van flung the trout into the Pranther. The riverman dove after it, surfacing a moment later with it in one webbed hand. A grave nod and he was gone.

"What's toward?" Riwhin called from the bushes. The baron was glad to see he'd had sense enough to don armor and to carry his bow with an arrow nocked and ready. He was a good deal less glad to see Elise behind Rihwin; he wished she wouldn't always run toward trouble. Frowning, he told them what had happened.

Rihwin said, "That Trokmê must hate you indeed, to work so hard for your destruction. Or perhaps he fears you."

Gerin laughed bitterly. "Why should he? I doubt I'm more than a pebble underfoot to him—a sharp pebble, aye, but a pebble nonetheless."

Hooves thuttered on the bridge called Dalassenos' Revenge. Rihwin half drew his bow, expecting more Trokmoi. But it was only a dour courier in the black and gold of the Empire, a leather message pouch slung over one shoulder. He headed south fast as his lathered horses would take him. "Make way!" he shouted, though no one blocked him.

"Just once," Gerin said, "I'd like to see one of them have more to say than 'Make way!' It's no more likely than a wolf climbing trees, though."

The Fox disliked Elabon's courier corps. All the barons north of the Kirs saw it as part of the thin web binding them to the Empire, and they were right. The couriers carried news faster than anyone else, but only on imperial business.

Later that day another courier came south at the same headlong pace. Gerin called after him for news. He got

none. They refused even to gossip, fearing it might somehow compromise them. Cursing, Gerin hurried his own
northward pace.

Rihwin, as it happened, did not know of the aoratos plant
or its uses. "And that is passing strange," he said, "for I
thought surely the Collegium's herbalists were aware of the
properties of every plant that grows within the Empire."
He took the little bush from Van and studied it. "I must
say it seems ordinary."

"Which is likely why no one's bothered with it here,"
Van said. "On the plains it stands out a good deal more."

"I must try it tonight," Rihwin said.

"The taste is foul," Gerin warned him.

"What if it is? If the effects are as interesting as claimed,
I may be on the brink of discovering a whole new vice."
He gave a voluptuary's leer, but spoiled it by winking.

"If you were half the carpet knight you pretend to be,
you'd have debauched yourself to death years ago," Gerin
said.

"And if you were as sour as you let on, you'd long since
have pickled in your own juice," Rihwin retorted, a shot
with so much justice that Gerin chuckled and owned himself beaten.

He stood first watch that night. By sunset he had grown
so edgy that he decided to chew some aoratos leaves himself, regardless of their flavor. He felt fatigue flow away
as the juice coursed through his veins. The curious extra
sense the plant conferred showed him a squirrel asleep in
its nest high in an aspen tree, a fox stalking a vole, a
nightjar whipping after fluttering moths. The ghosts seemed
troubled; thanks to his added perception, Gerin could
almost make out the cause of their alarm, but in the end
it eluded him.

He did not know whether he'd swallowed more leaves
this time or this was a more potent aoratos, but its effects
were still strong in him when he woke Rihwin. They made
the baron reluctant to seek sleep at once. He was also
curious to learn what the southerner would think of the
plant.

"Pah!" Rihwin almost choked on the first mouthful, but
choked it down. "A gourmet's delight it is not." He chewed

more leaves. A few minutes passed. His breath began to whistle more quickly through his nostrils. His voice grew soft and dreamy. "How bright Tiwaz is, like polished silver!" After another moment: "Is that a ferret over there, Gerin?" He pointed into the darkness.

The baron felt his own mind reach out. "I think it is."

"Remarkable. And the ghosts—hear them wail!"

They talked idly for a while, trying with scant success to find some everday sensation comparable to that induced by the aoratos. "This is foolishness," Gerin said at last. "If there were half a dozen things like it, it would not be marvelous at all."

"Astutely reasoned," Rihwin answered, his tone mildly sarcastic. "From that, it would follow—" He paused in midsentenced, exclaimed, "The ghosts are gone!"

They were, fled away as suddenly and completely as if driven to shelter by the rising sun. The gloom outside the campfire's glow seemed somehow strange and flat. Surrounded by this great stillness, the cry of a hunting owl came shockingly loud.

Gerin's surprised senses were still groping for an explanation when Rihwin, now feeling the aoratos more strongly than did the baron, whispered, "I know why they fled. Look north."

Looking was not what was required, but Gerin understood. The blood froze in his veins as he sensed the approaching demon. Only the aoratos plant let him do so; without it, the flying monster would have stayed unseen, undetected, until it descended on the travelers like a hawk stooping on roosting fowl.

The huge demon drew swiftly nearer, like a stone hurled from a god's hand. Even with the aoratos, its shape was hard to define. Gerin was most reminded of the jellyfish that floated in the Greater Inner Sea, but the analogy was imperfect, for Balamung's sending—the baron had no doubt it was such—surveyed with three bright, pitiless eyes the landscape over which it sailed. For mouth it had a rasping sucker disk, set with hundreds of tiny curved teeth. The edges of its gross body blurred and wavered, like a stone seen through running water.

Still, while in this plane it had to be vulnerable to

weapons, however fearsome its appearance. Though fear gripped him, Gerin strung his bow and set an arrow in it. His fingers worked more of themselves than under his conscious direction.

But the demon halted well out of bowshot. The baron's heart sank. He saw no way to lure it into range before it began a killing rush too swift to give him a good shot. Whistling tunelessly, Rihwin glanced from bow to demon.

The creature gave no sign of immediate attack. It seemed as uncertain as the men it faced. Words formed in the baron's mind: "How do you know of me? The man-thing who sent me forth promised easy meat, not warriors with weapons to hand."

For no reason Gerin understood, Rihwin was grinning. "Nor is that the only way in which your master deceived you," he said. He spoke softly to avoid waking Van and Elise, who could not sense the demon; it felt his ideas as he and Gerin perceived its.

"I name no man-thing master!" Its thought dinned in Gerin's head. More quietly, it asked, "And how else am I deceived?"

"Why, by thinking you can do us harm, when you cannot so much as touch us," Rihwin answered airily.

"How not?" the demon asked. Gerin was tempted to do the same. They had no protection against it, as it surely knew.

But Rihwin was not perturbed. "Consider," he said: "To reach us, you first must traverse half the distance, not so?"

"What of it?" the demon snarled.

"Then you will travel half the remaining interval, and then half of that, and half that, and so on forever. You may come as close as you like, but reach us you never will."

Gerin felt the demon muttering to itself as it pursued Rihwin's chain of logic. It did not seem very intelligent; relying on invisibility and ferocity, it had rarely needed much in the way of wits. At last it said, "You are wrong, man-thing, and my showing you this will be your death." Terrifyingly quick, it was twice as close as before. It halted for a moment. "Do you see?"

It halved the gap again, paused to show itself—and Gerin drove his arrow cleanly through its central eye.

It screamed like a woman broken on the rack and was gone, fleeing back to whatever plane Balamung had summoned it from. Gerin thought that agony-filled cry had to wake everything for miles, but only he and Rihwin seemed to hear it. Van and Elise slept on, and all was unchanged out in the darkness. No, not quite—the ghosts returned, their murmurs now far less fear-filled than before.

The baron picked up the denuded aoratos bush. He hefted it thoughtfully. "Thank the gods for this little plant," he said to Rihwin. "Without it, we'd've been nothing but appetizers for that devil."

"At the moment I am still too terrified to move, let alone think about anything so abstract as giving thanks. You have an unpleasant and powerful enemy, my fellow Fox."

"I've already told you that. Didn't you believe me before? As for fear, you handled yourself better than I did—I thought we were done for till you stalled the demon."

Rihwin shrugged. "That paradox always did intrigue me. I first heard a variation of it posed at the Collegium, purportedly to demonstrate that a longtooth could never catch its prey, even were the victim five times slower than it."

"It's logically perfect, but it can't be true. Where's the flaw?"

"I haven't the faintest idea, nor did my instructor. Your elucidation with the bow seemed as elegant as any."

Gerin tried to sleep. He was too keyed up to find rest quickly. He was still awake when Rihwin passed the watch to Van, and listened to his friend's sulfurous oaths at not having been waked to help fight the demon. Van was still grumbling complaints into his beard as his comrades at last gave in to slumber.

The next morning, Gerin let Elise drive for a while and tried to get more sleep in the back of the wagon. He knew Van had managed the trick on the way south. Now he wondered how. Every pothole was magnified tenfold when felt all along his body, and rumbling wheels and creaking axles did nothing to help his repose. Red-eyed and defeated, he came forward to take the reins again.

Traffic was light, for which he gave thanks. He wished Van had been able to buy a pair of Shanda horses instead of just the one. The shaggy little animal pulled magnificently. It seemed never to tire.

Its harnessmate the gray gelding was willing enough, but lacked the steppe beast's endurance. It exhaustedly hung its head at every rest stop. Gerin was afraid its wind would break if he pushed it much harder.

From the chariot Rihwin was sharing with him, Van pointed up the road at an approaching traveler and said, "Someone's coming in one awful hurry."

"Probably another whoreson of a courier," Gerin said. He reached for his bow nonetheless.

A courier it was, whipping his horses as if all the fiends of all the hells were after him. The beasts' scarlet, flaring nostrils and lathered sides said they had been used so for some time. "Way! Clear the way!" the courier shouted as he thundered past.

He was gone in the blink of an eye, but not before Gerin saw the long Trokmê arrow lodged in the crown of his broad-brimmed hat. North of the Kirs, the blow had fallen.

Rihwin stared blankly at the dismayed looks his friends wore; like Gerin, Elise and Van had recognized that arrow for what it was. Elise hid her face in her hands and wept. When the baron put an arm around her, he almost steered the wagon into Rihwin's chariot.

"Careful, captain," Van said.

Gerin's laugh was shaky. "Here I am trying to make Elise feel better, and look at me."

"Will someone please tell me what the trouble is?" Rihwin asked plaintively.

Gerin did, in a couple of curt sentences. Despite the gray gelding's exhaustion, he urged more speed from his horses.

"That's good thinking," Van called. "You can bet there's a mob a few hours or a day behind that courier, all of them hightailing it south as fast as they can go. Best make haste while the road's still clear."

"A pox! I hadn't even thought of that." Gerin added another worry to his list. He tried to comfort Elise, who was still sobbing beside him.

She shook his arm away. "I wish I had never left—I should be with my father." She cried even harder.

"I know," he said quietly. "But no one can change what you did, not god or man. All we can do now is wait to see how things are north of the Kirs and not borrow trouble till we know." *Wonderful,* he told himself, *you talk as if you thought you really could do it—and if your own guts knot any tighter, you can use them for lute strings.*

Despite his own doubts, his words seemed to reach Elise. She raised her tear-streaked face, trying without much success to smile. As the hours passed and the Kirs loomed ever taller on the horizon, a spurious calm came to the northbound travelers. They talked of life in the capital, legends from Kizzuwatna, swordfish-fishing on the Bay of Parvela south of Sithonia—anything except the Trokmoi and what was happening on the far side of the mountains.

As Van had guessed, they soon began meeting refugees fleeing the Trokmê invasion. The first one they saw brought a sardonic smile to Gerin's face: there stood Carus Beo's son, tall in his chariot. He used his whip with more vigor than the baron thought he still had. He shot passed Gerin's party without recognizing them.

The Marchwarden of the North was but the precursor of a steadily swelling stream of fugitives, many with better reasons to flee than his. The warriors who appeared had the look of defeated troops: they straggled south in small, dejected parties, and many were wounded. Now and again Gerin saw a minor baron among them, sometimes leading his family and a small party of retainers, more often alone, haggard, and afraid.

The Fox kept hoping to find a man he knew, so he could stop him and grill him at length. For two days he was disappointed. On the third, he spied a merchant who had been to Fox Keep two or three times, a man called Merric Forkbeard. The trader was still leading a string of donkeys, but their packsaddles were all empty. Gerin looked in vain for the two youths who had accompanied Merric in times past. When Merric heard the baron call his name, he pulled off the road to share what word he had. He took a skin of wine. His hands shook as he raised it to his lips. He had only a few more years on him than did Gerin, but looked to have added another ten in the past few days: his thin face, which Gerin remembered as full of quiet humor, was gray and drawn, his eyes haunted.

"I can't tell you as much as I'd like, Fox," he said,

running fingers through thinning sandy hair. "Six days ago, I was on the road between Drotar's holding and Clain the Fluteplayer's—a good bit southwest of your keep, I guess that is—when I saw smoke ahead. It was the plague-taken woodsrunners, burning out a peasant village and acting as if not a soul in the world could stop them. I turned around and headed south—and ran into an ambush." He bit his lip. "That's when I lost my nephews. They died cleanly— I think."

Gerin tried to express his sympathy, but Merric brushed it aside. "It's done, it's done," he said tiredly. He took another pull at the wineskin, went on, "I will say you're the last man I ever expected to see south of the mountains."

"I was looking for help against the Trokmoi, though I didn't find much."

"Even if you had, it would do you little good."

"What? Why?"

"I came through the pass hours ago. Even then, officers and men were rushing about, making ready to seal it off. What use would your aid be, trapped on this side of the Kirs?"

Gerin stared at him, aghast. "Hours ago, you say?"

"Aye."

"Then I have no time to waste bandying words with you, I fear. The gods keep you safe, Merric, and may we meet again in happier times." The baron twitched the reins and got his wagon into motion. Van and Rihwin followed close behind in the northerner's chariot.

Merric watched them speed north. "I don't think I'm the one who needs the gods for my safety," he muttered to himself.

Now Gerin could show the gray gelding no pity. Once north of the Kirs, he might be able to replace it, but unless he forced an all-out effort from it now, all such problems would cease to matter.

The rich southern countryside flashed by in a blur. To the north, the Kirs grew ever taller. Their crowns of snow were smaller than they had been twenty days before. High summer was drawing near.

The stream of fugitives continued to thicken, clogging

the road and stretching the baron's nerves tighter. Yet had that stream failed, all his hope would have vanished with it, for he would have known the pass was sealed.

He raced through the grimy town of Fibis, past its crucifixes, and into the foothills, now cursing desperately at every slight delay. The gray began to fail. Its nostril flared to suck in great gulps of air and its sides heaved with the effort it was making, but it plainly could not keep up the killing pace much longer. Gerin felt its anguish as keenly as if it were his own. Strange, he thought, how in the end all his hopes rode not on his own wit or brawn, but on the stamina of a suffering beast.

Much too slowly, the pass drew near. Another party of refugees appeared ahead, blocking the roadway and forcing the Fox to the verge. No, these were not refugees—they were the garrison troops who had manned the pass. They marched south in good order, spears neatly shouldered. If they were pulling out, the pass would be closed very soon. Even curses failed Gerin—had he come so far to miss by so little?

At last the gap came into sight. The baron's heart descended from his throat when he saw it was still unblocked. But at his approach an officer stepped into the road, backed by a double squad of archers. The officer stepped forward with a salute, introduced himself as Usgild son of Annar. "I am most sorry, sirs, lady. No travel is permitted beyond this point. We are but minutes from ending contact with the north, as it is under strong barbarian attack."

"I know—that's why I'm here." Gerin quickly outlined his need.

Having heard him out, Usgild shook his head. "I cannot take the responsibility for delaying a measure vital to the safety of my Empire." As if to underscore his words, his archers nocked arrows.

"Can nothing persuade you?" Gerin asked, hearing the finality in Usgild's voice. *Perhaps,* he thought frantically, *I can bribe him.* But he knew that had to be futile. Usgild seemed honest. Even if he wasn't, Gerin did not have enough money to buy him.

Nonetheless, he rummaged through his pockets—and his fingers closed on the tiny bronze Imperial Hand the agent

Tevis had left behind in Grizzard's tavern. He drew it forth and displayed it on his upturned palm. "Can nothing persuade you?" he repeated: "Not even this?"

He was afraid Usgild would doubt his right to the token, but the officer sprang to attention at the sight of the most potent official talisman the Empire knew. "My lord, I had no idea—"

"Never mind all that," Gerin said, determined to give him no chance to wonder. "Send a man at once to hold things up until we are through."

"Hanno!" the officer bawled. One of his archers raced for a chariot.

Gerin decided more, not less, effrontery would make him seem genuine. "My supplies are a bit low. I could use some field rations, and also"—he held his breath—"a fresh horse to replace this poor creature."

Usgild was beyond questions. "At once." Under his efficient direction, his men met Gerin's needs. A sturdy bay stallion replaced the gelding, which barely had the strength to be led away. Soldiers stowed square loaves of journeybread, salt beef, smoked sausages, and lumps of pale, hard cheese in the back of the wagon. They and their commander eyed the Fox with almost servile respect, doing his bidding as though they thought their lives were hanging in the balance. They probably did, Gerin thought sourly— an Imperial Hand was no one to trifle with.

He wondered why Tevis had seen fit to give him the emblem of his office. Could a Hand have realized the barons, in their way, served the Emperor too? It was hard to credit a southern man with such breadth of vision, but then Tevis, whatever else he had been, was no ordinary southerner.

Usgild broke into Gerin's thoughts. "My lord, may I ask your mission in the north?"

"I intend to seek out and slay the wizard who controls the Trokmoi." For the first time Gerin spoke simple truth, and for the first time Usgild looked unbelieving. The baron hardly blamed him, as he himself had no idea how to put an end to Balamung.

The soldier Hanno returned. Flicking a salute to Gerin, he said, "Imperial Hand or no, sir, if I were you I'd hustle down the pass. You've got some wizards mighty peeved at you. They were about halfway through their spells when I told them to hold up, and they're not what you'd call pleased about having to wait and start over."

A party like Usgild's must have been covering the northern end of the pass. The gap through the Kirs, so congested and noisy when Gerin had come south, was achingly empty and silent. The Empire's fortresses stared, empty-eyed, at wagon and chariot moving lonesomely where hundreds of men, beasts, and wains usually passed.

Half a dozen sorcerers paced the battlements of their sparkling, glassy towers. They too glowered down on the baron and his comrades. Though they were too high and too far for him to read their faces, the very snap of their robes in the breeze bespoke annoyance.

As soon as he was past, the wizards began their spells anew, moving in sharp, precisely defined patterns and chanting antiphonally. Their voices, thin and high in the vast quiet, followed Gerin a long way down the pass.

"I know that spell," Rihwin said, "but to think of using it on such a scale. . . ." His voice trailed away. He urged his dapples out in front of the wagon.

The commander of the pass had been no fool: to stop southbound traffic he had posted at the gap's northern outlet not a token force of archers but a solid company of spearmen and charioteers. They were needed. The road stretching north was full of fugitives, shouting, begging, threatening, gesticulating, but leaderless and not quite daring to rush the orderly ranks of gleaming spearheads standing between themselves and the southland. The din was dreadful.

Or so Gerin thought for a moment. Then the earth shook beneath the wagon. The sub-bass roar of endless tons of cascading stone left his ears stunned and ringing. A dust-filled blast of wind shrieked out of the pass behind him. It caught a couple of birds and sent them tumbling through the air. Guardsmen and refugees cried out in terror, but no sound from a merely human throat could pierce the avalanche.

"Looks like I'm home for good," Gerin said. No one could hear him either, but what did that matter? The fact itself seemed clear enough.

X

As inconspicuously as he could, Gerin made his way through the shaken solidery. No one tried to stop him. If any of the imperial troops had, he would have shown them the Hand. He was glad he did not have to. He did not want to find out how they would react to the symbol of a regime which had just marooned them on the wrong side of the mountains.

Those who had fled their homes and lands in the face of the Trokmê onslaught now parted before Gerin, stepping aside like wolves in the presence of a longtooth. Any man going north of his own free will had to be of superior stuff, not to be hindered by the likes of them.

Rihwin let the baron catch up to him, then said, "You will surely need a fighting tail later. Why not start collecting it now?"

Gerin shook his head. "These are the ones who ran first and fastest. I might be able to shame some into coming with me, but they'd likely disappear again at the first sign of a red mustache."

"Right you are, captain," Van said. "Later we'll run into some who got honestly beat: bushwhacked like poor Merric, or just too many woodsrunners and not enough of them. That bunch will be aching for revenge, or a second chance, or what have you. They'll be the ones we take along."

"The two of you make good sense," Rihwin said, adding thoughtfully, "There's more to this business than meets the eye."

They rolled through Cassat not long before nightfall, fighting heavy southbound traffic all the way. The town was nearly deserted. Most of its soldiers and the folk who catered to them must have fled with Carus Beo's son. Looters prowled through abandoned shops and taverns, seeking valuables, drink more potent than water, or perhaps just shelter for the night.

At most times, Gerin would have been after them sword in hand. To his way of thinking, they were worse than

Trokmoi: scavengers, preying off the misfortunes of others. Now he had more important concerns. He drove by, wanting to put as much distance as he could between the rats' nest Cassat had become and his camp for the night.

Only Nothos' crescent was in the sky when the sun went down. Math was a day and a half past new and lost in the glow of sunset. Tiwaz would not rise till midnight, and ruddy Elleb less than two hours before the next sunrise.

"Strange, not to have the Kirs staring us in the face," Elise remarked.

Her three companions round the campfire nodded. To Gerin, it was not only strange but wonderful. For the past couple of days, the mountains and the sealing of the pass had loomed over him like a death sentence. Now he felt reprieved. Tomorrow he would need to start thinking of Balamung and the Trokmoi again but, as he drew in a deep breath of cool night air made flavorful by the fire's smoke, he deliberately suppressed such worries.

Some responsibility, though, had to stay with him. "We need to be really careful on watch tonight," he said. "Some of the fools on the run will be more afraid of the Trokmoi than the ghosts. They'll likely be on the move tonight. And who knows? The woodsrunners may be this far south already."

Travelers in the night there were, but no Trokmoi and no problems, at least during the baron's watch. But when he woke the next morning to the sound of Rihwin's fervent cursing, he knew something had gone wrong. "What now?" he muttered, groping for his sword.

"The plague-taken wine's gone sour!" Rihwin said. "It's no better than vinegar."

"Great Dyaus above, from the howl you raised I thought it was Balamung come in person. Worse things have happened than sour wine, my friend."

"So have better ones. You cannot know what torment my year at Ricolf's was, away from the sweet grape."

"Aye, and look at the trouble you got into, once you had it back," Van said.

Rihwin ignored him. "By the gods, I'd thought a year's separation long enough, but here I am, bereft again."

"If you *must* have you precious wine," Gerin snapped,

"are you not mage enough to call it back from vinegar? If not, why did I ask you to come with me?"

Rihwin refused to notice the expasperation in Gerin's voice, but eagerly seized on his idea. "Your wits are with you, my fellow Fox! I learned that spell—" ("Naturally," Elise murmured, so low only Gerin heard) "and it's easy to cast."

As usual, the southerner was quick to fit action to thought. He rummaged through his gear, producing a packet of grayish powder and a minor grimoire. Gerin was relieved to see him checking the spell before he used it, but still felt a gnawing sense of unease. Things were moving too fast, and out of his control.

Rihwin fed tinder to the nearly dead embers of the fire, coaxing them back into flame. He sprinkled a few drops of the turned wine onto the fire, chanting an invocation in Sithonian. The gray powder followed. It produced an aromatic cloud of smoke. Rihwin chanted on: ". . . and to thee, O great Mavrix—"

Gerin's unease became alarm, but too late. With a whistling hiss, the summoned god, in all his effeminate finery, stood before Rihwin. "So!" Mavrix screeched, bouncing with wrath. "You are in league with this miscreant, and have the gall to seek my aid?" The furious deity pointed a finger at Gerin; somehow it did not seem strange that the digit should lengthen till it thumped the baron's chest.

"I will never help you, wizard! Never! Never!" Mavrix shouted, dancing around the little fire in a sort of wardance. "And you shall never have the chance to ask my aid again. Mortal wretch, now and forevermore you have forfeited your right to work sorcery, and be thankful I leave you the remainder of your pustulent life!

"Take that, ox-goad!" the god added for Gerin's benefit. He stuck out a long pink tongue like a frog's, made a gesture street urchins often used in the capital, and vanished.

"What was all that in aid of?" Rihwin asked, white-faced.

"I told you before, the god and I had a disagreement not long ago."

"Disagreement forsooth! The next time you have a disagreement with a god, my dear Gerin, please let me know

in advance so I can take myself elsewhere—*far* elsewhere."
Rihwin tried to resume his interrupted spell, stopped in
confusion. "A pox! The pestilential godlet did it! I still know
every spell I ever knew, but I can't use them. No wine,
no magic . . ." He seemed ready to burst into tears.

So, for the moment, was Gerin. He had gone south with
high hopes, and returned with—what? A suddenly useless
wizard and some sour wine. *No, fool, wait*, he told himself before his mood altogether blackened—*there's Elise,
and she's worth troubles a dozen times worse than these*.
His gloomy side added: *or she will be, if troubles no worse
than these at all don't kill you first.*

The Elabon Way continued packed with refugees. They
fled south toward a safety that no longer existed, carrying
on their backs or in handcarts such pitiful belongings as
they had salvaged. Pushing north against them was so slow
that at last, much against his will, Gerin decided to leave
the highway and travel on back roads. Though less direct,
he hoped they would also be less traveled.

His hopes were justified most of that day. He made
better progress than he had since he'd first seen that
accursed imperial courier. But as the first cool evening
breezes began to blow, what must have been the whole
population of two or three farming villages jammed the
narrow track on which he was traveling.

The peasants had their women, children, and meager
possessions in ramshackle carts driven by oxen or asses.
They drove their flocks of cattle and sheep before them.
When the baron tried to tell them the way through the
Kirs was blocked, they listened in dull incomprehension,
as if he were speaking some foreign tongue, and continued on their way.

The same thing happened three more times in the next
two days. Gerin's pace slowed to a crawl. Once more he
had the feeling the whole world was against him. He was
brusque even with Elise, and so churlish toward Rihwin
and Van that the outlander finally growled, "Captain, why
don't you shut up and do us all a favor?" Shame-faced, the
Fox apologized.

Later that day, Gerin heard a commotion ahead, but

thick woods and winding road kept its nature hidden. He, Van, and Rihwin reached for their weapons. But when the path opened out into a clearing, they put them down—there would be no fighting here. Instead of Trokmoi, they had come upon yet another group of peasants taking flight and the local lordlet trying to talk them out of it. Or so Gerin thought at first. A moment's listening showed him the noble had given up on that and was telling them what he thought of them for going.

"You cheese-faced, goat-buggering, arse-licking whores' get—" The noble's command of invective was marvelous; even Van listened in wide-eyed admiration. The fellow's appearance complemented his delivery. He was a solidly made man of about thirty-five; he had a fierce red face with one eye covered by a leather patch, thick brows, and a tangled black beard. He wore a bearskin cape over broad shoulders and massive chest, and carried a brace of scabbardless swords on his belt. "Lizard-livered, grave-robbing sodomites—"

The abuse rolled off his tenants like water from oiled leather. They were going whether he liked it or not. Despite the three troopers and two chariots he had at his back, there were at least twenty men in the exodus, each with scythe, mattock, or pitchfork close at hand. Gerin wished they would have been as ready to take up arms against the Trokmoi.

As the peasants began to move, the minor baron noticed Gerin. "Who in the five hells are *you*?" he growled. "Why aren't you on the run like these pissweeds here?"

Gerin named himself and his friends. He asked, "Are the woodsrunners so close, then, to send your villeins flying?"

"Close? I've yet to see one of the pox-ridden bandits, for all they've sent these dungheaded clods a-flying, aye, and most of my fighting men too. I've seen partridges with more heart in 'em than *they* showed." He spat in utter contempt and slowly began to calm. "I'm Nordric One-Eye, in case you're wondering—lord hereabouts, not that I look to have much left to be lord over."

"Friend Nordric," Rihwin said, "would it please you to fare north with us and take vengeance on the barbarians who have caused such chaos?"

Nordric lifted an eyebrow at the southerner's phrasing, but the notion of hitting back at the Trokmoi was too tempting for him to resist. "Please me? Great Dyaus above, I'd like nothing better! Those sheep-futtering, louse-bitten woodsrunning robbers—"

He rumbled on for another couple of angry sentences. Then he and one of his men climbed aboard one chariot and the other two soldiers into the second. His driver, Gerin learned as they began to travel, was Amgath Andar's son; one of the last pair was Effo and the other Cleph, but the Fox was not sure which was which. Neither of them said much. Nor, for that matter, did Amgath.

That did not surprise Gerin. Nordric talked enough for four. Not only that, he kept peppering his speech, even on the most innocuous subjects, with fluent, explosive profanity.

Rihwin steered close to Gerin. "It's as well for him he's short an eye—otherwise they'd surely style him Nordric Swillmouth."

The baron grinned and nodded. He was still glad to have Nordric along. He did not think the foul-mouthed baron would shrink from a fight, or his men either. Facing Trokmoi in battle had to be less terrifying than confronting an angry Nordric afterwards.

Though armed, Nordric and his men carried few provisions. Gerin had resupplied from imperial stores at the pass, but he knew what he had would not feed eight people long. The food would go even faster if he gathered more followers. That meant spending time hunting instead of traveling, something he resented but whose necessity he recognized.

More companions, though, also meant more men to stand watch. Freed from the need to break his sleep with a watch in three, Gerin spent the early evening sitting by the fire with Rihwin. He studied the southerner's grimoires with a desperate intensity that he knew was almost surely futile. Still, he persisted. The vengeful Mavrix had taken Rihwin's power to work magic, but not, it seemed, his ability to pass on what he knew.

"Here." Rihwin pointed to an incantation written in the sinuous Kizzuwatnan script. "This is another spell for the destruction of one's enemies when a bit of their spittle, hair, or nail parings is in one's possession."

"How does it differ from the more usual one, the one I would have set on the fair Namarra?"

"It has the advantage of needing no elaborate preparation, but is more dangerous to the caster. Unless perfectly performed, it will fall on his head rather than the intended victim's."

"Hmm." The spell looked simple enough, involving only a couple of genuflections and some easy passes with the left hand. But as Gerin studied its verbal element, his first enthusiasm faded: the Kizzuwatnan text was one long tongue-twister, full of puns, subtle allusions to gods he barely knew, constantly shifting patterns of rhyme and rhythm. He almost passed at once to the next charm. Then, stung by the challenge and artistry of the ancient versicle, he stopped and read it again and again, until it was fairly well lodged in his mind.

"I have it," he said at last, adding, "I think. What's next?"

"Here is one I've always found useful. It keeps horses' hooves sound and strong, and helps prevent all sorts of lameness."

"Yes, I can see where that would be a good thing to know. Ah, good, it's in Sithonian, too. Let me have a closer look—" And soon the veterinary magic was also stored in the baron's capacious memory.

The next day dawned luminously clear. The sun leaped into a sky of almost southern clarity and brilliance. The fine weather pleased Gerin less than it might have under other circumstances. In such heat, armor became an itchy, sweaty torment, but trouble was too close to chance removing it.

Thus the baron, longing for relief from the sweltering day, was glad to hear the rush of river water ahead. But almost at the same instant, he became aware of other sounds rising above the stream's plashing: the clash of bronze on bronze, the deep battle cries of Elabonian fighting men, and the higher, wilder yells of the Trokmoi.

Van was driving Rihwin's chariot. When he caught the noise of combat, his head jerked up like that of a dog suddenly taking a scent. "A fight!" he shouted, his voice pure glee. "The gods beshrew me, a fight!"

He sent the light car bounding forward with such a rush that he almost pitched the startled Rihwin into the roadway. Nordric and his driver were right behind, the stocky baron swearing sulfurously. On his heels were his liegemen, leaving Gerin to bring up the rear.

The Fox cursed as fervently as Nordric, but for a different reason. The last thing he wanted was to expose Elise to the risks of war, but he had no choice. "For Dyaus' sake, stay in the wagon and don't draw attention to yourself." He handed her his bow and quiver. "Use them only if you have to."

Black willows grew along the riverbank. Under their low spreading branches a grim drama was under way, with seven southerners battling twice as many Trokmoi. The Elabonians had accounted for four woodsrunners, but three of their own number were down and the survivors desperately fighting back to back at the water's edge when unexpected rescue arrived.

The Trokmoi shouted in dismay as Gerin's band leaped from chariots and wagons and loosed murder among them. Van was a thunderstorm, Gerin and Rihwin a pair of deadly snakes, striking and flickering away before being struck in return. Nordric's men fought with dour competence, but the petty baron himself brought the worst terror to the barbarians.

At last come to grips with the foes who had turned his life upside down, he went berserker-mad, his ruddy features darkening to purple, incoherent cries of raw rage roaring from his throat, spittle flecking his beard with white. Swinging a sword in each meaty hand, he rampaged through the Trokmoi, oblivious to his own safety as long as he felt flesh cleave and bones shatter beneath his hammerstrokes. The Trokmoi broke and ran after half of them had fallen. All but one were cut down from behind by the vengeful Elabonians. An arrow from the wagon brought down the last of them, who had outdistanced his pursuers—Elise once more proving her worth.

The onslaught was so sudden and fierce that Nordric's man Cleph was the only Elabonian badly hurt. He had a great gash in his thigh. Gerin washed it with wine and styptics and bound it up, but the bleeding would not stop.

Cleph was pale and clammy, and seemed partly out of his wits.

"You're going to have to tie off his leg," Van said.

"I hate to," Gerin answered. "If I leave the tie on for more than a few hours the leg may go gangrenous, and if I take it off he'll probably start bleeding again."

"Look at him, though. He'll damn well bleed out on you right now if you don't do something in a hurry," Van said. Shaking his head, Gerin applied the tourniquet. The flow of blood slowed to a trickle, but Cleph remained semiconscious, muttering curses under his breath against demons only he could see.

Nordric's battle-demon, on the other hand, deserted him after the fight was done. A man in a daze, he wandered across the small field of combat, staring at the results of his own butchery. "Dip me in dung and fry me for a chicken," he grunted, apparently not much believing what he saw.

"Friend Nordric, must your every phrase have an oath in it?" Rihwin asked.

"That's not so—" Nordric began, but his driver Amgath interrupted him.

"I fear it is, my lord," he said. "Remember what happened when Holgar the Raven bet you a goldpiece you couldn't go a day without saying something vile? 'You son of a whore, you're on!' you said, and forfeited on the spot."

The four footsoldiers Gerin and his comrades had saved were glad to take service with him. Two of them had lost brothers to the Trokmoi and another a cousin. They were all burning to retaliate. "The worst thing about dying here," said one, "would have been knowing we'd only taken a woodsrunner apiece with us."

Elise found herself less troubled over the Trokmê she'd slain than she had been at Ikos, which in turn troubled her. That evening she said to Gerin, "I don't understand it. He was only running away, and the driver back at the Sibyl's shrine was trying to kill us, but the first death left me sick for days, and now I feel almost nothing: only that I did what I had to do."

"Which is nothing less than true," the Fox said, though he knew it did not help much.

He stood a late watch, and a strange one in that no moons were in the sky: Tiwaz was new that night, Elleb a thin crescent, golden Math a fatter one, and pale, slow-moving Nothos just past first quarter. By an hour past midnight it was cool, quiet, and amazingly dark. Countless dim stars the baron had never seen before powdered the sky with silver, their light for once not drowned by the moons.

Cleph died early the next day. He had never really come to himself after the shock of the wound, and whenever the tourniquet was loosened it began to bleed again. They hastily buried him and pressed on.

Two men joined them that day, half a dozen more on the next, footsoldiers all. Of necessity, Gerin was reduced to a pace a walking man could keep. He wondered it the added numbers were worth the delay, and considered moving ahead with chariots alone. Van and Nordric were all for it. Rihwin advised caution. Events soon proved him right.

The baron's fighting tail was emerging from forest into cleared fields when a wild shout from ahead made them all grab for weapons. Just out of bowshot waited a force of Trokmoi of nearly the same makeup as their own: four chariots and a double handful of retainers afoot. About half the northerners wore plundered Elabonian armor. The others were in their native tunics and trousers, except for one tall, gaunt barbarian who was naked but for shield and weapons.

Gerin heard a growl go up behind him. He knew the men at his back were wild to hurl themselves against the Trokmoi. But he did not want to fight at this moment, against this foe. The little armies were too evenly matched. Even if he won the battle, he would be defenseless against the next band of woodsrunners he happened across.

The Trokmê seemed to have similar thoughts, which puzzled the baron. Most northerners fought first and questioned later. He watched, bemused, as the chief winded a long, straight horn. He was no trumpeter, but Gerin recognized the call he had blown: parley.

He waved an agreement, got down from the wagon, and walked alone into the field. He ignored the scandalized murmurs of his men. Those stopped abruptly when Van announced, "The next one of you who carps will be carp stew." His huge right fist, fingers tight round the sweat-stained leather grip of his mace, was a persuasive argument.

The northerner met Gerin halfway between their men, empty hands outstretched before him. Plump for a woodsrunner but cat-courteous, the Trokmê bowed low and said, "I am Dagdogma the son of Iucharba, who was the son of Amergin the great cattle-thief, who was the son of Laeg the smith, who was . . ." Gerin composed himself to wait out the genealogy, which, if it was like most others, would go back ten or twelve generations to a god.

Sure enough, Dagdogma finished, ". . . who was the son of great Fomor himself." He waited in turn.

Gerin did not think it wise to reveal his true name to the barbarian. "Call me Tevis," he said, picking the first name he thought of. Like Dagdogma, he spoke in Elabonian.

"The son of—?" Dagdogma prompted politely.

"Nobody, I fear."

"Ah well, a man's a man for all he's a bastard, and a fine crew you have with you. Not that we couldn't deal with them, but I'm thinking 'twould be a shame and a waste of my lads and yours both to be fighting the now."

Gerin studied Dagdogma, suspecting a trick. Things he had not noticed at first began to register: the Elabonian women's rings the Trokmê had jammed onto his little fingers, the gleaming soft leather boots he wore instead of the woodsrunners' usual rawhide, the booty piled high in his chariots. The baron suddenly understood. This was no northern wolf, just a jackal out to scavenge what he could with as little effort as possible.

The Fox was filled with relief and contempt at the same time. His talk with Dagdogma went quickly and well since, each for his own reasons, neither man had any stomach for fighting. The Trokmê trotted back to his men. He moved them off along a forest track running west, clearing the way north for Gerin and his troop.

But Gerin's own warriors were unhappy he had talked his way past the Trokmoi instead of hewing through them. "I came in with you to kill the whoresons, not pat 'em on the fanny as they go by," said one of the men who had joined just that day. "If you're going to fight your fool war like that, count me out. I'd sooner do it right."

He stamped away, followed by four more footsoldiers of like spirit. Van looked questioningly at Gerin, asking with his eyes whether to bring them back by force. The baron shook his head. He had no use for unwilling followers.

In turn, he eyed Nordric curiously; he'd expected the hot-tempered lordlet to leave him the moment he ducked a confrontation. Nordric spat. He said. "That was just a pig in a red mustache, and scarce worth the slaughter. There'll be real fighting soon enough—I think you draw bloodspilling like honey draws flies."

Just what I need, Gerin thought, but he had the uneasy feeling Nordric was right.

As he and his band moved north the next day, signs of the devastation the Trokmoi were working became more frequent: corpses by the roadside (some Elabonian warriors, some woodsrunners, and all too many serfs hacked down for the sport of it), empty peasant villages (some abandoned; others gutted, smoking ruins), livestock wantonly slaughtered and now rotting in the sun, fields of wheat and oats trampled into ruin or torched, and a good many keeps overthrown. A couple of castles now flew northern banners. Some of the Trokmoi, at least, had come to stay.

Their raiding parties were everywhere—bands of half a dozen men or so, under no real leadership, out more for the joy of fighting and the hope of booty than for Balamung or the conquest of the world. The Trokmoi seemed surprised to see a sizable party of Elabonians under arms. They gave them a wide berth.

The farther north Gerin went, the fewer refugees he came across. Most of those who had fled had already fallen to the barbarians, perished on the road, or made their way south. The few fugitives he did encounter could tell him little. They had been skulking in the woods for days now. None wanted to join him.

His homeland's agony brought torment to the Fox. How could he alleviate it even if he beat Balamung? "Twenty years of peace will hardly repair this," he said bitterly that night, "and when has the border ever known twenty years of peace?"

Only the moons, almost evenly spaced across the sky, were above all strife. Nothos had been nearly due southeast at sunset, Math a day past first quarter, Elleb just at it. Rushing toward his three slower siblings, Tiwaz was now a fat waxing crescent. As twilight deepened, the fourfold shadows they cast spread fanwise from men, chariots, and trees. The ghosts began their senseless night whispers.

Although Gerin's troop was still traveling by back roads, Elise began to recognize the cast of the land the next morning. Pointing to a keep crowning a hillock ahead, she said, "That holding belongs to Tibald Drinkwater, one of my father's vassals. We must be less than a day from home!"

The Fox had not dared hope he could come this far unscathed. An unfamiliar confidence began to grow in him. It was rudely dashed when he drew closer to Tibald's keep and discovered it had been abandoned and looted and its palisade torn down.

A little later, the path they were following merged with the Elabon Way. Without hesitation, Gerin led his band onto the highway. They sped north for the castle of Ricolf the Red. Van left Rihwin's chariot and joined the Fox. He took over the driving; Elise, despite her protests, was relegated to the rear of the wagon. If they traveled openly through country held by their foes, they had to do so in battle order; one of the new footsoldiers took Van's place with Rihwin.

As Van tested the edge of one of his chakrams with a callused forefinger, he said softly, "Captain, if Ricolf's holding has fallen, you'll look a right fool coming up on it in the open like this."

"If Ricolf's holding has fallen, I'll be in too much trouble to care how I look."

The last time Gerin traveled this stretch of road, it had been too dark and he was going too fast to pay much attention to landmarks. By now, though, Elise was on land she had known since birth. "As soon as we round this next bend, we'll be able to see the keep," she said.

"Aye, there it is," Van said a moment later, "and the red banner still flying, too. But what's all that folderol around the moat—tents and things?" He drew up the wagon. Gerin waved the rest of his little force to a halt.

"It's a Dyaus-accursed siege camp, that's what it is," the baron said. "Who would have thought it from the Trokmoi? Freeze, blast, and damn Balamung! Still, though, I think we may be able to give them a surprise." He climbed down from the wagon and talked briefly with his men. They nodded and readied themselves.

The Trokmoi had set up their perimeter just out of bowshot from the ramparts of Ricolf's castle, intending to starve it into submission. A scallop in the outer edge of the moat showed where they had tried to hurry matters by filling it and storming the walls. That, plainly, had failed.

No one raised an alarm as Gerin and his men drew close. As the baron had noticed, the woodsrunners did not seem to think an armed party could belong to anyone but themselves. But sooner than the Fox hoped, a sharp-eyed Trokmê raised a shout: "Esus, Taranis, and Teutates! The southrons it is!"

Quick as he was, he was too late. Gerin's men were already rushing forward, foot and chariotry alike. A flight of fire arrows sent trails of smoke across the sky. The arrows landed on the woolen fabric of the Trokmê tents. A second flight followed the first; a couple of archers had time for a third release before they had to reach for spear and sword to defend themselves from the barbarians, who came rushing from the siege line to meet this new threat.

The Trokmoi hurled themselves into battle with their usual ferocity. These were no fainthearts like Dagdogma and his crew, but Gerin's attack cast them into confusion. And after the first few moments, they had no leader to direct their courage. Van took care of that. He sent a chakram spinning into the throat of a gilded-helmed noble. It cut him down in the midst of a shouted order.

"What fine things chakrams are!" Van told Gerin as he readied another knife-edged quoit. "I can cast them and drive at the same time." As he had in the capital, he handled the wagon as if it were a chariot. The baron, who had both hands free, felled two barbarians with well-placed arrows.

Battle madness seized Nordric harder now than it had by the river. Disdaining even his sword, he leaped from his chariot, seized a Trokmê, and broke him over his knee like a dry stick. An instant later he was down himself, caught in the side of the head by the flat of a northerner's blade. Three Elabonian footsoldiers held off the Trokmoi until he was on his feet and fighting again.

Leaderless or no, the woodsrunners badly outnumbered Gerin's men. He was beginning to wonder if he'd bitten off more than he could chew when, as he'd hoped, their camp began to blaze. Many of them pulled out of the fight in dismay. They tried to fight the flames or salvage what belongings and booty they could.

Then Ricolf's drawbridge thudded down. He and his men fell on the barbarians from the rear. Ricolf and a few of his followers had harnessed their chariots. Their arrows spread destruction through the northerners.

The battle was suddenly a rout. The Trokmoi fled singly and in small groups, turning to loose an occasional arrow but not daring to stand and fight. Ricolf and his charioteers rode a short distance in pursuit, but had no real mass of fugitives to chase. They soon reined in.

Then the men from the besieged castle were all over Gerin's troopers. They squeezed their hands, pounded their backs, and yelled congratulations and thanks. But their jubilation faded as they recognized first Rihwin and then Gerin and Van. Curiosity replaced it. That grew tenfold when Elise stuck her head out of the wagon. Many shouted happily to see her, but as many seemed confused.

Ricolf returned from the hunt. His jaw dropped when he caught sight of Rihwin, who was having a hurt arm attended to. "What are *you* doing here?" he growled. Rihwin flinched. He started to stammer a reply, but Ricolf paid no heed. He had just seen Gerin, Van, and his daughter.

Gerin waited in some apprehension, not sure what the older baron's reaction would be. Ricolf got down from his chariot, speechless and shaking his head. He folded Elise into his arms, then turned to the Fox. "I might have known trouble would lure you back, kidnapper," he said; Gerin was relieved to hear no anger in his tone. "Your timely return has an explanation, I'm sure?"

"Would you hear it now?"

"This very instant. If any man is entitled, I am."

Having recovered some but not quite enough of his usual

aplomb, Rihwin suggested, "Perhaps to cool his throat after his exertions, my fellow Fox could use a cup of wine—" He stopped abruptly. The glare Ricolf turned on him was frightening.

"Rihwin, you are a fine young man in many ways," Ricolf said, "but if ever I hear the word 'wine' in your mouth again, I vow it will have my fist there for company."

So, unmoistened, Gerin plunged into the tale. His comrades did not let him tell it unhindered, but he controlled the flow of it, and it went well. He saw Ricolf's men, many of whom had given him hard looks when he began, coming round as he spoke. When he was done, Ricolf stayed silent a long time. He finally said, "Do you know, I believe you. No one would make up such an unlikely story."

"The last person who said something like that was Valdabrun," Gerin told him.

"From what I remember of my brother-in-law, he has trouble believing the sun comes up each morning. He misses a good deal of the juice in life." A twinkle in his eye, Ricolf asked Elise, "Do you mean to tell me you'd rather have this devious wretch than a forthright warrior like Wolfar?"

She kissed the Fox by way of answer.

Ricolf turned to Gerin. "Frankly, Fox, I thought you had more sense than to get involved in a tangle like this one."

"Frankly, so did I."

"Hmm. A year ago I had Elise's wedding plans firmly in hand, and now I seem to have very little to say about them. As I recall, Gerin, you said something about 'a mind of her own.' You were right, the gods know. This, though, I say and mean: I think you will make my daughter a good husband, but there will be no rushed wedding for fear of what the future may bring. If it should bring ill, such a wedding had better never happened. When the Trokmoi are driven away, that will be time enough."

"I can't quarrel with you," Gerin said. He saw disappointment cross Elise's face, but Ricolf's demand was only just under the circumstances.

Van said, "Ricolf, would you put a fist in *my* face if I asked for a mug of ale?"

"In your face?" Ricolf laughed. "You're like the thousand-pound thrush in the riddle, who perches where he pleases.

Things are a bit tight—the damned barbarians have been sitting outside for some days. We're a long way from being starved out, though. Come along, all of you. We'll see what we can do."

"You spoke of Wolfar in jest a moment ago," Gerin said. "What happened to him after I, ah—?"

"Left suddenly? When he woke up (which wasn't soon; you're stronger than you think), he tried to beat down the door of my chamber and have me send all my men after you at once. I'd have done it, too, were it not for the note Elise left behind," Ricolf said.

Elise looked smug. Gerin pretended not to notice.

Ricolf went on, "When I said no, things grew unpleasant. Wolfar called me an oathbreaker and worse. He said he'd pull my castle down around my ears for me. After that, I told him he could take his carcass away while he still had ears of his own. I see what you meant about him, Gerin: he can be mild as milk when it suits him, but cross him and he raves."

"It's the streak of wereblood in him," Gerin said. "It runs thinly in many families on both sides of the Niffet, you know, but strong in his." He told Ricolf what had happened to Wolfar when Nothos and Math were full together.

The older baron frowned. "I had not heard of that. If I had, I'd never have asked him here. Lucky such conjunctions are rare."

For all their joy over driving away the Trokmoi, neither Gerin's men nor Ricolf's could work up much revelry. The day was drawing to a close. Both bands were exhausted. Even Van, as dedicated a roisterer as was ever born, contented himself with little more than the single mug of ale he had asked of Ricolf. Men gnawed at smoked beef and hard bread, cheese and sun-dried fruit. Then they sought bedrolls or fell asleep where they sat. Gerin woke in Ricolf's great hall at sunrise the next morning, still holding the same half-empty cup over which he'd dozed off.

The day passed in watchful waiting. Everyone expected the Trokmoi to try to restore their siege. But the morning slipped by with no sign of the barbarians. Tiwaz rose at noon, overlooking only peace. Elleb followed a couple of hours later. He was trailed at hourly intervals by Math and pale Nothos, and all was still quiet.

"I think you may have driven them away for a while," Ricolf said to Gerin. The Fox pointed to heaven, wishing Ricolf's words into the ear of Dyaus.

As men began to realize the woodsrunners would not be back at once, they began the celebration they'd been too worn to unleash the night before. Gerin and Ricolf quickly saw they could not stop it: the warriors needed release. The barons did what they could, ordering a few reliable men to stay sober and stand sentry lest the Trokmoi dare a night attack.

Among the troopers Gerin chose was Amgath Andar's son, Nordric One-Eye's driver. Nordric himself happened to be close by. He reinforced the Fox's orders: "Keep your eyes open, you son of an unwed she-moose, or I'll wear your family jewels on a necklace."

"Does he always use his men so?" Ricolf whispered to Gerin.

"No. Usually he's worse."

Someone by the main gate got out a mandolin and began to play. Gerin thought fleetingly of Tassilo and Rihwin, and of how a couple of foolish drunks had changed his life. Leaving Elise tomorrow, he thought, would be harder in its own way than facing the Trokmoi: that he had done many times. But only once had he left the woman he'd come to love, and then in hands he thought safe. Now, even behind Ricolf's sheltering walls, Elise was in nearly as much danger as he.

When one of Ricolf's men passed him an earthen jug of ale, he gave it back still corked. He knew drink would only lower his spirits further. He watched as Van came up with his clay flute to accompany the mandolin-player. The man who had offered Gerin ale soon joined them with one of the long horns the Trokmoi favored. That surprised the Fox; few Elabonians played the northern instrument. The music was loud and cheery, but powerless to expel Gerin's gloom.

The sun sank and was forgotten. Most of the men in the holding gathered by the gate. Song followed bawdy song. Sentries shouted refrains from the stations on the wall. When too many throats grew dry at once, Van spun things along with a tale of his days on the plains of Shanda, a

story of high daring and higher obscenity. Then the soldiers roared into another ballad.

To escape the gaiety he could not share, Gerin wandered
into the castle's great hall. Dyaus' altar had no offering
before it now, nor were the benches crowded with feasters. One warrior snored atop a table. His head rested in
a puddle of dark, sticky ale. In a corner, another trooper
was kissing the bare breasts of a serving maid. Neither he
nor his partner paid the Fox any mind.

Gerin walked through the dark hall, kicking at rushes
and bones. Once in the corridor beyond, he stopped and
looked about: which sconce's torch, he wondered, had he
used to flatten Wolfar? Was it the one by that much-scarred
wooden door, or its neighbor a few feet down the hallway?
Unable to recall, he turned a corner—and almost ran into
Elise.

Later he realized he must have been trying to find her,
searching for the one happiness he'd found in a collaps-
ing world. At the moment, no thoughts intruded. She was
warm in his arms. Her lips and tongue met his with the
same desperation he felt. "Where—?" he whispered, strok-
ing her hair.

"Follow me."

It was, he thought, the chamber in which he'd slept on
his way south. That seemed fitting, somehow. He chuckled under his breath. Elise made a questioning sound. He
shook his head. "It's nothing, love."

The straw of the matress rustled as he drew her down.
She softly cried out beneath him, three times: first in pain,
then in wonder, and then, at last, in joy.

When she rose to leave, the pain of separation was nearly
more than Gerin could bear. She bent down for a last kiss,
said softly, "Come back to me," and was gone. He was sure
he would toss for hours after the door closed behind her.
Almost at once, though, he fell into a deep and dreamless sleep.

XI

It was nearly noon the next day before the Fox and his companions began the last leg of their journey. He left the wagon behind. Ricolf lent him his own stout three-man chariot, and with it a lean, weathered man named Priscos son of Mellor, his driver and shieldman.

Gerin suspected Ricolf guessed what had happened the night before, why he'd left the celebration so early. It showed in no overt way but, as the Fox made small talk with the older man while getting ready to leave, he felt an acceptance, a closeness between them of a different sort from their earlier friendship. He was glad. Ricolf's good opinion mattered to him.

Elise's farewell was wordless. He tasted tears on her lips as they kissed goodbye. He, Van, and Priscos climbed into Ricolf's chariot; Nordric and Amgath were beside them, as were Rihwin and Effo, the survivors of the fighting tail the Fox had recruited along the way, and a few volunteers from Ricolf's holding. They were twenty-two in all, with four three-man and five two-man chariots.

Priscos clucked to the horses. The little army started to move. The gatekeepers lowered the drawbridge. One of them caught Gerin's eye as he passed. "What are you running off with this time, my lord?" he asked.

"Nothing you don't see, Vukov," the Fox answered, pleased he remembered the fellow's name. He doubted the gatekeeper had had a happy time the morning after Elise left. He turned for a last glimpse of her, but the cramped confines of the gatehouse already blocked his view.

Priscos was a man of few words, most of them about horses. "You don't see many Shanda beasts hereabouts," he remarked. "Where did you come by this one?"

"What's the name of that town in the mountains, Gerin?" Van asked.

"Cassat."

"Aye. That's where I picked him up. Cheap, too—the clod of a horse-trader didn't know what he had. He's been a rare worker."

"They're ornery, I hear," Priscos said. He went on, more to himself than Gerin or Van, "Reckon I can handle that, though." Gerin was sure he could. Priscos had an air of quiet competence he liked.

As the sun sank, they camped by what had been the border station between Ricolf's land and Bevon's. Now the square wooden building which had housed Ricolf's guardsmen was only charred ruins. *One more debt to pay*, the baron thought, *among so many*.

The ghosts were strange that night. Their keenings and wailings were more intense, and also more nearly understandable, than the Fox had ever heard. One in particular flitted round him as if drawn like moth to flame. For all its efforts, he could neither make sense of what it would tell him nor recognize its pallid form in the flickering firelight.

"That is an uncanny thing," Rihwin said, watching the wraith's frantic but vain efforts to communicate.

"Likely it's like a Shanda spirit, seeking to lure you away from the light so it can drink your blood," Van said.

Gerin shook his head. "I feel no harm in it, even if I can't understand what it would say. Besides, Van, every ghost in the north country must have had a glut of blood by now."

To that the outlander had no reply but a grave nod.

Remembering the fraternal strife tearing Bevon's barony even before the Trokmoi invaded, Gerin wanted to cross it in a single day if he could. He did not want to camp inside it: if he could expect night marauders anywhere, Bevon's tortured land would be the place.

And tortured it was. The Fox's band passed two battlefields before the sun was high in the southeast. The woodsrunners had plundered both fields, but all the bloated, naked corpses seemed to be Elabonians. Here brother had fought brother, and fought with a hate greater than they turned against the Trokmoi.

As he surveyed the second meadow filled with bodies, Gerin's face was stony and full of bitterness. "Poor fools," he said. He wondered if his words were not an epitaph for all the northland.

Whichever brother had won the war, he had not enjoyed

victory long. A lot of the keeps still standing were held by
small bands of Trokmoi. They hooted in derision as they
saw Gerin's force go by, but did not move against it. "They
think us beneath contempt," the Fox said to Van, "and
perhaps we are."

"Honh! The next time I care what a woodsrunner thinks
will be the first."

A bit more than halfway through Bevon's barony, they
passed a roadside holding destroyed in a way Gerin had
never imagined before. The timbers of one whole wall of
the palisade lay like jackstraws in the bailey, as if kicked
in by a monster boot. The stone keep itself was a pile of
broken rubble.

Something white stuck out from under one limestone
slab. As the baron drew closer, he saw it was the skeleton
of a human hand and arm, picked clean of flesh by scavengers. No one, Elabonian or Trokmê, garrisoned this keep.

"This is the work of your Balamung?" Rihwin asked.

"He's not mine. I wish with all my heart I'd never heard
of him," Gerin said, but he had to nod as he spoke. His
warriors eyed the shattered keep with awe, fear, and
wonder. Hand-to-hand fighting against the Trokmoi was all
very well, but how could they hope to hold against sorcery like this? Even Nordric was grim and quiet.

"I wonder why such powerful wizardry has not been used
further south," Rihwin said. "Few castles could stand against
it, yet here, so close to the Niffet, is the first sign we've
had of anything more than a simple barbarian invasion."

"What difference does it make?" Gerin said bleakly,
staring once more at the blasted holding.

"Maybe none, maybe a great deal. One explanation I
can think of is that your northern mage may have so much
trouble trying to lay low one particular keep—I name no
names, mind you—that he has had little leisure to help his
men elsewhere."

Gerin gave him a grateful look. The line of hope the
southerner had cast him was thin, but he was all but drowning in despair. Anything that buoyed his spirits was welcome.

His renewed optimism and his hope of crossing Bevon's
lands in one day both collapsed not long after noon. His

band came to the top of a low rise. There they stopped in horror and dismay. For the next three or four miles, the Elabon Way and most of the surrounding landscape had been brutally wiped out of existence. All that was left was a ruined expanse of raw-edged muddy craters, some a hundred feet across and twenty deep. They overlapped one another in the mangled earth, as if the same giant who had pulverized the keep had then amused himself by pelting the ground with thousands of huge boulders. But there were no boulders, no visible explanation of how the devastation had been committed.

Chariots were not built to cross such terrain. Twice Gerin and his band had to stop to mend wheels battered by half-buried fragments of roadbed and treetrunk, and once more to fix the axle of Nordric's car when it broke.

Van repaired it with bronze nails, leather lashings, and a large measure of hope. He said, "It may hold, and then again it may not. All we need now is for a horse to break a leg in this mess."

Gerin's fingers moved in a protective sign. "May the ears of the gods be closed to you."

They barely managed to escape the ruined land before the sun set. All four moons were low in the east, slow-moving Nothos being most nearly full and Tiwaz still closest to first quarter.

That night the ghosts were louder and more insistent than Gerin had over known them. Again, one in particular tried to deliver some message to him; again, he did not understand. Although he failed, something in him responded to the ghost, as if it was the shade of someone he had once known well. Irked by the riddle he could not solve, he pored over Rihwin's grimoires until sleep overtook him.

He and his men came on another band of desolation not far into the lands of Palin the Eagle. This was worse than the one before: the ravaged area held several streams and ponds. Their water made the trek a nightmare of slimy, clinging mud.

In some places, chariots sank axle-deep in the muck. The warriors had to get out and slog through it on foot to lighten the load enough to let the horses move the cars at all. Men and beasts alike were filthy and exhausted when at last they reached flat, solid ground. To his disgust, Gerin found several fat leeches clinging to his legs.

Though some daylight was still left, the Fox decided to camp when he came to an unfouled creek in which to wash. Most of his men, spent by the day's exertions, collapsed into slumber almost at once.

Only Rihwin kept any semblance of good cheer. That surprised Gerin. He had expected the southern dandy to be dismayed at his present unkempt state.

"Oh, I am, my fellow Fox, I am," he said with a grin when Gerin asked, "but what, pray, can I do about my plight save laugh? Moreover, I truly begin to think Balamung has wreaked all this havoc for no other purpose than sealing aid away from your lands. Did you not tell me a mage was warding your keep?"

"Aye, or so I hope, at any rate: Siglorel Shelofas' son. He's southern-trained, true, but I don't know how long he can stand against one such as Balamung. For one thing, he drinks too much."

"By your reckoning, so do I, yet did it keep you from bringing me along on this mad jaunt? Also, never forget that while crisis makes cravens of some, in others it burns away the dross and leaves only their best."

"From your mouth to Dyaus' ear," Gerin said, touched again by Rihwin's efforts to reassure him. What the southerner was saying held just enough sense to keep him thoughtful, too: maybe Balamung did have some unknown reason to fear him. *And maybe*, he told himself, *I'll do as Van says and flap my arms and fly to Fomor*. Neither was likely.

Despite the gift of fowls' blood, the ghosts were a torrent of half-seen motion, a clamorous murmur of incomprehensible voices. The spirit which had visited Gerin on the two previous nights returned once more. He could see its ill-defined features writhing in frustration as it failed again to impart its tidings.

"You know, captain," Van said, "I may be daft, but I think the poor wraith even looks a bit like you." Gerin shrugged. For one thing, though the ghosts were extraordinarily immanent of late, they remained cloudy and indistinct. For another, the Fox, like most folk in the Empire and the lands it knew, had only a vague idea of his features. Mirrors of polished bronze or silver were uncommon and expensive; even the best gave images of poor quality. He probably had not seen his own reflection more than a dozen times since taking over his father's barony.

The holding of Raff the Ready, Palin's vassal who had guested Gerin and Van on their way south, was only a burnt-out shell. The little pond beside it was rubble-choked and fouled with the bodies of men and beasts. Gerin viewed the ruins with sadness, but little surprise. Too many years of peace had led Raff to neglect his walls. He could not have put up much of a fight, not in his dilapidated keep.

Late that afternoon, the Fox passed from Palin's land and entered his own once more. The roadside guardhouses on either side of the border were deserted, but had not been burnt. The borderstone itself had been uprooted by the Trokmoi. Gerin cursed when he saw its moss-covered runes effaced by fylfots chipped into the rock, as if Balamung was claiming the land for his own.

So, perhaps, he was. Gerin and his band had not gone far before they tripped some sorcerous alarm the wizard had planted. A misty image of the black-robed sorcerer appeared in the road before them. "Back, are you, Fox, in spite of it all? Well, you'll have no joy of it. My lads will see to that, and soon." With a scornful laugh, the projection vanished.

"The spell your enemy placed here was plainly set to react to you and no one else," Rihwin said. "In which case—"

Gerin finished for him: "—there's sure to be another charm in action now not far away, telling a few hundred woodsrunners to come down and make an end of me. Well, what can I do but go on? Balamung has thrown away the advantage of surprise in his vainglory, for whatever that's worth."

Arms at the ready, they moved ahead as the sun sank low in the west. As they passed a tiny crossroads, a whoop from behind some brush told them they had been seen. Archers nocked arrows; spearmen tightened grips on their weapons.

They did not have long to wait. Chariots and infantry together, a veritable army thundered down the cross road toward them. At its head was Wolfar of the Axe. His hairy features split in a bloodthirsty grin when he recognized the Fox. "What luck! It's the wench-stealing sodomite himself!" he roared to his men. Then, to Gerin: "I'll make a capon of you, to keep you from having such thoughts again!"

Had Wolfar's rancor against the Fox driven him into the arms of the Trokmoi? Gerin would not have thought that even of his western neighbor, yet here he was.

There was scant time for such thought. Gerin shot at Wolfar but missed. His arrow tumbled one of the men behind Wolfar out of his chariot. Rihwin and the other bowmen let fly too, dropping a couple of other men and sending a chariot down in crashing ruin as one of its horses was hit. But to stand and fight was madness, for Wolfar had easily ten times Gerin's force.

"North!" the Fox shouted to his followers. "We'll outrun the footsoldiers, at least, and meet him on more even terms."

North they fled in the gathering dusk. Wolfar howled hatred close behind. Arrows flew up. Almost all went wide—the jouncing chariots made poor shooting platforms.

"Captain," Van shouted in Gerin's ear, "what in the five hells is that up ahead?"

Only his will kept the baron from hysterical laughter. Whatever else Wolfar was, he was shown to be no traitor. "What does it look like? It's the wizard's bully-boys, come to finish us off. We're on the horns of a dilemma, sure enough, but maybe, just maybe, they'll gore each other instead of us."

The leader of the Trokmoi was an immensely tall, immensely fat blond barbarian who filled most of a three-man chariot by himself. He stared in dismayed amazement at the force of chariotry bearing down on him. Instead of the small band he'd expected, this looked like the leading detachment of an army as large as his own.

He frantically reined in, shouting, "Deploy, you spalpeens! Don't be letting 'em get by you, now!" The Trokmoi shook themselves out into a wide line of battle, some afoot, others still in their cars.

But Gerin did not intend to take evasive action. He and his men stormed toward the center of the Trokmê line, hoping to slash through and then let the northerners and Wolfar's men slaughter each other to their hearts' content. But the Trokmoi were too many and too quick to be broken through so easily. They swarmed round the Fox's chariots, slowing the momentum of his charge and stalling him in their midst.

Their huge leader left his car to swing a great bludgeon with deadly effect. He crushed the skull of Rihwin's chariot-mate, then lashed out at Priscos. Gerin's driver took the blow on his shield. It all but knocked him from the chariot. The baron chopped at the Trokmê with an axe. The barbarian, quicker than his girth would have suggested, ducked the stroke.

A horse shrieked as a woodsrunner drove a dagger into its belly.

For a moment, Rihwin was close by Gerin. "We've got to get out of here!" he cried.

"If you have any notion how, I'd love to hear it," Gerin said.

A barbarian tried to climb into his chariot. Van hit the man in the face with a chakram-braceleted forearm. He screamed through a torn, blood-filled mouth and fell away.

Then, suddenly, the pressure of the woodsrunners on Gerin's beleaguered band slackened as Wolfar hurled himself into the sea of Trokmoi after the man he hated. "He's mine, you arse-lickers! He's mine!" he roared.

The barbarians turned to meet this new and much more dangerous threat. Gerin tried to extricate his men from the now three-cornered battle. It was not easy. The Trokmoi had not forgotten them, and to Wolfar's men the woodsrunners were only obstacles blocking the way to their real target.

Unnoticed by anyone in the melee, the sun sank below the horizon. As it set, the four moons rose within seconds of one another, all of them full. The last time that had happened had been close to three centuries before Elabon's capital was founded.

Huge tides swamped low-lying coastal areas, drowning small towns and wrecking great ports. Prophets the world around cried doom.

And in those lands where the taint of wereblood ran

through a folk, no moons at quarter or crescent counteracted the pressure to change shape exerted by the light of a full moon's disk. Those with only the thinnest, most forgotten trace of wereness were now liable, indeed compelled, to take beast form.

Hills off to the east briefly shielded the battlefield from the rays of the rising moons. Then they topped the low obstacle and washed the fighters in their clear, pale light. Gerin was trading axe-cuts with a scrawny, green-eyed Trokmê who fought without armor when his foe dropped his weapon, bewilderment and alarm on his face.

The Fox had no idea what was happening to him, but was not one to let any advantage slip. His stroke was true, but the northerner ducked under it with sudden sinuous ease. The Trokmê's body writhed, twisted . . . and then the baron was facing no Trokmê, but rather a great wildcat. It spat fury and leaped at him.

He had no time to wonder if he had lost his mind. Razor-sharp claws tore at the bronze facing of his shield, snarling jaws full of jagged teeth snapped at his arm. He brought his axe crashing down between the mad eyes of the cat, felt its skull splinter under his blow. Hot blood spattered his arm. The carcass lay still a moment, twitching.

Gerin stared in disbelief. The awful wound he had inflicted healed before his eyes. Bones knit, skin and fur grew together as he gaped. The wildcat's eyes opened and caught sight of him. It yowled, gathered itself for a second spring—and was bowled over and spun to the ground by an outsized wolf. They rolled away, locked in a snarling, clawing embrace.

The battlefield was a world gone mad. At first the Fox thought some spell of Balamung's, intended for his destruction, had gone awry. He soon realized the chaos was far too general for anything of that sort.

Then, quite by accident, he saw the four full moons. Understanding came, but brought no relief, only terror. Nearly half the fighting men had gone were, in one beast-shape or another. The field was littered with corselets, greaves, and helms they escaped when the change came over them. The were-creatures fought former friends, foes, and fellow beasts with an appalling lack of discrimination.

A bellow of red rage from beside Gerin made him whip his head around, fearful lest Van too was falling under the influence of the moons. Not so: the outlander, in dispatching one of Wolfar's men who had remained both human and combative, had taken a cut on his forearm.

More and more, those who kept their human form left off fighting one another and banded together against the ravening werebeasts. At the baron's side were three Trokmê foot soldiers, but neither they nor he had any leisure in which to quarrel.

The werebeasts were so lithe and fast, they found it easy to slip through the quickest human guard and fasten claws or fangs on flesh. Even when they were killed, men gained only momentary respite from their onslaught. Within seconds of taking the most ghastly wounds, they grew whole once more.

Men caught away from their fellows were for the most part quickly killed. One pair of exceptions was Nordric One-Eye and his driver Amgath. Their chariot had foundered in the middle of the field when Van's repairs failed at last and the car's axle broke beneath it.

The werebeasts made short, dreadful work of their horses, but Nordric was in full berserker rage, and fast and savage as any shape-changer. With one mighty stroke of his sword he cut a leaping werewolf in two, then seized its tail and hurled the spouting hindquarters far away. "Live through *that*, you backscuttling demons' get!" he shouted.

Still, had the werebeasts not battled each other with the same ferocity they gave those who had not changed, they would have made short work of them all. As it was, boar stomped and tusked wolf, a pair of wildcats sprang at a stag. The stag tossed one away with a wicked swipe of its antlers, but went to its knees as the other reached its back. Then the werewolf was beset in turn by a gigantic badger.

The shape-changers, Gerin noted, seemed to keep the same body weight they had possessed as men. A couple of hawks far too heavy to fly stumped about the battlefield. Their cruel beaks gaped as they screamed challenge to all and sundry. Nor were they long without foes. A wolf attacked one, a fox the other. Between beaks, talons, and battering wings, both soon had cause to regret it.

The majority of the werebeasts were wolves, foxes, or wildcats, but deer, boar, bear, badger, and wolverine were all commonly represented. Along with these mundane creatures, though, were several oddities. One of Wolfar's men must have had some Urfa blood in his past, for a miniature but combative were-camel, moaning, snorting, and spitting, struck shrewd blows with its forefeet at the carnivores assailing it.

Off to one side lay a tremendous salmon, a corselet still round the middle of its body. It flopped and gasped in the air it could not breathe. It could not die, either, because of the vitality of its wereblood.

In the convulsions of the field, two transformed creatures stood out. One was the wolf which had been Wolfar. His passion against Gerin was so fierce that he kept it in beast shape. He fought to force his way through the press and close his jaws on the Fox's throat. His howls of fury held almost understandable curses buried within them.

Yet even the were-Wolfar gave way before a great tawny longtooth which, from its bulk, must have been the animal shape of the swag-bellied Trokmê commander. It flailed its way through the imbroglio with hammerlike blows of its paws, blows that sent even werebeasts reeling back, stunned.

The monster cat came up to the stalled chariot in which Nordric and his driver still held out. Amgath snapped his long lash at it, hoping to keep it at a distance. It squalled in pain and anger but, instead of being repulsed, ran at him. He dropped the whip and grabbed a short thrusting-spear. Too late. A single cuff crushed his face and broke his neck.

The longtooth's rush overturned the chariot and tumbled Nordric among the ravening werebeasts. Gerin was sure he was doomed. In an instant, though, he was on his feet, a sword in either hand. His curses pierced the cacophony of beast-noises around him. He seemed to face every way at once, flashing blades keeping death at bay. He drove off one werebeast after another. Trokmoi and Elabonians shouted together.

Their cheers turned to groans as he went down, a wildcat clinging to his back. Van leaped from the chariot and ran to his rescue. The wolf that had been Wolfar bounded toward him, slavering jaws agape, yellow eyes blazing hatred.

The outlander was ready when it sprang. A blow of his spiked mace shattered its skull. The wereflesh healed with unnatural speed, but Van was past by the time the wolf regained its feet. He kicked the cat away from Nordric. It lashed out at the first thing it hit, another, even bigger, wildcat. While they tried to gut each other with raking claws, Van hauled Nordric erect. Side by side, they fought their way back to the chariots.

Nordric was battered and bleeding, but still full of fight. Gerin and Van had to hold him back from throwing himself once more against the were-longtooth that had killed Amgath.

"There's no vengeance to gain against a beast you cannot kill," Gerin said. "He'll be in human shape again, you know—maybe you'll meet him then." Nordric let himself be persuaded, a true measure of the punishment he had taken.

Wolfar's chief lieutenant, Schild Stoutstaff, had not gone were. Now he began to rally to himself such of his overlord's men as were left. The Trokmoi, too, gravitated toward a pair of their nobles.

Gerin thought it a good time to vanish discreetly from the field. Followed by all his surviving men—Rihwin and Nordric in the former's chariot and three more warriors in another car—he edged toward the cover of the woods.

Their departure went unmarked by still-struggling men, but one werebeast saw. The wolf that was Wolfar bayed angrily and started to lope after them. Before he could clear the battlefield, the longtooth knocked him down from behind. It tried to bury its fangs in were-Wolfar's neck. The werewolf tried to twist free, but his foe's great weight held him down.

Wolfar writhed, wriggled, and clamped his teeth on one of the longtooth's forelegs. Bones crunched. The longtooth screamed. It tore at the wolf's belly with its hind feet. Wolfar let go, but only to snap at the longtooth's throat. Any greater purpose was forgotten in the fighting madness now gripping him. Outmatched physically, he was nearly the longtooth's match because of the fury that drove him.

Gerin thanked the gods he and the poor handful of followers left him had made good their escape. Giving quiet directions to Priscos, he guided them north through a web of tiny trails. No one who had not lived in the barony could have followed them in the dark.

At last he judged it safe to stop. The din of battle had long since died behind him, but the night was far from still. More than the usual number of animals ranged the woods. Many were men caught in the open by the werenight and now running wild, bloodlust in their souls.

That led to another thought: what hell was the werenight playing in keeps under siege—especially in Castle Fox (always assuming it had not fallen)? "Don't worry about it, captain," Van said when Gerin spoke aloud. "Whatever's going on inside, it's just as bad out, and that you can bet on. Balamung or no, the Trokmoi'll be in no shape to take advantage of things tonight. Maybe a weresnake will swallow the cur and solve our problem for us."

"Such happy endings happen more often in romances than in fact, I fear," Gerin said, but the outlander had heartened him.

Something else occurred to Rihwin: "Great Dyaus above! I wonder what's happening south of the mountains?" The Fox shied away from that idea. With even a small part of its populace turned were, the capital's narrow, winding streets and dark alleys would be a worse jungle than any forest through which he'd pass. He thought of Turgis and hoped the innkeeper was safe.

Not so the Sorcerers' Collegium. He started to send a curse down on its head, then stopped, suddenly ashamed of himself. "Now I understand why the southern wizards offered me no help!" he exclaimed. "They must have known this was coming, and been making ready to meet it. Sosper as much as told me so. No wonder they needed to keep every man they had in the southlands."

Despite exhaustion, Gerin found sleep hard to come by. So did his men: they were all in pain from wounds taken fighting the Trokmoi, Wolfar's warriors, or the werebeasts.

Also, the light of the four full moons seemed to allow the ghosts fuller access to this plane than at more normal times. They floated round the campfire, sometimes darting up to one or another of the men to try to give such advice as each thought important. Thanks to the moons, they were sometimes able to make themselves understood, but that understanding did not always make their listeners see why the wraiths deemed their news important.

"What possible difference does it make to me that the price of barley in the capital dropped two coppers a bushel three days ago?" Rihwin demanded. The spirit that told him did not explain.

The ghost that had been straining for days to get through to Gerin drifted toward him again. "Captain, I take oath it looks like you," Van said. "Face a little wider, maybe, but leave out that and what looks like a broken nose and it could be your twin—"

"Father Dyaus above!" Gerin whispered. "Dagref, is it you?" He moved to embrace his slain brother's shade, but it was like trying to hold a breeze.

The ghost withdrew a few paces, slowly and sadly shaking its head. Gerin recalled that gesture well. His older brother had always used it when the Fox did something foolish.

The memory brought sudden tears to the baron's eyes, though he and Dagref had not always been close. Dagref was half a dozen years older, while Gerin, as he approached manhood, found the soldier's life Dagref took to so naturally did not suit him at all. *Or so I thought then*, Gerin said to himself: *here I am living it*.

The lips of Dagref's ghost were moving, but the Fox still could not make out any words. He heard his brother's voice in his mind, but so windblown and blurred by echoes that he could not grasp Dagref's meaning. "Once more," he begged.

The wraith grimaced in exasperation, but started over. This time its meaning, or a sentence of it, was clear: "You still don't keep the stables as clean as our father would have liked," Dagref's ghost said. It shook its head again in the gesture so familiar to Gerin, then, satisfied it had finally got across what was necessary, disappeared into the darkness, leaving Gerin more bewildered than before.

"What did it say?" Van asked. Gerin told him. Van tugged at his beard, gave the Fox a quizzical look. "It's hounded you for days to let you know you're a scurvy excuse for a housekeeper? Tell me, captain, was your brother crackbrained?"

"Of course not." The news Dagref's ghost had given was plainly important to it. Gerin cursed himself for failing to see why. He turned the ghost's enigmatic words over and over in his mind, but came no closer to understanding them.

Half a night's sleep brought no new insight. He was glad, though, when he woke, to see the sun shining through the trees to the east and all the moons gone from the sky.

"You look like death warmed over," Van said. "There's dried blood all over your face."

The baron scrubbed with his fingers, saying, "I must have done enough tossing and turning to open up a cut or two." He pounded left fist into right palm. "Damn everything, what was Dagref trying to tell me?"

He got no good answer to that, either from his own wits or from his comrades when he put the riddle to them. "Perhaps he wants you to have a good storage place for my cheap barley," Rihwin suggested. Gerin glared at him, but it made as much sense as anything else.

Not long after they left camp, they came upon the mangled and partially eaten carcass of a brown bear. Beside it slept a naked Trokmê. Awakened by their approach, he leaped up and fled into the woods, red hair streaming behind him.

Rihwin stared in disbelief. "No man could—"

"And no man did," Van said grimly. "Look at the tracks: bear and wildcat. It shouldn't have been too hard. In were shape, the woodsrunner would have taken no hurt. Then he had his feast, curled up afterwards—and changed back when the moons set."

The forest path was punctuated by random death: another bear, horribly torn; a Trokmê with his throat ripped out; a pair of Elaboninan warriors so mutilated as to appall even Gerin's hard-bitten crew; a crofter's cottage, its flimsy door torn from leather hinges, a blackened puddle of blood luring flies at the threshold. Gerin did not need to look to be sure no one was alive inside. He hoped the deaths there had been quick.

Live Trokmoi still lurked in the woods. An arrow from hiding grazed the side of Gerin's helm. He and Rihwin shot blindly into the undergrowth. The sniper, unhurt, let fly again, hitting Priscos' left arm just below the shoulder. The driver cursed and tore out the arrow, then ripped at his tunic for cloth to bandage the wound.

The rest of the Elabonians jumped from their chariots. They ran for cover, then stalked the barbarian sharpshooter. The Trokmê, no fool, held his well-concealed position until he had what he thought was a good shot at Van. But in his cramped quarters he could not draw bow to his ear, only to his chest. The outlander's stout cuirass turned his shaft.

Van shouted in rage and rushed at the thicket from which the arrow had come. The Trokmê fled. A blow of Van's mace felled him from behind before he had taken ten strides. Like a charging longtooth, the outlander was deadly quick in a short rush.

He surveyed the sniper's corpse without a hint of remorse. "A pity the craven bushwhacker didn't die slower," he said. "If he wanted to fight, he should have come at us like a man."

Gerin had planned and executed enough ambushes in his time to keep a discreet silence.

When they returned to the chariots, Priscos was matter-of-fact. "Did you get him?" he asked. At Gerin's nod, he said, "Good," and jerked the reins to get the horses moving north again.

They returned to the Elabon Way no more than a couple of hours' journey south of Fox Keep. Gerin was sickly aware he was returning without even the ragtag army which had set out from Ricolf's holding. The werenight had seen to that. His main hope now was that it had disrupted Balamung's men more than the Elabonians.

Then that hope died too. A shout rang out from the flanking forest: "Here's more o' the buggers!" A score and more of footsoldiers charged from the woods, spears ready to cast, swords bared.

But the Fox was still reaching for his bow when he realized the cry had been in his own tongue, not the woodsrunners'. And when the onrushing warriors spotted him (or more likely spied Van and his distinctive armor), they stopped so abruptly that one man stumbled and fell to his knees. Then they came on again, but now in friendship and joy, raising a cheer to chill the heart of any Trokmê in earshot.

Gerin recognized them as Drago the Bear's men; their commander was one of Drago's chief retainers, Fedor the Hunter. The Fox did not know Fedor well. He usually stayed behind at Drago's keep as deputy when his overlord went to Castle Fox. But Gerin had never been gladder to see anyone than this heavyset, scar-faced warrior.

Fedor led his men up to the Fox. "We thought you dead, my lord," he said accusingly. "The Trokmoi and their cursed wizard claimed you were, when they tried to get me to yield the Castle of the Bear to them."

"Drago's holding stands?" Gerin said. "You beat back an attack the wizard led himself? Great Dyaus, Fedor, how? His magic has leveled more keeps than I can count."

"Oh, he tried to shake the holding down after I said no to him, so he did. Fires and smokes and flying demons and I don't know what all. But the Castle of the Bear is good and solid, and it sits on bedrock. As for the rest"—he shrugged with the same stolidity Drago would have shown—"we were inside and they were outside, and that's the way it stayed. The wizard's lightnings blasted one breach, but no woodsrunners came through it alive. They paid a lot more than half the butcher's bill, my lord. After a while, they'd had enough and went away."

Listening to the bald report, Gerin decided Fedor had not had the imagination to see he had no chance. And, going on phlegmatically where a more perceptive man would have despaired, he had endured. *Something to be said for dullness after all*, the Fox thought.

But Fedor was not yet done. "You need not look so surprised, my lord. Fox Keep still holds too, you know."

The baron's heart gave a great bound within him. "No," he said softly. "I did not know."

"Aye, it does." Fedor seemed oblivious to the impact his news had on the Fox. "They're under siege, true, but they managed to sneak a messenger to us through the woodsrunners' lines: some trick of your wizard Siglorel, I understand. Sixty men set out from the Castle of the Bear two days ago, but after last night—" He shrugged again. "For a while I thought I'd lost my wits, but I was too busy staying alive to worry about it."

"Weren't we all?" Gerin said.

Thanks to the footsoldiers, the final approach to Fox Keep was slower now, but Gerin would not have traded them for all the treasures of Ikos. A final fear gripped him: that the keep had fallen after its messenger went out. Then Van pointed north. "Right on the skyline, captain—the very tip of your watchtower. And I think"—he squinted—"aye, I think it's your banner atop it."

As his men exulted, Gerin tried to follow his friend's pointing finger. He had to say, "Your eyes are better than mine." But that Van saw what he claimed, the baron had no doubt. He had surmounted every stumbling block now, save the last . . . putting an end to the mightiest mage the world had seen in two thousand years. And even as he quickened his pace toward his castle, he realized he still had no idea how to do that.

XII

Castle Fox had taken a fearful beating, Gerin saw as he and his men sped toward it. Part of one wall had fallen, to be replaced by a lower, makeshift bulwark of timbers and earth. For some reason, the logs of the palisade were painted a sour dark green. Though the watchtower still stood, gaps had been bitten into some of the upper stonework of the keep.

Still, on the whole the Trokmê investment was a shabby job. Mighty sorcerer or no, Balamung was only a woodsrunner when trying to besiege a holding his magic could not flatten. He knew nothing of engines or stratagems, but had to rely on the ferocity of his troops—and ferocity counted for little against a fortress with determined defenders. Broken bodies littered the ground below the palisade. Here as at the Castle of the Bear, their bravery and inexperience were making the Trokmoi pay more than their share of blood.

But what ferocity could do, it would. Just out of bowshot from the palisade, Balamung harangued his men, nerving them to yet another charge against outwall and gate. Despite the repeated maulings the Elabonians had given them, despite the horrors of the werenight just past, they waved their weapons and cheered at his speech, for all the world like so many outsized, destructive children.

The Fox's men on the palisade caught sight of Gerin before the Trokmoi did. Their yells made Balamung pause in mid-word. He looked up. An evil orange glow lit his eyes. His voice sounded inside the Fox's head, scornful and exasperated at the same time: "It's infernally hard to kill that you are. Well, so long as you're here, you can watch your fine castle die, for I'm fresh out of patience with your puppydog of a wizard, indeed and I am."

The lean sorcerer gave quick orders to his men. Fifty or so loped toward the Fox ("Just to make sure you don't joggle my elbow, now," Balamung said). The rest advanced on the palisade. The baron found their discipline remarkable—and alarming. He'd hoped his sudden advent would draw all the barbarians from the walls and free his men inside to sally against them.

The first arrow hissed past his head. Another found the breast of one of Rihwin's proud dapples. The southerner's chariot slewed, flipped over. He and Nordric, both veterans of such mishaps, landed lightly. They were on their feet at once to face the oncoming Trokmoi.

More arrows flew past. The Fox shot a couple in return. Then he yelled to Priscos, "We'd all better get down. The horses will just have to take their chances."

The driver chewed his lip, unhappy at the thought of abandoning the beasts but knowing not all spills ended so luckily as Rihwin's. He pulled to a halt, his long face doleful. Sword in hand, he followed Gerin and Van to the ground.

He ran to the horses. Evading a snap from the Shanda pony, he slashed through their traces and slapped both beasts' rumps with the flat of his blade. They galloped away, leather straps trailing. Priscos gave Gerin a wintry grin. "All right, my lord, I expect I'm ready now."

The baron had no time to answer—the Trokmoi were upon them. He glimpsed a hurled stone just in time to flick up his shield and knock it aside. A wild-haired northerner, naked but for a helm and one greave, thrust at his legs with a short pike. He skipped aside.

Van rammed his own, longer, spear into the Trokmê's belly. He jerked it free with an expert twist. Bloody entrails came with it.

At first, progress toward Fox Keep was not hard. Though outnumbered almost two to one by the Trokmoi Balamung sent to hold them off, the Elabonians had better weapons and armor than their foes. But soon the lack of order the baron had looked for before began to cost his relieving force. More and more Trokmoi gave up the attack on the palisade and ran toward the hand-to-hand fighting they loved so well. Their wizard leader cursed shrilly and tried to bend them to his will again, but had little luck. Wizard or no, leader or no, he could not change the habits of the proud, wild folk he led.

A tall noble in brightly burnished scale-mail confronted the Fox. "It's Dumnorix son of Orgetorix son of—" he began. He got no farther, for an arrow—a Trokmê arrow, by its length and fletching—suddenly sprouted in his throat and sent him spinning to the ground.

Then the baron was facing a woodsrunner who must have learned his swordplay from an Elabonian. Forsaking the usual slashing style of the Trokmê, he thrust wickedly at Gerin's face, belly, and face again. His wrist was quick as a snake. But Rihwin sprang to Gerin's side. His slim blade darted at the Trokmê. Unable to stand against two such swordsmen, the barbarian sprang back among his comrades.

Both sides slowed to a brief, panting halt. Not fifteen feet from the Fox, a sweaty barbarian leaned on his spear. He was picking his teeth with a gory forefinger. He caught Gerin's eye and grinned. "Good fighting." And in truth, that was all the twisted corpses, the gashed limbs, the terror and agony meant to him: a sport, something to enjoy and at which to excel.

Gerin wearily shook his head. Too many on both sides of the border felt thus.

Someone threw a stone. Someone else cast a spear. The heat of battle again grew to a boil. Shouting like men struck mad, a wedge of Trokmoi slammed into the middle of Gerin's thin line, splitting his force in two.

The larger half, led by Nordric, made for the repaired breach in the palisade. That, thought Gerin, was largely because his berserker comrade saw more Trokmoi there than anywhere else. Nordric and his companions fought their way into range of covering arrows from the palisade. Its defenders cheered their every forward step.

For his own fragment, which included Van, Rihwin, and Priscos, the baron had another goal: Balamung himself. The black-robed mage, hood flung back to show his face, stalked menacingly round the palisade. Under one arm he carried the Book of Shabeth-Shiri. The codex was bound in light, fine-grained leather, perhaps tanned human hide.

No arrow bit the wizard, though the men on the palisade sent many his way. Some flared into brief blue flame, others flew wild, others simply vanished. Arrogant and contemptuous, Balamung stood, dry, under a rain of death. He opened the Book of Shabeth-Shiri and began to chant. Even fighting desperately a furlong away, Gerin felt the power the wizard gathered, saw the air around him shimmer with pent-up energies. His hair tried to prickle upright under his helm.

The Trokmoi who had been assaulting the wall of the palisade on which the spell would fall sprinted away for their lives. Balamung's chant rose to a crescendo. He shouted in the dread Kizzuwatnan tongue, paused, shouted again.

Sheets of red flame flowed from his fingertips. The fire engulfed the wall of the palisade. Gerin watched in awe and consternation. Not even ashes, he thought, could remain when that incandescent flood receded. But the palisade withstood the fiery bath unharmed, still the same sour green which had bemused the Fox before.

"I think your own wizard has won a point," Rihwin said, parrying a spearthrust. That was a notion new to Gerin. It had not occurred to him that the ugly paint might be a sorcerous defense.

Balamung shouted in frustrated wrath. His flapping black cloak gave him the aspect of a starveling vulture. He loped toward the repaired section of the palisade, crying to Siglorel, "Southron fool, you'll pay for not bending the knee to me!" Less than a bowshot from where Gerin battled his minions, the Trokmê mage opened his fell grimoire and began another spell.

Redoubling their efforts, the baron and his men tried to close with the wizard while his sorcery distracted him. But they had all they could do to stay alive; pushing forward against the barbarians was impossible.

The Fox could only watch as fire shot once more from Balamung's hands. It caught and clung to the untreated timbers of the improvised barricade—and to the back of a woodsrunner not quick enough to get away. A human torch, he shrieked and fell and burned. Gerin's men within Fox Keep braved arrows to beat at the flames with hides and pour water and sand on them, but could not douse the wizardfire.

Then Siglorel, clad in robes no less black than Balamung's, appeared at the top of the burning stretch of palisade. As Rihwin had said, when faced with the supreme challenge of his life he turned his back on the alepot and fought Balamung's spells to a standstill. Now he worked with unhurried skill, ignoring the missiles flying around him. His fingers flashed in intricate passes. As his hands fell when his spell was done, the flames fell too, leaving the bulwark smoldering but intact.

"You dare to show yourself in my despite?" Balamung hissed. Gerin shuddered at the malice in his voice. Siglorel gave his foe a tired, grave nod. "Then dare—and die!" Balamung's arm swept down. Lightning cracked from a clear sky. A flick of Siglorel's hand sent the bolt smashing harmlessly to the ground.

The backlash of energies from the wizards' duel—and simple fear, too— held Trokmoi and Elabonians frozen where they stood, unwilling witnesses to a struggle more dire than any in which they fought. Balamung was clearly the stronger. The lightnings he hurled crashed ever closer to his enemy, his whirlwinds spun up great clouds of choking dust that all but hid the palisade, his demons flew shrieking through the winds and dove on Siglorel like huge bat-winged falcons.

No levinbolt, though, seared through Siglorel's heart, no wind seized him and flung him to his doom (though the warrior who had been at his side had time for but one brief scream of terror as Balamung's tornado tore him from Castle Fox), no demon drank his blood. Face gone dead white from strain, hands darting now here, now there like those of a man wracked by fever, Siglorel somehow kept an ever-tightening circle of safety round himself.

Once or twice he even managed to strike back. Balamung contemptuously swatted aside his lightnings, as if they were beneath his notice. The end, Gerin saw, was inevitable. Balamung cursed in balked outrage as his weaker opponent evaded destruction again and again, but each escape was narrower, each drained more of Siglorel's waning strength.

Then the Trokmê wizard chuckled terribly. He briefly checked the Book of Shabeth-Shiri. At his gesture, a plane of pulsing violet light sprang into being on either side of Siglorel. As Balamung brought his hands toward each other, the planes of force he had created began to close upon

his antagonist. Siglorel tried to check the inexorable con-
traction, but all his knowledge, all his cantrips, were of no
avail against the ancient, mighty sorcery Balamung commanded.

Ever nearer each other drew the planes of force, so that
now Siglorel held them apart not with his magic, but by
the power of his strongly muscled arms and shoulders. The
desperate tableau held for half a minute, no more; then
only a crimson smear lay between the glowing planes.

Gerin expected his own life to be similarly crushed away,
but Balamung, a cat toying with a helpless mouse, took too
much pleasure in the baron's dismay to end the game so
quickly. Full of noxious confidence, his voice sounded in
the baron's ear: "First you can watch your fine keep fall.
Then I'll get round to dealing with yourself—if my lads
have not done it for me."

That seemed likely. Gerin and Van fought back-to-back
much of the time now. Many of the warriors who had
accompanied them were gone. Attacked at the same time
by one Trokmê with a sword and two more with spears,
Priscos went down while Balamung was speaking. Rihwin
and Gerin killed the spearmen, but Priscos lay where he
had fallen.

Balamung began another spell. A clot of black smoke
rose before him. It quickly began to take shape and solidity.
Even after his invocation ceased, that which he summoned
continued to grow.

The demon was roughly anthropoid, but twice the height
of any man, and broad in proportion. Forced to bear its
huge mass, its short thick legs were bowed, but they carried
it well enough. Its huge arms, hanging almost to the ground,
ended in grasping, taloned hands. Its skin was black and
green, and wet like a frog's. It was grossly male.

Its chinless lower jaw hung slack, showing row on row
of saw-edged teeth. A bifurcated tongue lashed in and out.
The demon had no nose, only red slits to match the banked
fires of its eyes. Above those eyes, its forehead sloped
straight back. Its batlike ears swiveled and twitched at every
sound.

Obeying Balamung's shouted command, it waddled
toward Castle Fox. The Trokmoi scattered before it. As he

watched it near the keep, Gerin saw a plume of smoke curl up from within the palisade. One of the outbuildings was alight, whether from Balamung's magic or a mere fire-arrow he did not know.

The wizard saw it too. He laughed. "You'll no more be putting your betters in the stables to sleep, will you now?"

At their mage's order, the Trokmoi raked the palisade with arrows, forcing its defenders to keep their heads down. A few Elabonians shot back. Two arrows pierced the demon. It wailed and gnashed its teeth, but did not slow.

Then Nordric rushed at it, a sword in either hand, curses rising even over its cries. All the barbarians around him had fled at the demon's onset, but in his blind fury he knew only the attack. The demon stopped as he charged. It was confused, no doubt, to see a human running toward it.

Then confusion gave way to a full-throated bellow of pain and rage, for Nordric's first stroke ripped into its thigh. Purplish-red ichor spurted from the wound. Gerin and the Elabonians cheered frantically, and were joined by more than a few Trokmoi not happy with the unholy ally Balamung had given them.

But the demon, faster than its bulk suggested, slipped by Nordric's next rush. An arm longer than he was tall snaked out. A huge hand seized him in a chest-crushing embrace. No last oath passed his lips as his swords fell from nerveless fingers. The demon brought the fresh-killed dainty to its mouth. The horrible jaws slammed shut. The monster flung what was left of the broken body behind it and resumed its advance on the palisade.

Reaching the repaired section of wall, it grasped a charred timber near the top. Enormous muscles bunched under its glabrous hide. The timber groaned, screamed, and came loose with a splintering crash. The demon tossed it aside, grabbed another and pulled it free, then another and another.

More arrows thudded into its flesh, but so thick were its muscles that they guarded its vitals almost as well as a corselet. The Trokmoi shouted in excitement as they saw the barrier torn apart.

When the breach was all but complete, an Elabonian with more courage than sense attacked the demon with a spear. A heavy forearm knocked aside his weapon. The demon lashed out with a broad, flat foot. The Elabonian's body, torn nearly in two by that terrible kick, flew through the air to land well within the courtyard of Fox Keep.

Balamung cried out once more in whatever fell tongue he used to control the monster he had summoned. It turned away from the keep, moved ponderously toward Gerin and his embattled comrades. The smoke from the burning stables grew thicker as the warriors who had been fighting the flames abandoned that task to meet the Trokmoi swarming into the breach.

More afraid of their hideous partner than the men they were facing, the woodsrunners who had opposed the Fox gave way as the demon neared. Out of the corner of his eye, Gerin saw Van closely studying the oncoming monster. The tight smile on the outlander's face puzzled him until he realized his friend had at last found a foe to overawe him.

Then shouts from the keep made every head whirl. The demon, bat-ears unfurled to the fullest extent, turned to meet the new challenger bearing down on it. Duin the Bold, mounted on a horse and carrying the biggest spear he could find, had rammed his way through the Trokmoi at the breach. He thundered toward the monster, shouting to draw its attention from Gerin and his companions.

The part of the Fox's mind which, regardless of circumstances, observed and recorded fine details, now noted that Duin was not riding bareback. He sat on a rectangular cloth pad cinched tight round the horse's middle. His feet were in leather loops depending from either side of the pad.

Duin rode straight at the demon, which gathered itself to meet him. His lance, powered by the hard-charging horse, plunged deep into the monster's belly. The improvised stirrups kept him atop his mount and added even more impact to the blow. The gore-smeared bronze spearpoint jutted from the demon's back.

Its roar of agony filled the field. Though blood bubbled over its lips, it plucked Duin from his horse and slammed him to the ground. He lay unmoving. The demon's shrieks faded to gurgles. It swayed, toppled, fell. Clawed fingers opened and closed on nothing, then were still.

But Balamung did not let the Trokmoi dwell on the defeat of his creature. "Have no fear, lads," he said. "I'm after having more of the beasts, which they'll not find easy to stop. And look: the palisade's broken, and there's fire in the courtyard. One more good push and we'll need push no more." He opened the Book of Shabeth-Shiri, began again the dreadful invocation which had called the demon from its plane.

Gerin looked from the congealing smoke of the Trokmê's magic to the smoke puffing up from the stables—the stables where Balamung had slept three years before, the stables which, as his brother's ghost had reminded him, had not been well cleaned from that time to this.

Sudden wild hope burned through him. If a single one of Balamung's hairs was buried in the old dry straw of the burning outbuilding—and if his own memory still held the spell he had learned from Rihwin more out of sheer annoyance from any expectation it would ever be of use . . . "What have I to lose?" he muttered to himself, and began.

A woodsrunner leaped at him when he dropped his sword and shield. Van stretched the man lifeless in the dirt. The outlander had no idea what his friend was doing, or indeed whether he still had all his wits, but would guard him as long as breath was in his body.

Chanting in the harsh Kizzuwatnan tongue, left hand moving through passes fast as he dared, the Fox went to his knees in the first of the three required genuflections. As he rose, he remembered the words of the Sibyl of Ikos, words he had thought filled only with doom. Confidence tingled along his veins, warm like wine. He grinned savagely. Aye, he was bowing to the mage of the north, but he did not think Balamung would appreciate the compliment.

That newfound confidence almost made him careless. His tongue stumbled in a particularly intricate passage of the spell. For a moment, his body filled with frightening heat. But he recovered and raced on, driving to be done before Balamung could finish his own magic and realize himself attacked. He bowed for the last time, shouted the last Kizzuwatnan curse, and stood. If he had blundered, he would soon be dead, either from the recoil of his spell or the overwhelming power of his foe.

He had won the race. Balamung was still incanting, his demon materializing before him. Half a minute passed in anticlimax. Gerin watched his enemy in baffled despair. Then the fire in the stables reached the two or three hairs still left from the wizard's visit long before.

Balamung paused for an instant, brushing a sleeve of his robe across his forehead as if to wipe away sweat. Then little yellow flames licked at the robe, and at his flesh as well. Smoke poured from his body.

The half-formed demon vanished.

Balamung screamed, a cry of utmost anguish that stirred horror though from the throat of a foe. The wizard beat at his flaming chest with arms no less afire. He knew the author of his destruction the instant his dreadful eyes seized the Fox's. A clawlike hand speared at Gerin for a final malediction. Flame dripped down the pointing index finger before the spell was cast.

The all-consuming fire left of Balamung only gray flakes of ash. The wind tossed them high in the air and blew them away. He had read his stars aright: no man would ever know his grave, for there was nothing of him to bury.

And with him burned the Book of Shabeth-Shiri. That evil tome, which had survived so long, seemed at the end more tenacious of life than the wizard who briefly owned it. Only slowly did the flames grip its pages. Gerin would have taken oath that he saw those pages flutter and rustle in an almost sentient effort to put out the fire and escape their fate. But the spells Shabeth-Shiri had amassed in ancient days now turned to smoke one by one, and as each was destroyed the power of the Book grew less. At last the fire engulfed it altogether, and it was gone.

A strange pause followed; neither side could quite believe Balamung had truly perished. Gerin's men in Fox Keep recovered first. Shouting, "The Fox! The Fox!" they battered their way through the dismayed Trokmoi at the breach and rushed toward the baron and his few remaining comrades. The woodsrunners scattered before them.

Drago the Bear took Gerin in an embrace that hurt even through armor. Right behind him were Rollan, Simrin Widin's son, and most of the borderer crew. They were thinner and dirtier than the Fox remembered, but still men to be reckoned with, and happier than he had ever seen them.

Gerin had hoped their onslaught, coupled with the death of the wizard at his moment of triumph, would send the Trokmoi fleeing for the Niffet. But a northern chieftain stopped the rout before it began. He cut down with his own hand a barbarian running past him. "Are we men or snot-nosed weans?" he roared. "It's but southrons we're fighting, not gods. They bleed and they die—and it's not many of 'em are left to be killed!"

The Trokmoi sensed the truth in his words. So, with sinking heart, did the Fox. Though magic had failed the barbarians, edged bronze might yet suffice. "We haven't enough men to fight in the open here. Back to the castle before they cut us off," he commanded. "Keep the best order you can."

Drago began to protest. He looked from the regrouping barbarians to the white scar over Gerin's eye and thought better of it. For the first hundred yards or so, the retreat went smoothly. Then the Trokmoi gave a hoarse cheer and charged.

Direct as always, Van went straight for the northern leader, reasoning that his death might kill the spirit he'd given his men. But not even the outlander's might let him bull his way through the Trokmoi. Their noble commander declined combat. Like few barbarians Gerin knew, he was aware he had more value for his band than his sword-arm alone.

The baron and his men were within the shadow of the palisade when Rihwin swore and fell, an arrow through his calf. An axe-wielding Trokmê leaped in for the kill. Though prone, Rihwin turned the first stroke with his shield. Before the woodsrunner could make a second, Drago speared him in the side. Gerin's burly vassal slung Rihwin over his shoulder like a sack of turnips. He ran for the breach with the rest of the Elabonians.

Thus, through the gap torn in the palisade, Gerin re-entered Fox Keep, the outbuildings afire before him, the Trokmoi hard on his heels. Cursing the noble who had rallied the northerners, he shouted for pikemen to hold the gap.

The barbarians outside the keep listened to the passionate oratory of their self-appointed leader. With much argument and wasted motion, they formed a ragged line of battle. "At 'em!" the noble cried. Now he led the charge himself.

Arrows and javelins took their toll of the onrushing barbarians, but they did not waver. They slammed into the thin line the Fox had built against them.

Spear and shield, sword and corselet kept them out. Van was everywhere at once, smiting like a man possessed, bellowing out a battle-song in the twittering tongue of the plains. He hurled his spear at the leader of the woodsrunners and cursed foully when he missed.

He took out his rage on the Trokmoi nearest him. Blood dribbled down the leather-wound handle of his mace and glued it to his hand. As always, Gerin fought a more wily fight, but he was in the front line, his left-handed style giving more than one woodsrunner a fatal half-second of confusion.

When at last the Trokmoi sullenly pulled out of weapon-range, though, Gerin realized how heavy his losses had been. Simrin Widin's son was on his knees, clutching at an arrow driven through his cuirass into his belly. Fandor the Fat lay dead behind him, along with far too many others. Almost everyone who could still wield a weapon was at the breach, and almost everyone bore at least one wound.

Shouts of alarm came from the watchtower and two sides of the palisade. "Ladders! Ladders!" The few defenders still on the wall raced to the threatened spots. One ladder, another, went over with a crash, but already red-mustached barbarians were on the walkway. They fought to hold off the Elabonians until their comrades could scale the wall for the final, surely victorious assault on Fox Keep.

Gerin knew such weariness as he had never felt before. He had endured the terrors of the werenight, slain a wizard more deadly than the world had known for a score of centuries . . . for what? An extra hour of life. Merely for the lack of a few men, his holding would fall despite all he had done. A double-bladed throwing axe hurled from the walkway flashed past him. It buried itself in the blood-soaked ground.

But instead of pressing home their attack, the Trokmoi cried out in despair and fear. The Fox's troopers shouted in sudden desperate urgency. The barbarians on the wall fled back to their scaling-ladders and scrambled down them, trying to reach ground outside the keep before its defenders sent their escape routes toppling.

Bewildered, the baron looked south and saw the most unlikely rescue force conceivable thundering toward Fox Keep. Wolfar of the Axe, in man's shape once more, still had with him a good third of the two-hundred-man army he had led before the werenight. Gerin more than half expected Wolfar's men to ignore the Trokmoi and attack him, but they stormed down on the barbarians, the blood-thirsty baron at their head.

The Trokmê noble tried to rally his men yet again. Wolfar rode him down. At his fall, the woodsrunners broke and ran, flying in all directions. They had already taken one assault from the rear, and had kept their courage after Balamung died just as his triumph seemed assured. Now courage failed them. They threw away weapons to flee the faster. Most ran for the Niffet, and most never reached it, for Wolfar's warriors fought with savagery to match their overlord's.

Gerin did not let his men join the pursuit. He kept them drawn up in battle array at the breach, unable to believe his long-time enemy would not try to deal with him next. Their numbers were near even, though Wolfar's men were fresher. But when Wolfar returned from the killing-ground, he and his vassal Schild stepped over the contorted bodies of the Trokmoi who had died before the palisade to approach Fox Keep unarmed.

"I ought to cut your liver out, Fox," Wolfar said by way of greeting, "but I find I have reason to let you live."

The notion galled Wolfar so badly, he could go no further. Schild spoke for his chief, over whom he towered— he was as tall and lean as Wolfar was short and stocky, and was one of the few men serving under Wolfar whom Gerin respected. He said, "As you can guess, once we pulled ourselves together after whatever madness struck last night"—Gerin started to explain the werenight, but decided it could wait—"we came north after you. But a little south of here, we caught a woodsrunner fleeing your keep. He told us you'd killed their wizard, the one you warned me of not long ago. Is it true?"

"Aye, it's true. Dearly bought, but true."

"Then you've earned your worthless life," Wolfar said, looking toward the corpse of the demon Duin had killed. It was already starting to stink. "You've done a great thing, damn you, and I suppose I have to let it cancel what's between us from the past." He started to offer Gerin his hand, but could not bring himself to do it. The Fox knew there was still no liking or trust between them.

That was not so of their men—soldiers from both sides broke ranks to fraternize. In their shared victory over Balamung and the Trokmoi, they forgot the enmity that had existed between them. Though he did not want to do it, Gerin felt he had no choice but to invite Wolfar and his troops to help man Castle Fox and make it defensible once more.

To the baron's secret disappointment, Wolfar accepted at once. "A holding with too few soldiers in it is almost worse than none at all," he said. "I worry about my own keep; the men I left behind rattle around in it like dried beans in a gourd—do they not, Schild?"

"Hmm?" Schild gave him an unclassifiable look. "Aye, my lord, the garrison there is very small indeed."

As Wolfar's men filed into the holding, Gerin assigned them duties: some to the palisade, others to help some of his own men plug the breach, still others to help the wounded or fight the fires still flickering in the outbuildings. Wolfar did not object to his dispositions. He seemed content to let the Fox keep overall command inside Fox Keep.

Gerin was glad to find that Rihwin's injury was not serious. "You're not hamstrung, and the arrow went clear through your leg. Otherwise we'd have to cut it out, which is nothing to be taken lightly," the baron told him. "As is, though, you should heal before long."

"If I put spikes on my wrists and ankles, do you think I'll be able to climb trees like a cat?" Rihwin asked, adjusting his bandage.

"I see no reason why not."

"Odd," Rihwin murmured. "I never could before."

"Go howl!" Gerin threw his hands in the air and went off to see to other injured men. If the southerner could joke at his wound, he would soon mend.

Had they taken place at any other time, Gerin would have reckoned the next days among the most hectic of his life. As if was, they scarcely stood comparison to what had gone before.

True, four days after Balamung's fall, the Trokmê chieftain who had turned longtooth in the werenight led an attack on Fox Keep. By then, though, the breach in the palisade was repaired, and the holding had fresh supplies drawn from the countryside. Nor did the woodsrunner have patience for a siege. He tried to storm the walls, and was bloodily repulsed. He himself jumped from a scaling ladder to the palisade walkway. Wolfar took his head with a single stroke of the heavy axe that gave him his sobriquet.

Then the ladder went crashing over. Half a dozen Trokmoi tried to leap clear as it fell. The ladders that stayed upright long enough for the barbarians to come to grips with the Elabonians were few. After their leader was slain inside the keep, they lost their eagerness for the fight.

In a way, that second attack by the Trokmoi was a gift from the gods. It further united Wolfar's men and Gerin's against a common foe, and again reminded them how petty their old disputes were now. A good lesson, Gerin thought. He regretted that the province north of the Kirs had not learned it sooner.

Wolfar, surprisingly, seemed to take the lesson to heart. He did not much try to hide his animosity toward Gerin, but he did not let it interfere with the running of the keep. He never mentioned Elise. He was as cordial as his nature allowed toward the baron's men, and insisted on praising Fox Keep's ale, though by now it was coming from the barrel-bottom and full of yeast.

Gerin would sooner have seen him surly. He did not know how to react to this new Wolfar.

For Schild, on the other hand, his admiration grew by leaps and bounds. When the Fox learned from a prisoner of a band of Trokmoi planning to raft over the Niffet,

Wolfar's lieutenant led a joint raiding party to ambush the barbarians as they disembarked. The ambush was a great success. The Trokmoi paddled back across the river after leaving a double handful of men dead on the shore.

On the raiders' return, Wolfar was so lavish in their praise and so affable that Gerin's suspicion of him redoubled. But beyond this uncharacteristic warmth, the thick-shouldered baron as yet showed no hint of what was in his mind.

"He's given me every reason to trust him," Gerin told Van one night, "and I trust him less than ever."

"Probably just as well for you," Van said. Gerin was not sorry to find his worries shared.

Word of Balamung's death spread quickly. It raised the Elabonians' spirits but disheartened their foes, who had leaned on the wizard's supposed invincibility. Two days after the defeat Schild had engineered for the band of south-bound barbarians, a large troop of Trokmoi came north past Castle Fox. Except for keeping out of bowshot, they ignored the keep, intent on returning with their booty to the cool green forests north of the Niffet.

Another large band came by a day later, and another two days after that. As if the appearance of the third group of retreating Trokmoi had been some sort of signal, Wolfar stumped up to the Fox in the great hall and said abruptly, "Time we talked."

Whatever Wolfar had been hiding, it was about to come into the open. Of that Gerin felt sure. Stifling his apprehension, he said, "As you wish. The library is quiet." He led his western neighbor up the stairs.

Wolfar seemed less disconcerted by his strange surroundings than Gerin had hoped. "What a bastardly lot of books you have, Fox!" he said. "Where did you pick them all up?"

"Here and there. Some I brought back from the southlands, some I've got since, a few came from my father, and a couple I just stole."

"Mmm," Wolfar said. Then he fell silent, leaning back in his chair.

At last Gerin said, "You said you wanted to talk, Wolfar. What's on your mind?"

"You don't know, Fox?" Wolfar sounded honestly surprised.

"If it's Elise, she won't marry you, you know. She'd sooner bed a real wolf."

"As if what she wanted had anything to do with it. Still, she's only a—what word do I need?—a detail, maybe."

"Go on." Now Gerin was genuinely alarmed. This cold-blooded calculator was not the Wolfar he had expected, save in his utter disregard for anyone else. The Fox wanted to keep him talking until he had some idea of what he was dealing with.

"I'd thought better of you, Gerin. We don't get along, but I know you're no fool. You have no excuse for being stone blind."

"Go on," Gerin said again, wishing Wolfar would come to a point.

"All right. On this stretch of the border, we have the only two major holdings that didn't fall. Now tell me, what aid did we get from the Marchwarden of the North or our lord Emperor Hildor?" Wolfar tried to put mockery in his voice, but managed only a growl.

"Less than nothing, as well I know."

"How right you are. Fox, you can see as well as I— better, I suppose, if you've really read all these books— the Empire hasn't done a damned thing for us the past hundred years. Enough, by all the gods! With the confusion on the border—and deep inside, too, from some of the things you've said—the two of us could be princes so well established that, by the time Elabon moved its fat arse against us, we'd be impossible to throw out, you and I!"

No wonder Wolfar had changed, Gerin thought, whistling softly. Anyone carrying that big an idea on his shoulders *would* change, and might buckle under the strain of it. Something else bothered the Fox too, but he could not place it. "What would you have us be princes of?" he asked. "Our side of the border is so weak the Trokmoi can come down as they wish, with or without their wizard. For now, we can't hope to hold them."

"Think, though. We can channel their force into whatever shape pleases us. Save for them, we're the only powers on the border now, and we can use them against whoever stands against us."

That idea Gerin liked not at all. He wanted to drive

every woodsrunner back across the Niffet, not import more as mercenaries. He said, "After a while, they'd decided they'd sooner not be used, and act for their own benefit, not ours."

"With their sorcerer gone, they could never hurt us, so long as we kept up enough properly manned and alert keeps," Wolfar argued. His elaborate calm worried Gerin more than any bluster or nervousness.

But at last he had it, the thing Wolfar was trying to hide. The blank look Schild had given his overlord, a few odd remarks from Wolfar's men . . . everything fell together. "Wolfar," he asked, "what were you doing on my land, away from your properly manned and alert keep, when you ran into me just before the werenight?"

"What do you mean?" Wolfar's deep-set eyes were intent on Gerin.

"Just this: you've tried to bury me in a haystack without my noticing. It almost worked, I grant you—you're more subtle than I thought."

"You'll have to make yourself plainer, Fox. I can't follow your riddles."

"Very well, I'll be perfectly clear. You, sir, are a liar of the first water, and staking everything on your lie not being found out. Your keep must have been sacked, and almost at once, or you'd still be in it, not trotting over the landscape like a frog with itchy breeches. In fact, you're as homeless as a cur without a master."

Wolfar took a long, slow breath. "Reasoned like a schoolmaster, Fox. But your logic fails you at the end."

"Oh? How so?"

Heavy muscles rippled under Wolfar's tunic. "I do have a home keep, you see: this one." He hurled himself at Gerin.

The Fox sprang from his seat and threw a footstool at Wolfar's head. Wolfar knocked it aside with a massive forearm. Like a crushing snake, he reached out for the Fox. In the first moment of fighting, neither man thought to draw sword. Their hatred, suppressed these past few days, blazed up out of control, too hot for anything but flesh against flesh, Gerin mad as Wolfar.

Then Wolfar kicked the Fox in the knee. He staggered

back, hearing someone shriek and realizing it was himself. The bright pain cut through his bloodlust. When Wolfar roared forward to finish him, he almost spitted himself on Gerin's blade.

His own was out the next instant. Sparks flew as bronze struck bronze. Wolfar used his sword as if it were an axe, hacking and chopping, but he was so quick and strong Gerin had no time for a telling riposte. His movement hampered by his knee, he stayed on the defensive, awaiting opportunity.

It came, finally: a clever thrust, a twist of the wrist, and Wolfar's blade and one finger went flying across the room. But before the Fox could pierce him, Wolfar kicked the sword from his hand and seized him in a pythonic embrace.

Gerin felt his ribs creak. He slammed the heel of his hand against Wolfar's nose, snapping his head back. In the capital they claimed that was often a fatal blow, but Wolfar merely grunted under it. Still, his grip loosened for an instant, and Gerin jerked free.

He wondered briefly what was keeping everyone from bursting into the library and pulling the two of them apart. They were making enough noise to scare the Trokmoi in the woods, let alone the men in the castle. But no one came.

Wolfar leaped for a sword. Gerin tackled him before he could reach it. They crashed to the floor in a rolling, cursing heap. Then, like a trap, two horn-edged hands were at the Fox's throat. Almost of their own accord, his reached through Wolfar's thick beard to find a similar grip. He felt Wolfar tense under it.

Gerin tightened his neck muscles as he had learned in the wrestling schools of the capital, tried to force breath after precious breath into his lungs. The world eddied toward blackness. In one of his last clear moments, he wondered again why no one was breaking up the fight. Then there was only the struggle to get the tiniest whisper of air and . . . keep . . . his . . . grip . . . tight . . .

After that, all he knew was the uprushing welcoming dark.

The first thing he realized when his senses returned was

that he was no longer locked in that death embrace. His throat was on fire. Van and Schild Stoutstaff bent over him, concern on their faces. He tried to speak. Nothing came from his mouth but a croak and a trickle of blood.

He signed for pen and parchment. After a moment's incomprehension, Van fetched them. Quill scratching, Gerin wrote, "What happened?"

As reading was not one of his many skills, Van held the scrap of parchment in some embarrassment. Seeing his plight, Schild took it from him. "'What happened?' " he read. "My lord Gerin, you are the only man who knows that."

Gerin looked a question at Van.

"Aye, Wolfar's dead." The outlander took up the tale. "When he and you went up to have your talk, the rest of us sat around the great hall wondering what would come of it. Then the racket started. We all looked at each other, hoping it was something simple, say a demon from one of the hells or Balamung back from the fire.

"But no, sure as sure, it was you two going at each other. We could have had a fight down there to match the one up here. If anybody had tried going up the stairs, that's just what would have happened. So, though nobody said much, we figured whoever came out would rule here, and anyone who didn't like it or couldn't stand it would be free to go, no hard feelings. And we waited.

"And nobody came out.

"Finally we couldn't stand it any longer. Schild and I came up together. When we saw you, we thought you were both dead. But you breathed when we pried Wolfar's hands off your neck, and he'll never breathe again—you're stronger than I gave you credit for, captain."

Gerin sat up, rubbing his bruised throat. Looking at Schild, he managed a thin whisper. "You knew Wolfar was tricking me with his talk of a keep he could go home to, and you helped him do it."

Van barked a startled oath, but Schild only nodded. "Of course I did. He was my overlord; he always treated me fairly, harsh though he was. He was not altogether wrong, either—it's long past time for us to break away from the Empire's worthless rule, and I cannot blame him for wanting the power he saw here for the taking."

Schild looked Gerin in the eye. "I would not have called you 'my lord,' though, did I not think you would do a better job with it." Slowly and deliberately, he went to one knee before the Fox. Van followed, though his grin showed how little he thought of such ceremonies.

Dazed more ways than one, Gerin accepted their homage. He half-wished he could flee instead. All he'd ever wanted, he told himself, was to read and think and not be bothered. But when the responsibility for Castle Fox fell on him, he had not shirked it. No more could he evade this greater one now.

He looked at his books, wondering when he would find time to open them again. So much to be done: the Trokmoi ousted, keeps restored and manned, Elise wed (a solitary bright thought among the burdens), Duin's stirrups investigated (which reminded him how few horses he had left), peasants brought back to the land . . . Dyaus above, where was there an unravaged crop within five days' journey?

He climbed to his feet and walked toward the stairs. "Well," he said hoarsely, "let's get to work."

AFTERWORD

When in the early 1970s Poul Anderson reissued *The Broken Sword* after it had been out of print for some years, he noted that, without changing the plot, he had cleaned up the writing. I didn't fully understand when I read his afterword: he'd published *The Broken Sword*, hadn't he? How could it need cleaning up?

Now the shoe is on the other foot. *Werenight* was written in bits and pieces from 1976 to 1978 (often in time stolen from my dissertation); it first appeared in 1979 broken into two parts, titled by the publisher *Wereblood* and *Werenight*. The same publisher also tagged me with the pseudonym Eric Iverson, on the assumption no one would believe Harry Turtledove, which is my real name.

And now it's time for the book to see print again. When I looked over the manuscript, I discovered, as Anderson and no doubt many others had before me, that I'm a better craftsman than I used to be. Without interfering with the story or characters I invented in my younger days, I have taken this chance to cut adjectives, adverbs, and semicolons, and generally tighten things up, and I've changed a couple of bit-players' names where I'd used others that struck me as too similar to them in later fiction. All in all, this is the book I would have written then if I'd been a better writer. I hope you enjoy it.

—Harry Turtledove, October 1992

Prince
of The North

I

Gerin the Fox eyed the new logs in the palisade of Fox Keep. Even after five years' weathering, they were easy to pick out, for they'd never been painted with the greenish glop the wizard Siglorel had concocted to keep Balamung the Trokmê mage from burning the keep around him. The stuff worked, too, but Balamung had slain Siglorel even so. Gerin knew something of magecraft himself, but he'd never been able to match Siglorel's formulation.

In front of those new logs, a handful of the Fox's retainers sat on their haunches in a circle. Gerin's four-year-old son Duren ran from one of them to the next, exclaiming, "Can I roll the dice? Will you let me roll them now?"

Drago the Bear held the carved cubes of bone. Rumbling laughter, he handed them to Duren, who threw them down in the middle of the gamblers' circle. "Haw! Twelve! No one can beat that," Drago said. He scooped up his winnings, then glanced toward Gerin. "The boy brings luck, lord."

"Glad to hear it," Gerin answered shortly. Whenever he looked at his son, he couldn't help thinking of the boy's mother. When he'd wed Elise, he'd been sure the gods had granted him everlasting bliss. He'd thought so right up to the day, three years ago now, when she'd run off with a traveling horseleech. Only the gods knew where in the shattered northlands she was these days, or how she fared.

The Fox kicked at the dirt. Maybe if he'd noticed she wasn't happy, he could have done things to make her so. Or maybe she'd just tired of him. Women did that, and men, too. "The great god Dyaus knows it's too late to do anything about it now," he muttered.

"Too late to do anything about what, Captain?" Van of the Strong Arm boomed as he came out of the stables. The outlander overtopped Gerin's six feet by as many inches, and was nearly twice as thick through the shoulders, too; the red-dyed horsehair plume that nodded above his helmet only made him seem taller. As usual, he kept his bronze corselet polished almost to mirror brilliance.

"Years too late for us to do anything about getting imperial troopers up here," Gerin answered. He was the sort who guarded private thoughts even from his closest friends.

Van spat on the ground. "That for imperial troopers. It was too late for those buggers five years ago, when the carrion-stinking Empire of Elabon shut all the passes into the north sooner than help us keep the Trokmoi out."

"Dyaus knows we could have used the imperials then," Gerin said. "We could use them still, if they'd come and if—"

"If they'd keep their hands off what's yours," Van finished for him.

"Well, yes, there is that," Gerin admitted: he was given to understatement.

Van wasn't. He snorted, back deep in his throat. "Honh! 'There is that,' he says. You think the Emperor of Elabon would be happy with the title you've gone and taken for yourself? You know what he'd do if ever he got his hands on somebody who styled himself the Prince of the North, don't you? He'd nail you to the cross so the ravens could sit on your shoulders and pick out your eyes, that's what."

Since Van was undoubtedly right, Gerin shifted the terms of the argument. He did the same thing whenever he and his friend wrestled, using guile to beat strength and weight. In wrestling as in argument, sometimes it worked and sometimes it didn't. He said, "I'm not the only one in the northlands with a fancy new title since Elabon abandoned us. I'd have company on the crucifying grounds."

"Aye, so you would," Van said. "What's Aragis the Archer calling himself these days? Grand Duke, that's it. Honh! He's just a jumped-up baron, same as you. And there's two or three others of your Elabonian blood, and as many Trokmoi who came south over the Niffet with Balamung and stayed even after the wizard failed."

"I know." Gerin didn't like that. For a couple of centuries, the Niffet had been the boundary between the civilization of the Empire of Elabon—or a rough, frontier version of it, at any rate—on one side and woodsrunning barbarians on the other. Now the boundary was down, and Elabon's abandoned northern province very much on its own.

Van tapped Gerin on the chest with a callused forefinger. "But I tell you this, Captain: you have the loftiest title, so he'd nail you highest."

"An honor I could do without," the Fox said. "Besides, it's quarreling over shadows, anyhow. Elabon's not coming back over the mountains. What I really need to worry about is the squabbles with my neighbors—especially Aragis. Of the lot of them, he's the ablest one."

"Aye, he's near as good as you are, Captain, though not so sneaky."

"Sneaky?" Since Gerin's devious turn of mind was what had earned him his Fox sobriquet, he couldn't even deny that. He changed the subject again: "You're still calling me 'Captain' after all these years, too. Is that the sort of respect the Prince of the North deserves?"

"I'll call you what I bloody well please," Van retorted, "and if one fine day that doesn't suit your high and mightiness, well, I'll up and travel on. I sometimes think I should have done it years ago." He shook his head, bemused that after a lifetime of wandering and adventure he should have begun to put down roots.

Gerin still did not know from what land his friend had sprung; Van never talked of his beginnings, though he had yarns uncounted of places he'd seen. Certainly he was no Elabonian. Gerin made a fair representative of that breed: on the swarthy side, long-nosed and long-faced, with brown eyes and black hair and beard (now beginning to be frosted with gray).

Van, by contrast, was blond and fair-skinned, though tan; his bright beard was that improbable color between yellow and orange. His nose had been short and straight. These days it was short and bent, with a scar across the bridge. His bright blue eyes commonly had mischief in them. Women found him fascinating and irresistible. The reverse also applied.

"Roll the dice?" Duren squealed. "Roll the dice?"

Van laughed to hear Gerin's son say that. "Maybe we'll roll the dice ourselves later on, eh, Captain? See who goes to Fand tonight?"

"Not so loud," Gerin said, looking around to make sure their common mistress wasn't in earshot. "She'll throw

things at both of us if she ever finds out we do that sometimes. That Trokmê temper of hers—" He shook his head.

Van laughed louder. "A dull wench is a boring wench.
I expect that's why I keep coming back to her."

"After every new one, you mean. Sometimes I think
there's a billy goat under that cuirass, and no man at all,"
Gerin said. Van might have settled in one place, but his
affections flew wild and free as a gull.

"Well, what about you?" he said. "If her temper doesn't
suit you, why don't you put her on a raft and ship her back
over the Niffet to her clansfolk?"

"Dyaus knows I've thought about it often enough," Gerin
admitted. After Elise left him, he'd thought about swearing off women forever. No matter what his mind said,
though, his body had other ideas. Now he laughed, ruefully. "If either of us truly fell in love with her, we'd be
hard-pressed to stay friends."

"Not so, Captain," Van answered. "If one of us fell in
love with her, the other would say take her and welcome.
If we both did, now—"

"You have me," Gerin admitted. He kicked at the dirt,
annoyed at being outreasoned even in something as small
as this. But if you couldn't grant someone else's reason
superior when it plainly was, what point to reasoning at all?

Van said, "I think I'll roll the dice myself for a while.
Care to join?"

"No, I'm going to take another pass at my sorcery, if
you know what I mean," Gerin said.

"Have a care, now," Van said. "You're liable to end up
in more trouble than you know how to get out of."

"Hasn't happened yet," Gerin answered. "I have the
measure of my own ignorance, I think." He'd studied a bit
of magic in the City of Elabon as a young man, back in
the days when people could travel back and forth between
the northlands and the heart of the Empire, but had to
give up that and history both when the Trokmoi killed his
father and elder brother and left him baron of Fox Keep.

"I hope you do," Van said. Pulling broken bits of silver from a pouch he wore on his belt, he made for the
dice game. Before he could sit down, Duren sprang at him
like a starving longtooth. He laughed, grabbed the boy, and

threw him high in the air three or four times. Duren squealed with glee.

Gerin made for a little shack he'd built over in a back corner of the courtyard. It was far enough from the palisade that, if it caught fire, it wouldn't burn down the castle outwall along with itself. Thus far, he hadn't even managed to set the shack ablaze.

"Maybe today," he muttered. He was going to try a conjuration from a new grimoire he'd bought from a lordlet to the southwest whose grandfather might have been able to read but who was himself illiterate and proud of it. As with most spells in grimoires, it sounded wonderful. Whether results would match promises was another question altogether.

The codex of the grimoire had silverfish holes on several of its pages, and mice had nibbled its leather binding while it lay forgotten on a high shelf in a larder. The spell in which Gerin was interested, though, remained unmutilated. In a clear hand, the mage who'd composed it had written, "A CANTRIP WHICH YIELDETH A FLAMING SWORD."

That *yieldeth* had made Gerin suspicious. Along with wizardry and history, he'd studied literature down in the City of Elabon. (*And where*, he wondered, *will Duren be able to learn such things, if he should want to?* The answer was mournfully clear: *in the northlands, nowhere.*) He knew Elabonian hadn't used those archaic forms for hundreds of years, which meant the author was trying to make his work seem older than it was.

But a flaming sword . . . false antique or no, he reckoned that worth looking into. Not only would it make ferocious wounds, the mere sight of it should cast terror into the hearts of his foes.

He hefted the bronze blade he'd use. It was hacked and notched to the point where it would almost have made a better saw than sword. Bronze was the hardest, toughest metal anyone knew, but it wasn't hard enough to hold an edge in continued tough use.

Gerin had the crushed wasps and bumblebees and the dried poison oak leaf he'd need for the symbolic element of the spell. Chanting as he worked (and wearing leather gauntlets), he ground them fine and stirred them into melted butter. The grimoire prescribed olive oil as the basis for the paste, but he'd made that substitution before and got by with it. It was necessary; the olive wouldn't grow in the northlands, and supplies from south of the High Kirs had been cut off.

He was readying himself for the main conjuration when someone poked his head into the hut. "Great Dyaus above, are you at it again?" Rihwin the Fox asked. His soft southern accent reminded Gerin of his student days in the City of Elabon every time he heard it.

"Aye, I am, and lucky for you at a place where I can pause," Gerin answered. If anyone had to interrupt him, he preferred it to be Rihwin. The man who shared his ekename knew more magic than he did; Rihwin had been expelled from the Sorcerers' Collegium just before his formal union with a familiar because of the outrageous prank he'd played on his mentor.

He walked into the hut, glanced at the sword and the preparations Gerin had made for it. He'd stopped shaving since he ended up in the northlands, but somehow still preserved a smooth, very southern handsomeness. Maybe the big gold hoop that glittered in his left ear had something to do with that.

Pointing to the wood-and-leather bucket full of water that stood next to the rude table where Gerin worked, he said, "Your precautions are thorough as usual."

Gerin grunted. "You'd be working here beside me if you took them, too." Rihwin had been rash enough to summon up Mavrix, the Sithonian god of wine also widely worshiped in Elabon, after Gerin had earned the temperamental deity's wrath. In revenge, Mavrix robbed Rihwin of his ability to work magic, and left him thankful his punishment was no worse.

"Ah, well," Rihwin said with an airy wave of his hand. "Dwelling on one's misfortunes can hardly turn them to triumphs, now can it?"

"It might keep you from having more of them," Gerin replied; he was as much given to brooding as Rihwin fought shy of it. He'd concluded, though, that Rihwin was almost immune to change, and so gave up the skirmish after the first arrow. Bending over the grimoire once more, he said, "Let's find out what we have here."

The spell was no easy one; it required him to use his right hand to paint the sword blade with his mixture while simultaneously making passes with his left and chanting the incantation proper, which was written in the same pseudoarchaic Elabonian as its title.

He suspected the mage of deliberately requiring the left hand for the complex passes to make the spell more difficult, but grinned as he incanted: being left-handed himself, he was delighted to have his clumsy right doing something simple.

The painting and passes done, he snatched up the sword and cried, "Let the wishes of the operator be accomplished!"

For a moment, he wondered if anything would happen. A lot of alleged grimoires were frauds; maybe that was why this one had sat unused on a shelf for a couple of generations. But then, sure enough, yellow-orange flames rippled up and down the length of the blade. They neither looked nor smelled like burning butter; they seemed more the essence of fire brought down to earth.

"That's marvelous," Rihwin breathed as Gerin made cut-and-thrust motions with the flaming sword. "It—"

With a sudden foul oath, Gerin rammed the sword into the bucket of water. A hiss and a cloud of steam arose; to his great relief, the flames went out. He cautiously felt the water with a forefinger. When he discovered it remained cool, he stuck in his hand. "Cursed hilt got too hot to hold," he explained to a pop-eyed Rihwin. "Oh, that feels good."

"Which, no doubt, is the reason we fail to find blazing blades closely clenched in the fierce fist of every peerless paladin," Rihwin answered. "Many a spell that seems superb on the leaves of a codex develops disqualifying drawbacks when actually essayed."

"You're right about that," Gerin answered, drying his hand on the thigh of his baggy wool breeches. Everyone in the northlands wore trousers; the Trokmê style had conquered completely. Even Rihwin, who had favored southern robes, was in breeches these days. Gerin inspected his left palm. "I don't think that's going to blister."

"Smear butter or tallow on it if it does," Rihwin said, "but not the, ah, heated mixture you prepared there."

"With the poison oak leaves and all? No, I'll get rid of that." Gerin poured it out of its clay pot onto the ground. After a bit of thought, he scooped dirt onto the greasy puddle. If the sole of his boot happened to have a hole, he didn't want the stuff getting onto his skin.

He and Rihwin left the shack. Shadows were lengthening; before long, no one would want to stay outdoors. Ghosts filled the night with terror. A man caught alone in the darkness without sacrificial blood to propitiate them or fire to hold them at bay was likely to be mad come morning.

Gerin glanced to the sky, gauging the hour by the moons. Nothos' pale crescent hung a little west of south; golden Math, at first quarter looking like half a coin, was about as far to the east. And ruddy Elleb (pinkish white now, washed out by the late afternoon sun), halfway between quarter and full, stood well clear of the eastern horizon. The fourth moon, quick-moving Tiwaz, would be a waning crescent when the serfs went out to work just after sunrise tomorrow.

As if Gerin's thinking of the serfs he ruled had brought them to new life, a mournful horn blew in the village close by Fox Keep, calling men and women in from the fields.

Gerin looked at the moons again, raised one eyebrow in a characteristic gesture. "They're knocking off early today," he remarked. "I think I may have to speak to the headman tomorrow."

"He'll not love you for making him push the other peasants harder," Rihwin said.

Who does love me, for any reason? Gerin wondered. His mother had died giving birth to him; maybe because of that, his father had always been distant. Or maybe his father simply hadn't known what to do when he got himself a thinker instead of a brawler.

His son Duren loved him, aye, but now it was his turn to have trouble returning that love, because whenever he saw Duren, he thought of Elise. She'd loved him for a while, until passion cooled . . . and then just disappeared, with only a note left behind begging him not to go after her. It was, in fact, very much the way she'd fled with him from her father's keep.

He didn't feel like going into any of that with Rihwin. Instead, he answered, "I don't care whether Besant Big-Belly loves me or not." That, at least, was true. "I do care that we grow enough to get through the winter, for if we don't, Besant will be big-bellied no more."

"He would say, did he dare, that all the peasants would be bigger-bellied did they not have to pay you a fourth of what they raised," Rihwin observed.

"He could say it to my face, and well he knows it," Gerin returned. "I'm not a lord who makes serfs into draft animals that happen to walk on two legs, nor do I take the half some barons squeeze from them. But if I took nothing, who would ward them from the chariot-riding wolves who'd swoop down on them?"

He waited for Rihwin to say something like, "They could do it for themselves." He was ready to pour scorn on that idea like boiling water splashing down from the top of a palisade onto the heads of attackers. Farmers didn't have the tools they needed to be fighters: the horses, the chariots, the swords, the armor. Nor did they have the time they needed to learn to use those tools; the endless rhythms of fields and livestock devoured their days.

But Rihwin said, "My fellow Fox, sometimes you don't know when you're being twitted."

Denied his chance to rend Rihwin with rhetoric, Gerin glared. He walked around to the front of the castle. Rihwin tagged along, chuckling. As they went inside, another horn sounded from a more distant village, and then another almost at the edge of hearing. Gerin said, "You see? If one village knocks off early, they all do it, for they hear the first horn and blow their own, figuring they don't want to work any harder than the fellows down the trail."

"Who *does* like to work?" Rihwin said.

"No one with sense," Gerin admitted, "but no one with sense will avoid doing what he must to stay alive. The trouble is, not all men are sensible, even by that standard."

"If you think I'll argue with that, you're the one who's not sensible," Rihwin said.

❖   ❖   ❖

The great hall of the castle occupied most of the ground floor. A fire roared in the stone hearth at the far end, and another, smaller, one in front of the altar to Dyaus close by. Above the hearth, cooks basted chunks of beef as they turned them on spits. Fat-wrapped thighbones, the god's portion, smoked on the altar. Gerin believed in feeding the god well; moreover, after his brush with Mavrix, he figured he could use all the divine protection he could get.

Two rows of benches ran from the doorway to the hearth. In winter, seats closest to the fire were the choice ones. Now, with the weather mild, Gerin sat about half-way down one row. A couple of dogs came trotting through the rushes on the rammed-earth floor and lay at his feet, looking up expectantly.

"Miserable beggars," he said, and scratched their ears. "I don't have any food myself yet, so how can I throw you bones and scraps?" The dogs thumped their tails on the ground. They knew they got fed sooner or later when people sat at those benches. If it had to be later, they would wait.

Van and Drago the Bear and the other gamblers came in, chattering about the game. Duren frisked among them. When he saw Gerin, he ran over to him, exclaiming, "I rolled the dice a lot, Papa! I rolled double six twice, and five-and-six three times, and—"

He would have gone down the whole list, but Van broke in, "Aye, and the little rascal rolled one-and-two for me, and sent me out of that round without a tunic to call my own." He shook a heavy fist at Duren in mock anger. Duren, safe beside his father, stuck out his tongue.

"The dice go up, the dice go down," Drago said, shrugging shoulders almost as wide as Van's. From him, that passed for philosophy. He was a long way from the brightest of Gerin's vassals, but a good many more clever men managed their estates worse. Since Drago never tried anything new, he discovered no newfangled ways to go wrong.

Gerin called to one of the cooks, "We have enough here to begin. Fetch ale for us, why don't you?"

"Aye, lord prince," the man answered, and hurried down into the cellar. He returned a moment later, staggering a little under the weight of a heavy jar of ale. The jar had a pointed bottom. The cook stabbed it into the dirt floor so the jar stood upright. He hurried off again, coming back with a pitcher and a double handful of tarred leather drinking jacks. He set one in front of everybody at the table (Duren got a small one), then dipped the pitcher into the amphora, pouring and refilling until every jack was full.

"Take some for yourself, too," Gerin said; he was not a lord who stinted his servants. Grinning, the cook poured what looked like half a pitcher down his throat. Gerin slopped a little ale out of his mug onto the floor. "This for Baivers, god of barley," he intoned as he drank.

"This for Baivers," the others echoed as they poured their libations. Even Van imitated him: though Baivers was no god of the outlander's, the deity, whose scalp sprouted ears of barley instead of hair, held sway in this land.

Rihwin made a sour face as he set down the mug. "I miss the sweet blood of the grape," he said.

"Point the first: the grape doesn't grow in the northlands and we've lost our trade south of the High Kirs," Gerin said. "Point the second: when you drink too much wine, dreadful things happen. We've seen that again and again. Point the third: wine lies in Mavrix's province, and have you not had your share and more of commerce with Mavrix?"

"True, all true," Rihwin said sadly. "I miss the grape regardless."

The cooks came round with bowls of bean-and-parsnip porridge, with tiny bits of salt pork floating in it to give it flavor. Like everyone else, Gerin lifted his bowl to his lips, wiped his mouth on his sleeve when he was done. South of the High Kirs, they had separate squares of cloth for cleaning your face and fingers, but such refinements did not exist north of the mountains.

Off the spit came the pieces of beef. While one cook carved them into man-sized portions, another went back to the kitchen and came out with round, flat, chewy loaves of bread, which he set in front of each man at the table. They'd soak up the juices from the meat and get eaten in their turn.

Gerin patted the empty place between Van and him.

"Put one here, too, Anseis. Fand is sure to be down before long."

"Aye, lord prince," the cook said, and did as he was asked.

Duren started tearing pieces from his round of bread and stuffing them into his mouth. Gerin said, "If you fill yourself up with that, boy, where will you find room for your meat?"

"I'll put it someplace." Duren patted his stomach to show the intended destination.

Just as the cook who was carving the beef started loading steaming gobbets onto an earthenware tray, Fand did come down from Castle Fox's living quarters into the great hall. Gerin and Van glanced over at each other, smiled for a moment, and then both waved her to that place between them.

"Och, you're still not after fighting over me," she said in mock disappointment as she came up. Beneath the mock disappointment, Gerin judged, lay real disappointment. She might have resigned herself to their peacefully sharing her, but she didn't like it.

Hoping to get her off that bloodthirsty turn of thought, Gerin called for a servant to pour her a jack of ale. He handed it to her himself. "Here you are."

"I thank you, sure and I do." Her Elabonian held a strong Trokmê lilt. She was a big, fair woman, not too much shorter than the Fox, with pale skin dusted with freckles wherever the sun caught it, gray-blue eyes, and wavy, copper-colored hair that tumbled past her shoulders. To Gerin, men of that coloring were enemies on sight; he still sometimes found it odd to be sharing a bed with a woman from north of the Niffet.

Not odd enough to keep me from doing it, though, he thought. Aloud, he said to Fand, "Should I have put you on a boat across the river after all?"

"'Twould have been your own loss if you had," she retorted, tossing her head so the torchlight glinted in her hair. One thing she had was unshakeable self-confidence—and why not, when two men such as they danced to her tune?

Gerin said, "My guess is still that you stuck a knife into the fellow who brought you south over the Niffet."

"I've told you before, Gerin dear: I brought my own self over, thinking life might be more lively here. Och, and so it has been, not that I reckoned on yoking myself to a southron—" she paused to half turn and make eyes at Van "—let alone two."

"*I'm* no Elabonian," Van boomed indignantly, "and I'll thank you not to call me one. One fine day I hitch a team to a chariot or just go off afoot—"

"How many years have you been saying that?" Gerin asked.

"As many as I've been here, no doubt, less maybe one turn of the fastest moon." Van shook his head, forever bemused he could stay in one place so long. "A tree, now, has need of growing roots, but a man—?"

"A man?" Fand said, still trying to stir up trouble. "You'll quarrel over whether you're a southron or no, but not over me? What sort of man is that after making you?"

"You should remember well enough from last night what sort of man I am." Van looked like a cat that had fallen into the cream pitcher.

Fand squeaked indignantly and turned back to Gerin. "Will you be letting him speak to me so?"

"Aye, most likely I will," he said. If she got fed up and left them both, he'd be sorry for a while, but he knew he'd also be relieved. He didn't feel like a screaming fight now, though, so he said, "Here comes the meat."

That distracted her. It distracted him, too. He drew his dagger from his belt and started carving strips off the bone in front of him and popping them into his mouth.

The dagger, like the rest of his personal gear, was severely plain, with a hilt of nothing more splendid than leather-wrapped bone. But it had good balance, and he kept the edge sharp; sometimes he used plainness to conceal effectiveness.

Van, by contrast, had the hilt to his knife wrapped in gold wire, with a big topaz set into the pommel. For him, flamboyance served the same purpose self-effacement did for Gerin: it disguised the true warrior beneath. Being dangerous without seeming so, Gerin had found, made the danger double.

Thinking thus, he glanced over at Fand, who was slicing

with her own slim bronze blade. Was she disguising something? He snorted and took a long pull at his ale. No, concealment wasn't in her nature. But he'd thought as much about Elise, and where had that got him?

Duren said, "Papa, will you help me cut more meat?" He had a knife, too, but a small one, and not very sharp. That helped keep him from getting cut, but it also kept him from eating very fast.

Gerin leaned over and sliced off several strips for him. "Splash water on your face when you're done," he said. He remembered how surprised and delighted he'd been to discover the elaborate hot and cold baths the City of Elabon boasted. North of the High Kirs, as best he knew, there was only one tub, and it wasn't at his holding. Not without a pang, he'd gone back to being mostly dirty most of the time.

Fand made eyes first at Van, then at him. "Och, a woman gets lonely, that she does."

"If you're lonely with the two of us to keep you warm at night, would you try a bandit troop next?" Van said.

She cursed him in the Trokmê language, Elabonian not being satisfying enough for her. Van swore back in the same tongue; he'd traversed the gloomy forests of the Trokmoi before he swam the Niffet (towing his precious armor behind him on a makeshift raft) and splashed up inside Gerin's holding.

"Will you be letting him speak to me so?" Fand demanded of the Fox once more.

"Probably," he answered. She picked up her drinking jack and threw it at him. She had more fury than finesse. It splashed down behind him and sprayed ale onto a couple of the hounds quarreling over bones. They separated with a yelp. Fand sprang to her feet and stomped upstairs.

"Not often dull around here," Van observed to no one in particular.

"It's not, is it?" Gerin said. "Sometimes I think I'd find a bit of dullness restful." He hadn't known much, not since he came back over the Kirs to take over his father's holdings and especially not since the Trokmoi and their wizard Balamung invaded the northlands. Balamung was dead now, without even a grave to hold him, but too many Trokmoi still raided and settled on this side of the Niffet, adding one more volatile element to already touchy politics.

Gerin emptied his own jack in a fashion more conventional than Fand's, went over to the amphora, and poured it full again. Some of his vassals were already swilling themselves into insensibility. *If I want dull*, he thought, *all I need do is listen to the talk around this table.* Dice, horses and chariots, crops, women . . . no new ideas anywhere, just old saws trotted out as if they were fresh-minted from pure gold. He longed for the days when he'd sat in students' taverns, arguing sorcerous techniques and the shape of the historical process.

Rihwin the Fox knew the pleasures of intellectual conversation, but Rihwin also knew the pleasures of the wine jar or, that failing, the ale pot. He might complain about having to pour down ale, but that didn't stop him from doing quite a lot of it. And, at the moment, he had a serving girl on his lap. He would have done a better job of fumbling at her clothes had his hands been steadier.

Van knew his letters; he'd made a point of learning them when he discovered Elabonian could be written. He even spoke well of its alphabet; Gerin gathered he'd run across other, more cumbersome ways of noting down thoughts in his travels. But learning his letters did not make him interested in quoting poetry, except for informational content, let alone analyzing it.

As for Gerin's own vassal barons, most of them thought reading a vaguely effeminate accomplishment (he wondered why; even fewer women than men were literate). They'd learned better than to say so to him, and had learned he was a good fighting man in spite of having a room that stored several dozen scrolls and codices. But that didn't mean they grew interested in thinking, too.

Gerin sighed and drank more ale himself. Sometimes he thought slipping back into near barbarism easier than trying to maintain the standards of civilization he'd learned south of the High Kirs. *Which is the way civilization falls apart,* said the part of him that had studied history.

After one more jack of ale, he didn't feel like arguing with that part any more. Rihwin and the girl had wandered off. Drago the Bear snored thunderously on the floor, and took no notice when one of the dogs walked over him. Duren was asleep, too; the little boy had curled up, cat-like, on his bench.

Van, on the other hand, was wide awake and looked more sober than Gerin felt. The Fox raised an eyebrow at him. "What would you?" he asked. "Shall we roll the dice after all?"

"For the lass, you mean?" Van shook his massive head. "You go to her tonight, if you've a mind to. She'd sweeten up for me in a bit, I expect, but I haven't the patience to get through the shouting that'd come first. I'll drink a bit more and then maybe sleep myself."

"All right." Gerin lifted Duren off the bench. His son wriggled a little, but did not wake. As he carried Duren upstairs, the Fox was grateful for the banister he'd added to the stairway when he came back from the south. With it, he was much less likely to trip and break not only his neck but the boy's.

He set Duren on the bed in his own chamber, hoping his son would wake up if he had to piddle in the night. Otherwise, the mattress would need some fresh straw.

With Duren in his arms, the Fox hadn't been able to carry a lamp or a taper up to the bedchamber with him. That left it black as a bandit's heart inside. He stumbled over some wood toy or other that he'd carved for Duren and almost fell on his face. Flailing his arms, he managed to keep himself upright and, with a muttered curse, went out into the hallway.

A couple of failing torches cast a dim red light there, enough, at least, to let him see where he put his feet. The walk to the next chamber was a matter of just a few steps. He rapped on the door, wondering if Fand had fallen asleep. If she didn't answer, he'd go back to his own bed.

But she did: "Which of you is it, now?"

Maybe it was the ale, but Gerin felt mischievous. He deliberately deepened his voice and put on a slight guttural accent: "Which d'you think?"

He heard her take three rapid strides toward the door. She threw it open and blazed, "Van of the Strong Arm, if you're after thinking y'can—" Then, by the torchlight and the brighter flame of the candle beside her bed, she realized it wasn't Van standing there. She scowled at Gerin. "You're a right devil to befool me so, and I ought to be slamming the door on the beaky nose of you."

He looked down that member at her. "Well?" he said when she didn't do as she'd threatened.

"Well, indeed," she said, and sighed. "Must be I'm the fool, for taking up with a southron man—worse, for taking up with a southron man and his great galoon of a friend, the both of them at once. Often enough I've said it, but—" Her face softened. "Since I am the fool, you may as well come in."

She stood aside to let him pass, closed the door behind him. She kept the room scrupulously neat; it was, by all odds, the cleanest part of the castle. Gerin knew the tunics and skirts and drawers in the cedar chest against the wall would all be folded just the same way. Beside that chest, her sandals and shoes stood in precise pairs. He lavished that much care only on his weapons, where it could be a matter of life or death.

Fand must have been mending a tunic when he knocked: it lay on the wool coverlet to her bed. Candlelight glistened from the polished bone needle she'd used. She picked up the tunic, set it on the chest. She nodded toward the candle. "Shall I blow it out?"

"Please yourself," he answered. "You know I like to look at you, though."

That won him a smile. "You southrons are sweeter in the tongue than men of my own folk, I'll say so much for you. Maybe there's the why of my staying here. A Trokmê chief, now, he'd just tell me to be after spreading my legs and waste no time about it."

Gerin's skeptical eyebrow rose. "My guess is that any man who told you such a thing would be likelier to get a knife in the brisket than anything else."

"Sure and that's the very thing he got, the black-hearted omadhaun," she said. "Why d'you think a puir lone woman would come to your keep at sunset, seeking shelter from the ghosts? Had his kin caught me, they'd have burned me in a wicker cage, that they would."

He knew she was right—that or some other equally appalling fate. South of the High Kirs, they crucified their miscreants. He reckoned himself merciful: if a man needed killing, he attended to it as quickly and cleanly as he could. But he'd killed his share and more, these past few years.

His other thought was that Fand calling herself a poor lone woman was about as accurate as a longtooth claiming it was a pussycat. At need, she likely could have shouted down the ghosts.

She cocked her head to one side, sent him a curious look. "What is it you're waiting for? I've no knife the now, nor even a needle."

"And a good thing, too, I say." He took a step toward her, she one toward him. That brought them together. Her face lifted toward his, her arms went round his neck.

She was cross-grained, quarrelsome, cantankerous—Gerin had never settled on just the right word, but it lay somewhere in that range. On the wool coverlet, though . . . she bucked like a yearling colt, yowled like a catamount, and clawed his back as if she were part wolverine.

In a way, it was immensely flattering. Even when he'd pleased Elise, which hadn't been all the time (nor, in the end, nearly often enough), she'd given little sign. With Fand, he had no room for doubt there. But a passage with her sometimes put him more in mind of riding out a storm than making love: the pleasure he felt afterwards was often tempered with relief for having got through it.

Their sweat-slick skins slid against each other as he rolled off her. "Turn over," he said.

"Turn over, is it?" she said. "Why tell me that? You're not one of those who-do-you-call-them—Sithonians, that's it—who like boys and use their women the same way. And I'm not one for that, as well you know." But, the warning delivered, she did roll onto her belly.

He straddled the small of her back and started rubbing her shoulders. The warning growls she'd let out turned to purrs. Her flesh was warm and firm under his hands. "Is that too rough?" he asked as he dug in with his thumbs.

She grunted but shook her head; her bright hair flipped back and forth, with a few shining strands covering his fingers and the backs of his hands. "You've summat here we never found north o' the Niffet," she said. "Sure and there may be more to this civilization you're always after prating of than I thought or ever I came to Fox Keep."

He wondered if he should tell her the best masseur he'd ever known, down in the City of Elabon, was a Sithonian who would have been delighted to do more with him than merely rub his back. He decided against it: the more people in the northlands who cherished civilization, for whatever reason, the better off the war-torn country would be.

As Gerin's hands moved from her shoulders down her spine, he moved down, too. After a bit, Fand exclaimed sharply, "I told you, I'm not one for—" She broke off, then giggled. "What a sneak of a man y'are, to put it in the right place from the wrong side." She looked back at him over her shoulder. "Different this way."

"Better? Worse?" Even in such matters, even at such a time, he liked to know exactly how things went.

But she laughed at him. "How can I tell you that, when we've hardly begun?" They went on, looking for the answer.

Gerin woke the next morning when Duren got out of bed to use the chamber pot. The light in the bedchamber was gray. The sun hadn't risen yet, but it would soon. Gerin got out of bed himself, yawned, stretched, and knuckled his eyes: the ale he'd drunk the night before had left him with a bit of a headache.

"Good morning, Papa," Duren said.

"Good morning," Gerin answered, yawning again; he woke up slowly. He tousled the boy's hair. "I'm glad you're using the pot. Are you finished? My turn, then." When he was through, he pulled on the tunic and trousers he'd tossed on the floor after he came back from Fand's room. They didn't have any new spots he could see, so what point in changing? People were more fastidious on the other side of the High Kirs, but not much.

Duren underfoot like a cat, Gerin walked down the hall to the stairs. Snores came from Fand's chamber. Louder snores came from Van's, one door further down. In the great hall of the keep, some of the Fox's vassals were already up and stirring; others lay bundled in blankets on straw pallets. The fire in the altar still burned, holding night ghosts at bay.

The doors that led out into the yard stood open, to give the great hall fresh air and clear out some of the smoke from the cookfires. Gerin picked his way through the warriors and went outside. In the east, Tiwaz's thin crescent stood low in the brightening sky. The other three moons had set.

Torches smoked along the palisade. Even so, Duren, who had followed his father into the yard, whimpered and said, "I don't like the ghosts yelling in my ears, Papa."

To Gerin, the cries of the night spirits were not yells but whimpers and faint wails, none of them understandable. As he had fires lit and had given the ghosts blood in the great hall, they were not likely to do him or Duren harm. He set his jaw and endured the cries he heard only with his mind's ear. Children, though, were supposed to be more sensitive to the spirits than adults.

A couple of minutes later, the first rays of the rising sun touched the top of the tall watchtower that stood above the keep. The ghosts sounded frightened for an instant, then vanished back into whatever gloomy haunt was theirs while the sun ruled the sky.

"A new day," Gerin said to Duren. "This is the time for living men to go abroad in the world." He patted the boy's back, heartening him against the terror that fluttered with the ghosts.

Van of the Strong Arm came out a few minutes later, whistling loudly but off-key. Smoke poured from windows and doorways as the cooks built up the fire to heat the morning porridge. Van squinted as a strand of smoke stung his eyes. "There ought to be a way to cook your food without smoking everyone who eats it as if he were a sausage," the burly outlander complained.

Gerin narrowed his eyes, too, but not at the smoke. *There ought to be a way* was a phrase that always set him thinking. Sometimes nothing came of it, but sometimes things did. He said, "Remember the newfangled footholders Duin the Bold came up with so he wouldn't go over his horse's tail if he tried to ride? Maybe we could find a new way to get rid of smoke, too."

"Remember what happened to Duin? He got himself killed with his newfangled scheme, that's what. Me, I'd sooner fight from a chariot any day." For all his wandering, for all the strange things he'd seen and done, Van remained at heart a profoundly conservative man.

Gerin had more stretch to him. "I think this business of riding to war will end up coming to something: a horse alone can cross terrain where a chariot can't go. But you have a special trouble there—where will you find a beast to bear your bulk?"

"I've never been small; that's a fact," Van said complacently. "From the rumbles in my belly, though, I'll be thin if I don't put something in there soon. They'll have bread and meat from last night to go with the porridge, won't they?"

"If they don't, they'll be looking for a new master by this time tomorrow," Gerin answered. Van clapped his big hands together and hurried back inside.

The morning proved busy. Gerin always kept someone in the watchtower. Life had been dangerous enough before the Trokmoi swarmed south over the Niffet. Now danger could come from any direction at any time. When the lookout's horn blew, men up on the palisade reached for their weapons; the gate crew got ready to pull up the drawbridge and defend Castle Fox against barbarians or men of Elabon.

But after he winded the horn, the watchman cried, " 'Tis but a single man approaching—a trader, by the look of him."

Sure enough, the fellow was no harbinger of a ravening horde: he drove a two-horse team from a small, neat wagon. "Dyaus give you a good day, sir," Gerin greeted him when he rolled into the courtyard. The Fox glanced at the sun. "To get here so early in the day, you must have spent last night in the open."

"That I did, lord prince," the man answered. He was small and neat himself, with a shortsighted gaze and hands with long, slim fingers. "I bought a couple of chickens from a peasant—likely a serf of yours—and their blood in a trench warded me against the ghosts. Otes son of Engelers I am, maker and purveyor of jewelry of all descriptions, and also ready to do tinker's work if you have pots and such that need patching."

"Aye, we have a few of those," Gerin said. "If you know the secret of proper soldering, you'll make a bit of silver before you leave here. I've tried, but without much in the way of luck. But jewelry, now—hmm." He wondered if he could find a piece Fand would like at a price that didn't make his own thrifty soul quail.

Van came up to the wagon and, from the thoughtful look on his face, might have had the same idea. But what he said was, "You're not the least brave man I ever met, Master Jeweler, if you take your wares through this bandit-raddled countryside alone."

Otes Engelers' son dipped his head to the outlander. "You are gracious, sir. I traveled up into the Fox's lands from those of Aragis the Archer. Few bandits try to make a living in your holding, lord Gerin, or in his—few who aren't vassals styling themselves barons, at any rate." He smiled to show that was meant as a joke.

"Aye, Aragis is a strong man." Gerin let it go at that. One of these days, he and Aragis were liable to fight a war. The prospect would have bothered him less had he been less afraid he might lose.

"Show us these jewels of yours," Van boomed.

Otes, as he'd said, had adornments of all descriptions, from polished copper with "gems" of glass paste to gold and emeralds. Before he'd opened all his little cedar chests to display the baubles inside, Fand came out of the castle to admire them with her two men. Suddenly she pointed to a brooch. "Isn't that pretty, now?" she breathed. "Sure and it must be Trokmê work. It fair puts me in mind of my auld village on the far side of the Niffet, that it does."

Smiling, the jeweler picked it up and held it in the palm of his hand. It was a circular piece, about three fingers broad, decorated with spirals half silver and half inlaid, polished jet. "As a matter of fact, my lady, I made this one myself, and I'm as Elabonian as they come," Otes said. "That it is from a northern pattern, though, I'll not deny."

" 'Twould suit the very tunic I have on me," Fand said, running a hand across the dark blue woad-dyed linen. She looked from one of her paramours to the other.

Van, who'd quarreled with her the night before, weakened first. With a cough, he said, "Master Otes, perhaps you'll be good enough to tell me what outrageous price you're asking for this chunk of tin and dirt."

"Tin?" Otes screeched. "Dirt? Are you blind, man? Are you mad? Feel the weight of that metal. And look at the

care and the workmanship I put into the piece, shaping
the tiny slivers of jet one by one and slipping each into
its place—"

"Aye, tell me more lies," Van said.

Sensing that the dicker would go on for some time, Gerin
took his leave. He figured he had time to walk out to the
village by Fox Keep, talk with Besant Big-Belly about knocking off too early, and be back before Van and Otes had
settled on a price. He knew how stubborn Van could be, and
the jeweler looked to have mule's blood in him, too.

But before the Fox could walk out over the drawbridge,
the lookout in the watchtower winded his horn again. He
called down, "A chariot approaches, lord Gerin, with what
looks to be a Trokmê chieftain and two of his men."

"Just a chariot?" Gerin shouted up. "No army attached?"

"I see only the one, lord," the lookout answered. A
moment later, he added, "The chieftain is holding up a
green-and-white striped shield: he comes under sign of
truce."

Gerin called to the gate crew, "When you spy him, give
him sign of truce in return. We'll see what he wants."
Before the invasions, he'd have attacked any northerners
he caught on his holding. Now the Trokmoi were powers
south of the Niffet. However much it galled him, he had
to treat with them.

"Who comes?" one of the men at the gate called to the
approaching chariot.

"It's Diviciacus son of Dumnorix I am, liegeman to
himself himself, the great chief Adiatunnus son of Commus,
who's fain to have me bring his words to Gerin the Fox,"
the chieftain answered in Elabonian that lilted like Fand's.
"No quarrel, no feud, stands between us the now."

The Trokmoi had slain Gerin's father and brother. As
far as he was concerned, that put him eternally at feud with
them. Moreover, he reckoned them deadly dangerous to
the remnants of civilization that survived in the northlands
after Elabon had cut the province loose. But in a narrow
sense, Diviciacus was right: no active fighting went on
between Adiatunnus' men and those of the Fox.

Dropping into the Trokmê tongue, Gerin said, "If it's
the Fox you're seeking, I am he. Aye, I grant the truce

between your chief and my own self. Come sit yourself by my hearth, drink a stoup of ale, and tell me Adiatunnus' words at your comfort and leisure."

Diviciacus beamed. He was a tall, thin, pale man with a lean, wolfish face, clean-shaven but for a straggling mustache of bright red. He wore a checked tunic and baggy wool trousers tucked into boots; a long, straight bronze sword hung from his belt. The other warrior in the chariot and its driver might have been poured into the same mold as he, save that one of them had sandy hair and mustache, the other blond.

Inside the smoky great hall, Diviciacus gulped down his first jack of ale, wiped his mouth on his sleeve, belched loudly, and said, "Sure and you're after living up to the name you have for hospitality, lord Gerin, that y'are."

Gerin could take a hint. He filled the Trokmê's drinking jack again, then said, "And what would Adiatunnus wish with me, pray?" The northern chieftain controlled several holdings a fair distance south and west of Fox Keep. Of all the Trokmoi who'd settled south of the Niffet, he was probably the most powerful, and the most adept at riding—and twisting—the swirling political currents of the northlands.

Diviciacus came to the point with barbarous directness: "Himself wants to know if you're of a mind to join forces with him and squeeze the pimple called Aragis off the arse of mankind."

"Does he?" Gerin said. In a way, that was logical: Aragis blocked Gerin's ambitions no less than Adiatunnus'. In another way . . . "Why wouldn't I be more likely to combine with a man of my own blood against an invader?"

"Adiatunnus says he reckons you reckon Aragis more a thorn in your side than his own self." Diviciacus smiled at the subtlety of his chief's reasoning, and indeed it was more subtle than most northerners could have produced. The envoy went on, "Forbye, he says that once the Archer is after being cut into catmeat, you can go your way and he his, with no need at all for the twain of ye to clomp heads like bull aurochs in rutting season."

"He says that?" Gerin didn't believe it would work so; he didn't think Adiatunnus believed it, either. Which meant—

He was distracted from what it meant when Duren came in and said, "I'm bored, Papa. Play ball with me or something."

"A fine bairn," Diviciacus said. "He'd have, what—four summers on him?" At Gerin's nod, the Trokmê also nodded, and went on, "Aye, he's much of a size with my youngest but one, who has the same age."

Gerin was so used to thinking of Trokmoi as warriors, as enemies, that he needed a moment to adjust to the notion of Diviciacus as a fond father. He supposed he shouldn't have been taken aback; without fathers, the Trokmoi would have disappeared in a generation (and the lives of all the Elabonians north of the High Kirs would have become much easier). But it caught him by surprise all the same.

To Duren, he said, "I can't play now. I'm talking with this man." Duren stamped his foot and filled himself full of air, preparatory to letting out an angry screech. Gerin said, "Do you want my hand on your backside?" Duren deflated; his screech remained unhowled. Convinced his father meant what he said, Duren went off to look for amusement somewhere else.

"Good on you for training him to respect his elders, him still so small and all," Diviciacus said. "Now tell me straight how you fancy the notion of your men and those of Adiatunnus grinding Aragis between 'em like wheat in the quern."

"It has possibilities." Gerin didn't want to say no straight out, for fear of angering Adiatunnus and of giving him the idea of throwing in with Aragis instead. The Fox reckoned Aragis likely to be willing to combine with the Trokmê against his own holdings; no ties of blood or culture would keep Aragis from doing what seemed advantageous to him.

"Possibilities, is it? And what might that mean?" Diviciacus demanded.

It was a good question. Since Gerin found himself without a good answer, he temporized: "Let me take counsel with some of my vassals. Stay the night here if you care to; eat with us, drink more ale—by Dyaus I swear no harm will come to you in Fox Keep. Come the morning, I'll give you my answer."

"I'm thinking you'd say aye straight out if aye was in your heart," Diviciacus said dubiously. "Still, let it be as you wish. I'll stay a bit, so I will, and learn what you'll reply. But I tell you straight out, you'll befool me with none o' the tricks that earned you your ekename."

Since persuading the Trokmê not to leave at once in high dudgeon was one of those tricks, the Fox maintained a prudent silence. He suspected Diviciacus and his comrades would use the day to empty as many jars of ale as they could. *Better ale spilled than blood*, he told himself philosophically.

Fand came in, wearing the silver-and-jet brooch just above her left breast. Diviciacus' eyes clung to her. "My leman," Gerin said pointedly.

That recalled to Diviciacus the reason he'd come. "If you've allied with us so, why not on the field of war?" he said, hope for success in his mission suddenly restored.

"As I said, I'll talk it over with my men and tell you in the morning what I've decided." Gerin went out to the courtyard, where Van was practicing thrusts and parries with a heavy spear taller than he was. The outlander, for all his size, moved so gracefully that he made the exercise seem more a dance than preparation for war.

When Gerin told him what Adiatunnus had proposed, he scowled and shook his head. "Making common cause with the Trokmê would but turn him into a grander threat than Aragis poses."

"My thought was the same," Gerin answered. "I wanted to see if you saw anything on the other side to change my mind." Van shook his head again and went back to his thrusts and parries.

Gerin put the same question to Drago. The Bear's response was simpler: "No way in any of the five hells I want to fight on the same side with the Trokmoi. I've spent too much time tryin' to kill them buggers." That made Gerin pluck thoughtfully at his beard. Even had he been inclined to strike the bargain with Adiatunnus, his vassals might not have let him.

He went looking for Rihwin to get one more view. Before he found him, the lookout called, "Another man approaches in a wagon."

"Great Dyaus, three sets of visitors in a day," Gerin exclaimed. Sometimes no one from outside his holding came to Fox Keep for ten days, or twenty. Trade—indeed, traffic of any sort—had fallen off since the northlands went their own way. Not only did epidemic petty warfare keep traffic off the roads, but baronies more and more either made do with what they could produce themselves or did without.

"Who comes?" called a warrior up on the palisade.

"I am a minstrel, Tassilo by name," came the reply—in, sure enough, a melodious tenor. "I would sing for my supper, a bed for the night, and whatever other generosity your gracious lord might see fit to provide."

Tassilo? Gerin stood stock-still, his hands balling into fists. The minstrel had sung down at the keep of Elise's father, Ricolf the Red, the night before she went off with Gerin rather than letting herself be wed to Wolfar of the Axe. Just hearing Tassilo's name, and his voice, brought those memories, sweet and bitter at the same time, welling up in the Fox. He was anything but anxious to listen to Tassilo again.

But all the men who heard the minstrel name himself cried out with glee: "Songs tonight, by Dyaus!" "Maybe he'll have ones we've not heard." "A lute to listen to—that'll be sweet."

Hearing that, Gerin knew he could not send the man away. For his retainers, entertainment they didn't have to make themselves was rare and precious. If that entertainment made him wince, well, he'd endured worse. Sighing, he said, "The minstrel is welcome. Let him come in."

When Tassilo got down from his light wagon, he bowed low to the Fox. "Lord prince, we've met before, I think. At Ricolf's holding, was it not? The circumstances, as I recall, were irregular." The minstrel stuck his tongue in the side of his cheek.

"Irregular, you say? Aye, there's a good word for it. That's the business of a minstrel, though, isn't it?—coming up with words, I mean." Being moderately skilled in that line himself, Gerin respected those who had more skill at it than he. He eyed Tassilo. "Curious you've not visited Fox Keep since."

"I fled south when the Trokmoi swarmed over the Niffet, lord prince, and I've spent most of my time since then down by the High Kirs," Tassilo answered. He had an open, friendly expression and looked as much like a fighting man as a singer, with broad shoulders and a slim waist. In the northlands, any traveling man had to be a warrior as well, if he wanted to live to travel far.

"What brought you north again, then?" Gerin asked.

"A baron's daughter claimed I got her with child. I don't think I did, but he believed her. I thought a new clime might prove healthier after that."

Gerin shrugged. He had no daughter to worry about. He said, "The men look forward to your performance tonight." Lying a little, he added, "Having heard you those years ago, so do I." The minstrel could sing and play, no doubt about that. The Fox's memories were not Tassilo's fault.

After a few more pleasantries, Gerin strode out over the drawbridge and headed for the peasant village a few hundred yards away. Chickens and pigs and skinny dogs foraged among round huts of wattle and daub whose thatched conical roofs projected out far enough to hold the rain away from the walls. Children too young to work in the fields stared at Gerin as he tramped up the muddy lane that ran through the middle of the village.

He stuck his head into Besant Big-Belly's hut, which was little different from any of the others. The headman wasn't there, but his wife, a scrawny woman named Marsilia, sat on a wooden stool spinning wool into thread. She said, "Lord, if you're after my man, he's out weeding the garden."

The garden was on the outskirts of the village. Sure enough, Besant was there, plucking weeds from a patch of vetch. Not only did he have a big belly, he had a big backside, too, which at the moment stuck up in the air. Resisting the urge to kick it, Gerin barked, "Why have you been blowing the horn with the sun only halfway down the sky?"

Besant jerked as if Gerin had kicked him after all. He whirled around, scrambling awkwardly to his feet. "L-lord Gerin," he stuttered. "I didn't hear you come up."

"If you don't want more unexpected visits, make sure

you work the full day," Gerin answered. "We'll all be hungrier come winter for your slacking now."

Besant gave Gerin a resentful stare. He was a tubby, sloppy-looking man of about fifty in homespun colorless save for dirt and stains here and there. "I shall do as you say, lord prince," he mumbled. "The ghosts have been bad of late, though."

"Feed them more generously, then, or throw more wood on the nightfires," Gerin said. "You've no need to hide in your houses from an hour before sunset to an hour past dawn."

Besant nodded but still looked unhappy. The trouble was, he and Gerin needed each other. Without the serfs, Gerin and his vassal barons would starve. That much Besant Big-Belly knew. But without the barons, the little villages of farmers would be at the mercy of Trokmoi and bandits: peasants with pitchforks and scythes could not stand against chariots and bronze armor and spears and swords. The headman did his best to ignore that half of the bargain.

Gerin said, "Remember, I'll be listening to hear when you blow the horn come evening." He waited for Besant to nod again, then walked off to see how the village fared.

The gods willing, he thought, the harvest would be good. Wheat for bread, oats for horses and oatmeal, barley for ale, rye for variety, beans, peas, squashes: all grew well under the warm sun. So did row on row of turnips and parsnips, cabbage and kale, lettuce and spinach. Gardens held vetch, onions, melde, radishes, garlic, and medicinal herbs like henbane.

Some fields stood vacant, the grass there lengthening for haymaking. Cattle and sheep grazed all the way out to the edge of the trees in others. A couple of lambs butted heads. "They might as well be barons," Gerin murmured to himself.

The peasants were hard at it as usual: weeding like Besant, repairing wooden fences to keep the animals where they belonged, unbaling straw to repair a leaky roof—all the myriad tasks that kept the village going. Gerin stopped to talk with a few of the serfs. Most seemed content enough. As overlords went, he was a mild one, and they knew it.

He spent more time in the village than he'd intended; the sun was already sinking toward the treetops when he headed back to Fox Keep. *No, Besant won't blow the horn early tonight, not with me here so long*, he thought. *We'll have to see about tomorrow.*

When he returned to the castle, the cooks were full of praise for the way Otes son of Engelers had fixed half a dozen pots. The Fox nodded approvingly. The large sale the jeweler had made to Fand (or rather, to Van) hadn't kept him from doing the other half of his job. On seeing Otes himself, Gerin invited him to stay for supper and pass the night in the great hall. By the way he grinned and promptly accepted, the neat little man had been expecting that.

In the great hall, Tassilo was fitting a new string to his lute and plucking at it to put it in proper tune. Duren watched him in pop-eyed fascination. "I want to learn to do that, Papa!" he said.

"Maybe you will one day," Gerin said. Stored away somewhere was a lute he'd had as a boy. He'd never been much good with it, but who could say what his son might accomplish?

After supper, Tassilo showed what he could do. "In honor of my host," he said, "I shall give you some of the song of Gerin and the dreadful night when all the moons turned full together." He struck a plangent chord from the lute and began.

Gerin, who had lived through that dreadful night five years before, recognized little of it from the minstrel's description. Much of that had to do with the way Tassilo composed his song. He didn't create it afresh from nothing; that would have overtaxed even the wits of Lekapenos, the great Sithonian epic poet.

Instead, like Lekapenos, Tassilo put his song together from stock bits and pieces of older ones. Some of those were just for the sake of sound and meter; the Fox quickly got used to hearing himself called "gallant Gerin" every time his name was mentioned. It saved Tassilo, or any other poet, the trouble of having to come up with a new epithet every time he was mentioned in the story.

And some of the pieces of old songs were ones Gerin had heard before, and which didn't perfectly fit the tale Tassilo was telling now. The bits about battling the Trokmoi went back to his boyhood, and likely to his grandfather's boyhood as well. But that too was part of the convention. More depended on the way the minstrel fit the pieces together than on what those pieces were.

All the same, Gerin leaned over to Van and said, "One thing I remember that Tassilo isn't saying anything about is how bloody frightened I was."

"Ah, but you're not a person to him, not really," Van replied. "You're gallant Gerin the hero, and how could gallant Gerin be afraid, even with every werebeast in the world trying to tear his throat out?"

"At the time, it was easy," Gerin said, which won a laugh from Van. He'd been through the werenight with Gerin. "Bold Van," Tassilo called him, which was true enough, but he hadn't been immune to fear, either.

And yet, the rest of Tassilo's audience ate up the song. Drago the Bear, who'd gone through his own terrors that night, pounded on the table and cheered to hear how Gerin had surmounted his: it might not have been true, but it sounded good. Duren hung on Tassilo's every word, long after the time he should have been asleep in bed.

Even the Trokmoi, whose fellows had been on the point of putting an end to Gerin when the chaos of the werenight saved him, listened avidly to the tale of their people's discomfiture. Well-turned phrases and songs of battle were enough to gladden them, even if they came out on the losing side.

Tassilo paused to drink ale. Diviciacus said to Gerin, "Give me your answer now, Fox, dear. I've not the patience to wait for morning."

Gerin sighed. "It must be no."

"I thought as much," the Trokmê said. "Yes is simple, but no needs disguises. You'll be after regretting it."

"So will your chief, if he quarrels with me," the Fox answered. "Tell him as much." Diviciacus glared but nodded.

When Gerin, who was yawning himself, tried to pick up Duren and carry him off to bed, his son yelled and cried enough to make the Fox give it up as a bad job. If Duren wanted to fall asleep in the great hall listening to songs, he'd let him get away with it this once. Gerin yawned again. *He* was tired, whether Duren was or not. With a wave to Tassilo, he headed for his bedchamber.

What with Fand and Van in the next room, the noise up there proved almost as loud as what the minstrel made, and even more distracting. Gerin tossed and turned and grumbled and, just when he finally was on the point of dropping off, got bitten on the cheek by a mosquito. He mashed the bug, but that woke him up again. He lay there muttering to himself until at last he did fall asleep.

Because of that, the sun was a quarter of the way up the sky when he came back down to the great hall. Van, who was just finishing a bowl of porridge, laughed at him: "See the slugabed!"

"I'd have gotten to sleep sooner if someone I know hadn't been making such a racket next door," Gerin said pointedly.

Van laughed louder. "Make any excuse you like. You outslept your guests, no matter what. All three lots of them are long gone."

"They want to get in as much travel as they can while the sun's in the sky. I'd do the same in their boots." Gerin looked around. "Where's Duren?"

"I thought he was with you, Captain," Van said. "Didn't you take him up to bed the way you usually do?"

"No, he wanted to listen to Tassilo some more." Gerin dipped up a bowl of porridge from the pot over the fire, raised it to his mouth. After he swallowed, he said, "He's probably out in the courtyard, making mischief."

In the courtyard he found Drago the Bear pouring a bucket of well water over the head of Rihwin the Fox. Both of them looked as if they'd seen the bottoms of their drinking jacks too many times the night before.

"No, I've not seen the boy all morning," Drago said when Gerin asked him.

"Nor I," the dripping Rihwin said. He added, "If he made as much noise as small boys are in the habit of doing, I'd remember seeing him . . . painfully." His eyes were tracked with red. Yes, he'd hurt himself last night.

Gerin frowned. "That's—odd." He raised his voice.

"Duren!" He put two fingers in his mouth, let out a long, piercing whistle that made Rihwin and Drago flinch.

His son knew he was supposed to come no matter what when he heard that call. He also wasn't supposed to go by himself too far from Castle Fox to hear it. Wolves and longtooths and other wild beasts roamed the woods. So, sometimes, did wild men.

But Duren did not come. Now Gerin began to worry. Maybe, he thought, the boy had gone off to the peasant village. He'd done that alone once or twice, and got his backside heated for it. But often a boy needed a lot of such heatings before he got the idea. Gerin remembered he had, when he was small.

He walked over to the village, ready to thunder like Dyaus when he found his son. But no one there had seen Duren, either. A cold wind of dread in his belly, Gerin went back to Castle Fox. He sent men out in all directions, beating the bushes and calling Duren's name. They came back scratched by thorns and stung by wasps, but without the boy.

Duren was missing.

II

Gerin paced between the benches in the great hall, making Rihwin and Van and Drago move out of the way. "One of those three must have snatched him," he said: "Diviciacus or Tassilo or Otes. I can't believe Duren would go wandering off where we couldn't find him, not of his own accord."

"If you're right, Captain, we've eaten up a lot of the day looking around here," Van said.

"I know," Gerin answered unhappily. "I'll go out and send others in chariots as well, even so; if Dyaus and the other gods are kind, one of us will catch up with our—guests." He spat the last word. Guest-friendship was sacred; those who violated it could expect a long, unhappy time in the afterlife. Unfortunately, though, fear of that didn't paralyze all rogues.

"Who'd want to steal a little boy?" Drago the Bear growled. His big hands moved in the air as if closing round a neck.

Gerin's more agile wits had already started pursuing that one. "Diviciacus might, to give Adiatunnus a hold on me," he said. "I don't think Adiatunnus would have ordered it— who could guess ahead of time if the chance would come up?—but I don't think he'd turn down a gift like that if it fell into his lap."

"Duren might give him a hold for now, but he'd get nothing but grief from you later," Van said.

"Aye, but since I turned him down for a joint move on Aragis, he's liable to think he'd get only grief from me anyhow," the Fox answered, thinking, *He's liable to be right, too*. Aloud, he went on, "Speaking of Aragis, Otes the jeweler came from his lands. And Aragis might not turn down a hold on me, either."

"You're right there, too," Drago said, making more choking motions.

"You're leaving out Tassilo," Van said.

"I know." Gerin kicked aside a dog-gnawed bone. "I can't think of any reason he'd want to harm me."

"I can," Rihwin the Fox said.

"Can you indeed?" Gerin said, surprised. "What is it?"

Rihwin coughed; his smoothly handsome face went a couple of shades pinker than usual. "You'll recall, lord, that when last you made the acquaintance of this Tassilo, I was in the process of, ah, disqualifying myself from marrying the fair Elise. I hadn't tasted wine in too long, you understand."

"Disgracing yourself is more like it," Van said, blunt as usual. Gloriously drunk, Rihwin had stood on his head on a table at Ricolf the Red's and kicked his legs in the air . . . while wearing a southern-style toga and no drawers.

He coughed again. "Perhaps your word is more accurate, friend Van, though not calculated to make me feel better about the incident or myself. Be that as it may, I resume: Elise having found you no more to her taste, lord Gerin, than her father did me, she might possibly have engaged the services of this minstrel to rape away the boy for her to raise."

Gerin bit down on that like a man whose teeth closed on a worm in an apple. Ever since Elise left him, he'd done his best not to think about her; whenever he did, it hurt. He had no idea where in the northlands she was, whether she was still with the horse doctor with whom she'd gone away, or even whether she still lived. But what Rihwin said made enough sense that he had to ask himself those questions now.

Slowly, he answered, "Aye, you're right, worse luck; that could be so." He plucked at his beard as he weighed odds. "I still think the Trokmoi are likeliest to have stolen Duren, so Van and I will go southwest after them. Which way did Tassilo fare?"

"West, toward the holding of Schild Stoutstaff, or that's where he told the gate crew he was heading," Drago answered.

Gerin grunted. If Tassilo had Duren with him, he might well have lied about his chosen direction. Or he might not have. Schild had been the leading vassal to Wolfar of the Axe. He wasn't a deadly foe to Gerin, as Wolfar had been, but he was no great friend, either. Though he'd acknowledged the Fox his suzerain after Gerin killed Wolfar, he forgot that whenever convenient. He might shelter Tassilo, or at least grant him safe passage.

"All right, Rihwin," Gerin said. "You ride west to Schild's border, and past it if his guards give you leave. If they don't—" He paused for effect. "Tell them they, and their overlord, will have cause to regret it."

Rihwin nodded. "As you say."

"Now, Otes," Gerin said.

Again, Drago answered: "He said he was heading east along the Emperor's Highway, to see if Hagop son of Hovan had tinker's work for him. He didn't think he'd sell Hagop much in the way of jewelry: 'skinflint' was the word he used, I think."

"For Hagop, it's a good one," Gerin said judiciously. "All right, you go after him, then."

"I'll do that, lord," Drago said, and strode out of the great hall. Gerin was as sure as if his eyes could follow that Drago was heading for the stables to hitch his team to his chariot, and that he'd ride out after Otes the minute the job was done. To Drago, the world was a simple place. His liege lord had given him an order, so he would follow it. Gerin sometimes wished he couldn't see all the complications in the world around him, either.

Van said, "You'll want me to ride with you, eh, Captain? We'll need a driver as well, if we're to take on Diviciacus and his friends on even terms."

"You're right on both counts," Gerin said. He thought about adding another chariot and three-man team of warriors, too, but decided against it. Van was worth a couple of ordinary men in a fight, and the Fox did not denigrate his own skill with his hands. And Raffo Redblade, who'd been driving for them for years, hadn't earned his ekename by running from fights. The Fox added, "And we'll send Widin Simrin's son south to ask what Aragis knows. Van, find him—he'll be in the courtyard somewhere—and get him moving, too."

The decision made, Gerin took his armor down from the wall and put it on: bronze greaves first, then leather cuirass faced with scales of bronze, and last of all a plain pot of a helmet. None of it was polished; none of it looked the least bit fancy—the Fox left that to Van. But his own gear was sound. It did what he wanted it to do: it kept edged and pointed metal from splitting his flesh. As far as he was concerned, nothing else mattered.

He slung his quiver over his shoulder, took down his bow, and then grabbed his shield. That was a yard-wide disk of leather and wood, with bronze edging to keep swordstrokes from chewing it up.

Most Elabonian warriors had gear much like the Fox's. Some men went in for gold or silver ornamentation, but he wanted nothing of the sort: curlicues and inlays could catch and hold a point, while rich armor made a man a special target on the battlefield.

With his outlandish armor, Van of the Strong Arm was always a target on the battlefield, but no one yet had been able to strip his crested helm and two-piece corselet from him. Along with his spear, he carried a sword, a mace, and several daggers. He was also a fine archer, but did not use the bow in combat, affecting to despise slaying foes from afar as unmanly.

"Foolishness," Gerin said, as he had many times before. "As long as you're alive and the other fellow isn't, nothing else matters. You get no points for style, not in war you don't."

Van brandished his spear. "Captain, that's never been a problem." His grin showed only a couple of broken teeth, more evidence (as if more were needed) he was more dangerous with weapons in hand than anyone he'd run up against.

Practical as usual, Gerin went into the kitchens and filled a leather sack with twice-baked bread that would keep indefinitely (and that needed someone with good teeth to eat it) and strips of smoked mutton even tougher than the bread. If he had to fight from the chariot, the sack would go over the side. If he didn't, he and Van and Raffo could travel for a few days without worrying about supplies.

Gerin shouldered the bag and carried it out to the stables. Raffo, a gangling young man with pimples along the margin of his beard, looked up from hitching the horses to either side of the chariot shaft. "Be good to get out on the road, lord Gerin," he said, getting the animals into the double yoke and securing them to the shaft with straps that ran around the front of their necks.

"It would be better if we were going out for a different reason," Gerin said heavily. Raffo's face fell; he'd forgotten that. The Fox had given up on expecting tact from his men. They were, he sometimes thought with something approaching despair, only a couple of steps more civilized than the Trokmoi. Improving that was a matter for generations, not just years; even keeping them from falling back into barbarism often seemed none too easy.

He stowed his shield on the brackets mounted on the inside of the car. It made the side wall higher. Van walked into the stables then. His place in the chariot was on the right side. He set his shield into its stowage place, too, and grunted approvingly when he saw the sack of supplies.

"That's good," he said. "Now we'll just need to buy a fowl from the peasants if we camp out in the open, or bleed out our prey if we go hunting: have to give the ghosts something, after all."

"Aye." Gerin's voice was abstracted. "The chase won't be easy. Diviciacus and his friends have half a day's start on us, and more than one road they can choose to go back to Adiatunnus—and we don't even know they have my boy." He wanted to scream in rage and fear. Instead, he grew more quiet and withdrawn than ever; he was not one to show worry on the outside.

"Only one way to find out," Van said.

"True, true." Gerin turned to Raffo. "Are you done harnessing the beasts?" By way of answer, the young driver vaulted into the car. The Fox clapped him on the back. "Good. Let's travel."

The six-spoked wheels began to spin. The bronze tires on those wheels rattled and clattered as they bounced over pebbles. Gerin felt every tiny thing the wheels went over, too. Had he not needed the most speed he could get, and had he not thought he might have to fight to get Duren back, he would have taken a wagon instead. But the chariot it had to be.

"A day of standing in this car and we'll wobble on solid ground like sailors coming off a ship long at sea," he said. The chariot rumbled out through the gateway, over the drawbridge, and away from Fox Keep.

"Speak to me not of sailing," said Van, who had done

his share of it. "You're not likely to get seasick in the car here, and that's a fact—a fact you can thank the gods for, too. I've puked up my guts a time or three, and I've no wish to do it again."

"South and west," Raffo said musingly. "Which road would they have taken, lord Gerin? Would they have fared south down the Elabon Way and then gone straight west toward Adiatunnus' castle? Or do you think they went along the lesser roads that run straighter between here and there?"

The Fox rubbed his chin as he considered. At last he said, "If they're going down the Elabon Way, Widin will come on them, for he's taking that road toward Aragis' holding."

"He'd be one against three," Van pointed out.

Gerin grimaced. "I know. But he wouldn't be foolish enough to attack them. If they have Duren, and he finds out about it, he'll get word back to the keep. We can plan what to do next—go to war with Adiatunnus, I expect."

"I didn't think you wanted to do that yet, lord Gerin," Raffo said.

"I don't," Gerin answered, "but I will. But if we go the same way Widin has, we narrow the search more than I want. I aim to throw my net as wide as I can, hoping to catch something in one strand of the mesh."

"Aye, makes sense to me," Van said, which eased the Fox's mind somewhat: his burly friend had a keen eye for tactics, though Gerin reckoned himself more adept in planning for years ahead.

Raffo steered the team down a way that headed toward Adiatunnus' lands. Within a couple of minutes, the clearing where Gerin's serfs scratched their living from the soil disappeared behind the chariot. Forest closed in on either side of the road, which, but for the ruts from wagons and chariots, might have been a game track. Branches reached out and tried to slap the Fox in the face.

He held up an arm to turn them aside. Whenever he went down a back road like this one, he was struck by how lightly civilization rested on the northlands. The stink of the castle midden, and the bigger one in the peasant village, were out of his nostrils now; the woods smelled green and growing, as if man with his stinks had never come this way. In the virgin pines and elms, robins sang sweetly, chickadees twittered, and jays cried their harsh, metallic calls. A red squirrel flirted its tail as it clambered up a tree trunk.

But Gerin knew better than to idealize the forest, as some Sithonian poets (most of whom had never set foot outside the City of Elabon) were wont to do. Wolves ranged through the woods; in hungry winters they'd go after flocks or the herders who tended them. Longtooths would take men as they would any other prey, winter or summer. And the aurochs, the great wild ox of the forest, was nothing to take lightly—a few years before, Gerin had almost died under the horns and trampling hooves of a rogue bull.

He motioned for Raffo to stop the chariot. With a puzzled look, the driver obeyed. But for the bird calls and the soft purling of a stream somewhere off out of sight, silence closed down like a cloak. To the Fox, who was comfortable with only himself for company, it felt pleasant and restful.

Van, though, quickly started to fidget. He pulled a baked-clay flute from a pouch on his belt and began playing a tune whose notes ran in no pattern familiar to Elabonian music. "That's better," he said. "Too bloody quiet here."

Gerin swallowed a sigh and tapped Raffo on the shoulder. "Let's get going again. I'd sooner listen to jingling harness than to Van's tweedles."

"Aye, lord Gerin. Now that you mention it, so would I." Raffo flicked the reins. The horses snorted resentfully—they'd started cropping the grass that grew between the ruts—and trotted down the road.

At the next village, Gerin asked the serfs if they'd seen the chariot full of Trokmoi come past. They all shook their heads, as if they'd not only not seen such a thing but never heard of it, either.

The Fox scowled. "We're too far north or too far south, and Dyaus only knows which: that or they've gone down the Elabon Way as Raffo feared." He pounded his fist on the chariot rail in frustration.

"Too far north'd be my guess," Van said. "The track we were on curved, I think, till it ran nearer west than southwest."

"I didn't note that myself, but you're most often right about such things," Gerin said. "Raffo, the next road we come on that heads south, you take it till it crosses one leading in the direction we really want to go." *Or until it peters out*, he thought: not all paths connected to others.

The peasants watched as their overlord rode out of the village. Though still on land he ruled directly rather than through one of his vassal barons, he seldom came here save when collecting what was due him each fall. He wondered what the serfs thought of this unexpected appearance. Most likely, they were relieved he hadn't demanded anything of them.

Shadows lengthened as the chariot rattled and rumbled through woods that seemed to grow ever thicker. "I wonder if this road ever does join up with anything else," Van said.

"If it doesn't pretty bloody soon, we're going to have to turn back and head for that last village to buy a couple of chickens," Gerin said. "I don't want to have to count on just fire to keep the ghosts away."

Raffo pointed with his free hand. "Looks like more light up ahead, lord Gerin. Might be only a meadow, mind you, but it might be fields, too, and fields mean another village."

It was fields; Gerin felt like cheering. No sooner had the chariot emerged from the woods than the quitting horn called the peasants in from their labor. The Fox looked around. "Yes, I know this place—Pinabel Odd-Eyes is headman here. I'm used to coming here from the west, though, not out of the north."

Pinabel's left eye was blue, his right brown. Brown and blue both widened when Gerin rolled into the center of the village. Pinabel bowed very low. "L-lord prince, what brings you here?" he stammered.

The nervousness he showed made Gerin wonder what sort of cheating he was doing, but he'd have to worry about that later. "My son's been kidnapped," he announced baldly. Pinabel and the other serfs who heard exclaimed in dismay; family ties mattered to them, not least because those were almost all too many of them had. He went on, "I think three Trokmoi who visited Fox Keep yesterday may have taken him."

That brought more murmurs from the peasants. They were even more afraid of the Trokmoi than of night ghosts, and with reason: the ghosts could be propitiated, but the woodsrunners ravaged as they pleased. But when Gerin asked if Pinabel and the others in the village had seen the chariot Diviciacus and his comrades were riding, they all denied it.

He believed them, much as he wished he thought they were lying. Pinabel said, "They might have gone through by way of the next road south. It's very great, I hear, though I have never traveled far enough to see it."

"Maybe." Gerin didn't have the heart to tell the headman that next road was just another muddy track. Like most serfs, Pinabel had never traveled more than a few hours' walk from where he was born.

"Will you stay with us till morning, lord prince?" Pinabel asked. "Night comes soon." He gestured to the east, where Elleb, only a day before full, had already risen. Math hung halfway up the sky, while Nothos, almost at first quarter, showed near enough where south lay. And in the west, the sun was near the horizon. When it set, the ghosts would come out.

But Gerin shook his head. "I want to push on as long as I may—every moment may prove precious. Sell me two chickens, if you would, so I can give the ghosts blood when they come."

"Aye, lord prince." Pinabel hurried away. He returned a couple of minutes later with a pair of hens, their legs tied with strips of rawhide. Gerin gave him a quarter of a silverpiece for them: probably more than they were worth, but the smallest bit of money he had in the pouch at his belt. Pinabel Odd-Eyes bowed himself almost double.

As the chariot bounced away, Raffo observed, "Most lords would have said, 'Give me two chickens' there."

That hadn't occurred to Gerin. He said, "Those birds aren't remotely part of the dues Pinabel's village owes on its land. I have no right just to take them from him."

"Neither does any other Elabonian lord with his serfs, if I understand your ways aright," Van said. "The thing of it is, most wouldn't let that stop 'em."

"You're probably right," Gerin said with a sigh. "But the

way I see it, I owe my peasants fair dealing, just as they
do with me. If I don't give it, how can I expect to get it
in return?"

"Often enough you won't get it in return, no matter what
sort of dealing you give," Van said.

"You're right." The Fox sighed again. "But when I don't,
I'm not soft on that, either." Gerin was scrupulously fair.
Anyone who thought him weak on that account soon
regretted it.

"If I don't stop now, lord Gerin, we'll not have time to
make ready to meet the ghosts," Raffo said, pointing to the
western skyline. The sun, red as hot copper, had to be just
on the point of setting.

Gerin thought about pushing on for another furlong or
two, but regretfully decided Raffo was right. At his nod,
the driver reined in. Gerin jumped down and gouged out
a trench in the soft dirt by the side of the road. That did
the edge of his dagger no good, but it was the only digging tool he had. Van handed him the trussed fowls. He
cut off their heads, one after the other—the knife was still
sharp enough for that—and let their blood spill into the
trench.

None too soon: he still held the second hen over the
hole when the ghosts came. They were, as ever, indistinct;
the eye would not, could not, grasp their shape. They
buzzed round the blood like carrion flies, soaking up vitality
from it. Because he'd given them the gift, they were not
fierce and angry and terrifying as they would have been
otherwise, but tried to give him good advice in return.

He could not understand them. He had never been able
to, save on the werenight, when his brother's shade managed to deliver a message of truly oracular obscurity—
though he'd been able to use it later to destroy Balamung
just when the opposite result looked far more likely.

Van bent over a firebow, twirling a stick with a rawhide
lace to start a blaze for the evening. He shook his head
like a man bedeviled by gnats. "I wish they'd quit yowl-
ing in my mind," he grumbled, but then he grunted in
satisfaction. "Here we go, Raffo—feed me tinder, a bit at
a time. You know how."

"Aye." Raffo had been crumbling dry leaves. He poked

some into the hole where the stick from the firebow spun.
Van breathed gently on the sparks he'd started, hoping to
fan them rather than blowing them out. "You have it!" Raffo
said, and gave him more tinder to feed the new little
flames. With the fire well and truly started, he passed Van
larger twigs to load on. Soon the thick chunk of branch
on which the outlander had used the firebow would also
catch.

"I wish it were that easy all the time," Van said. "Gut
those birds, Fox, and pluck 'em, so we can get ourselves
outside them. They're better fare than what we brought
with us."

"You're right there." The plucking job Gerin gave the
hens was quick and decidedly imperfect. He didn't care;
he was hungry. He picked out the birds' hearts, livers, and
gizzards from the offal to roast them over the fire, then
threw the rest of the guts into the trench with the blood.

He, Raffo, and Van drew stems of grass for the night
watches. Few bandits dared the ghosts to travel by night,
but Gerin was not the sort to take unnecessary chances—
the necessary ones were quite bad enough. And the beasts
of the forest, being without souls themselves, took no notice
of the night spirits. They usually did not attack travelers
encamped in the woods, but you never could tell.

Van drew the short stem, and chose the first watch.
Gerin and Raffo drew again. This time Raffo won, and
picked the watch that led to dawn. "Since I get to have
my sleep broken up, I may as well take what I can get of
it," Gerin said, and wrapped himself in a blanket—as much
to keep off the bugs as for warmth, for the night was mild.

Van shook him awake with the cheerful insouciance of
a man who'd already done his share of a job. "Nothing
much doing, Captain," he said while Gerin tried to break
free of the fog that shrouded his wits. Van took off the
helm, corselet, and greaves he'd worn through his watch,
cocooned himself in his blanket, and was snoring by the
time the Fox began to think himself awake.

Gerin put on his own helmet and sword, but did not
bother with his cuirass. He paced back and forth, not willing
to sit down until he was sure he wouldn't doze off. The
fire had died into embers. He fed it twigs and then

branches and brought it back to briskly crackling life. That drove away some of the ghosts flittering near, and reduced their murmur in his mind.

By the time he'd taken care of that, he felt more confident he could stay awake. He walked to the edge of the circle of firelight and sat down with his back to the flames. His night vision, almost ruined when he'd stoked them, slowly returned.

The moons had wheeled a good way through the sky. Nothos was nearing the western skyline, Math well west of south—when her golden gibbous disk sank below the horizon, it would be time for the Fox to rouse Raffo. Elleb, looking like a bright new bronze coin, neared the meridian.

Here and there in the forest, birches mingled with ash and oak and pine. By the light of the moons and the nightfire, their pale trunks seemed almost to gleam against the darker background.

Gerin wished his ears could grow more sensitive to the dark the way his eyes did. Off in the distance, a barn owl hooted. The Trokmoi thought the souls of dead warriors inhabited the pallid night birds. The Fox had his doubts about that, but he'd never tried a sorcerous experiment to find out one way or the other. He spent a while trying to figure out how such an experiment might be run, and what he could do if he found the Trokmoi were wrong. Making the arrogant woodsrunners doubt themselves in any way was likely to be worthwhile.

"You know," he said to himself in a low voice, "the midwatch isn't so bad after all. I don't get enough time of my own, with no one havering at me to do this or decide that right this moment." In small—or sometimes not so small—doses, he relished solitude.

Perhaps three parts of his four-hour watch had gone by when a coughing roar not far away roused him from contemplation, or rather jerked him out of it by the scruff of the neck. No one could ignore a longtooth's hunting cry; a man's blood knew it meant danger. One of the horses let out a frightened snort. The Fox found his left hand on the hilt of his sword without conscious memory of how it had got there—not that a sword would stop one of the great hunting cats if it chose to hunt him.

The longtooth, to his vast relief, came no closer to the campsite. "Well," he muttered, "I'm not sleepy now." He felt as if he'd had ice water splashed over him. When a nightjar swooped down to grab one of the moths fluttering around the fire, he almost jumped out of his skin.

He woke Raffo as soon as Math set. The driver looked toward the west, saw the moon was down, and nodded in approval. "No one ever said you weren't one for right dealing, lord," he said blurrily around a yawn.

Gerin wrapped himself in his blanket once more. He kept an eye on Raffo to make sure the younger man wouldn't go back to sleep as he almost had. Raffo, though, took watch-standing seriously, and paced about as the Fox had. Gerin feared he himself would have trouble dozing off again but, in spite of his worries, quickly drifted away.

The rising sun made him rise, too. His eyes came open just as the ghosts vanished for the day. He got to his feet, feeling elderly. Van was still snoring. Gerin roused him cautiously; the outlander's first waking act—especially when he was disturbed—was usually to grab for a weapon.

This time, though, he seemed to remember where he was, and came to himself without violence. He headed for the forest, saying, "Either I go off behind a bush or I burst where I stand."

"I watered the grass on watch, so I don't have that worry," Gerin said, buckling on his right greave. Raffo harnessed the horses.

The chicken bones and guts were already beginning to stink. The travelers moved upwind before they gnawed on bread and smoked meat. "Are we ready?" Raffo asked, looking around the little camp to make sure nothing had been forgotten. Gerin looked, too; if they had left something behind, he would have blamed himself.

They climbed into the chariot, Raffo driving, Gerin behind him on the left, Van on the right. Raffo flicked the reins. The horses started forward. When they came to a stream, Raffo let the animals have a brief drink. Gerin scooped up some water in the palm of his hand, too, and freshened what he carried in the waterskin at his belt.

At the next road that ran west, Raffo swung the chariot onto it. A little village lay not far from the crossroads. The appearance of their lord so early in the day was a prodigy for the peasants. When he asked if they'd seen Diviciacus and his comrades the day before, one of the men nodded. "Aye, just before noon it were," he said. A couple of other people nodded.

The Fox scowled; he was on the right track, aye, but no closer to the Trokmoi than when he'd set out. If they were traveling hard, maybe they had a reason. "Did they have a boy with them?" he asked, and then amplified that: "My son, I mean."

The serfs looked at one another. "Didn't see no boy, lord," answered the fellow who'd spoken before.

That wasn't what Gerin wanted to hear. Had the Trokmoi cut Duren's throat as if he were some sacrifice to the night ghosts, then dumped the corpse by the side of the road? Horrid dread filled him: his father, his brother—now his son, too? If that was so, he vowed he'd not rest till every red-mustached robber south of the Niffet was dead or routed back to the northern woods. Even as he made it, he knew the vow to be impossible of fulfillment. He spoke it in his mind, all the same; it would give his life a target.

"Take everything you can from the horses," he told Raffo, his voice harsh. "Now we have to catch them before they win back to Adiatunnus' lands."

"Aye, lord Gerin." But Raffo sounded doubtful. "They have a long lead, though. Gaining enough ground won't be easy, the more so as we may have to keep casting about for the road they took."

"I know that," Gerin growled. "But I'll have answers from them if I have to wring out each word with hot pincers."

Van thumped him on the shoulder. "Easy, Captain, easy. We don't even know they ever had the lad, mind you."

"But they must have—" Gerin stopped, shook his head. Assuming something was so because you thought it had to be was one of the flaws in logic that made the savants in the City of Elabon laugh. He took a deep breath and said, "You're right. We *don't* know they had him."

He wondered if he ever would, or could, know. Had Diviciacus and his crew killed Duren and tossed his body into the woods, scavengers would make short work of it (he knew too well that his son had only a little meat on his bones). When he'd charged out after the Trokmoi, he'd figured he or Drago or Rihwin or Widin would catch up with Duren's kidnappers, rescue the boy, and return in triumph to Castle Fox. Now he realized he'd been making assumptions there, too. Uncertainty, in a way, felt even worse than being sure of Duren's death would have. How long could he go on wondering without going mad?

Then he thought that, after a while, he wouldn't be uncertain any more. He'd have to reckon Duren dead if he wanted to keep on living himself.

"Push them," he said to Raffo. This time, the driver did not answer back. He flicked the whip over the horses' backs. They leaned into the harness, pushed their pace up to a fast trot.

The chariot rolled through another peasant village and then drove by the small keep of Notker the Bald, one of Gerin's vassal barons. "Aye, lord Gerin," Notker called from the palisade, "they came by here yesterday, sometime past noon, but they showed shield of truce, just as they had on the way to your castle, so I thought no more about it."

"Did they have Duren with them?" Gerin asked. Two sets of serfs had already answered no to that, but the Fox put the question again anyhow. Maybe, he thought with what he knew to be irrationality, a noble would have noticed something the serfs had not.

But Notker shook his head. "Your son, lord?" he said. "No, I saw him not. What then? Is it war between the woodsrunners and us despite the truce sign?"

"By the gods, I wish I knew." Gerin tapped Raffo on the shoulder to drive on before Notker asked any more questions he couldn't answer.

Toward the middle of the afternoon they passed the boundary stone that had marked the border between Gerin's holdings and those of his southwestern neighbor, Capuel the Flying Frog. No one had seen Capuel since the werenight; Gerin sometimes wondered if his ekename had been a clue to a were strain in his family and he'd turned toad when all the moons rose full together. More likely, though, the Trokmoi had slain him.

The boundary stone lay on its side these days, ruining

the charms for peace and prosperity that had been carved into it. Whether that was cause or effect Gerin did not know, but Capuel's former holding knew no peace these days. None of his vassals had been able to take any kind of grip on the land. The Fox held some of it himself, Trokmoi had overrun a couple of keeps, and the rest was given over to banditry.

The first peasant village the chariot passed was only a ruin, some of the houses burned, the rest falling to pieces from lack of care. Some grain grew untended in weed-choked fields, but before another generation passed no sign would be left that man had ever lived here.

"Captain, we may need to stop to hunt toward sunset, and I don't mean for the Trokmoi," Van said. "Who's going to sell us a chicken in country like this?"

Gerin didn't answer. He knew Van was right but didn't want to admit it, even to himself. Stopping to slay an animal with whose blood to propitiate the ghosts would make him lose time on Diviciacus, not gain it.

The next village was still inhabited, but that did the travelers no good. Only a handful of people remained in what had been a fair-sized hamlet. When one of them spotted an approaching chariot, he let out a yell full of fear and desperation. Everyone—men, women, children—fled from fields and houses into the nearby woods.

"Wait!" Gerin shouted. "I just want to ask you a couple of questions." No one paid him any attention.

He looked helplessly to Van. The outlander said, "You ask me, Captain, these poor buggers have got themselves trampled too often lately to take chances when somebody who looks like a warrior comes by."

"No doubt you're right," the Fox answered, sighing. "Doesn't say much for the state the northlands are in, does it?"

"Your serfs don't run from you, lord Gerin," Raffo said.

"That's so," Gerin said, "but there's more to the northlands than my holdings—and if I took in these lands, I'd do it by war, so the peasants here wouldn't get the chance to learn I treat them decently. They'd just go on running when they saw me coming."

Raffo didn't answer. Unless he should be involved in fighting to gain control of land beyond Gerin's holding, it was too remote to matter to him. That made him typical, not otherwise, which saddened Gerin: he tried to think in larger terms.

Van said, "You're not the only baron—excuse me, Captain: prince—the serfs don't flee. What Aragis does to the ones who run that he catches makes all the others think three times before they try it."

"He's a hard man," Gerin agreed. "Harder than need be, I think. But it may be that hard times require a hard man. Who can tell for certain?"

"Do you know what your trouble is, Captain?" Van said.

"No, but I daresay you're going to tell me," the Fox answered, raising that eyebrow of his. Every so often, Van found a flaw in him, rarely the same one twice. The infuriating thing was that more often than not he had a point.

"Your trouble, Captain, is that you're so busy trying to understand the other fellow's point of view that you don't give enough heed to your own."

Gerin clutched his chest and lurched in the chariot, as if pierced by an arrow. Van's chuckle rumbled deep in his chest. That was a hit, though, and the Fox knew it. He said, "Understanding the other fellow has its uses, too. Sometimes he may even be right."

"And what does that have to do with the price of tin?" Van said. "All you really need worry about is that he does what you have in mind."

"Are you sure you're not really a Trokmê after all?" Gerin asked mildly. That earned him the glare he'd expected.

The chariot rattled past a burned-out keep. Perched atop one of the charred logs sat a fat bustard. Van tapped Raffo on the shoulder, pointed. The driver pulled back on the reins; the horses stopped and began to graze. Van reached for Gerin's bow. "I saw the bird—will you let me do the hunting?" he asked.

"Go ahead," the Fox answered. Van might think slaying men with the bow an effete way to fight, but he was a fine archer nonetheless.

The outlander strung the bow. Gerin handed him an arrow. He dropped down from the chariot and slid toward the bustard, light on his feet as a stalking longtooth. The bustard grubbed under its wing for mites. Van got to within twenty paces before he stood still, nocked the shaft, drew the bow, and let fly.

The arrow hit the bustard just below where it had been scratching. It let out a startled squawk and tried to fly, but tumbled off its log into the ditch that had not served to protect the palisade. Van scrambled in after it. When he came out again, he carried the bird by the feet and wore an enormous grin.

"Well shot," Gerin said, pleased the hunt had been so successful—and so brief. "Blood for the ghosts and supper for us."

"The very thing I was thinking," Van said.

Before long, sunset forced the travelers to a halt. Gerin and Van got out of the chariot and, one with sword, the other with spear, moved cautiously through the woods on either side of the road until Gerin came upon a small clearing screened off by trees. He hurried back to the dirt track, whistled to let Van know he'd found what he was after.

"You've got a place to keep us away from prying eyes, do you?" the outlander said, slipping out from between a couple of oaks. Despite his bulk, he moved so quietly that Gerin had not heard him till he spoke.

"Indeed I do. In my own lands, I wasn't much worried about making a fire out where anyone could see it. Here, though, it might draw serfs on the run, bandits—who knows what? Why take the chance?" The Fox turned to Raffo. "Unharness the horses. We can lead them back to the clearing, too; the way's not badly overgrown."

"Aye, lord Gerin." Raffo freed the animals from the central shaft; he and the Fox led them away to tether them in the clearing.

Van joined them a few minutes later. "I dragged the chariot off the road and into the bushes," he said. "It won't be so easy to see now."

"Good." Gerin nodded. "And if one of the horses goes lame, now we know we can hitch you to the shaft in its stead. Maybe we'll let the horse ride in your place in the car."

"I thank you, Captain," Van said gravely. "Always good

to see how you look out for the welfare of them that serve you, so it is."

Suspecting he'd come off worse in that exchange, Gerin dug a trench to hold the blood from the bustard Van had killed earlier in the afternoon. When the bird had bled out, he frowned. "I hope that will be enough," he said. "We'd better build the fire bigger than we would have otherwise, or we'll have dreadful dreams all through the night."

After the sun went down, the ghosts did buzz gratefully around the offering the travelers had given them, but they rose from it faster than the Fox would have liked to see, as if they were men getting up from the table still hungry. They also braved the light and heat of the fire to gain more vital essence from the cut-up chunks of bird Gerin, Van, and Raffo were roasting.

The Fox drew first watch. After he woke Raffo for the middle stint, he fell asleep almost at once. His dreams *were* dreadful: monsters rampaging over the northlands, with men in desperate and what looked like losing struggle to drive them back. At first, in one of those almost-conscious moments dreams sometimes have, he thought he was harking back to the werenight. But he soon realized that was not so; these monsters seemed more appalling than mere wild beasts armed with the remnants of human wit that still clung to them.

When Van shook him awake at sunrise, he rose with such alacrity that the outlander gave him a curious look and said, "You're not apt to be so cheerful of a morning."

"Bad dreams," Gerin muttered, sliding a foot into a sandal.

"Aye, I had 'em, too." Van shook his head. "All manner of horrid creatures running loose—the gods grant I had a sour stomach or some such, to make me see such phantoms in my sleep."

The Fox paused with the sandal strap still unfastened. "That sounds like the same dream I had," he said slowly.

"And I," Raffo agreed. "I wouldn't have minded spending more time on watch and less in my blanket, and how often do you hear me say something like that?"

They hashed it out over breakfast, each recounting what he remembered of his dreams. As best Gerin could tell, they were all the same. "I don't like that," he said. "The omen is anything but good." His fingers shaped a sign to turn aside ill luck. The sign worked well enough for small misfortunes. Whatever misfortune lay ahead, he feared it would not be small—with Duren missing, it was already large. He offered the sign as a man without food in his house will offer a neighbor a stoup of water: not much, but the best he can do.

Van said, "If it is an omen, we won't be able to escape it, whatever it may prove to mean. One way or another, we'll get through." He seized his spear, made a sudden, savage thrust, as if to dispose of any troublesome foretellings.

The Fox wished he could match his friend's confidence. Van had never found anything, even the werenight, he couldn't overcome with brawn and bravery. Gerin trusted his own power less far. He said, "Let's get on the road."

They passed another couple of mostly deserted villages that day, and a wrecked keep. And, about noon, the Fox saw on a distant hill a building that wasn't quite a keep but was far stronger and more elaborate than anything a serf would need. Raffo saw it, too, and scowled blackly. "If that's not a bandits' nest, you can call me a Shanda nomad."

"That's what it is, all right, and right out in the open, too." Gerin spat into the dirt of the road to show what he thought of it. "Everything's going to the five hells when bandits set themselves up like barons."

"Who do you think the first barons were?" Van said. "Bandits who got rich, most likely. That's how it was a lot of places, anyhow."

"Insulting my ancestors, are you?" Gerin said. "I'd be angrier if I didn't know you were probably right. Even so, one fine day we're going to come down here and burn these bandits out before they get the chance to turn into barons."

"We're getting close to the lands Adiatunnus holds," Raffo said. "He's liable not to like that."

"Aye, he might have in mind to use these buggers, whoever they are, as a buffer between him and me," Gerin agreed. "That he has it in mind, though, doesn't mean it will happen so."

The sun had slid more than halfway down toward the west when the chariot clattered up to a new border stone standing by the side of the road. The boulder was carved not with Elabonian designs or letters, but rather with the fylfots and spirals the Trokmoi favored. In the roadway itself stood a couple of red-mustached northerners, one with a spear, the other with a sword. The one with the spear called in lilting Elabonian, "Who might you be, coming to the lands of the great chief, Adiatunnus his own self?"

"I might be anyone. I am Gerin the Fox," Gerin answered. "Did Adiatunnus' liegeman Diviciacus pass this way?"

"He did that." The border guard gave Gerin a look more curious than hostile. "And I'm after thinking it's fair strange, Fox, for you to be after him so. Have you changed your mind, now, over the matter anent which Diviciacus was sent forth for to talk with you?"

"I have not," Gerin answered at once, which made both Trokmoi scowl. "But neither am I at feud with Adiatunnus, nor with any of his. Does peace hold between us, or not?" He reached for the bronze-headed axe in its rest on the side wall of the chariot. Van hefted his own spear, not in a hostile way but thoughtfully, as if to find out how heavy it was.

It certainly made the Trokmoi thoughtful. The man who had spoken before said, "Sure and you've no need to be fighting us, now. For all Diviciacus ranted and carried on about what a black-hearted spalpeen you were, Fox—these are his words, mind, and none o' my own—he said not a whisper of faring forth to fight."

"As I told him I had no quarrel with Adiatunnus," Gerin agreed. "But tell me this—when Diviciacus rode through here, did he have with him in the chariot a boy of four summers? Not to put too fine a point on it, did he have my son? Before you answer, think on this: if you lie, we shall be at feud, and to the death."

The two northerners looked at each other. This time, the one who had the sword replied: "Fox, by Esus, Taranis, and Teutates I swear he did not." That was the strongest oath the Trokmoi used, and one they did not swear lightly. The fellow went on, "If we aimed to go to war with you, we'd up and do it. Stealing a child, now?" He spat. "Bad cess to any man who's after trying such a filthy thing."

"Aye," the other warrior said. "Did one of ours do such to you, Fox, we'd hand him back nicely tied and all, for you to do with him as you thought best. You could make him last days so, and wish every moment he'd never been born. I've two lads and a girl of my own, and I'd use the same way any ogre of a man who so much as ruffled a hair on their heads without my leave."

His anger and sincerity were unmistakable. Maybe Adiatunnus had set him and his friend here just because they lied so well, but Gerin couldn't do anything about that, not without an army at his back. He said, "I shall believe you, but remember what I said if you've not spoken truth."

"Och, but we have, so we've nought to fear," the fellow with the sword said. "I hope you find the bairn safe, Fox."

His friend nodded, adding, "Since you're apt to be spending the night in the open, would you want to buy a hen from us, now?"

"You probably stole it," Gerin said without rancor. "That's what all you Trokmoi south of the Niffet are—just a bunch of damned chicken thieves."

"Indeed and we're not," the northerner with a spear answered indignantly. "We came south because you Elabonians are after having so many things better and better than chickens to steal."

Since that was nothing but the truth, Gerin could not even argue with it. He tapped Raffo on the shoulder. His driver slewed the chariot in the narrow roadway and started east, back toward Castle Fox. "Sensible," Van said. "This set of woodsrunners seemed friendly enough, but we'll want to put some distance between them and us all the same. One of their higher-ups is liable to decide we're worth hunting through the night."

"My thought exactly," Gerin agreed. "Raffo, go by back roads while the day lasts, so long as they lead north or east. If we stay on the main track, I think we're asking for trouble."

"Aye, lord Gerin," Raffo said, and then, after a moment, "I'm sorry we didn't find your son."

Gerin sighed. "So am I. I have to pray that Rihwin or Drago or Widin had better luck than we did." He tried not to think about what might be happening to Duren. Too many of the pictures his imagination came up with were black ones.

"We were so sure the Trokmoi had run off with him, too," Van said. Another man might have put that, *You were so sure*— Like any proper friend, the outlander shared responsibility as well as credit.

"We'll know more when we get back to the castle," the Fox said, wondering how he'd keep from going mad till then.

Rihwin the Fox spread his hands. "Lord Gerin, Schild Stoutstaff's border guards declined to give me leave to pass into their overlord's land. For whatever it may be worth, they say Tassilo did enter that holding, but that they saw no sign of any small boy with him."

"For whatever it may be worth," Gerin repeated. "If he had Duren trussed up in the back of the wagon, it may be worth nothing at all. Or, on the other hand—" He gave up, shaking his head in frustration and dismay. He'd hoped he'd find answers at Fox Keep, not just more questions, but questions seemed in better supply. Turning to Widin Simrin's son, he asked, "Any luck with you?"

Widin was a young man, but wore his beard long and forked, an antique style. He shook his head. "The same as Rihwin, lord prince. Aragis' borderers say they'd not seen Rihwin—nor Tassilo nor Otes, either—but would not give me leave to enter their lord's land."

Drago the Bear said, "As for Otes son of Engelers, lord Gerin, far as I can tell he's just vanished off the face of the earth. No trace of him eastwards, that's certain."

"Well, what happened to him?" Gerin growled. But he knew that could have a multitude of answers, too. The jeweler might have run into bandits, he might have been taken ill and laid up at some little peasant village which Drago had gone right past, or he might have decided not to fare east after all. No way to be certain, especially now that Drago the Bear had decided to give up the trail and return to Fox Keep. Gerin might have wished for more diligence from him, but he'd done what he was told, which was about what he was good for.

As if uneasily aware his overlord was dissatisfied with

him, Drago tried to change the subject: "Lord Gerin, you shouldn't let Schild get by with the insolence he shows you these days. He bent the knee and set his hands in yours after you slew Wolfar, but you'd never know it by the way he acts. He has his nerve, he does, keeping your vassals off his land when he's properly a vassal his own self."

"In law, you're right," Gerin said. "Trouble is, we haven't much law north of the High Kirs. So long as he hasn't warred on me or attacked my lands when I was busy elsewhere, I've always had more important things to do than forcing him to heel."

"But when it's your son, lord prince?" Widin asked softly.

Gerin sighed. "Aye, now it's my son—not that Tassilo seems to have had him. I'll send Schild a courier with a letter: his border guards won't hold back a courier under my orders to take the message to their lord."

"They'd better not, anyhow," Drago said. "'Twould be against all polite usage." Down in the heart of the Empire, Gerin thought, Drago would have made a perfect man of law: he lived in a world where precedent bulked more real and larger than reality. That often served him well—it saved him the trouble of thinking, which was not his strength, anyhow. But when he had to confront something new and unusual, he might as well have been unarmed.

Rihwin the Fox said, "I hope the mere sending of a letter will not offend Schild's, ah, delicate sensibilities."

"You mean, will he get angry because my courier can read and he can't?" Gerin asked. Rihwin nodded. Gerin said, "It shouldn't be a problem. Schild may not have much in the way of learning, but he doesn't hate people who do—unlike some I could name." *Some who are my vassals*, he thought.

"If you did want to make him worry about you, Captain, you could use one of those serfs you've taught their letters," Van said.

"Makes me worry, too," Drago muttered, just loud enough to let Gerin hear.

"No, I try not to let word of that leak out of the holding," Gerin said. "The time's not ripe, not yet."

"Still don't know why you started that crazy business anyhow, lord," Widin said.

"Why? Because there's too much ignorance running around loose in the northlands, that's why," Gerin said. Widin and Drago both stared at him in incomprehension. Van shook his massive head; he'd known what the Fox was up to for years, and hadn't complained about it, but that didn't mean he approved.

Even Rihwin, who was himself not only literate but possessed of a formal education better than Gerin's, seemed dubious. "One of the things of which the serfs remain cheerfully ignorant is their own miserable lot," he remarked. "Let them learn to think, to reason, and they will surely wonder at the justice of an order which keeps them in their huts and the barons who rule them in grand keeps like this one."

"They wonder at that anyhow," Gerin said. "The northlands have never been free from peasant revolts, and that's only grown worse since the Trokmoi came over the Niffet. But my serfs, among them the ones I've taught, have stayed loyal where those of other lords rose."

"Belike that's so—for now," Van said. "But often, too, it works out that a man who's too hungry and worn to rise up will go on working where even a pack mule would drop dead. Give that same man a bit of hope, now, and a full belly, and then try to crack the whip on him . . . well, you'd better have a good place to hide, is all I have to tell you."

Gerin clicked his tongue between his teeth. That had some truth to it; his own reading of history said as much. But he answered, "I have to take the chance. If I don't, this whole land will slide back into barbarism in two generations' time, and the only way you'll be able to tell Elabonians from Trokmoi will be by black mustachios in place of red."

"I'm not ignorant," Drago said indignantly. "Hearing I am all the bloody time wears thin, lord Gerin. I know how to war and raise horses and keep order in my own holding. What else do I need?"

"Suppose there's a drought and you need magic done to get some rain?" Gerin asked.

"I hire a mage, of course."

"Where do you suppose the mage learned his art? If he's any good, at the Sorcerers' Collegium down in the City of Elabon. But northlands mages can't do that any more—we're cut off, remember. If we want to have another set of mages come along to replace the ones who die, we'll just have to find some way to train them ourselves. That means reading and writing, too, you know."

Drago scowled. "You don't argue fair, Fox."

"There I must disagree," Rihwin said. "Lord Gerin's arguments strike me as logical enough—and logic also seems to me to be a civilized appurtenance worth preserving. The question is whether the risks inherent in seeking to make civilized men of serfs outweigh the benefits to be gained from that course if successful."

Gerin abruptly sickened of the dispute. "A murrain on it," he growled. "The only thing that truly matters now is who has Duren and what they're doing to him. I said the same thing before we all set out searching, but I hoped we'd know something when we came back to Fox Keep. Instead, here we are sitting along this same cursed table five days later, and just as ignorant as the moment we set out."

Rihwin gave him a sidelong glance. "Where chariots rumbling down roadways and men beating bushes fail, sorcery might serve. I speak purely in the abstract, you understand, my own abilities along those lines having been raped away by the angry god, but the possibility deserves mention."

"It would deserve more mention if I were more of a wizard." Gerin sighed. "Oh, aye, you have the right of it, and I'll try, but I've essayed such magics before, and never yet found what I was looking for. And by the time we can find a proper mage and bring him here, the trail will have grown cold."

"Attempting a spell while convinced it will fail is the surest way to guarantee such failure," Rihwin said.

"I know that, too, but I find optimism hard to come by when I see no good reason for it." The Fox wished he could cast aside his gloom. As Rihwin had said, he would have been a better wizard—*though never a good one*, he thought—without it. But it was as much a part of him as the scar over his left eye.

Just then, Fand came into the great hall. She pointed to Rihwin and Widin and Drago. "I know they had no luck," she said. "Are you after finding your lost boy, and him so small and all?"

"No," Gerin said, and the one word pressed the weight of defeat and despair more heavily onto his shoulders.

"Och, the black shame of it, to be snatching children," Fand said. She meant it, Gerin judged, but hers was a nature that held the troubles of others in mind for only a little while before returning to her own concerns: "And fair lonely I was, too, with both my men off on a sleeveless errand. Still and all, though, they might have brought something back with them to make amends for being gone so long." She looked hopefully from Gerin to Van.

The outlander answered first: "Maybe I should bring my hand across your greedy backside. Does that seem fair, when you think on what we were about?"

When Van spoke in that rumbling tone of warning, as if he were an earthquake about to happen, sensible men walked soft. But Fand was nothing if not spirited herself. She shouted, "Greedy, is it, to be asking a simple question of you? Often enough there's a question you ask of me, aye, and with the understanding my answer had better be yes, too, or I'd be sorry for it. And you call me greedy? A pox take you!"

"If a pox did take me, where would I likely get it?" Van retorted.

"You've been staying with me too long," Gerin murmured. "That's the sort of crack I'm apt to make."

Fand didn't hear him. She let her wrath fall on Van: "You? Who knows where you'd be likely to come by the pox? You think I don't know you'll cover anything with a slit, like a billy goat in the springtime? I've more to fear from your wanderings than you from mine. Go on, now, tell me I'm a liar."

Van turned the color of the embers smoldering on the hearth. "That's the way of a man," he sputtered. Drago, Rihwin, and Widin nodded. So did Gerin, though he was less inclined to make a tomcat of himself.

"Och, I know that." Fand tossed her head in fine disdain. "But since it is, why blame me for what'd be the fault of your own self?"

Gerin worked so hard to choke down laughter that he had a coughing fit. Van wasn't the only one who'd spent a lot of time with him. No toga-wearing Sithonian sophist could have done a neater, more logical job of punching holes in the outlander's gibe than Fand just had.

Van looked his way. "Will you not come to my aid?" he asked plaintively, as if alone on the field and beset by a host.

"I think our lady here was greedy, too, but as for the rest, you got yourself into it, and you can get yourself out." Gerin rose and headed for the stairs. "As for me, I'm going to see what sort of search spells I can use to try to find my son."

Bass and alto shouts, like angry kettledrum and horn, followed him up to his library. He knew of no greater hoard of books anywhere in the northlands, yet he also knew how inadequate the collection was. There were hundreds of grimoires, for instance, but he owned fewer than ten. With them he had Lekapenos' epics, a few codices of history, a couple on natural philosophy, a treatise on horsemanship, another on war, a school set of Sithonian plays (many of them crumbs from Lekapenos' banquet)—and that was all. So much knowledge stored away in volumes he would never see, let alone own . . . thinking of his own ignorance saddened him.

He went through the grimoires one after another, looking for a spell that would let him see either who had taken Duren or where his son was now. He found a fair number of them, but had to dismiss most out of hand. Some were beyond his limited abilities as a mage. Some required ingredients he could not hope to obtain: dried sea-cow flipper from the Greater Inner Sea, for instance.

And too many needed wine. Even if it hadn't been unavailable, he would have been afraid to use it. The last thing he wanted was to attract the angry notice of Mavrix.

"I wonder if ale would do?" he muttered, running a finger down the closely written column of a cantrip that looked promising except for prescribing a silver bowl full of wine as the scrying medium.

A sentence near the end of the spell leaped out at him: *Whereas the aspect of Baivers god of barley is dull, sodden, and soporific, whilst that of Mavrix lord of the sweet grape (to whom the cry of* Evoii! *rings out) sparkles with wit and intelligence, the ill-advised operator who seeks to substitute ale for wine will surely have cause to regret his stupidity.*

"It was only an idea," the Fox said, as if talking things over with the author of the grimoire. That author was a Sithonian; though the Fox's copy was an Elabonian translation, he'd already found several scornful references to the westerners who had conquered and then been all but conquered by the more anciently civilized land, and equally short shrift given to other Elabonian gods.

Gerin plucked at his beard as he thought. Substituting butter for olive oil had worked out well enough. No matter what this snooty Sithonian said, using ale in place of wine could also succeed. And he was and always had been on good terms with Baivers. He picked up the grimoire, saying, "I'll try it."

He had a silver bowl; it had been at Fox Keep since his grandfather's day. He'd been thinking about melting it down along with the rest of the odd bits of silver in the keep and starting his own coinage. Now he was glad he'd never got round to doing that. And ale, of course, was easy to come by.

He took the bowl and a pitcher of the strongest brew in his cellar out to the shack where he essayed his magics. Before he began the conjuration, he took a while studying the text of the spell, making sure he could slip in Baivers' name and standard epithets for those of Mavrix. He nodded to himself: that ought to work. He didn't think he'd need to modify any of the mystical passes that accompanied the charm.

"I bless thee, Baivers, god of clear sight, and call upon thee: lift the darkness of night," he intoned, and poured the silver bowl half full of golden ale. He smiled a little when he thought of that; mixing gold and silver, even symbolically, ought to make the spell work better.

As often happened, the sound of his chanting drew Rihwin, who stood in the doorway to see what he was up to. Gerin nodded to him and set a finger to his lips to enjoin silence. Rihwin nodded back; he knew a man working magic did not need and sometimes could not tolerate distraction.

Again, the wizard who had written the grimoire made

the operator perform the more difficult passes with his left hand. Again, Gerin gratefully accepted that, because it made the spell easier for him. Soon, he thought, the ale would turn clear as crystal and he would be rewarded with a glimpse of Duren's face, or at least of his surroundings.

He caught himself yawning in the middle of the spell. *What's wrong?* he thought. He couldn't say it aloud; he was in the middle of the chant. As if from very far away, he watched his sorcerous passes grow languid, listened to his voice turn fuzzy. . . .

"Lord prince! Lord Gerin!"

With a great effort, the Fox opened his eyes. Anxious faces crowding close blocked light from the smoking torches that lit the great hall. Gerin's eyebrows came down and together—last he remembered, he hadn't been in the great hall, and torchlighting was hours away.

"What happened?" he croaked. He discovered he was lying in the rushes on the floor. When he tried to sit up, he felt as if he'd forgotten how to use half his muscles.

Among the faces peering down at him was Rihwin's. "Would that you could tell us, lord Gerin," the southerner answered. "You fell asleep, or perhaps your spirit left your body—however you would have it—in the middle of the spell you were using. We've tried from that time to this to rouse you, but to no avail till now."

"Aye, that's the way of it," Drago agreed. "We didn't know what in the five hells to do next—stick your foot in the fire, maybe."

"I'm glad it didn't come to that," Gerin said. From Rihwin, the suggestion might have been a joke. Drago, though, had neither the wit nor the temperament for jokes. When he said something, he meant it.

That odd, unstrung feeling was fading. Gerin managed to get to his feet. Van, ever practical, gave him a jack of ale. "It's not enchanted, Captain, but it's pretty good," he said.

Gerin gulped down half the jack before he choked and spluttered. "That's it," he said. "That's what went wrong. This time, the chap who wrote the grimoire was smarter than I am. He warned that Baivers' influence on the spell was soporific, and that's just what he meant."

"The Elabonian pantheon is so dismayingly stodgy," Rihwin said. Like many of his educated countrymen, he preferred the Sithonian gods to those native to Elabon.

But Van said, "Honh! Remember how much joy you had of Mavrix." Rihwin flinched but was honest enough with himself to nod, acknowledging the justice of the hit.

"Never mind any of that," Gerin said; his wits were beginning to work more clearly again, and his body to seem as if it might be fully answerable to him after all. "I've learned something from this escapade, which may in the long run make it worthwhile."

"What's that?" Van asked, a beat ahead of the rest.

"That whatever magic I can do isn't going to let me find my son. And find him I will." Gerin counted stubbornness a virtue. If you kept hitting at a problem, sooner or later it was likely to fall down. He went on, "Using ale for wine in the spell might have knocked me out, but, by Dyaus, there are eyes that never sleep."

"Not by Dyaus," Drago said. "By Biton, you mean, or do I mistake you?"

"No, you have the right of it," Gerin said. "I'll fare forth to the Sibyl at Ikos. Her verse will tell me what I need to know." He hesitated, then added, "If I can understand it, of course."

III

After the Empire of Elabon conquered the land between the High Kirs and the Niffet, the Elabonians pushed an all-weather highway, the Elabon Way, north from the town of Cassat to the river so they would always be able to move troops against invaders or rebels.

No large numbers of imperial troops had been seen in the northlands for generations before Elabon severed itself from its province north of the Kirs, but the highway remained: far and away the best land link the northlands boasted. Even barons who did little else maintained the stretch of the Elabon Way that ran through their territory: if for no other reason than to make sure they collected tolls from travelers along the road.

"Hard on the horses' hooves," Van remarked as the wagon rumbled onto the flag-paved roadbed.

"So it is," Gerin said. "Nothing to be done about it, though, unless you want to throw away the road whenever it rains for more than two days straight. Getting a wagon through hub-deep mud isn't much fun."

"Can't argue with that," Van agreed. "Still, we don't want the animals lamed or stonebruised, either."

"No. Well, we won't push them hard, not when it's a five days' run to Ikos," Gerin said. "As a matter of fact, the horses aren't what worries me most."

"You always have something to worry about—you'd be worried if you didn't," Van said. "What is it this time?"

"Ricolf the Red's would be a logical place to stop for the third night," the Fox answered. "Or it would have been the logical place—" His voice trailed away.

"—if Ricolf weren't Elise's father. If Elise hadn't up and left you," Van finished for him. "Aye, that does complicate your life, doesn't it?"

"You might say so," Gerin agreed dryly. "Ricolf's not my vassal. When Elise was with me, there seemed no need, and afterwards I hadn't the crust to ask it of him. Nor has he ever sought my protection; he's done well enough on his own. When Elise was with me, I had a claim on his keep once he died. Now that she's gone, I suppose Duren is the rightful heir: she's Ricolf's only legitimate child, and none of his bastard sons lived."

"Which means Duren is Ricolf's only grandson, too," Van said. "He'll need to know about the boy disappearing. Or let me put it another way—he'd have cause to quarrel with you if you rode by without saying so much as a word."

Gerin sighed. "I hadn't thought about it quite like that, but I fear you're right. I'm his guest-friend from years gone by, but it'll be bloody awkward just the same. He thinks Elise never would have run off if I'd done . . . Dyaus, if I'd known what I should have done, I'd have done it. He won't think better of me for letting Duren be kidnapped, either."

"Captain, you feel bad enough about that all by yourself—you won't hardly notice anyone else piling on a little more."

"Only you would think of making me feel better by reminding me how bad I feel now." The method was, Gerin admitted to himself, nicely calculated to suit his own gloomy nature.

Sitting beside him on the wagon's bench, Van stretched and looked about with an almost childlike delight. "Good to be out on the road again," he said. "Fox Keep's all very well, but I like having new things to see every minute or every bend in the road—not that the Elabon Way had many bends in it, but you take my meaning."

"So I do." The Fox looked eastward. Quick-moving Tiwaz, now a day past first quarter, had raced close to Nothos, whose pale gibbous disk was just rising over the tree-covered hills. He shook his head. Just as Tiwaz gained on Nothos, so troubles seemed to gain on him with every day that passed, and his own pace was too slow to escape them.

"There's a pleasant thought," Van said when he spoke his conceit aloud. "Tell you what, Fox: instead of sleeping in the open tonight, what say we rest at the next serf village we come upon? They'll have ale there, and you'll be better for drinking yourself drunk and starting off tomorrow with a head that thumps like a drum. Then at least you'll know what ails you."

"I know what ails me now," Gerin said: "Duren's missing. What I don't know is what to do about it, and that eats at me as much as his being gone." Nevertheless, he went on reflectively, "Headman at the next village south is Tervagant Beekeeper. His ale doesn't have the worst name in the lands I hold."

Van slapped him on the back, nearly hard enough to tumble him out of the wagon. "The very thing. Trust me, Captain, you'll be better for a good carouse."

"That's what Rihwin thought, and he ended up with his robe round his ears and his pecker flapping in the breeze."

Even so, the Fox reined in when they rolled up to Tervagant's village. The headman, a nervous little fellow who kept kneading the front of his tunic with both hands as if it were bread dough, greeted the arrival of his overlord with ill-concealed alarm. "W-what brings you so far south, l-lord prince?" he asked.

"My son's been stolen," Gerin answered flatly. Tervagant's eyes widened. The news, the Fox saw, had not reached the village till this moment. He set it forth for the headman and the crowd of listeners—mostly women and children, for the men still labored in the fields—who gathered round the wagon.

"Lord prince, I pray the gods give you back your boy," Tervagant said. Everyone else echoed his words; noble and peasant shared the anguish a missing child brought. The headman's hands fell away from his tunic. His face, which had been pasty, gained color. *Another one who's glad I'm not looking into his affairs*, Gerin thought. He wondered just how many village headmen had little schemes of their own in play. One of these days, he'd have to try to find out.

Not today, though. Tervagant ducked into his hut, came out with a ram's-horn trumpet. He glanced at Gerin for permission before he raised it to his lips. The Fox nodded. Tervagant blew a long, unmusical blast. Some of the peasants looked up from their work in surprise: the sun was low in the west, but not yet brushing the horizon. The men came in happily enough, though.

"Shall we kill a pig, lord prince?" the headman asked.

"Aye, if you can without hurting yourselves," Gerin answered. The thought of fat-rich pork made spit rush into his mouth. He added, "The blood from the beast will give the ghosts what they want, too."

"Some of the blood," Tervagant corrected thriftily. "The rest we'll make into blood pudding." In good times, serfs lived close to the edge. In bad times, they—and the nobles they supported—fell over it. They could afford to waste nothing.

The pig, like any other, was half wild, with a ridge of hair down its back. Tervagant lured it to him with a turnip, then cut its throat. He had to spring back to keep it from tearing him with its tushes. Blood sprayed every which way as the beast ran through the village until it fell over and lay kicking.

"That'll keep the ghosts happier than if the blood went into a nice, neat trench," Van said.

The fire the villagers made was big enough to hold a fair number of ghosts away by itself. They butchered the pig, baked some of it in clay, and roasted the rest. Living up to his ekename, Tervagant went into his hut, came out with a pot full of honey, and glazed some of the cooking meat with it. The delicious aroma made Gerin hungrier than he had been before.

Along with bread, ale, and berries preserved in more of Tervagant's honey, the pork proved as good as it smelled. A sizable pile of rib bones lay in front of Gerin when he thumped his belly and pronounced himself full. Van had found a pointed rock and was cracking a leg bone to get at the marrow.

"More ale, lord prince?" one of the peasant women asked.

"Thank you." He held out the cup they'd given him. She smiled as she filled it for him. She was, he noticed, not bad-looking, with light eyes that told of a Trokmê or two in the woodpile. She wore her hair long and unbraided, which meant she was unmarried, yet she was no giggling maid.

When he asked her about that, her face clouded. "I had a husband, lord prince, you're right, I did, but he died of lockjaw year before last."

"I'm sorry," Gerin said, and meant it—he'd seen lockjaw. "That's a hard way to go."

"Aye, lord prince, it is, but you have to go on," she said.

He nodded solemnly; he'd had quite a bit of ale by then. "What's your name?" he asked her.

"Ethelinda, lord prince."

"Well, Ethelinda," he said, and let it hang there. Now she nodded, as if he'd spoken a complete sentence.

After supper, Tervagant waved Gerin and Van into a couple of huts whose inhabitants had hastily vacated them. "The gods grant you good night, lord prince, master Van," he said.

"Me, I intend to give the gods some help," Van said. While he'd been sitting by the fire and eating, a couple of young women had almost come to blows over him. Now he led both of them into the hut Tervagant had given him. Watching that, Gerin shook his head. Too bad no one could find a way to put into a jar whatever the outlander had.

And yet the Fox was not altogether surprised to find Ethelinda at his elbow when he went into the hut the headman had set aside for him. "You've no new sweetheart?" he asked her. Some lords took peasant women without thinking past their own pleasure. Along with hunger, though, that was the sort of thing liable to touch off an uprising. As usual, Gerin was careful.

But Ethelinda shook her head. "No, lord prince."

"Good." Gerin had to duck his head to get into the hut. It was dark inside, and smelled strongly of smoke. He shuffled in, found a straw-filled pallet with his foot. "Here we are."

The straw rustled as he sank down onto it, then again when Ethelinda joined him there. She pulled her long tunic off over her head; that was all she wore. Gerin took a little longer getting out of his clothes, but not much. By the way she clung to him, he guessed she'd been telling the truth about having no sweetheart; he didn't think anyone had touched her so for a long time.

That made him take care to give her as much pleasure as he could. And, at the last moment, he pulled out and spurted his seed onto her belly rather than deep inside her. He thought he would make her grateful, but she said, "What did you go and do that for?" in anything but a happy voice.

"To keep you from making a baby," he answered, wondering if she'd made the connection between what they'd just done and what might happen most of a year later. Every time he thought he had the measure of serfs' ignorance, he ended up being startled anew.

Ethelinda knew that connection, though. "I wanted to start a baby," she said. "I hoped I would."

"You did?" Gerin rolled off her and almost fell off the narrow pallet. "Why?"

"If I was carrying your baby, I could go up to Fox Keep and you'd take care of me," she answered. "I wouldn't have to work hard, at least for a while."

"Oh." Gerin stared through the darkness at her. She was honest, anyhow. And, he admitted to himself, she was probably right. No woman had ever claimed he'd put a bastard in her; he was moderate in his venery and, to keep such things from happening, often withdrew at the instant he spent. But he would not have turned away anyone with whom he'd slept.

Maybe you shouldn't have pulled out, the darker side of him murmured. *With Duren gone, you're liable to need an heir, even if he is a bastard.*

He shook his head. Sometimes he got trapped in his own gloom and lost track of what needed doing. He couldn't let that happen, not now. His son depended on him.

Ethelinda sat up and reached for her tunic. "Do you want me to go away, lord prince?" she asked.

"We'll be crowded on this bed, but stay if you care to," Gerin answered. "The night's not so warm that we'd be sticking to each other wherever we touched."

"That's so," she agreed. "I always did like having somebody in a bed with me. That's how I grew up, with all my brothers and sisters and my father and my mother while she was alive, all packed tight together. Sleeping just by yourself is lonely." She tossed the tunic to the dirt floor. "And besides, who knows what might happen later on?"

What happened was that Gerin slept the night through and didn't wake up till after sunrise, when Ethelinda rose from the pallet and finally did put her tunic back on. When she saw his eyes open, she gave him a scornful glance, as if to say, *Some stallion you turned out to be.*

He bore up under that without getting upset; unlike Van, he didn't wear some of his vanity in his trousers. He looked around the peasant hut for a chamber pot. When he didn't see one, he got up, dressed quickly, and went off into the bushes by the village to relieve himself. The reek that rose from those bushes said he was but following the peasants' practice.

When he came back, Van was standing outside the hut he'd been given, tweedling away on his flute. The two women who'd gone in there with him both clung to him adoringly. His grin was smug. The Fox felt like throwing something at him, but contented himself with saying, "Time we got moving. We can eat as we travel."

"As you will." Van walked over to the horses, which were tethered to the low branches of a maple. "You harness the leader, then, and I'll see to the off beast. You're so hot to be on the road, the two of us together'll get us on our way in a hurry."

That afternoon, the wagon rolled into the holding of Palin the Eagle. Palin, who had Trokmoi on his western flank, acknowledged Gerin as his suzerain and, because he'd needed the Fox's help more than once against the woodsrunners, was more sincere about his submission than Schild Stoutstaff.

Not far into Palin's land, Gerin and Van came upon a belt of devastation: for several miles, the Elabon Way and the land to either side of it had been cratered by Balamung's destructive sorcery. Now that weeds and shrubs had had five years to spread over the craters, they looked less raw and hideous than they had when they were new, but the ground remained too broken for farmers to work.

The Elabon Way itself was in fair repair. That was at Gerin's order; he did not want the main road south from Fox Keep to remain a ruin. The repairs, he knew, did not come up to the standard the Elabonian Empire had set when it pushed the highway north to the Niffet. With the resources of a realm behind them, the imperial artisans had built to last, with a deep bed of gravel and stone, stone flags cemented together, and good drainage to either side of the roadway.

With peasant levies working in time snatched from their fields, the Fox hadn't had a prayer of matching such construction. Cobblestones and gravel did give the rebuilt stretch of the Elabon Way a surface that, while it was hard on hooves, did not turn into gluey mud whenever rain fell.

"Strange," Gerin said as the wagon jounced along over the uneven surface: "Whenever I travel this stretch of road, I remember trying to fight my way north over it just before the werenight."

"You're not likely to forget that," Van agreed. "Me, I find it strange to travel the same stretch of road more than once. I'm too used to seeing something new every day to be easy with the idea of going back and forth, back and forth. Boring to see the same hills on the skyline every day. I want to find out what's on the other side of them."

"Those hills?" Gerin pointed west. "They shelter Trokmoi and bandits."

"Not what I meant," Van said. "Captain, you've no poetry in you, and that's a fact."

"I suppose not. I do the best I can without it, that's all."

Toward evening, they passed the keep of Raff the Ready, where they'd guested on their last trip south to Ikos. No guesting at Raff's tonight; the keep had fallen to the Trokmoi, and nothing but tumbled ruins remained. Gerin shook his head, remembering the fine meal Raff had fed him. Tonight it would be hard bread and sausage and sour beer and whatever they managed to hunt up to keep the ghosts happy.

A red fox scurried across the road in front of the wagon. It paused by a clump of hound's-tongue, sitting up on its haunches with its own tongue lolling out as it watched the horses and men. Van tapped Gerin on the shoulder. "Rein in. Let me grab the bow and we'll have our evening's offering."

"What? Where?" Gerin said.

Van pointed to the fox. "Right there. Are you blind, not to see it?"

Gerin stared, first at the fox, then at his friend. "You're enough like a brother to me that I often forget you're not Elabonian born. It's not our custom to kill the animals that give us our ekenames. All my luck, such as it is, would run away if I tried to slay a fox."

"You wouldn't," Van said. "I would."

"I'd be abetting you." Gerin shook his head. "In the spirit world, it would count for the other."

"The spirit world will do more than count if we don't find something with blood in it pretty soon," Van grumbled. "Looks like all the peasants hereabout have fled, and a night in the open with only a fire to hold the ghosts at bay is nothing to look forward to."

"Something will turn up." Gerin sounded more confident than he felt. But hardly more than a minute after he'd spoken, he spotted a big, fat gray squirrel sitting on the topmost branch of an oak sapling that really should have been cleared away from the side of the road. Now he did rein in. Van had seen the squirrel, too; he was already reaching into the back of the wagon for the bow.

The bowstring thrummed as he let fly. The squirrel toppled out of the little tree and lay feebly kicking on the mossy ground below. It had stopped moving by the time Van walked over and picked it up. He hefted it in his hand. "It should serve," he said.

"Not a whole lot of meat, but what there is will be tasty baked in clay," Gerin said. "If you'd shot at the fox, the gods might not have put the squirrel in our path."

"If they're so grateful for me being good, why didn't they put a nice fat buck in that tree instead of a rat with a fuzzy tail that won't give us two good bites apiece?"

"Abandoned scoffer," Gerin said, though he had to fight to get words past the laughter that welled up when he pictured an antlered stag perched atop a sapling. "Show some respect for the gods of Elabon."

"I give them as much as they deserve and not a bit more," Van said. "I've done enough traveling, seen enough gods to know they're stronger than I am, but I'll be switched if I can see that some of 'em are a whole lot smarter than I am."

Gerin grunted, remembering Mavrix's long, pink tongue flicking out like a frog as the deity had mocked him and taken away Rihwin's sorcerous ability. "You may have something there, though you'll not be happier for it if some god hears what you've said."

"Ifsobe that happens, I'll just go on to someplace else

where the writ of Elabonian gods doesn't run," Van said. "The thing about gods is, they're tied to the lands of those that worship them, and me"—he thumped his chest—"I'm not."

"Just like you to be so sure you'd get away," Gerin said, but then something else occurred to him. "Gods can travel, though, as their worshipers do—look at the way the Sithonian deities have taken hold in Elabon. And, I fear, we'll have Trokmê gods rooting themselves here in the northlands now that the woodsrunners have made homes south of the Niffet."

"You're likely right; I hadn't thought of that," Van said. "Not a crew I'd be happy with as neighbors: their yen for blood is as bad as the one the Trokmoi have themselves. I should know; the woodsrunners were all set to offer me up till I got free of them."

"Yes, you've told that tale," Gerin said. He shook his head. "One more thing to worry about." Trouble was, he seemed to add to that list almost every day. He halted the wagon. As long as he and Van had an offering for the ghosts for tonight, he wouldn't worry about any of the things on that list till tomorrow.

Splitting the night into two watches rather than three left the Fox and Van yawning as they started traveling a little past sunrise. "I'm slower than I should be, and that's not good," Gerin said. "When we cross Bevon Broken-Nose's holding, we'll need all our wits about us."

"Bevon Broken-Land would be a better name for him, that's certain," Van said.

"Can't argue with you there," Gerin replied. Bevon's sons had been squabbling over their father's holding five years before. Bevon himself was still alive, but universally ignored beyond a bowshot from his keep.

Gerin pointed ahead. "There we are. That's progress, if you like."

"Your fort, you mean? Aye, I expect so. It's about the only thing that keeps the Elabon Way open through Bevon's lands, anyhow."

Despite a wooden palisade, the building wasn't a keep in the proper sense of the word: no stone castle sat inside the wall, only a blockhouse also of wood. Gerin had run up the fort and put a garrison in it less than a year after the werenight, to make sure the road stayed clear. Bevon and all four of his sons had protested furiously, but couldn't unite even to get rid of the Fox's men.

"One day soon, Captain, you'll just quietly claim the land along the road as part of your own holding, won't you?" Van said. "Without your patrols, it'd be the howling wilderness it was before you put your men here—and it's like you to let the facts talk before you open your mouth yourself."

"That has been in my mind lately, as a matter of fact." Gerin gave his friend a look half respectful, half annoyed. "I like it better when no one else can pick out what's in my mind."

"Live in a keep for a while with a man and he will rub off on you." Van added, "However much he doesn't care to," in the hope—which was realized—of making Gerin scowl.

A three-chariot patrol team came north up the Elabon Way toward the fort. Seeing the wagon, they made for it instead, to see who was on the road. Gerin waved to one of the men in the lead car. "Hail!" he called loudly. "How fares the road, Onsumer?"

"Lord Gerin!" the bulky, black-bearded man called back. "I thought that was your wagon, though I'm just now close enough to be sure. We had a quiet run down to Ricolf's border and back, so the road is well enough." His face clouded. "But what of you? Is this the business Widin Simrin's son spoke of?"

"My son being stolen, you mean? Yes," Gerin said. "All my searches went awry, those after the men who might have taken him and the one round Fox Keep as well. I'm off to Ikos, to learn if the Sibyl can see farther than I did."

"Dyaus and Biton grant it be so," Onsumer said. The driver and warrior who shared the car with him nodded vigorously.

"I can but hope," Gerin said. "Widin told me he learned nothing new on his run down here. Have you had word of anything unusual from Bevon's sons? One of them, I suppose, could have arranged to kidnap Duren, though I'd not have thought any of them had the wit to plan such a thing."

Onsumer shook his head. "No, lord Gerin, nothing of the sort. I think the lot of them are too busy trying to slaughter one another to worry about outsiders, even ones they hate. We haven't had an attack on the fort in close to a year, but the strife among the brothers never ends."

"You're probably right," Gerin said. "All the barons in the northlands squabbled among themselves and didn't pay heed to the Trokmoi till it was too late. I wonder if we Elabonians learned the joys of faction fighting from Sithonia."

"I wouldn't have the faintest idea about that," Onsumer said. He was a good enough soldier, and far from stupid, but all he knew of the wider world he'd heard in minstrels' songs.

He got the horses moving again. "Good luck to you," Onsumer called as the wagon rolled by. His comrades waved to Gerin. Then they turned around and headed back toward the fort.

An hour or so later, Van pointed to a column of black smoke rising in the distance. "Somebody's burning his neighbor out there, or I miss my guess."

"Better they battle each other than my men," Gerin said, "but better still if they didn't battle at all."

"Honh! What are the odds of that?"

"On the face of it, not good," Gerin admitted. "Still, it used to happen. Elabon, not so long ago, was a single empire stretching from the Niffet east past the Lesser Inner Sea into the seething river plains of Kizzuwatna. Now it's falling apart. When the Emperor and his court think more of putting gold in their own belt pouches now than worrying about where the Empire will be a generation hence, that happens."

"It's not just the ones at the top," Van said. "It's everyone who's strong, out to get rich off the ones who aren't and to put a fist in his strong neighbor's eye."

"Aye, that's the way of it," Gerin said. "In the early days, they say, Elabonian warlords would go back to the plow once they'd won a war." He grinned wryly. "Of course, who knows what tales of those early days are worth?"

Near the southern edge of Bevon's unhappy holding lay another belt of devastation from Balamung's sorcery. As before, the wagon bounced roughly over the equally rough repairs Gerin had had the local peasants make. Van said, "Remember how Bevon's sons tried to stop you from fixing the road, each of them screaming he'd do it himself?"

"Oh, yes." The Fox's laugh was less than mirthful. "And if I'd waited for that, I'd be waiting still, and so would Duren's grandson."

When Gerin had come into Ricolf the Red's holding five years before, only a couple of guards kept watch at the border. Now a fort like the one he'd built on Bevon's land stood strong to keep out bandits—and perhaps to keep out his own men as well. The thought saddened him.

A guardsman strode out from the open gateway of the fort to ask his business. The fellow started slightly when he recognized Gerin and Van. Gerin started slightly, too; he had no idea what this warrior's name was, but he'd been at the border on that other journey, too. The Fox remembered those first days when he'd known Elise and snuck her out of her father's keep as vividly as if they were just past. Now that only ashes lay between him and her, he often wished he could forget. Somehow that only made him remember more intensely.

"Lord prince," Ricolf's man said, his voice polite but wary. "What brings you to the holding of Ricolf the Red? Is it the matter your vassal—what was his name?—spoke of some days past?"

"Widin Simrin's son," Gerin supplied. "Yes, it has to do with my son—Ricolf's grandson. We've had no luck finding him—I'm for the Sibyl at Ikos, to see if Biton will grant her sight of where the boy might be."

"May it prove so," the guard said. "Since it's but you and your comrade here, and no host in arms behind you, pass on, lord prince."

"No host in arms behind me?" Gerin said angrily. "Does Ricolf look for one? I've no quarrel with him, but I may, by Dyaus, if he keeps thinking that way."

"You had no quarrel with Bevon, either, yet your men stay on his land against his will. We don't want that happening here."

"Ricolf ought to get down on his knees and thank me for that," Gerin ground out. "If my men didn't keep order along the Elabon Way, you'd have more trouble spilling into this holding than you dream of. But Ricolf keeps his own house quiet, and needs no help from me."

"Just pass on," the guard said.

Gerin flicked the reins so violently, the horses sprang forward with startled snorts. Van said, "A good thing we're away. I thought you were going to jump down and murder that fellow."

"For a counterfeit copper, I would have." Gerin rubbed at the scar over his eye. He was sure it was white now; it always went dead pale when he got furious. "Worst of it is, the fool's only echoing what Ricolf says."

"Would you sooner we didn't stop of Ricolf's holding, then?" Van asked.

"Now that you mention it, yes." But the Fox sighed. "Has to be done, though—as you say, Duren's his grandson, after all. I expect I'll get through it. I wouldn't show my face in his holding if I thought he seriously meant me harm— not without that host in arms behind me, anyhow."

"The gods grant it doesn't come to that."

"Yes." Gerin wasn't thinking of the gods alone. If he ever did have to take on Ricolf, his former father-in-law was only too likely to call on Aragis the Archer for aid. Having Aragis extend his power northward was the last thing Gerin wanted. For that reason as well as for Duren's sake, he'd speak softly to the older baron. So he told himself, anyhow.

The sun tinged the western sky with colors like the belly of a salmon. Gerin imagined he felt the ghosts stir, though they would not truly emerge until after sunset. And from the castle ahead came a boy's cry from the watchtower: "Who comes to the holding of Ricolf the Red?"

All was so much as it had been five years before that the hair on Gerin's arms tried to prickle up. He felt himself caught in time, like an insect in the sticky sap of a pine tree. Insects so stuck rarely got loose. The Fox knew the trouble here lay in his own mind, but knowing did little to help him get free, either.

He shouted back toward the keep, giving his own name and Van's—just as he had then. But then Ricolf had been eager to let him in; they'd become friends on Gerin's earlier journeys south. Now? Who could say what Ricolf thought now?

Whatever it was, the drawbridge lowered, thick bronze chains rattling and squealing over the spokes of the winch as the gate crew turned it. The horses' hooves drummed like thunder when they walked across the timbers over the moat. Water plants added touches of green there, but the smell said that Ricolf's men used the barrier to empty their slop jars.

Ricolf the Red stood in the bailey near the gate, waiting to greet Gerin. He was a broad-shouldered, thick-bellied man heading toward sixty, his manner still vigorous and his hair still thick, though now mostly white rather than the Trokmê-like shade that had given him his sobriquet. When he opened his mouth to speak, Gerin saw he'd lost a front tooth since the last time they'd met.

"Guest-friendship is a sacred trust," Ricolf said, his deep voice younger than his years. "With that trust in mind, I greet you, Fox, and you also, Van of the Strong Arm. Use my keep as your own while you stay here."

"You are gracious as always," Gerin said. Ricolf hadn't sounded particularly gracious; he sounded more like a man doing a duty he didn't much care for. Gerin thought more of him for that, not less. Sometimes his own sense of duty was all that kept him going.

"Pah! This for graciousness." Ricolf kicked at the dirt. "I hear something's amiss with my grandson, and I want to know everything there is to know about it. First Elise, now Duren—" He shook his big, hard-featured head. "I wasn't the luckiest man born, to link my family to you."

"That's not what you thought when you gave me your daughter," Gerin answered as steadily as he could; as always, anger and longing surged in him when Elise came to the front of his mind. He went on, "The gods know I am not a perfect man. Will you entertain the notion that Elise may not have been a perfect woman?"

"The notion does not entertain me." Ricolf kicked at the dirt again. "Well, we'll speak of that later. What's your pleasure for supper? We killed a sheep this afternoon, so there's mutton, or we can chop a couple of hens down to size if the two of you would rather."

"Mutton," Gerin and Van said in the same breath. The Fox added, "We've been traveling a good deal these past few days, and mostly supping on the fowls we've killed as blood-offerings for the ghosts."

"Thought as much," Ricolf answered, "but I figured I owed you the choice." He was indeed meticulous in observing the rituals of guest-friendship.

Inside Ricolf's great hall, fat-wrapped bones smoked on Dyaus' altar. At the cookfire, servants roasted ribs and chops. A big bronze pot boiled busily above it. Van stabbed a finger toward it. "That'll be the tongue and tripe, the lungs and lights?" he asked.

"Aye," Ricolf said. "Which of the dainties do you care for most?"

"The tongue," the outlander answered at once. "Have you got any rock salt to scatter on it?"

"I do that," Ricolf answered, a Trokmê turn of phrase he probably would not have used before he got woodsrunners for neighbors. "The holding has several good licks, one of them near big enough to mine salt from."

Had Ricolf's holding been Gerin's, he suspected he would have mined salt and sold it to his neighbors. The only concern Ricolf had beyond his own borders was foes who might come at him. Past that, he was content with his land as he found it. Gerin wondered if he himself would ever be content with anything.

Bread and ale and meat distracted him from such worries. He gnawed roasted mutton from ribs, then tossed them to the dogs. Tripe was slippery and gluey under his knife, chewy in his mouth. The kidneys' strong smell cut through the smoke that filled the hall and foretold their flavor.

He stuffed himself full, but Van outdid him. Ricolf watched the outlander with awe tinged by alarm. He said, "Dyaus, I'd forgotten how you put it away. You could eat a man out of his barony."

"There's a deal of me to keep fed," Van replied with dignity. "Would you pass me the pitcher of ale? Ah, thank you, you're very kind." He poured from the pitcher into a delicately carved rhyton, part of the great stock of southron goods Ricolf had laid on to impress the band of suitors for Elise's hand. Elise was gone. The drinking horns, the even more elaborately carved bathtub, and other such things remained, and probably lacerated Ricolf's spirit whenever he saw or used them.

Van poured the horn of ale down his throat, hardly seeming to swallow. He filled it again, drained it with the same ease. By the look Ricolf gave him, the older man expected him to slide under the table at any moment. Instead, he got up and spoke softly to one of the young women who'd fetched food. Gerin listened to her giggle and was not surprised when, a little later, she and the outlander went upstairs together.

The Fox wished he could have gone upstairs, too, even alone, but Ricolf's eyes held him. The white-haired baron said, "Your harvests must have been good in spite of everything, or you'd not be able to afford to keep him around."

"I don't begrudge him his appetites," Gerin answered. "Not any of them. The rest of his spirit is in proportion."

"As may be, as may be." But Van was not what Ricolf wanted to talk about, and Gerin knew it. Ricolf stared down at his own drinking horn for a while before he went on, "Well, Fox, what in the five hells happened?"

"With Duren, you mean? You've heard everything I know about that," Gerin answered. "Someone snatched the boy, and when I find out who he was, he'll be sorry for the day his father woke up with a stiff one in his breeches."

"Oh, no doubt." Ricolf drank, smacked his lips, brought his fist down onto the table. "You'll track the whoreson down and make him pay. You're bloody good at all that sort of thing. Prince of the North these days, are you? I'll not deny you've earned the title. You hold more land—or control it, which amounts to the same think—than anyone else in the northlands save maybe Aragis and one or two of the cursed Trokmoi, and you run it better, too."

"You're generous." The Fox also took a pull at his ale. He could feel it buzzing inside his head. Maybe that was what made him burst out, "I wish I were shut of the whole business, and just left to be what I'd like."

"So do we all," Ricolf said. "But you do it well, like it or no. Which brings me to what I'd truly learn: how was it you didn't do as well by Elise?"

Gerin wished he were drunk enough to fall asleep—or a good enough mime to pretend he was that drunk. But he wasn't, not either one—and he knew he owed Ricolf an answer. He drank some more, as much to give himself time to think as for any other reason. Ricolf waited, patient and stubbornly unmoving as a boulder.

"I suppose part of it was that her life at Fox Keep wasn't as different as she'd hoped from what she had here," Gerin said slowly. He snorted air out through his nose. Wherever Elise was now, she'd surely found a different life. Whether it was better was a different question altogether.

"Go on," Ricolf said.

"You know what the first flush of passion is like," Gerin said. "It masks everything bad or even boring about whomever it lights on. After a while, though, you can wake up and realize this isn't what you had in mind. I—suppose that's what Elise did."

"None of it your fault, eh?" Ricolf's rumbling baritone flung sarcasm as a catapult flung stones.

"I didn't say that," Gerin answered. "Looking back, I guess I took a lot for granted. I figured everything was all right because she didn't complain out loud—and I've always been one who doesn't necessarily expect things to be perfect all the time, so I didn't worry so much when they weren't. I think perhaps Elise did after we fell in love, and when things got rocky, they looked worse to her than maybe they really were. If I'd realized that sooner . . . oh, who knows what I'd have done?"

Ricolf chewed on that with the air of a man finding something on his plate other than what he'd expected. Now he drank and thought a while before he spoke: "I respect that knack you have, Fox, for looking at yourself and talking about yourself as if you were someone else. Not many can do it."

"For this I thank you," Gerin said.

"Don't." Ricolf held up a big-knuckled hand. "The trouble with you is, you don't know how to do anything *but* stand back from yourself, and from everybody around you. You talked about how my daughter might have felt after passion cooled, but what about you? Did you go back into that keep inside your head, the one you mostly live in?"

"You shame me," Gerin said quietly.

"Why? For asking a question?"

"No, because the answer is so likely to be yes, and you know it very well." If sarcasm had stung, truth cut like a knife, the more so for being unexpected.

Ricolf yawned. "I'm getting old to sit around drinking half the night," he said. "Come to that, I'm getting old for anything else, too. Only a handful of serfs on this holding who were born before I was. One winter not so far from now lung sickness will get me, or I'll fall over with an apoplexy. That wouldn't be too bad—quick, anyhow."

"You're strong yet," Gerin said, alarmed for his host. Few men spoke so openly of death, lest a god be listening. "If you do go out, you'll go fighting."

"That could happen, too," Ricolf said. "I'm not as fast nor as strong as I was, and there's plenty of fighting around. And what becomes of the holding then? I'd hoped to last long enough to pass it on to Duren, but now—"

"Aye, but now," Gerin echoed. If Ricolf died heirless, his vassal barons would brawl over the holding, just as Bevon's sons had been doing for so long further north. And Ricolf's neighbors would be drawn in, Aragis coming up from the south, the Trokmoi from the west perhaps biting off a chunk . . . and the Fox did not see how he could stand aloof. He even had a claim of sorts to the barony.

As if picking that from his head, Ricolf said, "Aye, a couple of my vassals might think well of you because you were wed to Elise. More of 'em, though, are likely to think less of you because she ran off. And if she ever came back here wed to a man with a fighting tail of his own—"

Gerin upended his drinking horn, poured the last draft down his throat. That thought, or rather nightmare, had crossed is mind, too, most often of nights when he was having trouble sleeping. He said, "I have no notion how likely that is, nor what I'd do if it happened. A lot would depend on who and what the fellow was."

"On whether you thought you could use him, you mean." Ricolf spoke without rancor. He drained his own rhyton, then pushed to his feet. "I'm going up to bed. Do you want to come along, so I can show you the chamber I've set aside for you? The keep's not packed with suitors now; I don't have to give you one of the little rooms down here off the kitchens."

"I'll come," Gerin said, and rose, too. Ricolf carried a lamp as they went up the stairs. He didn't say anything. The Fox counted that something of a minor triumph. He'd been dreading this interview since the day Elise left him, and he seemed to have got through it.

Ricolf opened a door. As Gerin walked through it into the little bedchamber the lamplight revealed, the older man asked quietly, "Do you miss her?"

Another knife in the night. Gerin said, "Yes, now and then. Quite a lot, sometimes." He stepped into the room and shut the door before Ricolf could stab him with any more questions.

South of Ricolf's holding, the land grew debatable once more. Gerin and Van traveled in armor, the Fox keeping his bow ready to hand. The Elabon Way seemed all but deserted. That suited Gerin fine: the fewer people he saw, the fewer people who saw him. He knew too well how vulnerable the wagon was to a good-sized band of raiders.

The roads that ran into the Elabon Way from east and west were dirt tracks like the ones up in the Fox's holding. Pieces of the Elabon Way were just dirt here, too; peasants had prised up the paving stones for the houses, and maybe barons for their keeps, too. That hadn't been so the last time Gerin visited Ikos, five years before.

He said, "Taking stones from the roadway used to be a crime that would cost a man his head or put him up on a cross. A good law, if you ask me; roads are a land's life-blood."

"No law left up here but what comes from the edge of a sword," Van said. "Most lands are like that, when you get down to it."

"South of the High Kirs, Elabon isn't, or wasn't," Gerin said. "Law counted for more than might there, for a lot of years. It was even true here for a while. No more, though. You're not wrong about that."

They rolled slowly past another connecting road. At the crossroads stood a granite boulder carved with pictures showing where the road led: a crude keep surrounded by farms and horses. "That's not the one we want, eh, Captain?" Van said.

"No. We're looking for an eye with wings—that's Biton's mark. We're not far enough south to come to it yet, I don't think. I hope it will still be there; some of the crossroads stones I thought I remembered from my last trip to the Sibyl aren't here any more."

"You were paying attention to stones?" Van shook his head in disbelief. "Far as I could see, you were so busy panting over Elise, you didn't have eyes for anything else."

"Thank you, my friend. I needed that just now, I truly did," Gerin said. The visit with Ricolf had left him glum enough. If Van was going to rub salt in the wounds, they'd sting even worse.

But Van, perhaps mercifully, kept quiet after that. Like Gerin's, his eyes went back and forth, back and forth. Every time the wagon went by a clump of bushes or some elm saplings growing closer to the road than they should have, he shifted the reins to his left hand so he could grab his spear in a hurry if he needed it.

The Fox soon became certain some crossroads stones were missing: he and Van rolled past a hollow in the ground that showed where one had recently been removed—so recently the grass hadn't filled in all the bare dirt. "Someone's losing trade on account of that," he said sadly. "I wonder if he even knows."

About halfway between noon and sunset, Gerin spied the winged eye he sought. "I'd have guessed it'd be there," Van said. "You steal it, you're fooling with a god, and what man with a dram of sense does that?"

"How many men have sense?" Gerin returned, which made his comrade grunt. He added, "Not only that, how many are wise enough to realize they're stealing from Biton and not just from some petty lordlet?"

"They don't know beforehand, they'll find out pretty soon," Van said, which was likely enough to be true that Gerin had to nod. The farseeing god looked after what was his.

The wagon swung east down the road that led to the Sibyl and her fane. Gerin remembered the lands away from the Elabon Way as poorer than the baronies along the main north-south route. They didn't seem so now. That wasn't because they'd grown richer. Rather, the holdings along the chief highway had suffered more from the Trokmoi and from the nobles' squabbles among themselves.

When Elabon conquered and held the northlands, the road that bore the Empire's name had also been one of the chief routes along which colonists had settled. Farther from the Elabon Way, the folk native to the land were more in evidence. They were dark like Elabonians, but slimmer and more angular, their faces full of forehead and cheekbones.

Old customs lingered away from the highway, too. Lords' castles grew scarce; most of the peasant villages held freeholders, men who owed no part of their crop to a baron. Gerin wondered how they'd fared when Trokmê raiders swooped down on them: they had no lords to ride to their defense, either.

The freeholders measured him and Van with their eyes when the travelers paused in a village to buy a hen before evening caught them. "You're for the Sibyl, then?" asked the man who sold it to them. His Elabonian had a curious flavor to it, not quite an accent, but old-fashioned, as if currents of speech had swept up the Elabon Way, too, but never reached this little hamlet.

"That we are," Gerin answered.

"You've rich gear," the peasant observed. "Be you nobles?"

Van spoke first: "Me, I'm just a warrior. Anyone who tries taking this corselet off my back will find out what kind of warrior I am, and won't be happier for knowing, either."

"I can take care of myself, too," Gerin said. Peasants without lords had to defend themselves, which meant they needed weapons and armor. Robbing people who already had them seemed a likely way to acquire such.

If that was in the peasant's mind, he didn't let on (*but then, he wouldn't*, Gerin thought). He said, "Aye, the both of you have that look. Go on, then, and the gods watch over you through the night."

As soon as they were out of earshot, Gerin spoke to Van, who was driving: "Put as much space between that village and us as you can. If you find a side road just before sunset, go up it or down it a ways. We'll want to camp where we can hide our nightfire."

"Right you are," Van said. "I'd have done the same thing without your saying a word, mind, but I'm glad you have the same thoughts in mind as I do. On your watch, sleep with your bow, your sword, and your shield and helm where you can grab them in a hurry."

"If I thought I could, I'd sleep in armor tonight," the Fox said. Van grunted out a short burst of laughter and nodded.

They traveled until the ghosts began to wail in their ears. Then, setting his jaw, Gerin sacrificed the hen to calm the spirits. A boulder shielded the light of the fire from the little track down which they traveled to get off the main road to Ikos.

Gerin had the first watch. Nothos and Tiwaz stood close together, low in the east at sunset: both were approaching full, though swift-moving Tiwaz would reach it a couple of days sooner than Nothos. Math would not rise until almost halfway through his watch, and Van alone could commune with Elleb, for the ruddy moon would stay below the horizon till after midnight.

The Fox moved as far away from the fire and the blood-filled trench near it as the ghosts would allow: he wanted to be sure he could spot trouble coming down the road from the village where he'd bought the chicken. His bow was strung, his quiver on his back and ready for him to reach over his shoulder and pull out a bronze-tipped shaft.

Sure enough, just about the time when golden Math began peeping through the leaves of the trees, he heard men coming along the road from the west. They weren't trying very hard to keep quiet; they chattered among themselves as they ambled eastward.

They all carried torches, he saw when they came to the crossroads. Even so, the ghosts bothered them. One said, "This havering is fair to drive me mad. An we don't find them soon, I'm for my hut and my wife."

"Ah, but will she be for you in the middle of the night?" another asked. The lot of them laughed. They paused at the narrow track down which Gerin and Van had gone. A couple of them peered toward the Fox. He crouched lower behind the bush that concealed him, hoping the light of three moons would not betray him to the peasants. Maybe their own torchlight left them nightblind, for they did not spy him. After some muttered discussion, they kept heading east down the main road.

Perhaps half an hour later, they came straggling back. Now their torches were guttering toward extinction, and they hurried on toward their village. "Mayhap 'tis as well we found the whoresons not," one of them said; Gerin recognized the voice of the fellow who'd sold him the hen. "They'd have slain some or ever we overcame them."

"We need arms," somebody answered.

"Belike, but we need men to wield them, too," the hen-seller replied. "You were in the fields, and saw them not: a brace of proper rogues, ready for aught. We'd have given the ghosts our own blood had we broiled ourselves with them, I tell you."

As the peasants withdrew, the argument got too low-voiced for Gerin to follow. The peasant who'd sold him the chicken was right; he and Van would have sold their lives dear. Even so, he was nothing but glad the farmers or robbers or whatever they reckoned themselves to be hadn't found him and his comrade. No matter how dearly you sold your life, you could never buy it back.

The Fox drew back down the path toward his camp. He didn't think the locals would come out again, and he proved right. When Math had traveled a little more than halfway from the horizon to the meridian, he woke Van and told him what had passed.

"Expected as much," the outlander answered, setting his crimson-crested helm on his head and adjusting the cheekpieces. "They had that look to 'em, so they did. Not likely they'll be back, not so late in the night."

"No." Gerin got out of armor as Van donned it. "Wouldn't do to count on that, though."

"Hardly." Van's rumbling chuckle had next to no breath behind it. "Tell you something else, Captain: on the way home, we make sure we roll through this place around noontime, so we're none too close to it the night before or the night after."

"Can't argue with you." Gerin yawned enormously. "Haven't the wit to argue with anything right now, I just want to sleep. If I get killed while you're on watch, I'll never forgive you."

"Nor have the chance, either," Van said, chuckling again. Gerin crawled under the blanket, conceding him the last word.

He awoke unmurdered the next morning to the savory smell of toasting sausage. Van had built the fire up from embers and was improvising breakfast. The flames sputtered and hissed as grease dripped down into them. Gerin accepted a sharp stick with a length of hard sausage impaled on it, burned the roof of his mouth when he tried to take a bite while it was still too hot to eat, swore, and then did manage to get the meat down.

Van finished before he did, and harnessed the horses while he was getting into his cuirass and greaves. A jay perched on a branch of a spruce seedling screeched at the outlander all the while. He pointed at it. "You'd best be quiet—some lands I've been through, the folk reckon songbirds good eating." As if it understood him, the jay shut up.

"Elabonians eat songbirds now and again," Gerin said. "We catch 'em with nets, usually, not with bow and arrow."

"Aye, that makes sense," Van said. "They're so small and swift, you'd need to be a dead shot to hit 'em, and you'd waste a slew of arrows." He fastened a last strap. "Come along, Captain. Let's be off."

The forest deepened and took on a new aspect as they rolled on toward Ikos. Perhaps, Gerin thought, taking on an old aspect was a better way of describing it. Elabonian traders and explorers, back in the days before Ros the Fierce brought the northlands under imperial control, described them as almost unbroken forest from the High Kirs to the Niffet and all the way west to the Orynian Ocean.

Around the Sibyl's shrine at Ikos, that ancient forest survived undisturbed. Some of the gnarled oaks and deep green pines might have been saplings when the men round what would become the City of Elabon were still unlettered barbarians. Some of them might have been saplings before the Kizzuwatnans in their river valleys scratched the world's first letters onto clay tablets and set them in an oven to bake.

Maybe the shaggy beards of moss hanging from many of those trees helped muffle sound, or maybe some lingering power clung to the forest: some of the trees that grew there, at any rate, Gerin had never seen outside these confines. Whatever the reason, the woods were eerily still. Even the squeak and rattle of the wagon's ungreased axles seemed diminished. Far above the roadway, branches from either side interlaced, cutting off a good part of the daylight and turning the rest cool and green and shifting.

"If we could drive the wagon under the sea, it might look like this," Gerin said.

"Maybe so." Van kept craning his neck, looking up, down, all around. "I don't like this place—and I don't think it likes people, either. It wishes we weren't here, and so do I."

"I'd argue with you, if only I thought you were wrong." Gerin kept not quite hearing things pacing alongside the road as if tracking the wagon, not quite seeing them no matter how quickly he turned his head toward what he hadn't quite heard.

Van mused, "I wonder what would happen if, come a dry summer, some lord sent his peasants in here with axes and torches."

Gerin wondered if the forest and the things that dwelt in it understood Elabonian. He feared they did, for all at once the cover of branches over the road grew thicker and lower, while most of those branches suddenly seemed full of thorns. The very roadway narrowed, with trees—many of them full of thorns, too—crowding close, as if ready to reach out and seize the intruders. Once or twice he was sure he saw eyes staring balefully at him from behind the leaves, but he never got a glimpse of the creatures to which they were attached.

Nervously, he said, "You were just joking there, weren't you, my friend?"

"What? Oh, aye." Van was more than bold enough against any human foe, but how could even the boldest man fight a forest? Eyeing the growing number of encroaching branches, he went on, "All this lovely greenery? In truth, it would be a dreadful shame to peel even one leaf off its stem."

For a long moment, nothing happened. But just when Gerin was about to grab for his sword and start slashing away at the aroused trees and bushes, everything returned to the way it had been. The sun played through breaks in the overhead canopy, the road widened out again, and the trees went back to being just trees. Whatever had been moving along with the wagon went away, or at least became altogether silent.

"Whew!" Van muttered under his breath. "Place must have decided I was just joking after all—which I was, of course." He added that last in a much louder voice.

"Of course you were," Gerin agreed heartily. Then his voice fell: "All the same, we'll spend tonight in one of the lodgings round Ikos, not in this wood. That will further prove we mean no harm to the powers here."

Van's eyes met his. The two men shared one thought: *It will also keep anything in the forest that's still angry from coming down on us.* The words hung unspoken in the air. Gerin didn't want to give any of those possibly angry things ideas they didn't have already.

The sun was low in the west behind Gerin and Van when they topped a rise and looked down into the valley wherein nested Biton's gleaming white marble shrine and, leading down from within it, the rift in the earth that led to the Sibyl's chamber.

"Last time we came this way, we camped in the woods," Van said. "As you say, though, better to pay the scot at one of the inns down there tonight." A little town had grown up in front of the Sibyl's shrine, catering to those who came to it seeking oracular guidance.

"Aye, you're right." Gerin sighed. He didn't like silver going without good cause. Come to that, he wasn't over-fond of paying silver even with good cause. But he did not want to spend a night in these uncanny woods; they were liable to shelter worse things than ghosts. He twitched the reins and urged the horses forward.

When he'd visited Ikos before, the town in front of the shrine had been packed with Elabonians from both the northlands and south of the High Kirs, Sithonians, Kizzuwatnans, Trokmoi, Shanda nomads, and other folk as well. A big reason Gerin had preferred to camp in the woods then was that all the inns had bulged at the seams.

Now, as the wagon rolled into town, he found the dirt streets all but empty. Several of the inns had closed; a couple of them, by their dilapidated look, had been empty for years. The innkeepers who survived all rushed from their establishments and fell on him and Van with glad cries. Gerin hardly needed to haggle with them; they bid against one another until he got his lodging, supper, and a promise of breakfast for half what he'd expected to pay.

The taproom in the inn was all but deserted. Apart from Gerin and Van, only a couple of locals sat at the tables, drinking ale and telling stories they'd probably all heard a thousand times. The innkeeper brought ale and drinking jacks to his new guests. "And what would your pleasure for supper be?" he asked, bowing as low as if the Fox had been Hildor III, Emperor of Elabon.

"Not chicken," he and Van said, much as they had at Ricolf's.

"You've traveled some way, then, and spent nights in the open." The innkeeper pursed his lips to show he sympathized. "I killed a young pig this afternoon. I was going to smoke and salt down the flesh, but I do some lovely chops flavored with basil and thyme and wild mushrooms. It's a splendid dish, if I say so myself, and one I don't have the chance to prepare as often as I'd like these days. True, the cooking of it takes a while, but where have you gentlemen to go in the meantime?"

Gerin and Van looked at each other. They nodded. The Fox said, "Your trade has fallen off since the Trokmoi swarmed over the Niffet and the Empire shut the last passage up from the south."

"Good my sir, you have no idea." The innkeeper rolled his eyes. "Sometimes I think all of us left here make our living by taking in one another's washing. The shrine has fallen on hard times, that it has, and every one of us with it."

"Does the old Sibyl still live?" Gerin asked. "I'd not expected to find her breathing when I was last here five years ago. Now nothing would surprise me."

"No, Biton took her for his own last year," the innkeeper answered. "The god speaks through a younger woman now.

'Tis not that the quality of oracle has suffered that's cost us trade"—he made haste to reassure the Fox—"only that fewer folk now find their way hither."

"I understand." Gerin drained his jack dry. The innkeeper hastened to refill it. Gerin drank again, sighed with something close to contentment. "Good to relax here, away from the ghosts, away from robbers in the night, with only the worries that brought me here to carry on my shoulders."

"That my humble establishment is able to ease your burdens does my heart good," the innkeeper declared.

"To say nothing of your coin hoard," Gerin said dryly.

The innkeeper turned his head to one side and coughed, as if mention of money embarrassed him. Then he paused, plainly listening over again to what Gerin had said a moment before. "Robbers in the night, good my sir? So men begin to hold the ghosts at bay and the gods in contempt?"

"Men on the very road that leads here," the Fox said, and told of the free peasants who'd looked to arm themselves at his and Van's expense. "They didn't come on us, for which Dyaus be praised—and Biton, too, for watching over us—but they weren't out there in the darkness just for the journey. I heard them speak; I know what I'm talking about."

"Sometimes I think the whole world is guttering down toward darkness, like a candle on the last of its tallow," the innkeeper said sadly. "Even my dreams these days are full of monsters and pallid things from the underground darkness. At night in my bed I see them spreading over the land, and poor feeble men powerless to do aught against them."

Gerin started to nod: here was another man who shared his gloomy view of the world. Then he gave the innkeeper a sharp look. "I too have had dreams like that," he said.

"And I," Van put in. "I tell you the truth—I mislike the omen."

"Maybe the Sibyl will shed light on it." Gerin did his best to sound hopeful, but feared his best was none too good.

IV

The horses were curried till their coats gleamed and hitched to the wagon waiting when Gerin went out to the stables to reclaim them. He tipped the groom who'd cared for them, saying, "You did more here than was required of you."

"Lord, you're generous beyond my deserts," the fellow answered, but Gerin noticed he did not decline the proffered coin.

Every other time Gerin had visited the Sibyl's shrine, the area around the fenced forecourt had been packed with wagons, chariots, and men afoot, and with all the visitors passionately eager to put their questions to Biton's oracle as soon as possible. The only way to get in quickly—sometimes the only way to get in at all—was to pay off one of the god's eunuch priests.

The Fox had prepared himself for that eventuality. At his belt swung two medium-heavy pouches, one an offering for the temple, the other (though the word would not be used in public) a bribe for the priest who would conduct him to the shrine.

He soon discovered he was going to save himself some money. When he and Van came to the gate in the marble outwall, only three or four parties waited ahead of them. Just a few more rolled up behind the wagon. Instead of shouting, cursing chaos, the oracle-seekers formed a single neat line.

Van recognized what that meant, too. "Let's see the priests try to squeeze anything past their due out of us today," he said, laughing.

To their credit, the priests did not try. They took the suppliants one group at a time, leading away their animals to be seen to while they consulted the Sibyl. Everything ran as smoothly as the turning spokes of a chariot wheel. Gerin wished all his visits had gone so well. He also wished this particular visit hadn't been necessary.

A plump, beardless fellow in a robe of glittering cloth

of gold approached the wagon. Bowing to Gerin and Van, he said, "Gentles, you may call me Kinifor. I shall conduct you to the Sibyl and escort you from her chamber once the god has spoken through her." His voice was pleasant, almost sweet, not a man's voice but not a woman's, either.

Thinking of the mutilation eunuchs suffered, Gerin always felt edgy around them. Because the mutilation was not their fault, he always did his best to conceal those feelings. He swung a plump leather sack into Kinifor's equally plump hand. "This is to help defray the cost of maintaining your holy shrine."

The eunuch priest hefted the bag, not only to gauge its weight but to listen for the sweet jingle of silver. "You are generous," he said, and seemed well enough pleased even without any special payment straight to him; Gerin wondered if the temple would see all the money in the leather sack. The priest went on, "Descend, if you will, and accompany me to the temple."

As Gerin and Van got down from the wagon, another priest, this one in a plainer robe, came over and led the horses away. The travelers followed Kinifor through the gate and into the fenced-off temenos surrounding the shrine. The first thing the Fox saw was a naked corpse prominently displayed just inside the gateway; hideous lesions covered the body. Gerin jerked a thumb at it. "Another would-be temple robber?"

"Just so." Kinifor gave him a curious look. "Am I to infer from your lack of surprise that you have seen others Biton smote for their evil presumption?"

"Another, anyhow," Gerin answered. "With the chaos that's fallen on the northlands since the last time I was here, though, I wondered if your god was up to the job of protecting the treasures here from everyone who'd like to get his hands on them."

"This is Biton's precinct on earth," Kinifor said in shocked tones. "If he is not potent here, where will his strength be made manifest?"

Perhaps nowhere, Gerin thought. When the Elabonians conquered the northlands, they'd taken Biton into their own pantheon, styling him a son of Dyaus. But the Trokmoi brought their own gods with them, and seemed to care little for those already native to the land. If they prevailed, Biton might fail for lack of worshipers.

Van cast an appraising eye on the treasures lavishly displayed in the courtyard before the temple: the statues of gold and ivory, others of marble painted into the semblance of life or of greening bronze, the cauldrons and mixing bowls set on golden tripods, the piled ingots that reflected the sun's rays in buttery brilliance.

The outlander whistled softly. "I wondered if I misremembered from last time I was here, but no: there's a great pile of stuff about for your god to watch over, priest."

"The farseeing one has protected it well thus far." One of Kinifor's hands shaped a gesture of blessing. "Long may he continue to do so."

The white marble temple that housed the entrance to the Sibyl's cave was in a mixed Sithonian-Elabonian style, a gift of Oren the Builder to win the favor of Biton's priesthood—and the god himself—not long after the northlands came under Elabonian sway. The splendid fane, elegantly plain outside and richly decorated within, was surely magnificent enough to have succeeded in its purpose.

Seemingly out of place within all that gleaming stone, polished wood, and precious metal was the cult image of Biton, which stood close by the fissure in the earth that led down to the cavern wherein the Sibyl prophesied. The temple was a monument to Elabonian civilization at its best, to everything Gerin labored to preserve in the northlands. The cult image was . . . something else.

As he had the last time he visited the shrine, the Fox tried to imagine how old the square column of black basalt was. As he had then, he failed. This was no realistic image of the god, carved with loving care by a Sithonian master sculptor or some Elabonian artist who had studied for years in Kortys. The only suggestions of features the column bore were crudely carved eyes and a jutting phallus. Yet somehow, perhaps because of the aura of immeasurable antiquity that clung to it, the cult image carried as much impact as any polished product of the stonecutter's art.

"Seat yourselves, gentles," Kinifor said, waving to the rows of pews in front of the basalt column, "and pray that the lord Biton's sight reaches to the heart of your troubles, whatever they may be."

The eunuch sat beside Gerin, bowed his head, and murmured supplications to his god. The Fox also prayed, though unsure how much attention Biton paid to petitioners' requests. Some gods, like Mavrix, seemed to listen to every whisper addressed to them, even if they did not always grant requests. Others, such as Dyaus the father of all, were more distant. He didn't know where in that range Biton fell, but took no chances, either.

As soon as he finished his prayer, he glanced up at the cult image. Just for a moment, he thought he saw brown eyes staring back at him in place of the almost unrecognizable scratches on the basalt. He shivered a little; he'd had that same odd impression on his last visit to the shrine. Biton's power might not reach far, but it was strong here at its heart.

Puffing a little, a plump eunuch priest climbed up out of the fissure in the earth that led down to the Sibyl's chamber. Behind him came a grizzled Elabonian with a thoughtful expression on his face. With a nod to Gerin, he strode out of the temple and away to reclaim his team and vehicle.

Kinifor said, "Nothing now prevents us from seeking the wisdom Biton imparts through his sacred Sibyl. If you will please to follow me, stepping carefully as you descend—"

On his previous visit, Gerin had had to fight for his life against Trokmoi dissatisfied with what they heard from the oracle. He looked down to see if bloodstains still remained in the cracks between the tesserae of the mosaic floor. He saw none, which pleased him.

Kinifor stepped into the cave mouth. Gerin followed. Darkness, illuminated only by torches not nearly close enough together, swallowed him. The air in the cave felt altogether different from the muggy heat he'd endured in the temple: it was damp but cool, with a constant breeze blowing in his face so that the atmosphere never turned stagnant.

Kinifor's shadow, his own, and Van's swooped and fluttered in the torchlight like demented birds. Flickering shadows picked out bits of rock crystal—or possibly even gems—embedded in the stone of the cave walls. One glint came red as blood. "Was that a ruby we just passed?" Gerin asked.

"It could be so," Kinifor answered. "Biton has guided us to many treasures underground."

"Is it your god or your greed?" Van asked. Kinifor spluttered indignantly. The outlander laughed at the priest's annoyance. Just then they came to a branch of the cave that had been sealed up with stout brickwork. "What about that? Didn't you have to wall it up because your prying roused things that would better have been left asleep?"

"Well, yes," Kinifor admitted reluctantly, "but that was long ago, when we were first learning the ways of this cave. The bricks say as much, if you know how to read them."

Gerin did. Instead of being flat on all sides, the bricks bulged on top, as if they were so many hard-baked loaves of bread. That style had come out of Kizzuwatna in ancient days, not long after men first gathered together in cities and learned to read and write and work bronze. He took a long look at those bricks. They couldn't possibly reach back so far in time . . . could they?

After that first long look came a second one. Loaf-shaped bricks had not held their popularity long in Kizzuwatna: they required more mortar to bind them together than those of more ordinary shape. Some of the mortar on these, after Biton only knew how many centuries, had begun to crack and fall away from the bricks; little chips lay on the stone floor of the cave.

The Fox pointed to them, frowning. "I don't remember your wall there falling apart the last time I came this way."

"I hadn't noticed that," Kinifor confessed. "Some evening, when no suppliants seek the Sibyl's advice, we shall have to send down a crew of masons to repair the ravages of time." His laugh was smooth and liquid, like the low notes of a flute. "If the barrier has sufficed to hold at bay whatever lies beyond it lo these many years, surely a few days one way or the other are of scant import."

"But—" Gerin held his tongue. The eunuch priest was bound to be right. And yet—this wasn't a slow accumulation of damage over many years. Unless he and Kinifor were both wrong, it had happened recently.

The rift wound deeper into the earth. Kinifor led Gerin and Van past more spell-warded walls. Several times the Fox saw more loose mortar on the ground. He would have taken oath it had not been there when he'd last gone down to the Sibyl's chamber, but forbore to speak of it again. Kinifor, plainly, did not intend to hear whatever he had to say.

The priest raised a hand for those who accompanied him to halt. He peered into the chamber that opened up ahead, then nodded. "Gentles, you may proceed. Do you seek privacy for your question to the Sibyl?"

Privacy would have cost Gerin an extra bribe. He shook his head. "No, you may hear it, and her answer, too. It's no great secret."

"As you say." Kinifor sounded sulky; most people who thought a question important enough to put to the Sibyl also thought it so important that no one other than Biton and his mouth on earth could be trusted with it. Gerin had been of that opinion on his latest visit. Now, though, he did not mind if the priest listened as he enquired about his son's fate.

Kinifor stepped aside to let the Fox and Van precede him into the Sibyl's underground chamber. As before, Gerin marveled at the throne on which she sat. It threw back the torchlight with glistening, nacreous highlights, as if carved from a single black pearl. Yet contemplating the oyster that could have birthed such a pearl sent his imagination reeling.

"It *is* a new Sibyl," Van murmured, very low.

Gerin nodded. Instead of the ancient, withered crone who'd occupied this chamber on all his previous journeys to Ikos, on the throne sat a pleasant-faced woman of perhaps twenty-five in a simple white linen dress that fastened over her left shoulder and reached halfway between her knees and ankles. She nodded politely, first to Kinifor, then to those who would question her.

But when she spoke, she might have been the old Sibyl reborn. "Step forward, lads," she said to Gerin and Van. Her voice was a musical contralto, but it held ancient authority. Though the Fox and the outlander were both older than she, they were not merely lads but babes when measured against the divine power she represented. Gerin obeyed her without hesitation.

Coming to the crone on that seat had seemed natural

to him. Finding a new, young Sibyl there made him think for the first time of the life she led. Biton's mouth on earth was pledged to lifelong celibacy: indeed, pledged never even to touch a whole man. Here far below the ground she would stay, day upon day, the god taking possession of her again and again as she prophesied, her only company even when above the earth (he assumed—he hoped—she was allowed out of the chamber when no more suppliants came) eunuchs and perhaps serving women. Thus she would live out however many years she had.

He shivered. It struck him more as divine punishment than reward.

"What would you learn from my master Biton?" the Sibyl asked.

Gerin had thought about how to ask that question all the way south from Fox Keep. If the god got an ambiguous query, the questioner was liable to get an ambiguous reply; indeed, Biton was famous for finding ambiguity even where the questioner thought none lurking. Taking a deep breath, the Fox asked, "Is my son alive and well, and, if he is, when and where shall we be reunited?"

"That strikes me as being two questions," Kinifor said disapprovingly.

"Let the god judge," Gerin answered, to which the priest gave a grudging nod.

Biton evidently reckoned the question acceptable. The mantic fit came over the young Sibyl, harder than it had with the old. Her eyes rolled up in her head. She thrashed about on the throne, careless of her own modesty. And when she spoke, the voice that came from her throat was not her own, but the same powerful baritone her predecessor had used—Biton's voice:

> "The Sibyl's doom we speak of now
> (And worry less about the child):
> To flee Ikos, midst fearful row
> (Duren's fate may well be mild).
> All ends, among which is the vow
> Pledged by an oracle defiled."

The god left his mouth on earth as abruptly as his spirit

had filled her. She slumped against an arm of the throne in a dead faint.

Kinifor said, "Gentles, the lord Biton has spoken. You must now leave this chamber, that the Sibyl may recover and ready herself for those who come here next."

"But the Sibyl—or Biton, if you'd rather—said next to nothing about the question I asked," Gerin protested. "Most of that verse had more to do with you, by the sound of it, than with me."

"That is neither here nor there," Kinifor said. "The god speaks as he will, not as any man expects. Who are you, mortal, to question his majesty and knowledge?"

To that Gerin had no answer, only frustration that he had not learned more from the query over which he'd pondered so hard on the journey down from his keep. He took what coals of comfort he could: Biton had urged him not to worry. But what if that was because Duren was already dead, and so beyond worry? Would the god have mentioned him by name if he was dead, especially when Gerin had not named him? Who could say what a god would do? Where the Fox had done his best to prevent ambiguity, it had found him out. Dismayed, he turned to go.

Van pointed to the Sibyl, who remained unconscious. "Should the lass not have come back to herself by now? You'd not bring new folk down here if they were to find her nearer dead than alive."

Kinifor opened his mouth, perhaps to say something reassuring. But before he did, he too took another look at the Sibyl. A frown crinkled the unnaturally smooth skin of his face. "This is—unusual," he admitted. "She should be awake and, if a priest is here with her, asking what the god spoke through her lips."

Gerin started to take a step toward her, then remembered the conditions under which she served Biton: any touch from him, no matter how well-meaning, brought defilement with it. He wondered if that was what the last line of her prophecy meant, then stopped worrying about prophecy while she sprawled unconscious. He asked Kinifor, "Do you want to tend to her while we make our own way back up to the temple?"

He might as well have suggested burning down the fane. "That cannot be!" the eunuch priest gasped. "For one thing, you might well lose your way, take a wrong turning, and never be seen again. For another, some turns lead to treasures not displayed above ground. No one not connected with the cult of Biton may turn his eyes upon them."

"I know what Biton does to those who would be thieves," Gerin protested, but Kinifor shook his head so vehemently that his plump jowls wobbled.

Van, as usual, spoke to the point: "Well, what about the wench, then?"

Kinifor went over to her, put a hand in front of her nose and mouth to make sure she was breathing, felt for her pulse. When he straightened, his face held relief as well as worry. "I do not believe she will perish in the next moments. Let me guide you back to the surface of the earth, after which she shall, of course, be properly seen to."

"Honh!" Van said. "Seems to me you care more about Biton's gold and gauds than about his Sibyl."

Kinifor answered that with an injured silence which suggested to Gerin that his friend had hit the target dead center. But this was the priest's domain, not his, so he let Kinifor lead him out of the Sibyl's chamber and back up the length of the cave to Biton's temple. Still grumbling and looking back over his shoulder, Van reluctantly followed.

To give Kinifor his due, he hurried along the stony way, pushing his corpulent frame till he panted like a dog after a long run. Surprisingly soon, light not from torches showed ahead, though the priest's body almost obliterated it as he climbed out of the cave mouth. Gerin came right after him, blinking until his eyes grew used to daylight once more.

"About time," rasped the tough-looking fellow who waited impatiently for his turn at the oracle. "Take me down there, priest, and no more nonsense."

"I fear I cannot, sir," Kinifor answered. "The Sibyl seems to have suffered an indisposition, and will not be able to reply to questioners at least for some little while."

That brought exclamations of dismay from the other eunuchs within earshot. They hurried to Kinifor to find out what had happened. He quickly explained. Two of Biton's servitors hurried down into the cave mouth. "If she has not yet returned to herself, we shall bring her out," one of them said as he disappeared.

The Elabonian warrior whose question was delayed shouted, "This is an outrage!" When no one paid any attention to him, he shouted viler things than that. His face turned the color of maple leaves in fall.

Gerin looked down his long, straight nose at the man. "Do you know what you remind me of, sirrah?" he said coldly. "You remind me of my four-year-old son when he pitches a fit because I tell him he can't have any honied blueberries till after supper."

"Who in the five hells do you think you are, to take that tone with me?" the fellow demanded, setting his right hand on the hilt of his sword.

"I'm Gerin the Fox, Prince of the North," Gerin said, matching the gesture with his left hand. "You should be thankful I don't know your name, or want to."

The red-faced man scowled but did not back down. Gerin wondered if he would have to fight in Biton's shrine for the second time in two visits. The temple complex had guards, but most of them were outside the fane keeping an eye on the treasures displayed in the courtyard and on any visitors who, careless of Biton's curse, might develop itchy fingers.

Then, from the entrance to the shrine, someone called, "Any man who draws his blade on Gerin the Fox, especially with Van of the Strong Arm beside him, is a fool. Of course, you've been acting like a fool, fellow, so that may account for it."

The angry Elabonian whirled. "And what do you know about it, you interfering old polecat's twat?" he snarled, apparently not caring how many enemies he made.

The newcomer strode toward him. He was a tall, lean man of perhaps forty, with a forward-thrusting face, a proud beak of a nose, and dark, chilly eyes that put Gerin in mind of a hunting hawk's. He said, "I'd be the fool if I didn't make it my business to learn all I could of Gerin the Fox. I am Grand Duke Aragis, also called the Archer."

The angry color drained from the face of the impatient warrior as he realized he'd caught himself between the two strongest men in the northlands. With a last muttered curse, he stomped out of the temple, though he took care to step wide around Aragis.

"Well met," Gerin said. He and Aragis were rivals, but not open enemies.

"Well met," Aragis answered. He turned his intent gaze on the Fox. "I should have thought I might find you here. After word of your son, are you?"

"Aye," Gerin said stonily. "And you?"

"On business of my own," Aragis said.

"Which is none of *my* business," Gerin suggested. Aragis nodded—once; he was not a man given to excess. Gerin said, "Have it as you wish. Whatever your question is, you may not be able to put it to the Sibyl, any more than that big-mouthed ruffian was."

"Why not?" Aragis asked suspiciously. The idea that Gerin should know something he didn't seemed to offend him.

Before the Fox could answer, the two priests who had gone down to see how the Sibyl fared came back up into the temple. They carried her between them, her face white and her arms dangling limply toward the ground. "Does she live?" Gerin called to them in some alarm.

"Good sir, she does," one of the eunuchs answered. "But since her senses do not return to her, we'll take her to her own dwelling"—he nodded his head to show in which direction from the shrine that lay—"and minister to her there. At the very least, she can rest more comfortably in her bed than in the underground chamber. Surely, though, the lord Biton will aid in her recovery." That would have come out better had it sounded more like assertion and less like prayer.

"Why should the lord Biton care?" Van asked, blunt as always. "Down below there, he sounded like he was getting out of the prophecy game."

"You rave, good sir, and tread the edge of blasphemy as well," the priest answered. He looked for support to Kinifor, who had heard the Sibyl's last prophecy.

The eunuch who had accompanied Gerin and Van made a strange snuffling sound, almost one a horse would produce, as he blew air out through his lips. Slowly, he said, "The verses may lend themselves to the interpretation proposed. Other interpretations, however, must be more probable."

Even such a halfhearted admission was enough to shock the other two priests. Clucking to themselves, they carried the unconscious Sibyl away.

Kinifor said, "I begin to fear there will be no further communing with the lord Biton this day. Perhaps everyone here would be well advised to return to his inn, there to await the Sibyl's return to health. We shall send word directly that occurs, and shall seek no further fee for your inquiries."

"You'd better not." Aragis put as much menace into three words as Gerin had ever heard. "And if the wench ups and dies, I expect my silver back."

The eunuch twisted his hand in a gesture to turn aside the evil omen. "The lord Biton would not summon two Sibyls to himself in such a short span of time," he said, but his words, like the other priest's, lacked confidence.

People filed out of the shrine, muttering and grumbling to themselves. Kinifor went out to let those who waited in the courtyard know they would be disappointed in their hope for an oracular response. Their replies, like those in the temple, ranged from curious to furious.

With rough humor, Aragis turned to Gerin. "What did you ask her, anyway, to put her in such a swivet? To marry you?"

Gerin growled down deep in his throat and took a step toward the Archer. Unlike the fellow who'd started to move on him, though, he mastered himself. "I ought to just tell you it's none of your cursed business," he said, "but since you already know why I'm here, what's the point? I asked after my son, as you've figured out for yourself."

"That's a bad business," Aragis answered. "The whoreson who did it may come to me, seeking advantage from it. By Dyaus, if he does, I'll run up a cross for him, and you'll have the boy back fast as horses can run. I swear it."

"If it happens so, I'll be in your debt," the Fox said. "I'd be lying if I told you the idea that you had something to do with it was never in my mind."

Aragis scowled. "Because we're the two biggest, we circle round each other like a couple of angry dogs—I don't trust you, either, as you know full well. But I did not have my hand in this, and I will not seek to profit from it, come what may. Would you, were it my lad?"

"I hope not," Gerin said. Aragis chewed on that, then slowly nodded. He looked sincere, but his face, as Gerin had already seen, showed what he willed it to, not necessarily what he felt. That was useful for a ruler, as Gerin knew—his own features were similarly schooled.

Van said, "All right, Archer, if you don't care to circle and watch and not trust, suppose you do tell us why you came up to Ikos, so long as it's not life or death for your holding that we know."

For a moment, Aragis was nonplussed. Gerin hadn't been sure he could be. Then his usual watchful expression returned as he considered the outlander's words. At last he said, "Fair enough, I suppose. I rode here because I've had bad dreams; I hoped—I hope still—the Sibyl could put meaning to them."

"What sort of dreams?" Gerin's curiosity was as dependable as the changing phases of the moons.

Aragis hesitated again, perhaps not caring to show a rival any weakness. But after another pause for thought, he murmured, "If I can't understand them, you bloody well won't, either." He raised his voice to answer the Fox: "They've been filled with horrid things, monsters, call them what you will, overrunning my lands—overrunning the rest of the northlands, too, for all I could tell." He grimaced and shook his head, as if talking about the visions made him see them again.

"I too have had this dream," Gerin said slowly.

"And I," Van agreed.

"And the innkeeper from whom we've taken rooms," Gerin said. "I did not like the omen when it was Van and I alone. Now with four—" He checked himself. "Four I know of, I should say—I like it even less."

"Wherever else we rub, Fox, I'll not argue with you there." Aragis ran a hand down to the point of his graying beard. "Did the Sibyl say anything to you of this before she had her fit? What verse did she speak?"

"Why don't you ask him how big his is, as long as you're snooping?" Van said.

Like most men, Aragis seemed a stripling when set

against the burly outlander. But he had no retreat in him. He reached for the sword that hung on his belt. Before Van could grab any of the lethal hardware he carried, Gerin held up a hand. "Hold, both of you," he said. "Aragis, you know what the question was. The answer has nothing to do with you, so I can give it without fear you'll gain from it." He repeated the oracular response.

Aragis listened intently, still rubbing his chin and now and then plucking at his beard. When Gerin was done, the other noble gave a grudging nod. "Aye, that's nought to do with me, and might even hold good news about Duren mixed in there. But what of the rest? I've never heard— or heard of—a reply so filled with doom. No wonder the Sibyl wouldn't wake up after she delivered it."

"I wonder if it's got summat to do with the dreams we've had," Van said.

Aragis and Gerin both looked at him. As if animated by a single will, their hands formed the same sign to turn away evil. "Off with you, omen," Aragis exclaimed. The Fox nodded vehemently.

Van said, "It's not much of an omen talk and finger-twitching'll turn aside."

"The little vole will turn and bite in the eagle's claws," Gerin answered. "One time in a thousand, or a thousand thousand, he'll draw blood and make the bird drop him. With omens, you never know which ones you can shift, so you try to shift them all."

Now it was Van's turn to look thoughtful. "Might be something to that, I suppose. I know what I'd sooner do, though, now that the Sibyl's not going to give you what you're after."

"And what's that?" Gerin asked, though he thought he knew the answer.

Sure enough, Van said, "Go back to the inn and hoist enough beakers of ale that we don't care about omens or Sibyls or anything else."

"If there's nothing for us here, we should head straight off to Fox Keep," Gerin said, but he sounded doubtful even to himself.

Van looked at the sun. "You want to start up the road just a bit before noon, so we can camp for the night in the middle of the haunted wood? Begging your pardon, Captain, that's the daftest thought you've had in a good-ish while."

Gerin prided himself on his ability to admit mistakes. "You're right, it is. And if we're stuck with spending another day at the inn, how better to pass it than with a carouse?"

He looked doubtfully at Aragis. Polite talk with his main rival in the northlands was one thing, a day of drinking with him something else again. Aragis studied him with the same question on his face. The Fox realized that, while he and the self-styled grand duke were very different men, their station gave them common concerns. That was disconcerting; he hadn't tried mentally putting himself in Aragis' shoes before.

After a moment of awkward silence, the Archer resolved the problem, saying, "The way back to my holding is straight enough, and I'll be free of the woods well before sunset if I start now, so I think I'll head south."

He stuck out his hand. Gerin clasped it. "Whatever comes, I hope we get through it without trying to carve each other's livers," he said. "The only one who'd gain from that is Adiatunnus."

Aragis' eyes grew hawk-watchful again. "I hear he sent to you. You were worried whether his men stole your boy. You're telling me you didn't join forces with him."

"That's just what I'm telling you," Gerin answered. "The five hells will vomit forth the damned before I join hands with a Trokmê."

He waited for Aragis to say something like that. Aragis didn't. He only nodded to show he'd heard, then walked off to reclaim the chariot or wagon in which he'd come to Ikos.

"Cold fish," Van said judiciously. "Not a man who makes an easy enemy, though, or I miss my guess."

"You don't," the Fox answered. "We've met only a couple of times before, so I don't have his full measure as a man, but what he's done in building up his holding speaks for itself. And you heard what he had done after his men hunted down a longtooth that had been taking cattle from one of his villages?"

"No, somehow I missed that one," Van said. "Tell me."

"He had an extra strong cross raised, and nailed and lashed the beast's carcass to it as a warning to others of its kind—and, more to the point, as a warning to any men who might have thought about trifling with him."

"Mm. It'd make me think twice, I expect," Van said. "Well, let's amble after him and get back our animals."

The beasts and the vehicles they drew waited outside the walled courtyard around the temple. By luck, the low-ranking priest who'd taken the wagon by the gate stood close to it now; that meant Gerin didn't have to convince someone else he wasn't absconding with the property of another. As he climbed in, he pointed to a thatch-roofed wooden cottage not far away. "Is that where the Sibyl lives when she's not prophesying?" he asked.

"So it is, good my sir," the priest answered. His smooth face held worry. "I saw her carried there not long since, and heard rumors and tales so strange I know not what to believe: even those who brought her seemed confused. Did the mantic trance take her for you?"

"It did. In fact, she lost her senses just afterwards, and did not get them back again as she usually does." Without repeating the oracular verse, Gerin told the priest what had happened in the underground chamber.

The corners of the eunuch's mouth drew down even further. "Biton grant she recover soon," he exclaimed. "Never has the good god seen fit to call two Sibyls to himself so quickly. The temple suffers great disruption while the search for a new maid to speak his words goes on."

"To say nothing of the fees you lose when the oracle is quiet," Gerin said, remembering sacks of silver he'd pressed into priests' pudgy palms.

But, in injured tones, the eunuch replied, "I did say nothing of those fees." Perhaps he was genuinely pious. Stranger things had happened, Gerin supposed. He twitched the reins, urging the horses back toward the inn.

The innkeeper and the head groom met him in front of it. "You'll honor my establishment with another night's custom?" the innkeeper asked eagerly, adding, "I trust all went well for you with the Sibyl? I gather there was some sort of commotion in the temple?" Like anyone else, he delighted in gossip.

"Not in the temple—under it," Van said. Gerin let him tell the tale this time. The outlander was a better story-teller than he, anyhow. When Gerin told what he knew, he did it baldly, laying out facts to speak for themselves. Van embellished and embroidered them, almost as if he were a minstrel.

When he was through, the innkeeper clapped his hands. Bowing, he said, "Good my sir, if ever you tire of the life you lead, which I take to be one of arms, you would be welcome to earn your bread and meat here at my inn, for surely the stories you spin would bring in enough new custom to make having you about a paying proposition."

"Thank you, sir, but I'm not quite ready yet to sit by the fire and tell yarns for my supper," Van said. "If you'll fetch Gerin and me a big jar of ale, though, that'd be a kindness worth remembering."

Seeking to be even more persuasive, Gerin let silver softly jingle. The innkeeper responded with alacrity. He shouted to his servants as Gerin and Van went inside and sat in the taproom. Grunting with effort, two men hauled a huge amphora up from the cellar. Right behind them came another fellow with a flat-bottomed pot full of earth. The Fox wondered at that until the two men stabbed the pointed base of the amphora down into the pot.

"It won't stand by itself on a wooden floor, don't you see?" the innkeeper said. "And if the two of you somehow empty it, you won't be able to stand by yourselves, either."

"Good. That's the idea," Van boomed. "You have a dipper there, my friend, so we can fill our jacks as we need to? Ah, yes, I see it. Splendid. If we do come to the point where we can't walk, you'll be kind enough to have your men carry us up to our beds?"

"We've done it a few times, or more than a few," said one of the men who'd lugged in the amphora. "For you, though, we ought to charge extra, seeing as you're heavy freight." He looked ready to bolt if Van took that the wrong way, but the outlander threw back his head and laughed till the taproom rang.

The innkeeper hovered round Gerin like a bee waiting for a flower to open. The Fox didn't take long to figure out why. He'd jingled silver, but he hadn't shown any. Now he did. The innkeeper bowed himself almost double as he made the coins vanish—no easy feat, for he was almost as round as some of the temple eunuchs.

Once paid, he had the sense to leave his guests to themselves. Van filled two jacks, passed one to Gerin. He raised on high the one he kept. "Confusion to oracles!" he cried, and poured the red-brown ale down his throat. He let out a long sigh of contentment: "Ahhhh!"

Gerin also drank, but more slowly. Halfway through, he set down his jack and said, "The poor Sibyl seemed confused enough already. I hope she's come back to herself."

"Well, so do I," Van admitted. He clucked impatiently. "Come on, Captain, finish up there so I can pour you full again. Ah, that's better." He plied the dipper. Before upending his own refilled jack, he went on, "I wonder if, for a woman with juice in her like the new Sibyl looks to have, letting the god fill you makes up for long years without a man to fill you. Not a swap I'd care to make, anyhow."

"I had the same thought myself, when I saw her in the chamber in place of the crone who'd been there time out of mind," Gerin answered. "I don't suppose Biton would speak to anyone who wasn't willing to listen, though."

"Mm, maybe not." Van kicked him under the table. "What shall we drink to this round?"

Without hesitation, Gerin raised his jack and said, "Dyaus' curse, and Biton's, too, on whoever kidnapped Duren." He emptied the jack in one long pull, his throat working hard. Van shouted approval and drank with him.

After a while, they stopped toasting with each round and settled in for steady drinking. Gerin felt at the tip of his nose with thumb and forefinger. It was numb, a sure sign the ale was beginning to have its way with him. Suddenly, half drunk, he decided he didn't feel like sliding sottishly under the table.

Van filled his own jack, lowered the dipper into the amphora, and brought it, dripping, toward Gerin's. When he turned it so the dark amber stream poured into the jack, it quickly overflowed. He scowled at the Fox. "You're behindhand there." Only the care with which he pronounced "behindhand" gave any clue to how much he'd poured down himself.

"I know. Go on without me, if you've a mind to. If I drink myself stupid today, I'll drink myself sad. I can feel it coming on already, and I have plenty to be sad about even with my wits about me."

The outlander looked at him with an odd expression. Gerin needed a moment to recognize it; he hadn't often seen pity on his friend's blunt, hard-featured face. Van said, "The real trouble with you, Captain, is that you don't let go of your wits no matter how drunk you get. Me, I'm like most folk. After a while, I just stop thinking. Nice to be able to do that now and again."

"If you say so," Gerin answered. "I've lived by and for my wits so long now, I suppose, that I'd sooner keep 'em about me all the time. I'd feel naked—worse than naked—without 'em."

"Poor bastard." Van had drunk enough to make his tongue even freer than it usually was. "I tell you this, though: a long time ago I learned it was cursed foolishness to try and make a man go in a direction he doesn't fancy. So you do what you feel like doing. Me, I intend to get pie-eyed. Tomorrow morning I'll have a head like the inside of a drum with two Trokmoi pounding on it, but I'll worry about that then."

"All right," Gerin said. "You've touched wisdom there, you know."

"Me? Honh!" Van said with deep scorn. "I don't know from wisdom. All I know is ale feels good when it's inside me, and I feel good when I'm inside a wench, and a nice, friendly fight is the best sport in the world. Who needs more?"

"No, really." The Fox had enough ale inside him to make him painfully earnest. "So many folk aren't content to let their friends"—he almost said *the people they love*, but knew with accurate instinct that that would have been more than Van could put up with—"be what they are. They keep trying to make them into what they think they're supposed to be."

Van grunted. "Foolishness," was all he said. He plied the dipper yet again, then burst into raucous song in a language Gerin didn't know.

The outlander went to the jakes several times over the

course of the afternoon as the ale extracted a measure of revenge. When he came back from the latest of those visits, he zigzagged to the table like a ship trying to tack into port against a strong wind. His chair groaned when he threw his bulk into it, but held.

Even after more drinking, he was able to paste an appreciative smile on his face when a servitor brought over flatbread and a juicy roast of beef. He used his eating knife to carve off a chunk that would have done a starving longtooth proud, and methodically proceeded to make it disappear, lubricating the passage with ale.

After so many years' comradeship, the outlander's capacity no longer amazed Gerin, even if it did still awe him. The innkeeper watched Van eat and drink with amazement, too: glum amazement that he hadn't charged more, if the Fox was any judge. Gerin did his best to damage the roast, too, but, beside Van's, his depredations went all but unnoticed.

Twilight faded into night. Torches, their heads dipped in fat for brighter flames, smoked and crackled in bronze sconces. Gerin drained his jack one last time, set it upside down on the table, and got to his feet. He moved slowly and carefully, that being the only sort of motion he had left to him. "I'm for bed," he announced.

"Too bad, too bad. There's still ale in the jar," Van said. He got up himself, to peer down into it. "Not a lot of ale, but some."

"Don't make me think about it," the Fox said. "I'm going to have a headache in the morning as is; why bring it on early?"

"You!" Van said. "What about me?" Pity showed on his face again, this time self-pity—he had indeed drunk titanically, if he'd managed to make himself maudlin.

Gerin climbed the stairs as if each were a separate mountain higher than the last. Triumph—and a bellyful of ale—surged in him when he got to the second story. The floor seemed to shift under his feet like the sea, but he reached the room he shared with Van without having to lean against the wall or grab at a door. That too was triumph of a sort.

He rinsed out his mouth with water from the pitcher

there, though he knew it would be a cesspit come morning anyhow. Then he undressed and flopped limply onto one of the beds. He pulled off his sandals, hoping Van wouldn't choose the same bed and squash him when—if— the outlander made it upstairs.

Sometime in the middle of the night, the Fox sat bolt upright in bed, eyes staring, heart pounding. His head was pounding, too, but he ignored it. The horror of the dream that had slammed him out of sodden slumber made such merely fleshly concerns as hangovers meaningless by comparison.

Worst of all, he couldn't remember what he'd seen— or perhaps the darkness of the dream had been so absolute that even imaginary vision failed. Something dreadful was brewing somewhere in the dark.

The room in which he lay was dark, too, but not so dark that he could not see. Light from all the moons save Elleb streamed in through the window, painting crisscrossing shadows on the floor. In the other bed, Van snored like a bronze saw slowly cutting its way through limestone.

Just as Gerin tried to convince himself the dream, no matter how terrifying, had been only a dream and to go back to sleep, the outlander stirred and moaned. That he could move at all amazed the Fox; the room reeked of stale ale.

Van shouted—not in Elabonian, not in words at all, but like an animal bawling out a desperate alarm. One of his big hands groped for and found a knife. He sprang to his feet, naked and ferocious, his eyes utterly devoid of reason.

"It's all right," Gerin said urgently, before that mad gaze could light on him and decide he was the cause of whatever night terror Van faced. "It's only a dream. Lie down and sleep some more."

"A dream?" Van said in a strange, uncertain voice. "No, it couldn't be." He seemed to shrink a little as consciousness came back. "By the gods, maybe it was at that. I can hardly believe it."

He set the knife back on the floor, sat down at the edge of the bed with a massive forearm across his eyes. Gerin understood that; now he noticed his own throbbing head, and Van's had to be ten times worse. The outlander stood again, this time to use the chamber pot. Gerin also understood that. "Pass it to me when you're done," he said.

"I thought I was lost in a black pit," Van said wonderingly. "Things were looking at me, I know they were, but I couldn't see even the shine of their eyes—too dark. How could I fight them if I couldn't see them?" He shuddered, then groaned. "I wish my head would fall off. Even the moonlight hurts my eyes."

"I had a dark dream, too, though I don't remember as much of it as you do," Gerin said. Analytical even hung over, he went on, "Odd, that. You've drunk much more than I have, yet you recall more. I wonder why."

"Captain, I don't give a—" Van's reply was punctuated by a frightened wail that came in through the window with the overbrilliant moonlight. The Fox recognized the innkeeper's voice, even distorted by fear.

More than his headache, more than his own bad dream, that fear kept him from falling back to sleep. Van said nothing but, by the way he tossed and fidgeted, he lay a long time wakeful, too.

Breakfast the next morning was not a happy time. Gerin spooned up barley porridge with his eyes screwed into slits against the daylight. Van drew up a bucket of water from the well outside the inn and poured it over his head. He came back in dripping and snorting, but turned aside with a shudder from the bowl of porridge the innkeeper offered him.

The innkeeper did his best to seem jolly, but his smiles, although they stretched his mouth wide, failed to reach his eyes. Little by little, he stopped pretending, and grew almost as somber as his suffering guests. "I have some word of the Sibyl, good my sirs," he said.

"Tell us," Gerin urged. "You'll give me something to think about besides my poor decrepit carcass." Van did not seem capable of coherent speech, but nodded—cautiously, as if afraid the least motion might make his head fall off.

The innkeeper said, "I hear she still lies asleep in the bed where the priests put her, now and again thrashing and crying out, as if she has evil dreams."

"I wonder if hers are the same as mine and Van's," Gerin said: "darkness and unseen things moving through it."

"I saw—or rather, did not see—the same last night." The innkeeper gave a theatrical shiver. His eyes flicked over to Dyaus' altar by the fireplace. The king of the gods might hold the ghosts at bay, but seemed powerless against these more frightening seemings that came in the night.

Van made a hoarse croaking noise, then said, "I wonder what Aragis dreamt last night." He didn't quite whisper, but used only a small piece of his big voice: more would have hurt him.

"Are you sure you won't eat something?" Gerin asked him. "We'll want to do a lot of traveling today, to get beyond the wood and also past that peasant village where they hunted us in the night."

"I'm sure," Van said, quietly still. "You'd make a fine mother hen, Captain, but if I put aught in my belly now, we'd just lose time stopping the wagon so I could go off into the woods and unspit."

"You know best," the Fox said. The porridge was bland as could be, but still sat uncertainly in his own stomach, and lurched when he stood up. "I do think we ought to go upstairs and don our armor, though. However much we hurt, we're liable to have some handwork ahead of us."

"Aye, you're right," Van answered. "I'd be happier to sit here a while—say, a year or two—till I feel I might live, or even want to, but you're right." With careful stride, he made his way to the stairs and up them. Gerin followed.

The rasps and clangs of metal touching metal made the Fox's head hurt and, by Van's mutters, did worse to him. "Don't know how I'm supposed to fight, even if I have to," Gerin said. "If I could drive somebody away by puking on him, I might manage that, but I'm not good for much more."

"I feel the same way," Van said, "but no matter how sick I am, if it's a choice between fighting and dying, I expect I'll do the best job of fighting I can."

"Can't argue with that," Gerin said. "If you think I'll be looking for a fight today, though, you're daft."

"Nor I, and I'm a sight fonder of them than you are," Van said. "The thing of it is, a fight may be looking for you."

"Why do you think I'm doing this?" Gerin shrugged his shoulders a couple of times to fit his corselet as comfortably as he could, then jammed his bronze pot of a helm over his head. Sighing, he said, "Let's go."

"Just a moment." Van adjusted the cheekpieces to his own fancy helm, then nodded. By his pained expression, that hurt, too. Anticipating still more future pain, he said, "And we'll have to listen to the cursed wagon wheels squeaking all the rest of the day, too."

Gerin hadn't thought of that. When he did, his stomach churned anew. "We've got to do something about that," he declared.

"Stay here a while longer?" Van suggested.

"We've stayed too long already, thanks to you and your carouse. Curse me if I want to spend another useless day here because you drank the ale jar dry—and I helped, I admit it," the Fox added hastily. He plucked at his beard. Thinking straight and clear through a pounding headache was anything but easy, but after a few seconds he snapped his fingers. "I have it! I'll beg a pot of goose grease or chicken fat or whatever he has from the innkeeper. It won't be perfect, the gods know, but it should cut the noise to something we have hope of standing."

Van managed the first smile he'd risked since he woke up. He made as if to slap Gerin on the back, but thought better of it; perhaps he imagined how he would have felt had someone bestowed a similar compliment on him in his present delicate condition. "By the gods, Captain, it can't hurt," he exclaimed. "I was thinking we'd have to suffer the whole day long, and no help for it."

"No point in suffering if you don't have to," Gerin said. "And I can't think of a better way to use wits than to keep from suffering."

The innkeeper produced a pot of chicken fat without demur, though he said, "There's a cure for a long night I never ran across before."

"Aye, that's just what it is, but not the way you mean." The Fox explained why he wanted the fat. The innkeeper looked bemused, but nodded.

Gerin crawled under the wagon and applied a good coat of grease to both axles. When he came out and stood up again, Van said, "We'll draw flies."

"No doubt," Gerin said. "After a while, it'll go bad and start to stink, too, and somebody will have to scrub it off. For today, it'll be quieter. Wouldn't you say that's worth it?"

"Oh, aye, you get no quarrel from me there." Van's laugh was but a faint echo of his usual booming chortle, but it served. "Thing of it is, I'm usually the one with no thought but for today and you're always fretting about tomorrow or the year after or when your grandson's an old graybeard. Odd to find us flip-flopped so."

The Fox considered that, then set it aside. "Too much like philosophy for early in the day, especially after too much ale the night before. Shall we be off?"

"Might as well," Van said. "Can I humbly beg you to take the reins for the first part of the go? I don't think you hurt yourself as bad as I did."

"Fair enough." Gerin clambered onto the seat at the front of the wagon. The reins slid across the calluses on his palms. Van got up beside him, moving with an old man's caution.

"The lord Biton bless the both of you, good my sirs," the groom said.

Gerin flicked the reins. The horses leaned forward against their harness. The wagon rolled ahead. It still rattled and creaked and jounced, but didn't squeak nearly as much as it had. Van looked wanly happy. "That's first rate," he said. "With even a bit o' luck, I'll feel like living by noon or so."

"About what I was hoping for myself," Gerin said. He drove out of the stable yard and around to the front of the inn. The wagon wasn't as quiet as all that, but it was enough quieter than it had been to satisfy him.

The innkeeper stood by the entryway and bowed himself double as the wagon passed him. "The lord Biton bless the both of you," he said, as the groom had. "May you come again to Ikos before long, and may you recall my humble establishment with favor when you do."

"They didn't used to act like that before the Empire blocked the last pass through the Kirs," Gerin murmured. "Then they had guests up to the ceiling and sleeping in the horses' stables, and they hardly knew or cared whether they saw anyone in particular again."

"Reminds me of a story, Captain, indeed it does," Van said, a sure sign he was feeling better. "Have I told you how they get the monkeys to pick pepper?"

"No, I don't think I've heard that one," Gerin answered. "How do they—"

He got no further, for the horses gave a snort of alarm and reared in terror. Trying to fight them under control, Gerin thought their unexpected motion the reason the wagon swayed beneath his fundament as if suddenly transformed to a boat bobbing on a choppy sea. Then Van shouted "Earthquake!" and he realized the whole world was trembling.

He'd felt earthquakes once or twice before, years ago. The ground had twitched, then subsided almost before fear could seize him. This quake was nothing like those. The shaking went on and on; it seemed to last forever. Through the roar of the ground and the creaking of the buildings in the town of Ikos, he heard cries of fear. After a moment, he realized the loudest of them was his own.

A couple of inns and houses did more than creak; they collapsed into piles of rubble. And when the Fox looked down the street toward the temple of Biton, he saw with horror that the gleaming marble fane was also down, along with great stretches of the wall that protected the holy precinct.

When the earth finally relented and stood still, Gerin realized his hangover was gone; terror had burned it out of him. He stared at Van, who stared back, his usually ruddy face fishbelly white. "Captain, that was a very bad one," the outlander said. "I've felt quakes a time or two here and there, but never any to compare with that."

"Nor I," Gerin said. The ground shook again, just enough to send his heart leaping into his mouth. He scrambled down from the wagon and ran toward the nearest fallen building, from which came pain-filled shouts. Van ran right beside him. Together they pulled away timbers and plaster until they could haul out a fellow who, but for a couple of cuts and a mashed finger, had taken miraculously little hurt.

"All the gods bless you," the man said, coughing. "My wife's in there somewhere." Careless of his own injuries, he began clawing at the wreckage himself. Gerin and Van worked with him. Men and women also came running from buildings that had stayed upright.

Then someone screamed, "Fire!" Flames born in the hearth or on Dyaus' altar or of some flickering lamp were loose and growing. Black smoke, thin at first but all too quickly thicker, boiled up to the sky—and not just from the downfallen inn where the Fox labored. Every wrecked building was soon ablaze. The shrieks of those trapped under beams rose to a new and dreadful pitch.

Along with everyone else, Gerin fought the fires as best he could, but there were not enough buckets, not enough water. Flames grew, spread, began to devour buildings the earthquake had not tumbled.

"Hopeless," Van said, coughing and choking against the smoke that now streaked his face with soot. "We don't get away, we're going to cook, too, and the wagon and horses with us."

Gerin hated to retreat, but knew his friend was right. He looked again toward Biton's overthrown temple. "By the gods," he said softly, and then shivered when, as if the gods were listening, the ground shook again. "I wonder if the Sibyl foresaw this when she prophesied yesterday."

"There's a thought." Van's face lit up. "And here's another: with the wall down and the temple guards likely either squashed or scared to death, what's to keep us from scooping a wagonload of gold out of the holy precinct?"

"You're braver than I am if you want to chance Biton's curse," Gerin said. "Remember the corpses we've seen of those who tried stealing from the temenos?" By Van's expression, first sulky and then thoughtful, he hadn't remembered, but did now. Gerin went on, "But let's head over there anyhow. We ought to see if we can do anything for the poor Sibyl. If I know those greedy priests, they'll be so worried over the temple and their treasures that they're liable to forget her—and she may not even be aware to remind them she's alive." The thought of her lying in the rubble, trapped and unconscious and perhaps forgotten, raised fresh horror in him: he could not imagine a lonelier way to die.

"Right you are, Captain." Now Van got into the wagon and took the reins without hesitation; maybe the shock of the earthquake had made him forget his morning-after pains, too. Gerin scrambled up beside him. The horses snorted, both in fear and from the billowing smoke. The Fox counted himself lucky that they hadn't bolted when the fires started. He was anything but sorry to get away from the flames himself.

Along with so much else, the gold-and-ivory statues of Ros and Oren had fallen in the earthquake—fallen and shattered into the pieces from which they were made. Oren's head, its features plump and unmemorable but decked with a crown heavy with gold and sparkling with rubies, sapphires, and emeralds, had bounced or flown out beyond the overthrown marble wall that delimited Biton's precinct.

Gerin and Van looked at each other, the same thought in both their minds. So much gold—Whispering a prayer of propitiation to Biton, the Fox leaped down from the wagon. He seized the image of the dead Emperor's head, ready to cast it aside at the first sign of the curse striking home (and devoutly hoping that would be soon enough). Grunting at the weight of gold, he picked up the head and crown and chucked them into the back of the wagon.

"We won't need to fret about money for a bit," Van said, beaming, and even the abstemious Fox could only nod.

The quake struck so early in the day that hardly anyone had yet come in hope of hearing the Sibyl's prophetic verse. Only one wagon and one chariot had their horses tethered out in front of the dwelling the Sibyl used as her own. The cottage still stood, while chunks of the marble wall around the temple precinct had come down with gruesome result on the priest who the day before had tended Gerin's team.

Seeing the Sibyl's dwelling intact made the Fox hesitate. "Maybe we should just head for home," he said doubtfully. "Those fellows over there will be able to take care of her without violating ritual." He pointed through a gap in the wall toward figures running around by the ruined temple.

Van looked that way, too. His eyes were sharper than Gerin's, perhaps because, unlike the Fox, he spent no time peering at faded script in crumbling scrolls. He grabbed the mace off his belt. "Captain, you'd better look again. Whatever those things are, you don't want 'em tending the Sibyl."

"What are you talking about? They must be priests, and they—" Gerin's voice broke off as, squinting, he did take another look. He saw priests, all right, but they were down on the ground, not one of them moving. Over them bent pallid shapes hard to make out against the white marble of the temple. They didn't quite move or look like men, though.

One of them raised his head and saw the wagon. The bottom of his—its?—face was smeared with red. Gerin didn't think the thing was hurt. The blood around its mouth likelier said it had been—feeding.

As Van had seized the mace, so Gerin grabbed for his bow. The pale, bloodstained figure loped toward the wagon. The Fox remained unsure whether it was man or beast. It carried itself upright on two legs, but its forehead sloped almost straight back above the eyes (which were small and themselves blood-red) and its mouth was full of teeth more formidable than anything Gerin had seen this side of a longtooth.

Ice ran down his back. "The quake must have knocked down the underground walls, the warded ones," he exclaimed. "And these are the things the wards held back."

"Belike you're right," Van answered. "But whether you are or not, don't you think you'd better shoot that one before it gets close enough to take a bite out of us? Whatever it was eating before doesn't seem to have filled it."

Staring at the pallid monster, Gerin had almost forgotten he was holding his bow. He pulled an arrow from his quiver, nocked, drew, and let fly in one smooth motion. The monster made no effort to duck or dodge; it might never have seen a bow before. The arrow took it in the middle of its broad chest. It clawed at the shaft, screaming hoarsely, then crumpled to the ground.

The scream drew the attention of a couple of other monsters. *How many of them had lived underground?* Gerin wondered. *And for how long?* Whatever the answer was, the things were above ground now, and looked to be out for revenge against the men who had forced subterranean life on them for so long—and on any other men they could sink their teeth into.

Before the monsters rushed the wagon, a charge by a

squad of temple guards distracted them. They attacked the guardsmen with the ferocity of wild beasts. The guards had spears and swords and armor of bronze and leather. The monsters looked to be faster and stronger than anyone merely human.

Gerin got but a brief glimpse of the fight, which looked to be an even match. "If we mix ourselves up in that, all we'll do is get killed," he said to Van. "More of those cursed things keep swarming up out of what's left of the temple."

"Well then, let's snatch the Sibyl and get out of here before they find her and figure she'd make a tasty snack," Van said. In other circumstances, that would have seemed rough humor. Remembering the blood round the mouth of the monster he'd shot, Gerin thought the outlander was just stating a probability.

He jumped down from the wagon when Van reined in by the Sibyl's dwelling. The door stood ajar, perhaps knocked open by the earthquake. Gerin ran inside.

Had the quake not thrown pots from shelves and lamps from tables, the cottage would have reminded the Fox of one inhabited by a prosperous peasant. Tapestries enlivened whitewashed walls; the furniture looked better made than most. That hadn't kept stools from falling down, though, or the clay oven in one corner of the cottage from cracking.

The Sibyl lay on her bed, unconscious still, in the midst of chaos. As Gerin stepped toward her, the ground trembled beneath his feet once more. That was almost enough to send him fleeing out of the cottage in terror of offending Biton. But, he reasoned, earthquakes were not in the province of the farseeing god. Had he angered Biton, the deity would have shown his displeasure more directly.

He stooped beside the Sibyl, who still wore the thin linen dress she'd had on in the chamber beneath the ruined temple. He wondered if his touch would bring her to herself. She stirred and muttered as he lifted her, but her eyes stayed closed. He hurried back out through the doorway.

"Good thing the monsters are still battling in there," Van said when he returned. "A wench in your arms is pleasant even if you're not having her, but worthless to fight with."

"Scoffer," Gerin said. But the rising noise of combat

inside the temple precinct warned him he had no time to swap banter with Van. As gently as he could, he set the Sibyl in the back of the wagon. Again she muttered but did not wake. He took his seat beside Van, snatched up his bow and quiver once more. Nocking another arrow, he said, "Let's get out of here."

"Right you are." Van twitched the reins. The horses bolted ahead, glad to have an outlet for their fear. As the wagon rattled past a gap in the fence, a monster came through. Gerin shot it. It fell with a roar. Van pushed the horses up to a gallop. Skirting the burning town of Ikos, the wagon plunged into the old woods.

V

Not long after noon, the Sibyl came back to herself. By then, the travelers were more than halfway through the strange forest that guarded the road to Ikos. Gerin had expected trees fallen across that road, perhaps other signs of upheaval from the earthquake. He discovered none. As far as the woods were concerned, the temblor might never have happened.

"Good," Van said when he remarked on that. "Maybe the trees'll swallow up those creatures, too, when they come swarming out of Ikos."

"Wouldn't that be lovely?" Gerin said. "Likely too much to hope for, though, because—" He broke off as the wagon shifted under his fundament. It wasn't, as he'd first feared, yet another quake: rather, he found when he looked back into the bed of the wagon, the Sibyl had gone from lying to sitting up. He nodded to her. "Lady, I bid you good day."

Her eyes showed nothing but confusion. "You are the pair for whom I prophesied just now," she said, her voice also halting. Though it suited her appearance well, hearing it once more gave Gerin a small shock: after Biton had spoken through her, he'd almost forgotten she had a voice of her own.

"Not 'just now,'" he said, wondering how he could let her know what had happened while she lay unconscious. "That was yesterday; you've been in Biton's trance for more than a whole day."

"Impossible. It never takes me so," she said angrily. But a moment later, she looked confused again. "Yet if you do not speak truth, why am I on the point of bursting? Halt a moment, I pray you." Van reined in. The horses, glad of a breather, began nibbling grass by the side of the road.

Gerin got down and went around to the back of the wagon. He held out a hand. "Here, lady, I'll help you down so you can ease yourself."

She recoiled as if he'd proposed helping her down so he could ravish her. "Are you mad?" she demanded in a voice like winter. "I may have no contact whatever with any entire man. Were I to do so, I'd be Sibyl no longer."

The Fox sucked in a long breath. She hadn't figured out how she'd got into the wagon. He could hardly blame her, but it didn't make what he had to say come any easier: "Lady, I fear that to save your life I had to touch you. The gods know I'm sorry for it, but I saw no other way." He repeated the oracular verse she had given him, and explained the morning's horrors.

The more he talked, the paler the Sibyl grew. "Lies," she whispered. "It must be lies. You've ruined me, and now you seek to twist my own words against me and make me believe you did it for my own good?" Her head whipped around like a hunted animal's; her eyes lit on the gold and ivory head of Oren the Builder. Gerin had thought she was already white as could be, but discovered he was wrong. "You—took this?" she demanded. "And the lord Biton did not strike you dead?"

A flip answer came to Gerin's mind; he stifled it before it passed his lips. "Lady, he did not. When I took it, it lay outside the bounds of the holy precinct. As I said, the earthquake knocked everything into confusion. The temple itself no longer stands. What happened to the chamber where you prophesied I could not say, but the quake must have knocked down the warded walls that kept those monsters from coming to the surface."

Van turned and said, "For all you know, Fox, it might have been the other way round. Remember the bits of mortar we saw at the base of those walls when Kinifor led us down to the lady? The things might have been trying for years to breach the magic that held 'em in check, and when they finally did it, that could've made the earth shake."

"You're right; it could have happened so," Gerin agreed. "But whichever way it was doesn't matter." He gave his attention back to the Sibyl. "Lady—have you a name, by the way?"

She'd been listening to him and Van talk back and forth as if they were madmen whose madnesses by chance coincided. She snapped back to herself when the Fox asked her that question, but needed a moment to find an answer for it. At last she said, "I was called . . . Selatre. They took the name from me when I became Biton's mouth, but I recall it was mine." The bitter curve of her lips was anything but a smile. "I may as well wear it again, for thanks to you I'll serve the god no more. If all you say is true, better you should have left me to die there."

"Lady . . . Selatre . . . I pray I'm wrong, but I don't think I am, when I tell you the only things left alive in Ikos by sunset tonight will be the ones that came out from under Biton's fane. How deep and wide the caves run, how many monsters there are—I know none of that. But I couldn't leave you in your cottage to perish from their teeth and claws, not when the question I put to you was what made you swoon away," Gerin said.

Selatre said, "If you think saving me was a favor, you're wrong. Lost, polluted . . . how can I hope to make my way in the world again, now that you've taken away my reason for being?"

"You made your way in it before you were Sibyl," Van said roughly. "And plenty of people go on living who've taken worse hurts than you. Go into the woods, water the ferns, and come back and we'll feed you bread and sausage and ale. Things always look cheerier with food in your belly, and you must be hungry as a longtooth after sleeping the day around."

Selatre sniffed at the homely advice, but, perhaps because nothing better occurred to her, nodded after a moment. Gerin started to offer his hand again, but the first motion made her shrink back with such dismay that he stopped before it was well begun. Instead, he ostentatiously stepped away from the wagon and let her clamber down by herself.

"What do we do if she tries to run to Ikos on her own?" he whispered to Van when she walked in among the bushes by the side of the road.

"If the jade's that foolish, let her go," the outlander answered. "Me, I don't think she is."

Gerin got out the food Van had promised the Sibyl. She took longer to come back than he'd expected, and he wondered if she had slipped away. The idea of pursuing her through the uncanny forest was far from appealing. But just when he was beginning to worry he might have to, she returned, her face unreadable. He pointed to the meal he'd fixed from the travel supplies, but did not try to give it to her. If she didn't want to be touched, that was her affair.

She did manage a quiet word of thanks, then fell on bread and sausage and onions and ale as if she'd gone without food for ten or twenty days, not just one. She was still eating when, faintly, from far down the road to the west came a snarling roar that wasn't bear or longtooth or wolf or any beast Gerin had heard before. The hair on his arms and the back of his neck prickled up even so.

Van said, "That's one of the things from the caves, if you ask me."

Selatre put down the piece of bread she'd been gnawing. "A terrible sound," she said, shuddering. "I've heard it in my nightmares. Now, perhaps, I begin to believe you."

The innkeeper had said she seemed to be having evil dreams. *That was this morning*, Gerin thought, amazed. It seemed an age ago, in a different world. Given all that had changed between then and now, maybe it was.

The Fox said, "We've seen monsters in our dreams, too—and seen them in the flesh today, in the temple compound."

"And if we don't want to see more of them in the flesh, I think we'd better get rolling again," Van said. "If I had to guess, I'd say they're likely not after us in particular right now, just out exploring, finding out what aboveground is like after being down below so long. But if they come on us, I don't think they'd stop with a cheery good day, if you take my meaning."

Gerin stood aside to let Selatre scramble into the wagon by herself. Getting her back to Fox Keep was going to be awkward if she thought any accidental bump the equivalent of a violation. Of course, if that was how she felt, she was already convinced he'd violated her, and he couldn't do anything about it. He chewed on the inside of his lower lip. No time to worry about any of that now. Once they were safe away from Ikos would be soon enough.

He said to Van, "I'll drive for a while now. You can rest your head."

"It's all right," the outlander answered. "Since the ground

started shaking, I haven't hardly noticed my poor aching noodle."

"The same with me," Gerin said. "It's not the cure for a long night of drinking I'd choose, though."

"Nor I, Fox, nor I." Van started to laugh, but broke off: another one of those snarling roars cut through the stillness of the woods. The outlander yanked on the reins, then reached around behind him into the wagon for the whip. He cracked it just above the horses' backs. Gerin thought that was laying it on thick; the animals seemed alarmed enough to run hard just from the fierce sound of the roar.

Selatre said, "Have a care, please. You almost touched me when you were groping back here." She sat huddled in a far corner, as if certain Van had intended to grope her.

"Lady—Selatre—we're not out to do you harm or throw you down in the roadway and have you or anything of the sort." The outlander sounded as if he were holding on to his patience with both hands. "For one thing, Gerin and I both prefer willing wenches. For another, or if you think I'm lying about the first, we could have had our way with you four times each before you woke up."

"I know that," she answered quietly. "Any touch, though, pollutes me, not just a lewd one. Lord Gerin, I grant you meant well when you plucked me from my cottage, but I'd sooner you had not done it. To lose that sense of union with the god, to know he will never speak through me again because I am his pure vessel no more . . . life stretches long and empty ahead of me."

The Fox exhaled through his nose in impatient anger. "Lord Biton would have spoken through you no more whether we came to your dwelling or not. If we hadn't, you'd have been monster fodder before another hour went by. And that, if you ask me, is a short and empty life, save perhaps when speaking about a monster's belly, which would have been quite comfortably full."

He twisted around to see how Selatre took that. He didn't want to flay her with words; after all, she was suddenly cast into a situation she'd never imagined and for which she'd never prepared. If he'd hit too hard, he was ready to backtrack and apologize.

But, to his surprise, she returned the ghost of a smile.

"Next to being devoured, I suppose rescue may be a better choice. Very well; I do not blame you for it—much."

"Lady, I thank you." He could have—given his nature, he easily could have—freighted that with enough sarcasm to make it sting. This time, though, it came out sincere. The Sibyl—no, the ex-Sibyl—was trying to adjust; he could at least do the same.

Shadows were lengthening when they came out of the haunted forest that surrounded Ikos and into woods like those in the rest of the northlands. The transition point was easy to spot: as soon as they returned to the normal woods, the earthquake showed its effects again, not least with a couple of toppled trees stretched across the roadway.

Moving those trunks would have taken half a village of serfs. Van drove around them through the undergrowth. As he did so, he said, "Wouldn't have wanted to try this back a ways. You go in there, who knows if you come out again?"

"I like that," Selatre said. "You were willing enough to send me off into those woods when I needed to make water. Did you hope you would be rid of me?"

Van coughed and spluttered. "No, lady, nothing like that at all. If I thought of it at all, I thought you were holy enough to have nothing to fear."

"So I may have been, once," Selatre said, gloom returning. "No more."

They rode on a while in silence after that. Eyeing the sinking sun, Gerin said, "We might do well to look for that spot after we came through the free peasant village. They won't know what we're about until we roll past them early tomorrow morning."

"If they're not all downfallen from the quake," Van added. "Only thing I worry about there, Captain—not counting the ghosts, for we've little to give 'em—is monsters on our trail."

"The ghosts will keep them from traveling at night. . . ." Gerin's voice trailed away. "I hope," he finished, realizing he had no way of knowing what—if anything—the ghosts could do to the horrid creatures from the caves.

"*We* can't go on traveling all night," Van said. "Whether the ghosts let us or not, we'd ruin the horses, maybe kill 'em. So stopping's still our best plan, and I think you picked a good place for it."

To the Fox's admiration, Van recognized the little side road down which they'd turned a few nights before. Gerin recognized it, too—once he was on it. But the landmarks looked different coming west from the way they had going east, and he might well have driven right past the junction.

The outlander got busy making a fire. Bow in hand, Gerin walked through the woods in search of a blood offering for the ghosts. When the light began to fade alarmingly before he'd found either bird or beast, he began turning over stones and pieces of bark. He grabbed a fat, long-tailed lizard before it could scuttle back into hiding. It twisted in his grasp and bit his finger hard enough to draw blood from him, but he held on and, swearing, carried the creature to camp.

Van gave it a dubious look. "That's the best you could come up with?" he asked, and made as if to get up himself. But the sun was down by then, and the ghosts beginning to haver. Scowling against their cries, he said, "Cut its throat, quick. It has to be better than nothing."

Gerin made the sacrifice, then flipped away the lizard's writhing body. He peered down into the trench he'd dug. The blood seemed hardly enough to dampen the dirt at the bottom. He wondered if he should have kept hunting till he found a creature with more to give the ghosts.

But in spite of the paltry offering, the night spirits seemed no more vicious than they had at other times when he'd camped in the open. Mildly puzzled but not inclined to complain at his good fortune, he pulled a sack of supplies from the back of the wagon. Selatre accepted the small loaf of hard-baked bread he held out to her, but was careful not to let her fingers brush his when she took it.

He forgot to be irked, exclaiming, "Lady, I wonder if the holiness you bring from Ikos—the last holiness left of Ikos, I fear—isn't helping hold the ghosts at arm's length."

"I am holy no more," she answered bleakly.

"You're the Sibyl no more, true," Gerin said, "but I wonder if the other is so. You didn't abandon Biton; he chose to leave you. How could that be your fault?"

She looked startled, and did not answer. She looked

startled again when Gerin and Van drew straws to see who would take first watch and who second, but shook her head at her own foolishness. "Of course that's needful here," she said, half to herself. "Who would do it for you?"

"We didn't bring any temple guards along, that's certain," Van said. He got up and paced about; Gerin had won his choice, and decided to sleep through the first watch. The outlander went on, "Here, lady, you can take my blanket till I wake up the Fox; then I expect he'll let you have his."

"You're generous, both of you," the Sibyl said, watching Gerin nod. Even so, she made sure she placed herself on the far side of the fire from him before she wrapped the checked square of wool around her and settled down for the night.

Van needed to shake and prod and practically pummel Gerin before he'd wake. The outlander pointed over across the embers to Selatre. With a grin, he said, "She's human enough—she snores." The grin disappeared. "Now how am I supposed to wake her and get my blanket back without making her think I've got rape on my mind? That's what she thinks of touching, plain enough."

"You can have mine if you like," Gerin said.

"Too small for my bulk; you know mine's bigger than the usual," Van said. "I'll take it if I have to, but I'd really like to roll up in my own."

Gerin did some thinking. With his wits midnight-slow, it wasn't easy. At last, though, he said, "Here, I have it." He rose creakily and poked around under a tree until he found a long, dry stick. Then he went over to the Sibyl and tapped her with it until she jerked awake and sat up.

"How dare you lay hands on—" she began. Then she realized Gerin hadn't laid hands on her. Faint firelight and the beams of all the moons but Elleb (which hadn't yet risen) showed her confusion. "I see," she said at last, inclining her head to Gerin. "Your friend wants his blanket back, not so? And you found a way to let me know without touching me. I wonder if I would have done as well." She unwrapped herself and stood. "Here you are, Van of the Strong Arm."

As Van came to strip off his armor and claim the blanket, Selatre stepped back to make sure they didn't bump even by accident. She looked away till he was settled. Then, instead of taking Gerin's blanket at once, she said, "Let me walk off into the woods for a moment first."

She didn't go far because of the ghosts (whose wails seemed to Gerin to get worse while she was away), and came back as fast as she'd promised, but Van was snoring by the time she returned. He'd said Selatre snored, too, but the Fox doubted she came anywhere close to the thunderous buzz he produced.

The former Sibyl wrapped herself in Gerin's blanket and wiggled around on the ground, trying to find a comfortable position. She kept squirming for some time, while Gerin walked back and forth waking up. Finally Selatre said, "I can't sleep right now."

"Nothing too out-of-the-way about that, I suppose, not when you lay in your bed through the day and the night and into the next day again," Gerin said.

"I can still hardly believe that." Selatre looked up into the sky. After a moment, Gerin realized she was studying the moons. When she spoke again, her voice held wonder: "Tiwaz is closer to Math than he should be, and has sped farther past golden Nothos. What you say there must be so, which argues for the truth of the rest of your tale."

"Lady, I told you no lies, nor did Van." The Fox was nettled; here he'd risked his life to save her, and she still wondered if he was nothing more than a kidnapper? That irritation came out in the sneer with which he said, "I trust you don't find yourself polluted by mere talk with a man?"

She flinched as if he'd slapped her. "By no means," she answered tonelessly. "However—" She turned her back on him and started to wrap his blanket around her once more.

"I'm sorry," he said, scraping a shallow trench in the ground with the hobnailed sole of his sandal. "I shouldn't have said that. Talk all you care to; I'll listen."

He wondered if she'd pay any attention to him; he would not have blamed her for ignoring him after that gibe. But, slowly, she turned back to him, eyeing him with the same grave attention she'd given the moon not long before. "You will forgive me when I say that (knowing little of men in general and barons in particular) you strike me as unusual?" she asked.

His laugh held little mirth. "Since everyone in the northlands says as much, why should you be any different?"

"I meant no insult," Selatre said. "The word of you that came to Ikos after Biton laid his hand on me and made me Sibyl held no reproach: indeed, you were on the whole well thought of for trying to hold to the standards of the Empire of Elabon even after Elabon abandoned the northlands."

"Nice to know someone somewhere had some notion of what I was about," Gerin said. "More than my vassals do, I think." With a deliberate effort of will, he forced his thoughts from that gloomy track and changed the subject: "How did it happen that Biton chose you through whom to speak?"

"I'd known he might since I became a woman," Selatre answered. "For though I was normal in every other way, my courses never began, which is a sign of the farseeing one's notice in the villages round his shrine. But Biton's mouth on earth had served him so long I never dreamt he might one day call her to himself at last—or that his eye would fall on me to take her place."

"How did you know you were the one he wanted?" Gerin asked.

"He came to me in a dream." Selatre's eyes went far away, looking through the Fox rather than at him. Slowly, she continued, "It was the realest dream, the most lifelike, you can imagine. The god—touched me. I may say no more. I've never felt anything like that dream for realness, save, very much the opposite way, with horror rather than delight, the evil dreams I've had of late."

Gerin nodded. "I've had those myself. They're worse than any I've known before, that's the truth." He wondered if she experienced them even more vividly because of her intimate contact with Biton and things of the spirit generally. Not knowing any way to find an answer to that, he chose a different question: "Did you go and proclaim yourself at the temple, then?"

"No. I would have, but the very next day the priests came to my village instead. Biton had sent some of them dreams of me, and they sought me out."

"Ah," the Fox said. Had the dream come to Selatre

alone, he might have thought it sprang from her imagination, but if the priests also knew the farseeing god had chosen her to succeed the ancient Sibyl, not much room was left to doubt Biton had sent it.

Endlessly curious, the Fox found a chance to put a question he'd never expected to be able to ask: "What is it like when Biton speaks through you? What do you feel or think or whatever the word is?"

"It's not—like—anything else I know," Selatre answered. "When the mantic fit takes hold of me, of course, I know nothing at all; I always have to ask the priest, if one is there with me, what my response was. But while the god's power is coming over me, before he takes me fully—" She didn't go on, not with words, but she shivered, and her eyes were full of longing. At last she added, "And now no more, never again. No more."

Her voice wept. Suddenly Gerin believed in his belly that she would sooner have died than be rescued at the cost of losing that link with Biton; it struck him as almost like losing a lover or a husband. But with the temple cast down and monsters loose on the northlands, the link was surely lost anyhow. Had he not believed that, he would have drowned in guilt.

Maybe Selatre conceded the point, however reluctantly, for she said, "And now that it is to be no more, what, lord Gerin, do you see life holding for me at Fox Keep? What would you have me do?"

Gerin had his mouth open to reply before he realized he had no idea what to say. What place had he, had the keep, for Biton's former Sibyl? Serving woman, apt to be pawed by his vassals and his guests? Could she return to peasant life after time spent with the god? He doubted it.

And then, just as he was about to confess ignorance, inspiration struck. "Do you have your letters?" he asked.

"No—Biton spoke to me direct, not through scribblings," she answered. "But I always thought I might like to learn."

"I'd be glad to teach you," he said. "One of the things that goes into keeping up the standards of the Empire of Elabon, as you called it, is having a grasp of time and place that goes farther than what you—or I, or anyone—can keep in your head. The more people who read and write, the more who can get that wide knowledge civilization needs. I teach as many folk as I can."

"As may be," Selatre said. "But what has it to do with whatever my life at Castle Fox would become?"

"I have a fair store of books at the keep," Gerin answered. "Oh, any bibliophile south of the Kirs would laugh himself silly to hear it called such, but I do have several dozen scrolls and codices, and I get new ones—old ones other folk don't care about, most of the time—now and again. I had in mind for you, if you think it would suit, to take charge of them, learn what's in them and where it can be found, make new copies as they're needed or if someone asks for such: not likely, I admit, in the state the northlands are in, but stranger things have happened. What say you?"

She was silent a long time, so long he began to fear he'd somehow insulted her after all, even if he'd just intended to find her a place where she could be useful and one that might keep her from some of what she would surely see as indignities. Then, at last, she said, "I am not ashamed to tell you I must apologize, lord Gerin."

"Why?" he asked, startled. "For what?"

"In spite of everything you've said, you have to understand I had trouble fully crediting your reasons for snatching me from Ikos," she answered. "Once you had me back at Fox Keep, who could guess what you might do with me? In truth, I could guess, and my guesses frightened me." Her laugh came shaky, but it was a laugh. "And instead of putting me in your bed, you'd put me in your library. Do you wonder that I needed a moment before I found a way to answer you?"

"Oh," Gerin said. "Put that way, no." He too took a while groping for words before he went on, "Lady, enough women are willing that forcing one who's not has always struck me as more trouble than it's worth. But folk who have wits and can use them are precious as the tin that hardens copper to bronze. I judge you may be one of that sort. If you are, by Dyaus, I'll use you."

"Fair and more than fair," she said, then seemed to surprise herself with a yawn. "Perhaps I shall sleep more, after all. My heart is easier than I thought it could be."

"I'm glad of that," Gerin said as she wrapped herself in his blanket again. She seemed to have forgotten the creatures still issuing from the cave under Biton's temple. He remembered, but forbore to remind her. Let her rest easy while she could.

The free peasant village whose men had hunted Gerin and Van through the night on their way to Ikos was a sorry place when they and Selatre rode up to it at midmorning the next day. Half the houses had fallen down in the earthquake; several bodies lay sprawled and stiff on the grass, awaiting burial.

"If they'd built stronger, they'd have come through better," Van said, unwilling to waste much sympathy on folk who would have robbed and maybe murdered him.

"Maybe so," Gerin said, "but maybe not, too. Stronger houses might still have fallen—look at Biton's temple. And if they did, they'd have crushed whoever was inside them. This way, a lot of people probably managed to crawl out of the wreckage."

"Mm, something to that, maybe," Van admitted. "All the same, I won't be sorry to see this place behind me." He started to urge the horses up from a walk to a trot.

"No, wait," Gerin said, which made the outlander grunt in surprise and send him a disbelieving look. He explained: "The lady there has but the one linen dress, which is all very well for prophesying in but not what you'd want to wear day in and day out. I was thinking we might stop and buy another here, something of sturdy wool that would do until we got back to Castle Fox."

"Ah. There's sense to you after all. There usually is, but this time I wondered." Van reined in.

Several of the villagers were in the fields; earthquake or no, tragedies or no, the endless routine of tillage had to go on. The women and children and few men who stayed by the houses swarmed toward the travelers' wagon. "Noble sirs, spare us such aid in our misfortunes as you can give," a woman cried. Others said the same thing in different words.

The Fox stared down his nose at them. "By Dyaus, you're better disposed to us now than you were when you came after us in the night to take our armor and swords."

"And mace," Van added, hefting the viciously spiked weapon in question. If the peasants had any thoughts of trying to attack now, the blood-red reflections of the sun off those bronze spikes did a good job of dissuading them.

The older man who'd sold the travelers a hen spoke for his people: "Lords, we all have to live as best we can, so I shan't go grizzling out I'm-sorries, though I expect you wish the five hells would take us. But would you see us cast down like this?"

"You don't have it as bad as some," Gerin said: "The temple at Ikos crashed in ruins yesterday." The peasants wailed, some in genuine horror and distress, others, Gerin judged, in fear that, with the temple ruined, no one would ever again use the road from the Elabon Way to Ikos. That was, he thought, a good guess. He went on, "In aid of which, I present to you the lady Selatre, who was till yesterday the Sibyl at Ikos, and whom we rescued from the wreckage of the place."

The villagers gasped and exclaimed all over again. The Fox got down from the wagon to let Selatre descend without—the gods forfend!—touching him; Van shifted on the seat to make her way out easy. The peasants stared at her and muttered among themselves. At last one of them called to her, "Lady, though the temple be fallen, why did you not stay and wait for its repair?"

Selatre cast down her eyes and did not answer. Gerin looked for some gentle way to break the news of the eruption of the monsters from the caves below the fane. While he was looking, Van, who minced few words, said, "If she'd stayed, she'd have been eaten. The same is liable to happen to the lot of you in the next few days, so you'd better listen to what we have to say."

He and Gerin, as was their way, took turns telling the tale of what had happened back at Ikos. When they were through, the fellow from whom they'd bought the chicken, who seemed to be a village spokesman, said, "If you didn't have the Sibyl with you, I'd reckon you were makin' up the tale to pay us back with a fright for wanting to lift the bronze off you."

"And since the lady is here, what do you believe?" Gerin demanded in no small exasperation. "You'll find out soon enough whether we lie, I can tell you that. You've made a point of getting arms and armor, however you do it. When those creatures come, you'll need them. Don't leave them sitting wherever you've got them hidden; wear the mail, and take the spears and swords out into the fields with you."

"Take bows, too," Van said. "These monsters aren't what you'd call clever, from the little we saw of 'em. They don't know arrows. Every one you kill from long range is one you won't have to fight up close. I'd say they're stronger and faster than people, and they have nasty teeth."

The details the Fox and Van gave were enough to begin to convince the villagers they weren't just trying to frighten them. "Maybe we'll do as you say," the old man said after looking over his comrades.

"Do whatever you bloody well please," Gerin said. "If you don't care about your necks, don't expect me to do your worrying for you. All I'd like to do before I get out of here is buy a proper wool dress for the lady. I'll pay silver for it, too, though the gods alone know why I'm dealing justly with folk who aimed to deal unjustly with me."

When he said "silver," three or four women ran into their houses—those that still stood—and brought out dresses. None of them seemed to the Fox to stand out from the others; he turned to Selatre. She felt of them and examined the stitching with the air of a woman who had done plenty of her own spinning and weaving and sewing. Gerin remembered she had been a peasant before she was Sibyl: she knew of such things.

"This one," she said at last.

The woman who'd produced it tried to set a price more or less equal to its weight in silver. Gerin, who parted with precious metal reluctantly at best, let out a loud, scornful laugh. "We don't have to buy here," he reminded her. "Other villages must have seamstresses who've not been stricken mad." After that, she quickly got more reasonable; he ended up buying the dress with only a slight wince.

"Have you also a pair of drawers you might sell?" Selatre asked.

The woman shook her head. "Don't wear 'em but in winter, to help keep my backside warm." Selatre shrugged; likely it had been the same where she grew up, too.

"Do you want to put the dress on here, where you'll have more in the way of privacy?" Gerin asked her.

"I'd not thought of that," she said. "Thank you for doing it for me." She ducked into one of the peasant huts, soon returning wearing the wool dress and with the linen one under her arm. Some of the aura of the Sibyl's cave left her with the change of clothes; she seemed more intimately a part of the world around her, not so much a waif cast adrift by circumstance. Maybe she felt that, too; she sighed as she stepped around Gerin to stow the linen dress in the wagon. "It's as if I'm putting away part of my past."

"The gods willing, you have long years left ahead of you," Gerin answered. He meant it as no more than a polite commonplace, but it set him wondering. With monsters not only loose on the world but emerging from the ruins of Biton's temple, who could judge the will of the gods?

Van spoke to the villagers: "Remember what we told you, now. How sorry you'll be in a few days depends on whether you listen to us or not. You take no notice today, you won't have the chance to be sorry and wish you'd paid heed."

"And the lot of you, you're just driving away and leaving the trouble behind your wheels," said the older peasant who spoke for the peasants.

He had some reason to sound bitter. Peasants stayed with their land; a journey to the next village was something strange and unusual for them. But Gerin said, "If what I fear is true, you'll just see the creatures before us; there may well be enough to torment all the northlands."

He did not convince the peasant, who said, "Aye, but you're a lord; you can hide behind your stone walls." He gestured to the buildings of the village, some of them fallen and even those still standing none too strong. "Look at the forts we have."

To that the Fox found no good reply. Once Selatre was aboard the wagon, he climbed in, too. Van clucked to the horses and flicked the reins. The animals snorted and began to walk. The wagon rolled out of the peasant village.

When they'd gone a couple of furlongs, Selatre said, "The man back there was right. He and his have no way to shelter against the creatures that come forth against them."

"I know," Gerin answered sadly. "I have nothing I can do about it, though. Did I stay to fight, I'd die, and so would they, and so I'd do them no good, and myself only harm."

"I saw as much," Selatre said. "Otherwise I'd not have waited to speak until the villagers could not hear. But that's a callous way to have to look at the world."

"Lady, the world's a hard place," Van said. "Begging your pardon, but I'm thinking you've not seen a whole lot of it. Well, now you will, and much of what you see, I fear, will leave you less than joyful."

Selatre didn't answer. Gerin couldn't tell whether that was because she disagreed with Van but was too polite to say so or because she agreed but didn't care to admit it. His opinion of her good sense had risen a notch, though, for the way she'd held her tongue where speaking out would have embarrassed him.

They returned to the Elabon Way that afternoon. Selatre exclaimed in pleasure at seeing Biton's mark on the stone that marked the side road. Then, remembering what had happened back at Ikos, she sobered once more. Gerin said, "I'm sorry the stone reminded you of the temple, but I must say you're taking it bravely."

"In part, I suppose, what happened back there still seems unreal, not least because I wasn't awake to see and feel it myself," she answered. "And I lived most of my life in a village not much different from the one we went through. I know life can be hard."

Van urged the horses onto the stone slabs of the Elabon Way. The drum of their hoofbeats, so different from the muffled clopping they'd made on the dirt side road, caught Selatre's notice. She exclaimed in wonder: "Here's a marvel! Who would have thought you could cover over a roadway and use it the whole year around? No mud here."

"That's why they made it so," Gerin agreed. "You catch on fast."

"The work it must have taken," Selatre said. "How far does it run?"

"From the Kirs up to the Niffet," the Fox said. "In the old days, they could command and have folk heed." He clicked his tongue between his teeth, remembering the troubles he had keeping the stretch of the Elabon Way under his control even partly and poorly repaired.

Van said, "Seems to me, Captain, every time we come north toward your holding, we're in the midst of trouble. Last time, we were heading into the teeth of the Trokmoi, and now we're stormcrows ahead of those—things—coming out of Ikos."

"We'd better stay ahead of them, too," Gerin said. "Otherwise we won't make it back to Fox Keep." He pointed to the horses. "We have to get the best we can from them without making them break down. Getting stuck somewhere could prove downright embarrassing."

"That's one word for it," Van said, "and a politer one than I'd choose, too."

Gerin had hoped to reach some lordlet's castle by nightfall; all at once, the idea of sleeping behind walls too high to be easily climbed developed a new and urgent appeal. But the approach of sunset found the wagon on the road with no keep in sight, only a peasant village. The Fox glumly bought a chicken and pushed the horses forward until the first stirrings of the ghosts reluctantly made him stop.

"No sooner than we start out tomorrow, we'll ride past three keeps," he grumbled as Van spun his firebow. The outlander made fire with his usual skill; Gerin killed the fowl, drained its blood as an offering, then gutted it and did a hasty job of plucking before he cut it in pieces for cooking.

"That's the way of things, Captain, so it is," Van agreed. He turned to Selatre. "Ah, thank you, lady—is that wild basil you've found?"

"Yes." She set the herb on the ground so he could pick it up and rub the chicken with it before he put the meat over the flames.

Gerin drew first watch. Selatre curled up in his blanket and tonight fell asleep almost at once. When she began to snore (something Van had mentioned, but not a noise the Fox had thought to associate with someone a god sometimes possessed), the outlander sat up. Gerin jerked in alarm. "I thought you were gone, too," he said reproachfully.

"I nearly was, before I thought of something that woke me right up again," Van said. "Mind you, Fox, I'm not saying a word against aught you've done since the earthquake—you'd best understand that. But—"

"What is it?" Gerin asked, suspicion in his voice. Anyone who prefaced his remarks by denying he was going to criticize always ended up doing just that.

"Well, Captain, all well and good we rescued the Sibyl here, even if she won't let herself be touched by the likes of us. All well and good—better than well and good—you've figured out a place for her at Castle Fox if she picks up her letters as you hope. But we're bringing back with us a lass who's young and not the least comely I've seen— *and what will sweet Fand say to that?*"

"Oh, father Dyaus." Gerin didn't know in detail the answer to that question, but contemplating it was plenty to make his head start aching. "She'll wonder which of us aims to throw her out of the keep, and she won't think a finger's breadth past that—which will end up tempting me to throw her out even if the notion hadn't crossed my mind till now."

"Just what I was thinking, Captain. Hard to have lustful thoughts about a woman who'd turn blue if you brushed her hand while you passed her a drumstick, but will Fand see it the same way? I ask you."

"Not likely." One of the serfs in Besant's village was a decent potter, not for any fancy ware but for serviceable cups and jars. Gerin had the feeling he'd be busy soon: when Fand got upset, crockery started flying. The Fox scowled at his friend. "Thank you so much. I wasn't going to have any trouble staying awake through my watch anyhow. Now I wonder if I'll ever sleep again."

Van started to bark laughter, then abruptly stopped. "Might not be safe sleeping in the same bedchamber, and that's a fact, seeing how she stuck a knife into that Trokmê."

"Mm—there is that." Gerin tried to look on the bright side: "Maybe she'll take it all in good part, or maybe she'll be so offended when we bring in Selatre that she'll get up on her hind legs and take the next boat over the Niffet."

"Since when did Fand ever make anything easy, outside the bedroom, I mean?" Van said. He didn't wait for an answer—which was as well, for Gerin had none to give him—but lay down again and soon began to snore loud enough to drown out Selatre.

After a while, what precisely had happened at Ikos began to blur in Gerin's mind with the tale he told of it at every peasant village and lord's holding up along the Elabon Way. The disbelief he met was so strong that sometimes he began to doubt his own memory. Only when he looked to the former Sibyl at his side was he reassured he hadn't imagined it all.

"They're a pack of fools," Van said after the travelers rolled out of the keep of one of Ricolf's vassals.

"Oh, I don't know," Gerin answered resignedly. "Had someone come to Fox Keep with our tale, would you have believed it?"

"They'll find out soon enough whether we're telling the truth," Van said. "And they'll be sorry they think we aren't."

The outlander's pique lasted through a midday meal at the holding of Ricolf himself. Van, though, so loved to spin stories that telling Ricolf about what had happened at Ikos restored his good humor. Ricolf said, "Aye, we felt the quake here, and lost crockery in it, but I'd not looked for word so weighty as what you bring."

Seeing his former father-in-law at least willing to take him seriously, Gerin said, "You'd be wise to start thinking of ways to keep your peasants safe from the monsters as they spread, either by making sure they have a keep they can flee to or by posting armed men among 'em."

"Ah, Fox, you should have been a schoolmaster after all," Ricolf said, smiling not quite enough to take the sting from his words. "You're so good at telling everyone else what he should do; if only you'd try telling yourself as well."

"What's that supposed to mean?" Gerin said.

Instead of answering directly, Ricolf got up from the table and walked out of the long hall into the courtyard. Gerin followed him. Ricolf paused by the well. Gerin started feeling foolish as he walked up to him; if the older baron wanted to make a pleasantry at his expense, he should have ignored it. But he hadn't, and now he'd lose more face by turning around and walking away than by going on.

"What did you mean by that?" he repeated.

"I believe you may not know, so I'll answer straight," Ricolf said. "Anything at all can happen to a person once; the gods delight in keeping us confused so we remember we're not so wise nor so strong as they are. But when a man does something twice, that says more about him than about the way the knucklebones fall."

"You call that a straight answer?" Gerin said. "Dyaus preserve me from a twisty one, then—or Biton, if you aim to take the Sibyl's station now that she's let go of it."

"The Sibyl enters in, sure enough," Ricolf answered, leaning back against the stonework of the well. "This is the second time now, Fox, you've snatched away women you had no proper business taking, Elise being the first."

Gerin exhaled in annoyance. "What was I supposed to do, Ricolf? Leave the Sibyl to be devoured by those— things? If I'd come here with that tale, you'd have found some other way to connect it to your daughter . . . and to blame me for it. It's not as if I'm in love with Selatre."

"As I recall, you weren't in love with Elise, either, not when you took off with her," Ricolf said. "You were just bearing her to her uncle south of the Kirs. But those things have a way of changing."

"Ricolf, however our holdings have sometimes rubbed these past few years, have I ever used you with less than the courtesy any man owes the father of his wife?" Gerin asked. He waited for Ricolf to shake his head before he went on, "Then within that courtesy, I have to tell you you've got your head stuck right in the dung heap."

He took a wary step back. If Ricolf drew blade on him, he wanted room in which to fight. He had no great worries about holding off the older baron, but he wanted to be able to hold him off in a way which suggested to Ricolf's warriors that he wasn't trying to murder their overlord, merely protect himself.

Ricolf stared as if he doubted his own ears. A flush turned his face as red as his hair had once been (Elise had had skin like that, the Fox remembered—transparent as a Trokmê's). Then, to Gerin's relief, a snort escaped his lips and turned into a guffaw. "All right, Fox, you win that one," Ricolf wheezed, but he added, "For now, anyhow. A year or two down the road, we'll see who laughs last."

"Oh, go howl," Gerin said.

"I'm done, I'm done." Ricolf pacifically held up his hands. "Dyaus forbid I should try to tell you anything when you already know all that's been written or thought by every wise man since the gods decided they'd like to have a ball they could kick around and made the world to give themselves something interesting to do: besides swiving one another, I mean, and if that gets stale for a man after a while, it likely does for the gods, too."

"Not by the tales that are told of them," Gerin answered, but he let it go at that; Ricolf waxing philosophical struck him as unlikely enough to make a challenge unwise.

And indeed, Ricolf's next words were utterly mundane: "With all this hurrah behind you, you'll be all in a sweat to get back to Fox Keep, so I don't suppose you'll stay the night. You'll be wanting a trussed fowl, then, or some such, to hold the ghosts out of your head."

"Aye, that would be kind of you," the Fox agreed. "Do you know, though, Selatre seems to calm them—not altogether, but partway—by herself. I suppose it's because she was Biton's intimate for so long."

"Does she?" Ricolf's tone irked Gerin, but not enough to make him rise to it. The older baron shrugged and said, "I'll see what sort of bird the kitchen crew can scare up for you."

Instead of a hen, Ricolf's cooks presented Gerin with a trussed duck that tried to bite his hand and quacked furiously when he stowed it in the back of the wagon. It kept quacking, too. "Can't say as I blame it," Van remarked as he got onto the wagon's seat himself. "I wouldn't be happy if anybody did that to me, either."

"Can you tie something around its beak?" Gerin asked Selatre when the duck went right on making a racket after the wagon rolled out of Ricolf's keep and headed up the Elabon Way once more.

"Oh, let it squawk. What else can it do, poor thing?" Selatre said. Since she was in the back of the wagon with it and had to endure more of the noise than Gerin did, and since Van had already said more or less the same thing, the Fox let her have her way. Nonetheless, by the time the sun neared the western horizon, he looked forward to lopping off the duck's head for more reasons than just keeping the ghosts happy.

When they stopped to camp for the night, he steered the wagon off the road to a little pond that had enough saplings growing close by to screen it away from the casual glance of anyone on the road by night. Van got down and began gathering dry leaves and twigs for tinder.

Gerin descended, too. He went around to the back of the wagon and said to Selatre, "Hand me out that pestiferous duck, if you please. We'll eat him tonight, but he's already had his revenge. My head aches."

The ex-Sibyl seemed merely practical, not oracular, as she picked up the duck by the feet and held it out to Gerin, warning, "Be careful as you take him. He'll do his best to bite; he won't just quack."

"I know." Trying to take the duck from Selatre without touching her as he did so didn't make things any easier for Gerin, but he managed, and didn't bother mentioning the extra awkwardness. If that was how Selatre was going to be, he'd accept it as best he could.

Once he had the duck, he set it on the ground. He made himself stand by and not offer Selatre a hand as she got down from the wagon, wondering all the while how long he'd need before not offering aid became automatic for him. Then Selatre stumbled over a root, exclaimed, and started to fall. Altogether without thinking, Gerin jumped forward and steadied her.

"Thank you," she said, but then stopped in confusion and jumped back from him as if he were hot as molten bronze.

"I'm sorry," he said, though apologizing for having kept her from hurting herself struck him as absurd.

She shivered as she looked down at the arm he'd grabbed, then nodded with the same sort of deliberation Gerin had shown when he kept himself from helping her down a few moments before. "It's all right," she said. "However much I try to stay away from them, these things will happen now that I'm so rudely cast into the world. I may as well do my best to get used to them."

The Fox bowed. "Lady, on brief acquaintance I thought you had good sense. Everything you do—this especially— tells me I was right."

"Does it?" Selatre's laugh came shaky. "If that's so, why do I feel as if I'm casting away part of myself, not adding on anything new and better?"

"Change, any change, often feels like a kick in the teeth," Gerin answered. "When the Trokmoi killed my father and my elder brother and left me lord of Fox Keep, I thought the weight of the whole world had landed on my shoulders: I aimed to be a scholar, not a baron. And then—" He broke off.

"Then what?" Selatre asked.

Gerin wished he'd managed to shut up a few words earlier. But he'd raised the subject, so he felt he had to answer: "Then a few years ago my wife ran off with a horseleech, leaving me to raise our boy as best I could. His kidnapping was what made me come to Ikos."

"Yes, you've spoken of that." Selatre nodded, as if reminding herself. "But if you hadn't come, by everything else you've told me, the creatures that dwelt in the caves under Biton's temple would have killed and eaten me after the earthquake."

"If the earthquake would have happened had I not come," Gerin said, remembering the words of doom in the last prophecy Biton had issued through Selatre's mouth.

Van came around the wagon. "I've already got the fire going," he announced. "Are you going to finish off that duck, or do you aim to stand around jabbering until the ghosts take away what few wits you have left?" He turned to Selatre. "Take no notice of him, lady, when he gets into one of his sulks. Give him a silver lining, as you did, and he'll make a point of looking for its cloud."

"To the hottest of the five hells with you," Gerin said. Van only laughed. The nettle he'd planted under Gerin's hide stung the worse for bearing a large measure of truth.

The Fox dug a trench in the ground with his dagger, then drew sword and put an end to the duck's angry squawking with a stroke that might have parted a man's head from his shoulders, much less a bird's. He drained the duck's blood into the trench for the ghosts. Van took charge of the carcass. "It'll be greasy and gamy, but what can you do?" he said as he opened the belly to get rid of the entrails.

"Gamy or no, I like the flavor of duck," Selatre said. "Duck eggs are good, too; they have more taste than those from hens."

"That's so, but hens are easier to care for—just let 'em scavenge, like pigs," Gerin said. He glanced around. "Even though we were slow with the offering, the ghosts are still very quiet. Lady, I think that's your doing, no matter that we happened to touch again."

Selatre cocked her head to the side, listening to the ghosts as they wailed and yammered inside her head. "You may be right," she said after she'd taken their measure. "I remember them louder and more hateful than this when I was still living in my village, before Biton made me his Sibyl. But I am Sibyl no more; the god himself said as much, and your touch sealed it—" She shook her head in confusion; the dark hair that had spilled over one shoulder flew out wildly.

Gerin said, "I don't think holiness is something you can blow out like a lamp. It doesn't so much matter that I touched you—certainly I didn't do it with lust in my heart, or aiming to pollute you. What matters is that the god touched you. My touch is gone in an instant; Biton's lingers."

Selatre thought about that and slowly nodded, her finely molded features thoughtful. Watching her in the firelight, Gerin decided Van had been right: she was attractive enough to make Fand jealous. Was she more attractive than the Trokmê woman? Their looks were so different, the comparison didn't seem worthwhile. But that it had even crossed his mind made him wonder if Ricolf hadn't been wiser back at his keep than the Fox had thought at the time.

He scowled, angry at himself for so much as entertaining that notion. Selatre said, "What's wrong? You look as if you just bit into something sour."

Before he could come up with anything plausible, Van saved the day, calling, "Come over here by the fire, both of you, and bite into something that's going to be gamy and greasy, like I said before, but better all the same than a big empty curled up and purring in your belly."

The duck was just as Van had predicted it would be, but Gerin fell to gratefully even so. A full mouth gave him the excuse he needed for not answering Selatre's question, and a full belly helped him almost—if not quite—forget the thoughts which had prompted that question in the first place.

The wagon came out from behind the last stand of firs that blocked the view toward Castle Fox. "There it is," Gerin said, pointing. "Not a fortress to rival the ones the Elabonian Emperors built in the pass south of Cassat, but it's held for many long years now; the gods willing, it'll go on a bit longer."

Selatre leaned forward in the rear of the wagon to see better, though she was still careful not to brush against the Fox or Van. "Why are most of the timbers of the palisade that ugly, faded green?" she said.

Van chuckled. "The lady has taste."

"So she does." Gerin refused to take offense, and answered the question in the spirit in which he hoped it had been asked: "It was a paint a wizard put on them, to keep another wizard from setting them afire."

"Ah," Selatre said. Thin in the distance—Gerin did not allow trees and undergrowth to spring up anywhere near the keep; if anyone set ambushes, he'd be that one—a horn from the watchtower said the wagon had been seen.

He twitched the reins and rode forward with a curious mixture of anticipation and dread: seeing his comrades again would be good, and perhaps some of them had word of Duren. But the trouble he expected from Fand cast a shadow over the homecoming.

"We were free peasants in the village where I grew up; we owed no lord service," Selatre said. "Not much of what we heard about Elabonian barons was good, and I came to have a poor opinion of the breed. You tempt me to think I may have been wrong."

Gerin shrugged. "Barons are men like any others. Some of us are good, some bad, some both mixed together like most people. I'm bright enough, for instance, but I worry too much and I'm overly solitary. My vassal Drago the Bear, whom you'll meet, isn't what you call quick of wit and he hates anything that smacks of change, but he's brave and loyal and has the knack of making his own people like him. And Wolfar of the Axe, who's dead now, was vicious and treacherous, if you ask me, but he'd never shrink from a fight. As I say, we're a mixed bag."

"You speak of yourself as if you were someone else," Selatre said.

"I try sometimes to think of myself that way," the Fox answered. "It keeps me from making too much of myself in my own mind. The fellow who's sure he can't possibly go wrong is usually the one who's likeliest to."

A couple of men came out of the gate and waved to the approaching wagon: squat Drago with slim Rihwin beside him. "Any luck, lord?" Drago called, raising his voice to a shout.

"What did the Sibyl say?" Rihwin asked, also loudly.

"We're still the ripple of news furthest out from where the rock went into the pond," Van said.

"So we are." Gerin nodded, adding, "I like the picture your words call to mind." Behind them and in every other direction, others would also be spreading word of what had happened at Ikos. Soon the whole of the northlands would know. But for now, there was a dividing line between those who did and those who didn't, and he and Van were on it.

He raised his voice in turn to answer his vassals: "By your leave, I'll tell the tale in the great hall and not sooner. That way I'll have to retell it only once, and there's a good deal to it."

"Is that Duren in the wagon behind you?" Rihwin asked.

Drago's sight had begun to lengthen as he aged. Today, that served him well. "No, loon," he said. "That's a man grown. No, I take it back—a woman?" The Fox didn't blame him for sounding surprised.

Rihwin's agile wits let him leap to a conclusion that wouldn't have occurred to Drago. "You've caught up with Elise?" he said loudly. "Did she steal the boy away, lord Gerin?" That his wits were agile, of course, didn't necessarily mean he was right.

At that moment, Gerin wished he'd kept quiet. The rumor would be all over the keep, all over the serf villages, and would spread faster than the truth could follow it. "No, it's not Elise," he said, even louder than Rihwin had spoken. "This is the lady Selatre, who up till bare days ago was Biton's Sibyl at Ikos."

Warriors up on the palisade, who'd already begun to gossip about Rihwin's speculation, abruptly fell silent. Then they started buzzing again, more busily than before. Maybe Rihwin's wild guess wouldn't go everywhere after all, Gerin thought: the truth was so much stranger that it might take precedence.

He drove the wagon over the drawbridge and into the keep, then got down from it. Van slipped off from the other side. They both stood back to let Selatre descend with no risk of touching either of them.

Gerin introduced his vassals to her one by one. He wondered how good she'd be at matching unfamiliar names to equally unfamiliar faces; that often gave him trouble. But she coped well enough, and showed she knew who was who when she spoke to the men. The Fox was impressed.

Widin Simrin's son asked the question they all had to be thinking: "Uh, lord Gerin, how did you come to have the holy Sibyl riding with you?"

"You felt the earthquake a few days past?" Gerin asked in turn.

Heads bobbed up and down. Drago said, "Aye, we did, lord. Like to scare the piss out of me, it did. We lost some pots, too, and spilled ale from a couple of broken jars." He sighed in sorrow at the misfortune. Then he scratched his head. "Has that aught to do with the lady here?"

"It has everything to do with the lady here," Gerin said. Van nodded, the crimson horsehair plume on his helm drawing eyes to him. The Fox went on, "Let's all go into the great hall. I hope not all the ale spilled." He waited until reassured on that before finishing, "Good, for I'll need a mug or two to ease my throat as I—and Van, and the lady Selatre—tell you what happened, and why she's here."

He waved toward the entrance to the castle. Drago and Widin and Rihwin and the rest hurried inside. Selatre waited till they'd gone through the door before she too went in. Even if she'd consciously decided not to let getting touched every once in a while bother her, she aimed to avoid it where she could.

Gerin did not go into the great hall until even Selatre was inside. He told himself that was politeness, and so it was, but it was also anxiety: he put off for a moment the likelihood of confronting Fand.

He knew that was foolish: putting off trouble, even for a little while, wasn't worth the effort, and often made it worse when it finally came. But knowing that and facing up to a screaming fight with Fand were two different things. At last, bracing himself as if walking into a winter wind, he walked into the great hall.

His stiff pose eased as his eyes adjusted to the gloom within: Fand had to be still upstairs. "Took you long enough," Van rumbled, though he no doubt had the same concern. "If you'd stayed out there much longer, the ale would've been drunk by the time you got around to joining us."

"Can't have that." Gerin went over to the jar and dipped a jack full. He wet his throat, then told what had happened on the way to Ikos and after he and Van had got there. His vassal barons muttered angrily when he spoke of the peasants who'd hunted him in the night. He shook his head. "I was angry at the time, too, but it all fades away when you set it alongside what came later."

He spoke of the trip down to the Sibyl's cave and of the disturbing oracular response Biton had delivered through Selatre's lips. His listeners muttered again, this time with the same dread he'd felt when those doom-filled words washed over him. Selatre broke in, "I remember lord Gerin and Van coming into my underground chamber, but nothing after that, for the mantic trance had possessed me."

Gerin went on with the rest of the story: Selatre's continued and abnormal unconsciousness, the meeting with Aragis in the temple, the carouse afterwards (now that his hangover was gone, Van grinned in fond memory), and the earthquake the next morning.

Sometime while he was going through all that, Fand came down and sat beside Drago the Bear. Maybe the vassal baron's bulk kept Gerin from spotting her right away, or maybe he'd kept from looking toward the stairs on purpose. But she leaned forward when he spoke of the monsters that had emerged from the ruins of Biton's temple. Again, he had his listeners' complete and dismayed attention. Fand kept quiet while he spoke of the battle the creatures had had with the temple guards in the sacred precinct.

Then he said, "We'd gone back there, Van and I, because our innkeeper said the Sibyl still hadn't come to her senses. After the quake, we feared her cottage would burn like so many buildings in the town of Ikos. Since we'd been responsible for pitching her into the fit, we thought we should make amends for it if we could. As it happened, her dwelling hadn't caught fire, but the monsters would have made short work of her if we hadn't got there when we did."

Fand stirred but still did not speak. Selatre said, "I woke up in their wagon some hours later, with my world turned all topsy-turvy."

Actually hearing Selatre seemed to draw Fand's notice to her. The Trokmê woman leaned forward, her chin on her hands, intently studying the former Sibyl. Then, to Gerin's dismay, she got to her feet and looked from him to Van. In a voice low but no less menacing because of that, she said, "And which of you was it, now, who was after wanting to trade me for the first new bit o' baggage you chanced upon, like a wandering tinker mending a pot in exchange for a night's rest and a bit o' bread in the morning?"

"Now, lass, didn't you listen to the Fox?" Van usually had no trouble with women, but now he sounded nervous, which didn't help. "It wasn't her body we had designs on, just saving her life."

"Likely tell," Fand snarled. "Sure and you'd have been just as eager to go back for her had she been old and toothless, not young and toothsome, sure and you would."

Gerin had thought himself the most sarcastic soul in the northlands; saying one thing and meaning another was a subtle art more often practiced south of the High Kirs. But wherever Fand had picked it up, she was dangerously good at it. And her furious question made the Fox ask himself if he would have headed back toward the fane to rescue Selatre's crone of a predecessor. He had to admit he didn't know, and that troubled him.

"Is this your wife, lord Gerin, thinking I'm some sort of menace to her?" Selatre asked. "I hope that is not so." Now she looked as if she doubted anew all the assurances she'd come to trust on the road north from Ikos.

"My leman, rather, and Van's," the Fox answered. Selatre raised an eyebrow at his domestic arrangements, but he ignored that; he'd worry about it later. Fand, as usual, was immediate trouble. To her, he said, "I'll thank you to keep a civil tongue in your head. By the gods, I did what I did for the reasons I said I did it, and if you don't fancy that, you can pack up and leave."

"Och, you'd like that, now wouldn't you?" Fand was low-voiced no more; her screech drove Drago from the seat close by her. "Well, lord Gerin the Fox—and you too, you overthewed oaf"—this to Van—"you'll not be rid of me so easy as that, indeed and you won't. Use me and cast me forth, will you?"

She picked up her drinking jack and threw it at Gerin. It was half full; a trail of ale, like a comet's tail, followed it as it flew. The Fox had been expecting it, so he ducked in good time—you needed battle-honed reflexes to live with Fand.

Van tried again. "Now, lass—"

She snatched the dipper out of the jar of ale and flung it at him. It clanged off the bronze of his cuirass. He was vain about his gear; he looked down in regret and anger at the ale that dripped to the floor.

"I ought to heat your backside for that," he said, and took a step forward, as if to do it on the spot.

"Aye, come ahead, thrash me," Fand fleered, and stuck out the portion of her anatomy he had threatened. "Then tomorrow or the day after or the day after that you'll be all sweet and poke that cursed one-eyed snake o' yours in my face—and I'll bite down hard enough to leave you no more'n a newborn wean has. D'you think I wouldn't?"

By the appalled look he wore, Van thought she would. He turned to Gerin for help in quelling this mutiny. The Fox didn't know what to say, either. He wondered if Fand would storm out of the castle, or if he'd have to throw her out. He didn't really want to do that; for all her hellish temper, he liked having her around, and not just because he slept with her. Till Duren was kidnapped, she'd watched over him as tenderly as if she'd given birth to him. Her wits were sharp, too, as he sometimes found to his discomfort.

Right now, though, he wouldn't have minded putting a hard hand to her behind, if only he'd thought that would make matters better. Unfortunately, he thought it would make them worse. If force wouldn't help and she wouldn't listen to reason, what did that leave? He wished he could come up with something.

Then Selatre got to her feet. She dropped a curtsy to Fand as if the Trokmê woman had been Empress of Elabon and said, "Lady, I did not come here intending to disrupt your household in any way: on that I will take oath by any gods you choose. I am virgin in respect of men, and have no interest in changing my estate there; as lord Gerin and Van of the Strong Arm both know, any touch from an entire man would have left me religiously defiled before—before Biton abandoned me." Her brief hesitation showed the pain she still felt at that. "I tell you once more, I am not one like to steal either of your men from you."

Where Gerin and Van had fanned Fand's fury, Selatre seemed to calm her. "Och, lass, I'm not after blaming you," she said. "By all 'twas said, you had not even your wits about you when these two great loons snatched you away. But what you intend and what will be, oftentimes they're not the same at all, at all. Think you I intended to cast my lot with southron spalpeens?"

"I'm no southron," Van said with some dignity.

"You're no Trokmê, either," Fand said, to which the outlander could only nod. But Fand wasn't screaming any more; she just sounded sad, maybe over the way her life had turned out, maybe—unlikely though that seemed to Gerin—regretting her show of temper.

"And what am I?" Selatre said. She answered her own question: "I was the god's servant, and proud and honored he had chosen me through whom to speak. But now he has left me, and so I must be nothing." She hid her face in her hands and wept.

Gerin was helpless with weeping women. Maybe that explained why he got on with Fand as well as he did—instead of weeping, she threw things. He knew how to respond to that. He hadn't known what to do when Elise cried, either, and suddenly wondered if that had been one of the things that made her leave.

He looked to Van, who made an art of jollying women into good spirits. But Van looked baffled, too. He jollied women along mostly to get them into bed with him; when faced with a virgin who wanted to stay such, he was at a loss.

Finally the Fox went into the kitchens and came back with a bowl of water and a scrap of cloth. He set them in front of Selatre. "Here, wash your face," he said. She gulped and nodded. Van beamed, which made Gerin feel good; he might not have done much, but he'd done *something*. It was a start.

VI

A chariot came pounding up the road toward Fox Keep. The driver was whipping the horses on so hard that the car jounced into the air at every bump, threatening to throw out him and his companion. "Lord Gerin! Lord Gerin!" the archer cried.

The Fox happened to be on the palisade. He stared down in dismay at the rapidly approaching chariot. He was afraid he knew what news the onrushing warriors bore. But he had been back in Fox Keep only five days himself; he'd hoped he might have longer to prepare. Hopes and reality too often parted company, though. "What word?" he called to the charioteer and his passenger.

They didn't hear him over the rattling of the car and the pound of the horses' hooves, or spy him on the wall. The chariot roared into the courtyard of the keep. The driver pulled back on the reins so sharply that both horses screamed in protest. One tried to rear, which might have overturned the chariot. The lash persuaded the beast to keep all four feet on the ground.

At any other time, Gerin would have reproved the driver for using the horses so; he believed treating animals mildly got the best service from them. Now, as he hurried down from the walkway across the wall, such trivial worries were far from his mind. "What word?" he repeated. "Tomril, Digan, what word?"

Tomril Broken-Nose tossed the whip aside and jumped out of the chariot. "Lord Gerin, I'm here to tell you I beg your pardon," he said.

"You didn't come close to killing your team for that," the Fox answered.

"Oh, but we did, lord prince," Digan Sejan's son said. "Tomril and I, we both thought you were babbling like a night ghost when you came up the Elabon Way warning folk of those half-man, half-beast things that were supposed to have gotten loose from under some old temple or other—"

"But now we've seen 'em, lord Gerin," Tomril broke in, his eyes wide. "They're ugly, they're mean, they've got a taste for blood—"

Now Gerin interrupted: "And they must be up at the bottom of Bevon's barony by now, or you wouldn't have seen them. What news do you have from Ricolf's holding?"

"About what you'd expect," Tomril answered. "They're loose there, too, the cursed things, and ripping serf villages to bits."

"Oh, a pestilence," Gerin said wearily. "If they're in Ricolf's holding, and Bevon's, they'll be here, too. How are the peasants supposed to grow crops if they're liable to be killed in the fields or torn to pieces in their beds?"

"Curse me if I know the answer to that one," Tomril said. "Things I've seen, things I've heard, make me think these creatures are worse than the Trokmoi, and harder to get rid of, too."

"They don't care a fart about loot, neither," Digan chimed in. "They just kill and feed and go away—and in the woods, they're clever beasts, and not easy to hunt."

"I hadn't thought of that, but you're right," Gerin said. "How many Trokmoi have we disposed of because they stayed around to plunder or loaded themselves down with stolen gewgaws till they couldn't even flee?"

"A good many, lord." Tomril touched the hilt of his sword in fond reminiscence. Then he scuffed the ground with a hobnailed sandal. "Won't be so with these monsters, though. They've got teeth and claws and enough of a man's cleverness to be more dangerous'n wolves ever dreamt of, but they aren't clever enough—I don't think so, anyways—to steal the things we make."

"Maybe they're too clever for that," Gerin said. His warriors stared at him in incomprehension. He didn't try to explain; struggling against the black depression that threatened to leave him useless took all he had in him. After he'd ridden out the Trokmê invasion, he'd begun, now and then, to have hope that he might keep something of Elabonian civilization alive north of the High Kirs. Now even a god seemed to have abandoned the land, leaving it open for these monsters from underground to course over it.

Rihwin came up in time to hear the last part of the

exchange between Gerin and the two troopers. He said, "Lord Gerin, meseems these creatures, however horrific their semblance, should by virtue of their beastly nature be most vulnerable to magic: nor are they likely to have sorcerers of their own to help them withstand the cantrips we loose against them."

"The cantrips *I* loose against them, you mean," Gerin said, which made Rihwin bite his lip in embarrassment and nod. Gerin went on, "A really potent mage might be able to do what you say. Whether I can is another question altogether. I tell you frankly, I'm afraid of spells of bane, mostly because I know too well they can smite me instead of the ones at whom I aim them."

"A man who recognizes his limits is wise," Rihwin said, which made Gerin snort, for if he'd ever met a man who had no sense of limit whatever, that man was Rihwin.

Gerin paced up and down in the courtyard. At last he stopped and made a gesture of repugnance. "I won't try those spells," he said. "That's not just for fear of getting them wrong, either. Even if I work them properly, I'm liable to end up like Balamung, consumed by evil magic that's overmastered me."

Rihwin studied him judiciously. "If any man could work spells of bane without their corrupting him, I reckon you to be that man. But whether any man can do such is, I concede, an open question."

"Sometimes open questions are best left unopened," Gerin said. What he would do if faced by disaster complete and unalloyed he did not know; he muttered a silent prayer to Dyaus that he would not have to find out. Aloud, he went on, "What we need to do first, I think, is summon the vassals, fare south, and see if we can't teach those creatures fear enough to make them learn to stay away from lands I hold."

"As you say, lord prince," Rihwin agreed cheerfully. "I look forward to sallying forth against them." He mimed shooting a bow from the pitching platform of a chariot.

The Fox did not look forward to sallying forth. He felt harassed. He'd never wanted to be baron of Fox Keep, and once he became baron willy-nilly he'd never delighted in war for its own sake, as so many men of the northlands did. After the Empire of Elabon abandoned the northlands, his main aim had been to maintain its legacy in the lands he ruled. Fighting all the time did nothing to further that aim, but failing to fight meant dying, so what was he to do?

Rihwin said, "Of course, you also must needs take into account the possibility that the Trokmê clans north of the Niffet will seize the chance to strike south on learning of your deployment toward the opposite side of your holding."

"Thank you so much, bright ray of sunshine," Gerin said. "And I have to worry about Schild Stoutstaff, and Adiatunnus, and where in the five hells my son has disappeared to, and more other things than I have fingers and toes to keep track of."

"Lord Gerin, that's why the Sithonians devised counting boards," Rihwin said with a sly smile. Gerin stooped, picked up a clod of dirt, and flung it at him. Rihwin ducked. His smile got wider and even more impudent. "Ah, my fellow Fox, I see you've been taking lessons in deportment from your lady."

"Grinning and ducking won't save you now," Gerin exclaimed. "You'd better run, too." He chased Rihwin halfway round the keep, both men laughing like boys. Gerin finally stopped. "You're made of foolishness, do you know that?"

"Maybe I am," Rihwin said. "But ifsobe that's true, what does it make you?"

"Daft," Gerin answered at once. "Anyone who'd want to run a holding, let along the beginnings of a realm, has to be daft." He sobered quickly. "I'll have to send out word to my vassal barons to gather here with as many armed men as they can bring. That can't wait. If it does, we'll have other visitors than our warriors."

Fand stood in the doorway to her chamber and shook her head. "No, Fox, I don't care to have you in here this evening, so back to your own bed you can go."

Gerin scowled at her. "Why not? This is three times running you've told me no, and I know you've said aye to Van at least twice." One reason the two friends had stayed friends and not quarreled over Fand was that she'd always treated them pretty evenhandedly—till now.

"Because I don't care to, is why," she said, now tossing her head so her hair flew about in coppery ringlets. "And if that's not enough of an answer to suit you, why, to the corbies with you."

"I ought to—" he began.

"Ought to what?" she broke in. "Have me by force? Och, you can do it the once, belike; you're bigger nor I am, and stronger, too. But your back'd never be safe after that, nor had you better sleep but behind barred door. For that I'd take vengeance if it cost the life of me."

"Will you shut up, you idiot woman, and let me get a word in edgewise?" he roared in a startlingly loud voice—loud and startling enough to make Fand give back a pace. "I was trying to say, before you started screeching at me, that I ought to know what you think I've done wrong so I can figure out whether I really meant it or if I should try to make amends."

"Oh." Fand came as close to seeming subdued as she ever did. After a moment, she sighed. "It's not that you don't mean well, indeed and it isn't. But haven't you had enough to do with women to know that if you need to ask a question like that, the answer'll do you no good?"

Elise had said things like that, not long before she left him. He hadn't understood then, and didn't altogether understand now. "I don't fancy guessing games," he said slowly. "Usually you tell me whatever's in your mind—more than I want to hear, sometimes. Why not now?"

"Och, it's late at night, and I'd sooner sleep than have a row with you the now," Fand said. "Go on to your own bed, Fox. Maybe tomorrow I'll feel kinder toward you—who knows?" Then, because she was honest in her own fashion, she added, "Or maybe I won't."

Evasion made Gerin angry; when he wanted to know something, he kept digging till he found out. "Tell me what you're thinking," he growled. "If I've done something wrong, I'll find a way to make it right."

"You do try that, I'll own; you're just enough and to spare, for a fact," Fand said. "This time, though, 'twill not be so easy for you, I'm thinking." She shut her mouth tight then, and gave him a stubborn look that warned she'd say no more.

More than her words, the set of her face finally told Gerin what she meant. He clapped a hand to his forehead. "You're still sizzling because I brought Selatre to the keep," he exclaimed.

"And wouldn't you be, now, if I was after coming back here with a big-thewed, big-balled Trokmê man with a fine yellow mustache on him?" she said. "Och, puir fellow, by the side o' the road I found him, starving and all. Sure and I didn't fetch him back to sleep with him, even if he will be living in the castle from here on out." She did a wicked parody of his explanation of how he'd come to bring Selatre to Castle Fox, and topped it off by assuming an expression innocent and wanton at the same time.

Gerin hoped he managed to disguise his startled laugh as a cough, but wouldn't have bet money on it. "You have the tongue of a viper, do you know that?" he said. It pleased her, which wasn't what he'd had in mind. He went on, "By the gods, I haven't set a hand on her since she got here. I don't mean I haven't tried to take her to bed, I mean I literally have not touched her. So I don't know why you keep wanting to have kittens about it."

"Foosh, I know you've not touched her." Fand tossed her head in fine contempt. "But can you tell me so easy you've not wanted to?"

"I—" Gerin lied with few qualms when he dealt with his neighbors; only a fool, he reckoned, told the bald truth on all occasions. But lying to his leman was a different business. He ended up not answering Fand at all.

When she saw he wasn't going to, she nodded and quietly shut the door between them. The bar on her side did not come down; he could have gone in.

He stood in the hallway for a minute or so, then muttered, "What's the bloody use?" He went back to his own chamber and lay down. He was still awake when pale Nothos rose in the east, which meant midnight had come and gone. Eventually he slept.

Van sang in the stables as Raffo readied the chariot to go out on campaign. Gerin had always looked on war as an unpleasant part of the business of running a barony, but now the idea of escaping from Castle Fox for a while suited him fine.

When he said as much, Van stopped singing and started to laugh. "What's so stinking funny?" the Fox asked irritably.

"You're that glad to get away from sweet Fand, are you?" Van said, laughing still. "This I tell you: she's as happy to have you gone as you are to be going. Not just her eyes are green; she's jealous enough to spit poison like some of the snakes they have in the jungles of the east."

"I already saw that for myself, thank you very much," Gerin said. He wished Van hadn't brought it up where Raffo and a good many other men as well could listen, but after a moment he realized that didn't matter: the only people in his holding who hadn't heard about how well Fand liked his coming back with Selatre were deaf, and their friends had probably drawn pictures in the dirt for them. Fixing the outlander with a baleful stare, he ground out, "And how is it she hasn't stayed angry with you? You had as much to do with getting Selatre here as I did."

"Oh, no doubt, no doubt," Van admitted. Just then Raffo climbed into the chariot. Van followed him, setting his shield in the bracket on his side of the car.

Gerin did the same on his side. "You were saying?" he prompted when Van showed no sign of going on.

"I was, wasn't I? Well, how do I put it?" Van fiddled with his weapons to give him time to gather his thoughts. Raffo flicked the reins and got the horses going. As they passed from the stable out into the courtyard, the outlander said, "I guess the nub of it is, she believes me when I tell her I'm not out to bed Selatre. You she's not so sure about."

"I don't know what I have to do," Gerin said wearily. "I've told Fand and I've told her—"

"Not that simple, Captain, and you likely know it as well as I do," Van said. "Me, I'm a wencher and not a lot more, and Fand, she suits me well enough, though the gods know I'd sooner she didn't have that redheaded temper of hers. You and Fand, though . . . but for bed, damn me to the hottest one of your five hells if I can see where the two of you fit together."

"She came to Fox Keep at the right time," Gerin answered.

"Oh, I know that," Van said. "After Elise up and left,

any woman would have done you for a while, just to let you remember you're a man. But I'd not expected this to last so long." He laughed again. "I figured you'd sicken of quarreling with her and leave her all to me, not that I know whether I could stand that myself."

"You have all of her now, seems like, without my having any say at all," the Fox answered, less than delighted his friend had seen into him so clearly.

"So I do, and I still don't know whether I can stand it." The outlander sighed. "What made it work so well, the three of us I mean, is that Fand has more than enough venom for any one man, but she's bearable when she has two to spread it on. Of course, it helps that neither of us is the jealous sort."

"No." Gerin let it go at that. Had he cared more for Fand, he thought, he would have been more likely to be jealous, too, but he didn't care to say as much straight out. He did add, "Another thing that helps is that she's lickerish enough for the two of us together. I think she'd wear me out if I had to try to keep her happy by my lonesome."

"You're getting old," Van said, to which the Fox mimed throwing a punch, for his friend was no younger. Then Van sighed again, and went on, "One more thing to worry about." He stopped, seemed to listen to himself, and guffawed. "By the gods, I've been with you too long, Captain. I'm even starting to sound like you."

"Believe me, I like the idea even less than you do," Gerin answered, and Van pretended to wallop him. Up ahead at the reins, Raffo snickered.

The chariots rolled south down the Elabon Way in no particular order, now bunched together, now strung out in a long line. Sometimes the Fox's warriors sang or swapped jokes, sometimes they kept them to themselves. Gerin knew the Empire of Elabon had imposed stricter discipline on its soldiers when it was strong, but he didn't know how the trick was done. By all the evidence, Elabon didn't know anymore, either.

Even though he was still in his own holding, he kept a wary eye on the woods and brush to either side of the Elabon Way. If the monsters from Ikos had been seen in Bevon's holding (not that Bevon held much of it), they might be loose in Palin's lands, too—and they might have come farther north than that.

Serfs in the fields stared as the chariots bounced past them. A few took no chances, but dropped their hoes and stone-headed mattocks and ran for the safety of the trees. After the chaos the northlands had endured the past five years, that did not surprise the Fox, but it left him sad. Here he and his comrades fared forth to protect the peasants, and they seemed to feel they needed protecting from their overlords.

Thanks to Gerin's forethoughtfulness, the little army had several hens among the baggage. They also had enough axes to cut plenty of firewood for a good-sized blaze. Between the offering and the fire, the evening ghosts were hardly more than a distraction.

"We'll set pairs of sentries out all night long in a triangle," Gerin said. "I won't have us assailed without warning."

Van took charge of roasting the two chickens they'd sacrificed. He was the logical man for the job: not only was he as good a roadside cook as anyone else, he was also no one to argue with when he passed out pieces of meat, for there weren't enough to go around. Those who went without chicken made do with hard-baked biscuits and smoked meat, cheese, and onions. Everyone drank ale.

Gerin tossed a gnawed thighbone into the fire. He chewed at a biscuit about as tough as his own teeth. "I wonder if this came from Ros the Fierce's reign, or just Oren's," he said after he managed to get a mouthful down.

"You have no cause to make complaint against Oren the Builder," Rihwin said, "for the image of him you fetched back from the fane at Ikos leaves you perhaps the richest man in the northlands."

"Aye, gold is good to have, I'll not deny," Gerin said. "That's not the way I expected to come by it, but you hear no complaints from me."

Some of the warriors rolled themselves in their blankets as soon as they'd finished eating. Others stayed up a while to talk or roll knucklebones by the light of the fire. Van snarled in angry dismay when he lost three throws in a row; his luck usually ran better than that. Then he lost again, and stood up from the game. "Enough is enough," he declared.

"Well, if you won't gamble with us, what about a tale?" Widin Simrin's son said. He had his own reasons for being willing to call off the game: a nice little pile of silver gleamed in front of him.

Everyone who heard the suggestion spoke up for it all the same, especially the men from outlying keeps who seldom got the chance to hear Van yarn. The outlander coughed and plucked at his beard. "Which tale shall I give you?" he asked. "You pick one for me."

"How about the one about how they teach the monkeys to pick pepper?" Gerin said. "You were going to start it a few days ago, but we got interrupted. And if I've not heard it, my guess is that few others here have."

From the way the warriors exclaimed, none of them knew the story. "So I've not told it in all the time I've been at your keep, eh, Captain?" Van said. "Nice to know I've not yarned myself dry, and that's a fact. All right, here goes: the tale of the way they teach monkeys to pick pepper."

Before he started the story, he paused to swig ale and lubricate his throat. That accomplished, he said, "This is what I saw in Mabalal, which is a hot, damp country a good ways east and south from Kizzuwatna. Take the muggiest summer day you've ever known here, imagine it ten times worse, and you'll start to know what the weather there is like.

"Now maybe it's on account of the weather, but a lot of the folk of Mabalal are what you'd have to call lazy. Some of 'em, I swear, would just as soon lie with their mouths open in the rain as get up and find themselves a cup to drink from—but that's no part of the tale.

"If you want to know what pepper trees are like, think of willows—they look much like 'em, right down to the clusters of fruit. The trouble with 'em is, they grow on the steepest hillsides and cliffs, so people have a beastly time getting to 'em to take away the pepper."

"Probably why it costs so much by the time it gets here," Gerin said.

"Likely so, Captain. Now the folk of Mabalal are lazy, like I said. If we had to hope for them to climb hillsides and cliffs to gather the pepper fruits, it'd cost more than it does, I tell you true. What they do instead is get the monkeys to work for 'em, or maybe trick 'em into it would be a better way to put it."

"What's a monkey?" asked a warrior from an isolated keep, a man who never went more than a couple of hours' walk from his holding unless on campaign.

"A monkey is a beast about the size of a half-year babe that looks like a furry, ugly little man with a tail," Van answered patiently. "They live in trees, and have thumbs on their feet as well as their hands. They're clever and mischievous, almost like children, and they cause a lot of trouble stealing things and ruining them.

"The other thing about monkeys is, they like to do what people do—and the folk of Mabalal, who live with 'em the same way we do with dogs and cats, know it. There are whole bands of these monkeys, mind you, that live in the rough country where the pepper trees grow. So when the Mabalali want to get themselves some pepper, what they do is this: they go down to the foothills below the rough country and pick all the fruit off some of the trees there. Then they dump piles of the fruit in little clearings they've made close by, and they pretend to up and leave.

"Now, all the while the monkeys have been watching them from the high ground. The monkeys go and they pick the fruits from the pepper trees, and then they come down and they drop them in the clearings just the same way they'd seen the men do it. Sometimes they'll steal the fruit the Mabalali have left, sometimes they won't. Either way, the Mabalali get the pepper, and they get it without having to do the hard work themselves. So you see, sometimes being lazy isn't such a bad thing after all."

The warriors buzzed appreciatively, as they would have at any tale well told. For them it was a pleasant way to pass the time and a story to remember so they could tell it in turn. Gerin also liked it on those terms, but it set him thinking in a different way, too. "I wonder how many useful things have come from men's being too lazy to keep on doing things the same old hard way," he mused.

"Give me a for-instance, Captain," Van said.

That made the Fox scratch his head. At last he said, "Take the fellow who thought of the wagon. Wouldn't you bet he was sick of hauling things on his back?"

"Ah, I see what you're saying," Van said. "Likely so."

"And the fellow who first brewed ale, what was he sick of?" Rihwin asked. With a grin, he answered his own question: "Seeing straight, I suppose."

Gerin and Van both laughed at that, but Drago the Bear drew in a sharp, disapproving breath. "No man first brewed ale," he said flatly. " 'Twas the gift of the god Baivers, and any who don't want his anger had best remember it."

Rihwin opened his mouth for what Gerin was sure would be a reply taken straight from the philosophers of the City of Elabon. Before that reply could emerge, Gerin forestalled it: "Rihwin, my fellow Fox, I trust you do recall the difficulties you had with Mavrix god of wine not so long ago?"

"Well, yes, I do," Rihwin said reluctantly. "I did not believe, however, that you of all people in the northlands would stifle the full and open discussion of ideas of all sorts. I—"

Gerin took him by the arm. "Here, walk with me," he said in a tone that brooked no argument. When the two men were as far from the fire and the blood offering as the wailing of the ghosts would let them go, Gerin continued in a low voice, "For all your study, one thing you never learned: there's a time and a place for everything. If you want to start arguments about the nature and powers of the gods, don't do it when you're heading out on campaign. I want my men's thoughts focused on two things: working with one another and slaughtering any monsters they happen across. Does that make sense to you?"

"I suppose so," Rihwin said, though he sounded sulky. "Yet you would be hard-pressed to deny that in theory—"

Gerin cut him off again, this time with a sharp chopping gesture of his left hand. "Theory is wonderful," he said. "What we have here is fact—if the men quarrel among themselves, they won't fight well. You do anything more to make them fight worse than they would otherwise and I'll leave you behind at the first keep we come to, or at a peasant village failing that. Do you understand me?"

"Oh, indeed." Rihwin angrily tossed his head; firelight glinted from the gold hoop in his left ear. "You're a hard man when you take the field, lord prince Gerin the Fox." He loaded Gerin's title with scorn.

"War is too important a business to be slack with it,"

Gerin answered, shrugging. "Will you do as I say and not stir up disputes among the gods, or shall I leave you? Those are your choices, sirrah."

Rihwin sighed. "Let it be as you say. You'd do better, though, if you learned to ease men into doing your will rather than hammering them into it."

"No doubt." Gerin sighed, too. Rihwin had nothing wrong with his wits, only a dearth of common sense. "And you'd do better if you thought more before you started talking or doing things. We all try to be the best men we can, and we all fail in different ways. Which watch do you have tonight?"

"The middle one." Rihwin's mobile features assumed an expression of distaste.

"There, you see?" Gerin said. "If your head held as much sense as a cabbage, you'd be asleep already instead of standing here arguing with me. Go curl up in your blanket."

"The power of your reasoning ravishes me yet again," Rihwin cried. Gerin snorted and made as if to kick him in the backside. The transplanted southerner lay down and soon fell asleep. Gerin had the midwatch, too, but stayed awake a good deal longer.

When the Fox's chariots rolled down into Bevon's holding, all the local barons shut themselves up right in their keeps and prepared to stand siege. "You just want to bite out another piece of our land," one of them called from his palisade when Gerin came up to the wall.

"That's not so," Gerin answered, wondering if the white rag he bore would protect him from the lordlet's archers. As he had so many times before, he spoke of the monsters that had erupted from the caves beneath Biton's temple.

And, as had happened too many times before, he met only disbelief. The petty baron laughed scornfully. "You're supposed to be clever, Fox. I'd have thought you could come up with a better excuse than that to come down on your neighbors."

"Have it as you will." The Fox knew he sounded weary, but couldn't help it. "You'll find out soon enough whether I'm telling the truth. When you learn I am, maybe you'll remember some of what I've said." He turned and walked back to the chariot where Van and Raffo waited. No one shot at him, so he just rode on.

Down at the southern border of Bevon's holding, Ricolf's men were no longer wary of the force Gerin used to hold the Elabon Way open. They'd seen the monsters for themselves—seen more of them than the Fox had, as a matter of fact. He spent the first couple of hours after he arrived asking questions.

"Some of the creatures are smarter than others, lord prince, seems like," one of Ricolf's troopers said. "I've seen a couple carrying sword or axe, and one even with a helm on its ugly head. But others'll either charge or run off, just like wild beasts."

"Interesting." Gerin plucked at his beard. "How many of them are there, would you say, and how much damage have they done?"

"How many? Too many, that's sure," the trooper said. "As for damage, think how much fun wolves would be if they had more in the way of wits, and hands to let them get into things doors and gates keep them out of."

Gerin thought about it. He didn't like the pictures that painted themselves in his mind. Elabonians were in the habit of calling Trokmoi wolves because of their fierce raids, but they had humanly understandable motives: they were out for loot and captives as well as slaughter for its own sake. Beasts that hunted and killed without grasping, let alone using, the concepts of mercy and restraint were daunting in an altogether different way.

The Fox thanked Ricolf's man and went back to pass the word to his own warriors. "One thing's certain," he said when he'd given them the grim news: "These creatures won't act like a regular army of men. They aren't an army at all, not really. Instead of trying to storm up the Elabon Way in a mass, I look for them to spread through the woods by ones and twos and maybe packs—no larger groups or bands or whatever you want to call them."

"If that's so, lord Gerin, we might as well not have brung these here chariots," Widin Simrin's son said.

"For fighting, you're right," the Fox answered, letting his young vassal down easy. "But we'd have been another two or three days on the road if we'd footed it down here."

Widin nodded, abashed. Drago the Bear said, "What'll you have us do with the cars, then? We can't go into the woods with 'em, that's certain, and you say the woods is where we'll find these things." He shook his head in somber anticipation. "You're going to make foot soldiers out of us, I know you are."

"Do you see that I have any choice?" Gerin asked. "Here's what I'm thinking: we'll split up by chariot crews, with teams of three crews sticking together in teams. That'll give each team nine men, which should be enough to hold off even a pack of the creatures. At the same time, we'll have eight or ten teams spreading out along the border between Bevon's and Ricolf's holdings, and that ought to give us a chance to keep a lot of the beasts from slipping farther north."

"What about the ones that are already over the border?" Van asked. "How are you going to deal with them?"

"Bevon's vassals, or rather Bevon's sons' vassals, will slay some of them," Gerin said. "That should convince them the things are real and dangerous. As for the others, we'll just have to hope there aren't too many."

"Fair enough," Van said, to Gerin's relief. The Fox's great fear—one he didn't want to speak aloud to his followers—was that, like the Trokmoi, the monsters would permanently establish themselves in the northlands. If men couldn't rid the woods of wolves, how were they to be free of creatures cleverer and more vicious than wolves?

He divided his men into teams of nine, and appointed a leader for each band. He had contrary misgivings about naming Drago and Rihwin: the one might miss things he ought to find, while the other got in trouble by being too inventive. But they were both better than anyone else in their bands, so he spoke their names firmly and hoped for the best.

He ordered half the teams to head east from the Elabon Way, the other half west. "We'll go out for three days, hunt for a day, and then come back," he said. "Anybody who's not back to the road in seven days' time and hasn't been eaten to give him an excuse will answer to me."

Eastbound and westbound forces headed out from the highway; the Fox and his chariot crew were in the latter.

At first each half of the little army tramped along as a single body, the better to overawe any of the local nobles who might be tempted to fare forth against them. Men chattered and sang and, after a while, began to grumble about sore feet.

When morning had turned to afternoon and the sun sank toward the horizon, Gerin turned to the team headed by Widin Simrin's son. "You men go back and forth through the woods hereabouts," he said. "The rest of us will push on, then leave another team behind, then another, and another, so when we're through we'll have men all along the border. Do you see?"

"Aye, lord," Widin answered. "That means at the end of our reach, though, so to speak, we won't be able to search for as long as we will here closer to the Elabon Way."

"True enough," the Fox said, "but I don't know what we can do about it. Travel takes time, and there's no help for it." He nodded approvingly to Widin; that was a much better point than the one he'd raised before. Gerin hadn't worked the implications of his strategy through so logically himself. "When we get back to Fox Keep, would you be interested in learning to read and write?"

"No, lord prince," Widin replied at once. "Got better things to do with my time, I do—hunting and wenching and keeping my vassals and serfs in line." He sounded so sure of himself that Gerin subsided with a sigh and did not push the question.

With Widin's team left behind, the rest tramped on. They took a game track through a stand of oaks and emerged on the far side at the edge of cleared fields in which peasants labored. The peasants stared at them in horror, as if they were so many monsters themselves, then fled.

Their cries of terror made Gerin melancholy. "This holding has seen too much war," he said. "Let's push ahead without harming anything here: let them know not every warrior is out to steal what little they have."

"A wasted lesson if ever I heard one," Van said. "The next band through here, so long as it isn't one of ours, will treat them the way they expect us to." Gerin glared at him so fiercely that he hastened to add, "But we'll do it your way, Captain—why not?"

Evening came before the Fox reckoned the time ripe to detach another piece of his force. Along with the men he had with him, he tossed knucklebones to see who would stand watch through the night. He felt like cheering when he won the right to uninterrupted sleep. No sooner had he cocooned himself in his blanket and wriggled around a little to make sure no pebbles poked his ribs than he knew nothing of the world around him.

A hideous cry recalled him to himself: a wailing shriek part wolf, part longtooth, part madman. He sat up and looked around wildly, wondering for a moment where he was and what he was doing here. His gaze went to the heavens. Tiwaz, nearly full, stood high in the south; ruddy Elleb, a couple of days past fullness, was in the southeast. Crescent Math had set and Nothos not yet risen. That put the hour a little before midnight.

Then all such mundane, practical thoughts vanished from his head, for the dreadful call again rang through the woods and across the fields. Some men started up from their bedrolls, grabbing for bow or sword. Others shrank down, as if to smother the cry with the thick wool of their blankets. Gerin could not find it in himself to blame them; the scream made him want to hide, too.

In a very small voice, someone said, "Is that the cry these monsters make?"

"Don't know what else it could be." Van sounded amazingly cheerful. "Noisy buggers, aren't they? 'Course, frogs are noisy, too, and a frog isn't hardly anything but air and legs."

Gerin admired his friend's sangfroid. He also admired the way the outlander had done his best to make the creatures from the caves seem less dangerous; he knew they were a great deal more than air and legs.

The frightful cry rang out yet again. "How are we to sleep with that racket?" Widin Simrin's son said.

"You roll up in your blanket and you close your eyes," Gerin said, not about to let Van outdo him in coolness. "We have sentries aplenty; you won't be eaten while you snore."

"And if you are, you can blame the Fox," Van put in, adding, "Not that it'll do you much good then."

Off in the distance, almost on the edge of hearing, another monster shrieked to answer the first. That sent ice walking up Gerin's back, not from terror at the faraway cry but because it said the creatures that made those dreadful sounds were spreading over the northlands. Gerin wondered how many more were calling back and forth farther away than he could hear.

The one nearby kept quiet after that. Exhaustion and edgy nerves fought a battle over the Fox; exhaustion eventually won. The next thing he knew, the sun was prying his eyelids open. He got up and stretched, feeling elderly. His mouth tasted like something scraped off the bottom of a chamber pot. He walked over to a tree, plucked off a twig, frayed one end of it with the edge of his dagger, and used it to scrub some of the vileness from his teeth. Some of his men did the same, others didn't bother.

Rihwin, who'd grown up south of the High Kirs, was so fastidious that even frayed twigs didn't completely satisfy him. As he tossed one aside, he said, "In the City of Elabon they make bristle brushes for your mouth. Those are better by far than these clumsy makeshifts."

"If you like, you can teach the art to one of the peasants who makes big brushes for rubbing down horses," Gerin said. "We might be able to sell them through the northlands—not many southern amenities to be had here these days."

"My fellow Fox, I admire the wholeheartedness of your mercenary spirit," Rihwin said.

"Anyone who sneers at silver has never tried to live without it." Gerin looked around. "Where'd Van go?"

"He walked into the woods a while ago," Widin said. "He's probably off behind a tree, taking care of his morning business."

The outlander returned a few minutes later. He said. "When you're done breaking your fast, friends, I want you to come with me. I went looking for the spot where that thing made a racket last night, and I think I found it."

Several of the men were still gnawing on hard bread and sausage as they followed Van. He led them down a tiny track to a clearing perhaps a furlong from the camp. The carcass of a doe lay there. Much of the hindquarters portion had been devoured.

A scavenging fox fled from the carcass when the men

came out of the woods. Van said to Gerin, "I hope your name animal hasn't ruined the tracks I saw. I'd be liable to think ill of it if it has, and I know you wouldn't like that." He walked over to the doe, grunted. "No, looks like we're all right. Come up a few at a time, all of you, and have a look at what the ground shows."

Gerin was part of the first small group forward. When he got close to the dead doe, Van pointed to a patch of bare, soft dirt by the animal. The footprints there were like none the Fox had ever seen. At first he thought they might be a man's, then a bear's—they had claw marks in front of the ends of their toes. But they didn't really resemble either. They were—something new.

"So this is the spoor we have to look for, is it?" he said grimly.

"Either that or someone's magicking our eyes," Van answered. "And I don't think anybody is."

The Fox didn't think so, either. He waited till all his men had seen the new footprints, then said, "They have claws on their hands, too. Now that we know what their tracks look like, let's get moving and see if we can't hunt down a few."

The warriors were quiet as they trooped back to the campsite. Now they had real evidence that Gerin and Van hadn't made up the tale about the monsters. They'd believed them already, likely enough, in an abstract way, but hearing about something new and terrible wasn't the same as seeing proof it was really there.

A couple of hours after they started tramping west, Gerin detached another band of men from his force to scour the area where they were. The rest slogged on; grumbles about aching feet got louder.

Around noon, Rihwin said, "Lord Gerin, something which may be of import occurs to me."

"And what is that?" Gerin asked warily. You never could tell with Rihwin. Some of his notions were brilliant, others crackbrained, and knowing the one bunch from the other wasn't always easy.

Now he said, "My thought, lord prince, is that these may in sooth be creatures of the night, wherein we heard the two of them giving cry. For does it not stand to reason that, having lived an existence troglodytic lo these many years,

perhaps even ages, their eyes, accustomed as they must be
to darkness perpetual, will necessarily fail when facing the
bright and beaming rays of the sun?"

"Troglo—what?" Van said incredulously, no doubt speaking for a good many of the Fox's warriors.

Gerin was well-read and used to Rihwin's elaborate
southern speech patterns, so he at least understood what
his fellow Fox was talking about. "Means 'living in caves,'"
he explained for those who hadn't followed. To Rihwin, he
said, "It's a pretty piece of logic; the only flaw is that it's
not so. Van and I saw the things fighting the temple guards
in broad daylight the morning of the earthquake, and heard
one behind us coming out of Ikos later that same day. Their
eyes work perfectly well in sunlight."

"Oh, a pox!" Rihwin cried. "How dreadful to see such
a lovely edifice of thought torn down by hard, brute fact."
He sulked for the next couple of hours.

The Fox detached another team late that afternoon, and
camped with his remaining two teams not long afterwards.
The night passed quietly, much to his relief. Standing first
watch was not so onerous—better that than being torn from
sleep by a horrible screech, at any rate.

Early the next morning, he gave Rihwin's team their area to
patrol. "Good hunting," he said, clapping his ekenamesake
on the shoulder.

"I thank you, lord Gerin," Rihwin answered, and then,
"Do you know, there are times when I wonder how wise
I was to cast aside my life of wealth and indolence in the
southlands for an adventurous career with you."

"There are times when I wonder about that, too," Gerin
said. "A lot of them, as a matter of fact. What you're saying
now is that your heart wouldn't break if you didn't happen to run across any monsters?"

"Something like that, yes."

"I feel the same way, believe me," Gerin said, "but if
we don't go after them, they'll end up coming after us. I'd
sooner make the fight on my terms, and as far from my
keep as I can."

"I understand the logic, I assure you," Rihwin said. "The
argument takes on a different color, however, when it moves
from the realm of ideas to the point of affecting one

personally. Logicians who cling to abstract concepts seldom run the risk of being devoured."

"No matter how much they may deserve it," Gerin added, which won him a glare. He gave Rihwin another encouraging swat. For all the southerner's talk, Gerin didn't worry about his courage. His common sense was another matter, or would have been if he'd had any to speak of.

The Fox led his own team westward. Alarmed at their advance, a young stag bounded out of a thicket. Van pulled an arrow from his quiver, nocked, and let fly, all in close to the same instant. "That's a hit!" he shouted, and hurried forward to where the stag had been. Sure enough, blood splashed the grass. "Come on, you lugs," the outlander said to his companions. "With a trail like this to follow, a blind man'd be eating venison steaks tonight."

They ran the deer down about a quarter of an hour later. It lay panting on the ground, too weak to run any further; Van's arrow stood in its side, just back of the heart. It tried to struggle to its feet, but could not. Its large brown eyes stared reproachfully at the warriors. Van stooped beside it. With one swift motion, he jerked up its head and cut its throat.

Together, Van and Gerin tackled the gory job of butchering the stag. "Next stream we come to, I wash," Gerin declared.

"You may not need to wait for a stream, Captain," the outlander answered, pointing west. The weather had been fine, but clouds were beginning to roll in off the distant Orynian Ocean. "That could be rain."

"So it could." The Fox glowered at the clouds, as if he could hold them back by sheer force of will. "If it starts raining, how are we supposed to track anything? By the gods, how are we even going to keep fires going to help hold the ghosts at arm's length?" His rising bad temper even extended to Van. "And why couldn't you have killed this deer closer to sunset, so we could use its blood as an offering to the spirits?"

Van stood tall and glared down at him. "Are you going to complain that the grass is green instead of blue, too, or will you help me get the meat off this beast?" As usual, his comrade's bluntness showed Gerin where he'd stepped over the line from gloomy to carping. He nodded shame-facedly and fell to work.

Raffo said, "I have a thought, lord Gerin." He waited for the Fox to grunt before he went on, "What say we post ourselves in hiding around the offal there and see if it doesn't lure one of the creatures we're seeking? The stink of blood might draw 'em."

"We're already farther west than any of the other teams," Gerin said musingly. "It would mean pushing on a ways further tomorrow, but why not? As you say, the lure is good: might as well be a grub on a fish hook. Aye, we'll try it— but I still want to go and find water."

"And I," Van agreed. His arms were bloody to the elbows.

"We'll be back as soon as we may," Gerin said. "Set your ambush, but remember to know what you're shooting at before you let fly."

He and Van found a creek a couple of furlongs west of where the stag had fallen. Just as they came up to the bank, a kingfisher dove into the water, to emerge a moment later with a minnow in its bill. Something else—a frog or a turtle, Gerin didn't notice which—splashed into the creek from a mossy rock and didn't come out again.

The stag's blood had already started to dry; scrubbing it off wasn't easy. "We need some of the soap they make from fat and ashes south of the High Kirs," Gerin said, scraping one arm more or less clean with the nails of his other hand. "Maybe I'll try cooking a batch myself when we get home to Fox Keep."

"The stuff's too harsh for my liking," Van answered. "It takes off the top layer of your hide along with the dirt." He looked at Gerin. "You have a splash of blood by your nose, Fox. . . . No, on the other side. There, you got it."

"Good." Gerin gave a theatrical shiver. "That water's cold." He glanced westward again. The dirty gray clouds were piled higher there. "And before too long, more than my arms'll get wet. That does look like rain coming. The serfs will be glad of it, but I wish it would have held off till we were under a roof again."

"Weather won't listen, any more'n a woman will," Van said. "Let's head back and see if Raffo's brainstorm came to anything."

"We'd have heard if it did," Gerin answered. But he followed Van back toward the rest of their team. They could hold their ambush till it was time to set up camp for the night, he decided. Turning to his friend, he added, "It occurs to me now—too late, of course—that pile of guts might draw something besides monsters. If a longtooth decides it wants a meal, I hope they have sense enough to let it eat its fill."

"You're right," Van said. "I'm just glad Rihwin's not with us. He's a fine chap, mind you, but he hasn't the sense you need to cart guts to a bear, so why should a longtooth be any different? If you ask me—"

Gerin didn't have the chance to ask Van anything. A racket broke out ahead, the shouts of men and the hideous shriek they'd heard in the night. He jerked his sword out of its sheath, Van pulled the mace from the loop at his belt on which it hung, and the two of them pounded toward the tumult as fast as their legs would carry them.

"It's us!" Gerin yelled as he ran. "Don't shoot—we're not monsters." Whether any of the men was cool-headed enough to note and heed his cry was an open question.

Because he thought that way, the arrow that hissed between him and Van neither surprised nor infuriated him. He had a moment to be glad it had missed them both, then burst through the bushes into the little open space where the stag had died and been butchered.

Several of his men had already emerged from cover, too. "The thing went that way," Raffo exclaimed, pointing south. "We all shot at it, and hit it at least twice, maybe three times." What he'd seen suddenly seemed to sink in. His eyes went wide and staring. "Lord Gerin, forgive me that I ever doubted your words, I pray you. The creature is all you said it was, and more and worse besides."

"Yes, yes," Gerin said impatiently. "Enough jabbering— let's catch it and kill it. Lead on, Raffo, since you know the way."

Looking imperfectly delighted with the privilege he'd been granted, Raffo plunged into the woods. The trail was easy to follow, blood and tracks both. Before long, Gerin could hear the monster crashing through the undergrowth ahead. "The things have weaknesses after all," Van panted.

"They aren't woodswise like proper beasts, and they aren't what you'd call fast, either."

"You don't know about that," Gerin answered. "How fast and careful would you be with two or three arrows in you?" Van didn't answer, from which Gerin concluded he'd made his point.

With a roar, the monster sprang out from behind an elm tree. Four men shot arrows at it. Two of those missed; excitement could ruin anybody's aim. The creature screamed when the other two struck. But despite them, and despite the other shafts that pierced it, it rushed at its pursuers.

Its claws scraped against the bronze scales of Gerin's corselet. He could feel the force behind them, even if they did not wound; as he'd guessed, the monster was stronger than a man. He slashed with his sword. The thing screamed again.

Van clouted it with his mace. The blow would have crushed the skull of any man. It knocked the monster to the ground, but it got up again, blood streaming from the dreadful wound to the side of its head. Cursing in half a dozen languages, Van smote it again, even harder than before. This time it fell and did not rise again.

"Father Dyaus above," said a warrior named Parol and called Chickpea after a wart by his nose. Gerin's heart pounded in his chest. He felt as if he'd fought against a Trokmê rather than hunted a beast. The monster's strength, even badly wounded, accounted for some of that. More, though, came from how much the thing resembled a man.

"Will you look at it?" Raffo said in wondering tones. "Take the ugliest scoundrel you've ever seen—old Wolfar, for instance—and make him five times as ugly as he really was, every which way, I mean, and you've just about got this thing here."

"Oh, not quite everything," Parol said. "I wouldn't mind being hung so good, and that's no lie."

That comment aside, Raffo's remark was to the point. Gerin had noted how manlike the monsters were from the moment he set eyes on them. Then, though, he hadn't had the leisure to examine one closely; he'd been more concerned about getting away from Ikos with his life and Van's and the Sibyl's.

Squat, muscular, hairy—the thing did resemble Wolfar, he thought, unkind to his old enemy though he'd killed him five years earlier. But Wolfar, except when he turned werebeast, had not been armed with claws on hands and feet both, and even as a werebeast his teeth had hardly matched the ones filling the monster's long, formidable jaws.

Above those jaws, its features were also a vicious parody of mankind's: a low nose with slit nostrils; large eyes set deep under heavy ridges of bone; thick hair, almost fur, rising to a crest on top of its head and nearly disguising how little forehead it had.

"There it is," Gerin said. "Dyaus above only knows how many of these things are spreading over the northlands."

"Are they all of the same sort as this one?" Raffo asked.

"Some of 'em are likely to be females or bitches or woman monsters or whatever the right name is," Parol put in.

"They're ugly enough so it'd only matter to another monster." Raffo made a gesture of distaste. "What I meant was, is this one pretty much like the others? You'd get a different notion of what people were like from Van's corpse and the one I'd like to make out of that weedy little jeweler who may have run off with Duren."

"Otes." Gerin heard the growl in his own voice as he supplied the name. How could he properly search for his son when catastrophe was overtaking all the northlands? More and more, he feared he'd never again see Duren alive. But Raffo's question raised a serious point. "I haven't had enough experience with them to answer that, though Ricolf's man said some seemed smarter than others," he said. "One way or another, we'll all find out before long."

The warriors trooped back to where they had slain the deer, leaving the monster's body where it lay. "We may as well camp, as Raffo said," Van remarked. "No point in pushing further in the little daylight left."

When evening fell, the ghosts were very quiet. "Likely gorging on the creature's blood," Gerin said. He looked up to the sky. Math should have been at first quarter, with Tiwaz and Elleb rising in the early hours after sunset, but he saw only clouds. The wind was picking up. "We'll have trouble gauging watches tonight, and it feels like rain, to boot."

"I'm not looking forward to tramping along through the mud," Van said. "We won't be able to do much in the way of looking for monsters, either, not with rain making it hard for us to see our hands when we stretch our arms out at full length."

"Aye, you're right," Gerin said morosely. "I hadn't thought so far ahead yet." The gobbet of venison on which he was gnawing suddenly lost a good deal of its flavor. How was he supposed to set a perimeter to keep the monsters out of his holding if they could shamble past fifty paces away without getting noticed?

For that matter, if other nobles in the northlands didn't fight them as hard as he would himself, how was he supposed to keep the monsters out of his holding at all? The most obvious answer to that was depressing: maybe he couldn't. He hadn't had much hope of besting Balamung, either, but he'd persisted and come through. He had to believe he could do the same again.

He stood an early watch, then rolled himself in his blanket and fell asleep at once in spite of his worries. When he woke, he looked around in confusion—why was everything still dark? Then a raindrop landed on the end of his nose, and another in his hair.

The rain started pattering down in earnest a few minutes later. Men swore sleepily and rigged makeshift tents from their blankets and saplings pressed into service as tent poles. In spite of those, the rest of the night was chilly, wet, and miserable.

Day came with rain falling steadily from a leaden sky. The fire had gone out. Some of the venison from the night before had been cooked; along with hard bread, it made a decent enough breakfast, but not as good as it would have been, hot and juicy from the flames.

The warriors donned their armor and squelched off westward. Gerin felt as if he were moving inside a circle perhaps a bowshot across; the rain curtained away everything beyond that distance. Every so often, he or one of his comrades would slip in the mud and get up covered with it. Little by little, the rain would wash him clean once more—until he slipped again.

Echoing what Van had said the night before, Raffo

grumbled, "How are we supposed to search in this? We'll
be lucky if we can keep track of ourselves, let alone the
cursed monsters."

Gerin did not answer, for he feared his driver was right.
With rain and clouds concealing sun and landmarks, he
wasn't even altogether sure he was still heading west. "Have
to wait to see which half of the sky gets dark first," Van said.
"Then we'll have a notion of how to head back toward the
Elabon Way, anyhow, if not just where we'll strike it."

Raffo said, "Poor old Rihwin. He could be sitting under
one of those red tile roofs south of the High Kirs that he
never gets tired of talking about, with wenches to fetch
him meat and grapes and wine. And he was silly enough
to trade all that for this life of luxury." He shook himself
like a wet dog to show what he meant.

Just thinking of being dry made Gerin wish he were
somewhere other than tramping through the mud. He said,
"May the next puddle you step in be over your head." As
if to turn his words into a magic-powered curse, he waggled
his hands in mock passes.

He'd almost stopped paying attention to the circle of
relatively clear vision in which he moved: one piece of
damp, dreary ground seemed much like the next. Looking where he put his feet so he wouldn't go into a puddle
over his head himself struck him as more important than
anything else.

Then Raffo gasped, half in horror and half in amazement. The sound was plenty to jerk Gerin's head up.
Splashing through the wet grass and mud came a band of
eight or ten monsters.

They spied Gerin's men at about the same moment as
Raffo saw them. A bulky male, evidently the leader of the
band, swept out his arm to point at the warriors. He
shouted something; through the rain, Gerin could not tell
whether it was real words or just an animal cry. Whatever
it was, the rest of the creatures got the idea. With hoarse
roars, they charged the Fox's men.

In such dreadful weather, bows were useless. Gerin
stooped to pick up a stone the size of a goose egg. He flung it
at the oncoming monsters, then yelled, "Out sword and at
them!" A moment later, his own blade slid from its scabbard.

A stone flew past his head. One of the creatures, at any rate, had wit enough to think of it as a weapon. Then the fight was at close quarters, the savagery and strength of the monsters well matched against the armor and bronze weapons Gerin's warriors carried.

With his long, heavy spear, better made for use afoot than from a chariot, Van had an advantage over his monstrous foes: he could thrust at them long before they closed with him. But when he sank the leaf-shaped point deep into the belly of one screaming creature, another seized the spearshaft and wrenched it out of his hands. He shouted in shock and dismay; long used to being stronger than any man he faced, having an opponent who could match him in might came as a jolt.

The monster dropped the spear; it preferred its natural weapons to those made by art. But when it sprang at Van, he stove in its head with an overhand blow from his mace. He needed no second stroke; the fight with the creature the day before had warned him to put all his power into the first one.

Gerin got only tiny glimpses of his friend's fight—he had troubles of his own. The monster that faced him was female, but no less unlovely and fierce on account of that. He felt as if he were fighting a wolf bitch or female longtooth, and knew none of the hesitation he might have felt against a woman warrior.

He slashed at the monster. It skipped back. It knew the sword was dangerous to it, then. The Fox went after it, slashed once more. This time the monster ducked under the blade and rushed him. He got his shield up just in time to keep it from tearing out his throat. It was very strong; when it tried to pull the shield off his arm, he wondered if his right shoulder would come out of its socket. The shield strap held, but barely.

Even in the pouring rain, the monster stank with a reek halfway between the musky smell of a wild beast and a human body that had never been bathed. Something else was there, too, a musty smell, perhaps the residue of long years—of countless generations—of life underground.

The Fox slashed again, and scored a bleeding line across the creature's rib cage. It squalled in fury and stopped trying to tear away his shield. But it did not turn and flee, as a wounded animal likely would have done. Instead, it went back to the attack, this time rushing at Gerin and knocking him off his feet, then springing on him as he lay in the mud.

Again his shield saved him, fending the monster away from his face and neck. He hissed in pain as its claws raked down his arm. But, though he was untaloned himself, his sandals had bronze hobnails to help him grip the ground. He kicked at the monster, and hurt it again.

He dropped his sword; it was too unwieldy for this work. Had he not been able to get at his dagger, or had he dropped it while yanking it from its sheath on his belt, he would have died. As it was, he stabbed the monster again and again.

It shrieked, first shrilly, then with a bubbling undertone as bloody froth burst from its mouth and nose. For once, Gerin wished he were not lefthanded; his blows to the right side of the creature's body had pierced a lung, but not its heart. Now, though, it wanted escape. He stuck out a leg in a wrestler's trick and tripped it when it tried to flee. It went down with a splash.

He half leaped, half rolled onto its back, stabbing again and again in an ecstasy of loathing, fury, and fear. The monster was as tenacious of life as any wild beast, that was certain. He'd put enough holes in it to make a sieve before it finally stopped trying to break free.

He didn't know whether it was dead. He didn't care—it was out of the fight for a good long while. He snatched up his sword again, scrambled to his feet, and hurried to give aid to his comrades.

Several of them were down, as were most of the monsters. Raffo and Parol Chickpea together battled the big male that had led the pack. It sprang on Parol. He screamed hoarsely. Gerin used the sword like a spear, stabbing the monster from behind. It wailed and tried to turn on him. Raffo's blade met its thick neck with a meaty *chunnk*. Blood spurted. Head half severed, the monster pitched forward onto its face and lay still.

When their leader fell, the couple of creatures still on their feet gave up the fight and fled. Gerin's warriors did not pursue them; they had enough to do finishing the monsters on the ground and seeing to their own wounded. One man was dead, Parol's driver, a likable young fellow called Delamp Narrag's son. Several others had bites and slashes of greater or less severity. Binding them up in the rain wasn't easy.

"You're bleeding, Fox," Van remarked.

Gerin looked down at his clawed arm. "So I am. I hope we come to a village before long, so I can pour beer into those cuts and cover them over with lard. If they're anything like cat scratches, they're liable to fester."

"You're right about that." Van looked over the little battlefield. "Well, we beat 'em back. They're not as tough as armored warriors. That's something, anyhow."

"Something, aye." Now that he wasn't fighting for his life, the Fox noticed how much that arm hurt. "But I'd not want to be a peasant, even one with a mattock or scythe, and have one of those things spring at me from out of the woods. If I were lucky and hit it a good lick, it might run off. But if I missed that first stroke, I'd never get a chance to make a second one."

"You're right about that, too," Van said. After a moment's reflective pause, he added, "One of the ones that got away fled north."

"I saw it go. I was trying not to think about it," Gerin said wearily. "That's one past us, certain sure. I wonder how many more there are that we've never seen. Even the one is too many."

"And you're right about that," Van said. "If you're so bloody right all the time, why are we in this mess?" Gerin had no good answer for him.

VII

Rihwin walked mournfully through the courtyard, a bandage plastered over his left ear and tied round his head to hold it in place. "Can't you take that off yet?" Gerin asked him. "We've been back here ten days now, so you can't still be bleeding, and the wound didn't fester, or you'd have taken sick long since."

"Oh, I could, if that were all there was to it," Rihwin answered. "The sad truth is, though, that I'm uglier without the bandage than with it."

Gerin clapped a hand to his forehead. "You're vainer than a peacock, is what you are. If you hadn't worn that gold hoop in your ear, the monster down in Bevon's holding never would have had the chance to hook a claw on it and tear it out. And a torn ear's not the worst thing in the world, anyhow. I've seen plenty of men with worse, and that's a fact."

Rihwin's mobile features twisted into a dolorous frown. "But my earlobe has shriveled up and withered. In the southlands, surgeons had ways of repairing such wounds, for those who could bear the pain. Many did, as a ruined ear does one's appearance no good. Henceforward, I'm liable to be styled Rihwin One-Ear, not Rihwin the Fox. But who in this benighted country is familiar with such techniques? Not a soul, unless I'm much mistaken."

"I fear you're right," Gerin said. "Your southern surgeons may have had practice at such work, but we don't wear earrings here." He paused a moment, his curiosity awakening. "How do the southern surgeons go about their work with ears, anyhow?"

"First they ply the patient well with wine and poppy juice, to dull his senses as much as they can," Rihwin answered. "They also have his friends hold him, mind you— I've done that duty a time or two. Then they cut loose a flap of flesh from behind the ruined ear, open up what remains of the earlobe so it's raw and bloody, and sew the two together. After they grow into one—for they will, once

410

they exchange blood—the surgeon cuts off the base of the flap and behold! One has a new ear, perhaps not so fine as the original article but far better than the miserable nub I have left."

Gerin eyed him speculatively. "Do you know, my fellow Fox, in my years up here on the frontier, I've done my share of rough healer's work: drawing arrows, stitching wounds, setting bones, what have you. The men I've treated haven't done any worse than anyone else's patients. If you like, I might try to rebuild your ear for you."

Rihwin went into a sudden and hasty retreat, holding his hands out before him as if to fend off Gerin. "I thank you, but no. Not only do you lack some of the essentials (for where will you find wine and poppy juice here in the northlands?), but, meaning no disrespect, you have neither witnessed nor essayed the procedure in question."

"But you described the procedure so clearly," Gerin said, half to alarm Rihwin, half in real disappointment. "I feel as if I could give you something better than the stub you have now. If I were to sketch in ink the shape of a proper earlobe here on the side of your neck—"

Rihwin retreated further. "No thank you," he repeated. "Now, I grant that I cannot wear a bandage forever, but if I were to let my hair grow long, in half a year it would conceal the mutilation, thus obviating the need for surgery."

"I suppose you could do that," Gerin admitted. "Why didn't you think of it a while ago, instead of whining about how your looks were ruined forever?"

"I didn't have such incentive to devise an alternative until this moment," Rihwin answered with a sheepish grin. "Compared to the prospect of being carved upon by an inept and inexperienced butcher—again, meaning no disrespect—going through life with but one earlobe suddenly seems much less unattractive." Rihwin was self-absorbed, but not stupid. He fixed Gerin with a suspicious stare. "And you, sirrah, manipulated me into coming up with that alternative."

"I did?" Gerin was the picture of innocence. "All I wanted was to try my hand at surgery."

"I know," Rihwin said darkly. "I am certain the procedure would have been quite interesting—for you. And for me—how much I should have enjoyed it—is another matter altogether."

"If you hadn't wanted something done about it, you shouldn't have described *how* to do something about it in such loving detail," Gerin said.

"Believe me, my fellow Fox, I shall not be guilty of repeating the error," Rihwin said. "I suppose you should have been as eager to follow through had I suggested you repair the ear by thaumaturgic means."

"Now, there's an idea!" Gerin exclaimed. "You know, that really ought to be within my power, such as it is. It wouldn't involve much, just a straightforward application of the law of similarity. And you still have your right ear intact to serve as an exemplar. What could be more similar to a man's left ear than his own right? Let's go over to that little shack of mine and—"

Rihwin fled.

Selatre read, "In this year, the fifth of his reign, the Emperor Forenz, the second of that name"—she paused to sound out a word she didn't run across as often as the usual opening formula of a chronicle's annual entry; she read *that* with confidence—"increased the tribute on the Sithonian cities. And the men of Kortys gathered together and thought how best they might revel—"

Gerin blinked and leaned over to check the scroll in front of her. "That's 'rebel,'" he murmured.

She looked at the passage again. "Oh. So it is." She let out a small, embarrassed laugh. "It does change the meaning, doesn't it?"

"Just a bit." Gerin started to reach and to touch her hand in added praise, but thought better of it. Selatre made little fuss over accidental contact these days, but she remained unhappy about anything that wasn't an accident. He went on, "Even with the slip, you're doing marvelously well. You've picked up your letters as fast as anyone I've ever taught."

"Letters are simple," she said. "Seeing how they fit together and make words is harder." She looked around the room that served Castle Fox as a library. "And so many words there are to read! I'd never imagined."

Now Gerin laughed, bitterly. "When I look at them, I see how few there are. It's a good collection for the northlands—for all I know, it may be the only collection in the northlands—but it's a chip of wood drifting on the sea of ignorance. I studied down at the City of Elabon; I know whereof I speak."

"As may be," Selatre said. "When Biton abandoned me, I thought I would be empty of knowledge, of the feeling of knowledge passing through me, forevermore. This is a different sort from what the god gave directly, but it's worthy in its own way. For that I thank you."

She hesitated for a moment, then set her hand on top of his, very lightly, before she jerked it back. Gerin stared at her. Then a snarl of rage, a noise like ripping canvas, jerked his gaze to the doorway. Fand had chosen that moment to walk by. The fury on her face was frightening. Gerin waited for her to scream at him, but she stalked away instead. That worried him more than her usual firestorm would have.

"I'm sorry," Selatre said. "Your leman does not favor me, and I've gone and made matters worse."

"Not that much worse," he answered. "Things have been going, mm, imperfectly well for a while already."

She sighed and said, "I must confess, I don't altogether understand. If things between you and her have not gone well, as you tell me, why do you still seek her bedchamber?"

He felt his face heat. From anyone else, that question would have got nothing more than a sharp, *None of your affair*. With Selatre, though, he tried to be as honest as he could. Maybe that sprang from lingering awe and respect for the oracular role she'd once had, maybe just because, by her nature and not Biton's, she called forth such honesty. After a little thought, he said, "Because what goes on in the bedchamber, as you say, is one of the few good things we have left between us. Has been one of the good things, I should say."

Selatre caught the distinction. "Has been but is no more, do you mean?"

"I suppose I do." The Fox gnawed on the inside of his lower lip. "You've seen children balance a board or a branch on a rock and make a game out of going up and down, up and down?"

"Of course," she answered. "I've played that game myself. Haven't you?"

He nodded, then went on, "Van and I have played it with Fand, these past couple of years. But staying in balance, the two of us with one woman, isn't easy, any more than keeping the board in balance on a stone is. And I seem to be the one who's falling off." He laughed, ruefully but without much anger. "I shouldn't be surprised that's happening, not when Fand has a temper like boiling oil. I ought to be surprised we've kept the balance as long as this."

"You would have kept it longer, if not for me," Selatre said. "She thinks you're out to have me take her place."

"I know she does," Gerin said. "That isn't what I intended when I brought you here to Castle Fox."

She studied him. For a moment, he thought the fathomless wisdom of Biton still looked out through her eyes. Then he realized the wisdom he saw was her own, which made it no less intimidating. "Do you intend that now?" she asked. Even if he'd intended to evade, she didn't make it easy; though she hardly had her letters, she used words with a precision the rhetoricians down in the City of Elabon might have envied.

"By Biton or Dyaus—whichever you'd rather, Selatre— I swear I do not want you to take Fand's place in my life," he answered steadily. "If you think I am in the habit of swearing false oaths, you can best judge my likely fate in the world to come."

"Only a fool mocks the gods, and whatever else you may be, lord Gerin, you are no fool," Selatre said. "For that, and for the truth you've shown me thus far, I will believe you."

"And for that I thank you," the Fox said.

"Shall we return to the chronicle?" Selatre asked. "There, with the words before us on the parchment, we have less room for misunderstanding."

"That is probably a good idea." Gerin listened to her read. Every sentence seemed to come with more confidence than the one before it. Now that she'd grasped the principle, she was showing she could apply it. Some men took

years to reach the place where she'd come in moonturns.
Some men gave up in dismay and never got there at all.

He was proud of her, and pleased with himself for having
guessed so well where she would fit into the life of Fox
Keep and the human fabric of the holding as a whole. She
and Fand didn't fit; Van had foreseen that more clearly than
he had himself. And Van and Fand still seemed to be
getting along as well as Fand ever got on with anyone.

Under the usual busy stir of his thoughts, Gerin
remembered something else as well—Selatre had reached
out and taken his hand. He didn't know how much that
meant; he didn't know if it meant anything. Of one thing
he was sure: he wanted to find out.

Rain plashed down on Castle Fox, filling puddles in the
courtyard and turning the ditch around the palisade to the
muddy beginning of a moat. Harvest lay far enough ahead
for the peasants to look on the storm with relief rather than
alarm.

In any other year, that would have made Gerin do the
same. Now a cloud-filled sky and curtains of water kicking
up myriad splashes everywhere only raised his hackles; the
wet weather reminded him too vividly of the storm that had
rolled through the day his band of warriors fought the pack
of monsters.

Planting his feet with care on the slippery steps, he
mounted to the palisade and peered south. He could see
the peasant village near the castle. The broad thatched roofs
of the huts there would keep most of the rain away from
the walls of wattle and daub, but he knew serfs would be
patching them with fresh mud after the downpour rolled
away eastward.

Beyond the village, at the edge of visibility through the
rain, lay the woods. Gerin wished he could peer inside
them, see into each windfall and cave, under each fallen
tree. He feared monsters sheltered in some of them. He
did not have the men he would have needed to form a
cordon around his entire border, but without such a cordon,
how was he supposed to hold off the creatures?

He was thinking so hard, he did not notice anyone
coming up to join him until footfalls jarred the timbers

beside him. Van wore a conical hat of woven straw that kept the rain off his face. "Wondering what's out there, Captain?" the outlander asked.

"I know what's out there," Gerin answered glumly. "I'm wondering how close it is and how soon we'll have to worry about it right here. But as a matter of fact, when you asked I was wishing bronze were cheaper."

"Begging your pardon, Fox, but I have to tell you I don't follow that one," Van said.

"If bronze were cheaper—if we had more copper and especially more tin—we could afford to make more weapons. Then the peasants could have 'em, and that would give them a better chance of killing the monsters instead of getting eaten."

"Mm, likely you're right." Van's features turned blunter and harder as he frowned in thought. "But even if you are, I'd lay you five to one that a lot of your vassal barons wouldn't fall in love with the idea of giving their serfs swords and spears and helms and cuirasses."

"For fear the arms would get turned on them instead of the monsters, you mean?" Gerin asked. Van nodded. So did the Fox. "Not many of my vassals need to worry overmuch, I think; they know I don't put up with some of the things that go on in other holdings. But if the idea ever spread through the northlands, I'll not deny a good many barons would have cause to fear their peasants would revolt. I can think of half a dozen I'd rise against in an instant if someone put a sword in my hand."

"Oh, aye, more than that." Van's big head bobbed up and down again. "But here's a question for you, Fox: suppose you put swords and spears in the hands of a lot of your serfs. When the time comes to pay the dues they owe you, aren't they going to go after your collectors instead of handing over the grain and ale and such? They'll be protecting themselves, so why should they go on paying you to do it for them?"

"That's—a good question," Gerin said slowly. "They all turn into villagers like the ones who tried to waylay us, is that what you're saying?"

"That's just what I'm saying," Van agreed.

Gerin thought for a while. "Do you know, it's very likely

they would," he said at last. "The way of life we have here looks as it does because bronze is so scarce and costly. Peasants can't afford to get their hands on arms and armor: not enough bronze to go around. Things would be different if there were."

"Better? Worse?"

"Damn me to the five hells if I know," Gerin answered. "But different they'd surely be. Like those footholders Duin the Bold came up with a few years ago, before he died in the fight against Balamung: what with everything else that's gone on since, I haven't had the chance to explore what all they're good for, but it's plain they make riding a horse and staying on its back a lot easier than that ever was before. If you can really fight from horseback, what point to chariots?"

"Maybe *you* can fight from horseback," Van said. "You're a good-sized man, aye, but alongside me you're a stripling. The horse that could bear my weight, especially in armor" —he slapped his broad, bronze-covered chest—"hasn't been foaled yet. If it's not the chariot, I'm a foot soldier."

"That's not the point," Gerin said. "Chariots are like any of the rest of our weapons; they're scarce and hard to come by. More men could be warriors if they just had to lay hold of a horse and some arms rather than a team and a car to go with it."

"Then you'd best start showing them those footholders and what to do with 'em," the outlander answered. "We're going to need as many warriors as we can muster, and that soon, too."

"I know—sooner than I can train them into being proper horsemen, the more so as I'm nowhere near a proper horseman myself." Gerin sighed. "If only that monster of Balamung's hadn't killed Duin when he kicked out. Our little pepperpot would have had all of us riding whether we wanted to or not."

"He rode ideas even harder than you do, and that's a fact," Van said. "You're better at picking the ones to ride, though; I give you so much."

"Such generosity," Gerin said in tones far drier than the weather. "Suppose I did teach a good many men, barons and peasants both, to ride and fight from horseback . . ."

His voice trailed away. Actions had inevitable consequences; on that philosophers and historians agreed. The trick was to reason out what they might be before you acted, instead of getting caught by surprise later.

His best guess was that large numbers of warriors on horseback would prove as revolutionary as large numbers of bronze weapons in the hands of the serfs. If one lord in the northlands succeeded in forming a good-sized force of cavalry as opposed to chariotry, the rest would have to imitate him or go under. Since a man wouldn't need as many resources to maintain a horse as he would for a team and chariot, vassal barons' holdings could shrink until, after a couple of generations, it might be hard to tell a poor baron from a prosperous peasant.

Gerin had been teaching bright serfs their letters. Did he really want to arm them, too? Was he ready to unleash more great change on a land that had seen too much too fast of late?

For the moment, the decision was out of his hands. The monsters were forcing the pace of change, not he. But if they were put down at last—

Van cleared his throat, bringing the Fox's thoughts back to the here and now. The outlander said, "Captain, what is it you've done to put Fand in such a swivet? Last night she was going on about the sheep's eyes you were casting at Selatre till I all but had to hit her over the head with an ale jar to make her leave off."

"I've done nothing of the sort," Gerin said indignantly. "I've spent time with her, aye, but I have to if she's to learn her letters and be able to go through the books in the library and find out what's in them. You hit the mark there at the start—having Selatre here hasn't set right with Fand, and she blames me, not you, that Selatre's here."

"She said you were pawing Selatre when she walked by the library the other day," Van said, doubt in his voice. "Not that I'd care to believe Fand over you, mind, but she says she saw it with her own eyes."

"She didn't," Gerin insisted. "You think Selatre would stay here for a moment if I tried pawing her? As a matter of fact, she put her hand on mine, not the other way round."

"*Selatre* touched *you*?" Van said, giving the Fox a sharp stare. "Honh!" The noise was not a word, but carried a world of meaning nonetheless.

Gerin wished his friend were not so tall; it made trying to look down his nose at Van likelier to give him a crick in the neck than to overawe the outlander. He said, "Fand's hardly speaking to me anymore. Are you going to start in and speak for her?"

"Not a chance," Van said. "Ever since I got too big for my mother to tell me what to do, I've lived just as I pleased, and I'm a great believer in letting everyone else do the same thing. But if you think I'll pretend to be blind to what goes on around me, you can think again on that, too."

The Fox rolled his eyes. "Do you know *why* she touched me? She was glad I'd taught her her letters; they fill up some of the emptiness she feels now that Biton speaks to her no more. That's all."

"That may be why she says she did it, but the fact remains—she did it, she didn't have to do it, and she hasn't done it with anybody else," Van says. "Me, I'd say that means it's not all, not even close to all."

"That's—" Gerin felt fury rising in him. He seldom lost his temper, but results were memorable when he did. But before he exploded like a tightly stoppered pot left too long in the fire, he paused to wonder why he was getting so angry so fast. When he did, the anger evaporated. "That's— possible," he said in a small voice.

Van studied him with approval. "You're honest with yourself, that I will say for you. And suppose it's not just possible but so? What will you do then?"

"You ask good questions. That's a better question than I have an answer for right now." One corner of Gerin's mouth quirked up in a wry smile. Suppose Selatre was coming to care for him? Could he come to care for her in return? After falling in love with Elise and then watching that love crumble to ashes, he wondered if he dared let himself become vulnerable to a woman again. In some ways, going into battle against the monsters was easier. There, at least, he knew what he had to do to come through unhurt.

Van said, "Mind you, Fox, I have nothing against the

lass. Too quiet for my taste, but I'm a roisterer born and you're not. But I do want to know you're doing what you're doing with your eyes open."

"I don't even know," Gerin said heavily. "I tell you this much, though: just as you find Selatre too quiet, a couple of years of life with Fand have left my ears ringing, and that's the truth."

"Ah, it's not so bad," Van said. "She shouts, you shout back. After the yelling's done, you futter a couple of times and all's right till the next go-round."

"We've done that more than once, she and I," Gerin said. "Too many times more than once, as a matter of fact. That sort of thing gets wearing in a hurry, at least for me."

"Ah, Fox, you pay fancy prices for pepper and cloves and the gods only know what all else to make your food taste interesting, and you want the rest of your life dull as oatmeal porridge without even salt."

"My food won't stick a knife in me if it doesn't like the way I've cooked it," Gerin retorted. "And I wouldn't mind the rest of my life turning dull for a while. These past few years, what with one thing and another, it's been too bloody lively to suit me."

Van yawned an enormous, sarcastic yawn.

Nettled, Gerin said, "For that matter, you great barrel-brained oaf, I've never heard you speak Fand so fair. Here's a warning: if she throws me over, she'll aim her whole self straight at you. Are you ready for that?"

"I can handle her," Van said, confidence throbbing in his voice. Gerin wondered if he was as smart as he thought he was.

A peasant brought the Fox the news he'd been dreading. The fellow arrived in the back of a chariot along with Notker the Bald and his driver. He looked stunned, not only at traveling that way and faring so far from his home but also, Gerin thought, for deeper reasons: his own face might have borne that expression of disbelieving amazement just after the ground at Ikos stopped shaking.

"It's happened?" the Fox asked Notker.

"Aye, lord Gerin," his vassal returned. "This fellow here made it to my keep day before yesterday from his village next to the lands of Capuel the Flying Frog. I thought you'd best listen to his story, so I fetched him hither." His lined face made him look even more worried than he sounded.

"Monsters?" Gerin asked.

"Monsters, aye, and worse," Notker said. Gerin had not imagined there could be worse. Notker pointed to the serf he'd brought to Fox Keep. "This here is Mannor Trout, lord—he's the best fisherman in his village, which is how he got his ekename and likely why he's alive today." He nudged Mannor. "Tell the lord prince the tale you told me."

The peasant brushed a lock of dark hair back from where it had flopped down onto his forehead. "Aye, lord Notker," he said in rustic accents. His voice rang oddly flat, as if he held all emotion back from it to keep from having to remember the terror he'd known. "My village is southwest of here, you know, close to the border of your holding, and—"

"I know," Gerin said impatiently. "I rode that way not long ago, in search of my son Duren. I don't recall seeing you, though."

"You didn't, nor I you, though the talk of you going through lasted for days," Mannor said. "I was off fishing then, too." He drew himself up with pride, or at least its memory. "I bring in enough from the streams that they don't begrudge me staying out of the fields. They didn't, I mean." He shivered; that passionless tone he'd been using threatened to flee, leaving him naked against whatever it shielded him from.

"So you were at the stream the day I passed through your village, and you were at the stream this other day, the one you're going to tell me about," Gerin said, wanting to move the tale along without making Mannor face more than he could stand.

The serf nodded. That lock of hair fell onto his forehead again. This time he let it stay. He said, "I was having a day to beat all days, if you know what I mean, lord prince. Every time I stuck a new worm or a grub on my hook, I'd catch me a big tasty one, I would. Weren't much past noon when I had me 'bout as much as I felt like hauling back. Reckoned I'd eat some, trade me some to other folk, smoke me some for winter, and salt down the rest: we've a good lick close by, we do."

"All well and good," Gerin said. "So you were carrying your fish back to the village—through the woods, is that right?"

"Just like you say," Mannor agreed. "I get myself inside maybe two furlongs of the fields and hear the most horrible racket you ever put ear on in all your born days. Wolves howling, longtooths caterwauling—put 'em all together and they ain't a patch on this. I drop my fish and run up to see what I can see."

"Monsters in the village." Gerin's voice was as flat as the peasant's.

"Monsters, aye, but that's not all," Mannor said. "There was monsters, but there was Trokmoi, too, and they was workin' together to wreck and kill, Dyaus drop me into the hottest hell if I lie."

Notker nodded, his face now even grimmer: he'd already heard the tale. Gerin stared in horrified dismay. He'd imagined a great many catastrophes; he was good at it. But never in his blackest nightmares had he dreamt the creatures from the caves under Biton's temple would—or could—make common cause with his human foes.

"How do you mean, working together?" he demanded of Mannor. "Were the Trokmoi using the monsters for hunting dogs, to drive people out for destruction?" Adiatunnus was clever, no way around that. Perhaps he or one of his men had figured out a way to tame the monsters.

But the serf shook his head. "Some of the things, they was just goin' around bitin' whatever they could get their teeth into, like they was wolves or summat like that. But some, they was carryin' swords and spears and even talkin' some kind of growly talk with the red mustaches. They were uglier than the woodsrunners, but otherwise I didn't see much to choose between 'em."

"Can you confirm this?" Gerin asked Notker. It wasn't so much that he disbelieved Mannor as that he so much wanted to disbelieve him.

His vassal said, "No, lord prince. As soon as I heard the story, I figured you had to give ear, too. But do you think it's one he'd make up?" The Fox didn't, but he wished Notker hadn't made him realize he didn't.

Almost unnoticed by both of them, Mannor went on,

"Two o' the things, they caught my little boy. They was squabbling over him like dogs over a bone till a Trokmê, he seen what was happening and he takes his axe and chops the body in half." Quietly, hopelessly, he began to weep.

"Here," Gerin said, tasting the uselessness of words. "Here." He put an arm around the serf's shoulder. Mannor's tears soaked hot through his tunic. He held the man, and held his own face even harder, to keep from breaking down and blubbering along with him. Hearing what had happened to the serf's son reminded him all too vividly of all the things that might have happened to Duren. That he did not know which—if any—had befallen the boy only let him exercise his ability to envision disasters.

"What do we do with him, lord Gerin?" Notker asked.

The Fox waited until Mannor had cried himself out, then said, "First thing to do is get him good and drunk." He pointed the serf toward the entrance to the long hall of the keep. "Go on in there, Mannor; tell them I said to give you all the ale you can drink." He shoved Mannor in the direction of the doorway; the man went as if he had no will of his own left. Gerin turned back to Notker. "We have to see if he can live with this now. He has to see for himself, too. It won't be easy; he'll carry scars no less than if he'd been wounded in war, poor fellow."

"You know about that, lord prince," Notker said. The Fox nodded. These days, he had no family left: his father and brother slain, his wife run off, and his son stolen.

As he'd grown used to doing, he resolutely shoved that grief and worry to the back of his mind. More immediately urgent worries took precedence. He said to Notker, "The Trokmoi and monsters didn't assail your keep?"

"No, lord," Notker answered. "First I heard of them coming over the border from Capuel's—Dyaus knows why we still call it that, with nobody in charge there these past years—was when Mannor brought word. The gods only know what's happened since, mind you, but you'd reckon raiders and yon creatures could move faster than a grief-crazy serf if they had a mind to."

"That you would." Gerin rubbed his chin in perplexity.

Notker shared that perplexity. "Not like what you'd look for from the woodsrunners, neither. The Trokmoi, when they hit you, they mostly hit you like a man going into a woman: they want to get in as deep as they can as fast as they can."

"True enough." Gerin made an abstracted clucking noise, then suddenly held up one finger. "I have it, I think. Adiatunnus is a sneaky beggar, and smart, too—though not half so smart as he thinks he is. He's cobbled up some kind of deal with these creatures, but he doesn't know how well it's going to work. So he thinks he'll try it out small at first, and if it does what he hopes, why then he'll strike harder the next time. How does that sound to you?"

"Don't know if it's true," Notker said after some thought of his own. "Makes decent sense, though."

"In a way, it does," the Fox said. "But only in a way—that's why I called Adiatunnus half-smart. Now I'm warned. He'll be gathering his forces, collecting more monsters, doing whatever he thinks he needs to do. And do you know what I aim to do in the meanwhile?"

"What's that, lord?" Notker asked.

"I aim to hit him first."

The chariot hit a bump. Gerin's legs kept him smoothly upright without conscious thought on his part. "How am I supposed to administer my holding if I'm too busy fighting to pay heed to anything else?" he asked.

Van had adjusted as automatically as the Fox. He glanced over and answered, "I don't know the answer to that one, but let me give you one in return: how are you supposed to administer your holding if the Trokmoi and the monsters swarm out and take it away from you?"

"There you have me," Gerin said. "If I can't keep it, it isn't truly mine. But if I can't run it, it's hardly worth keeping." Schooling south of the High Kirs had left him fond of forming such paradoxes.

Van cut through this one with the ruthless economy he usually displayed: "If you still hold on to it, you can always fix it later. If it's lost, it's gone for good."

"You're right, of course," Gerin said, but the admission left him dissatisfied. Endless warfare would hurl his holding back into barbarism faster than anything else he could think of. But, as Van had said, everything else turned irrelevant if he didn't win each war.

Along with his regathered host of vassals, he rolled southwest down the same road he'd taken to Adiatunnus' border after Duren disappeared. This time, he wouldn't stop and exchange polite chitchat with the Trokmê chieftain's border guards. He'd go after Adiatunnus—and his monstrous allies—with all the might he had.

Notker the Bald brought his chariot up alongside Gerin's. He pointed ahead. "There's my keep, off to one side. At our pace, we'll make the village before sunset."

"So we will, and then roll through it," Gerin said. As soon as the sun had started to swing down toward the horizon from its high point in the sky, he'd ordered a couple of chariots out two furlongs ahead of the rest. The Trokmoi were often too impatient to set proper ambushes, and he suspected the monsters Adiatunnus had taken as allies would be even less skilled in the stratagems of war.

A puff of breeze from the west brought a whiff of something sickly sweet. Raffo turned and wrinkled his nose. "Phew! What's that stink?"

"Dead meat," Van answered.

The Fox nodded. "We're coming up on the village Mannor Trout got out of, or what's left of it. Mannor didn't lie, that's certain."

The closer they got, the worse the smell grew. Gerin coughed. The stink of carrion always made fear and rage bubble up in him: it called to mind the aftermath of too many fights, too many horrors.

The serf village, though, was worse than he'd expected. He'd been braced for sprawled, bloated corpses and charred ruins, and they were there. He'd looked for the livestock to be run off or slain, and it was. He'd known the crows would rise in a black cloud and the foxes slink off into the woods when he disturbed them, and they did.

But he hadn't reckoned on so many of the pathetic corpses looking as they'd been mostly devoured before the scavengers started on them. His stomach did a slow flip-flop. He should have realized the monsters wouldn't be fussy about where they got their meat. Intellectually, he had realized it. The implications, though, had escaped him.

Van said, "I had thought to round up a hen or two here, to give to the ghosts come sundown and to cook up for

us, too. But now I'm going to let that go. The gods alone
know what these hens have been pecking at since the
Trokmoi and their little friends went home."

Gerin's stomach lurched again. "Reasoned like a philoso-
pher," he said. Anthropophagy, even at one remove, was
worth fighting shy of. A few minutes later, a pig stuck its
head out of the bushes. No one shot at it. It was even
likelier than any surviving village chickens to have fed on
the bodies of those who had raised it.

After making sure no life remained in the village, Gerin
waved his arm. The chariots rattled on toward the border
with the holding of Capuel the Flying Frog. How much
of that now lay in the hands of the Trokmoi and the
monsters was anyone's guess. Few men said much about
what they'd seen in the clearing, but a new, grim sense
of purpose informed the force. They'd collect the payment
due, and more.

Just before sunset, a cock pheasant made the mistake
of coming out from the woods onto a meadow to feed. Its
ring-necked head came up in alarm when it saw, or perhaps heard, the chariots on the road. It began to run
rapidly, then leaped into the air, its wings thuttering.

Arrows hissed toward it. One of them, either cleverly
aimed or luckier than the rest, brought the bird tumbling
back to earth. "Well shot!" Gerin called. "Not only will it
feed the ghosts, it'll feed some of us, too."

"Aye, a pheasant's tasty, no doubt of that," Van said. "Me,
though, I'd sooner hang it a while to let it get properly
ripe before I cook it."

"Yes, I've seen you do that at Fox Keep once or twice,"
Gerin said. "I don't care for my meat flyblown, thank you
very kindly. Besides, we've no time for such fripperies
tonight. Bringing it down at all strikes me as a good enough
omen."

"Flyblown's not the point," Van replied. "Bringing out
the full flavor is. But you're right about today: we just pluck
it and gut it and put it over the flames or bake it in clay."

"Fuel for the fire," the Fox agreed. "It'll help us keep
going. And then we'll get into Adiatunnus' lands and set
some fires of our own."

❖   ❖   ❖

For all Gerin knew, the Trokmê guards at the border to Adiatunnus' holding might have been the same crew with whom he'd spoken when he came seeking Duren. This time, he didn't get a close look at them. As soon as they saw his force of chariotry approaching, they cried "The southrons!" in their own language and fled. They got in among the trees before any of his men could shoot them like the pheasant.

"Shall we stop and go after them, lord prince?" Raffo asked.

"No," the Fox answered. "We storm ahead instead. That way we get in amongst the woodsrunners faster than they have word we're coming."

The first village his men reached was inhabited by Elabonian serfs who had acquired new masters in the five years since the Trokmoi swarmed south over the Niffet. When they realized the men in the chariots were of their own kind, they came swarming out of their huts with cries of exultation.

"The gods be praised!" they shouted. "You've come to deliver us from the Trokmoi and from the—things." With that seemingly innocuous word, half their joy at seeing Gerin and his followers seemed to evaporate, boiled away in the memory of overpowering fear. One of them said, "The Trokmoi are bad enough, stealing and raping and all. But those things . . ." His voice guttered out like a candle.

"If you want to go, just pack whatever you can carry on your backs and run for my holding," Gerin said. "The peasants there will take you in. The ground is thin of men these days, with so much war and plunder. They'll be glad to have you, to help bring in a bigger crop."

"Dyaus bless you, lord," the serf said fervently. Then he hesitated. "But lord, how shall we travel with these things loose in the woods and ready to swoop down on us?"

"Take weapons, fool," Van said. "Anything you have is better than nothing. Would you rather be eaten trying to get away or stay here till the monsters come into your house and eat you in your own bed?"

"Truth to tell, lord," the serf said, taking no chances on the outlander's rank, "I'd sooner not be et at all."

"Then get out," Gerin said. "Now we've no more time

to waste gabbing with you. The Trokmoi and the monsters destroyed a peasant village in my land, just over the border from what used to be Capuel's holding. Now they're going to find out they can't do that without paying the price for it." He slapped Raffo on the shoulder. The driver flicked the reins of the chariot. The horses started forward.

The Fox put himself in the lead now, with Drago's chariot right behind. The Bear would reliably follow him, and wouldn't do anything foolish. That counted for more than whatever brilliant stratagems Rihwin *might* come up with, for Rihwin might just as easily do something to endanger the whole force.

The road opened onto another clearing, this one recently hacked out of the woods. In it stood three or four stout wooden houses, bigger and sturdier than the round cottages in which most serfs dwelt. "Those are Trokmê homes," Gerin said. "I've seen enough of them north of the Niffet."

"Let's get rid of the Trokmoi in 'em, then," Van said. One of those Trokmoi came out from behind a house. He stared in amazement that might have been comical under other circumstances at the Elabonians encroaching on what he'd come to think of as his land. That lasted only a couple of heartbeats. Then he let out a shout of alarm and dashed for shelter inside.

Gerin already had an arrow in the air. It caught the woodsrunner in the small of the back. He went down with a wail. Gerin caught Van's eye. "Try doing that with your precious spear," he said.

Another Trokmê came outside to see what the shouting was about. Gerin and Drago both shot at him—and both missed. He ducked back into the house in a hurry, slammed the door, and dropped the bar with a thump Gerin could hear across half a furlong.

"Fire arrows!" Gerin yelled.

A couple of chariots had firepots in them, half full of embers ready to be fanned to life. Others carried little bundles of straw soaked in pitch. While some of his men got real fires going, others tied the bundles to arrows, just back of the heads. Still others used shields to protect them from the Trokmoi, who started shooting at them from the windows of the houses.

Trailing smoke, the fire arrows flew toward the woodsrunners' shelters. Some fell short; some went wide—their balance was all wrong. But others stuck in wall timbers or the thatch of the roofs. Before long, smoke rose up from a dozen different places. The Trokmoi inside yelled at one another. Some of the voices belonged to women. One corner of Gerin's mouth twisted down, but only for a moment. The Trokmoi hadn't cared about women or children when they struck his holding. What did he owe them?

The fires on the roofs grew and spread. The women's cries rose to shrill shrieks, then suddenly stopped. Doors came open. Red- and yellow-mustached men charged out, half a dozen in all. Some had helms on their heads; two or three carried shields. They threw themselves at Gerin's troopers with no thought for their own survival, only the hope of taking some Elabonians with them before they fell.

"You'll not have our wives and daughters for your sport," one of them panted as he slashed at the Fox. "We're after slaying the lot of them."

Van's spear caught the woodsrunner in the side. The fellow wore no armor; it bit deep. Van twisted the shaft as he yanked it out. The Trokmê coughed bright blood and crumpled.

Gerin looked around. None of the other woodsrunners was still on his feet. One of his own men swore as he bound up a slashed arm. That seemed to be the only wound his warriors had taken—they'd so outnumbered their foes that they'd dealt with them three and four and five to one, and not all of them had been engaged by a long shot.

The houses kept on burning. Drago the Bear said, "That smoke's going to give us away."

"It's liable to," Gerin agreed, "though fire gets loose easily enough, and it's bloody hard to douse once it does. Adiatunnus and his lads will know something has gone wrong, but not just what—until we show up and teach 'em. Let's get moving again."

Before long, they came to another peasant village—or rather, what had been one. Now several monsters from under the temple at Ikos stalked among the houses. More of them tore at the carcasses of a couple of oxen in the middle of the village square. They looked up, muzzles and hands red with blood, as Gerin's chariot came into sight.

Two or three monsters ran straight for the chariot, as any fierce beasts might have. Gerin shot one of them: a lucky arrow, right through the throat. That made the others hesitate, more thoughtful than any beasts would have been.

But it also gave the rest of the monsters the chance to snatch up weapons: clubs, spears, and a couple of swords. Then they too rushed toward the Fox, their cries more like words than any he had heard from the creatures before.

He had a bad moment or two there. There were a lot more monsters than he had men in the two lead chariots. He was about to order Raffo to wheel the horses around and retreat when reinforcements came rattling up.

Some of the monsters kept on with the attack, again as beasts might have done. But others must have made the calculation he'd been on the brink of a short time before: they headed off into the woods, to fight another day.

When the skirmish was done, Gerin pointed to the deserted huts in the village and said, "Torch the place. If those things were denning here, we don't want to give them anyplace they can return to once we've gone."

More smoke rose into the sky. The Fox knew that whoever saw it would figure out something unusual was going on in the northeastern part of the land Adiatunnus had overrun. His lips skinned back from his teeth. He had reached the point where he was resigned to having a woodsrunner for a neighbor; Adiatunnus hadn't acted much differently from Capuel the Flying Frog and the other Elabonian barons he'd displaced. But if Adiatunnus consorted with monsters—

That led Gerin to another thought. As Raffo drove the chariot deeper into the Trokmê's territory, the Fox said to Van, "I wonder how the monsters came to align themselves with Adiatunnus. Most of the ones we saw in Bevon's holding wouldn't have had the wit to do such a thing."

"If I had to guess, Captain, I'd say there's smart ones and dumb ones, same as with people," the outlander answered. "Say the smart ones are as smart as dumb people: that'd make the dumb ones like wolves or longtooths or any other hunting beasts. The smart ones'd have the wit for something like banding together with the Trokmoi, and maybe even for bringing along some of their stupid friends." He laughed. "Makes 'em sound like half the folk we know, doesn't it?"

"More than half," Gerin said. Van laughed again. The Fox went on, "I wish we didn't have to waste time with all these little fights. I want to hit Adiatunnus as hard and sudden a blow as I can, but every skirmish we fight makes me slower to get to him and gives him more time to ready himself."

"Well, we can't very well say to the woodsrunners we run into—or still less to these monsters—'Sorry there, friend, we have more important things to do than slaughtering you right now. Can you hang about till we're on our way back?' "

Gerin snorted; when you put it that way, it was absurd. All the same, unease gnawed at him. Before he'd set out on this punitive raid, he'd seen it clearly in his mind: go into Adiatunnus' territory, strike the Trokmoi—and with luck kill their chieftain—and then fare home again. Reality was less clear-cut, as reality has a way of being.

Before long, his army rolled past the ruins of what had been a palisaded keep before the Trokmoi came south over the Niffet. The woodsrunners hadn't bothered repairing the timbers of the outwall; instead, they'd built a dwelling of their own in the courtyard between the wall and the stone keep, turning the place into a sort of fortified village.

A couple of Trokmoi were up on what was left of the wall, but they raised no alarm when Gerin's chariot came into sight. "Are they all asleep?" he demanded indignantly. He didn't like his enemies to act stupidly; it made him wonder what sort of ruse they were plotting.

But Van smacked one fist into the palm of his other hand. "Me, I know what it is, Captain: they think we're woodsrunners, too."

"By the gods, you're right." Gerin waved toward the distant stronghold. One of the Trokmoi waved back. The Fox frowned. "I don't fancy going in after them. They could have enough men to make that expensive—and it would cost us the speed and free movement the chariots give."

"More fire arrows?" Raffo said over his shoulder.

"Aye, and maybe a muzzle for a mouthy driver, too," Gerin answered, but he swatted the young man on the back to leave no doubt that was a joke. "We want to make sure none of them gets away, too, so what we'll do is—"

His chariot, and Drago's with it, pulled off the road a little past the keep the Trokmoi had altered. That might have perplexed the men on the battered wall, but not enough to make them cry out. Even when the first chariots of the Fox's main force came into view, they kept silent long enough to let the cars get well begun on forming a ring around the holding.

"Southrons!" The cry in the Trokmê language floated across weedy fields to Gerin's ears. "We've been cozened by southrons!"

So they had, and by the time they realized it, they were too late to do anything about it. The Elabonian warriors shot arrows at any woodsrunner who appeared on the palisade. Some of them also shot fire arrows at the wooden palisade itself and over it at the roofs of the houses it sheltered. The timbers of the palisade caught only slowly; the same was not true for the dry straw thatching of those roofs.

"Well, what'll they do now?" Van said as several thick plumes of gray-white smoke rose from the courtyard.

"Curse me if I know," Gerin answered. "I don't know what I'd do in that spot—try not to get into it in the first place, I suppose. But they don't have that choice, not anymore."

Some of the Trokmoi took refuge in the stone keep in the center of the courtyard—Gerin saw bits of motion through its slit windows. He wondered if that would save them; the door and all the furnishings within were wood, and liable to catch fire . . . and even if they didn't, so much smoke filled the air that anyone inside was liable to feel like a slab of bacon being cured.

The Trokmoi had let the ditch around the palisade alone; shrubs and bushes grew in great profusion in it. That would have made matters easier for anyone who tried to lay siege to the castle, but it helped those inside now. Some leaped off the wall—not just men but also women with their skirts flying up around them as they jumped—to land in those bushes and shelter there from fire and foe alike.

And the drawbridge thumped down. A double handful of woodsrunners in bronze armor stormed forth to put up the best fight they could. Gerin admired their gallantry even as his men thundered toward them. Fighting afoot against chariotry was like trying to spoon up sand with a sieve. The Elabonians rattled by, pouring arrows into their foes, and the woodsrunners could do little but stand and suffer.

They had one moment of triumph: an archer of theirs hit an oncoming horse in the neck. The beast crashed to the ground, dragging down its harnessmate and overturning the car the two horses pulled. Men tumbled over the ground like broken dolls. The three or four Trokmoi still standing raised a defiant cheer. Soon they were dead.

Of the Elabonians in the wrecked chariot, one also lay dead, his head twisted at an unnatural angle. Another writhed and groaned with a broken leg and other injuries besides. The third, Parol Chickpea, was on his feet and hardly limping. "By all the gods, I'm the luckiest man alive!" he cried.

Gerin was not inclined to argue with him, but said, "Whether it's so or not, don't boast of it. If you tempt the divine powers to take away what they've given, they're too apt to yield to that temptation."

He did what he could for the warrior with the broken leg, splinting it between two trimmed saplings. The fellow had to be tied aboard a chariot after that, though, which ruined the car's efficiency and made him cry out at every bump and pothole in the road—and the road seemed nothing but bumps and potholes.

"I should have brought a wagon to carry the wounded," the Fox said as they made camp that evening in the heart of the land Adiatunnus had seized. "I didn't want anything to slow us down, but here we are slowed down anyhow by all the fighting we've done—and we haven't really come to grips with Adiatunnus yet."

"Expecting a plan to run just as you make it asks a lot of the gods," Van said.

"That's so." Gerin fretted despite the admission. He always expected his plans to work perfectly; if they failed, that reflected unfavorably on him, since he had formed them. Life being as it was, few of them came to pass exactly as designed, which left him plenty for which to reproach himself.

Pale Nothos, nearly full, was the only moon in the sky: Math was just past new, and too close to the sun to be seen, while Tiwaz was a waning crescent and ruddy Elleb halfway between full and third quarter. It had been about there in its wanderings through the heavens when the Fox and his men slew the first monster down in Bevon's holdings, though rain clouds kept him from seeing it then.

Thinking of that monster made him think of the monsters that had joined Adiatunnus. He did not expect the Trokmoi themselves to sally forth against his men at night. He still hoped, though he didn't really believe, Adiatunnus hadn't yet learned of his attack. Even if the woodsrunners did know of it, sending men out by night was not something to be undertaken lightly.

But the monsters were something else again. He'd already seen that the night ghosts held no terror for them. They might well try to fall on his warriors when they had them at a disadvantage.

That made him double the watchstanders he'd placed out away from the main campfires. The men he'd hauled from their blankets grumbled. "Go back to sleep, then," he snapped. "If you'd rather be well rested and dead than sleepy and alive, how could I possibly presume to argue with you?" Stung by sarcasm, the newly drafted sentries went out to take their places.

Sure enough, monsters did prowl the woods and fields; their yowls and screams woke the Fox several times before midnight came. He'd grab for sword, shield, and helmet, realize the creatures were not close by, wriggle around till he was comfortable once more, and go back to sleep.

Then he heard screams that came not only from the monsters' throats but also from those of his own men. He snatched up his weapons and sprang to his feet. The night was well along; Elleb had climbed halfway from the eastern horizon to the meridian. But Gerin's eyes were not on the reddish moon.

Its light, that of Nothos, and the crimson glow of the embers showed two of his sentry parties locked in battle with the monsters, and more of the creatures running toward the warriors slowly rousing themselves round the fire.

Gerin shouted to distract a monster from an Elabonian who still lay on the ground snoring. The Fox envied the man's ability to sleep through anything, but wished he hadn't put it on display at that exact moment.

The monster swerved from the sleeping warrior and rushed at Gerin. Moonlight glinted from its teeth. Its clawed hands were outstretched to rend and tear. He was acutely aware of having only helm and shield; cool night air blew through his linen shirt and wool trousers, reminding him of what the monster's teeth and claws would do to flesh so nearly naked.

Instead of slashing, he thrust at the creature, to keep the full length of arm and sword between it and him. It spitted itself on the point of the bronze blade. He twisted the sword in the wound, then yanked it free. The monster screamed again, this time with the note of shocked surprise he'd heard so often from wounded men.

As it staggered, he thrust again, this time taking it right in the throat. Blood fountained, black in the light of the moons. The monster stumbled, fell, and did not rise again.

The Fox ran to the next closest fight he could find. He stabbed a monster in the back. It shrieked and whirled to face him, whereupon the trooper it had been fighting gave it a sword stroke almost identical to the one Gerin had used.

Though the monsters were individually more than a match for unarmored men, they had little notion of fighting save by and for themselves. That let the Elabonians slowly gain the upper hand on their attackers. And, like any beasts of prey, the monsters were not enthusiastic about taking on foes who fought back hard. They finally fled into the forest, still screaming in fury and hate.

"Throw some wood on the fire," Gerin said. "Let's see what needs doing here and do it."

As the flames leaped higher, the warriors went around finishing off monsters too badly hurt to run or even crawl away. Several men were also down for good. Gerin, Rihwin, and a couple of others who knew something of leechcraft did what they could for men who had been bitten or clawed.

"Lucky they didn't go for the horses," Van said, holding

out a gashed arm to be bound up. "That would have spilled the perfume into the soup."

"Wouldn't it?" Gerin said. "As is, we'll have some cars with two men in them rather than three. But you're right; it could have been worse."

"It could that," the outlander said; every once in a while, a Trokmê turn of phrase cropped up in his speech. "Me, I'm just as glad I won't be clumping along on foot when Adiatunnus and his jolly lads come after us in their chariots. That'll be tomorrow, unless Adiatunnus is blinder than I think."

"You're right there, too," the Fox said. "We could have run into them yesterday, easy as not. I'd hoped we would, as a matter of fact. All these little fights leave us weaker for the big one ahead."

Van nodded, but said, "We've hurt them worse'n they've done to us, though."

"I console myself with that thought," Gerin answered, "but drop me into the hottest hell if I know who can better afford the hurt, Adiatunnus or me. He brought a lot of Trokmoi south over the Niffet with him, the whoreson, and these monsters only add to his strength."

"We'll find out come the day," Van said, more cheerfully than Gerin could have managed. "For me, though, the only I thing I want to manage is some more sleep." He set down spear and shield, doffed his helm, wrapped himself in his blanket, and was snoring again while the Fox still stared indignantly.

Gerin could not put the desperate fight out of his mind so easily, nor could most of his men. Some still groaned from their wounds, while others sat around the fire and chatted in low voices about what they'd just been through.

The eastern sky turned gray, then pink, then gold. Tiwaz's thin crescent almost vanished against the growing light of the background against which it shone. The sun spilled its bright rays over the land. The Fox's men scratched shallow graves for their comrades the monsters had slain, then covered them over with stones to try to keep the creatures or other scavengers from molesting their remains. The corpses of the monsters, now stiff in death, they let lie where they had fallen.

Drivers harnessed chariots. "Let's get going," Gerin said. "What we do today tells how much this strike is worth."

The first peasant village through which they rolled was empty and deserted. Gerin thought nothing of that till his warriors had already passed the hamlet. Then he realized word of their coming had got ahead of them. If the peasants knew invaders were loose in Adiatunnus' lands, the Trokmoi would know, too.

"Well, we didn't really think we could keep it a secret this long," Van answered when Gerin said that aloud. The outlander checked his shield and weapons to make sure he could get at them in an instant. Gerin told Raffo to slow the pace. When the driver obeyed and the chariots behind came up close enough, he shouted the warning back to them. Then he thumped Raffo on the shoulder. His chariot rejoined Drago's in the lead.

Cattle, sheep, and a couple of horses grazed on a broad stretch of meadow. They looked up in mild surprise—and the herders with them in dismay—when Elabonian chariots began rolling out. The herdsmen fled for the woods, but they were a long way away.

"Shall we go after 'em?" Raffo asked. "By their red locks, they're woodsrunners."

"No, let 'em run," Gerin said. "They look like men who hardly have their breeches to call their own; they're no danger to us."

Van pointed across the meadow. More chariots, these drawn by shaggy ponies and painted with bright spirals and jagged fylfots, came rattling out of the woods there. The men in them were pale-skinned and light-haired, like the herders. Bronze shone ruddy in the morning sun. "You want folk dangerous to us, Fox, I think you've found them," Van said.

Before Gerin could so much as nod, Drago the Bear called from the other chariot: "What do we do now, lord?"

"Pull over to one side, begin to form line of battle, and clear the roadway so the cars behind us can deploy," Gerin answered. Raffo, who knew his mind well, already had the chariot in motion. Drago's driver conformed to his movements.

To Van, Gerin murmured, "Now we see how much

Adiatunnus has learned from a few years of fighting against Elabonians."

"Aye, if he's brought his own army in a great roaring mass, Trokmê style, he'll swarm down on us before our friends get here," the outlander said. "Let's hope he's set out scouts the way we have, and that they're waiting for their main body, too." He chuckled. "The fighting trick'll work against him this time, not for."

Much to Gerin's relief, the Trokmoi across the meadow didn't whip their horses into a wild charge. Instead, they too sidled out onto the grass almost crab fashion, as if wondering how many cars the Fox had with him and how soon those cars would arrive.

Gerin was wondering the same thing about the woodsrunners. Adiatunnus must have done a fine job of absorbing Elabonian military doctrine, for his supporters began coming out of the woods at about the same time as those of the Fox. The two lines of chariots stretched about to equal length on the meadow. Monsters stood between the cars of Adiatunnus' battle line. Gerin wondered whether that would do the Trokmê more good than harm; the ponies that pulled the chariots seemed nervous of these fierce new allies.

Adiatunnus cupped his hands and bellowed like a bull. Gerin knew that voice. At the same moment, Gerin raised his arm and then brought it down to point toward the Trokmê line. Drivers on both sides whipped their teams forward.

Chariot battles were generally fluid as quicksilver, and this one proved no exception. The herds in the broad field made teams swing wide to avoid them. The pounding of the horses' hooves, the rattle and thump of the cars, and warriors' hoarse, excited shouts panicked the sheep and cattle and made them run wild, spreading more confusion still.

Gerin plucked an arrow from his quiver, nocked, and let fly at Adiatunnus: if the chieftain fell, that would make his followers easier meat. Shooting from the jouncing platform of a chariot car—indeed, standing in the car without hanging on to the rail to keep from being pitched out on your head—was anything but easy, though endless practice let him do it without wondering how he managed. He cursed when the Trokmê did not fall.

An arrow hissed by his own ear; the woodsrunners were aiming at him, too. Here and there, men on both sides pitched out of chariots to sprawl in the thick green grass. Horses went down, too, and often made the cars they drew founder with them. Sometimes warriors would come up from those mishaps unhurt, and go on to fight as foot soldiers.

A monster loped toward Gerin's chariot. The creature was almost as fast as the horses, and much more agile. Unlike some the Fox had seen, it carried no weapons. Even so, it was clever enough to attack the beasts of burden rather than the men they hauled: the horses could not fight back, and if one of them went down, the chariot was apt to overturn, too.

The Fox shot at the monster from only a few yards' distance, and turned the air sulfurous when his arrow went wide. Van was on the wrong side of the chariot to attack the creature, and in any case could not reach it with his thrusting spear. The horses squealed and shied away from the monster as it came up on them.

Before Gerin could draw another arrow, Raffo lashed the monster across its outstretched arms with his whip. The thing screeched. The driver hit it again, *craack!*, this time across its muzzle, just missing one eye. The monster clapped a hand to the wound and fled.

Along with three or four other chariots, Gerin's overlapped the end of the Trokmê line. "Come on! We'll roll 'em up!" he shouted with fierce joy, and led his men around the enemy's flank. The chaos they created was marvelous to behold—and would have been more marvelous still had the woodsrunners' line not overlapped his on the other wing. But it did, and the whole battle spun round, a mad wheel of destruction.

The Fox found himself face-to-face with Adiatunnus. The Trokmê had lost his helm somewhere in the fighting; his bald pate glowed red from exertion and sun. His eyes, though, were cold and shrewd, "Well, lord Gerin," he said with a mocking salute, "we lie athwart your way home now, don't we?"

"You do that," Gerin answered in the Trokmê tongue, "but no more than we lie athwart yours."

Fighting ebbed as the leaders parleyed. Adiatunnus scowled; perhaps he'd hoped to panic Gerin, but he'd failed. He looked over the field. "You've hurt us about as bad as the other way round," he said. "Are you fain to go on, now, or shall we say enough and have done?"

Gerin gauged the field, too. The Trokmê chief had the right of it; the battle was drawn. The woodsrunners had wrecked Mannor Trout's village, but he'd had his revenge there: he'd hurt Adiatunnus' lands worse. Fighting till only a handful of men still stood had scant appeal to him, especially with the monsters on the loose.

"Enough—for now," he said reluctantly, "if you can hold those—things—to a truce to let us separate."

"That I can, though I'll thank you for not speaking ill of my friends and allies here," Adiatunnus said. "And 'for now' indeed—we'll have at each other again, I have no doubt. Och, and when we do, I'll be after having more in the way of friends and allies, but you, Fox—what will you do?"

Gerin pondered that question as the rival forces warily passed through each other. He was still pondering it when he crossed back over the border into his own holding, and when he came home to Fox Keep. Ponder as he would, though, he found no answer that satisfied him.

VIII

"My poor ear," Rihwin moaned for what had to be the five hundredth time. Gerin prided himself on being a patient man, but when his patience snapped, it snapped spectacularly.

"By all the gods, I'm sick to death of listening to your whining," he growled, and grabbed Rihwin. The southerner tried to twist free, but Gerin was the best wrestler in the northlands. He twisted one of Rihwin's arms behind his back and started frog-marching him toward the shack where he worked his magics.

"What are you doing?" Rihwin yelped.

"I am going to fix that ear of yours, one way or the other," the Fox said. Rihwin hadn't struggled hard till then, but he started to. Gerin twisted his arm up a little higher. Rihwin gasped as he felt his shoulder joint creak.

Inside the shack, Gerin slammed him down onto the one rickety chair in front of the table where he labored at his sorcery. He'd managed to overawe Rihwin, which wasn't easy. The southerner made no effort to bolt. In a small voice, he repeated, "What are you doing?"

"What I said I'd do: use the law of similarity to build that ear of yours back to where it's the same as the other one. The spell should be simplicity itself: what could possibly go wrong?"

Now Rihwin did try to rise. "I'd really rather not find out. Given the choice between a half-trained wizard—which, you must admit, is a charitable description of your talents—and keeping silent about my mutilation, I opt without hesitation for silence."

Gerin slammed him down again. "You've said that before, over and over. You've gone back on your word, too, over and over. Now, don't be a donkey—just sit there and I'll set you right in no time. Unless you'd rather I tried that operation you described—"

"No," Rihwin said hastily. "You're sure you know what you're doing?" He had the look of a man sitting down to gamble against a fellow notorious for using loaded dice.

"I know what I have to do," Gerin answered, which was not quite an affirmative. He flipped through the vellum pages of a codex until he came to a cantrip which was a general application of the law of similarity. Then he paused a while in thought. Suddenly he smacked one fist into the other palm. "The very thing!" he exclaimed. He turned to Rihwin. "I'm going out to find something to tailor the spell to your very problem. You'd better be here when I get back."

"What are you looking for?" Rihwin still sounded suspicious.

Gerin grinned triumphantly. "Earwigs."

"Well, father Dyaus, that's ingenious," Rihwin said. "Perhaps I *shall* be here when you return."

With that Gerin had to be content. He went out and started turning over stones in the courtyard. Under one not very far from the stables, he found several of the shiny, dark brown insects. They tried to crawl away, but he grabbed them and carried them back to the shack. "Even the little pincers on their posteriors will serve symbolically to represent the ring you wore in your ear."

"Why, so they will." All at once, Rihwin went from dubious to enthusiastic. "Don't fribble away the time. Get on with it."

Gerin got on with it, but first spent more time studying the spell in the grimoire. He knew his own inadequacy as a sorcerer, and also knew he would never get the chance to make two serious blunders. Fitting a general spell to a specific application required certain adaptations of both verse and passes. He muttered to himself, planning in advance the rhymes he'd use and the passes he'd have to change. The spell was intended to be simple, which meant most of the passes used the right hand. That hindered him more than it helped. He'd overcome the problem before, though, and expected to be able to do it again.

He felt confident as he launched into the chant. His right hand was clumsy, but seemed to be doing what he required of it. He poured rose water over the earwigs he'd imprisoned in a bronze bowl. They didn't drown quite as fast as he'd thought they would, but surely that degree of exactitude wouldn't matter.

"My ear feels strange," Rihwin remarked. He brought his hand up to the ruined flap of flesh. "You've not changed it yet, but the potential for change is manifestly there."

"Shut up," Gerin said fiercely, though Rihwin had given him good news. The donkey had to know he didn't need to be distracted, not when he was coming to the climactic moment of the spell. His right hand twisted through the last pass; he grunted in satisfaction at having done it correctly. He cut a red wool thread with a bronze knife he never used for any other purpose and cried, "Transform!"

"You've done it!" Rihwin said exultantly. "I can feel the change."

Gerin turned to see what his magic had wrought. He suffered a sudden coughing fit, and hoped his face would not betray him. He had changed Rihwin's ear, but not quite in the way he'd intended. It was indeed whole, but not pink and round: it was long and pointed and hairy.

He knew what had gone wrong. He'd called Rihwin a donkey, and then thought of him as a donkey when he'd spoken up at the wrong time. Somehow, the resentful thought had leaked into the conjuration and left his fellow Fox with a donkey's ear.

A fly buzzing around the inside of the shack chose that moment to light on the new-formed appendage. As a donkey's ear will, it twitched. The fly flew away. Rihwin started violently and clapped a hand to his head. The evidence, alas, was all too palpable. "What have you done to me, you muddler?"

"Muddled." Gerin kicked at the dirt floor of the shack, feeling smaller and more useless than the earwigs he'd drowned.

"Well, what are you going to do about it? You were going to give me an ear, you—you moldy pigeon dropping, not this—this excrescence." Gerin had never heard an unwounded man scream through three consecutive sentences before; in the abstract, the feat was to be admired.

"I'll try my best to set it right," Gerin said. "I should be able to manage a simple reversal of the spell." He reached for the grimoire.

"You said the spell itself would be simple, too," Rihwin reminded him. He wasn't screaming any more, but sarcasm sharp and sour as vinegar dripped from his tongue.

"So I did," Gerin admitted. "Look, if all else fails, I'll buy you a hat." That sent Rihwin's voice back into the upper registers.

Gerin tried to ignore him, though it wasn't easy. In theory, reversal spells were simple. Both the law of similarity and that of contagion applied and, since he'd just essayed the spell he wished to overturn, the links were temporally strong. On the other hand, given the sorcerous ineptitude he'd just demonstrated— He made himself not think about that. A magician needed to believe he'd succeed.

A magician also needs talent, part of him jeered. The rest of him made that part shut up. He plunged headlong into the first reversal spell he found. The more time he spent thinking about it, the more he'd hesitate later. If you fell out of a jouncing chariot, you needed to get back in and ride again.

By luck, most of the passes were for his left hand. He went through them with care, but not with confidence— he wondered when, if ever, he'd have confidence in his magic once more. Rihwin sat in the chair, arms folded, glaring stonily at him. Normally, having Rihwin keep quiet while he cast a spell would have been a blessing. As things were, it just disconcerted Gerin more.

He raced through the cantrip at a pace a practiced wizard would have hesitated to match. One way or another, he'd know soon. His fingers twisted through the last and hardest pass of the spell. "Let all be as it was!" he yelled.

"Something happened," Rihwin said. "I felt it." But he didn't raise his hand to discover exactly what it was. Maybe he was afraid. He asked Gerin, "Did you deck me out with an octopus tentacle?"

"I haven't even seen octopus tentacles since that Sithonian eatery I used to frequent in the City of Elabon," Gerin replied. He stared at the place where the donkey's ear had sprouted from Rihwin's head.

"That's not a responsive answer." Rihwin sighed theatrically. "Very well, since you won't tell me, I shall just have to find out for myself." Slowly, he brought his left hand up to his head. His eyes grew as wide as Gerin's. "It's *my* ear," he whispered. Then, even more amazed, he added, "And it's whole—isn't it?"

"It certainly looks that way," Gerin said. "Does it feel so, too?"

"By Dyaus, it does. How ever did you manage that?"

"If I knew, I would tell you." Gerin cudgeled his wits for an explanation. At last, he said, "The reversal spell must have undone your wound as well as my magic—that's all I can think of."

Rihwin felt of his ear. "There's the hole through which the hoop passed. You must be right, lord Gerin; like you, I can think of no other explanation that fits." Now that his ear was restored, he started to laugh. "My fellow Fox, you are the best bad magician I have ever known."

"I'll take that for a compliment." Suddenly Gerin started to laugh, too. Rihwin's elastic features showed curiosity. Gerin explained: "If I could do on purpose what I did by accident, think of the demand I'd be in from wenches who wanted to frolic and yet be wed as maidens."

Rihwin leered. "Aye, and think of the fee you could charge, too."

"I'm surprised women don't already have a magic like that," Gerin said. "Or maybe they do, and just don't let on to us men."

"It could be so," Rihwin agreed. He felt his ear again, as if not believing Gerin had, no matter how erratically, accomplished exactly what he'd said he'd do. "Now I have to wait until Otes or another jeweler passes through, so I can have a new hoop made to replace the one I lost."

"If you get your ear torn again on account of that foolish southron conceit, don't expect me to fix it for you," Gerin said.

"If I come to you again to have my ear fixed, I deserve to wear a donkey's in its place," Rihwin retorted. Gerin mimed taking an arrow in the ribs; Rihwin had won that exchange.

One of Gerin's warriors who held the Elabon Way open through Bevon's holding brought disquieting news back to Fox Keep. "Lord prince, it's said Bevon and two of his sons have made common cause with Adiatunnus—and with the monsters from Ikos," he said between swigs from a jack of ale.

"Said by whom?" Gerin demanded, not wanting to believe Elabonians could fall so low as to align themselves with the creatures.

"By Bevander, another of Bevon's sons," the soldier answered. "He came to us calling down curses on past enmity and saying he'd sooner cast his lot with you than with a bunch of things."

"I wonder what he meant by that," Gerin said, "the monsters, or his father and brothers?" The warrior who'd brought word started, then snorted as he was swallowing, which made him choke and spray ale over the tabletop.

Gerin plucked distractedly at his beard. He'd reckoned Adiatunnus' embrace of the monsters a hideous aberration. If more and more lords proved willing to use the creatures to further their own ends, they *would* gain a permanent place in the northlands. He wondered which lord who favored them they'd first end up devouring.

"What will you do, lord Gerin?" the soldier answered.

"Do about what, Captain?" Van called from the stairway. He and Fand were coming down into the great hall hand in hand. By the foolish grins on their faces, Gerin had no trouble imagining what they'd been doing up on the second floor. Fand smirked at him, just in case he had had trouble. She wanted to make him jealous—her door stayed closed to him these days.

He knew a certain amount of annoyance at the way she flaunted what she was up to, but jealousy stayed dormant. He wondered what that was telling him. To keep from having to think about it, he turned to the trooper and said, "Tell him what you just told me."

The trooper obeyed. Van scowled and rubbed at the scar that creased his nose. Fand poked him in the ribs, indignant at being forgotten. He let go of her hand and slipped his arm around her waist. She molded herself against him, but most of his attention was still on what he'd just heard. "Good question," he said. "What *will* you do, Fox?"

"I don't know yet," Gerin answered. "I begin to think I need allies myself. I wonder if the monsters have got to Schild's lands yet. If they have, he may be more likely to remember he's my vassal. And Ricolf will fight on my side, even if he isn't fond of me anymore."

"The Trokmoi south of the Niffet will range themselves with Adiatunnus, sure and they will," Fand said.

Gerin couldn't tell whether she was trying to be helpful or to goad him further. He gave her the benefit of the doubt. "I wouldn't be surprised if you're right. All the more reason for me to look for those who will help me struggle against them." He puckered his lips, as if at a sour taste. He hated having to rely on any power but his own. It left him too vulnerable by half. But he was already vulnerable, in a different way.

"Hagop son of Hovan—" Van began.

"—Is hardly worth having on my side, for he brings little force with him," Gerin interrupted. "I want to win this fight, not have it drag on forever." As he spoke, one way to do that came to mind. "If Grand Duke Aragis would make common cause with me, now—"

Van, Fand, and the trooper all stared at him. He didn't suppose he could blame them. Ever since Elabon abandoned the northlands and the Trokmoi entered them, he and Aragis had been most successful at building from the ruins of empire. He'd taken for granted that they would clash one day, and assumed Aragis had done the same— a notion their meeting at Ikos had only reinforced. But the monsters and the lords who would use them to augment their own power were a danger to Aragis no less than to Gerin.

At last Van said, "You don't think small, Captain. That much I give you."

The more Gerin looked at the idea, the more he liked it himself. "I see two problems," he said. "One is making sure we stay allies with Aragis and don't end up his vassals. He'll have the same concern about us, no doubt. It could make working together ticklish."

"Aye, I can see that one," Van said with a sage nod. "This setup of vassalage you Elabonians have makes you so sticky about rank and honor that it's a wonder you ever get anything done. What's the second?"

Gerin made a wry face. "Simply getting a messenger from Fox Keep to the Castle of the Archer. With all the monsters loose on the land between what I hold and what belongs to Aragis, I really should send a good-sized fighting force just to see to it that he hears my offer and I hear his answer. But I can't afford to do that, not now, not with the monsters and the Trokmoi and now Bevon and his sons ganging together against me."

"Send Rihwin," Van suggested. "Ever since you got him that one ear back, he's been talking both of mine off about—what does he call it?—your natural talent as a mage, that's right."

Remembering the near fiasco in the shack, the Fox said, "That only proves he's not as smart as he thinks he is." He plucked at his beard again. "I need to ponder this a bit more before I go and do it. It's not something I can just set in motion before I try to look at the places it may lead."

"Rihwin would," Van said. "But then, you already said what needs saying about him. Not that he's stupid, mind, but that he thinks he has your Dyaus' view of things, and he doesn't."

"I don't what?" Rihwin asked, coming into the great hall from the courtyard.

"Know your backside from a longtooth turd," Fand said. Gerin and Van hadn't put it so pungently, but it did a fair job of summing up their opinion.

Rihwin looked down over his shoulder at the part of him cited. "That's what I thought I had there," he said, as if in relief. "Trying to sit down on a longtooth turd strikes me as unaesthetic."

"As what, now?" Fand said. Her Elabonian was fluent, but that was not a word used every day in a frontier castle of a former frontier province of the decaying Empire of Elabon.

"Messy and smelly," Gerin translated for her. "He's making a joke."

"Is he? Then why doesn't he up and do it?" Fand said.

"I take a certain amount of pleasure at being insulted by so fair a lady," Rihwin said, bowing, "but only a certain amount." He turned on his heel and strode out.

"A pity you gave him back his missing ear," Fand said to Gerin. "Better you should have torn off the other one." She bared her teeth and looked every bit as savage as she sounded. The Fox was sure she meant to be taken literally.

He said, "What good would that do? Rihwin didn't listen with two ears and didn't with one, so why do you think he would with none?"

Fand stared at him, then gurgled laughter. "It's not just that y'are lefthanded, Fox, but sure and you think that way as well. How am I to stay angry at you, now, when you go sneaking round my temper with such silliness as that?"

Gerin didn't answer. As far as he was concerned, he hadn't done anything to deserve Fand's anger. His thoughts were another matter, but if men—and women, too—were scourged for their thoughts, every back in the northlands—no, every back in the world—would bear stripes.

Van said, "Will you send to Aragis, then, Captain?"

"I think so," Gerin answered. "But as I said, I'll weigh it a bit more before I make up my mind. I grudge the strength I'd have to send to make sure my embassy got through."

"Fair enough, I suppose," the outlander said, "but don't go weighing overlong. My gut warns me we haven't much time to squander."

If Van was worried, the situation could not be good; Van generally saw fighting as sport. Gerin had already thought matters bleak. Seeing his friend's concern, he wondered if he hadn't been too optimistic.

Rap, rap. Knocking on Fand's door, Gerin realized he hadn't been so nervous approaching a woman since he'd gone off into the woods with a serf girl at about the age of fourteen. If she told him no again, he vowed he'd have nothing more to do with her.

The door opened. Fand eyed Gerin with the same irresolution he felt. At last, with the hint of a smile, she said, "You're not one to give up easy, are you, now?"

"If I were, I'd either be dead or living in the southlands," Gerin answered. "May I come in?"

"Sure and you'd do better with more sweet talk, not just throwing it out so, like a sausage, *splash!* into the soup pot." Fand sounded a trifle irked. She didn't close the door in his face, though, as she had so many times lately. After a moment, she stepped aside and motioned for him to join her. She closed the door behind him, barred it.

A tunic lay on the bed, bone needle and thread halfway through a rip on one sleeve. Gerin turned the sleeve right side out so he could see how the repair would look. "That's fine work," he said.

"For which I thank you, though sewing by lamplight is more trouble nor it's worth, I'm thinking." Fand rubbed her eyes to show him what she meant. After an awkward pause, she went on, "But you didna come here to be talking of shirts." She sat down on the bed.

"No, I didn't." Gerin sat down beside her. "I came because I hoped we could end the quarrel between us."

"Because you wanted to futter me," Fand said. She didn't sound angry, though, as she had so often when she sent him away. She might have been talking about how the wheat was doing this year. After a moment, Gerin nodded; saying he didn't want her would have been a lie. Fand's mouth quirked in a wry smile. "Och, you're no seducer, are you now? But have your way this once, Fox. We'll see what we bring to it." She pulled the tunic she was wearing up over her head, then stood to slide off her brightly checked wool skirt.

Seeing her naked made the breath catch in his throat, as it always did. She was a splendid woman, and she knew it, which only made the impression stronger. Gerin undressed in a hurry. They got back down on the bed together.

They did their best to please each other. The Fox tried hard; he could tell Fand was doing the same thing. He rolled off her quickly afterwards, not wanting her to have to bear his weight any longer than she needed to. "I thank you," she said, and sat up.

Gerin lay on one side. He looked over to her and said, "It's no good any more, is it?"

She sighed. "If you're after knowing the answer, why d'you ask the question?"

"Saying the words, hearing them, makes it seem real somehow," he answered. "Besides, I might have been wrong." He swung himself over to the side of the bed, grabbed his breeches, and put them back on. As he fiddled with the waist string, he added, "I won't trouble you that way again."

" 'Twas no trouble," Fand said. " 'Twasn't much of

anything at all, if you take my meaning. And isn't that a strange thing, now? The gods know I looked for the two of us to break, but I thought 'twould be after a grand shindy we'd both remember all our days. But here we are, just— quits."

"Quits," Gerin echoed dully. He leaned over and kissed her, not on the mouth but on the cheek. "It was always lively while it lasted, wasn't it? If it's come to the point where it's not any more, as well we give it up."

"Truth there." Fand sent him an anxious look. "You'd not throw me out of Fox Keep because I'm your doxy no more, would you?"

He laughed. "And have Van come after me with that mace of his? Not likely. No, you're welcome to bide here as long as you like—provided you don't drive everyone around you utterly mad. That may not be so easy for you." He chuckled to show he didn't expect to be taken altogether seriously.

"Och, when I'm the only one right and the whole world beside me wrong, how can I not speak out plain?" But Fand laughed, too. "I ken what you'll tell me—you wish I'd find a way. Well, I'll try, indeed and I will. What comes of it we'll have to see."

He nodded and got to his feet. Walking to the doorway felt strange. He'd never parted from a longtime lover before. Elise had parted from him, and without a word of warning, but that wasn't the same thing. With his hand on the bar, he turned back and said, "Good-bye." The word came out funereally somber.

Maybe that crossed Fand's mind, too, for she said, "I've not died, y'know, nor yet headed back to the forests. I'll be down for porridge come the dawn, same as always." But she also seemed to feel the moment. "It won't be the same any more, will it?"

"No, but it's likely better this way. If we did go on long enough, we'd have ended up hating each other." Something of that had happened with him and Elise, though there it had been quiet and one-sided till it burst out when she left.

If he stayed by the door talking, he was liable to end up talking himself out of what he'd resolved to do. He swung up the bar. Fand came over to lower it after he left. She smiled a farewell as he stepped out into the hallway, closed the door after him.

From her chamber to his was only a few strides. In the moment he needed to step between them, Selatre came down the hall, probably on her way to the garderobe. She'd seen Fand's door close. She looked from it to Gerin and back again, then kept walking without a word or another glance.

His face heated. The kindest thing Selatre could think of him was that he'd just slaked his lust. He wanted to run down the hall after her and explain that he and Fand weren't going to do that sort of thing any more, but he didn't think she'd listen.

"What's the use?" he muttered, and opened the door to his own chamber. He closed it after himself, threw off his clothes, and flung himself down onto the bed. The straw-stuffed mattress shifted back and forth on the grid of rawhide straps that supported it. The slow, rolling motion made Gerin feel as if he were on a chariot just setting out.

In a little while, Selatre's soft footsteps came back up the hall as she returned to the chamber he'd given her. They didn't pause in front of Fand's doorway, nor in front of his. If anything, they sped up.

Silence returned. Outside, the moons wheeled through their endless dance: Tiwaz full, Elleb lost in the bright skirts of the sun, Math waxing between first quarter and full, Nothos waning from full toward third quarter. Gerin got up and stared through his narrow window at the multiple shadows the moons cast.

Nothos had climbed almost to his high point in the sky before the Fox finally slept.

After a couple of days of thought, Gerin did appoint Rihwin his envoy to Aragis the Archer. He would sooner have fared south himself, but dared not, not with so many things poised to go wrong close to home.

"Tell him how things are here," he said to Rihwin. "The alliance I offer is equal, neither of us to have any claim of superiority over the other. If he doesn't care for that, to the five hells with him. And Rihwin, my fellow Fox, my friend, my colleague—"

"Ah, now that you've sweetened it, here comes the gibe," Rihwin said.

"If you choose to take it as one, aye," Gerin answered. "To me, it was just going to be a remark your nature makes me make. What I was going to say is this: for Dyaus' sake, don't get cute."

"I?" Rihwin was the picture of offended dignity. "What could you possibly mean?"

"What I said. I've met Aragis. He has about as much laughter and merriment in him as a chamber pot does, but he's anything but stupid. Stick to the matter at hand with him and you'll do fine. Get away from it—start telling jokes, drink too much ale, anything of the sort— and all you'll earn from him is contempt. I don't want that to rub off on me, because you're going there as my agent. Is that clear?"

"If you don't care for the way I do things, send Drago the Bear," Rihwin said sulkily. "He'll do exactly as you say— he hasn't the wit to do anything else."

"That's why I'm sending you," Gerin answered. "But you need to understand what's riding on this, and that I don't want any of your japes and scrapes as you fare south. You may not be able to help it; I know they're in your blood. Do your best all the same."

Rihwin's features registered anger, resignation, and amusement, all in the space of a couple of breaths. At last he said, "Very well, lord prince. I shall essay the role of a sobersided nitpicker: in short, I shall model my conduct on you in all regards." As if that were not enough, he added, "To make the impression complete, I shall seek to carry off any nubile female relative the Grand Duke may happen to have." He cocked his head to one side to see what impression that had on Gerin.

The Fox started to scowl, started to curl his hands into fists, but gave up and threw them in the air while he broke out laughing. "You, sirrah, are incorrigible," he declared.

"I certainly do hope so," Rihwin answered blithely. "Now that we've settled how I'm to comport myself on this embassy, with how large a retinue am I to be entrusted?"

"Four chariots and teams feels about right to me," Gerin said. "Any more and you'd look like an invasion; any fewer and you're liable not to get through. What say you to that, my fellow Fox?"

"It strikes me as about the right number," Rihwin said. "If you'd said I was to go alone, I wouldn't have gone. Had you put me in charge of a dozen chariots rather than a dozen men, I'd have assumed you'd gone daft—more daft than usual, I should say."

"For this ringing endorsement of my faculties, I thank you," Gerin said. "Now go ready yourself. I want you to leave before sunset. The matter grows too urgent to admit of much more delay."

"If you and Aragis together can't control what happens in the northlands, who can?" Rihwin asked.

"Adiatunnus, perhaps," Gerin said. Rihwin looked startled, then made a sour face, and finally nodded. He began a prostration such as he might have offered to the Emperor of Elabon. Had he actually got down on his belly, Gerin would have kicked him in the ribs without hesitation. But he stopped with the obeisance half made and went off to get ready to travel.

Gerin felt better now that he'd made his decision. He was doing something, not waiting on Adiatunnus and the monsters to do something to him. That desire to see something, no matter what, happen had brought others down. He knew as much. But waiting to be ruined did not sit well with him, either.

He walked back into the keep from the courtyard. He didn't know how badly his raid had hurt Adiatunnus, but at the least it must have made the Trokmê thoughtful, for the Fox had had no reports of woodsrunners on his side of the border since. Not many monsters had gone after his peasants, either. To him, that made the raid something worth doing, too.

Van and Fand were sitting in the great hall, jacks of ale in front of them. Van gnawed on a mutton shank left over from the night before. When Gerin came in, Fand pushed herself closer on the bench to the outlander, as if to say the Fox couldn't take her away from him. But Gerin was mostly relieved not to have to look forward to their next tiff. If Van wanted to stay with her, he wouldn't stand in his friend's way.

He dipped up a jack of ale for himself and sat down across from the close-knit couple. After a pull at the jack, he told Van what he'd done.

The outlander considered it, nodded gravely. "If your pride won't keep you from working in harness with Aragis, it's probably the best move you could make."

"If it's between pride and survival, I know which to choose," Gerin said.

Fand sniffed. "Where's the spirit in that? A serf would say as much."

Gerin started to bristle, then reminded himself he didn't have to let her outrage him. "Have it however you'd like," he said. "I can only answer for myself." He drained the jack, set it down on the table in front of him, and got to his feet. "A very good morning to you both. Now, by your leave, I have other things to attend to."

As he headed for the stairway, he felt Fand's eyes on his back. She didn't say anything, though; maybe she was also reminding herself that they didn't have to quarrel. On the other hand, he thought, maybe she was just speechless that he hadn't risen to her bait.

Upstairs, he hurried down the hall toward the library. He'd been doing that ever since he came back from south of the High Kirs; when he was with his books, he could remember the scholar he'd wanted to become and forget the baron the gods had decided he would be. Had his footsteps grown quicker yet since he started teaching Selatre her letters? *Well, what if they have?* he asked himself.

She was waiting for him when he got there. She was not the sort to sit idle; she had a spindle and some wool, and was busy making thread. She smiled and put down the spindle when he came through the door. "Now for something my wits can work on, not my hands," she said, sounding as if she looked forward to the switch.

"More on the nature of the gods," Gerin said, pulling a scroll from the pigeonhole where it rested.

"Ah, good," she said briskly. "My own life was so bound up with Biton that I know less of the rest of the gods than I should, especially seeing how my circumstances have changed." She no longer sounded bitter, only matter-of-fact.

The Fox slipped the velvet cover from the scroll, worked

the handles until he reached the section he and Selatre were going to read. "Ah, today we come to the god—" His voice changed. "Here, read it for yourself."

"Mavrix," Selatre said, sounding out the name. She'd caught Gerin's sudden shift of tone. "Why does the Sithonian god of wine—what's the word I want?—disturb you?"

"Raise my hackles, you mean?" Gerin shivered. "We've had dealings, Mavrix and I. I'd guess the god's not happy with them, and I know I'm not. If it weren't for Mavrix, Rihwin would still be a mage. If it weren't— But never mind all that now; I can tell it another time. Just read me what our deathless author set down on parchment." Irony filled his voice. The scroll was a thoroughly humdrum compilation of the deities worshiped by the various peoples of the Elabonian Empire. He would gladly have replaced it with a more interesting volume on the same theme, had he been lucky enough to stumble across one.

Selatre was not yet at the point where she could appreciate fine points of style. She fought her way through words and sentences, seizing meaning as best she could. " 'Mavrix, the god of wine native to Sithonia,' " she read, " 'is also widely reverenced in Elabon. His votaries are even found north of the High Kirs, although all wine in that distant province is of necessity imported.' "

"The scroll says it, but I never knew of Mavrix's cult up here," Gerin said. "Still and all, when Rihwin invoked him in a minor magic, he appeared—not to do Rihwin's bidding, but to punish him for associating with me."

"And why did the god see fit to do that?" Selatre asked. Before the Fox could answer, she held up a hand. "Tell me another time, as you said. I resume: 'The cult of Mavrix is held in chief repute by those who have little happiness in their lives. In the release they take from wine and from the orgiastic nature of his worship, they find the pleasure otherwise lacking to them.' Does *orgiastic* mean what I think it does?"

"Every sort of excess?" Gerin asked. Selatre nodded. Gerin said, "That's what it means, all right. Go on; you're doing very well."

"Thank you." Selatre started reading again: " 'The Emperors of Elabon sometimes persecuted those who took part in Mavrix's rites when Sithonia was a newly acquired province. Like much else Sithonian, however, the god's cult has become an accepted part of Elabonian life in recent years, and the cry "Evoii!" is often heard all through the Empire.' "

"I've heard it," Gerin said. "If I never hear it again, I'll be just as glad. Mavrix is a powerful god, but not one whom I care to worship. I like order too well to be easy with the lawlessness the lord of the sweet grape fosters."

Selatre clicked her tongue between her teeth. "The lord Biton is also a patron of order and reason, so I understand what you are saying, and yet—may I read on?"

"Seems you already have, if you know what comes next in the scroll," Gerin said. "You read that with just your eyes alone, didn't you? Not many can do that so soon; quite a few have to say the words to themselves no matter how long they've been reading."

"You don't," Selatre said. "I tried to imitate you."

After a few seconds, he said, "I can't think of the last time anyone paid me a compliment like that. Thank you." He let out a wry chuckle. "Not that you're likely to find the way most folks go by looking to me for a guide."

"I think you have the better way," Selatre said, which produced a longer silence, especially since, as Gerin noted, she didn't qualify the comment with *here* or any such thing. She looked down at the scroll again and read some more: " 'Mavrix is also the god who chiefly inspires poets and other artists, and is the patron of the drama. His love for beauty is well known.' " She looked up from the scroll. "Those are worthy attributes for a god, I think."

"Oh, indeed." Gerin's voice was dry. "Our chronicler here, though, is a rather—hmm, how should I put it?—a reticent man, shall we say. Among other ways, the god's 'love for beauty' manifests itself as a passion for pretty boys."

He wondered how Selatre would take that, and whether she'd even understand what he was talking about. Both the Sithonians and their gods were fonder of pederasty than the northlands peasants among whom she'd spent her life until Biton chose her for his own. But she must have figured out what he meant, for she laughed heartily. Then, sobering, she said, "Is that written down in one of your other books? If not, it may be lost."

"Do you know, I'm not sure," Gerin answered. "You've just made me sure of one thing, though, not that I wasn't already: I couldn't have found anyone better to oversee this library."

"Now you compliment me," she said. "In turn, I want to thank you once more for bringing me here to tend your books. It's not the life I had, but it's far more than I had any reason to hope for."

This time, she didn't just set her hand on his, she clasped it, nor did she pull away when he returned the pressure. He started to lean forward to kiss her, then hesitated, not from lack of desire but out of a scrupulous sense of fairness. He said, "If you're drawn to me, think on why. If it's only because I'm the one who brought you out of Ikos and helped show you how to live in the wider world, think on whether that's reason enough."

She laughed at him. She couldn't have surprised him more if she'd burst into flame. "I am a woman grown, lord Gerin, and you are not my father." As was her way, she sobered fast. "What you are with the lady Fand is something else again, especially in light of what I saw the other night."

That sobered Gerin in turn. Slowly, he said, "The thing is dead. Aye, you saw me leave her chamber." He sighed. "Aye, we'd been to bed—what point denying it when it's so? We won't do that again—no sense to it, not when it was as it was. If she and Van get along, I wish them nothing but joy. If they don't, I probably ought to wish him a hide as hard and thick as his corselet."

"So you should." She smiled again, but not for long. "And is it because what you and Fand knew is dead that you now show an interest in me?"

"Maybe in part," he answered, which surprised her. He quickly added, "But only in small part, I'd say. More—far more—is that you are as you are. Believe me or not, as you will." One of his eyebrows rose, a sort of punctuation by expression. "Besides, you were the one who took *my* hand. I wouldn't have presumed to do such a thing, not with you being who you are."

"I noticed that," Selatre said. "You'd promised as much when you took me away from Ikos, but who knows what a man's promises are worth till they're tested? When I saw you meant what you said, I—" She didn't go on, but looked down at the scroll in front of her. Unlike Fand's, her skin did not usually show much color, but she flushed now.

"You decided you wanted to take the first step," Gerin said. Selatre kept her eyes on the scroll but, almost imperceptibly, she nodded.

Gerin plucked at his beard. What he'd known with Fand had gone beyond the pleasure of the bedchamber, but not far beyond; there was a core of himself he'd never yielded. He'd done that only once, with Elise . . . and after what came of that, he was wary—*no, frightened*, he told himself—of risking it again. But if he involved himself with Selatre, he would have to risk it; he could feel as much already.

Do you want to spend the rest of your days alone inside? he wondered. It was easier; it was safer; it was, in the end, empty.

"Are you sure?" he asked. Saying the words was almost as hard as going into battle.

Selatre nodded, a little less hesitantly. With something of the feeling of a man diving into deep water, Gerin leaned toward her. He wondered if she would know how to kiss; she'd said she'd been consecrated to Biton ever since her courses failed to start when she reached womanhood.

But her lips met his firmly; her mouth opened and her tongue played with his. It was, in fact, quite as satisfactory a kiss as he'd ever had. When at last they broke apart, he said, "Where did you learn that?"

"In my village, of course." She looked puzzled for a moment, then burst out laughing again. "Oh, I see—you expected me to be not just a maiden but ignorant as well. No. Some of the young men there couldn't have cared less that the god had set his mark on me. I knew I couldn't yield my body to them, but that doesn't mean I led an altogether empty life."

"Oh," he said in a small voice. "I hadn't thought of that. When you said Biton had chosen you, I suppose I thought you'd lived solitary from that time on."

"No," Selatre said again. "It wasn't like that, not until the god called to himself the Sibyl that was and chose me in her place—though only for a brief time." Her face clouded for a moment, then cleared. "But I must say you were right: if that time is ended, I have to live the rest of my life as best I can."

This time, she leaned toward him. The kiss went on and on. His arms closed around her. She stiffened when he cupped her breast with one hand. He took the hand away. "If you're not ready, just let me know," he said. He still wasn't sure how fast he wanted to charge ahead with her. Had he been a few years younger, lust would have overridden thought, but those days were past him, even if Van still sometimes thought more with his crotch than with his head.

Selatre said, "Having come this far, I think it's time to finish the job of returning me to the world. I've heard it can hurt the first time, but if you know hurt may be coming, it's easier to bear."

"I hope I won't hurt you, or not badly," Gerin said. "When I was down in the City of Elabon, another student there had a scroll on the proper way to deflower a maiden as gently as possible. What it said made good sense, though I confess I've never needed to use it till now."

"They write books about *that*?" Selatre said, her eyes wide. "If you had one of those in your library here, Gerin, think how many more people you could win to reading."

"You're right, I expect," he said, remembering the illustrations with which the scribe had enlivened the scroll. Then he noticed Selatre had called him by his name alone, without the honorific she'd always used before. It startled him for a moment. Then he laughed at himself. If they were about to be intimate, didn't she have the right to address him intimately?

He was never sure afterwards which of them got up first from the table in the library. They walked side by side down the hall toward his bedchamber. With any other woman, he would have slipped his arm around her waist. With Selatre, he still held back in spite of what they were going to the bedroom to do. If she wanted to touch him before then, she could.

They were three or four strides from the door when the lookout in the watchtower winded his horn. Gerin stopped dead. Grinding his teeth, he said, "Oh, a pestilence! Not *now*, by all the gods."

He couldn't read Selatre's face. Was that wry amusement there, or maybe relief? If they didn't seize the chance now, would she change her mind later? What was he supposed to do if she did? Pretend nothing had happened? Or—?

Then the lookout shouted, "Lord Gerin, Rihwin the Fox is heading back toward Fox Keep."

"What?" Gerin exclaimed, his worries about Selatre forgotten. "I only sent him out two days ago. He can't even have got out of the land I hold, let alone to Aragis' and back. Has he lost his wits? Has he lost his nerve?"

Selatre said, "You'd better go and see what that's about. Other things can wait for their own time."

"Yes," he said abstractedly. That sounded promising, even if she hadn't promised anything. He barely noticed. He was already trotting for the stairs. Selatre followed more slowly.

Gerin's trot went to a run as soon as he got down to the great hall. He dashed out into the courtyard, sprinted for the gate. Someone called from up on the palisade: "I see Rihwin and the chariot crews that went out with him, lord prince, but he's got more crews with him than just those. Not men I recognize, neither."

The drawbridge was already creaking down over the ditch around the palisade. Panting a little, Gerin waited impatiently for it to drop far enough to let him see out. At last, it did. Sure enough, there was Rihwin's chariot in the lead, but he was bringing back twice as many crews as he'd set out with.

No sooner had the drawbridge thumped into place than Gerin walked across it. The quicker he found out what madness Rihwin was perpetrating now, the quicker he could start figuring out how to deal with it—if it could be dealt with. He was getting tired of having to clean up Rihwin's messes, especially when they were as exquisitely mistimed as this one.

Seeing Gerin, Rihwin waved. "Hail, lord prince," he called. "The business of going to Aragis' holding just got easier."

Gerin waited till Rihwin got close enough so he wouldn't have to scream, then demanded, "What on earth are you talking about, you—jackanapes? How can you be gone two days and come back claiming success? And who are these ruffians you've brought along with you?"

He hadn't had much hope of cowing the irrepressible Rihwin, but he hadn't expected him to break out in guffaws, either. "Your pardon, lord prince," Rihwin said when he could speak, though he didn't sound a bit sorry. He went on, "Allow me to present acquaintances made on the Elabon Way: Fabors Fabur's son and Marlanz Raw-Meat, envoys sent by the Grand Duke Aragis the Archer to discuss terms of alliance with you."

"Lord prince," two of the strangers said together. After they bowed, one of them added, in a voice almost as deep as Van's, "I'm Marlanz." He was young, broad-shouldered, and burly, with the look of a man for whom fighting was a favorite sport. Fabors was older and, Gerin guessed, likely to be smarter (although sometimes men who looked like nothing but bluff warriors were a lot smarter than they seemed).

"Well," Gerin said. That was better than standing there with his mouth open, but not much. He tried again, but only, "Well," emerged once more. On a third effort, he managed coherent speech: "Well, lords, I would be lying if I said I wasn't glad to see you. You are most welcome. Come into my keep, you and all your comrades. Drink of my ale; eat of my meat; you shall be my guest-friends here."

"Lord prince, you are gracious," Fabors Fabur's son said. Marlanz Raw-Meat nodded vigorously. Fabors went on, "Should you ride south, know that my keep shall be as your own for as long as you care to use it."

"And mine," Marlanz agreed.

"Come, come," Gerin said, and stood aside so the chariots—both those that had started out with Rihwin and those that had come north with Aragis' vassals—could cross over the drawbridge and into Castle Fox.

Stable boys hurried out to take charge of the horses and chariots. They gaped, big-eyed, at the newcomers. Gerin's warriors crowded round him, lest the men who'd accompanied Marlanz and Fabors had treachery in mind.

Marlanz stared at Van. "I've heard tales of you, sir," he said, "and, knowing how taletellers lie, thought to measure myself against you. I see I'm liable to have put myself too high."

"If you can fight as well as you talk, sir, you'll do well enough for yourself, I expect," Van answered. Marlanz bowed. Van bowed back. Gerin was reminded of two big dogs sniffing at each other.

"Come, lords," he said again. As he crossed the threshold into the great hall, he called to the servants: "Ale for my guest-friends. Aye, and carve some steaks from that cow we slew last night, too, and set 'em over the fire."

"Just singe mine, light as you can," Marlanz put in. "I can't abide beef cooked all gray and tough as shoe leather."

The slab of meat the servants slapped down in front of Marlanz on a round of flatbread was so red and juicy that the Fox expected it to bellow in pain when he stuck a knife in it, but he attacked it with every sign of relish. Gerin had no trouble figuring out how he'd come by his ekename.

Selatre had been standing back by the stairway. Gerin waved her forward, patted the bench beside him. Fabors Fabur's son raised an eyebrow. "Have you at last wed again, lord prince?" he asked. "Word of this had not reached the Archer's Nest."

"Good name for a keep," Gerin remarked, unsurprised that Aragis kept close track of what he did—he made it his business to learn all he could of Aragis, too. To answer the question the Archer's man had put, he went on, "Lord Fabors, lord Marlanz, allow me to present you to the lady Selatre, who was Sibyl at Ikos until the earthquake overthrew Biton's shrine there and loosed the monsters long trapped under it."

Marlanz had started to bristle at being introduced to a woman rather than the other way round, but composed himself at once when he learned who Selatre was. "Sibyl," he murmured respectfully, bowing in his seat.

"Sibyl no more," she said. "Simply Selatre . . . and who Selatre is remains in large part to be discovered." Her eyes slid to Gerin. The arrival of the envoys had interrupted part of that discovery.

That arrival had also touched off enough commotion to

bring Fand down to find out what was going on. Her eyes narrowed when she saw Selatre beside the Fox; she came over and sat down next to Van. Gerin introduced her to Aragis' vassals as the outlander's companion. Van nodded at that, though he didn't seem quite certain he was pleased. Fabors Fabur's son looked thoughtful, but held his peace— here was more news that had not reached the Archer's Nest.

After the sharing of food and drink had made them his guest-friends, Gerin said to Fabors and Marlanz, "Well, lords, I know why you've come—on the same mission for which I sent Rihwin south. I daresay you'll have discussed it with him as you came here. What conclusions have you reached?"

"Lord prince, our overlord the Grand Duke Aragis sent us north with virtually the same terms for an alliance in mind as you gave to Rihwin the Fox—a fine fellow, I might add," Fabors said. "The Archer favors an equal alliance between himself and you for as long as that remains agreeable to both parties, overall command to depend on whether the fighting is north or south of Ikos."

"There's a nice touch," Gerin said approvingly. "I'd simply assumed we'd share the lead. Well, lords, as you say, I think we'll get along nicely. Since the earthquake, I've heard little from south of Ikos. Tell me how Aragis' lands fare, if you would be so kind."

Marlanz gulped down the ale in his jack before answering, "Imagine wolves in a hard winter, coming out of the woods to kill sheep and shepherds, too. Then imagine that ten times worse, and you'll have some idea of the state we're in. These cursed creatures have more wit than wolves, and they have hands, too, so nothing is safe from them. The serfs are afraid to go out into the fields, but staying huddled in their huts does 'em no good, either. I'm sure you know how that goes, lord prince."

"Only too well," Gerin answered grimly. His vassals in the great hall nodded. The Fox went on, "Have the more clever monsters joined together with any of Aragis' neighbors to make his life even more delightful?"

"No, lord prince," Marlanz and Fabors chorused. Fabors added, "When your vassal the lord Rihwin told us of their dealings with Adiatunnus—may he roast in the hottest hell forever—we both cried out in horror."

"That we did," Marlanz Raw-Meat agreed. "It speaks well of your strength here that you've held off such a dreadful combination where we faced only the monsters, yet Aragis saw the need to send us forth before you put your vassal on the road to look for his aid."

"Don't put too much into it," Gerin said. "It may just mean I'm more stubborn and less trusting of my neighbors than the grand duke."

"Meaning no offense to you, lord prince, I find that hard to picture," Fabors Fabur's son said. Marlanz nodded vigorously.

"I think you may have insulted your own lord rather than me, but have it as you will," Gerin said. "Since matters are as they are, I am going to propose that Aragis first send such chariotry as he can north to aid my forces against Adiatunnus, the monsters, and a few worthless, faithless Elabonians who have joined with them. If he can do that, how soon can he do it, and how many chariots can he spare from his own concerns?"

"Lord prince, I think he can do it, and I think he can send the cars not long after we return with word the deal has been struck," Fabors answered. "How many he can send, he shall have to judge for himself. He's spread his chariots and crews widely through the keeps of the lands he holds, and told his peasants to send up fire signals if their villages are attacked. Thus aid can reach them as soon as may be."

"That's not the worst ploy in the world for keeping the serfs safe," Rihwin said. "Why didn't you try something like it, my fellow Fox?"

"It's like covering your belly after somebody hits you, then moving one hand to your face when he hits you there," Gerin answered. "Or, if you'll let me change my figure of speech, I'd rather dig an arrowhead out of the wound than slap a bandage on it with the point still in there."

"You're a man of sense, lord prince," Marlanz Raw-Meat said. "The grand duke himself has been thinking hard about changing the way he's fighting the cursed creatures—says it's like being nibbled to death by fleas. Between his men and yours, we ought to have a force strong enough to really do something, not just try to hit back when things get done to us."

"That's my hope," Gerin agreed. "That's why I sought alliance with him." As Marlanz had said, even though Aragis was threatened only by monsters, he'd felt the need for help before Gerin, who also had the Trokmoi to worry about. Hitting back as hard as he could had let the Fox keep his foes off balance.

"Together, we'll smash them," Marlanz said, slamming his fist down onto the table so that drinking jacks jumped. Fabors Fabur's son nodded but did not speak. When it came to negotiating terms for the alliance, he seemed to have authority; Marlanz spoke with more weight on matters strictly military.

"Are we in accord, lords?" Gerin asked. Both of Aragis' envoys nodded. The Fox said, "Then shall we take oaths to bind us to our enterprise. I will take them with you as Aragis' representatives. I know he will expect them of me, as he and I have not always been on the best of terms since Elabon pulled out of the northlands."

"And you will expect them no less of him, you're saying," Fabors remarked. "He expected as much, and authorized us to swear on his behalf, binding him to the pact in the eyes of the gods. And you are correct: he does desire your oath as well."

"Cooperation first; trust can come later," Gerin said. "And whether he authorized it or not, the laws of similarity and contagion bind you to him and him to the pact; I am mage enough to work through them at need. I hope we shall have no need. By which gods would Aragis have us swear?"

"None out of the ordinary, lord prince," Fabors answered: "Dyaus the king of heaven, of course, and Biton for foresight—that his Sibyl is here will only lend the oath more force—and, because we're fighting not least to keep our serfs safe, Baivers and Mavrix as well."

A prickle of alarm ran through the Fox. "Would not Baivers suffice on his own? Mavrix and I . . . have not got on well in the past."

"So lord Rihwin told us," Fabors said. By the way his

eyes slid toward Rihwin, the tale had been juicy, too. But he took a deep breath and resumed: "Nonetheless, my suzerain was particular about wanting the lord of the sweet grape included in the oath. Baivers, said he, has power only over ale and barley, while Mavrix, along with being the god of wine, is also associated with fertility in general, and hence a protector of farmers."

That, unfortunately, made too much theological sense for Gerin to come up with a glib way around it. He remembered that he and Selatre had been reading about Mavrix when they acknowledged their attraction for each other; lust was also part of the Sithonian god's domain. Maybe that had been an omen. Gerin might not want anything to do with Mavrix, but if the converse didn't hold true, how was he supposed to oppose the god's will?

He sighed—he saw no way. "Let it be as the grand duke wishes," he said. "I have but one reservation: if he fails to send at least thirty chariots and crews, and if they fail to reach here within thirty days, I shall no longer reckon myself bound by the terms of the oath."

Fabors and Marlanz put their heads together and talked quietly with each other for a couple of minutes. At last Fabors nodded. "It shall be as you say."

Gerin and Aragis' envoys clasped hands and swore the oath, binding themselves and, through Marlanz and Fabors, Aragis to the terms upon which they'd agreed. Then the Fox called to the kitchen crew: "Slaughter us another cow. We'll burn the fat-wrapped thighbones on Dyaus' altar, that their savor may climb to heaven and make him look kindly on our cause."

"And we'll eat the rest ourselves," Van boomed.

"Remember, I'll want my portion barely cooked," Marlanz added hastily.

Gerin walked upstairs to his bedchamber carrying a lamp. He set each foot down in turn with deliberate care; he was a little drunk and very full. He opened the door, set the lamp on a chest of drawers, and started to take off his tunic. As soon as he'd undressed, he would blow out the lamp.

Someone knocked on the door. He almost got trapped

in the tunic's sleeves as he pulled it back down. Fabors Fabur's son had been spinning a long, involved explanation of why Aragis insisted on having Mavrix in the oath—so long and involved, in fact, that Gerin wondered if the real reason was that the Archer knew of his trouble with the god—and hadn't wanted to stop even when the Fox yawned his way out of the great hall. If Fabors was out there now wanting to natter away some more, Gerin aimed to teach him never to do anything so foolish again.

He threw the door wide. But the load he'd planned to dump on Fabors' head turned into a coughing fit, for Fabors wasn't standing out there. Selatre was.

Listening to him splutter, she asked, "Are you all right?" in tones of real concern. When he managed a nod, she said, "Well then, shall we go on from where we were, uh, interrupted this afternoon?"

"Are you sure?" he asked; she nodded in turn. He went on, "I didn't come to your chamber tonight because—" He came to a ragged stop, not sure how to go on.

"For fear I'd lost my nerve, you mean?" Selatre said.

"That's just it," Gerin said gratefully.

"I wondered why you stayed away," Selatre said. "The only two things I could think of were *that* on the one hand and that you didn't really want me on the other. I thought I'd better find out which it was."

"If you don't know the answer to that—" Gerin ran dry again. After a moment, he resumed: "If you don't know the answer to that, I'll just have to show you." He took a step to one side to let Selatre come into the bedchamber. He shut the door behind her, barred it, then glanced over to the flickering lamp on the chest of drawers. "Shall I blow that out?"

"However you'd rather," she answered after her usual grave consideration. "It certainly would have been light had we come here earlier in the day, though."

"So it would," he agreed. "Well, then—" Feeling foolish at echoing what she'd said a few moments before, he stepped forward, took her in his arms, and kissed her. As he'd discovered in the library, her knowledge of that portion of the game was enjoyably more than theoretical.

When their lips parted at last, she murmured, "Did you

learn that in the book you were telling me of? If you did, I'd like to read it."

"Er—no," he answered. "And, as I said, I don't have a copy here in Fox Keep."

"That's too bad," Selatre said, quite seriously. "You really should write down what you remember of it—and what you've learned other places as well." She brought her mouth toward his again.

After some long, pleasurable time, he led her over to the bed. He was sure she couldn't be altogether ignorant of what went on between men and women—after all, she'd grown up in a peasant hut which, if it was like all the other peasant huts he'd known, would have boasted one room and in that room one bed for the whole family. But knowing how things happened and having them happen to her might be two different matters, especially when, not long before, she hadn't been able to stand a man touching her at all, let alone in her most secret places.

She hesitated with her hands at the neck of her tunic. "Do you want me to blow out the lamp after all?" he asked.

Selatre shook her head, perhaps as much at herself as toward Gerin. Almost defiantly, she pulled the tunic up over her head, then kicked off her sandals and got out of her long wool skirt and the linen drawers she wore beneath it. Gerin had known she was well made, but hadn't realized how well. If he stared too much, he might fluster her. The only way to keep from staring was to undress himself. He did that, quickly, and lay down on the bed.

Selatre hesitated again before joining him there. The soft straw of the mattress rustled as her weight came down on it. "Forgive me," she said. "I am—nervous."

"No reason you shouldn't be, and every reason you should," he said. "First times come only once."

She nodded. "What did your book say we're supposed to do next?"

"Not any one thing in particular," he answered. "If I remember aright, it says I'm supposed to kiss you and caress you for a long time to make you easy in your mind and to help make your body ready for what we'll do after that." He smiled at her. "I'd want to do that anyhow."

He embraced her, drew her to him. She started to pull

back when their bare bodies met—that was touching of a different sort from what she'd known before. But she checked herself, managed a smile in return. When he kissed her, she kissed him back.

"That tickles," she said as his tongue slid down the smooth, soft skin of her neck. Then it found the tip of her right breast. "Ah," she murmured, a syllable all breath and no voice.

After some time, he let his mouth stray lower. The sound she made was half surprise, half pleasure. He'd forgotten about the book; he enjoyed what he was doing for its own sake.

"Oh, my," she said a little while later. "I'd expected one surprise, but two? Is that something you brought back with you from south of the High Kirs?"

"As a matter of fact, no," he answered. But then, who could guess what would be done in a peasant village outside of Ikos?

"Well, wherever you learned it, it's—" She didn't go on in words, but the pause and the delighted expression on her face said enough. After a moment, she added, "Could I do the same for you?"

"You could, but probably not for very long right now," Gerin said. "Let's try something else instead." He sat up on the bed. "Here, why don't you get onto my lap?"

She straddled him, which he hadn't expected quite yet; she did know the theory of what they were going to do. He took himself in hand. She lowered herself onto him, slowly and cautiously. "It doesn't hurt," she said, and then, a heartbeat later, "Wait. There."

"Yes," Gerin said. "Do you want to stop? No rush here." She shook her head. "All right, then," he said, and took hold of her buttocks, easing her down until he was fleshed to the root—that was what the racily illustrated scroll in the City of Elabon had recommended, and it seemed to work well. "Is it all right?" he asked.

"It didn't hurt as much as I thought it would," she said, nodding. "You were gentle. Thank you."

He kissed her and ran his hands over her body. When he was sure she'd meant what she said, he began to move inside her, slowly, a little at a time, not hurrying at all. His left hand slid down between her legs to add to her pleasure—or perhaps to create it, as few women were likely to find full joy from coupling itself their first time.

His own pleasure built slowly. He let that happen, rather than straining to quicken it. When at last it reached its peak, it was all the more intense because of the long, unhurried climb to get there. He closed his eyes and squeezed Selatre hard against him.

There was a little blood when she slid off him, but not much. He wondered what she'd thought. Not looking at him, she said, more than half to herself, "I'm so sorry for all the Sibyls who died without ever knowing this."

He set a hand on her bare shoulder. Instead of pulling away, she snuggled against him. He said, "I made two alliances today. This is the better one."

"Oh yes," she said. "Oh yes."

IX

Aragis' envoys rode out at dawn two days later. Gerin cordially loathed getting up with the sun, but made a point of seeing them off. He glanced up into the sky and pointed to golden Math, which, three days past full, was sliding toward the western horizon. "Lords, she makes her turn in nine-and-twenty days," he said to Marlanz and Fabors. "By the next time she reaches that phase, I hope to have the Grand Duke's chariots fighting alongside mine."

"We shall do everything in our power to make it so," Fabors Fabur's son said.

"Aye, that should give us time for travel and for gathering the men and cars," Marlanz Raw-Meat added. "I hope the Archer orders me north again. Fighting the monsters and the Trokmoi at the same time would be worth the candle, I think."

Gerin had seen a good many men, Trokmoi and Elabonians both (to say nothing of Van), who loved war for its own sake. He recognized that, but it baffled him every time he ran into it. He said, "I'd sooner not be fighting at all, but sometimes you have no choice."

Marlanz sent him a curious look. "Your hand's not cold in war, lord prince. You may not care for it, but you do it well."

He probably had as much trouble understanding the Fox as Gerin did with him—maybe more, if he didn't make a practice of trying to see into the minds of people different from him. Explaining seemed an unprofitable use of time to Gerin, who contented himself with answering, "If you don't do what needs doing, before long you won't have the chance to do anything at all." Marlanz weighed that— as Gerin had guessed on first meeting him, he was smarter than he looked—and finally nodded.

The drawbridge thumped down. Aragis' ambassadors and the warriors who had come north to protect them rolled across it and off toward the Elabon Way. The gate crew hauled the bridge back up. Visitors to Fox Keep were few in these days of disordered commerce, and who could say what lurked in the not too distant woods? For legitimate travelers, the bridge would come down again. Meanwhile, Castle Fox was fortress first.

Van came out of the keep, rubbing sleep from his eyes. "So they're on their way south, are they?" he said through a yawn. "We can use all the help we can find, and that's a fact."

"I know," Gerin answered. "I didn't like the way Adiatunnus mocked me at the fight in that clearing. We'll see how he laughs when he finds Aragis' chariots ranged beside mine."

"Aye, that'll be a good thing, no doubt about it." Van yawned again. "I want some bread and ale. Maybe they'll make my wits start working."

"The Urfa nomads in the deserts south of Elabon brew some sort of bitter drink that's supposed to keep a man awake if he's tired and wake him up if he's all fuzzy the way you are," Gerin said. He sighed. "Time was when Urfa came up to Ikos to talk with the Sibyl. We might have bought some of the berries from them. Now the oracle at Ikos is no more, and even if it were still there, the Urfa couldn't come up through Elabon to get to it."

" 'The oracle at Ikos is no more,' " Van repeated as he and the Fox walked back toward the great hall. He glanced over to Gerin. "The lady Selatre's still very much here, though."

"So she is," Gerin said. He and Selatre hadn't tried to keep their becoming lovers a secret—not that they could have even if they did try. Castle Fox had too many pairs of eyes, too many wagging tongues, for that. If he could, Gerin would have looked down his nose at Van. The outlander being considerably taller, he looked up it instead. "So what?"

"So nothing, Captain," Van said hastily. "May you and she have joy of it." He paused, then went on in a low-voiced mumble, "And may the gods grant that I keep up with Fand and don't decide to throttle her."

"There is that," Gerin observed. Fand hadn't said anything to him; one thing that had been plain to both of them was that whatever they'd had was dead. But when she looked from him to Selatre, *I told you so* gleamed in her green eyes. She *had* told him so, too, which only made the look on her face more irksome. On the other hand, Fand enjoyed getting people angry at her, so he refused to give her the satisfaction of showing his annoyance.

Van cut a chunk from the loaf of bread on one of the tables. The morning was cool; Gerin decided he'd rather dip up a bowl of barley porridge from the pot that sat above the fire on the hearth at the far end of the hall. He took a horn spoon, then set that and the bowl on the table while he got himself a jack of ale.

He'd just poured a little libation to Baivers when Selatre came downstairs. "Here, join us," he said. "Marlanz and Fabors have headed south to take Aragis word of the agreement."

"I thought it must be so when you made yourself wake so early," she answered, cutting herself a piece of bread as Van had done.

"I'm sorry," he said. "I didn't mean to wake you." He felt guilty; he hadn't slept the night through with a woman in his own bed for a long time, and probably hadn't been as quiet as he might have been. For that matter, he hadn't slept with anyone in his own bed since Duren disappeared, and that was . . . more than sixty days ago now, he realized with a small shock, reckoning up everything that had happened since.

"It's all right," she said. "The sun was up, so I would have been awake soon anyhow. That's how it always was in my village, and that's how it was at Ikos, too." She somehow managed not to make Gerin feel bad for preferring to sleep later when he could. After she'd poured ale for herself, she sat down right beside him.

Fand came into the great hall a little later. When she saw Gerin and Selatre together, she didn't bother with breakfast. She just walked over to Van and plopped herself down in his lap.

He'd been reaching for his ale. Instead, his arms went around her. "What do you think you're doing?" he spluttered.

Her arms went around his neck. "What do you think I'm doing, now?" she purred into his ear.

Van could resist anything except temptation. He did try:

"So early in the morning?" he said incredulously. Fand leaned closer still, whispered something Gerin couldn't quite catch into the outlander's ear. Whatever it was, it seemed to have the desired effect. Van snorted like a stallion and then, still holding Fand, stood up and carried her upstairs.

Gerin and Selatre stared after them. A moment later, a door—presumably the one to Fand's chamber—slammed shut. When Gerin and Selatre looked from the stairway to each other, they both started to laugh. "Oh, my," Gerin said. "She has a hook in him like a man fishing for salmon."

"Did she always act like that?" Selatre asked in a small voice. She sounded half bemused, half awed.

The Fox shook his head. "When she was with us both, she didn't—usually—try to use one of us to make the other jealous." He chuckled. "Drop me into one of the hells if she's not trying to make me jealous now that we're apart." He took Selatre's hand. "She'll have no luck there."

"I'm glad." Selatre squeezed him. *Not long ago*, he thought, *she'd have been mortally offended if I touched her at all*. Then he realized with the front of his mind that that change had of course started some days after Duren disappeared. Somehow he felt he'd known Selatre longer.

Rihwin the Fox came into the great hall for breakfast. He nodded to Gerin and Selatre as he ambled over to the pot of porridge. Though he'd formally courted Elise, he'd never made any permanent attachments since returning to the northlands with Gerin and Van, contenting himself with tumbling the occasional servant woman or peasant girl.

Catching Gerin's eye, Rihwin tugged at his left ear and brayed like a donkey. He'd done that a couple of times before, and succeeded in embarrassing Gerin. This time Gerin was ready for him. He said, "You do that very well. You must have had a good deal of ass in you even before I worked that magic to restore your ear."

Rihwin staggered, as if pierced by an arrow. That made some of the hot porridge slop out of his bowl and onto the hand that was holding it. Now wounded literally as well as metaphorically, he sprang into the air with a yelp. "See what you made me do?" he shouted at Gerin.

"I'm sorry, but I can't take the blame for that one,"

Gerin said. "You were a showoff long before you met me, and you've got yourself in trouble for it a good many times before, too."

As was his way, Rihwin calmed as quickly as he'd heated. "I'd be more inclined to resent that if it weren't true." He got himself a jack of ale, then bowed to Gerin and said, "May I sit by you and your lady, your supreme awesomeness?"

"Sit, sit," Gerin said, valiantly resisting the urge to throw something at him. In a way, Rihwin was like Fand: he could be infuriating, but he was never dull. Fortunately, though, he lacked Fand's flammable temper.

He threw himself bonelessly down onto the bench next to Gerin. For all his seeming insouciance, he had a keen sense of what made others comfortable; Selatre still didn't care to be touched, even by accident, by anyone save Gerin.

He took a swig from his jack of ale, then leaned forward so he could look past Gerin to Selatre. "As you are Sibyl no more, lady, let me prophesy for you now: many years of happiness. I suppose that also means happiness for this lout here"—he nodded at Gerin—"but we'll just have to put up with what we can't help."

"One fine day, I *will* throttle you," Gerin muttered. Rihwin dipped his head, as at some extravagant compliment. Gerin threw his hands in the air.

Selatre said, "I thank you for the wish, and may a god prove to have spoken through you."

"I don't think foolishness has a god, unless it be Mavrix in his aspect as king of the drunkards," Gerin said. He'd meant that for a joke, but it brought him up short once he'd said it. All he wanted was to ignore Mavrix and hope the god would do the same with him, but suddenly that didn't seem easy.

He got up and poured himself another jack of ale. He wasn't thirsty any more, nor did he want to get drunk to start the day. Maybe, though, by showing his loyalty to Baivers he could persuade Mavrix to leave him alone. But even as he quaffed the apotropaic ale, he had his doubts.

Neither the Trokmoi nor the monsters were so considerate as to wait for Aragis' men to arrive and help drive them away. Gerin's raid into Adiatunnus' holding did make the woodsrunner thoughtful, but didn't stop him. And as for the creatures, who could say whether the ones that attacked Gerin's villagers were aligned with Adiatunnus or not? Either way, the work they did was dreadful.

Herders began to disappear, along with their flocks. The monsters slew more livestock than they could eat. Wolves or longtooths seldom behaved so, but men often did. As the reports came in to Castle Fox, Gerin grew ever grimmer.

He did what he could to help his serfs cope with the new menace skulking through the woods. He ordered herdsmen to go forth in pairs, and always to be armed either with bows or with hunting spears. He gave permission for all his smiths to make spearheads and arrowheads in large numbers. With more and more serfs at least somewhat armed, they'd have a better chance of holding off the monsters when no chariot-riding nobles could come to their aid.

Some of his more conservative vassals grumbled at that. Drago the Bear said, "Who's going to take all those spears away when the monsters are gone, lord Gerin? They'll use 'em on each other, aye, and on us nobles, too, if we don't watch 'em careful—and we can't watch 'em careful all the time."

Having been through a similar argument not long before with Van, the Fox only nodded tiredly. "You're right," he said, which made Drago's eyes widen. Then he went on: "But if we go under because we didn't arm the serfs, we won't have to worry about what we do later, now will we?"

Drago chewed on that for a while—literally, for Gerin watched his jaws work beneath his unkempt mat of graying brown beard—then walked off without making any direct reply. Under his breath, though, he was muttering phrases like "newfangled foolishness" and "idiotic shenanigans." The Fox refused to let that worry him. Stones changed more readily than Drago, but the Bear did as he was ordered.

Getting spears and arrows into the hands of the serfs wasn't enough, and Gerin knew it. They might kill an occasional monster, and would be cheered no end by so doing, but they weren't fighting men. If Gerin wanted any crops brought in come fall, he and the rest of the nobles would have to ride forth and do what they could to hold the monsters away from the villages.

Leaving Selatre was a wrench. That in itself surprised him; getting away from Fand had often seemed a relief. He took his sorrow on departing as a good sign: with luck, it meant he and Selatre had more to join them together than the pleasures of the bedchamber. Fine as those were, in the end they weren't enough. You needed other bricks as well if you wanted to build something that would last.

When he'd brought Elise up to Fox Keep, he'd thought they'd made something that would last forever. One thing he hadn't yet known was that you needed to keep what you'd built in good repair. If you didn't, it would fall down on your head. He'd have to bear that in mind this time.

Such thoughts vanished from his head as the road jogged and Castle Fox vanished behind a stand of trees. "The monsters have been especially bad in the southwest," he said, grabbing for the rail as the chariot hit a pothole.

"That's no surprise," Raffo said over his shoulder. "They swarm into Adiatunnus' lands and then out against us."

"No doubt you're right," the Fox answered. "Wherefores don't much matter, though. Whatever the whys of it, we have to hurt the creatures badly enough to be sure the serfs can bring in the harvest. Fall's not that far away." He waved to the fields past which they were riding. The grain there was starting to go from green to gold.

Van dug a finger in his ear. "Am I hearing you right, Fox? You of all people saying wherefores don't matter? Either you've come down with a fever or—Wait, I have it. It must be love."

Gerin set a hand on the shaft of the war axe on his side of the chariot car. "I'd brain you, did I think you had any brains in there to let out."

"Aye, well, to the crows with you, too," Van said. Both men laughed.

As the chariots clattered by, peasants in the villages and out in the fields waved and cheered. They'd never been especially hostile to the nobles who ruled them; Gerin was a mild and just overlord. But they'd rarely seemed so glad to see armored men in chariots, either. *Worthwhile reminding them we do more than take their crops and futter their women,* Gerin thought.

Toward afternoon, one of the serfs did more than wave and cheer. He ran up to Gerin's chariot, the lead in a six-car force, shouting, "Help us, lord! Three of the creatures slaughtered our sheep, then ran back into the woods." He pointed to show the direction they'd taken, adding, "Remon hit one with an arrow, I think, but it kept running."

"Maybe we'll have a blood trail to follow, Fox," Van said. "Give us a better chance to hunt down the cursed things."

The peasant's eyes went wide. "You're lord Gerin?" he said, and bowed when the Fox nodded. That sort of thing had happened to Gerin before. Not all serfs knew what he looked like, for years could pass between his visits to any one village.

"Aye, I'm Gerin," he answered, and alighted from the chariot. Van stepped down after him. They waved the rest of the cars to a stop. Gerin pointed in the same direction the peasant had. "Three monsters just went in there. The villagers managed to wound one, so we may have blood to follow."

"Fox, what do you say the drivers stay with the cars?" Van put in. "If there're three of the things around, there may be more, and that'll let folk properly armed fight for the serfs if monsters pop out of the woods."

"Aye, let it be as you say," Gerin answered, which drew howls of anger from Raffo and the other drivers. He glared them into submission, wondering as he did so at the urge that made men eager to risk their lives fighting and irate when they lost that chance, even with an honorable excuse.

Van pulled his mace from his belt and trotted into the woods, saying, "Come on, you lugs. The more time we waste here, the farther the cursed creatures can run."

Along with the rest of the fighting crews, Gerin pounded after the outlander. Sweat quickly burst out on his forehead. Running in armor was hard work—doubly so for Van, whose fancy cuirass was a good deal heavier than the one the Fox wore. But the outlander moved as easily as if he'd been in a thin linen shirt.

"Here, hold up," Gerin called at the edge of the woods. He was panting a little, but hadn't ordered the halt on account of that. "Let's see if we can find spilled blood. That'll give us the way the monsters took."

Less than a minute later, Widin Simrin's son exclaimed, "Over here, lord Gerin!" The Fox and the rest of the warriors hurried to him. Sure enough, blood splashed the grass where he stood; more painted the dark green leaves of a holly bush.

Gerin and his men plunged into the woods. Along with the blood the monster was losing, they also had footprints in the soft earth to follow. They crashed through the brush shouting at the top of their lungs, hoping to frighten the monster and its fellows into breaking whatever cover they'd found.

"There!" Drago shouted. He used his sword to point. Gerin caught a glimpse of a hairy body between a couple of saplings. Parol Chickpea, fast with his bow, loosed an arrow at the monster. It bellowed, whether in pain or simply in rage the Fox could not tell. Along with his companions, he dashed toward the place where it had disappeared. The men spread out widely, not wanting to give it any chance to get away.

It sprang out from behind the pale trunk of a birch tree, almost in Van's face. The outlander shouted in surprise, but kept the presence of mind to get his shield up and protect his bare face and arms from the monster's claws and teeth. He smote the creature with his mace. Blood spurted as the viciously spiked head struck home. The monster snarled and wailed, but did not run. Gerin sprinted to come to the aid of his friend.

The monster wailed without snarling when his sword slash drew a red line across its rib cage. Half turning to meet him, it left itself open to Van, who hit it in the side of its head with all his massive strength. The creature crumpled.

"A stupid one," Van said, panting. "The ones with the wit to wield weapons are truly dangerous."

"Even the ones without are bad enough." Gerin looked down at the twitching corpse. "I don't see an arrow in this one, either, so the one the peasant hit must still be around here somewhere."

"I hadn't thought on that, but you're right," the outlander

said. "Let's get on with the searching, then." He slammed the head of his mace into the ground a couple of times to clean the monster's blood from the bronze spikes, then pushed on through the woods.

Not far ahead, two cries rang out, one from the throat of a monster, the other a deeper coughing roar that froze the Fox in his tracks for a moment, as it was meant to do. "Longtooth." His lips shaped the word, but no sound passed them.

The monster's scream rose to a high-pitched squall, then died away. The longtooth roared again, this time in triumph. Gerin rounded up his companions by eye. Ever so cautiously, they approached the place from which the roars had sounded. Twelve men were enough to drive off a longtooth at need, though doing so was always a risky business.

Gerin pushed aside the small-leaved branch of a willow sapling to peer out into a small clearing. At the far edge of the open space, the longtooth crouched over the monster's body.

"*That's* the one the peasant shot," Van breathed into Gerin's ear. The Fox nodded; part of an arrow shaft still protruded from the creature's left buttock. He wondered whether it had deliberately broken off the rest or the shaft had snapped as it ran through the woods.

The question was irrelevant now; the longtooth had seen to that. The great twin fangs that gave it its name were red with the monster's blood; it had torn open the creature's throat. Longtooths, fortunately, were solitary hunters—had they traveled in packs, they would have been an even worse plague than the monsters. This one, a big male, was almost the size of a bear, with massive shoulders and great taloned forepaws almost as formidable as its fangs.

It growled warningly at Gerin and the other warriors. The long, orange-brown hair on its neck and shoulders—not quite a lion's mane, but close—bristled up to make it look even larger and more threatening. Its little stumpy tail, the only absurd part of a thoroughly formidable creature, twitched to show its anger at being interrupted over a meal.

"Let's kill it," Parol Chickpea whispered hoarsely.

Up till then, Gerin had thought Parol's sobriquet came

from the large round wen by his nose. The comment, though, made him wonder if a chickpea was what Parol used to do his thinking. He said, "No, it's done us a favor. We'll just go on our way and see if we can find the last monster."

Parol grumbled at that, but went along when everyone else moved away from the clearing. Gerin was sure the longtooth would be contentedly feeding for some time. All the same, he didn't go very far from his followers, nor they from one another. The price of being wrong about what the great hunting cat was doing was too high to pay.

Perhaps because the warriors stayed tightly bunched together, they didn't flush out the last monster. After another hour's search, Gerin said, "I fear it's got away. The gods willing, though, it won't be back in these parts any- time soon—and if it is, it may run across that longtooth."

"That would be good," Drago rumbled.

"So it would," Gerin said. "A longtooth is more than a match for one of those things, or two, or even four. But if a pack of them set out to drive a longtooth from its prey, I think they could do it."

"Best thing to happen there is that they kill each other off," Drago said. Gerin nodded at that. Somehow, though, things seldom worked themselves out so conveniently, at least not where he was concerned.

The warriors made their way back toward the peasant village. When they came out of the woods, not only the serfs but also their drivers raised a cheer. The cheer got louder after Gerin yelled, "Two of the creatures dead," and did not subside when he admitted the third had escaped.

He gave Remon a silver buckle for wounding one of the monsters. The serf, a young, well-made man, puffed out his chest, stood very straight, and did his best to act like one of the warriors who'd accompanied the Fox. Gerin thought that at best unconvincing, but it seemed good enough to impress the young women of the village. To Remon, their opinion doubtless mattered more than his.

"Sun's going down," Van observed.

Gerin glanced westward. The outlander was right. Gerin suspected his friend had an ulterior motive for the remark— several of the young women had also noticed him—but decided not to make an issue of it. "All right, we'll pass the night here," he said.

The villagers brought out their best ale for the nobles in their midst, and roasted a couple of sheep the monsters had killed. The rest, Gerin was sure, would be smoked or sun-dried or made into sausages. Nothing went to waste. He'd seen oaks in the woods nearby. No doubt the hides, however torn, would be tanned and used for winter coats or capes.

Remon disappeared from the celebration with one of the pretty girls who'd exclaimed at his prowess with a bow. There was prowess and then there was prowess, Gerin thought.

Several of his comrades also found themselves companions for the evening. As Van headed off toward one of the huts with a young woman, he turned back to Gerin and said, "You sleeping alone tonight, Fox?"

"Yes, I think so," Gerin answered. "Another cup of ale and then I'll roll up in my blanket."

"All very well to be a one-woman man around the keep, Captain," the outlander said, "but you're not around the keep now."

"I don't tell you how to live your life, and I'll thank you for granting me the same privilege," Gerin said pointedly.

"Oh, I do, Captain, I do, but if I think you're a silly loon, you may be sure I'll tell you so." Van turned back to the girl. "Come along, my sweet. I know what to do with *my* time, by the gods." She went, not only willingly but eagerly. The Fox shook his head. Van had a gift, that was certain.

Van also reveled in variety. Gerin snorted. "If I need a different woman so soon after I found one, then I didn't find the right one," he muttered to himself.

"What's that, lord Gerin?" Drago stared owlishly. He'd put his nose into the ale pot a great many times. He'd sleep like a log tonight, and likely bawl like a hurt ox tomorrow with a head pounding fit to burst.

Gerin was just as well pleased the Bear hadn't caught what he'd said. He did his best to keep his private life private. In the tight little world of Fox Keep, that best often wasn't good enough, but he kept making the effort. And

Selatre, unlike Fand, did not strike him as one to relish trumpeting her affairs—in any sense of the word—to the world at large.

He glanced up into the sky. Only Elleb shone there, a day before full. Swift Tiwaz had just slipped past new, while Nothos was approaching it. And golden Math, almost at her third quarter, would rise a little before midnight.

Math was the moon that mattered now. If she returned to the waning gibbous shape she'd had when Fabors and Marlanz set out for Aragis' lands before the Archer's chariots came north—if she did that, then all of Gerin's carefully laid plans would go awry.

"In that case, I'll have to try something else," he said, again to Drago's puzzlement—and to his own, for he had no idea what that something might be.

The sweep through the southern part of his holding netted the Fox several slain monsters. More to the point, it showed the serfs—and the monsters, if they paid attention to such things—that he and his vassals would defend the villages in every way they could.

Parol Chickpea was the only real casualty of the sweep: one of the monsters bit a good-sized chunk out of his right buttock. Gerin heated a bronze hoe blade over a fire back at the peasant village from which they'd set out and used it to cauterize the wound. Parol bawled louder at that than he had when he was bitten, but the wound healed well. Then he had to endure being called Parol One-Cheek all the way back to Castle Fox.

Two days after he'd returned to the keep, Gerin was up on the palisade when a chariot came streaking up from the south. He started worrying the instant he spied it: no one bringing good news would be in such a hurry. In any case, it was too early to expect Aragis' men.

He hurried down from the palisade while the gate crew was letting down the drawbridge. "What's toward, Utreiz?" he asked when the chariot came into the courtyard.

Utreiz Embron's son was one of the leaders of the force holding the Elabon Way open through Bevon's holding: a slim, dark fellow, a better than decent swordsman, and a long way from foolish—a rather lesser version of Gerin, as a matter of fact. He scowled as he got down from the car, saying, "It's not good news, lord prince."

"I didn't think it would be," Gerin answered. "Tell it to me anyhow."

"Aye, lord." Utreiz spat in the dirt. "Bevon and two of his stinking sons—Bevonis and Bevion—came out in force against us, with monsters coursing alongside their chariots. For the time being, the road's cut."

"Oh, a plague!" Gerin cried. The outburst spent, his wits began to work. "Bevander's with us, though. That'll help. Have our men gone south to pull Ricolf the Red into the fight? Having the Elabon Way blocked hurts him no less than us."

"Lord, my guess is they have, but it would be only a guess," Utreiz answered. "I came north, thinking this something you had to know as soon as might be."

"You did right," Gerin said. "So Bevion and Bevonis are the two who went with Bevon to suck up to Adiatunnus and the monsters, eh? And Bevander is on our side, as I said. What about Bevon's fourth son?"

"You mean Phredd the Fat?" Utreiz spat again. "The gods only know what he's doing—he hasn't the slightest clue himself. He could be trying to train longtooths to draw chariots, for all I know. He's not in the fight, that much I can tell you."

"Too bad," Gerin said. "I was hoping he'd come in on Bevon's side. He'd hurt him worse by that than by joining us, believe me."

"The gods know you're right about that, lord, but so far he's sitting out," Utreiz said. "Can you send us men to help force the road open again?"

"A few, maybe," Gerin said unhappily. "I'm stretched too thin as it is. I wish some of the lordlets on the land that used to be Palin the Eagle's would do their share. No merchants will ever get to their keeps if the highway stays closed."

"I've sent men to several of them," Utreiz answered.

"Stout man!" Gerin thumped him on the back. "There aren't enough people who see what needs doing and then go ahead and do it without making a fuss and without asking anyone's leave."

Utreiz shuffled his feet like a schoolboy who'd forgotten his lessons and looked anywhere but at the Fox. Praise plainly made him uncomfortable—another way in which he resembled his overlord. "I'd best head back now," he said, and climbed into the chariot that had brought him north. "You send those men as soon as may be, lord. We could use 'em." He spoke to the driver, who got the horses going and rattled away. He hadn't even stopped for a jack of ale.

"Send those men as soon as may be," Gerin echoed, wondering where he was supposed to find men to send. If he could have conjured warriors out of the air, he would have used them against Adiatunnus. But he realized he would have to reduce the sweeps against the monsters for the time being, no matter how little he relished the prospect. He would lose a disastrous amount of prestige if Aragis had to force the road open.

Glumly, he tramped into the great hall. Selatre was in there, eating some sun-dried plums. She smiled a greeting and waved him over to her side. "Here, open," she said, and popped a prune into his mouth.

It was sweet, but not sweet enough by itself to sweeten his mood. He said "Thank you" even so; Selatre appreciated formal politeness. He studied her—she looked a trifle on the haggard side, but wryly amused at the same time. The combination tweaked his curiosity. "You've got something to tell me," he said. "I can see it in your eyes." He wondered if he was about to become a father again.

"Yes, I do," she said, and her tone made him all but sure of it. Then she went on, "Just another proof I'm Sibyl no more: my courses started this morning. I needed a moment, I confess, to figure out what was happening to me." Her mouth twisted. "One part of full womanhood I'd willingly have missed."

"Mm, yes, I can understand that," he said judiciously. He knew a certain measure of relief that he didn't have to worry about fatherhood at such an inconvenient time, and a different measure of relief that Selatre still seemed in a reasonably good humor. At such times, Fand could often make a longtooth flinch. But then, Fand's temper was certain to be uncertain.

"I didn't know this would happen when I came into your

bed, but it makes sense that it has," Selatre said. "Biton's law was that no woman who had known man could be his Sibyl. Now that we're lovers"—he admired the matter-of-fact way she brought that out—"no wonder I've lost what marked me as a possible Sibyl in the first place."

Gerin nodded. "That does make sense. And it's reasoned as nicely as any schoolmaster down in the City of Elabon might have done—not that they're in the habit of reasoning about such things."

Selatre stuck out her tongue at him. "What about the fellow who had that endlessly entertaining book?"

"He wasn't a schoolmaster," Gerin said with a snort. "Just an endlessly lecherous student. Now that I think back on it, a lot of us were like that." He waited for Selatre to make some sort of sharp reply to that, but she didn't. For once, her ignorance of men in general worked to his advantage.

The lookout in the watchtower let go with a long, discordant blast from his horn. "Chariots approaching out of the west, a pair of 'em," he bawled.

"Out of the west?" Gerin said. "I wonder who that is." He got to his feet. "Better go find out." He headed out toward the courtyard. Selatre followed.

"It's Schild Stoutstaff, lord," Parol Chickpea called from atop the palisade. "Shall we let him in?"

"Schild, is it?" the Fox said. Had he had ears like a real fox's, they would have pricked forward with interest. "Aye, by all means let him come in. I'll be fascinated to see what he wants of me."

"Why's that, lord prince?" Parol asked with a hoarse guffaw. "On account of he only remembers he's your vassal when he wants something off you?"

"That does have something to do with it, yes," Gerin answered dryly. The drawbridge lowered once more—*a busy day*, the Fox thought. A couple of minutes later, Schild and his companions rolled into the courtyard.

"Lord prince," Schild called, nodding to Gerin. He was a big, burly fellow, on the swarthy side, a few years older than the Fox, and had the air of one who trusted his own judgment and strength above any others. That alone made him less than the best of vassals, but Gerin understood it, for it was part of his own character as well.

"What brings you here?" he asked.

Schild jumped down from his chariot, surprisingly grace-ful for such a bulky man. He strode over to Gerin and fell to his knees in front of him, holding out his hands before him with their palms pressed together. "Your servant, lord prince!" he said, his eyes on the ground.

Gerin took Schild's hands in his, acknowledging the other man's vassalage and his own obligations as overlord. "Rise, lord Schild," he said formally. As soon as Schild was back on his feet, the Fox went on in more conversational tones: "You must need something from me, or you'd not choose to remember I'm your master."

"You're right, lord Gerin, I do." Schild didn't even bother correcting the Fox. "Those horrible things they say came up from under the ground are a hideous plague in my holding. My own vassals and I can't keep the serfs safe, try as we will. I have pride—you know that. I've buried it to beg aid of you."

"So now you'd be glad to see chariots cross from my holding to yours, eh?" Gerin waited for Schild to nod, then drove home the dart: "You wouldn't even let my men onto your land to seek my stolen son earlier this year—but you didn't need me then, of course."

"That's true. I made a mistake, and I may end up pay-ing for it, too," Schild answered steadily. He won Gerin's reluctant admiration for that; whether you liked him or not, you had to admit he held very little nonsense. Now he let loose a rueful laugh. "I have more to tell you about that than I did then, too."

"Do you?" Gerin's voice went silky with danger. As if of itself, his hand slipped to the hilt of his sword. Schild was no mean fighting man, but he gave back a step from the expres-sion on the Fox's face. "You had best tell it, and quickly."

"Aye, lord prince. You have to understand, I didn't know it at the time when your man came asking." Schild licked his lips. "That minstrel—Tassilo was his name, not so?— he came through my holding. You know that much already, I daresay. He didn't stop at my keep, though; he guested with a couple of my vassals before he passed out the other side of my lands. Lord Gerin, I learned not long ago he had a boy with him. If I'd known that then—"

"What would you have done, lord Schild?" Gerin asked, his quiet fiercer than a scream. "What would you have done? Sent Duren back to me? Or would you have kept him for a while, to see what advantage you might wring from him?"

"Damn me to the five hells if I know, Fox," Schild answered, formal politeness forgotten. "But I didn't have the chance to find out, which is likely just as well. Now I know, and now I'm here, and now I've told you."

"If I ever find out you lied to me about this—" Gerin let that drop. He had a score to settle with Schild even if Schild hadn't lied—but not now. Other things had to come first.

"Not here," Schild said. "I know what my life would be worth if I tried." He spoke with as much assurance as if he'd looked at rapidly approaching clouds and announced, "It looks like rain." Gerin had always done his best to give his neighbors the idea he'd be a dangerous man to cross. Seeing he'd succeeded should have been more gratifying than it was.

He said, "Duren came into your holding, then, and was alive and well when he went out again?"

"So far as I know, Fox, that's the way of it," Schild answered.

Selatre came up to Gerin, set a hand on his arm. "The prophecy Biton spoke through me said your son's fate would be mild. I'm glad we begin to see the truth of that now."

Schild's eyes widened when he realized who Selatre had to be, and then again when he realized what her touching Gerin was likely to mean. The Fox noted that without doing anything about it; his thought swooped down on Selatre's words like a stooping hawk. "Biton said Duren's fate might well be mild," he answered with a sort of pained precision he wished he could abandon, "not that it *would* be. We still have to see."

She looked at him. As if Schild—as if everyone but the two of them—had receded to some remote distance, she asked quietly, "You're afraid to hope sometimes, aren't you?"

"Yes," he answered, as if speaking to her ears alone. "Expect much and you're too often disappointed. Expect little and what you get often looks good."

Selatre made an exasperated noise. Before she could carry the argument further, though, Schild broke in: "Well, Fox, what can I expect from you?"

That hauled Gerin back to the world of chariots and monsters and red-mustached barbarians: not the world in which he would have chosen to spend his time, but the one in which the gods had seen fit to place him. He started calculating, and did not care for the answers he came up with. He'd been stretched too thin before he'd had to commit men to reopening the Elabon Way; he was thinner now. Fixing Schild with a glare, he growled, "Why couldn't you have forgotten you were my vassal a while longer?"

"Because I need your aid, lord prince," Schild answered, more humbly than the Fox had ever heard him speak.

He suspected a great deal of that humility was donned for the occasion, but that didn't mean he could ignore it. "Very well, lord Schild, I shall defend you with such forces as I can spare," he said. "I shall not do so, though, until you furnish me this year's feudal dues, in metal and grain and ale, for your holding. You haven't paid those dues lately; I hope you remember what they are."

By the sour look Schild gave him, he remembered only too well. "I knew you were a cheeseparer, Fox," he ground out, "so I started the wagons rolling as soon as I left my keep. They should be here in a day or two with the year's dues. To try to make up for its being my first tribute in a while, I even put in a couple of flagons of wine I found in my cellars."

"Don't tell Rihwin that," Gerin exclaimed.

"The way you're using me now, I hope they've gone to vinegar," Schild said, scowling still.

"If you want aid from your overlord, you'd best give him service with more than your lips," Gerin answered, unperturbed at Schild's anger. He went on, "Speaking of which, though you swore me fealty after I slew Wolfar of the Axe, you've given me precious little."

"I've demanded precious little till now, either," Schild retorted.

"That may be so, but the aid I send you is liable to cost me more than this year's dues alone," Gerin said. "My other vassals—my true vassals—pay what they owe whether they call on me for aid or not, for they don't know when they'll need me. Collecting all I'm due now would break you, so I shan't try, but what I take from you each year will go up hereafter—and if you don't render it, you'll see my chariots in ways you won't like so well as riding to your rescue."

Schild's expression was bright with hatred. "I wish Wolfar had wrung your neck instead of the other way round."

Gerin's blade hissed free. "You're welcome to try to amend the result, if you like."

For a moment, he thought Schild would draw, too. This once, the clean simplicity of combat looked good to him. If he slew Schild, the other's land would pass to him . . . and if he didn't, he wouldn't have to worry about alliances and feudal dues any more.

But Schild took a step back. Gerin did not think it was from fear. Few barons shrank from a fight on account of that—and the ones who did commonly had enough sense that they didn't go provoking their neighbors. The Fox's reluctant vassal said, "Even if I slay you and get out of this keep alive, I can't fill your shoes fighting the creatures, worse luck."

Gerin clapped a hand to his forehead in genuine amazement. He sheathed his sword. "An argument from policy, by the gods! For that I'll gouge you less than I would have otherwise—having a neighbor who can think will pay off for itself, one way or another."

"I have to think you're right about that," Schild answered. "I've got one, and it's costing me plenty."

That crack was almost enough of itself to make Gerin like him. The Fox said, "Come into the great hall, drink some ale with me, and we'll try to figure out what we can do for you." He'd turned and taken a couple of steps before he remembered Schild had been less than forthcoming about his son. He kept walking, but resolved not to like or trust his neighbor no matter what sort of cracks Schild made.

Schild poured ale down his throat. He watched Gerin warily, too; coming to the Fox for aid could not have been easy for him. "How many cars will you send?" he demanded. "And how soon will you send them? We're hurting badly, and that's the truth. If I'd thought we'd have anything to eat this winter—" He let that hang. No, asking for help hadn't been easy.

Gerin didn't answer right away. He'd been weighing the question even before Schild asked it. "I want to say eight, but I suppose I can spare ten," he said at last.

"What, why you tightfisted—" Schild cursed with an inventiveness and a volume that had men running in from the courtyard and coming down from upstairs to see what on earth had gone wrong now.

Van said, "You don't have a moat, Captain, but shall I chuck him in the ditch for you?"

"No," Gerin answered. "He's pitching a fit because he doesn't know all the facts yet. For instance," he continued with a certain amount of spite, "I haven't told him the chariots and crew I do send will have to be back here in fifteen days' time. They can sweep his holding, but they can't stay there and fight all the way up till harvest time."

"That does it!" Schild sprang to his feet. "I'm for my own lands again, but the gods. And to the five hells with you, Fox, and a murrain on your ten stinking cars and your fifteen stinking days. We'll manage somehow, and after we do—"

"Sit down and shut up." Every once in a while, Gerin could strike a tone that produced obedience without thought. He wished he could manage it at will—it was useful. This time it worked; Schild's knees folded and he sat back onto the bench. Gerin went on, "I can't send more than ten cars because I'm sending others south to open the Elabon Way: Bevon and two of his worthless sons have struck at it and driven my garrisons back. And I'll want the chariots home soon because Aragis the Archer and I have made alliance; he's bringing his forces north so we can strike at Adiatunnus and the monsters together. I want my force of chariotry at full strength for that. Now do you understand, lord Schild?"

"I understand you're the biggest bastard ever spawned in the northlands, lord Gerin," Schild answered, but the fire had gone out of his voice. He got up again, carried his jack to the pitcher of ale, poured it full, and drained it dry. Only after he'd wiped his mouth and mustache on the sleeve of his tunic did he give his attention back to the Fox. "You set me up for that tantrum, you son of a whore. You just wanted to see how loud you could make me yell."

"If it weren't so, I'd deny it," Gerin said. "In case you're interested, you yell louder than I thought you could."

"Truth that," Van put in. "I thought one of those monsters was loose in the keep when I heard you roar."

Schild looked from one of them to the other. "To the five hells with both of you. Now, when will you send out your chariotry?"

"As soon as I can," Gerin answered. "I'll send messengers today to my vassals who have keeps on the western side of my holding. As you'll have noticed, I haven't enough men here myself to make up ten cars, or anything close to that number. I would have, if I didn't need to order crews south against Bevon." He spread his hands. "I'm afraid that's what you get, lord Schild, for taking so long to make up your mind you're really in trouble. My men ought to be crossing your frontier about the time your tribute comes in to Fox Keep."

"Aye, I'd worked that out for myself, thanks," Schild said. "You're not an easy overlord to serve under, lord prince. I console myself by thinking you're fair in what you do."

"I'll take that," Gerin said.

The Fox lay beside Selatre, watching the lamp gutter toward extinction. Its red, dying flame cast flickering shadows on the wall of the bedchamber. He let one hand run idly down the smooth length of her torso. He'd felt sated after he made love with Fand. He felt happy now. It had been so long since he'd felt really happy after he'd made love that the difference struck him like a blow.

He wondered how he'd failed to notice when that happy feeling started to slip away while Elise shared his bed. Partly, he suspected, his own stupidity was to blame. And partly, he'd supposed it was simply part of their growing used to each other. That was probably stupid too, now that he thought about it.

When she'd bedded the horseleech after she ran off, had she felt happy afterwards? Gerin rather hoped so.

Selatre snuggled against him, which drove thoughts of
Elise, if not altogether out of his head, then at least back
into the dark corners where they belonged these days. She
laughed a little as she said, "The time when I thought no
man could touch me seems faraway now. I was foolish."

"No, you weren't." Gerin shook his head. "You were
doing what was right for you then. On the other hand, I'd
be lying if I said I wasn't glad you'd changed your mind."
He bent his head so he could kiss the sweet hollow place
where her neck met her shoulder.

"Your beard tickles," she said, and then, as if she weren't
changing the subject at all, "What I'm glad of is that my
courses are finally spent. I could have done without that
part of becoming a woman—I think I've said as much
before."

"Eight or ten times," Gerin agreed.

She poked him in the ribs. He jerked. For someone who
hadn't been allowed to touch a man for a long time, she
learned fast. Maybe she'd grown up with little brothers back
in her peasant village. Gerin had been a little brother. He
knew what pests they could make of themselves.

Selatre said, "One of the reasons I didn't care for my
courses is that they kept me from having you. I've grown
greedy so fast, you see."

"They don't have to keep men and women apart," Gerin
observed.

"No?" Selatre sounded surprised. Her mouth twisted.
"It would be messy."

"It can be," Gerin agreed. "You're apt to be dry then,
too. But"—he smiled a lopsided smile—"there are compen-
sations. I didn't want to seem as if I were forcing myself
on you this first time. You're finding out about so many
new things so fast, I thought I shouldn't burden you with
one more. The gods willing, we have plenty of time."

"I think I am very lucky here." Selatre snuggled closer
still. "I may have said that before, too—eight or ten times."
She gave him a look that said, *What are you going to make
of that?*

He knew what he wanted to make of it, and was hoping
he could rise to the occasion once more, when someone
came running up the hall toward the bedchamber. He

scowled; it was too late at night for anyone to bother him without excellent reason. Then the fellow outside shouted, "Lord Gerin, there are monsters loose in Besant's village!"

"Oh, a pox!" Gerin cried, and sprang out of bed. "I'm coming!" He scrambled into tunic and trousers, buckled on his sandals and grabbed his sword belt, and unbarred the door. Selatre barely had time to throw a blanket over her nakedness.

Gerin hurried downstairs, where his armor, with that of his vassals, hung from pegs on the side walls of the great hall. He got into his corselet, jammed his bronze pot of a helm onto his head, and put his shield on his right arm. Tonight he'd make do without his greaves. He snatched up his bow and a full quiver of arrows.

Van had already armed himself. "Come on, Captain," he said impatiently. "I've missed good fighting to wait for you."

"You must have been down here, to have got into your gear so fast," Gerin said.

"Aye, so I was, drinking ale, rolling the dice with a few of the lads—you know how it goes. When the drawbridge thumped down, I figured somebody'd gone and pissed in the porridge pot, and sure enough, in came this scream-ing serf, babbling of monsters. I sent one of the cooks upstairs for you, while those of us who were down here got weapons and went out to fight." With that, he trotted for the door himself, the Fox at his heels.

At the gate, one of the men there handed Gerin a blazing torch. "Against the ghosts, lord prince," he bawled. Gerin was grateful for his quick thinking, but felt overbur-dened as he pounded toward Besant Big-Belly's village.

Even with the torch, the night spirits assailed him as soon as he got outside the keep. Dark of night was their time, their element; they sent a chilling blast of hate and resentment down on a mortal who presumed to enter it without better apotropaic than fire alone.

He set his teeth and ran on. Beside him, Van muttered oaths, or perhaps prayers, in a language he did not rec-ognize. When those had no effect, the outlander shouted, "Be still, you cursed soulsuckers!" If any living man could awe the ghosts, Van would have been the one to do it. But no living man could.

Fortunately, Besant's village lay only a couple of furlongs from Fox Keep. Before the spirits could find all the chinks in the armor of Gerin's soul and slip cold mental fingers in to drive him mad, he was among the wattle-and-daub huts of the serfs. They'd given the ghosts the usual gift of sunset blood, and so were not haunted through the night. But things fiercer than phantoms assailed them now.

A man lay sprawled in the street. His blood darkened the dirt on which he'd fallen. His linen tunic was rucked up; monsters had been feeding on his legs and hindquarters before the warriors came to drive them off.

Gerin threw down his bow. In the dim light, shooting was useless. Math's crescent almost brushed the horizon, and even pale Nothos' fatter crescent, higher in the western sky, made distances seem to shift and waver, as if in a dream. His sword snaked free. This would have to be close-quarters work.

Screams from inside a hut with its door flung open told of a monster inside. Peering over the edge of his shield, Gerin ran in. The darkness was all but absolute, but his ears told him of the struggle there. Roaring, the monster turned from the serf it had been attacking to meet him.

He thrust at it with his sword. He couldn't have done more than pink it, for its cries redoubled. *Crash!* Something wet splashed in the Fox's face. The monster was staggering, though—the serf, with great presence of mind, had hit it over the head with a water jar. The Fox stepped close, stabbed again and again and again. The monster stumbled, recovered, fell.

"Dyaus bless you, lord prince," the serf and his wife cried in the same breath.

"And you, for the help you gave," he answered as he turned and rushed back out into the street. No time now for polite conversation.

Fighting the monsters was not like fighting human foes. That had both advantages and disadvantages. As Gerin had noted before, the creatures fought as individuals, not as part of a larger group. In the confused brawling in the darkness, though, his own men were hardly more organized. And the creatures neither cared anything for loot nor felt any shame at running away if they found themselves in danger they could escape by no other means. Full of notions about glory and honor and courage, Trokmoi would have held their ground and let themselves be killed where they stood.

Gerin caught the reek from a monster's body—a thicker, meatier smell than came from a man, no matter how long unwashed—and threw up his shield before the creature, just another shadow in the night, closed with him. He almost dropped the shield in surprise when a sword slammed against it.

The monster gave him the first unmistakable words he'd heard from one of their throats: "Die, man!" They were in the Trokmê tongue, and snarled rather than spoken, but he had no trouble understanding them.

"Die yourself," he answered in the same language. The monster had no shield, no armor, and no skill at swordplay to speak of. But it was very quick and very strong. When it beat aside his thrust, the blow almost knocked the sword from his hand.

He wondered if it could see better in the night than he could. After it and its ancestors had spent so many generations in a troglodytic life, that seemed likely. And, though it was very awkward with its sword, something let it thwart his strokes again and again.

"Here, Captain, I'm coming!" Van shouted. His heavy footfalls got closer fast.

The monster, though, did not wait to be attacked by two at once. It turned and scampered away toward the woods, faster than an armored man could hope to follow. The fighting died away not long after that, with the rest of the creatures either down or fled. Some of Gerin's troopers had been clawed or bitten, but none of them was badly hurt.

Besant Big-Belly sought out the Fox. The serfs in his village hadn't been so lucky. As lamentations and moans of pain rose into the night, the headman said, "We've three dead, lord prince, and several more, men and women both, who won't be able to work for some while. Dyaus and the other gods only know how we're to bring in enough crops to meet your dues come fall." He wrung his hands in anxiety.

It was, Gerin thought with a flash of contempt, utterly

characteristic of him to worry about the dues first and
people only afterwards. "Don't worry about it," he said, "If
I see the people here are making an honest effort, I won't
hold them to blame for falling a bit short of what they
might have done otherwise."

"You're kind, lord prince," Besant cried, seizing Gerin's
hand and pressing it to his lips. The Fox snatched it back.
He suspected the headman would use his generosity as an
excuse to try to slack off before the harvest or cheat him
afterwards, but he figured he had a decent chance of
getting the better of Besant at that game.

"Lord prince?" A hesitant touch on his arm: it was the
serf in whose house he'd fought. "I want to thank you, lord
prince. Weren't for you, reckon that hideous thing would've
et Arabel or me or maybe the both of us."

"Pruanz is right," the woman beside the peasant said.
"Thank you."

"Can't have my villagers eaten," Gerin said gravely. "They
never work as well afterwards."

Rihwin would have smiled at the joke, or at least recognized that it was one. It flew past Pruanz and Arabel,
a clean miss. "Words, they're cheap," Pruanz said. "Want
to give you something better, show we really mean what
we say."

"Pruanz is right," Arabel said. "You come back with me
to the house, I'll make you feel as good as I know how."
Even in darkness, he saw her twitch her hips at him.

"Lord prince, she's lively," Pruanz said. "You'll like what
she does."

Gerin looked from one of them to the other. They meant
it. He sighed. He'd taken his pleasure with peasant women
a good many times, but he didn't feel like it now, not with
Selatre waiting for him back at the keep. As gently as he
could, he said, "I don't want to take your wife from you,
Pruanz. I was just doing as a liege lord should, and I have
a lady of my own."

Pruanz didn't answer, but Arabel did, indignantly: "Well!
I like that! What does she have that I don't?" She rubbed
herself against the Fox. By the feel of her, she did indeed
possess all female prerequisites.

He was embarrassed enough to wish he'd left her and

her husband in the hut to be devoured. He managed to free his arm from Arabel and said to Pruanz, "The best way for the two of you to show you're glad you're alive is to bed each other."

Arabel let out a loud, scornful sniff. "Well! Maybe I should leave you to your fancy lady, lord prince, though I don't suppose she gets much use out of you, neither."

"Arabel!" Pruanz hissed. "That's no way to talk to him what saved us."

"And who saved *him*, smashing a jug over that horrible thing's head?" she retorted. "I expect that means you saved me, too." She all but dragged her husband back toward their hut. Gerin suspected his suggestion was about to be fulfilled, even if he'd given it to the wrong one of the pair.

He gathered up his troopers. They didn't have torches for the walk back to Fox Keep, but the ghosts were fairly quiet. *Why not?* he thought as he neared the drawbridge—the night spirits were no doubt battening on the new gift of blood they'd just received from the dead peasants and monsters.

Some of the warriors went off to bed right away. Others paused in the great hall for a jack of ale—or several jacks of ale—before they slept. After Gerin had put his armor and the bow he'd recovered back on their pegs, Van planted an elbow in his ribs, hard enough to make him stagger. "Fox, that's twice now lately you've turned it down when you had the chance to take some," he said. "You must be getting old."

"Oh, you heard that, did you?" Gerin looked up his nose at his taller friend, who stood there chuckling. "If you want to get much older, you'd be wise to tend to your own affairs and leave mine—or the lack of them—to me."

"Affairs, forsooth." Van drained his drinking jack, poured it full, drained it again. Then he headed for the stairs, a fixed expression on his face. For his sake, Gerin hoped Fand was in, or could be cajoled into, the mood. If she wasn't, or couldn't, she'd throw things.

"That's the closest they've come to here," Drago the Bear said, yawning. "I don't like it, not even a little bit." By his matter-of-fact tone, he might have been talking of a hot, sticky summer's day.

"I don't like it, either," Gerin answered. "I'm stretched far too wide—seems that's all I say lately. Men and cars off in Schild's holding, more of them down in the south fighting Bevon and his bastard boys—"

"They were born in wedlock, far as I know," said Drago, who could sometimes get the letter and miss the spirit.

"They're bastards all the same," Gerin said. "Lining up with the Trokmoi is bad enough, but anyone who lines up with the monsters deserves whatever happens to him. *I* intend to happen to Bevon and Bevonis and Bevion, but while I'm dealing with them, I can't be dealing with Adiatunnus and *his* monster friends. And if my men can't push Bevon off the Elabon Way, and if Aragis' troopers fail too, what then? I can't see anything—except us losing the war, I mean."

"Never happen," Drago said, and fell asleep at the table, his head in his hands.

Gerin wished he had his vassal's confidence—and naïveté. He knew only too well how easy losing the war would be; his nimble imagination, usually an asset, betrayed him with images of blood and defeat and treachery. So many ways things could go wrong. What he had trouble coming up with was ways they could go right.

He emptied his own drinking jack and went upstairs himself. He opened the door to his bedchamber as quietly as he could, expecting Selatre to be asleep. But he found the lamp lit and her sitting up in bed waiting for him. She wasn't spending the time idly, either; she'd gone down the hall to the library and fetched back a codex to read until he returned. She put it down and said, "Biton and the other gods be praised that you're all right. Every time you go out to fight now—"

"Not a scratch," he said, turning to bar the door. "We hurt the monsters worse than they hurt the village, so that's—well, not all right, but better than it might have been." He didn't want to talk about the skirmish; all he wanted to do was forget it. "What do you have there?"

She flipped back to the first leaf of parchment. "*On the Motions of the Moons*, by one Volatin of Elabon. It was the first volume I saw in the library, the reason being that you left it out on the table there instead of returning it to its proper niche." She fixed him with the severe look of a librarian whose sense of order had been transgressed.

"I'm sorry," he said; rather to his surprise, he found himself meaning it. "So you're trying Volatin, are you? What do you make of him?"

"Not much, I'm afraid," she admitted. "Endless numbers and curious signs you didn't teach me and other obscurities and oddments. What do they all mean?"

"They mean that if I'd looked through his book five years ago I'd have known the werenight was coming, for he showed it beyond doubt in those columns of numbers. But I just thought of the book as a curiosity I'd brought back from the City of Elabon, and so it sat idle and useless on my shelf." He scowled in self-reproach.

"What could you have done about the werenight had you known of it?" Selatre asked.

"Given that I was traveling when it happened, probably nothing," he said. "But it's made me pay close attention to the phases of the moons ever since. Ten—no, eleven—days from now, Math will be full, the day after that Elleb and Nothos, and the day after *that* Tiwaz. It's not quite a dreadful werenight like the one we had before—from what Volatin says, those come less than once in a thousand years. But men with a were streak in them will come closer to changing then than on any other night for a long time to come. It's—"

"—One more thing to worry about," Selatre finished for him.

He stared at her in surprise and delight. "Well, well," he said. "I didn't know you spoke my language."

"I'm learning," she said.

X

Three days after the monsters attacked Besant's village, the lookout in the watchtower blew a long blast on his horn and shouted, "A chariot approaches from the south!" A few minutes later, he added with some excitement, "It's Utreiz Embron's son, by the gods!"

Gerin was in the stables, fitting a new spoke to a chariot wheel. He dropped the knife with which he was making a final trim of the spoke. Raffo, who was helping him, said, "Well, we'll know one way or the other."

"That we will," Gerin answered, and hurried out into the courtyard.

Men were also bustling out from the keep itself: everyone in Castle Fox—everyone in Gerin's domain—had a vital stake in learning whether the Elabon Way had been reopened. Van caught the Fox's eye and said, "Wishing you luck, Captain."

"I'll take all I can get, thanks," Gerin said.

The drawbridge seemed to be crawling down. Gerin's hands folded into fists; his nails bit into his palms. At last, with a thump, the drawbridge met the ground on the far side of the ditch around the palisade. Utreiz's chariot thumped over it. Even before the warrior spoke, a great weight lifted from Gerin's heart, for he, his driver, and the other warrior in the car were all wreathed in smiles.

"Dyaus and all the gods be praised, we smashed 'em!" Utreiz cried. He tried to go on, but a great cheer from everyone in the courtyard drowned the rest of his words. Rihwin the Fox leaped up into the car and planted a kiss on the startled Utreiz's cheek. He had no designs on the other man's body; that was just a southern way of showing joy at good news. In the rougher northlands, though, it was best used with caution. "*Get* off me!" Utreiz said, and several other rougher things the hubbub mercifully muffled.

When the din died away a little, Gerin said, "Tell us all that befell. Maybe"—he glanced around pointedly—"we'll be able to hear you now."

"Aye, lord prince." Utreiz turned as if to push Rihwin out of the chariot, but Rihwin had already jumped down. Looking foolish, Utreiz resumed: "In one way, it was just as you said: Ricolf the Red and his men came up from the south to join us and Bevander against Bevon and his other two sons. Since they held the road, we had to sneak through the woods to the west to set up a common attack on the same day. We set out right at dawn, caught 'em by surprise worse than they did when they hit us and grabbed that stretch of road. Bevonis is dead. We caught Bevion; he offered me everything in the world not to let Bevander have him. Bevon, curse him, got away and holed up in his keep."

He had to shout the last part; cheering had erupted again. Through it, Gerin said, "Well done! The road is open, we have our men back from Schild's holding—"

"What's this, lord?" Utreiz asked, and Gerin realized he hadn't heard about Schild's cry for help.

He explained quickly, finishing, "You'd have been just as glad if the men I'd sent to Schild had stayed out a few days more, seeing as Rihwin was one of them. But all we have to do now is await Aragis' troopers." *And hope they come*, he added to himself.

"This splendid news calls for an equally splendid celebration!" Rihwin shouted, which raised more cheers from the warriors gathered in the courtyard around Utreiz. Even Gerin clapped his hands, not wanting to be thought a wet blanket. If his men felt like roistering where no fight impended, that was all right with him. But then Rihwin went on, "What say we break out the wine with which Schild was generous enough to buy our aid?"

Some of the troopers clapped again. Others—notably Van and Drago—looked to Gerin instead. "No," he said in a voice abrupt as an avalanche.

"But, my fellow Fox—" Rihwin protested.

Gerin cut him off with a sharp, chopping gesture. "No I said and no I meant. Haven't you had enough misfortunes with wine and with Mavrix, my fellow Fox?" He freighted Rihwin's ekename with enough irony to sink it.

Rihwin flushed, but persisted, "I hadn't intended to summon the lord of the sweet grape, lord prince, nor had I intended to do aught more with his vintage than sip it, and not to excess."

"No," Gerin said for the third time. "What you intend and what turns out have a way of being two different things. And I trust that gift of wine from Schild about as far as I'd trust so many jars full of vipers."

"What, you think the whoreson's out to poison us?" Van rumbled. "If that's so—" He didn't go on, not with words, but pulled his mace free and whacked the shaft against the palm of his left hand.

But Gerin shook his head and said, "No," yet again. Van looked puzzled. Rihwin looked as dubious as he had just before Gerin gave him an ass's ear in place of his own. Gerin went on, "What I mean is, I fear that Mavrix seeks a foothold in my lands." He explained how the Sithonian god of wine and fertility and creativity had repeatedly cropped up of late, finishing, "Given what's passed between the god and me—and between the god and Rihwin—these past few years, the less presence he has here, the happier and safer I'll feel. I didn't dare refuse the wine of Schild, for that would have offered Mavrix insult direct. But I shan't invite his presence by broaching those jars, either."

"I had not considered the matter in that light," Rihwin admitted after rather more thought than usual. "So far as men can, you may well have wisdom there, lord prince. But one thing you must always bear in mind: the lord of the sweet grape is stronger than you are. If it be his will that he establish himself in your holding, establish himself he shall, whether you will or not."

"I am painfully aware of that," Gerin said, sighing. "But what I can do to prevent it, I will. I'm on good terms with Baivers. Drink all the ale you please, Rihwin, and I'll say not a word. The wine jars stay closed."

"Sense, lord prince," Utreiz Embron's son said. Van nodded. After a moment, so did Drago. After a longer moment, so did Rihwin.

"Good," Gerin said. All the same, he quietly resolved to take the wine jars from the cellar—where they resided with the ale—and find a more secret place for them. Rihwin's intentions were surely good, but his actions lived up to them no more than anyone else's—less than those of a few people who crossed the Fox's mind.

The warriors trooped into the great hall, still loudly congratulating Utreiz. "It's not as if I won the fight all by my lonesome," he protested, much as Gerin might have in the same circumstances. Nobody paid any attention to him. He'd taken part in the victory and brought news of it, and that was plenty.

Seeing the invasion, servants hurried downstairs and into the kitchens. They quickly returned with ale (no wine; the Fox checked each amphora to be sure of what it held), meat from the night before, and bread to put it on. Some of the warriors called for bowls of the pease porridge that simmered in a big pot above the hearth.

The troopers made enough racket to bring people down from upstairs to see what was going on. Van caught Fand in his arms, planted a loud, smacking kiss on her mouth, and then sat down again, pulling her into his lap. He grabbed for his jack of ale. "Here, sweetling, drink!" he cried, almost spilling it down her chin. "We've beaten Bevon and his boys proper, that we have."

"Is it so?" she said. "Aye, I'll drink to that, and right gladly, too." She took the jack from his hand, drained it dry. Gerin wondered if she would have been so ready to toast a triumph over Adiatunnus—he, after all, was of her own folk, not just an Elabonian on the wrong side. The Fox shook his head. She'd never been disloyal to him that way. When Van kissed her again, she responded as if she meant to drag him upstairs in a moment—or possibly not bother with dragging him upstairs. But then she got off his lap to claim a drinking jack of her own and fill it full of ale.

Selatre came down into the great hall in the middle of that. She too got a jack of ale. Gerin stood to greet her, but hesitated to do so much as take her hand; she remained leery of publicly showing affection. Unlike many, she didn't assume her own standards applied to everyone: she watched Fand and Van with much more amusement than disapproval.

She sat down on the bench by the Fox. "I take it the news is good?" she said. Then she saw Utreiz. "Now I know the news is good, and what sort of news it is. We've beaten

Bevon and his sons and taken back the full length of the Elabon Way, not so?"

Gerin nodded. "That's just what we've done." He gave her an admiring look. "You don't miss much, do you? Next time I have to ride out in a sweep against the monsters, I think I'll leave you in charge back here."

For the first time since they'd become lovers—maybe for the first time since she'd come to Fox Keep—Selatre got angry at him. "Don't mock me with things you know I can't have," she snapped. She waved to the crowd of noisy, drinking warriors. "The only use they have for women is to tumble them, or maybe to have them fetch up another jar of ale from the cellar. As if they'd pay heed to me!" She glared.

Taken aback at her vehemence, the Fox said slowly, "I'm sorry. I don't suppose I meant that altogether seriously, but I didn't mean to mock you with it, either." He plucked at his beard as he thought. "If you wanted to badly enough, you could probably bring it off. All you'd need to do is remind them that you'd once been Sibyl and give them the feeling your eye for what needed doing was better than theirs even now."

"But that would be a lie," Selatre said.

Gerin shook his head. "No, just a push in the right direction. There's a magic to getting people to do what you want that doesn't show up in any grimoire. It uses what a person has done and who he is to show that he—or she— is apt to do well, or to come up with the right answer, or whatever you like, the next time, too. That's what I was talking about here. You *could* do it. Whether you'd want to or not is another question."

"Some of me is tempted," she said in a small voice. "The rest, though, the bigger half, wants no part of it. I'm not fond of having people tell me what to do, so I don't think I have any business giving orders to anyone else, either."

"Good for you," Gerin said. "I never intended to be a baron, much less somebody who calls himself a prince. I just aimed at being a scholar, studying what I wanted when I wanted to do it." Self-mockery filled his laugh. "What you aim at in life and what you end up with are often two very different things."

That made him think of the jars of wine Schild had sent him. They still sat down in the cellar, sealed and innocuous, and he'd move them somewhere safer yet as soon as he got round to it. But with Mavrix immanent in that wine, who could say how much his own aims mattered?

The moons coursed through the sky, Tiwaz swiftly, Nothos so slowly that his phase seemed to change but little from day to day, Elleb and Math in between. Gerin paid them close heed for two reasons: to gauge the time when the four moons would come full in the space of three days, and to see how many days Aragis the Archer had left to fulfill the promise his envoys had made.

Golden Math was two days past first quarter when word came to Fox Keep that the monsters had attacked a village near the southern boundary of Gerin's holding. Cursing under his breath—why wouldn't things ever hold still long enough for him to catch his breath?—he readied a force of chariotry and set out to sweep the countryside. He had no great hope of sweeping it clean, but refused to sit idly by and let the creatures hold the initiative.

The sweep actually went better than he'd expected. His warriors caught three monsters feeding on a cow they'd dragged down in the middle of a meadow close by the road. With joyous whoops, they sent their chariots jouncing over the grass to cut the monsters off from the safety of the woods. The creatures were slow to flee, too, staying at the carcass for a last couple of mouthfuls of meat before they tried to get away. Thanks to that, the Fox's men were able to bring them all down with no loss to themselves.

One of the monsters still tried to crawl toward the woods despite having taken enough arrows to give it the aspect of a hedgehog. Van got down from the car he shared with Gerin and smashed in its head with his mace. Then he and some of the other men began the gory business of reclaiming shafts from the bodies of the creatures.

Raffo turned to Gerin and said, "Here's another way keeping the trees well back from the side of the road did you a good turn, lord prince. If you'd let them grow up close, as other barons do, those stinking things might have made good their escape."

"That's true," Gerin said. "After a while, you sometimes get to wonder whether something's more trouble than it's worth, but when you see the work you've spent pay for itself, it reminds you that you might have known what you were doing all along."

The war party reached the ravaged village a little before sunset. The serfs there had fought back as well as they could; they'd lost a man, two women, and some livestock, but they'd also managed to kill a monster. Gerin sent his troopers out on a short foray into the forest surrounding the village, ordering them to be back in the open before night took them. That was one command he was sure they'd obey—no one wanted to meet the ghosts away from blood and fire.

A deadfall of branches and sticks caught the Fox's eye. "There's a likely place," he said, pointing.

Van and Raffo both nodded. "Aye, you're right," Van added, and probed the brush with his spear.

With a scream, a monster burst out and hurled itself at him. He held it off with his shield, though its charge forced him back two steps. Among them, he and Gerin and Raffo made short work of the creature. "Female," Gerin noted.

"Aye, so it was. Mean enough, all the same," Van said, sounding embarrassed at having to give ground. He sighed. "They're all mean enough, and to spare."

Inside the deadfall, something yowled—two somethings, by the sound. Gerin stared in dismay at Van. "It had cubs," he said, as if accusing his friend.

"Aye," the outlander answered, and then, after a moment, "No reason we should be surprised, I suppose. The creatures must have been having cubs for the gods only know how long, down in their caves. They'll have kept right on doing it now that they're aboveground. This one will have been pregnant before she got aboveground, come to that."

"So she will," Gerin said. The outlander was right, of course, but that didn't take away the startlement. The Fox dug into the deadfall, scattering brush in all directions. After a moment, Van and Raffo pitched in to help.

They soon uncovered the monster cubs. Gerin stared

at them in dismay. They looked like nothing so much as ugly, hairy babies. "What are you going to do with them?" Raffo asked, gulping a little. Oddly, that made Gerin feel a little easier: the driver didn't have the stomach just to kill them, either.

Van did. "Get rid of them," he said. "You know what they turn into."

"I don't know what to do," the Fox answered slowly. "Aye, I know what they turn into, but I'm still not sure how smart the monsters are. If they learn I'm slaying their cubs out of hand and understand that, it'll just make them worse foes of mine than they are already."

"Honh!" Van said, a noise of deep discontent. "How could they be?"

"I don't know, and I don't want to find out."

"Well, what will you do?" Van asked scornfully. "Take 'em home and make pets of 'em?"

"Why not? We have Fand back at Fox Keep. . . ." Gerin murmured. Actually, the idea tempted him, tweaking his curiosity. If you raised a monster among men, what would you get? A monster? A pet, as Van had said? Something not too far removed from an ugly, hairy man, or, for that matter, an ugly, hairy woman? If he'd had fewer things to worry about, if he'd had more leisure, if he hadn't been certain all his vassals would scream even louder than Van had, he might have tried the experiment. As it was— "I know what we'll do."

"What's that, lord?" Raffo asked.

"Nothing," Gerin said. "Nothing at all. We killed the female in battle—well and good. We won't—we can't—take the cubs back to Castle Fox. You're right about that, Van. But I won't just slaughter them, either. I'll leave them here. Maybe beasts will get them, or maybe, if the monsters do have something in the way of family feeling, they'll take them and raise them up. I'll leave that in the hands of the gods."

He hadn't asked whether Van or Raffo approved. Now he looked to see if they did. Raffo nodded. Van still seemed unhappy, but finally said, "You have a way of looking for the middle road, Fox. I suppose you found it here. Let's go back."

When they returned to the village, they found the other
chariot crews had also had good luck. They'd killed two
monsters, the only serious injury they'd taken being to Parol
Chickpea, who'd just recovered from his bitten buttock.
Now he was gray-faced, and had a bloody rag wrapped
around his left hand—he'd lost two fingers from it.

"How did that happen?" Gerin asked. "His shield should
have protected him there. He's right-handed, so he doesn't
have that hand out in the open the way I do."

"Just bad luck," Drago the Bear answered. "The monster
he was fighting gave a good yank at his shield, and it broke
away from the handgrip and lashing. Then the thing sprang
at him, and he stuck out his arm to keep from getting its
teeth in his neck instead. I hope he heals; he's lost a lot
of blood."

Gerin made unhappy clucking noises. "Aye, he's a good
fighter, and a long way from the worst of men." He kicked
at the dirt, feeling useless. "Would that the gods had never
let this plague of monsters loose on us. Every warrior, every
serf even, we lose is one we can't replace."

"That's all true, lord, but the creatures are here, and we
have to fend 'em off as best we can," Drago said. Gerin
wished he could muster that same stolid acceptance for
things he couldn't help.

The warriors started back toward the main road at dawn
the next day. They left Parol Chickpea behind; he'd taken
a fever, and was in no condition to spend a day in the
chariot. "We'll do the best we can for him, lord prince,"
the village headman promised. With that Gerin had to be
content. The serfs' herbs and potions were as likely to help
Parol as any of the fancier doctoring techniques that came
from south of the High Kirs. Unfortunately, they were also
as likely not to help.

When the dirt track the chariots were following ran into
the Elabon Way, Van pointed south and said, "More cars
heading up toward us, Captain."

The Fox hadn't looked southward; he was intent on
getting back to the keep. But his eyes followed Van's
pointing finger. His left eyebrow rose. "Quite a few cars,"
he said in surprise. "I hope Bevon hasn't rallied and driven

my men off the highway again." He let out a long sigh. "We'd better go find out." He tapped Raffo on the shoulder. The driver swung his chariot south. The rest of the cars in the war party followed.

Before long, Gerin realized he didn't recognize any of the approaching chariots. He also realized his band was badly outnumbered. If Bevon somehow had managed to pull off one victory, he might be on the point of another.

Then Van pointed again. "There in the second car, Fox. Isn't that tall, skinny fellow Aragis the Archer?"

"Father Dyaus," Gerin said softly. He squinted. "Your eyes are sharper than mine." Then he let out a whoop loud enough to make Raffo start. "Aye, it *is* Aragis—and see all the friends he's brought with him."

"A great whacking lot of them, that's for certain," Van said.

The more teams and chariots Gerin saw, the more thoughtful he grew. He started to regret that whoop of glee. Measured all together, his own forces comfortably outnumbered Aragis' army. But his forces were scattered over several holdings and doing several different things, which left him in a decidedly uncomfortable position here. If Aragis should decide to take advantage of his superior numbers here on the spot, affairs in the northlands would suddenly look very different, although Gerin would be in no position to appreciate the difference.

A bold front had served him well many times in the past. He tapped Raffo on the shoulder again. "Let's go down and give the grand duke proper greeting."

"Aye, lord prince." Raffo sounded a little doubtful, but steered the car toward the approaching host. The rest of the chariots in Gerin's war party followed. He heard some of his men muttering among themselves at the course he took, but no one challenged him. He had a reputation for being right. The next few minutes would show how well he deserved it.

He waved toward the oncoming chariots. Someone waved back: Marlanz Raw-Meat. A moment later, Fabors Fabur's son waved, too. Then Aragis also raised his hand to greet the Fox.

"Well met," Gerin called when he'd drawn a little closer

to Aragis' force. "You're in good time, and here with more
cars even than I'd looked for. Well met indeed. We were
just out driving the monsters back from one of my villages,
and slew several." *And left two to an unsure fate*, he added
to himself. Aragis didn't need to know about that. He would
surely have killed the cubs without a second thought.

"Good for you, lord prince," Aragis called back. "And
not only have I brought my men and my horses and my
cars, I have a present for you—two presents, as a matter
of fact."

"Have you now, grand duke?" The Fox hoped he
sounded fulsome rather than worried. An unscrupulous man,
which Aragis had a reputation of being, might reckon a
volley of arrows and a hard charge as presents.

But Aragis didn't order an attack. He reached down into
the car and held up a large, tightly tied leather sack. "Here's
one of them." Then he reached down again and lifted
something else, something heavier. His lips pulled back
from his teeth, partly from the effort and partly in a real
smile. "And here's the other."

From his arms, Duren squealed, "Father!"

Gerin prided himself on seldom being at a loss. His pride
suffered now, but he couldn't have cared less. "Duren," he
whispered.

Aragis couldn't possibly have heard that, but nodded
nonetheless. His driver reined in. He set Duren down on
the stone surface of the road. The boy ran to Gerin's
chariot.

The Fox jumped out of his car even though Raffo hadn't
stopped it. He staggered a little when he landed, and then
again when Duren ran into him full tilt. He picked up his
son and squeezed him so tight against his own corseleted
chest that he felt the air go out of the boy. "Father, why
are you crying?" Duren demanded indignantly. "Aren't you
glad to see me?"

"That's why I'm crying," Gerin answered: "Because I'm
glad to see you."

"I don't understand," Duren said.

"Never mind," Gerin told him. Aragis' chariot had come
up behind Duren. The Fox turned to the hawk-faced grand
duke and said, "You know I was afraid you'd taken the boy,

or rather kept him after someone else—it would have been Tassilo, wouldn't it?—took him. I never thought to get him back through you. To say I'm in your debt just shows how little words can mean."

"You've yet to open your other gift," Aragis said. He handed Gerin the leather sack without more explanation. When the Fox undid the knot in the rawhide lashing that held it closed, a foul stench escaped. He nodded; from the weight and heft of the sack, he'd expected it would hold a head. He looked inside, nodded again, and closed it. "Aye, that's Tassilo."

"I packed him in salt for some days after I—mm—took him apart," Aragis said. "I wanted you to be able to recognize him, to be sure he was dead."

Gerin picked up the sack and threw it into the grass by the side of the road. It bounced a couple of times and lay still.

"You gave him too easy an end, you ask me," Van told Aragis.

"I thought on that," Aragis admitted. "Still, though, while he kidnapped the boy, he didn't do anything worse while he had him. That may have been because he wanted to keep his value as hostage high, but whatever the reason, it's so. I let his end be easy on account of it."

"He's dead. That's all that matters," Gerin said. "No, not all." He squeezed Duren breathless again, then asked Aragis, "When did he come to you?"

"As the gods would have it, the day after I sent my vassals to you seeking common cause," Aragis said. "So any of the men here with me will attest." His driver and the other warrior in the car with him nodded, almost in unison.

"I see," Gerin said slowly. He wondered if the grand duke was telling the truth. Had he perhaps had Duren earlier, and contemplated using him against the Fox? Aragis was not a man to cross; no doubt his own vassals would support him. Duren wouldn't know, not exactly; four-year-olds had very strange notions of time. Gerin decided to let it lie for now.

"How fare you here?" Aragis asked. "Your own men down further south were full of stories of hard fighting to hold the road open."

"That's true, but we won the fight," Gerin said, doubly glad Aragis hadn't had to try forcing his way through Bevon's men—and quadruply glad Aragis hadn't tried and failed. The Fox went on, "We've had a few other small things happening, too," and with that airy understatement explained his sweeps through his one holding and the one Schild had so urgently requested.

"You've had a busy time of it," Aragis said, a statement so self-evidently true that Gerin didn't even bother nodding. The grand duke added, "I was taking the omens before I set out, and the bird's flight warned me I'd best leave early rather than late, so here you see me now. Try as I would, I couldn't make sense of why, but I accepted the reading all the same."

"I think you did well," Gerin said, and told him of the near werenight due in a few days.

Aragis' eyes narrowed. "Is that a fact?" he said, then shook his head. "No, I'm not doubting you, Fox. Just that, with so many things closer to home to keep track of, I never thought to worry about the moons."

"Sometimes the things you most need to worry about aren't the obvious ones," Gerin said. For some reason that made him think, not of the untouchably distant moons, but of Elise, who'd given no signs—no signs he'd noticed, anyhow—of discontent until one day she was simply gone.

Aragis said, "I have a hard enough time worrying about the things that are obvious. The rest I leave to the gods and clever fellows like you." His voice rang sardonic, but only slightly. He didn't worry about the long run or the wide picture as much as Gerin did. In the short term, and over the limited space of the northlands, his methods worked well enough.

"Let's head up to the keep," Gerin said. "We'll wait out the moons there, if that suits you, and then do our best to smash Adiatunnus. If his lands aren't a sanctuary for the monsters, we'll stand a better chance of controlling them."

"I wonder if we'll ever be able to do that," Aragis said gloomily. "The damned Trokmê's lands are nowhere near mine, but the stinking creatures plague me as bad as they do you, maybe worse. After we finish up here, I'll want you and yours to ride south and help me clear my hinterlands of 'em."

"That's why we made the pact," Gerin agreed, "though as you say I don't know if we'll ever be able to clear them completely now. Sometimes that strikes me as more a job for gods than for men."

"If prayer were the answer, every monster in the northlands would have died a hundred times by now," Aragis said.

"Isn't that the sad and sorry truth?" Gerin said. "But I wasn't thinking so much of prayer. The gods hear prayer for a double handful of thousands of different things every day. No wonder most of them aren't granted—grant one and a god rejects another in the granting. What's crossed my mind once or twice lately, though, is . . . evocation."

Aragis stared at him. So did his own men. He didn't blame any of them. The last time he'd been at all involved in evoking was five years before, when Rihwin summoned Mavrix to turn sour wine back into sweet. Rihwin hadn't intended to evoke Mavrix then, only to invoke him. When you let a god fully enter the material world, you ran a tremendous risk. Summoning the god was relatively easy. Controlling him once summoned was anything but.

"You have a reputation for not thinking small," Aragis said at last, "and I see it's well earned."

"Dyaus above, it's not something I *want* to do," Gerin exclaimed. "Why do you think I so want this alliance to succeed? If we can beat the Trokmoi and the monsters on our own, we won't have to think about calling on the gods. But if it comes down to a choice between losing the fight and trying one last great stroke to win it, which would you take?"

"Damn me to the five hells if I know." Aragis shook his head, as if Gerin had made him look at something he would sooner not have contemplated. "As you say, lord prince, let us hope the choice does not come down to that. Shall we ride on to your keep now, and ready ourselves for the fighting ahead?"

"I suggested as much a while ago, but we've been standing around here talking instead," Gerin said. He picked Duren up and started to set him in his own chariot.

"Wait, Papa, I have to piddle," Duren said. He started toward the bushes off to the side of the road. Gerin and

Van both went with him, the one with drawn sword, the other with heavy spear at the ready. Wild beasts and worse dwelt in the woods these days.

When Duren was done, Van grabbed him by the feet and carried him back to the chariot upside down. He squealed laughter all the way. Hearing that laughter lifted years from Gerin's heart. He nodded to Aragis, who nodded back. It was good to know there were depths to which some men in the northlands would not sink.

Having Duren in the car with him bouncing up and down made the trip back to Castle Fox one of the more enjoyable journeys Gerin had ever taken. Even having his son ask "Are we almost there yet?" with great regularity didn't, couldn't, come close to taking the edge off his happiness, not today.

When they got back to Fox Keep late that afternoon, the castle was shut up tight against them. Gerin would have been furious to find it any other way: the lookout would have seen a great many chariots, far more than had set out the previous morning, and had better have assumed they were hostile. The Fox rode up close enough for the warriors on the palisade to recognize him and called, "We're all friends here—Aragis the Archer has brought his men north. And look!" As Aragis had before him, he held Duren high.

The men on the wall cheered themselves hoarse. The drawbridge came down quickly, heavy bronze chain rattling over the winch. Van asked quietly, "Where are we going to put all of Aragis' men? The keep won't hold the lot of 'em, and besides—"

"I won't want all of them inside at once until I have more of my own troopers here to balance the scale," Gerin finished for him. "I don't see how I can keep from feasting 'em tonight, but after that . . ." Now he let his voice trail away.

"Look sharp," Van said. "Here's Aragis coming up."

The grand duke said, "Lord prince, we are allies, but not yet certain of each other, although you've been too polite to speak much of that. We've brought canvas and such; if it please you, most of my men will sleep outside the keep. You need have no fear. We'll set a watch against monsters and such, as we did on the road north."

Gerin dipped his head. "I thank you. You've just made my life easier."

"I thought that might be so." Aragis' smile was pleasant enough, but something hard remained under the surface. "I might have made other plans, did I not need your aid in the south as much as you need mine here—maybe more."

"Indeed," Gerin said. "I understand what you're saying. Your grandson will rule mine, maybe, or mine yours, but if we fight now, we both go under. We'll be wise to bear that in mind all through this campaign."

"My grandson will have his own worries," Aragis said. "I can't untangle mine right now, let alone his. But as you say, Fox, remembering we need each other is the best way to keep from going to war too soon."

It was probably the only way that would hold Aragis in check, Gerin thought. The Archer, by all evidence, was ruthlessly effective in pursuing his own interests. Reminding him that Gerin was part of those interests seemed eminently practical. Nodding, the Fox said, "Shall we go into the keep together? You'll guest with me, of course."

"Apart from my men, you mean? Aye, of course," Aragis answered. One thing his nature made easy: Gerin didn't have to waste time with polite-sounding explanations. Aragis saw through to the essence of things and accepted them for what they were.

Some of the men on the palisade came down to greet the Fox and his companions. Others held their posts, bows ready. Hearing the commotion, servants came out from the great hall to see what was happening. So did Fand and Selatre.

Seeing Fand, Duren jumped out of the chariot and ran to her. She scooped him up in an embrace, said to Gerin, "Och, you got him back! Good on you there."

"First thing that's gone right in a while," the Fox said. Then he glanced toward Selatre and corrected himself: "No, the second thing."

Duren wiggled out of Fand's arms. He pointed at Selatre. "Who is that lady? I've never seen her before." He looked thoughtful, which made him look amazingly like a miniature, beardless version of Gerin. "Is that my mama come back?" he asked, hope lighting his face brighter than the sun. He'd barely been toddling when Elise left Fox Keep.

"No, it's not," Gerin said gently, and the sparkle died in Duren's eyes. His father went on, "But do you know who it is? That's the lady who used to be the Sibyl down at Ikos, the one the god spoke through. Her name is Selatre. She lives at Fox Keep now."

"My vassals spoke to me of this," Aragis said, without giving any hint of how he felt about it.

Duren studied Selatre, then asked the child's natural question: "Why?"

Gerin had always tried to be as straightforward with his son as he could. That wasn't easy now, but he did his best: "Because the earthquake—do you remember the earthquake?" Duren nodded, eyes wide. Gerin continued, "The earthquake knocked down Biton's temple at Ikos, and it let loose the monsters from underground there. Van and I were afraid the monsters would kill Selatre and eat her, the way they do, so we rescued her and brought her to Castle Fox with us when we came back."

"Oh," Duren said. "All right." After a moment, he asked, "Why were you and Van at Ikos?"

"To ask the god to tell us through the Sibyl where you were," Gerin answered.

"Oh," Duren said again. "But I was with Tassilo." By his tone, that was as much a fact of nature as trees' leaves being green.

"But we didn't know you were with Tassilo," the Fox reminded him. "And even if we had known it, we didn't know where Tassilo was."

"Why not?" Duren asked, at which point Gerin threw his hands in the air.

He said, "Let's bring up some of the good ale from the cellar, slay an ox and some sheep, and rejoice that we have enough bold warriors here now to take on the Trokmoi and the monsters." *Or so I hope, at any rate*, he thought. *If we don't, we're in even more trouble than I reckoned on before.*

"Nothing finer than a good sheep's head, all cooked up proper, with plenty of ale to wash it down," Drago the Bear declared. Baron though he was, he had a peasant's taste in food.

The Fox looked to the sky. With sunset near, all the moons were up: Tiwaz at first quarter near the meridian, then Elleb halfway between first quarter and full, and then, close together and low in the east, Math and Nothos. Gerin shook his head. Five years earlier, he'd paid attention to the motions of the moons mostly to let him gauge the time by night; seeing them crawl together now sent a shiver of dread through him. This stretch, surely, would not approach the horrors of the werenight, but how bad would it be? No way to know, not yet.

He said, "The blood of the beasts slaughtered for our supper will hold the ghosts at bay. If you like, grand duke, we'll do some of the butchering outside the keep, that your men's encampment may also gain the boon of blood."

"A good thought," Aragis said. "Do it." He was so direct, he even used words like soldiers, sending forth no more than he needed to carry out his plans.

"Might we not broach even one of the jars of wine we have from Schild to help us rejoice in this alliance?" Rihwin asked.

"No," Gerin and Van said in the same breath. Gerin pretended not to see the curious look Aragis sent him for quashing the question so quickly. He was heartily glad he'd taken those jars out of the cellar and hidden them deep under straw in the stables. To Rihwin, he went on, "Ale suffices for the rest of us, so it will have to do for you, too." Rihwin's pout made him look positively bilious, but he finally gave a glum nod.

Duren kept running around the courtyard and in and out of the great hall, as if making sure things hadn't changed while he was gone. Every once in a while, his voice would rise in excitement: "I remember that!" He'd been gone a quarter of a year, no small chunk of a four-year-old's life.

Selatre came over to Gerin and said, "He's a promising boy."

"Thank you. I've always thought so," the Fox answered. "I just praise Dyaus and all the gods that he doesn't seem to have suffered badly in Tassilo's cursed hands. The minstrel must have reckoned he'd need him hale and not too unhappy as a hostage." That sparked a thought in him. He called his son over and asked, "How was it that you went away with Tassilo when he took you away from here?"

"He promised he'd teach me his songs and show me how to play the lute," Duren answered. "He did, too, but my hands are too small to play a big one. He said he would make me a little one, but he never did do that." And then, to the Fox's surprise, Duren started chanting what Tassilo had called the song of Gerin at his visit to Fox Keep. He did it better than he'd ever sung before he was kidnapped; in that, at least, the minstrel had kept his promise. It wasn't remotely enough.

One of the cooks came out and said, "Lords, the feast begins!" The warriors streamed into the great hall. Even with chairs and benches brought down from upstairs, it was still packed tight.

Fat-wrapped thighbones smoked on Dyaus' altar by the hearth. When a servant brought Gerin a jack of ale, he poured a libation to Baivers and the rest of the ale down his throat. A serving woman picked her way down the narrow space between benches, pulling rounds of flatbread from a platter piled high and setting one in front of each feaster in turn.

She would have gone faster had more than a few men not tried to pull her down onto their laps or to grab at her as she went past. One of them wound up with flatbread draped over his face instead of on the table before him. "I'm so sorry, noble sir," she said, very much as if she meant it.

A cook with a sheep's head on a spit carried it to the fire and carefully started singeing off the wool. "Oh, that will be fine when it's finished," Drago said. He thumped his thick middle. "Have to remember to save some room for it."

Servants with meat more quickly cooked—steaks and chops and roasted slices of hearts and kidneys and livers—came by and set the sizzling gobbets on top of the flatbreads. The feasters attacked them with belt knives and fingers. They threw gnawed bones down into the dry rushes that covered the floor. Dogs growled and snarled at one another as they scrambled for scraps.

Aragis the Archer raised his drinking jack in salute to Gerin, who sat across the table from him. "You're a generous host, lord prince," he said.

"We do what we can, grand duke," the Fox replied. "Once in a while, for celebration, is all well and good. If we ate like this every day, we'd all starve, serfs and nobles together, long before midwinter rolled around."

"I understand that full well," Aragis said. "Between war and hunger and disease, we live on the edge of a cliff. But by the gods, it's fine sometimes to step back from the edge and make life into what it was meant to be: plenty of food, plenty of drink—you brew a fine ale—and no worries, not for today." He raised his jack again, then drained it. A servant with a pitcher made haste to refill it.

Selatre turned to Gerin. Under the noise of the crowd, she said, "Surely there's more to life than a full belly."

"I think so, too," he said, nodding. "So does Aragis, no doubt, or he'd be content to stay in his castle and stuff himself. If you ask me, he'd sooner drink power than ale." But then, trying to be just, he added, "If you don't have a full belly, not much else matters. Years the harvest fails, you find out about that." He paused thoughtfully. "What civilization is, I suppose, is the things you find to worry about after your belly's full."

"I like that," Selatre said. Now she nodded. "Well said."

Van sat at Gerin's right hand, with Duren between them. He'd been talking with Fand, and missed Gerin's words. Selatre's brisk statement of approval caught his notice. "What's well said, Fox?" he asked.

Gerin repeated himself. Van thought it over—perhaps a bit more intensely than he might have at other times, for he'd emptied his drinking jack again and again—and finally nodded. "Something to that." He waved a big arm in a gesture that almost knocked a plate out of a servant's hands. "You Elabonians, you've a great many things past farming. I give you so much, that I do."

Fand rounded on him. "And what o' my own folk?" she demanded. "Sure and you're not with the southrons who call us woodsrunners and barbarous savages and all, are you now?"

"Now, now, lass, I said nothing of the sort. I didn't speak of the Trokmoi at all, just of the folk of my friend here," Van answered, mildly enough. Gerin breathed a silent sigh of relief; he'd seen trouble riding Fand's question as sure as rain rode a squall line. Then, to his dismay, the outlander, instead of leaving well enough alone, went on, "Though now that you ask me, I will say that, since I traveled the forests of the Trokmoi from north to south, I'd far sooner live here than there. More good things to life here, taken all in all."

"Would you, now?" In the space of three words, Fand's voice rose to a screech that made heads whip around. "Well, have some fine Elabonian ale, then!" She picked up her drinking jack and poured it over Van's head, then got up from the bench and started to stalk off.

Snorting and cursing and blinking because the stinging stuff ran down into his eyes, Van reached out a meaty hand and hauled her back. She squawked and swung at him. He blocked the blow with his other arm, slammed her down into her seat hard enough to make her teeth come together with a loud click. "Here, see how you like it," he said, and drenched her with his jack of ale.

She cursed him in Elabonian and the forest tongue, loudly and ingeniously. He just sat there grinning, which fanned the fires of her wrath.

"Go on, both of you, and dry yourselves off," Gerin said, uncomfortably aware a common role for a would-be peace-maker was taking arrows from both sides. "Van may say what he thinks—"

"I'd like to see anyone stop me," the outlander put in.

"Shut up, will you?" Gerin hissed at him before continuing, "—and you, lady, may agree or not, as you judge best. But if you drench someone, you shouldn't be surprised or even angry to get drenched in return."

He waited for her to flare back at him, but every once in a while logic reached her. This proved one of those times. "Aye, summat to that," she said, tossing her head so little drops of ale flew from her coppery hair. She looked warily at Van. "Quits for now?"

"Aye, for now." This time, the outlander got up first. Fand followed him. Gerin wondered if they'd look for a towel or the nearest bedchamber. He laughed a little. Even if Fand wasn't his woman any more, he still got involved in her quarrels.

After a while, Duren said, "Why aren't Van and Fand coming back?"

"I think they're probably making up their quarrel," Gerin answered, smiling.

"Seldom dull around this place, is it?" Aragis said. He was smiling, too, more than half in bemusement. "My keep is more, mm, sedate."

By which you mean anyone who doesn't think like you had best not let you know it, Gerin thought. But how the Archer ran his holding was his business. Duren curled up in the space Fand and Van had vacated and went to sleep. Gerin ruffled his hair and said, "Somebody finds it dull, anyhow." He stared down at the little boy, still hardly daring to believe he had him back again, then raised his jack to Aragis in salute. Returning Duren made up for a multitude of the grand duke's sins.

Presently Van and Fand did return. Fand looked rumpled. The outlander looked smug. They both looked surprised when they found Duren stretched out where they'd been sitting.

"Don't worry," Gerin said. "You can have your places back. I'll take him up to bed." He scooped up his son, who wiggled and muttered but did not wake.

Selatre drained her drinking jack, set it down, and brought a hand up to her mouth to cover a yawn. "I'm for my own bed," she announced. "I'll walk up with you, if that's all right."

"Your company is better than just all right, as you know very well," Gerin said. He lifted Duren up as high as he could, to keep the boy's dangling legs from catching any of the feasters in the head, and made his way toward the stairs. Selatre followed.

Duren sighed again when Gerin put him down in the bed they both used. Duren muttered something, but Gerin couldn't make out what it was. "He has the look of you," Selatre said.

The Fox nodded as he straightened up. "He has my coloring, certainly. I suppose his features are mostly mine, too." Gently, he pulled off his sleeping son's shoes and tossed them by the side of the bed. "After what happened, I hate to leave him alone, even for an instant."

"I don't blame you," Selatre said. "But if he's not safe here in your bedchamber, where can he be safe?"

"The way the world wags now? Maybe nowhere," Gerin said bleakly. "None of us is really safe these days." He took a couple of steps over to Selatre, put his arms around her, and kissed her. "We just have to do the best we can, that's all."

She nodded. "Do you think you could leave him alone long enough to come with me to my little chamber?"

He paused in some surprise before he answered: she hadn't invited him to her chamber before. After he'd given it to her, he'd stayed out of it, not wanting to infringe on the privacy he knew she craved. On the other hand, the two of them would need privacy from Duren now. She'd grown up with everyone sleeping and doing everything else in one big bed, but he hadn't. He slipped an arm around her waist. "I think I'll take that chance."

Afterwards, though, he quickly dressed and returned to his own room. Wanting to make sure Duren was safe was only part of that. Selatre's chamber lay on the south side of the hall, and its window faced south. Light from the moons streamed into the chamber and cast multiple shifting shadows. With what lay ahead, Gerin wanted to think about the moons as little as he could.

Golden Math came full first. That night passed well enough: Tiwaz was two days before full, ruddy Elleb and Nothos both one day before. All three of them had risen earlier than Math, and so their rays did much to diminish the one full moon's effect.

From the werenight of five years before, Gerin knew which of his men were vulnerable to taking beast's shape. The two he worried most about were Widin Simrin's son—who'd been just a boy at the time of the werenight—and Parol Chickpea. He wondered how Parol was, down in the serf village. Widin he locked away in the cellar with the ale; the youngster came through that first night unchanged.

He fretted more over Aragis' men than over his own, for they were an unknown quantity to him. He asked the Archer which of his men had the were taint, but Aragis was vague: "Lord prince, that's hard for me to answer, for my vassals were most of 'em at their own keeps the night of the werenight. The Trokmoi hadn't reached my lands yet, so we were still at ease. Afterwards, I had more urgent things to worry about than finding out which of my warriors had donned beast shape. I just didn't see the need."

Gerin looked down his nose at the grand duke. "Which means we're vulnerable now," he said in reproof as mild as he could make it. No, Aragis wasn't forethoughtful enough; when something had gone, he assumed its like would return no more.

As the next evening approached, the one on which Elleb and pale Nothos would be full and swift-moving Tiwaz and Math but one day to either side of it, he sent all of Aragis' men save the Archer himself, Marlanz Raw-Meat, and Fabors Fabur's son out to the tented encampment they'd made. If trouble broke out, he wanted it well away from the keep. To his relief, the only comment Aragis made was, "A sensible precaution, lord prince."

The Fox sent Widin Simrin's son to his shelter and mewed him up, saying, "If you don't change tonight, you probably won't tomorrow. But better safe—we'll enclose you then, too." Widin just nodded; he knew necessity when he saw it.

Tiwaz came up over the eastern horizon first, a day before full and not far from round. Then, as the sun set, Elleb and Nothos rose side by side. Gerin watched them from the palisade. No cries of alarm rent the air the instant the two full moons appeared, for which he gave hearty thanks. Golden Math soon followed. Because she moved through her phases more slowly than Tiwaz, her bright disk was even closer to a perfect circle than his.

When all four moons were in the sky and no screams of horror had come from within the keep or from the tents where Aragis' men sheltered, the Fox decided he could safely descend and eat supper. He'd been sensible enough to have plenty of ale brought up before he closed Widin in the cellar, so washing down his meat would not be a problem.

Aragis, who was already gnawing on beef ribs basted with a spicy sauce, greeted him with a wave and something not far from a sneer. "All quiet as the tomb here, lord prince. Seems to me you fretted over nothing."

Gerin shrugged. "Better to be ready for trouble and not

have it than to have it and not be ready, as happened at the werenight of the four full moons."

"Can't quarrel hard with that, I suppose," Aragis admitted. He took another big bite from the rib he was holding; grease ran down his chin. "Your cooks do a fine job indeed; I give you that without any argument."

"Glad something here makes you happy," Gerin answered. He waved to one of the kitchen servants for some ribs of his own.

"Only thing that bothers me about sitting here some days eating your good food is that we could have been out campaigning already, striking at the Trokmoi and the monsters," Aragis said.

"They'll be there, grand duke, never fear," Gerin said. The servant plopped a round of flatbread on the table in front of him, then set atop it several steaming ribs. He tried to pick one up, scorched his fingers, and stuck them in his mouth. Aragis hid a chuckle behind a swig of ale.

"I thought you were the patient sort, lord prince," Fabors Fabur's son said slyly, a gibe enough to the point to make Gerin's ears heat.

"I don't know why everyone is praising the food to the skies," Marlanz Raw-Meat grumbled. "They've cooked it to death, and that after I told them and told them I like it with the juice still in it."

Gerin stared over toward the gobbet of meat Marlanz was attacking. It might have been lightly singed on the outside, but juice and blood from it soaked the flatbread on which it lay. If Marlanz wanted it cooked less, he should have torn it off a cow as the beast ran by.

Before he could say as much, Gerin looked from the dripping chunk of meat to Marlanz himself. His beard seemed thicker and bushier than it had moments before, his teeth extraordinarily long and white and sharp. His eyes gave back the torchlight with red glints of their own.

"Meat!" he snarled. "Rrraw meat!" The backs of his hands grew hairier by the heartbeat.

"Your pardon," Fabors Fabur's son said, his voice rising to a frightened squeak as he slid down the bench away from his friend. Aragis' eyes were wide and staring. Van started to draw his sword, then slammed it back into its sheath.

Gerin understood that; he'd stopped his own hand half-way to the hilt of his blade. Unless struck with silver, werebeasts knit as fast as they were cut. He'd seen that, to his horror and dismay, during the werenight.

"Rrrraw meat!" Marlanz said again, and growled deep in his throat. His voice was hardly a voice at all—more like an angry howl.

"Give him what he wants," Gerin called quickly to the frightened-looking cooks. "Raw meat, and lots of it."

The men used that as an excuse to flee the great hall. Gerin hoped one of them, at least, would be brave enough to come back with meat. If not, Marlanz was going to try getting it from the warriors and women with whom he'd sat down to supper.

A cook, staggering under the weight of the haunch he carried on a platter, came slowly out of the kitchens. He did not bring the meat out to Marlanz, but set it down between the hearth and Dyaus' altar and then retreated much faster than he'd advanced. Gerin found himself unable to complain. That the fellow had come back at all was enough.

The Fox rose and edged past Marlanz, whose tongue lolled from jaws that had stretched remarkably to accommodate the improved cutlery they now contained. "Good wolf," Gerin said in a friendly way, as if he were talking to one of the keep's dogs. He looked around for those dogs, and did not see them—they'd all run outside as Marlanz began to change. They wanted no part of him. Gerin didn't, either, but he had less choice.

Grunting, he picked up the platter and carried it over to Marlanz. He bowed over it as if he were an innkeeper serving up an elaborate repast at some splendid hostelry in the City of Elabon. Indeed, his concern for his client's satisfaction was even more pressing than such an innkeeper's: none of their guests was likely to devour them if displeased with his proffered supper.

Marlanz looked from the dripping haunch to Gerin and back again. He bent low over the meat and sniffed it, as if to make certain no flame had ever touched it. Then, not bothering with the knife that lay on the table by the platter, he began to feed. That was the only word that seemed appropriate to Gerin—Marlanz tore off bite after bite with his teeth, worked his jaws briefly, and gulped down the barely chewed chunks. Meat vanished from the bone at an astonishing rate.

Gerin hurried back to the kitchens. "That haunch may not be enough," he warned. "What else have you?"

A cook pointed. "There's but half a pig's carcass, lord prince, that we were going to—"

"Never mind what you were going to do with it," Gerin snapped. Some of the doctors down in the City of Elabon reckoned eating raw pork unhealthy. That, as far as the Fox was concerned, was Marlanz's lookout. He grabbed the split carcass by the legs and lugged it out into the great hall.

As he came up to Marlanz, he realized that the offal from the carcass would have served just as well in the noble's present condition. He did not, however, have the temerity to haul the meat back from the kitchens. Instead, he set it on the table in front of Marlanz, who began destroying it with the same wolfish single-mindedness he'd shown on the chunk of beef.

"He can't eat all that," Van said as Gerin cautiously sat back down.

"You have my leave to tell him as much," Gerin said. "Go right ahead." Van sat where he was; he was as bold as any man ever born, but a long way from a fool. Fand set a hand on his arm, as if to congratulate him for his good sense. That surprised Gerin, who would have expected her to urge the outlander into any fight that came along.

"I'd have tried fighting him, lord prince," Aragis said, his eyes shifting back and forth from Gerin to Marlanz. "Your way is better, though. You're sorry to lose so much meat, no doubt, but you'd be sorrier losing men hurt or killed against a werebeast that can't be slain—and one who's a good vassal when in his proper shape."

"That last weighed heaviest on my mind," Gerin said.

"For which I am in your debt," Aragis said, "and Marlanz will be when he comes back to himself."

Marlanz wasn't quite in full beast shape, as he would have been during the werenight of five years before; he seemed rather a man heavily overlain with wolf. That made Gerin wonder if he possessed the full invulnerability werebeasts had enjoyed then. Some experiments, he'd found, were more interesting to think about than to try. And, as Aragis had said, Marlanz was a good fellow—and certainly looked to be a good warrior—when fully human.

The Fox wondered if he was going to have to get more meat still to set before Marlanz. As a werebeast, he ate like a wolf. Little by little, though, Marlanz slowed. He glared around at the unchanged men and women watching him, then picked up what was left of the pig carcass with mouth and pawlike hands and carried it over to a dark corner of the great hall. There he set it down while he heaped up rushes beside it into a sort of nest. He lay down in that nest, turned himself around a couple of times to accommodate its shape to his, and fell asleep.

"I hope he sleeps well," Gerin said sincerely. "Come sunrise tomorrow, he'll be a man again."

Selatre giggled. "And wondering mightily, too, how he happened to end up on the floor beside half—no, less than that now—a dead pig."

"Maybe we'll call him Marlanz Pork-Ribs," Rihwin said blithely.

Fabors Fabur's son sent him a serious look. "Van of the Strong Arm might possibly do that and have it taken in good part. For anyone less imposing, such chaffing is liable to be unwise."

"I think you're likely to be right," Gerin said. He too gave Rihwin a severe look. Sometimes Rihwin paid attention to such signals, sometimes he didn't. Gerin hoped this was one of the times he did, because he might end up very sorry if he got Marlanz angry at him.

"I hope that will be our only excitement for the night," Selatre said. Even Van, an incurable adventurer, nodded; the horrors of the werenight must have burned themselves into his memory for good.

Gerin said, "I'll check and see how Widin is doing." He went down to the door of the cellar, rapped on it, and asked, "Are you all right in there, Widin?"

"Aye, and still in my own shape, too," his young vassal answered. "May I come out now?"

"I don't see why not," Gerin answered. "Marlanz Raw-Meat's long since gone were; if the fit hasn't hit you by now, I don't expect it will tonight." He unbarred the door and released Widin.

"What sort of beast is he?" Widin asked.

"Wolf, like most northern werecreatures," the Fox said. "Actually, he's about half wolf and half man right now. He's gone to sleep in the rushes, guarding some meat like a hound. Come upstairs to the great hall, and you can see him for yourself."

He led Widin upstairs. Widin gave the sleeping Marlanz a wide berth, and did not turn his back on him even for a moment. That struck the Fox as eminently practical. A trooper who'd drawn palisade duty came to the entrance to the great hall and said, "Lord prince, a warrior of Aragis' wants us to let down the gate so he can have speech with you."

"Is he in his own proper shape, with no beasts with him?" Gerin asked after a moment's thought.

"Aye, lord, he is," the sentry answered. "The moons are so bright, nothing could hide, neither."

"We'll let him in, then," Gerin decided. He walked out to the gate and told that to the men who worked the drawbridge, adding, "but we'll raise the bridge again as soon as he's across it into the courtyard here." That would mean more work for the men, but he did not want to leave the keep open and vulnerable to whatever lurked under two full moons and the other two nearly full.

Down rattled the drawbridge. As soon as Aragis' warrior had crossed it, the gate crew hauled it back up again. The fellow came over to Gerin and sketched a salute. "Lord prince, I'm Rennewart Forkbeard, one of Aragis' vassals, as your man said." He was middle-aged, solid-looking, and wore his beard in the old-fashioned style his ekename described.

"What's toward in your camp out there?" Gerin asked. "You've had a man take beast shape, is that it?"

To his surprise, Rennewart shook his head. "No, it's not that. Oh, a couple of the lads are hairier than they have any business being, but they're all still their own selves, if you know what I mean. We aren't worried about 'em. No, the thing of it is, just a little bit ago we had a man walk into camp naked as the day he was born, and a deal bigger. He's not one of ours. We were wondering if he came from the keep here some kind of way, or maybe from your peasant village not far off."

"Why do you need to ask me?" Gerin said. "Why not just ask him?"

"Lord prince, the thing of it is, he won't talk—won't say a word, I mean," Rennewart answered. "Won't or maybe can't—I don't know which. We figured you'd know him if anybody did."

"Yes, I suppose I would," Gerin said, puzzled: his holding had a couple of deaf-mutes, but they lived in distant villages and had no reason to show up at Fox Keep in the middle of the night, especially naked. He plucked at his beard; his curiosity was tickled. "All right, Rennewart, I'll come out and look at him."

The walk from keep to camp was short enough that the ghosts did not much afflict him before he came to the area protected by the sacrifices Aragis' men had made. Most of them were awake, either on watch or aroused by word of the strange newcomer.

"We brought him into my tent, lord prince," Rennewart said, leading Gerin to it and holding the flap wide. "Here he is."

Gerin drew his sword before he went in, wary of a trap. But the inside of the tent was brightly lit by several lamps, and held only some blankets and, as promised, one naked man sprawling on them.

"I've never set eyes on him before," Gerin said positively. "I'd know him, were he from my lands." The fellow was almost Van's size, and just as well-thewed as the enormous outlander. He was swarthy and hairy, with a beard that came up almost to his dark eyes and a hairline that started just above them. "Who are you?" the Fox asked. "Where are you from?"

The naked man listened with every sign of attention—mute he might be, but he wasn't deaf—but didn't answer. Gerin tried again, this time in the Trokmê language. The fellow stirred on the blankets, but again gave no answer and no real sign he understood.

"We tried that, too, lord prince, with no better luck than you just had," Rennewart Forkbeard said.

"Go fetch my companion, Van of the Strong Arm," Gerin

said. "He knows more different languages than any other man I've met."

Rennewart hurried away, and soon returned with the outlander. Listening to the drawbridge go down and up, Gerin spared a moment's sympathy for the gate crew. Van stared at the naked man with interest. Like the Fox, he started off with Elabonian and the Trokmê tongue, and failed with both. Then he used the guttural language of the Gradi, who lived north of the Trokmoi, and after that brought no response he spoke in the hissing tongue used by the nomads of the Shanda plains. Those, at least, Gerin recognized. Van tried what must have been a dozen languages in all, maybe more. The shifting sounds of his words interested the naked man, but not enough to make him say anything past a couple of grunts. After a while, Van spread his hands. "I give up, Captain," he said, returning to Elabonian.

"Come to think of it, I have one other tongue," Gerin said, and addressed the naked stranger in Sithonian, a language he read more fluently than he spoke it. He might as well have saved his breath.

"He can hear," Rennewart said. "We saw that."

"Aye, and he's not altogether mute, anyhow," the Fox agreed. "But—" He paused, a suspicion growing in him, then said, "Maybe what he needs is a jack of ale. Could you bring him one, please?"

Rennewart sent him a first-rate dubious look, but brought the jack as asked. He handed it to Gerin, saying, "Here, you want him to have this, *you* give it to him."

Gerin took the couple of steps that brought him over to the naked man. He held out the leather jack, smiling invitingly. The stranger took it, gaped at it, but did not raise it to his lips. Quietly, Van said, "It's like he never saw one before."

"I'm beginning to think that's just what it's like," Gerin answered. He took back the jack, drank from it to show what it was for, and returned it to the naked man. The fellow drank then, clumsily, so ale trickled through his beard and dripped on the ground. He spent a moment thinking over the taste, then smacked his lips and gulped down the rest of the ale. He held out the jack to Gerin with a hopeful expression.

Gerin pulled him to his feet. "Here, come along with me," he said, and eked out his words with gestures. The naked man followed him willingly enough. So did Van and Rennewart, both looking curious.

The naked man jumped when the drawbridge thudded down, but went across it with the Fox. The feasters in the great hall stared at the newcomer; Gerin hoped Van didn't notice Fand's admiring glance. He gave the fellow another jack of ale, then took a pitcherful with him as he led the naked man down to the cellar from which he'd but lately released Widin.

Lured by the prospect of more ale, the stranger again accompanied him without protest. Gerin set the pitcher on the ground. As the stranger made for it, the Fox hurried out of the cellar, shut the door behind him, and dropped the bar. Then he went back up to the great hall, poured a jack of ale for himself, and gulped it down in one long draught.

"All right, Captain, what was that all about?" Van demanded when he thumped the jack down on the table. "You know something; I can see it in your face."

Gerin shook his head. "Come morning, I'll know something. Now I just suspect."

"Suspect what?" several people answered in the same breath.

"I suspect I just locked a werebeast in the cellar," Gerin answered.

Again several people spoke at once, Aragis loudest and most to the point: "But that was no beast—he was a man."

"And quite a man he was, too," Fand murmured, which drew her a sharp look from Van.

"When men go were, they take beast shape," the Fox said, filling his drinking jack again. "If a beast goes were, though, what would it become? A man, unless all logic lies. And look at this fellow—not just at how hairy he was, either. He had no idea how to be a man. He wore no clothes, he couldn't speak, he didn't know what a cup was for till I showed him. . . . As I say, we'll know for certain come morning, when we open the cellar door after moonset and see who—or what—is down there."

Aragis shook his head, still doubtful. But Selatre said,

"I like the notion. It might even explain how the monsters came to be: suppose a female beast turned woman long years ago, and a farmer or hunter found her and had his way with her and got her with child. Come morning, she'd be an animal once more, but who knows what litter she would have borne?"

"It could be so," Gerin said, nodding. "Or men as werebeasts might have mixed their blood with females of their beast kind. Either way, you're right—the get might be horrific. It's a better guess at how the monsters began than any that's crossed my mind." He raised his jack in salute to her cleverness.

"If you conceive by me, you'll know what you'll have, lass," Van said to Fand.

"More trouble than I'd know what to do with, I expect," she retorted.

"How d'you put a viper's tongue in such a pretty mouth?" he asked, and she looked smug.

The ale ran out not long after that, and no one seemed enthusiastic about going down to the cellar for more, not with the stranger down there. No one seemed enthusiastic about staying in the great hall, either, even if Marlanz had plenty of raw meat by his side as he slept. The kitchen helpers went to their quarters and barred the door. Everyone else went upstairs.

Gerin made sure the sun was well up—which meant full Elleb and Nothos would be well down—before he went downstairs the next morning. Even then, he went not only armed but ready to beat a hasty retreat.

He found Marlanz Raw-Meat back in fully human form, and just sitting up in the rushes, looking mightily confused at how he'd got there and even more confused at the pile of well-gnawed pig bones beside him. "How strong *do* you brew your ale, lord prince?" he asked. "Funny, though—it must have been a mighty carouse, but my head doesn't hurt."

"It wasn't ale—it was the moons," Gerin answered, and explained what had happened the night before.

Marlanz stared, then slowly nodded and got to his feet. "I'm told the same fit came over me, only stronger, at the great werenight five years gone by. I remember nothing of that night, either."

Van came downstairs then, also armed. He grunted in relief to see Marlanz without visible traces of lycanthropy, then said, "Shall we go down to the cellar and see what your wereman's become?"

That required more explanations for Marlanz. When they were through, Aragis' vassal pulled out his own sword and said, "Let's slay the appalling creature."

"If we can get it out of the keep without fighting, I'll be just as happy to do that," Gerin answered.

Marlanz stared, then realized he meant what he said. "You are the lord here," he said, in tones that implied he was willing to obey even if he wouldn't have gone about things thus himself.

"Take a shield off the wall and carry some of those bones of yours in it," Gerin told him. "Maybe they'll make the thing in the cellar as happy as they made you—and you didn't quite get all the meat off them."

Marlanz's stare turned reproachful, but he did as he was asked. Van said, "What if it's still a man down there?"

"We'll find him something else for breakfast," Gerin replied, which had the virtue of making both his companions shut up.

They went down to the cellar together. Gerin unbarred the door and pushed it open. "Father Dyaus above," Marlanz said softly—a medium-sized black bear sprawled on the dirt floor. The beast looked up at them in absurd surprise.

It did not growl, nor did the hair on its back rise. It didn't jump up and flee into the dark recesses of the cellar, either. "What's wrong with it?" Van demanded, as if he assumed Gerin would know.

And, for a wonder, Gerin did. "It's still got ale coursing through it from last night. That was a good-sized pitcher, and who knows when in man-shape it might have finished?" He paused, then chuckled. "I'm glad it's a friendly drunk."

Luring the bear upstairs with bones proved easy, though it wobbled as it walked. "I still say we ought to kill it," Marlanz grumbled as the gate crew let down the draw-bridge and the bear staggered off toward the forest.

"We didn't try killing *you* last night," Gerin reminded him.

"Lucky for you that you didn't," Marlanz said, drawing himself up with prickly pride. Gerin agreed with him, but wasn't about to admit it.

XI

The next night, only Tiwaz was full, with Elleb and Nothos a day past and Math two. This time, Gerin sent Marlanz Raw-Meat down to the cellar and locked Widin Simrin's son in the shack where he worked on his magics. To his great relief, neither Marlanz nor Widin changed shape, so he released them both when all four moons had risen into the sky.

The bear that walked like a man did not return to the camp of Aragis' warriors, either in man's form or its own. Gerin had wondered if a taste for ale would draw it back.

"Just as well it's staying away," said Drago, a Bear himself, when Gerin remarked on that. "We don't need a thirsty bear when we have a thirsty Fox." He sent Rihwin the Fox a sly look. Rihwin ostentatiously ignored him.

Late the next afternoon, Parol Chickpea came into Fox Keep, riding in the back of a peasant's oxcart. "By the gods, I'm glad to see you," Gerin exclaimed. "When I left you behind there, I feared you'd never come out of that village again."

"I feared it myself, lord, but I went were night before last, and here, look at this." Parol thrust the hand from which he'd lost a couple of fingers under Gerin's nose.

"I see what you mean," Gerin said. The wound, instead of being festering and full of pus, looked as if he'd had it for years. The rapid healing werebeasts enjoyed hadn't been able to restore his missing digits, but had done the next best thing. Somehow, the Fox doubted it would ever become a popular part of medicine all the same.

"The bite on my arse is better, too," Parol said confidentially, "but I don't suppose you want to see that."

"As a matter of fact, you're right," Gerin said. "I wasn't interested in your hairy bum before you had a chunk bitten out of it, and I'm not interested in it now, except to see if it makes you sit at a tilt."

"It doesn't, by Dyaus!" Parol was the picture of indignation till he noticed the smirk Gerin was trying to hide. He laughed sheepishly. "Ah, you're having a joke on me."

"So I am." Gerin felt embarrassed; jokes at the expense of Parol were too easy to be much fun. To make amends, he told the warrior something about which he'd just made up his own mind: "Now that we've passed through the little werenight, we'll start the move against Adiatunnus and the monsters come sunrise tomorrow."

Parol beamed. "Ah, that's very fine, lord. I owe those horrible creatures something special for all they've done to me, and I aim to give it to them."

"Stout fellow!" Gerin said. Parol was not the best fighting man he had, lacking both Rihwin's grace and cleverness on the one hand and Drago the Bear's indomitable strength on the other. But he was not in the habit of backing away from trouble, and that covered a multitude of sins.

The tents in which Aragis' men had passed the nights since they reached Fox Keep came down. The warriors stored most of them inside the keep, bringing along only a few in which they could crowd together in case of rain. Gerin was less worried about Aragis' men coming into Fox Keep than he had been when they first arrived. Not only had the grand duke shown he didn't intend treachery, but enough of Gerin's troopers had come into the area to put up a solid fight if Aragis suddenly changed his mind. The force that rolled southwest against Adiatunnus and the monsters had more of Gerin's men in it than Aragis'.

Leaving Fox Keep stirred mixed feelings in Gerin: hope that this fight, unlike the ones that had gone before, would yield decisive results; sorrow at leaving Selatre behind; and a separate mixture over Duren: sorrow at leaving him, too, but also joy that he was there to be left.

Aragis brought his chariot up alongside the Fox's. "You have a good holding here," he said. "Plenty of timber, streams where you need them, well-tended fields—you must get a lot of work out of your peasants."

Gerin didn't care for the way Aragis said that: it brought to his mind a picture of nobles standing over serfs with whips to make them sow and weed and harvest. Maybe such things happened on Aragis' land—he had a reputation for ruthlessness. The Fox said, "They work for themselves, as much as they can. I don't take a certain proportion of what they raise, whether that's a lot or a little. I take a fixed amount, and they keep whatever they produce above that."

"All very well in good years," Aragis answered, "but what of the bad ones, when they don't bring in enough to get by after you've gathered your fixed amount?"

"Then we dicker, of course," Gerin said. "If my serfs all starve giving me this year's dues, I'm not likely to get much out of them next year."

Aragis thought that over, then saw the joke and laughed. "I don't dicker with peasants," he said. "I tell them how it's going to be, and that's how it is. As you say, starving them is wasteful, but I always remember I come first."

"I believe that, grand duke," Gerin said, so innocently that Aragis again paused for a moment before sending him a sharp look. Smiling inside, Gerin went on, "I haven't had a peasant revolt since I took over this holding, and we've been through some lean years, especially the one right after the werenight. How have you fared there?"

"Not well," Aragis admitted, but his tone made that seem unimportant. "When the peasants rise up, we knock them down. They can't stand against us, and they know it. They've no weapons to speak of, and no experience fighting, either."

"But if they're going to fight the monsters, they'll need more weapons than they have, and if they spend a good deal of time fighting the monsters, they'll get some experience at that, too," Gerin said.

Aragis gave him a look that said he hadn't thought so far ahead, and wished the Fox hadn't, either. After a long silence, he answered, "You must be of the view that solving one problem always breeds another."

"Oh, not always," Gerin said blithely. "Sometimes it breeds two or three."

Aragis opened his mouth, closed it, opened it again, and finally shook his head without speaking. He tapped his driver on the shoulder. Gerin was not surprised when the grand duke's chariot dropped back behind his own. Van laughed a little and said, "Here you went to all the trouble of making an ally of the Archer, and now you do your best to drive him away."

"I didn't mean to," Gerin said. He sounded so much like Duren after he'd dropped a pot and broken it that he started to laugh at himself.

When the dirt road went through the woods, it narrowed so that the chariots had to string themselves out single file. It was wider in the cleared lands between the forests; the cars bunched up again there.

The peasants working the fields paused to stare as the chariots rolled by. Some of them cheered and waved. Gerin wondered what Aragis thought of that. From all he'd said, and from all the Fox had heard, he ruled his serfs by force. He was a hard and able man, so he'd got away with it thus far, but was his heir likely to match him? Only time would answer that.

Gerin noted that a fair number of peasants cultivated their wheat and barley and beans and peas and turnips and squashes with full quivers on their backs. As one of them moved down a row, he bent, picked up his bow, carried it along with him, and then set it down again. Herdsmen also carried bows, and spears in place of their staves. What they could do against the monsters, they were doing. But an unarmored man, even with a spear in his hands, was not a good bet against the speed and cleverness the creatures showed.

The Fox saw only one monster that first day of the ride southwest. The thing came out of the woods a couple of furlongs ahead of his chariot. It stared at the great host of chariotry rattling its way, then turned and swiftly vanished back between the beeches from which it had emerged.

"Shall we hunt it, Captain?" Van asked.

Gerin shook his head. "We'd be wasting our time. If we can beat Adiatunnus, we'll take their refuge away from the creatures. That'll do us far more good over the long haul than picking them off one and two at a time."

"Sometimes you think so straight, you cook all the juice out of life," Van said, but let it go at that.

As sunset neared, Gerin bought a sheep from a village through which he passed. That provoked fresh bemusement from Aragis, who, like a large majority of lords, was accustomed to taking what he needed from his serfs regardless of whether it was properly part of his feudal dues. The grand duke also seemed surprised when the Fox told some of his warriors to cut firewood rather than taking it from the serfs or putting them to work. But he did not question Gerin about it and, indeed, after a few minutes ordered his own men to help those of his ally.

With all four moons now past full, the early hours of the night were unusually dark. Although the evening was warm and sultry, Gerin ordered the fires kept burning brightly. "The last thing I want is for the monsters to take us unawares," he said, after which he got no arguments.

The dancing flames kept more men sitting around them and talking than would have happened on most nights. After a while, Drago the Bear turned to Van and said, "What about a tale for us, to make the time pass by?" To several of Aragis' men sitting close to him, he added, "You've never heard a yarnspinner to match him, I promise you."

"Aye, give us a tale, then," one of those troopers said eagerly, and in a moment many more—and many of Gerin's men as well—took up the cry.

Van got to his feet with a show of shyness Gerin knew to be assumed. The outlander said, "I hate to tell a tale now, friends, for after Drago's spoken of me so, how can I help but disappoint?"

"You never have yet," one of Gerin's men called. "Give us a tale of far places—you must've seen more of 'em than any man alive."

"A tale of far places?" Van said. "All right, I'll give you another story of Mabalal, the hot country where they teach the monkeys to gather pepper for 'em—some of you will remember my tale about that. But this is a different yarn; you might call it the tale of the mountain snake, even though it's really about the snake's head, as you'll see.

"Now, they have all manner of snakes in Mabalal. The plains snake, if you'll believe it, is so big that he even hunts elephants now and again; the only time the natives go after him is when he's fighting one of those huge beasts."

"What's an elephant?" somebody asked. Gerin knew about elephants, but had his doubts about serpents big enough to hunt them—although he'd never managed to catch his friend in a lie about his travels. After Van explained, the warrior who'd asked the question was loudly dubious about the elephant's snaky trunk, though Gerin knew that was a genuine part of its anatomy.

"Well, never mind," the outlander said. "This story's not about elephants or plains snakes, anyhow. Like I said, it's about mountain snakes. Mountain snakes, now, aren't as big as their cousins of the plain, but they're impressive beasts, too. They have a fringe of golden scales under their chins that looks like a beard, and a crest of pointed red scales down the back of their necks almost like a horse's mane. When they're burrowing in the mountains, the sound their scales make reminds you of bronze blades clashing against each other."

"Are they venomous?" Gerin asked; unlike most if not all of his companions, he was in part interested in Van's stories for their natural—or perhaps unnatural—history.

"I should say they are!" Van answered. "But that's not why the men of Mabalal hunt them—in fact, it'd be a good reason to leave 'em alone. The snakes sometimes grow these multicolored stones in their heads, the way oysters grow pearls, but these stones are supposed to make you invisible. That's what they say in Mabalal, anyhow.

"There was this wizard there, a chap named Marabananda, who wanted a snakestone and needed an axeman to help him get it. He hired me, mostly on account of I'm bigger'n any three Mabalali you could find.

"Marabananda wove gold letters into a scarlet cloth and cast a spell of sleep over them. Then he carried the cloth out to one of the mountain snakes' nests. The snake heard him coming—or smelled him, or did whatever snakes do—and stuck its head out to see what was going on. He held the cloth in front of it, and as soon as the mountain snake looked, it was caught—snakes can't blink, you know, so it couldn't get free of the spell even for a moment.

"Down came my axe! Off flew the head! The snake's body, back in its burrow, jerked and twisted so much that the ground shook, just like the earthquake that knocked down the temple at Ikos. And Marabananda, he got out his knives and cut into the head—and damn me to the five hells if he didn't pull out one of those shiny, glowing snakestones I was telling you about.

" 'I'm rich!' he yells, capering around like a madman. 'I'm rich! I can walk into the king's treasure house and carry away all the gold and silver and jewels I please, and no one will see me. I'm rich!'

" 'Uh, lord wizard, sir,' says I, 'you're holding the stone now, and I can still see you.'

"Well, Marabananda says this is on account of I'm just a dirty foreigner, and too unenlightened for wizardry to touch. But the Mabalali, he says, they're more spiritually sensitive, and so the magic will work on them. He wouldn't listen to me when I tried to tell him different. But I did talk him into not trying till dead of night, in case he was wrong.

"Around midnight, off he went. He would have had me come with him, but I'd already shown the magic didn't work on me. He got to the treasure, and—" Van paused for dramatic effect.

"What happened?" half a dozen people demanded in the same breath.

The outlander bellowed laughter. "Poor damned fool, the first guard who spied him going in where he didn't belong struck off his head, same as I did with the mountain snake. I guess it goes to show the snakestone not only didn't make old Marabananda invisible to the guard, it let the guard see something even the wizard couldn't."

"What's that?" Gerin got the question in before anyone else could.

"Why, that he was a blockhead, of course," Van replied. "When he didn't come back from his little trip after a bit, I figured it had gone sour for him and I got out of there before the royal guardsmen came around with a pile of questions I couldn't answer. I don't know what happened to the mountain snake's head after that. Just like life, stories don't always have neat, tidy endings."

By the way the warriors clapped their hands and came up to chatter with Van, they liked the story fine, neat, tidy ending or no. Aragis told him, "If ever you find life dull at Fox Keep, you can stay at my holding for as long as you like, on the strength of your tales alone." When Van laughed and shook his head, the grand duke persisted, "Or if you decide you can't stomach staying with your Trokmê-tempered ladylove another moment, the same holds good."

"Ah, Archer, now you really tempt me," Van said, but he was still laughing.

"I'm for my blankets," Gerin said. "Any man with a dram of sense will do likewise. We may be fighting tomorrow, and we will be fighting the day after."

Off in the distance, a longtooth roared. Some of the horses tethered to stakes and to low-hanging branches snorted nervously; that sound was meant to instill fear. It had made Gerin afraid many times in the past. Now, though, he found it oddly reassuring. It was part of the night he'd known all his life. The monsters' higher, more savage screeches he found far more terrifying.

Morning came all too soon, as it has a way of doing. The sun shining in Gerin's face made him sit up and try to knuckle sleep from his eyes. Where all four moons had been absent at sunset, now they hung like pale lamps in the western sky. Soon they would draw apart again, and Gerin would be able to stop worrying about their phases for a while—although he promised himself he'd check their predicted motions in the book of tables from time to time.

Drivers gulped hasty breakfasts of hard-baked biscuits, smoked meat, and crumbly white cheese, then hurried to harness their horses to their chariots. The warriors who rode with them, generally older men of higher rank, finished their breakfasts while the drivers worked. The food was no better, but time could be a luxury, too.

As soon as the chariots rolled out of Gerin's land into the debatable ground south and west of his holding, the troopers saw more and more monsters. The monsters saw them, too; their hideous howls split the air. The Fox wondered if they were warning their fellows—and Adiatunnus' men.

In the debatable lands between Gerin's holding and the territory Adiatunnus had taken for himself when the Trokmoi swarmed over the Niffet, brush and shrubs and saplings grew close to the road. The barons who'd owned that land before had been less careful of it than the Fox had with his. Now most of them were dead or fled. Gerin claimed much of their holdings, but the woodsrunners made his possession too uncertain for him to send woodsmen onto it.

The first arrows came from the cover of the roadside scrub a little past noon. One hummed past his head, close enough to make him start. He snatched up his shield and moved up in the car so he could hope to protect himself and Raffo both. "Keep going," he told the driver, and waved the rest of the chariots on as well.

"What?" Van said indignantly. "Aren't you going to stop and hunt down those cowardly sneaks who shoot without showing their faces?"

"No," Gerin answered, his voice flat. The unadorned word made Van gape and splutter, as he'd thought it would. When the outlander fell silent, the Fox explained, "I am not going to slow down in any way, shape, form, color, or size, not for monsters, not for Trokmoi. That's what Adiatunnus wants me to do, so he'll have more time to ready himself against us. I don't aim to give it to him."

"It's not manly, ignoring an enemy who's shooting at you," Van grumbled.

"I don't care," Gerin said, which set Van spluttering again despite their years of friendship. Gerin went on, "I am not fighting this war to be manly. I'm not even fighting it for loot, though anything I take from the Trokmoi helps me and hurts them. The only reason I'm fighting it is because I'll have to do it later and on worse terms if I don't do it now. Fighting it now means moving as fast as we can. We weren't quite quick enough the last time we struck at Adiatunnus. This time, the gods willing, we will be."

Van studied him some time in silence. At last the outlander said, "Me, I've heard you call Aragis the Archer ruthless a time or three. If he wanted to hang the same name on you, I think it'd fit."

"And what does that have to do with unstoppering the jar of ale?" Gerin asked. "I do what I have to do, the best way I can see to do it. You'd better pass up the little fight if you intend to win the big one."

"Put that way, it sounds good enough," Van admitted. He still looked unhappy, like a man forced to go against his better judgment. "When somebody shoots at me, though, I just want to jump down from the car, chase him till I catch him, and leave him as pickings for the crows and the foxes—no offense to you—and the flies."

"That's what the Trokmoi want us to do," Gerin answered patiently. "When you fight a war, you're better off not doing what your foe has in mind for you."

"You'll have your way here with me or without me," Van said, but then relented enough to add, "So you know, Captain, you have it with me—I suppose."

With that Gerin had to be content. By the time his army drew out of range of the archers, they'd had two horses and one man wounded, by luck none of them badly. *A small enough price to pay for avoiding delay*, he thought, relieved it was not worse.

He kept the chariots rolling almost up to the moment of sunset before stopping and sacrificing some of the hens he'd brought from Fox Keep. "Adiatunnus may know we're coming," he said, "but with luck he doesn't know we'll be in his lands so soon. We should start hitting him early tomorrow; we've made fine time coming down from my keep."

When the sun set, the night was very dark, for none of the moons would rise for more than two hours. That stretch of evening blackness would just grow over the next several days, too, till swift-moving Tiwaz sped round to the other side of the sun and began to illuminate the night once more. It worried Gerin. Because of the ghosts, his men could do little in the night, but he'd already seen that that did not hold for the monsters.

He took such precautions as he could, posting sentry squadrons all around the main area where his men and Aragis' rested. The Archer's troopers were inclined to complain about having their sleep interrupted. Gerin stared them down, saying, "When my warriors come south to your lands, we'll be under the grand duke's commands, and he'll make the arrangements he thinks best. Now the worries are mine, and I'll meet them in my own way."

He did not look to Aragis for support; this too was his worry. Had the Archer chosen to argue with him, he'd been ready to lose his temper in as spectacularly dramatic a way as he could. When he was through dealing with the grand duke's men, though, Aragis got up and said, "The prince of the north is right—he leads here. Anyone who doesn't fancy that will answer to him here and then to me after we go south." Out went the sentries without another word.

Gerin bundled himself in his bedroll and soon fell asleep. What seemed like moments later, shouts of alarm rang out from the sentries, and mixed with them the monsters' screams. The Fox had his helm on his head, his shield on his arm, and his sword in his hand and was on his feet and running toward the fighting before he fully understood where he was.

As soon as the situation did sink in, Gerin realized whoever led the monsters—whether that was Adiatunnus or some of the more clever creatures—knew how best to use them. Instead of attacking the troopers, who were armed and at least partly armored and could fight back, the monsters turned their fury on the long lines of tethered horses.

There dreadful din and chaos reigned. The horses screamed and kicked and bucked under the savage teeth and claws of their attackers. Some of them tore loose the lines by which they were tethered and ran off into the night. Every one that got away would have to be recaptured later—if Gerin and his men could manage that. At the same time, though, every horse that fled drew monsters away from the main point of the assault, which left the Fox unsure how to feel about the flight.

He had little time for feeling, anyhow—nothing to do but slash and hack and keep his shield up to hold fangs away from flesh and pray that in the darkness and confusion he didn't hurt any of his own men, or Aragis'. The fear-maddened horses were as appalled to have men close by them as monsters. Someone not far from Gerin went down with a muffled groan as a hoof caught him in the midsection.

He stabbed a monster that was scrambling up onto a horse's back—and leaving long, bleeding claw tracks in the beast's flanks. The monster howled and sprang at him. He slashed it. It screamed in pain and fled. The hot, coppery smell of its blood and the horse's filled his nose.

Pale Nothos was the first moon over the eastern horizon. By the time he rose, the warriors had managed to drive the monsters back into the wood from which they'd come. "Put more wood on the fire and start another one over here," Gerin shouted. "We have a lot of work to do yet tonight."

His army was still at it when Tiwaz, Elleb, and Math rose in a tight cluster a couple of hours after Nothos appeared. The men went out by squads to bring back the horses that had bolted, but that was the smaller part of what they needed to do. Treating the animals' wounds— and their panic—was a far bigger job. The drivers, men who dealt most intimately with their teams, did the greater part of the work. The rest of the troopers lent what help they could.

"I mislike everything about this," Gerin said gloomily. "Who knows what the beasts will do when they next face the monsters, or even smell them?"

"I'd not yet thought past this night," Aragis said. "Did we bring enough spare animals to make up for the ones we lost and those hurt too badly to pull a car?"

"I think so," the Fox answered; he'd been trying to run his own mental count, but confusion didn't make it easy. He looked at the hairy corpses scattered over the grass. "We hurt the monsters badly here; I don't think they'll try anything like that again. The question is, was the once enough?"

"We'll know come morning." Aragis yawned. "I don't know if we'll have any wits left by then, though. I'm dead for sleep, and I'm for my blanket."

"And I," Gerin said with a matching yawn. "One more thing for Adiatunnus to pay for—and he shall."

When the sun rose, Gerin stumbled over to a nearby stream and splashed cold water on his face to give himself a brittle semblance of alertness. Then he examined the horses the monsters had attacked. They looked worse by daylight than they had in the night, with blood dried on their coats and matted in their manes, with gashes the drivers had missed by the light of moons and fires, with mud slapped on the wounds the men had seen. He wondered how they would fare when they had to draw the chariots, but had no choice. He waved for the drivers to harness them.

Because the animals were sore and nervous, that took longer than it might have. But once they were hitched to the chariots, they pulled them willingly enough. Van drew a clay flute from a pouch on his belt and began a mournful, wailing tune that sounded as if it had come off the plains of Shanda. He assumed an expression of injured dignity when Gerin asked him to put the flute away for fear of frightening the horses.

The border post Adiatunnus had set up in imitation of Elabonian practice was empty and deserted; he must have got wind that Gerin was moving against him.

"We move straight on," the Fox commanded. "No stopping for loot anywhere. Until we run up against Adiatunnus' main force and smash it, we haven't accomplished a thing."

But when the army came to a peasant village, Aragis ordered his chariots out of the road to trample the wheat and barley growing in the fields around it. After a moment's hesitation, Gerin waved for his warriors to join the Archer's. "I hate to hurt the serfs," he said, "but if I strike a blow at the Trokmoi thereby, how can I keep from doing it?"

"You can't, so don't fret yourself," Van answered. "You go to war to win; you said as much yourself. Otherwise you're a fool."

The peasants themselves had vanished, along with most of their livestock. The army took a few chickens and a half-grown pig, set fire to the serfs' huts, and rolled on.

Perhaps the next village they came to had planted earlier than the first; the wheat and rye growing around it had already turned golden. That meant the crops were nearing ripeness. It also meant they would burn. The warriors tossed torches into the fields near the road, watched flames lick across them. The serfs would have a hungry winter. Gerin vowed to himself to work enough destruction in Adiatunnus' holding to make their Trokmê masters starve, too.

Every now and then, a red-mustached barbarian would peer out of the woods at the invaders. Gerin ignored those watchers; every man afoot was one he wouldn't have to face in a chariot. "I want to reach Adiatunnus before the sun sets," he said grimly. "Spending a night in his lands with the monsters prowling about sets my teeth on edge."

"Ah, but Captain, does he want you to reach him?" Van said. "You ask me, that's a different question altogether. If he can get the monsters to come out and soften us up again, you think he won't do it?"

"No, I don't think that," Gerin said. "But he pays a price

if he hangs back, too. The deeper we penetrate into his
lands, the more harm we do him, and the hungrier his
warriors and serfs will be come winter. It's a nice calculation he has to make: can he afford what we will do to
him for the sake of what the monsters might do to us
tonight?"

"You think he'll weigh the odds so—this much on this
side, that much on the other?" Van shook his head vehemently. "That's what *you'd* do, certain sure. But Adiatunnus,
he'll be watching the sky. As soon as he sees so much
smoke there that his fighters start screaming at him louder
than he can stand, he'll yell for them to jump into their
chariots and come at you. Whether that's today or tomorrow morning we won't know till we see the woodsrunners
drawn up in a meadow athwart our path."

"Or, better yet, till we catch them trying to get across our
path," the Fox said with a ferocious smile. "But you're likely
right; if you try to judge what the other fellow would do by
what you'd do yourself, you'll be wrong a lot of the time."

The army moved past the small keep Gerin had burned
out in his earlier raid. The castle at the keep's heart had
burned; the roof was fallen in, and soot covered the outer
stonework. No one moved on the walls. Gerin grinned
again. He'd struck Adiatunnus a blow there.

To his surprise, the Trokmê chieftain did not sally forth
against him while the sun remained in the sky. He'd pushed
close to the keep Adiatunnus had taken for his own and
to the woodsrunners' village that had grown up around it
by the time failing light at last made him halt. Behind him,
all the way back to the border of Adiatunnus' lands, lay
as broad a swath of devastation as the Fox could cut. Gerin's
eyes were red with the smoke he'd raised; his lungs stung
every time he breathed.

When he encamped, he treated the horses as if they
were pure gold come to life. He placed them and the
chariots in the center of the camp, with the warriors in a
ring around them and sentries out beyond the main force.
That meant spreading his men thinner than he would have
liked, but he saw no other choice. Without chariotry, what
good were the warriors? The Trokmoi would ride circles
around them.

Rihwin the Fox said, "The first of the moons will not rise tonight until even longer after sunset than was so yestereven."

"I know," Gerin said dolefully. "And the other three, moving more swiftly in their rounds than Nothos, will have gone farther still and will rise later still." He pronounced the words with a certain amount of gloomy relish; every now and then, he drew perverse enjoyment from imagining just how bad things could be.

Few men sought their blankets right after they ate. No one put weapons out of arm's reach. After one attack on the horses, another looked too likely to take lightly.

Twilight still lingered in the western sky when, in the black shadows of the woods, a monster screamed. Warriors who had tried to sleep snatched up swords and shields and peered about wildly, waiting for a sentry or perhaps a horse to cry out in agony.

Another monster shrieked, and another, and another. Soon what sounded like thousands of the creatures were crying out together in a chorus that sent icy fingers of dread running up Gerin's back. "Damn me to the five hells if I see any way to sleep through this," he said to Van, "not when I'm already on edge looking ahead to battle tomorrow."

"Ah, it's not so bad, Captain," the outlander said. When Gerin stared at him in some surprise, he explained, "I don't care how loud they scream at us. Last night, we taught 'em something they hadn't known before, else they'd be running out of the woods at us with slobber dripping off their fangs. Now with all the moons down'd be the best time for 'em to try. Me, I think they don't dare. They're just trying to make us afraid."

Gerin considered. All at once, the hellish cries seemed less terrifying than they had. "You may well be right," he said, and managed a laugh. "They aren't doing a bad job of it, either, are they?"

"It's nothing but a great pile of noise." Van refused to admit fear to anyone, most likely including himself.

"We won't stop staying ready for a fight, whether you turn out right or wrong," Gerin said. "That's the best way I know to make sure we don't have one."

The hideous chorus kept up all night long, and got

louder as the moons rose one by one. By then, though, most of the troopers had concluded the monsters were screaming to intimidate rather than as harbinger to an attack. Those not on sentry did manage to drop off, and their snores rose to rival the creatures' shrieks.

Gerin didn't remember when he dozed off, but he woke with a start at sunrise, having expected to pass the whole night awake. Most of the men were in the same state, complaining of how little they'd slept but grateful they'd slept at all. The horses seemed surprisingly fresh; an attack like the one of the night before might have panicked them, but they'd resigned themselves to the monsters' screams faster than the warriors who guarded them.

"Will we fight today?" Aragis asked rather blurrily; his mouth was so full of smoked sausage that he looked like nothing so much as a cow chewing its cud.

"We will," Gerin said with grim certainty. "If we don't, we penetrate to the heart of Adiatunnus' holding before noon, and torch the big Trokmê village that's grown up around the keep he's taken for his own. He won't let that happen; his own warriors would turn on him if he did."

"There you're right," Aragis said after a heroic swallow. "A leader who won't defend what's his doesn't deserve to keep it. My men will be ready." Gerin had the feeling the Archer primed his vassals for battle by making them more afraid of him than of any imaginable foe, but in his own savage way the grand duke got results.

Not half an hour after the chariots rolled out of camp, they passed the meadow where Gerin's forces and Adiatunnus' had dueled fewer than fifty days before. Some of the ruts the chariot wheels had cut were still visible; grass had grown tall over others.

Gerin had wondered if the Trokmê chieftain would pick the same spot to defend his lands as he had in the last fight. When Adiatunnus didn't, the Fox's anxiety grew. Fearing an ambush when the road went through the next stand of woods, he dismounted several teams of fighting men and sent them in among the trees to flush out any lurking woodsrunners. That slowed the rest of the army, and the searchers found no one.

Past that patch of forest, a broad stretch of clear land opened up: meadows and fields that led to Adiatunnus' keep, the Trokmê village, and the meaner huts of the Elabonian peasants who still grew most of the holding's food. Mustered in front of them was a great swarm of chariotry: Adiatunnus, awaiting the attack.

The Fox was lucky—he spotted the Trokmoi before they spied his car in the shadow of the woods. He ordered Raffo to a quick halt, then waved the chariots of his force up as tight together as they could go without fouling one another. "We'll need to be in line before the woodsrunners can sweep down on us," he said. "The gods be praised, they don't look all that ready to fight, either. My men will form to the left when we burst out into the open, Aragis' to the right. I expect we'll all be mixed together before the day is done—that's just a way of keeping us straight when we start. May fortune roll with us."

"May it be so," several troopers said together. Gerin thumped Raffo on the shoulder. The driver flicked the reins and sent the horses forward onto the meadow. A great shout rose from the Trokmoi when they caught sight of the chariot. They swarmed forward in a great irregular wave, hardly bothering to shake out into line of battle in their eagerness to close with their enemies.

"Look at 'em come," Van said, hefting his spear. "If we can get ourselves ready to receive 'em, we'll beat 'em to bits, even with the monsters running between their cars there."

"They don't care much for tactics, do they?" Gerin said. "Well, I've known that a great many years now. The trouble with them is, they have so much pluck that that's too often what decides things."

He nocked an arrow and waited for the Trokmoi and the monsters to come within range. Behind him, ever more chariots rumbled out of the woods to form line of battle. Each one drew fresh cries of rage from the woodsrunners. Gerin saw he had more cars than the woodsrunners did. Whether they'd all be able to deploy before the fight opened was another question.

When the Trokmoi closed to within a furlong, Gerin waved his arm and shouted "Forward!" at the top of his lungs. Chariots depended on mobility; if you tried to stand to receive a charge, you'd be ridden down.

Raffo cracked the whip above the horses' backs. The beasts bounded ahead. A chariot wheel hit a rock. The car jounced into the air, landed with a jarring thump. Gerin grabbed the rail for a moment; his knees flexed to take the shock of returning to earth.

He'd pulled all the way to the left, to be on the wing of his own force. That also meant he was far away from the track that led toward Adiatunnus' keep. The horses galloped through ripening rye, trampling down a great swath of grain under their hooves. The Fox's lips skinned back from his teeth in a predatory grin. Every stride the horses took meant more hunger for his foes.

An arrow hissed past his head. Adiatunnus' hunger was distant, something that would come with winter. Had that arrow flown a couple of palms' breadth straighter, Gerin would never have worried about it or anything else, again. Planning for the future was all very well, but you had to remember the present, too.

Gerin loosed the shaft he'd nocked, snatched another from his quiver, and set it to his bowstring. He shot once more. The Trokmoi were packed so closely, the arrow would almost surely do them some harm. He shot again and again, half emptying his quiver as fast as he could. The rest of the shafts he thriftily saved against more specific targets and urgent need.

His men had followed him on that wide sweep to the left, encircling the Trokmoi on that wing. Had Aragis taken the same course on the right, the woodsrunners would have been in dire straits. But Gerin's deployment order had left the Archer with fewer chariots there, and he commanded that wing with a blunter philosophy of battle than the Fox employed. Instead of seeking to surround the enemy, he pitched straight into them. Some of his men kept shooting at the Trokmoi, while others laid about them at close quarters with sword and axe and mace.

A monster ran at the chariot in which Gerin rode. It came at the horses rather than the men, and from the right side, where Van with his spear had less reach than the Fox with his bow. But the creature reckoned without Raffo. The driver's long lash flicked out. The monster howled and clutched at its face. Raffo steered the car right past it. Van thrust his spear into the monster's vitals, yanked it free with a killing twist. The monster crumpled to the ground and lay kicking.

A Trokmê driver whipped his team straight for the Fox. His car bore two archers, both of whom let fly at almost the same time. One arrow glanced from the side of Van's helmet, the other flew between the outlander and Gerin.

Gerin shot at one of the archers. His shaft also failed to go just where he'd intended it, but it caught the Trokmê driver in the throat. The reins fell from his fingers; he slumped forward over the front rail of the car. The team ran wild. Both of the archers grabbed for the reins. They were past before Gerin saw whether either one managed to seize them.

"Well aimed, Fox!" Van cried.

"It didn't do what I wanted it to do," Gerin answered. Uncomfortable with praise, he used bitter honesty to turn it aside, like a man trying to avert an omen he didn't care for.

"Honh!" Van said. "It did what it needed to do, which is what matters." That left Gerin no room for argument.

His hopes built as the battle ground on. The Trokmoi were ferocious, but not all the ferocity in the world could make up for a bad position—and, this time, he'd brought more men into the fight than Adiatunnus had. The monsters helped even the odds, but not enough.

He spied the Trokmê chieftain, not far away. "Well, you robber, you asked what I'd do next," he shouted. "Now you see."

Adiatunnus shook a fist at him. "To the corbies with you, you black-hearted omadhaun. You'll pay for this." He reached for his quiver, but found he was out of arrows.

Gerin jeered at him. He pulled out a carefully husbanded shaft, set it to his bow, and let fly. Adiatunnus realized he had no time to grab for his shield, so he threw up his arms. The arrow caught him in the meaty part of his right upper arm, about halfway between elbow and shoulder. He let out a howl any monster would have envied. The wound wasn't fatal, probably wasn't even crippling, but he would fight no more today.

Van swatted Gerin on the back, almost hard enough to pitch him out of the chariot onto his head. "Well aimed!" the outlander boomed again.

And again, the Fox did what he could to downplay praise. "If that had been well aimed, it would have killed him," he grumbled.

The Trokmoi tried to slam through Aragis' men. Had they succeeded, they'd have regained their freedom of movement. But Aragis' chariots were grouped more tightly than Gerin's, and the woodsrunners could not force a breakout. When they failed, they began falling back toward the cover of their village.

"We'll roast 'em like mutton!" Aragis' fierce, exultant cry rang over the battlefield, though the Trokmoi still fought back with fierce countercharges—they were beaten, but far from broken.

Gerin waved several chariots with him, trying to get between the Trokmoi and the haven they sought. Bad luck dogged the effort. An arrow made one of the Elabonian drivers drop the reins, and the horses, freed from control, chose to run in just the wrong direction. A pair of monsters sprang into another chariot; the mad fight that ensued there kept the car from going as he'd hoped it would. He never did find out why a third car failed to follow, but it did.

That left him with . . . not enough. The Trokmoi did not have to slow down much to get around the handful of chariots with which he tried to block their path, and then he was the one in danger of being cut off and surrounded. Cursing, he shouted to Raffo, "We can't go back, so we'd best go on. Forward!"

Like an apple seed squeezed out from between thumb and forefinger, the Fox and his followers fought their way free from the far side of the fleeing Trokmê force. Now he was on the right wing of the attack, and most of his vassals on the left. He'd foretold that things would get mixed up in the fight; being of an uncommonly orderly turn of mind, though, he hadn't expected the mixing to include himself.

He still had arrows left, and shot them at the retreating Trokmoi. Some of the woodsrunners had their cars pounding down the narrow lanes between their homes.

"Uh-oh," Van said. "Are you sure we want to go after 'em in there, Fox?"

Whenever Van urged caution, he had to be taken seriously. "Looks like a good way to get chewed to bits, doesn't it?" Gerin said after he'd taken a long look at the situation.

"Doesn't it just?" Van agreed. "We'll get a good many of 'em, and do the rest real harm, if we set the place afire. But going in there after the woodsrunners, you ask me, that's putting your prong on the block for the chopper."

Had Gerin been undecided before, the wince from that figure of speech would have been plenty to make up his mind. He waved his arms and shouted for his men to hold up and ply the Trokmê village with fire arrows. A good many Trokmoi, though, were thundering into the village between him and his vassals, so only a few of those vassals heard. And, while he was supposed to be in command of Aragis' men as well, they ignored him when he tried to keep them from pursuing the Trokmoi.

"Now what, lord prince?" Raffo asked as the chariots streamed past.

Gerin looked at Van. The outlander's broad shoulders lifted in a shrug. The Fox scowled. The only thing he could do that would let him keep his prestige among the Elabonian warriors was also the thing he'd just dismissed as stupid. "Go on," he shouted to Raffo. "If that's where the fight is, that's where we have to go."

"Aye, lord prince," Raffo said, and cracked the whip over the horses' backs.

It was as bad as Van had predicted, as bad as Gerin had thought it would be. Foundered chariots blocked several of the village lanes, robbing the Fox's force of mobility, the essence of chariotry. Some of the Trokmoi fought afoot, side by side with the monsters. Other men ran into the houses and shot arrows at the Elabonians from windows and doors, ducking back into cover after they'd shot.

And quite as fierce as the men were the Trokmê women. It was like fighting dozens of berserk Fands. They screamed and shouted. Under their pale, freckled skins, their faces turned crimson with fury and the veins stood out like cords on their necks and foreheads. Some threw stones; others used bows and swords like their men. They weren't merely unnerving; they were deadly dangerous.

"Back, curse it! Back and out!" Gerin shouted, again and again. "We'll throw everything away if we get stuck in this kind of fighting. Out and back!"

Little by little, his men and Aragis' began to heed him. But pulling out of the battle was harder than getting into it had been. Turning a chariot around in the crowded, bloody alleyways of the village was anything but easy; too often, it was next to impossible. Gerin wondered if going forward would have cost less than the withdrawal did.

A lot of the chariots had lost the firepots with which they'd begun the day's fighting. Still, before long, fire arrows sent trails of smoke through the air as they arced toward the thatched roofs of the Trokmê cottages. The weather had been dry. Before long, the straw on the roofs was blazing.

More chariots rampaged through the fields outside the village, wrecking the crops that still stood after the battle had gone through them. Through thickening smoke, Gerin saw Trokmoi fleeing into Adiatunnus' keep.

"Do you aim to lay siege to 'em?" Aragis the Archer asked. The grand duke's helmet was dented, maybe by a stone. The edge of the helm had cut him above one eye; when he healed, he'd have a scar like Gerin's.

"We can't take the keep by storm, however much I wish we could," Gerin answered. "We don't have the numbers, we don't have the ladders, and they'd be fighting for their lives. We can't starve them out, either. Adiatunnus will have more in his storerooms and cellars than we can draw from the countryside. We can send in fire arrows and hope to start a big blaze, but that's just a matter of luck."

"Aye, but we should try it," Aragis said. Nonetheless, he showed relief that Gerin did not intend to linger in Adiatunnus' country.

The Fox understood that. "You'll want to campaign against the monsters in your own lands as soon as may be, won't you?"

"As a matter of fact, that's just what's in my mind," Aragis said. "Harvest won't wait forever, and I'd like the woods cleared of those creatures before then . . . if that can be done. I'd not care to harm your campaign by pulling back from here too soon, but—"

But I will, if you don't pull back on your own hook soon enough to suit me. Aragis didn't say it—Gerin gave him credit for being a good ally, a better one than the Fox had expected—but he thought it very loudly.

"If it suits you, we'll spend the rest of the afternoon lobbing fire arrows into the keep in the hope of sending it all up in smoke, and then—then we'll withdraw," Gerin said. "We'll ravage more of Adiatunnus' lands as we go. By your leave, we'll stop at Fox Keep for a few days, to let me set up the defenses of my own holding while I'm in the south, and then I'll meet my end of the bargain."

"Couldn't ask for fairer than that," Aragis said, though his eyes argued that any departure later than yesterday, or perhaps the day before, was too late. But again, he held his peace; he recognized necessity, and recognized that against it any man struggled in vain.

The charioteers rode rings around Adiatunnus' keep, howling and shouting louder than the Trokmoi on the walls as they sent more fire arrows smoking through the air. Up on the walls of the keep with the woodsrunners were several monsters. Gerin hoped they and the Trokmoi would quarrel in the tight quarters, but had no way to make that happen.

Two or three times, thin columns of black smoke rose from within the keep. Whenever they did, Gerin's men, and Aragis' too, cheered themselves hoarse. But each time, the smoke thinned, paled, died. At last, as the sun sank ever lower in the west, the Fox called off the attack. He and his followers drew off toward the northeast, back in the direction from which they had come.

Wounded horses and men and monsters still thrashed and groaned and screamed on the battlefield. Now and again, an Elabonian chariot would halt so its crew could cut the throat of a horse or a monster or a Trokmê, or so the troopers could haul an injured comrade into their car and do for him what they could once they stopped to camp. Some of the injured cried out louder in the jouncing chariots than they had lying on the ground. Their moans made Gerin grind his teeth, but all he could do was keep on.

"One thing," Van said as they entered the woods from which they'd emerged to fight: "we won't have to offer much in the way of sacrifice to the ghosts tonight."

"That's so," Gerin agreed. "We gave them blood aplenty today. They'll buzz round the bodies the whole night long, like so many great carrion flies round a carcass—gloating, I suppose, that all those brave men joined their cold and gloomy world."

The chariots came out of the woods bare minutes before sunset. Gerin led them out into the middle of a broad meadow. "We stop here," he declared. "Van, I leave it to you to get the first fire going." He told off parties to go back to the forest and chop down enough wood to keep the fires blazing all through the night. Nothos would rise with a third of the night already passed, and the other three moons later still.

That accomplished, the Fox turned his hand to giving the wounded what help he could. As always in the aftermath of battle, he was reminded how pitifully little that was. He splashed ale on cuts to help keep them from going bad, set and splinted broken bones, sewed up a few gaping gashes with thread of wool or sinew, bandaged men who had ignored their hurts in the heat of action. None of what he did brought much immediate relief from pain, although some of it, he made himself remember, would do good in the long run.

More horses were hurt, too. He helped the drivers doctor them when he was done with the men. The men, at least, had some idea why they'd been hurt. The horses' big brown eyes were full of uncomprehended suffering.

He didn't know who'd ordered it, but the men had made the same sort of circle of fires they'd built the night before. He chose warriors who'd slept through the previous night undisturbed for sentry duty, and made himself one of them. He was tired down to the marrow of his bones, but so was everyone else.

"Did we win?" Van asked as he replaced the Fox for midwatch. "Did we do all you wanted done?"

"Aye, we won," Gerin said, yawning. "Did we do enough?" Yawning again, he shook his head and made for his bedroll.

"Wait, Captain." Van called him back. The outlander pointed to the woods, from which monsters were coming forth.

Sentries' shouts roused the camp. Swearing, men snatched at weapons and armor. Gerin found his sword in his hand. It wasn't magic; he just didn't remember drawing the weapon.

The monsters approached to the edge of bowshot, but no closer. "There aren't that many of them," Gerin remarked as the creatures began a chorus of their dreadful shrieks. Shriek they did, but they made no move to attack. After a while, the Fox said, "I think they're trying to put us in fear, nothing else but. A plague on 'em, says I. No matter how they scream, I'm going to get some sleep." He raised his voice: "All save the sentries, rest while you can. We'll have warning enough if they truly aim to come after us."

He rolled himself up in his blanket. The monsters' hideous outcry kept him awake a little longer than he would have been otherwise, but not much. Not even Mavrix the god of wine appearing before him would have kept him awake for long, he thought as sleep swallowed him.

He woke wondering why he'd worried about Mavrix, but shook his head at the pointlessness of that: sleepy minds did strange things, and there was no more to say about it. The monsters were gone. That didn't surprise him; with sunrise, the Elabonians could have started shooting at them with good hopes of scoring hits.

Not all the warriors had been able to sleep. Some of them shambled about as if barely alive. How they'd be after another day in the chariot was something about which the Fox tried not to think.

No help for it. After breaking their fast on hard bread and sausage and ale, they rolled northeast, back toward the Fox's holding. Knowing no large force lay directly ahead of them, they spread out widely over the countryside, doing as much damage to Adiatunnus' lands and villages and crops as they could with fire and their horses' hooves and the wheels of their chariots.

A victory, but not a perfect one. Gerin had hoped to smash Adiatunnus utterly; he'd hurt the Trokmê chieftain, literally and metaphorically, but not enough to seize much of his territory with any assurance of keeping it. Maybe the monsters had learned not to attack large bands of armed and armored men, but they hadn't been exterminated— and Adiatunnus' lands still gave them haven.

"Not enough," Gerin said under his breath. Van glanced over to him, but did not venture to reply.

Some of Gerin's vassals peeled off from the main force as they reentered his territory, off to their own castles and to protect their own villages. Most, though, stayed on the road to Fox Keep. Before long, they'd be riding south to help Aragis and fulfill Gerin's part of the bargain.

He'd wondered if the serfs would ask him whether he'd rid their villages of the monsters for good, and dreaded having to tell them no. Then the army passed through a village the creatures had attacked while he was deep in Adiatunnus' territory. That made him feel worse. He'd hurt the Trokmoi and the monsters, but he'd been mad to think he could root them out with a single victory.

He also wondered how much he and his men would accomplish down in the holding of Aragis the Archer. He feared it would be less than Aragis hoped, but kept that fear to himself. Whatever the grand duke's misgivings, he'd come north. The Fox saw no way to keep from reciprocating, not if he wanted to keep his good name.

The return to Castle Fox was subdued. The victory the army had won did not outweigh the men who would not come back, the complete triumph that had eluded the Elabonians.

Seeing Selatre again, squeezing her to him, was wonderful, but she quickly sensed that, past having come home alive and unhurt, Gerin had little to celebrate. That made her shrink back into herself, so that she seemed to stand aloof from the chaos in the stables although she was in the middle of it.

Van and Fand got into a screaming fight over what business the outlander had had going off to fight the Trokmoi. He clapped a hand to his forehead and bellowed, "You tell me not to tangle with them when the only reason you're here is that you stabbed the last woodsrunner daft enough to take you into his bed?"

"Aye, I did that, and I had the right of it, too, for he was of my own folk, for all that he was an evil-natured spalpeen to boot," she said. "But you, now, you're the Fox's friend, but you're after being my lover. So you see!"

Van shook his head—he didn't see. Gerin didn't see, either. If being Fand's lover turned Van into some sort of honorary Trokmê, by her own argument that gave him a special right to go to war against the woodsrunners. Fand was seldom long on logic; the gods seemed to have given her extra helpings of all the passions instead.

Duren hopped around, saying, "May I go fight too next time, Father? May I, please?"

"You're raising a warrior there," Aragis said approvingly.

"So I am," Gerin answered. He wasn't altogether pleased. Aye, any holding on the frontier—any holding in the northlands—needed a warrior at its head. But he hoped he would also be able to raise a civilized man, lest barbarism seize all the land between the Niffet and the Kirs and hold it for centuries to come.

The castle cooks dished out mutton and pork and bread and ale. The warriors ate and sought their bedrolls. Gerin stayed down in the great hall, hashing over the fight, till Duren fell asleep beside him. Then, as he had a few nights before, he carried his son upstairs to his bedchamber.

When he went back out into the hall, he found Selatre waiting there. She said, "If you were so worn you'd gone to bed with your son, I'd have walked back to my room, but since you're not—"

He caught her to him. "Thank you for being here when things don't look as good as they might." Even as he spoke the words, he realized he was doing his best to put a good face on the campaign from which he'd just returned. Things looked bloody awful.

Selatre ignored all that. She said, "Don't be foolish. If you hadn't been there for me, I'd be dead. Come on." She led him back to her chamber.

He took her with something approaching desperation. He hoped she read it as passion, but she wasn't one to be easily deceived. That she stayed by him when he needed her most was a greater gift than any other she could have given him.

Afterwards, he fell into a deep and dreamless sleep. When he jerked awake, Nothos' light streamed through the window, but not yet golden Math's: past midnight, then, but not far past. Beside him, Selatre was also sitting bolt upright.

"Something is amiss," she said. Her voice sent chills through him. For the first time in many days, she sounded like the Sibyl at Ikos, not the woman he'd come to love.

But no matter how she sounded, she was right. "I heard it, too," Gerin said. He stopped, confused. "Heard it? Felt it? All's quiet now. But—" He got out of bed and started to dress.

So did she. "I don't know what it was. I thought for a moment Biton touched me." She shook her head. "I was wrong, but it was more than a dream. I know that. And if it woke you, too . . ."

"We'd better find out what it was." Gerin held his sword in his left hand. How much good the blade would do against whatever had roused him and Selatre, he had no idea, but it couldn't hurt.

All seemed quiet in Fox Keep as he and Selatre tiptoed down the hall to the stairs. Van's snores pierced the door to Fand's chamber. Gerin smiled for a moment at that, but his lips could not hold their upward curve. A few warriors had fallen asleep in the great hall, maybe too drunk to seek their proper beds. Gerin and Selatre walked by. He looked this way and that, shook his head in the same confusion Selatre had shown. Whatever was wrong, it lay outside the castle proper. He didn't know how he knew, but he did.

Outside, sentries paced their rounds up on the palisade. The courtyard seemed as still as the keep. Gerin began to wonder if worry and nerves hadn't played tricks on Selatre and him at the same time. Then he heard footfalls—slow, erratic footfalls—coming up from the stables toward the entrance to the great hall.

"Stay here," he whispered to Selatre, but when he trotted round to the side of the keep to see who—or what—approached, she followed. She was not so close to him as to cramp him if he had to fight, so he bit down his annoyance and kept quiet.

He rounded the corner and stopped dead with a strangled snort of laughter. No wonder the footfalls had been as they were: here came Rihwin, gloriously drunk. Gerin wondered how Rihwin managed to keep up his footfalls without falling himself. His face bore a look of intense concentration, as if putting one foot in front of the other took everything he had in him. It probably did.

Gerin turned to Selatre in mingled amusement and disgust. "We might as well go back to bed, if this poor sot's the worst menace we can find."

"No. We stay," she said, again sounding like the Sibyl she had been. "More is here than we yet know. Can you not feel it?"

And Gerin could: a prickling of the hairs at the nape of his neck, a tightening of his belly, his mouth suddenly dry as dust. He'd felt like this in the instant when the ground began to shake at Ikos, when his body gave alarm but his mind hadn't yet realized why.

The ground wasn't shaking now, though he wouldn't have bet Rihwin could have told whether that was so. Nevertheless, the feeling of awe and dread built inside Gerin till he wanted to run or scream or smash something just to get relief. He did none of those things. Forcing himself to stillness, he waited for Rihwin's staggering progress to bring his fellow Fox to him.

Rihwin was so intent on walking, he didn't notice Gerin till he almost ran into him. "Lord pr-prince!" he said thickly, and gave such a melodramatic start that he nearly tumbled over backwards. "Mercy, lord prince!" he gasped, and then hiccuped.

Now Gerin drew back a pace, his nose wrinkling. "Feh!" he said. "Your breath stinks like a vineyard in pressing season."

"Mercy!" Rihwin repeated. He swayed as he stared owlishly at his overlord; standing in one place seemed about as hard for him as walking. His face was slack with drink, but alarm glittered in his eyes.

Then Gerin looked through him instead of at him, really hearing for the first time what he himself had said. "You've been at the wine Schild brought us, haven't you, my fellow Fox?" he asked softly. He'd let his sword trail to the ground. Now it came up again, as if to let the wine out of Rihwin.

"Mercy!" Rihwin squeaked for the third time. "I found it buried in the hay when we brought our—*hic!*—horses to the stables. I broached but two jars. Mer—*hic!*—cy!"

"That is it." Selatre's voice was firm and certain. "That is what we felt: the power of Mavrix loosed in this holding."

Gerin wanted to scream at Rihwin. Even in his fury, though, he remembered the hour, remembered the warriors and women and cooks and servants asleep inside Castle Fox. But although he hissed instead of shrieking, his fury came through unabated: "You stupid, piggish dolt. Thanks to your greed, thanks to the wine you're going to piss away over the course of the next day, you've made Mavrix notice us and given him a channel through which he can enter this land—and he hates me. What shall I do to you for that? How could Adiatunnus serve me worse than you just did?"

Tears ran down Rihwin's cheeks; they glistened in Nothos' pale light. "Lord prince, you're right," he mumbled. "I don't know what came over me. I shaw—*saw*—the jars there in the straw, and it as as conshu—con*su*ming fire blazed all through me. I had to drink, or die." Even sozzled, he spoke with elaborate southern phrasings.

"That's the fanciest way to call yourself a no-account, worthless drunkard I ever heard," Gerin said in disgust.

Selatre set a hand on his arm. She still used that gesture seldom enough to command attention when she did. "Wait," she said. "There may be more truth in what he says than you hear. Perhaps Mavrix inflamed his soul, as he put it, to open the way for the god to make his presence felt in the northlands once more."

"It could be so, lord prince," Rihwin exclaimed eagerly. "Though the lord of the sweet grape expunged all sorcerous ability from my spirit, he left intact my knowledge."

"Not that you haven't tried to drown it in ale—and now wine," Gerin snarled, still anything but appeased.

"I deserve that." Rihwin's voice was full of drunken earnestness. "But it is as your gracious lady said. Were Mavrix to seek entry to your holding, I am just the sort of insht—insh—in*stru*ment he would employ." He smiled in triumph at finally forcing out the difficult word.

"All right, it could be so," Gerin said grudgingly. "Shall I thank you for it? Great Dyaus above, I'm still trying to figure out whether we can survive it. As I said, as you know, the god loves me not, nor you either."

Rihwin hung his head. "That is true."

"The god has his purposes, and we have ours," Selatre said. "He will accomplish his come what may. We can't say the same, worse luck. What we have to seek is a way in which the god's purposes are met, and ours as well, and, having found it, coax him into accepting it."

Gerin looked at her gratefully. "Put that way, it might almost be done." But in the back of his mind, he heard, or thought he heard, the god laughing, laughing.

XII

Red-eyed and yawning, Gerin told the tale over breakfast the next morning to those who had been lucky enough not to sense the coming of Mavrix in the night. Beside him sat Selatre, also yawning. He was glad to have her there, for without her confirmation he doubted whether Aragis or Van, to say nothing of the rest, would have believed him. But at the same time he worried, for she sounded once more like Biton's Sibyl, not like his woman. He shook his head, bemused. Having lost Elise to a horseleech, would he lose Selatre to a god?

Aragis snapped him out of his reverie. The grand duke might not have been much for the long view, but he had a supremely practical grasp of the moment. "All right, lord prince, Mavrix is here among us, whether we like it or not," he said. "What do we do about it? Can we turn it to our own purposes?"

"I"—Gerin glanced at Selatre—"we, that is, think we may have found a way." One reason he was red-eyed was that he and Selatre had spent the last part of the night talking over that very question. He sighed. He didn't like the answer they'd come up with. "We are going to evoke the god, to bring him fully into the world here and bargain with him."

"Are you daft, Fox?" Van burst out. "Mavrix, he hates you. Bring him fully here and you just make it easier for him to squash you flat."

"This is the course of which you spoke when we met in the southern marches of your holding. A desperate one, if you ask me," Aragis said. But past that, he did not try to dissuade Gerin. Mavrix was not angry at *him*. And if the Sithonian god of wine did destroy the Fox in some lingering, interesting, and creative way, no one would be better positioned to take advantage of it than the grand duke.

Gerin tried to answer both men at once: "Mavrix will come, whether we want that or not. If we try to stand against it, he'll find more reasons to be angry. If we aid his path, we may satisfy him and still accomplish what we want. If not, we still may be able to control him." He looked at Selatre again.

She nodded. Voice hesitant at first, she said, "At the same time as lord Gerin evokes Mavrix, I—I shall try to bring into the world Biton, my former patron, my former— bridegroom." Even with her swarthiness, her cheeks darkened in embarrassment. But she went on, "Biton the farseeing is a god of order, of forethought, the opposite of most things Mavrix stands for. And Biton is old in the northlands, old. His power is rooted here, not new-come like Mavrix's. It may be that he can keep the lord of the sweet grape from the excesses that can accompany his rite."

"But, lass," Van said gently, "after what befell at Ikos, will the god hearken to your evoking?"

Selatre bit her lip. She'd asked the same question, just as morning twilight began to paint the eastern horizon with gray. "I don't know," she answered. "The only way to find out is to make the attempt."

"What if Biton won't come when you call him?" Aragis said. "What then?"

"Then we're left with Mavrix—undiluted," Gerin said after a moment seeking the right way to put it. "We'd be no worse off than if we didn't try to evoke Biton at all." *No better off, either*, his mind jeered, but he resolutely ignored his own gloomy side.

Aragis stuck out his chin. "I insist that you don't seek to bring the gods into the world until you fulfill your half of our agreement. If they wreak havoc on you, I'll also suffer on that account."

"But if we can persuade them to do as we'd like, we might be able to rid the land of monsters without any more fighting," Gerin said. "Have you thought on that, grand duke? Not just driving the creatures back into the woods so they're a lesser nuisance, but actually being rid of them for good and all. We can't make that happen; we're mere mortals. But the gods can do it, if they will. A risk, aye. But if things go as we design . . ."

"Besides which, thanks to Rihwin, Mavrix is already loose in the land, remember," Van said. "He can make mischief any time he chooses. Sometimes the best way to keep someone from moving on you is to move first your own self."

"Rihwin!" Aragis eyed Gerin. "With your name for being clever, lord prince, I can't believe you sent that sot to me as ambassador. Where is he, anyhow?"

"Still drunk asleep in his bed, I suppose," Gerin answered. "As for the other, there's something in what you say, but less than you think. He's brave and clever enough when he's sober, if short sometimes on common sense. But every now and then, things—happen—with him." He spread his hands, as if to say Rihwin's vagaries baffled him, too.

Aragis' hawk face was not made for indecision. Scowling, he said, "All right, Fox, I don't see how I can stop you short of war here, but this I tell you now: it had better work."

"That I already know," Gerin answered. "For my sake, for your sake, for the northlands' sake, it had better work—which is no guarantee it will."

"All right," Aragis said heavily, as if with his warning he washed his hands of whatever might result from the evocation. "When do you begin your wizard's work?"

"At noon," Gerin said, which made the grand duke gape.

"Noon is Biton's hour," Selatre added, "the time when the sun sees farthest. Mavrix is strongest by night, when his impassioned votaries cry 'Evoii!' Whatever chance his lesser strength by day gives us, we'll gladly take."

"Besides," Gerin said, "by noon Rihwin will be up—or I'll drag him out of bed, one. We'll need him in this business, too."

"The gods help you," Aragis said, a sentiment with a multitude of possible meanings.

Even by noon, Rihwin the Fox was not a happy man. His face was pasty and his eyes tracked with red; by the way he kept blinking in the sunshine, he found it much too bright to suit him. "I don't see why you're making *me* carry the jars of wine to your shack," he grumbled petulantly.

"Because if it hadn't been for you, we wouldn't have to be trying this," Gerin answered, his voice hard as stone. "Since the fault is yours, you can bloody well play the beast of burden." He brayed like a donkey. Rihwin flinched.

Selatre had laid an assortment of growing things on a makeshift stone altar in the shack: flowers, fir cones, duck's eggs. "We won't want to summon Mavrix solely as god of wine, but also as the god of increase generally," she said. "That may make him more restrained—or, of course, it may not." Among the flowers, she set the scroll that held a book of the Sithonian national epic by the great poet Lekapenos. "Mavrix also inspires the creation of beauty, as we've noted."

"As you've noted, you mean," Gerin said. "Most of this was your idea; you're the one who's studied Mavrix of late. Till that wine came into the holding, I was happy pretending he didn't exist." He turned to Rihwin. "Set that last jar down over there—carefully! Don't crack it."

Rihwin winced. "When you shout like that, you make my head feel as if it's about to fall off." After a reflective pause, he added, "I rather wish it would."

"Remember that the next time you try to drown yourself in a wine jar, or even one full of ale," Gerin said without much sympathy. He drew his dagger, cut through the pitch that sealed the stopper of one of the wine jars, and then worked in his knife blade and levered out the stopper.

The sweet bouquet of wine wafted from the jar. Gerin sighed with relief. He'd worried that the wine jar, or even both surviving jars, might have gone to vinegar. Had they been bad, he didn't know what he would have done. Drawing some of Rihwin's wine-soaked blood didn't seem like the worst idea in the world.

Gerin dipped up two cups of wine, one for himself, the other for Rihwin. "Don't drink yet," he growled as he handed Rihwin his. He looked over to Selatre and went on, "I still think we might be wiser to call on Biton first. Then his presence will also serve to check Mavrix."

But she shook her head, as she had ever since they began planning the evocation. "Biton has little reason now to hear any summons from me. But if I call on him with Mavrix already here, simple jealousy may help to lure him. Whatever the lord of the sweet grape seeks, the farseeing one is likely to want to thwart."

"You served the god; you know him best," Gerin said, yielding yet again. He, and after a moment Rihwin with him, approached the altar and poured a small libation, being careful not to mar the scroll of Lekapenos. "Thank you for your bounty of the sweet grape, lord Mavrix," Gerin declaimed in halting Sithonian, and sipped from his cup of wine.

Rihwin also drank. His eyes widened; he suddenly seemed several years younger, or at least less worn. "*Thank you for the sweet grape, lord Mavrix,*" he said, and then to Gerin, in more ordinary tones, "Nothing like letting a small snake bite you to ease the venom of a big one."

"Rihwin, your trouble is that you don't know how to keep any snakes small," Gerin said. Just to irk Rihwin, he waved the southerner to silence, not giving him a chance for a sharp retort. "Be still. I am going to summon the god."

He walked over to the altar, raised his hands high, and said, "I summon you to my aid, lord Mavrix, I who have drunk your wine, I who have met you in days past, I who am but a mere mortal imploring your assistance, I who am weak—" He humbled himself without shame. Measured against the might of a god, any mortal was weak.

The litany went on and on. Gerin began to wonder if Mavrix would let himself be evoked. The Sithonian god of wine had some of the deviousness of the principal folk that worshiped him. He might appreciate the irony of forcing Gerin to summon him and then refusing to appear. If that happened, the Fox intended to drink as much wine as he could hold and then ride south with Aragis.

But just when he became certain Mavrix had indeed set him up to fail, the god appeared in the crowded little shack, somehow without making it more crowded—gods had their ways. Mavrix's features were regular, exceedingly handsome, and more than a little effeminate. The god wore sandals and a fawnskin robe, and had a leopardskin tunic draped over his shoulders. In his right hand he carried a green, leafy wand tipped with ivory. A faint odor of grapes and of something else, harsher, ranker—perhaps old blood—rose from him.

His eyes were not like a man's eyes. They were two black pits that reflected nothing. When Gerin looked into them, he felt himself falling through infinite space, down and down and down. He needed a great effort of will to pull his senses back from those twin pits and say in a shaken voice, "I thank you for granting me your presence this day, lord Mavrix." He knew he'd just made a hash of the Sithonian grammar, which was likely only to win the god's contempt, but it couldn't be helped, not now.

Mavrix looked at—and through—him. He felt himself pierced by the god's gaze, almost as if by a sword. In a voice in perfect keeping with his appearance, Mavrix said, "Pleased, are you? Pleased? The vengeance I owe you, you should be quaking like an aspen leaf in a gale. I moved Schild Stupidstaff to give you wine in hope it would let me come here and take that revenge. And you are *pleased*?"

Selatre started her petition to Biton then. Gerin heard her speak of her own unworthiness to summon the god who had abandoned her, and then forgot about her. If he didn't give Mavrix all his attention, he would be ruined past any hope of Biton's redemption.

Gesturing toward the altar and the various gifts it contained, Gerin said, "If you so badly wanted your revenge, lord Mavrix, these would have brought you here. Did you truly need the gift of wine?"

"Aye, for two reasons," the god replied. "First, now that you have summoned me into the world at this place, I can act here more fully than I could otherwise. And second, while first fruits and such are mine, wine is *mine*, if you take my meaning. When I am called by wine, I am more truly myself than if evoked in any other way."

"By which you mean you can be vicious without regretting the consequences, blaming them instead on the strength of the wine," Rihwin said. "You—"

"Silence, worm," Mavrix said, and, although Rihwin's lips continued to move, no more sound came from them. It was an effect Gerin had often wished he could achieve. To Gerin, the lord of the sweet grape said, quite conversationally, "You'd think he'd learn his lesson, wouldn't you? And yet, having fallen foul of me once, he persists in risking my wrath yet again. As do you, I might add, and you are less a fribbler than he. Why is this?"

Gerin did not directly answer that. Instead, he pointed to the book of Lekapenos he had set on the stone. "You are not god of wine only, lord Mavrix. You are also patron of

beauty and cleverness. Is this not so?" He was remembering
more Sithonian than he'd thought he had in him.

Mavrix drew himself up to his full height, which was
much more than a man's, yet somehow did not break
through the ceiling of the shack. "No one would deny it,
little man. But you did not answer my question, and not
answering a god is yet another capital crime to set against
you." He gestured with his wand. It looked innocuous, but
in his hands it was a weapon more fell than any spear or
sword in the grip of the boldest, fiercest fighter.

Gerin's mouth went dry; he knew the power of that
wand. Forcing his voice to steadiness, he replied, "Lord
Mavrix, I had to answer in a roundabout way. Truly I know
your role in inspiring the folk of Sithonia to the peak of
artistic endeavor they once enjoyed. The reason I summoned you, lord, is that ugliness now blights the northlands.
If you look about here, if you see it, I pray you to banish
it for aesthetic reasons if no others."

"Seldom have I seen a fish wriggle on a hook as you
do," the god said petulantly. "Very well, I shall look." His
eyes lighted for a moment. Gerin saw in them shifting
scenes of the monsters' depredations. Then they became
deep pools of blackness once more. He sneered at Gerin.
"Ugly they are, but what of it? You savages in these cold,
grapeless lands treat each other as vilely as the monsters
use you. Why should I care what they do?"

Before Gerin could answer, Selatre let out a gasp of
startlement and delight, and Biton manifested himself in
the shack. Again, it somehow accommodated him without growing and at the same time without seeming
crowded. Gerin had wondered how the farseeing god
would appear, whether as the handsome youth of the
pediment reliefs on his overthrown shrine or the more
primitive image that was mostly eyes and jutting phallus.
To him, Biton seemed now the one thing, now the other,
depending on which was uppermost in his own mind at
any given moment.

Selatre gasped, "Thank you, farseeing one, for hearing
the prayer of your former servant who reveres you still."

"Loyalty is rare enough to deserve notice," Biton
answered in a voice that held the same slight rustic accent

as Selatre's, "the more so when it is retained even after it can no longer be returned."

Mavrix stared at Biton with undisguised loathing. His features shifted with divine celerity to suit his mood. Turning to Gerin, he sneered, "If you think summoning this boring backwoods bumpkin of a deity will somehow save you, I urge you to disabuse yourself of the notion."

"That's not why I called on him," Gerin answered. He bowed to Biton and said, "Farseeing one, the Sibyl begged your presence here for the same reason I evoked Mavrix lord of the sweet grape: to beg you to help rid the land of the monsters now infesting it. As they sprang from the caverns beneath your fallen fane, I dared hope you might consider them in some small measure your responsibility."

"Lord, I beg you to look about," Selatre added, "and see the destruction and disorder these monsters spread wherever they go."

As Mavrix had, Biton looked. Sometimes Gerin saw his head revolve on his neck in a manner impossible for mere flesh and blood, while at other instants what he perceived was a basalt stele spinning. In either case, though, Biton unquestionably had eyes—or at least an eye—in the back of his head.

When his image settled, he said, "This is most distressing. It seems the sort of chaos this foreign mountebank might favor." With an arm or with that phallus, he pointed at Mavrix.

"I?" Mavrix twisted in indignation, so that his leopardskin cape swirled gracefully about him. Gerin could not imagine him doing anything ungraceful. But he'd seen in previous encounters with Mavrix that the god had a temper. Mavrix's smooth voice turned into an angry screech: "Mountebank, is it? I'd think these monsters more your style—barbarous creatures they, fit only for a barbarous land. And after all, they haunted the caverns under your shrine. If you despise them so, why didn't you get rid of them? I suppose you lacked the power." He sneered dismissively.

Biton suddenly seemed wholly human to Gerin; perhaps the stone pillar that was his other guise could not properly express his wrath. "They are not my creatures!" he bellowed in a voice that reverberated through Gerin's head like the deep tolling of a great bronze bell. "My temple blocked them from coming forth and inflicting themselves on the upper world. In the caverns, they were part of nature, not a blight upon it. But when I saw the shrine would fall—"

"Farseeing one indeed," Mavrix interrupted, sneering still. "If it took you so long to notice that, you aren't much of a god."

"At least my senses aren't blinded by drunkenness, adultery, and incest," Biton retorted primly. "Half the time, you don't even know what you see; the rest of the time, you don't care."

Both gods started screaming. Gerin clapped his hands to his head, but it did no good. He was hearing Mavrix and Biton with his mind, not his ears, and they kept on dinning just as loud as before.

"Father Dyaus protect us," Rihwin mouthed silently.

"Don't invite him, too," Gerin exclaimed. "Aren't two squabbling gods enough to satisfy you?" He wanted to run, but he didn't think that would do any good, either. If Biton and Mavrix went at it with everything they had, the whole of the northlands might not be big enough to hold a safe haven. He'd hoped evoking both of them at once would help keep them under control. Instead, it seemed to be inflaming them.

"I thought this scheme mad from the outset." Rihwin moved his lips exaggeratedly and eked out his words with gestures, so Gerin could not mistake what he meant. "You are sorcerer enough to evoke the gods, but not enough to make them do your bidding once here. Better you should never have tried!" He clapped a hand to his forehead.

At that moment, Gerin would have been hard-pressed to argue with him. Mavrix thrust his ivory-tipped wand at Biton. Faster than thought, the farseeing god was stone again, and knocked the wand aside with his phallus. Mavrix howled in pain. Biton, anthropomorphic once more, laughed in his face. Mavrix stuck out a tongue longer and pinker than a human could have had.

Some philosophers called the gods men writ large. Gerin was reminded of nothing so much as small, squabbling boys writ large—but these small boys had superhuman strength and power.

"I should have listened to Aragis and waited," Gerin groaned.

"You should have listened to someone," Rihwin mouthed. With Mavrix distracted, he was faintly audible. "You're always so splendid at deducing what everyone else should do, but when anyone makes a suggestion to you, do you heed it? Ha!" In case his fellow Fox hadn't caught that, he repeated himself: "Ha!"

That held enough truth to sting. Gerin had always relied on his own judgment because he'd found none consistently better. More often than not, his judgment had served him well. But when he made a mistake, he did not commonly content himself with a small one.

"Oh, shut up," he growled nonetheless. "As if you've proved yourself worth listening to over the years." Rihwin gave back a gesture much used by street urchins in the City of Elabon.

Next to the way the gods were behaving, the argument between the two men seemed downright sedate. Mavrix used the same gesture Rihwin had, and stuck out his tongue again to boot. Still in human guise, Biton lifted his robe and waggled the phallus whose stone version had parried the fertility god's wand.

Mavrix laughed scornfully. "I've seen mice with more than that."

"For one thing, you're a liar. For another, who cares what you've seen?" Biton retorted. "I'd sooner look at things of consequence than the private parts of mice."

"I'd sooner look at things of consequence than *your* private parts," the lord of the sweet grape said. With another nasty laugh, he went on, "Some seeker after consequences you are, too, if you couldn't even tell your own chief temple was about to be overthrown."

"What is the blink of an eye against the great sweep of time?" Biton said. "The temple at Ikos stands for centuries yet to come; am I to be condemned for failing to notice the brief interval in which it is downfallen?"

Under less harrowing circumstances, Gerin might have found that interesting, or even hopeful. If Biton's temple at Ikos was to be rebuilt, that argued some sort of civilization would survive in the northlands. His own survival, however, seemed too problematic at the moment for him to take the long view he usually favored.

"Now that you mention it, yes," Mavrix answered. "Perhaps your true image should have a patch over that third eye—and one of the other two, as well."

"I'd almost welcome such," Biton snapped, "if it meant I did not have to see all the hideous things your monsters are working and shall work in this land."

"They're not my monsters!" Mavrix screeched. "Are you deaf as well as blind? They're not my monsters! Not! *Not!* They're hideous and ugly and revolting, and what they do is enough to make anyone with a dram of feeling puke right onto his shoes, thus." What Mavrix spewed forth had a bouquet richer than that of any wine Gerin had ever known— another area where gods enjoyed an advantage over men.

Not long before, Mavrix hadn't cared what the monsters were doing in—and to—the northlands. Gerin, though, hadn't blamed the god for them. Now that Biton had blamed him, he resented that more than he enjoyed making Gerin squirm. And if Gerin could bend Mavrix's course, even a little . . .

"Lord Mavrix, if you despise the monsters so, you could easily show lord Biton they have nothing to do with you by driving them out of the northlands," he said.

"Be quiet, little man," Mavrix said absently, and Gerin *was* quiet, as Rihwin had been before him. He had no choice in the matter. He exchanged a look of despair and alarm with Selatre. It had been worth a try, but not all tried succeeded.

Biton said, "Ah, lord of the sweet vomitus, so you do claim the creatures for your own."

"I do *not!*" Mavrix screamed in a voice that should have knocked Fox Keep flat. "Here, I shall prove it to you." He sucked in a theatrically deep breath, puffed out his cheeks, and turned purpler than any man could: Gerin thought of a divine frog with skin the color of wine. After that tremendous effort, the god exhaled hard enough to make Gerin stagger. "There! They're gone. Look all over the northlands, unseeing one, and you shall find not a single one of the disgusting creatures."

"Coming from you, drunken fool, any assertion requires proof," Biton growled. As it had before, his head began to spin independently of his body—or, alternatively, the stone pillar that was his body turned round and round. Suddenly he stopped and stared contemptuously at Mavrix. "You're as slovenly a workman as I might have guessed. Look there."

Something glinted for a moment in Mavrix's fathomless eyes. "Well, so I missed a couple of them. What of it?" He gestured. "Now they are here no more. Do you see? They are not mine!"

Biton continued his surveillance. His whirling head abruptly halted once more. "And again! You must in truth be the god of drunkenness, for you're sloppy as a drunkard. Look over yonder now."

Gerin wondered what sense Biton used to find the monsters, how he indicated to Mavrix where "over yonder" was, and how Mavrix turned his own senses in that direction, whatever it was. He also wondered just how Mavrix was getting rid of the monsters, and where they were going. Were he a god, he supposed he would know. As a man, he had to go on wondering.

"All right, those are gone, too." Mavrix stuck out his froggy tongue at Biton again. "*Now* do you see any more, lord with the eye in the back of your bum?"

Biton spun and searched. A moment later, he said triumphantly, "Aye, I do, you sozzled ne'er-do-well. What of those?"

Mavrix must have stretched his senses in the direction the farseeing god gave him, for he said, "And they are vanished, too, and so am I. Even with these few drops of wine to ease the path for me here, the northlands are a place I'd sooner leave than come to." He fixed his black, black eyes on Gerin. "Clever man—you were right. There are things uglier than you and your kind. Who would have thought it?" With that, he vanished.

Gerin found he could speak again. Being a politic man, the first thing he said was, "I thank you, lord of the sweet grape, and bless you as well." Then he turned to Biton. "Farseeing one, may I ask a question of you?" When the god did not say no, he went on, "Did Mavrix truly rid the northlands of the creatures that dwelt so long under your temple?"

He waited nervously, lest Mavrix hear him and return in wrath at having his power questioned. But the lord of the sweet grape evidently had been only too glad to leave the northlands for good.

Biton started to nod, then searched once more. When he stopped, he looked annoyed. "That wine-soaked sponge of a Sithonian god is too inept to deserve his divinity," he said.

The Fox took that to mean a monster, or a handful of monsters, still survived somewhere in the northlands. He wondered if Mavrix had left behind the cubs he'd spared—and if he would ever find out. In his humblest tones, he went on, "Lord Biton, would you be generous enough to complete what the lord of the sweet grape began?"

To his dismay, Biton shook his head. "I do not see myself doing that," the farseeing one said. "It is a task for men if they so choose. No, my duty now is to restore Ikos to what it was before the earth trembled beneath my shrine. Everything there shall be as it was—everything. The temple shall stand again without the agency of man, and the Sibyl shall be restored to her rightful place there, to serve as my instrument on earth." He gazed fondly at Selatre.

She looked from the god to Gerin and back again. Her voice trembling, she said, "But lord Biton, I no longer qualify to serve you in that way. In your last prophetic verse, you yourself called me an oracle defiled. Since that day, I have known the embraces of a man"—she glanced nervously toward Gerin once more—"and my courses have begun. I am no longer a fit tool for your work."

"Everything shall be as it was—everything," Biton repeated. "If I can rebuild my fane from tumbled stones, do you think I have not the power to restore your maidenhead, to make you a fit vessel for my voice?"

Selatre looked down at the ground. "I am certain you have that power, lord Biton," she murmured.

Gerin wished desperately for some way to attack Biton, but could imagine none. Unlike Mavrix, the farseeing god could not be duped into losing his temper, not by a man; he was far less vulnerable to earthly concerns than the earthy lord of the sweet grape. The Fox stared over at Selatre. Of course she would choose to go back to the god.

How could she not? She had been consecrated to him since she became a woman, had served him as Sibyl since her predecessor died. Sibyl was all she'd wanted to be; she'd resented being rescued from her residence by the temple after the earthquake; she hadn't been able to abide even the touch of a man for a long time after she was rescued.

True, she'd come to love him and he her, but what was that brief brightness when measured against the course for which her life had been designed? Now that she had the chance to return to that course, how could he blame her if she chose to take it?

Truth was, he couldn't. Having her go back to Ikos would tear him worse inside than he'd been torn when Elise left him. No matter what he'd felt about Elise, she'd no longer cared for him, else she'd not have gone. But he knew Selatre loved him still, as he'd come to love her. Only being certain she would be happier back at Ikos let him bear up under the thought of losing her. Even with that certainty, it was hard, hard.

Biton turned his farseeing eyes on Selatre. "You say nothing. Are you not honored, are you not pleased, that all shall be restored? Even as I speak to you, the shrine at Ikos returns to its proper state. It awaits your coming."

"Of course I am honored, lord Biton," she answered, very softly. "Whether I am pleased . . . Lord, have you the power to see what might be as well as what shall be?"

For a moment, Biton seemed a stone pillar to Gerin, and altogether unfathomable. Then he resumed his human appearance. "Even for me, a god, this is difficult," he replied, his voice troubled. "So many paths branch off from the true one, and then from one another, that losing oneself grows quickly easier the farther ahead one seeks to see. Why do you ask?"

"Because I would have you look down the path I would choose for myself," Selatre said. "You are a god; if you wish your will to be done, done it shall be. How can I, who shall live for a little and then die, oppose it? But—" She did not go on. Even thinking of declining an honor a god would confer on her took something special in the way of courage.

It also filled Gerin with hope as wild and desperate as his despair had been a moment before.

Biton's head began its boneless spin. This time it did not just revolve, but also grew misty, so Gerin could see the far wall of the shack through it. The farseeing god searched for what seemed a very long time; now and again, he would almost disappear altogether. Gerin started when Biton fully returned.

"You may live your life as you will," the god told Selatre. "My Sibyl is my bride, not my slave. I shall mark another, one who will be willing to serve me. I shall not tell you what may spring from your choice, but I say this: as with any other, make the best of it. And a word of warning— for mortals, there is no such thing as living happily ever after."

"I know that, lord Biton. Thank you. I will try to make the best of it." Selatre started to prostrate herself to the god, but Biton disappeared before her knees could touch the ground.

She and Gerin and Rihwin stared at one another, dazed. "I think we may have won," Gerin said in a voice that sounded disbelieving even to him. Then he remembered something more important to say than that. He turned to Selatre. "Thank you. I'll try never to make you sorry for choosing me over, over—" For one of the few times in his life, words failed him. She'd known what she was giving up. At last, huskily, he managed, "I love you."

"I've noticed that," she said, and smiled at his startled expression. "It's why I chose to stay with you, after all. You love me, while for Biton I'd just be—oh, not a tool, not quite, maybe something more like a favorite pet. It's not enough, not now that I've known better." Her own voice went soft. "And I love you, which did, mm, enter into my thinking." She smiled again, this time with a touch of mischief.

Rihwin said, "We have two jars of the blood of the sweet grape here, waiting—indeed, all but crying—to be drunk in celebration of our triumph."

"How right you are, my fellow Fox." Gerin picked up the jar they'd opened to summon Mavrix—and poured it out over Rihwin's head. The red-purple wine splashed him and Selatre, too, but it drenched Rihwin, which was what he'd had in mind. The southerner spluttered and squawked

and flapped his arms—which just splattered the wine more
widely—and rubbed at his eyes. Gerin didn't doubt they
stung fiercely—and didn't regret what he'd done, either.

"A waste, a criminal waste," Rihwin said, sucking at his
mustache so as to swallow every precious drop he could.
"Had it not been for my wine-bibbing, we would not have
seen the northlands freed from the vicious and horrible
curse of the monsters."

"Had it not been for your wine-bibbing," Gerin said
grimly, "we wouldn't have had to put our fate in the hands
of two gods, one of whom was already angry at me and
the other ready to get angry because I'd taken his voice
on earth as my woman. Aye, it turned out well. That's not
why I gave you the one jar of wine as I did—it was for
forcing us to take such a dreadful chance." He picked up
the other, unopened jar. "Because we succeeded, this one
is yours to do with as you will."

Rihwin bowed, dripping still. "You are a lord among
lords, my fellow Fox."

"What I am is bloody tired of having to worry every
moment of every day," Gerin said. "The gods willing"—a
phrase that took on new and urgent meaning after the
evocation—"I'll have maybe three days of peace now before the next thing, whatever it is, goes horribly wrong.
Come on, let's tell Aragis and the rest what we've done
here today."

Along with Van and Fand and Drago and Marlanz and
Faburs, Aragis the Archer stood at what Gerin thought of
as a "safe" distance from the shack. The word was a mis-
nomer, of course. Had the gods truly released their wrath,
nowhere in the northlands would have been far enough
from Fox Keep to escape—as the monsters had discovered.

Everyone pointed and exclaimed when they came forth.
Fand's voice pierced through the rest: "Did the sot spill
the wine and wreck your magic, now?"

"Not a bit of it," Gerin answered. "We summoned the
gods, and the monsters are no more."

That raised the hubbub quite a bit higher than it had
been. Van said, "But how can it be, Captain? You only just
went in there."

"What? Are you witstruck?" Gerin demanded. "We were

in the shack an hour at least, more likely two." He looked to Selatre and Rihwin for confirmation. They both nodded.

Without a word, Aragis pointed up into the sky. Gerin's eyes followed the track of the grand duke's finger toward the sun. He had to look away, blinking, but not before his jaw dropped in astonishment. By the sun's place in the sky, a couple of minutes might have passed, but no more.

"I don't understand it," he said, "but I was telling the truth, too. I suppose the bigger truth is, when you treat with gods, you can't expect the world they know to be the ordinary one we usually live in."

Aragis said, "I think you had better tell me in detail all that came to pass in there. I warn you, I am not satisfied with what you have said so far. It strikes me as likely to be a ploy to keep from having to honor your share of our terms of alliance. Are you saying the monsters are simply gone, thus?" He snapped his fingers.

"Let's go into the great hall and broach some ale, and I'll tell you everything I remember," Gerin said.

Rihwin held out the jar of wine Gerin had given him. "No, let's share this," he said. "As Mavrix is part of the tale, so should he also be part of the explanation." That made sense, but hearing it from Rihwin surprised Gerin. For his fellow Fox to share wine he could have kept for himself was not far from a revolution in human nature, and confirmed that something extraordinary had indeed happened inside the hut.

Divided among so many—and with a libation to the lord of the sweet grape—the one jar of wine did not go far, but Gerin savored every sweet drop; when he'd evoked Mavrix, he'd hardly tasted what he'd drunk. Aided by Selatre and the wine-soaked Rihwin, he explained everything that had passed in the hut.

When he was done, Van said, "Some of the yarns I've told are wild, but I hand it to you, Captain: that beats 'em all."

"Thank you—I think." Gerin could rely on his friend to believe him. Aragis the Archer was something else again. Gerin eyed the grand duke with some concern, wondering how he would react.

Aragis' jaw worked, as if he were chewing over the tale Gerin had told. At last he said, "It fits together well enough;

I give you so much. But how am I to know whether it's the truth or just a clever tale to get me out of your hair?"

"Send a team down to Ikos," Selatre suggested. "If they find no monsters on the way and discover Biton's shrine restored, you'll know we have not lied. It's not a long journey; four days, five at the most, will get your men to the temple and back. Then you won't have to guess—you will know."

Aragis' jaw went up and down again. After a moment, he dipped his head to Selatre. "My lady, that is a fine thought. We would not have left here much before my men could return from Ikos in any case. I'll do as you say, though I'll send more than one team south, on the off chance you're . . . mistaken." He was too courteous to suggest straight out that she was lying, but left the implication in place.

Once his mind was made up, he was not a man to waste time. Four chariots fared south toward Ikos that afternoon. Gerin gladly gave them supplies for the journey; he was confident about what they'd find there. He went to sleep that night wondering where the last of the monsters, the ones Mavrix had missed, still lurked in the northlands. Were they the cubs he'd spared? Solve that riddle and you'd deserve undying praise. The world being what it was, you probably wouldn't get it, but you'd deserve it.

Two days later, the lookout in the watchtower blew a long blast on his horn and shouted, "Lord prince, chariots approach out of the southwest." Gerin frowned; it was too soon for Aragis' men to be coming back, and the southwest . . . The sentry's voice cracked in excitement as he added, "Lord prince, they're Trokmoi!"

The Fox cupped his hands and called up to the sentry, "How many chariots? Are we invaded?" That would be a mad thing for Adiatunnus to try, but just because a thing was mad didn't mean it couldn't happen.

"No invasion, lord prince," the sentry answered, much to his relief. "There's just a handful of them, and they're showing the striped shield of truce."

To the gate crew and the men on the palisade, Gerin called, "We'll let one crew into the courtyard; the rest can

wait outside. If they try to follow, they'll never go home
again."

The Trokmoi uttered not a word of protest when Gerin's
troopers passed them those conditions. At the Fox's nod,
the gate crew let down the drawbridge, then grabbed for
bows and spears. A single chariot rattled and rumbled over
the bridge into Fox Keep. Gerin recognized one of the
woodsrunners in it. "I greet you, Diviciacus son of Dumnorix,"
he said.

"And I'm after greeting you as well, lord Gerin, though
I met some of your men closer than I cared for, these few
days past," the Trokmê answered. A long, ugly cut furrowed
his left arm and showed what he meant. He got down from
the car and bowed low to Gerin. "Lord prince, in the name
of Adiatunnus my chieftain, I'm come here to do you honor.
Adiatunnus bids me tell you he'll be your loyal vassal for
as long as you're pleased to have him so. Forbye, there're
tribute wains waiting to come hither so soon as your lord-
ship is kind enough to tell me you accept his fealty, indeed
and there are."

Gerin stared at Van. They both stared at Aragis. All three
men seemed bewildered. Gerin knew he was. He turned back
to Diviciacus. "What accounts for Adiatunnus' . . . change of
mind?" he asked carefully. "A few days past, as you said,
we were all doing our best to kill one another."

"Och, but that was then and this is now," Diviciacus
answered. He sounded bewildered, too, as if he'd expected
the Fox to know exactly what he was talking about. When
he saw Gerin didn't, he went on, "Himself was chewing
things over with one of the monsters—one o' the smart
ones, y'ken—the other day when lo! All of a sudden the
creature turns to smoke before the very eyes of him, and
then it's gone! All the others gone with it, too; not a one
left, far as we can tell. Will you say that's none o' your
doing, lord prince?"

The Fox didn't say anything for a moment. Now Aragis
bowed to him, almost as low as Diviciacus had. "Lord
prince, I think in your own way you have met the terms
of the alliance to which we agreed, which is to say, I doubt
the monsters now threaten my holding."

"Thank you, grand duke," Gerin said vaguely. He'd

known what Mavrix had said he'd done, of course, but knowing in the abstract and being confronted with actual results were two different things. Pulling himself together, he told Diviciacus, "Aye, the god worked that at my urging." In fact, the gods had worked that because they'd been quarreling with each other, but some things the Trokmê didn't need to know. "And so?"

"And so, lord prince," Diviciacus answered, "Adiatunnus has the thought in him that he'd have to be a raving madman to set himself against your honor, you being such a fine wizard and all. 'Diviciacus,' he tells me, 'not even Balamung could have magicked the creatures so,' and I'm after thinking he's right. If he canna stand against you, he'll stand wi' you, says he."

"So he'll stand with me, will he?" Gerin said. "I mean him no disrespect, but he's shown he's not to be trusted, that chieftain of yours. When he says he'll stand with me, he's more likely to mean he'll stand behind me, that being the best place from which to slide a dagger between my ribs."

Diviciacus sighed. "Himself feared you'd say as much, there being bad blood betwixt the two of you and all. He gave me leave to say this if you didna trust him: he'll give you his eldest son, a boy of twelve, to live with you here at this keep as hostage for his good behavior. The lad'll leave with the load of tribute I spoke of earlier."

"Will he?" Gerin pondered that. Adiatunnus could hardly offer more to show his sincerity. The Fox added, "Did your chieftain give you leave to take the oath of homage and fealty in his place?"

"He did that, lord prince, and I know the way you southrons do it, too." Diviciacus went to one knee before Gerin and held out his hands, palms together. Gerin set his hands to either side of the Trokmê's. Diviciacus said, "Adiatunnus my chieftain owns himself to be your vassal, Gerin the Fox, Prince of the North, and gives you the whole of his faith against all men who might live or die."

"I, Gerin, Prince of the North, accept the homage of Adiatunnus through you, Diviciacus son of Dumnorix, and pledge in my turn always to use him justly. In token of which, I raise you up now." The Fox did just that, and kissed Diviciacus on his bristly cheek.

The Trokmê beamed. "By Taranis, Teutates, and Esus I swear my chieftain Adiatunnus' fealty to you, lord prince."

Any oath less than the strongest one the Trokmoi used would have made Gerin suspicious of the chieftain. With it, he bowed in return, satisfied. "By Dyaus the father of all, Biton the farseeing one, and Mavrix lord of the sweet grape, I accept his oath and swear in turn to reward his loyalty with my own."

Diviciacus eyed him keenly; Adiatunnus had not dispatched a fool as his ambassador. "You Elabonians are always after swearing by Dyaus, but the other two aren't usually the gods you name in your frickfullest aiths. They'd be the ones who did your bidding for you, I'm thinking."

"That's my affair," Gerin said. The Trokmê was right and wrong at the same time: Gerin had indeed summoned Mavrix and Biton, but the gods did their own bidding, no one else's. If you were clever enough—and lucky enough— you might make them see that what you wanted was also in their interest. That once, the Fox had been clever and lucky enough. He never wanted to gamble on such bad odds again.

Aragis' chariot crews returned with word of Ikos miraculously restored and not a sign of monsters anywhere, and seemed miffed when everyone took their report as a matter of course. The day after they got back to Fox Keep, Aragis and his whole host set out for his holding in the south.

"Perhaps we'll find ourselves on the same side again one day," Aragis said.

"May it be so," Gerin agreed. He didn't quite care for the grand duke's tone. Had he been in Aragis' sandals, he would have worried about himself, too: with Adiatunnus as his vassal, his power and prestige in the northlands would soar . . . maybe to the point where Aragis would go looking for allies now, hoping to knock him down before he got too powerful to be knocked down. In Aragis' sandals, Gerin would have tried that. To forestall it, he said, "I almost wish I didn't have the Trokmê as my ally. He'd be easier to watch as an enemy than as someone who claimed to be my friend."

"There is that." Aragis rubbed his chin. "Well, we'll see how you do with him." With that ambiguous farewell, the Archer turned and went back among his own men. Gerin knew he would bear watching, too, no less than Adiatunnus. This once, his interests and the Fox's had coincided. Next time, who could say?

Gerin sighed. If he spent all the time he should watching his neighbors, where would he find time for anything else?

Not long after Aragis and his warriors left for the grand duke's lands, Duren came up to Gerin and asked, "Papa, are you angry at Fand?"

"Angry at Fand?" The Fox frowned. He often thought Fand counted any day where she didn't make someone angry at her a day wasted, but he didn't say that to his son. Duren liked Fand, and she'd never been anything but gentle with him. "No. I'm not angry at her. Why did you think I was?"

"Because you never go to her chamber anymore. It's always Van."

"Oh." Gerin scratched his head. How was he supposed to explain that to his son? Duren awaited a reply with the intense seriousness only a four-year-old can show. Slowly, Gerin said, "Fand has decided she likes Van better than she likes me. You remember how she and I would quarrel sometimes, don't you?"

Duren nodded. "But she quarrels with Van, too."

"That's true," the Fox said, "but it's—usually—a happy sort of quarreling. She doesn't treat you any differently now that she's just with Van instead of with him and me, does she?"

"No," Duren said.

"That's good." Gerin meant it; he would have quarreled with Fand, and in no happy way, had the boy said yes. He went on, "Now that Fand is with Van, Selatre is my special friend. Do you like her, too?" He waited anxiously for Duren's answer.

"Oh, yes," Duren said. "She's nice to me. She doesn't treat me like a baby, the way some people do just because I'm not big yet. And do you know what else?" His voice dropped to the conspiratorial whisper reserved for secrets. "She taught me what some of the letters sound like."

"Did she?" Gerin said. "I'll bet I know which ones, too."

"How can you know that?" Duren demanded in the tone children use when, as frequently, they assume their parents can't possibly know anything.

"Were they the ones that spell your name?" Gerin asked.

Duren stared at him. Every once in a while—not often enough—a parent will redeem himself by proving he does know what he's talking about after all. "How did you know?" the boy said, his eyes enormous. "Did you use magic?" Now that his father had got away with summoning two gods, he assumed Gerin was a mighty mage. The Fox, who knew how lucky he'd been, wished that were so but made a point of bearing firmly in mind that it wasn't.

He said, "No, I didn't need any magic for that. The letters of a person's name are almost always the ones he learns first, because those are the ones that are most important to him. Do you know what else?"

"No, what?" Duren breathed. He liked secrets, too, and was good at keeping them for a boy of his years.

"When Selatre came to Fox Keep—that was just a few days after Tassilo stole you—she didn't know her letters, either," Gerin said. "I taught them to her myself. So she should know how to teach you, because she just learned."

"Really?" Duren said. Then he looked doubtful. "But she reads so well. I can only read the letters in my name, and find them in other words sometimes. But I don't know what the other words say."

"It's all right. It's nothing to worry about," Gerin assured him. "You're still very little to know any letters at all. Even most grown people don't, you know. Selatre learned hers quickly partly because she's smart—just like you—and partly because she's a woman grown, and so when she reads something she understands what it's talking about. You can't always do that, because a lot of things that are in the words on the parchment haven't happened to you yet. Do you understand?"

"No." Duren's face clouded over. "I want to be able to do it now."

Gerin picked him up, tossed him in the air, and caught him as he came down. Duren squealed. Gerin spun him around and around and around. He squealed again. When Gerin set him down, he took a couple of staggering steps and fell on his bottom. Gerin was dizzy, too, but tried not to show it. He said, "Could you throw me up in the air and spin me around and around like that?"

"Don't be silly, Papa." Duren tried to get up, but seemed to have as much trouble walking as Rihwin had the night he broached the wine.

"Why not?" Gerin persisted. "Why can't you do that?"

"You're too big."

"That's right, and you're too little. When you're bigger, you'll be able to do things like that, and you'll be able to read easier, too."

Duren considered that, then said, "Spin me again!" Gerin happily obeyed, and enjoyed listening to the happy sounds his son made. This time, Duren didn't even try to stand up when Gerin put him on the ground. He lay there staring up at the sky; Gerin would have bet he saw it going round and round. Finally he made it back to his feet. "Again!" he demanded.

"No," the Fox said. "If you do too much of that, you can make yourself sick."

"Really?" Gerin watched his son think that over; the process was very visible. Duren obviously decided that was an interesting idea, and one worth exploring further. He spun away, laughing out loud.

Gerin laughed, too, but only for a moment. Duren could afford to live for the present—indeed, at his age, he could hardly do anything else. Gerin did not enjoy that luxury. His son was the only good thing he had left from his shattered marriage with Elise, and he loved the boy without reservation. But what would happen to Duren when he wed Selatre and had children by her? Minstrels sang songs about stepmothers, but how would he blame Selatre for wanting her own blood to advance? Who would end up whose vassal, and after how much hatred and strife?

With such unpleasant thoughts in his mind, he was almost embarrassed when Selatre came out of the great hall and walked over to him. "Why so grim-faced?" she asked. "The monsters are—wherever Mavrix sent them. They're not here, anyway. Ikos is risen again, I suppose with a new Sibyl. Adiatunnus is lying low, at least for now. You should be happy."

"Oh, I am," he said, "but not for any of those reasons."

She frowned, looking for the meaning behind his words. When she found it, she looked down at the ground for a moment; sometimes a compliment could make her as nervous as being touched once had. Then she said, "If you are so happy, why haven't you told your face about it?"

He clicked his tongue between his teeth. "I was trying to look into the future, and I don't have a god to guide my sight."

"Biton didn't guide me," Selatre said. "He just spoke through me, and I had no memory of what he would say. What did you see that troubled you so?"

Gerin wondered if he should have kept his mouth shut. But no: Selatre prized truth, partly from her own nature and perhaps partly also because so much raw truth had washed through her as the god's conduit. So, hesitantly, he explained.

"Yes, those are troubling thoughts," she said when he was done. "Much will depend on what sort of man Duren becomes, and on any other children who may appear." She glanced over to him, her head cocked to one side. "So you aim to wed me, do you? This is the first I've heard of it."

He coughed and sputtered; his ears got hot. "I did intend to ask you formally," he said; hearing how lame his voice sounded only made his ears hotter. "But yes, it has been in my mind, and it just—slipped out now. What say you to that?"

"Oh, I say yes, without a doubt," Selatre answered. He hugged her, glad past words that he hadn't been too clumsy for her to bear. But she still had that—measuring—look on her face. She said, "As long as you are looking into the future, what makes you bold enough to think *I* won't want to run off with a horseleech someday, as Elise did?"

"Oof!" he said, the air rushing out of him; she couldn't have deflated him any more thoroughly if she'd kicked him in the belly. "And we men like to think we're the cool and calculating sex." But he saw she wanted a serious answer, and did his best to give her one: "I've learned some things since I wed her, or I hope I have, anyhow. I know better than to take a wife for granted just because we've given each other pledges. Marriage is like, hmm, the palisade around this keep: if I don't keep checking to make sure the timber stays sound, it'll fall to pieces one day. That's most important. The other thing is, you suit me better than she did in a lot of different ways. I don't think the two of us will rub each other raw. And if we start to, I hope I'm wise enough now to try to make sure that doesn't get too bad. And I hope you are, too." He waited to see what she'd say to that.

Once more to his vast relief, she nodded. "Those are good reasons," she said. "If you'd given me something like, 'Because I think you're lovelier than the stars in the sky,' then I'd have worried."

"I do," Gerin said. "Think you're lovelier than the stars in the sky, I mean."

Selatre glanced away. "I'm glad you do," she answered quietly. "But while that's a fine reason to want to bed someone, it really isn't reason enough to wed. One fine day, you'd likely see someone else you think is lovelier than the stars in the sky—and then, what point in having married?"

"The one and only good thing about growing older that I've found is that I don't think with my crotch as much as I used to," he said.

"As much, eh?" Selatre stuck out her tongue at him. "I will put up with a certain amount of that, I suppose . . . depending on whom you're thinking about."

He slipped an arm around her waist, drew her to him. Not very long before, even trying that would have got him killed by the temple guards at Ikos. Even more recently, she'd have pulled away in horror, still thinking a man's touch a defilement. Now she molded herself to him.

As if to prove he hadn't been thinking entirely with his crotch, he said, "Duren tells me you're starting to teach him his letters."

"Do you mind?" Her voice was anxious. "I didn't think I had to tell you; you've always been one to want people to be able to read. And he's a good boy, your son. I like him. If he has an early start on his letters, they'll come easier for him. Learning them once I was all grown up, I sometimes thought my head would burst."

"Did you?" Gerin said. "If you did, you hid it very well. And you learned them very well, too—better than most of the people I've taught when they were younger. No, I don't mind. You're right—I'm glad he has a start on them. And I'm glad you like him."

Maybe he gave that some slight extra emphasis, or maybe Selatre was getting better at fathoming the way his mind worked. She said, "Aye, I can see how you might be."

She made a face. "I don't intend to act like a wicked stepmother in a tale, I promise you that." She paused for a moment, her expression thoughtful. "I wonder what the stepmothers in those tales intended. Is anyone ever wicked in her own eyes?"

"Do you know," Gerin said slowly, "there's a question that would keep the sages down in the City of Elabon arguing for days. When I first opened my mouth, I would have said of course some people seem wicked, even to themselves. But when I try to see through their eyes, I wonder. Balamung the Trokmê wizard set the northlands on their ear a few years ago, but he thought he was taking just revenge for slights he'd got. And Wolfar of the Axe—" He broke off and scowled; remembering Wolfar made him remember Elise, too. "Wolfar was out for his own gain, and didn't see one bloody thing wrong with that. You may be right."

"They probably saw you as wicked for trying to stop them," Selatre said.

"So they did," Gerin said. "Which didn't mean I didn't judge them wicked, or that they didn't need stopping."

"And you stopped them," Selatre said, nodding. "Did I rightly hear that you slew Wolfar in the library?" She gave him a different sort of sidelong look this time, as if to say that was not the proper use to which to put a chamber dedicated to preserving books.

"If I hadn't killed him there, he certainly would have killed me," Gerin answered. "That he didn't wasn't for lack of trying." His neck throbbed at the memory; Wolfar had come within an eyelash of strangling him. But he *had* strangled Wolfar, and in so doing won what passed for Schild's loyalty.

Selatre said, "If you hadn't slain him then, I probably wouldn't be alive today—the monsters would have caught me the day of the earthquake." Her laugh came shaky.

"Strange to think your own being depends on something that had happened years ago to someone you didn't know then."

"Aye, that is a curious thought," Gerin agreed. "Some Trokmê—or maybe more than one of the woodsrunners; I've never known for certain—twisted my life out of the path I'd planned for it when he—they—killed my father and my brother and left me baron of Fox Keep. If you dwell on the might-have-beens, it's like wandering through a maze."

"Might-have-beens strain even the powers of the gods," Selatre said. "Remember how Biton had to strain to see what might come from my going back to Ikos and my staying here with you?"

"I'm not likely to forget it," Gerin said with feeling. "I thought I'd lost you forever."

"Biton was kindly, perhaps in memory of how I'd served him before," Selatre answered. "But even if he hadn't been, how could you hope to set your will against a god's?"

"I couldn't," Gerin said, and let it go at that. The god's will had not been his principal concern; Selatre's had. With a lifetime devoted to Biton and bare days to him, she was only too likely to have chosen to return to what she'd always known. That she hadn't left made him grateful every time he looked at her. Most seriously, he said, "I'll do my best to make sure you're never sorry about your choice."

"You needn't worry about that," Selatre said. "The farseeing one will have made his own selection by now; with the temple at Ikos restored, he would not leave it without a Sibyl. I'm here because I wanted to be, and not because I have no other choice open to me."

Again Gerin kept part of his thoughts to himself. There was always another choice: the one Elise had taken. What he had to do now—what he had to do forever—was to make sure Selatre was too content at Fox Keep ever to want to leave it.

He hugged her again, but didn't think, as he had a little while before, of taking her up to his chamber and barring the door. Simple affection had its place, too. Maybe after all he could say some of what he'd thought: "If we work at it, it *will* turn out all right."

"Are you making prophecies now?" Selatre asked. "Perhaps I should have worried about whether Biton would take you back to Ikos and set you on the throne of pearl."

"Thank you, no," Gerin said. "I'm right where I belong, not doing what I'd hoped to be doing, maybe, but doing something that needs doing—and I'm just happy you think you belong here, too."

"That I do," Selatre agreed. "And now, if you're not going to drag me upstairs, I'll go up by myself and wade through that scroll on Kizzuwatnan hepatomancy I was trying to make sense of the other day."

"That one doesn't make much sense to me, either," Gerin said. "My guess is that it either didn't make much sense to the Sithonian who wrote it in the first place or to the Elabonian who put it into our language. I've tried foretelling a few times from livers of cows or sheep we've slaughtered, but what I divined had nothing to do with what ended up happening. Something's been lost somewhere, I think."

"Maybe it will come clear if I keep studying it," Selatre said, and headed back into the great hall.

Gerin smiled as he watched her go. Though she didn't put it the way he had, she also believed in working at something till you got it right. Even without hepatomancy, he knew a good omen when he saw one.

The way she'd teased him about dragging her upstairs he took for a good omen, too. With Elise, anything involving the bedchamber had been a deadly serious business. With Fand, he'd never known whether he was in for a grand time or a fight. Making love with someone neither earnest nor inflammatory was new to him, but he liked it.

Drifting after Selatre, he walked into the great hall himself. Van sat at one of the tables there, a roast chicken—mostly bones now—in front of him, a pitcher of ale within easy reach. He nodded to the Fox and said, "Grab yourself a jack, Captain, and help me get to the bottom of this."

"I don't mind if I do." Gerin sat down across from the outlander, who poured him a full jack.

Van raised his own and said, "To the Prince of the North—maybe one day to the King of the North!" He poured the ale down his throat, then stared sharply at Gerin. "You'd better drink to that."

"So I should," Gerin said, and obediently drank. He smacked his lips, partly tasting the ale, partly Van's words. King of the North? "If I'm lucky, my grandson may wear that title."

Van plucked at his beard. "I don't know, Fox. All's topsy-turvy here, and you're a young man yet. If you live, you may do it."

Gerin shifted uncomfortably on the bench, as if he'd got a splinter in his backside. "I don't know that I *want* to do it. A title like that . . . It'd be an open invitation to all the other lords in the northlands to gang together and pull me down."

"I don't know," Van repeated. "Me, I don't think Aragis would lift a finger against you, for fear you'd call down the gods and turn him into a lump of cheese, or some such. Same with Adiatunnus. And without them, who'd raise a proper fight?"

"They're wary of me now, aye," Gerin said, "but that'll fade by the time the first snow falls. I can't make myself king before then; I'm too weak. And taking the title when I haven't the strength to back it up—" He shook his head. "Aragis wants to be king. I think he'd fight for pride's sake if I went and put on a crown."

"Have it your way—you generally do," Van said. "From where I sit, looks like you could bring it off." He poured the last of the ale into his jack, drained it, got up, and headed for the stairs.

He'd left one of the wings on the roast fowl uneaten. Gerin pulled it off the carcass, gnawed on it thoughtfully. He shook his head after a little while, still convinced he was right. All the same, he sent a resentful look toward the stairway: Van had kindled his ambition, and he'd known just what he was doing, too.

"Not yet," Gerin said. His lands had suffered too much from the monsters, and from the fights with Adiatunnus. He wanted time to wed Selatre and to enjoy life with her (though the calculating part of his mind said being married to the former Sibyl of an Ikos now miraculously restored would also foster his prestige among his neighbors). No, not yet.

But who could say? The time might come.